ON THE GAMANT WORLDS—

The planet of Kayan, where Zadok, leader of the Gamant people and keeper of the *Mea Shearim*—the gateway to God—is about to face the greatest challenge to the future of the Gamant race. . . .

The desert world of Horeb, where the Old Believers are on the brink of rebellion against the terrorist rule of High Councilman Ornias, spokesman for the man who may be the true Mashiah or the long-prophecied Antimashiah. . . .

ON THE MAGISTERIAL BATTLE CRUISER *HOYER*—

where Captain Cole Tahn, serving the alien Magistrates, must decide whether to carry out orders which will bring fiery devastation to world after Gamant world. . . .

WITHIN THE FIELD OF THE *MEA SHEARIM*—

where those of the line of Ephraim will come face-to-face with beings of inconceivable power, beings who have chosen humankind as the tool with which they will redefine the very nature of existence. . . .

AN ABYSS OF LIGHT

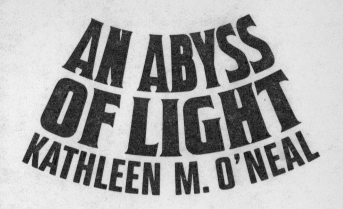

AN ABYSS OF LIGHT

KATHLEEN M. O'NEAL

DAW BOOKS, INC.
DONALD A. WOLLHEIM, PUBLISHER

375 Hudson Street, New York, NY 10014

First Printing, May 1990

1 2 3 4 5 6 7 8 9

PRINTED IN THE U.S.A.

ACKNOWLEDGMENTS

Many people share in the creation of this book. Personal discussions on the Problem of Evil with Gary Kessler, John Bash, Charles Kegley, Bruce Jones and Itrice Sanders form the cornerstones of my perspectives. Nonfiction works by Elie Wiesel, James H. Charlesworth, Nora Levin, Mircea Eliade, Edmond Jacob, and Gershom G. Scholem were indispensible for the background on history and mysticism. Those who seek a greater understanding of the symbolism found in *An Abyss of Light*, need look no further than their writings.

I also owe a debt of sincere gratitude to Shandel Gamer, Cori Wexler, Mary Stancavage, and Dixie King. For all the warm beers on cold days in Jerusalem. I haven't forgotten.

My sister, Karen Sue Jones, provided invaluable advice on child psychology and development. My editor, Sheila Gilbert, worked her magic on the manuscript. As always, her insights were superb.

Lastly, my husband, W. Michael Gear, is the unseen force behind this book. As friendly adversary on plot and character development, his heartbeat pounds here nearly as much as mine.

THE GREEK APOCALYPSE OF EZRA
Fragment, dated: 150 A.D. Old Earth Standard

And Ezra said, "It would be better if man were not born! The dumb beasts are better than man, for they do not have punishment."

And God said, "Ask Abraham your father what kind of son presses suit against his father?"

"As the Lord lives, I shall never stop pleading the case with you. Where are your former mercies, O Lord? Where your long-suffering? Who made Adam?"

"My immaculate hands."

"Was he not guarded by an angel? How was he deceived who was guarded by angels whom you commanded to be present whatever happened?"

And God said, "Count the stars and the sands of the sea and if you will be able to count these, then you will also be able to argue the case with me."

"Lord, I cannot count them. I bear human flesh. But neither will I stop arguing. Lord, Lord, where is your goodness?"

"Your sins exceed my kindness."

And Ezra saw a terrible darkness and night without stars or moon and he was much afraid. He wept bitterly.

PROLOGUE

Jeremiel Baruch ran a hand through his sweat-damp blond hair and leaned back tiredly against the blue chair. The ship's command cabin stretched in a white oval around him, windows dotting the hull. Three levels of computer screens displayed different colored information on the console in front of him. Rudy Kopal, his second in command, piloted the ship. A medium-sized man with brown curly hair and gray eyes, his straight nose rode atop full lips. He continually glanced sideways at Baruch, eyes measuring, worried.

"Jeremiel, for God's sake, this is suicide and you know it," he drawled softly, a sign of his upbringing on the planet of New Savannah.

"Maybe."

"What do you mean, 'maybe.' Some lunatic religious fanatic summons you from halfway across the galaxy—a lunatic you don't even know!—and you go running?" He shook his head, gritting his teeth. "You'd have never taken such chances three months ago. You'd have checked this out every which way—"

"I'll check after you drop me over Kayan."

"By then, old friend, I'll be long gone. What if it's a trap?"

"I've been in traps before."

"Sure, and I was there to pull you out. Me and about fifty thousand troops with battleships. This is a little different. A little scarier, if you know what I mean."

"Doesn't matter."

Rudy bowed his head and his nostrils flared. Jeremiel watched him with numb patience, feeling nothing but a terrible emptiness. It got harder every day to teeter around the edges of that chasm that had grown in his mind without falling in. Some deep part of his soul longed to lose itself in that inner pit of darkness. At least then the agony would end.

"Doesn't matter, for God's sake. *Doesn't matter!*" Rudy shoved Jeremiel's shoulder hard, spinning his chair around

11

so he could pin his eyes. "Do you think Syene was the only one who needed you? *Huh?*" He stabbed a finger toward one of the portals at the stars that had appeared as they slipped from light vault to regular space. "There's a million Gamants left in this galaxy running sick with fear from the Galactic Magistrates and you're the only man who fights to protect them. You're the only—"

"You're as good a commander as I am, Rudy. Better, probably. You can handle anything that comes up." At the mention of Syene's name, his stomach muscles had clenched tight, anguish welling to smother him. *Syene . . . what did I do to you?*

Rudy heaved an irritated sigh and flopped back into his chair, glaring through eyes as hard and glittering as stone. "I know you're hurting, Jeremiel. Everybody knows it. But you don't have the luxury of wallowing in your pain for a year. Without you in top shape, mentally and physically, this whole underground movement is liable to come toppling down around our ears. And you know what that means. Gamant culture and religion, everything we hold dear, gets wasted."

"I just need a short rest. Just a couple of months."

"You've already had two months. Are you sure you can pull yourself together in two more?"

"Rudy, don't—"

"*Goddamn it, Jeremiel!*" He shot to his feet and began furiously pacing the small cabin, black jumpsuit rustling in the sudden quiet. "I understand you need a reprieve. And, God knows, I'd take you anywhere in the galaxy you wanted to go. I'd guard your back from now till kingdom come, if you asked. *But this lunacy about Horeb . . .*" He turned suddenly, staring hard. "Why don't you let me take you somewhere else? Remember that backward little hole in the wall on Vensyl? Candlelit saloons and mountain peaks so high they seemed to pierce the clouds? They'd never find us there. I'll send a message to Merle Wells that we'll be gone for two months. She can handle any trouble that—"

He shook his head wearily. "No."

"Why the hell not? She's a damned fine commander."

"Horeb is undergoing violent upheaval. Gamants are killing Gamants. The Desert Fathers there have asked my help. I can't turn them down. If I don't help, who will? And the change will do me good. I won't have to stare at the same halls Sy . . ." His heart thundered, "we walked together every day. It'll give me time to—"

"Then let me go to Horeb with you? You *need* me! Your abilities with strategy and tactics have fallen to pieces and you damn well know it! Besides, you're going to want somebody you can depend on. You've had enough traitorous—"

"I don't . . . !" Jeremiel shouted, leaning forward menacingly as his inner chasm widened, threatening to swallow him up. *Dannon betrayed . . . don't think about him!* "I don't want to talk about it, Rudy. Leave it alone!"

Kopal massaged his forehead. "All right, but someday soon you're going to have to. And wouldn't you feel a hell of a lot better if it was me you had around to discuss it with? Me, who also knew and loved Syene?" He dropped his voice to a whisper. "Listen, I can help you with battle plans and training the troops on Horeb. I can—"

"Rudy," he breathed, suppressing the angry despair that stirred in him. "I—I just . . ." He saw Kopal clench his fists standing straighter, waiting. "I appreciate your offer. You're my best friend. But I *need* to go alone. It's what the Desert Fathers requested and I've no reason to turn them down."

"No reason? No reason except it would be goddamned easy to set up an ambush for one man. You think that billion notes the Magistrates have on your head isn't attractive? Half the galaxy would try to palm their brothers off as you if they thought they had a chance of collecting."

Jeremiel gave him a bare smile. "I'm to report to Zadok first. And if there's anyone I trust completely, besides you, it's Zadok. There's no question but that he has the best interests of Gamant civilization in mind. If there's the slightest bit of suspicion about the Horeb thing, he'll know."

"And what then?"

"What do you mean?"

Rudy spread his arms in exasperation. "*I mean*, if you find out the Desert Fathers have set you up, where are you? Trapped on Kayan amidst six Magisterial military installations and a few thousand soldiers. And I'll be long gone! You know I can't hang around in dangerous space."

"No, you can't." Jeremiel closed his eyes and rubbed the back of his neck. Rudy was right, of course. But somewhere deep inside he couldn't convince himself it mattered. Death could be lurking around the next turn and he just didn't care. Nothing in the universe mattered anymore. Nothing except a fatal mistake he'd made and the black chasm that swelled inside him to fill every moment of his life.

"And what about Tahn?" Rudy asked gruffly. "He's still waiting out there. If he gets a whiff of where you've gone, he'll be on you like ducks on a june bug."

A prickle climbed Jeremiel's spine. Tahn was the most brilliant commander in the Magisterial military. Six times in the past year, he'd almost caged the Underground fleet. Only desperate acts on Jeremiel's part had saved them. But the day was coming, he knew, when without more troops and ships to join the Gamant cause, Tahn would win. "It'll be harder to find me on foot, than when I'm surrounded by ten battle cruisers."

"Don't be so damned sure. You can move a hell of a lot faster in space than through a forest."

"Horeb's a desert."

"Well . . . through sand dunes, then. The point is—"

"I get your point."

Rudy slammed a fist against the hull of the ship. The thud rang ominously. "Do you? I'm not leaving you alone, Jeremiel. That's all there is to it. You can't offer yourself up as a sacrificial—"

"*I'm* not *offering. And* you're *leaving!* If that's the last order you ever obey from me, you're going to—"

"Damn it!" Rudy cursed imploringly as he squeezed his eyes closed and pleadingly tipped his chin to the ceiling. Sweat glistened on his olive skin, soaking the ends of hair that stuck to his forehead. Against the white hull behind him, he looked like some tortured savior.

Haggardly, Jeremiel rested his chin on his chest, exhaling tiredly. "I'll call if I need you."

"Sure. Sure, you will. *If you can.* And what if me and all your forces are locked around Giclas or Pitbon and can't get back to you for months?"

He lifted a hand nonchalantly. "I'll make do as best I can. There are always places to hide. I'll—"

"You'll what?" Rudy demanded. "Duck into some cave and pray to God that when you have to come out for supplies nobody recognizes you? Steal a fast transport and fly hell-bent for the Lysomian system where you know you've got friends, worried every second the Magistrates are going to spot you and you'll place everybody there in jeopardy?"

"I'll figure something out."

Rudy bent down, bracing his hands on Jeremiel's chair arms, to stare him in the eyes. He met that hot challenge with equanimity, feeling like an observer rather than a participant in the affair. It took only a few seconds of glaring before Rudy's gaze softened, going from fiery to worried sick. He straightened, walking to a portal to stare out at the stars. Kayan floated just ahead, a magnificently lush blue-green world covered with streaks of clouds. "I'm fighting a losing battle, aren't I?"

"But you're doing it well."

Rudy turned, giving him an annoyed smile. He pointed a finger sternly, but his voice came out low, affectionate. "If you get yourself killed, you'll force me to blast half the goddamned sector to find the culprit. Remember that, will you?"

"I will."

They stared at each other a moment, exchanging a silent communication of friendship, then Rudy strode quickly across the cabin and gripped him roughly by the arm, jerking him out of his chair. Scrutinizing him grimly, he embraced Jeremiel so hard it forced the air from his lungs.

"Take whatever time you need to heal yourself. Then call and I'll come running."

Jeremiel tightened his arms around his friend's midsection. "Just a couple of months, Rudy. That's all I need."

CHAPTER 1

Apartment houses stood empty, doors banging in the hot wind sweeping the dirt streets. Abandoned possessions loomed like sentries in the gaping sockets of windows, free to anyone, the owners long vanished. Lifeless. This far section of the capital city of Seir lay in ruins, black clouds of smoke billowing in the silent blue sky.

Rachel Eloel ran up Izhar Street, clutching her eight-year-old daughter's hand in a death grip. Long black hair streamed out behind her.

"Mommy, I'm scared."

15

"Don't cry, Sybil," she whispered shakily. "Dear God, please don't cry."

"Are they coming after us? Those bad men?"

"Yes, sweetheart. You must be very quiet."

The sun dipped in and out between the roofs of burned buildings, lighting her path with a false brightness promising no hope. Old yards, thick with withered grass, led to what had been the homes of friends. She knew the names so well, she unconsciously whispered them as she passed: Leashno, Tarin, Wexler. Dead trees, silence and desolation, had the world gone mad? *God? Where are you?*

A chant of harsh voices carried on the wind and Rachel shuddered. Planetary marines. Rounding a corner, she spied a tumbled pile of rubbish. Dragging Sybil, she shouldered through the head-high refuse, pushing to the back and crouching in the dense shadows of the overhanging building. Petrolon boxes and stinking cans surrounded them, the smells of rotting fish and sour milk strong.

Sybil brushed brown curls from her face and looked up through wide, afflicted eyes. "Where's Daddy?"

"I don't . . . He's home, baby. It's all right. We'll see him soon."

"Why didn't he come get us when the bad men burned the temple?"

Rachel's heart rose into her throat. She wiped sweaty palms on her long blue robe. This was the week of Sighet, the holy week celebrating the freedom of the Gamant people from the horrible labor camps of the wicked Edom Middoth. Yet all the temples on Horeb stood closed . . . save one. Adom Kemar Tartarus held his blasphemous ceremonies at his magnificent palace, while hundred of laborers finished the new temple to Milcom. People prostrated themselves daily before the growing structure. *Dear God, how could they? Traitors!* She and Shadrach had risked death to hold an illegal Sighet celebration in the basement of an abandoned and ruined temple on the outskirts of town. An ugly thing, the broken structure looked like the fanged mouth of some beast. That morning, the fourth day of Sighet, they'd been feasting when the military forces of the Mashiah stormed their sanctuary, firing blindly into the crowd.

"Mommy? Why didn't Daddy come when the bad men—"

"He . . . he had to go home, Sybil. We'll ask him when we get there, all right?"

16

"You're lying to me, aren't you?" Sybil whispered anxiously. "Don't lie to me. I need to know if—"

"Hush! I'm not lying to you. I—I—"

"Can we go see him? I want my daddy now."

Rachel stroked her daughter's tangled hair and kissed her forehead. "Soon, baby. We just have to sit here quietly for a little while longer . . ." Her voice faded, terror taking over as her ears picked up sounds from the street. Boots against stone. The hum of a rifle.

"Over here!" someone shouted.

Rachel froze as the thudding of footsteps swelled closer. Sybil's eyes widened and she twined fingers in Rachel's blue sleeves.

"Mommy, what . . ."

Rachel clamped a hand over her mouth, not realizing the force she used. When the child scratched her viciously, whispering, "Don't! Hush!" Sybil's tiny head flailed, face twisting. Then she sank down to her mother's lap, refusing to look at her, but Rachel could feel the tears soaking her robe.

"I'm sorry, Sybil. Please, I didn't mean to—"

"Come out!" a harsh male voice demanded. "I know you're there. I can smell you filthy demon worshipers. Come out before I shoot!"

Quaking, Rachel shoved Sybil behind her, tucking her in a dirty box stained all over with mold and holding a finger to her lips. The little girl's eyes filled with tears. She reached out, silently pleading. Tiny fingers worked in a gesture of "take me, take me." Rachel mouthed the words, "no," and "quiet."

"Damn you! I know you're there. Hear this?" The hiss of a pulse rifle switched to full charge met her ears.

"Mommy—"

"Here!" Rachel shouted, stumbling over a crate. "Don't shoot. I'm coming." Quickly, she shouldered through the trash to stand in a shaft of sunlight penetrating between the tall buildings. Her dark hair fluttered wildly in a gust that swirled red dust up to the charred rooftops before whirling away.

The marine in front of her lowered his rifle, clicking the charge down a notch as a sadistic smile curled his lips. He stood over six feet with blond hair and sleepy blue eyes. His green formfitting uniform was splattered with crimson stains.

"Well, well, you're not what I expected." He turned and

17

yelled over his shoulder, "Hey, Charlie, come see what I've found."

Rachel locked her trembling knees, forcing herself to stand straight, defiant, as a stocky sergeant with dark hair and a bulbous nose trotted around the corner and stopped dead in his tracks. "Holy father! *It's her*, isn't it?"

"Hell, yes," the blond responded. "I think. You're Eloel, aren't you?"

She steeled herself. Had the Mashiah sent them after her? Did he know she'd escaped the temple holocaust? "No."

"The hell you aren't. I know you from the spectrum prints." The marine fingered the trigger of his rifle.

She clamped her trembling jaw. They had prints? But the rebel faction had been so careful. Behind her, she heard Sybil wail softly, barely audible. Terror flooded her veins. She'd witnessed what the planetary marines did to children of the Old Believers. Seen with her own eyes their tiny bodies explode in flares of violet.

"Look!" Rachel shouted, stepping forward. "I don't know who you think I am, but I'm a loyal follower of the Mashiah. What do think you're doing, hunting down innocent citizens—"

"If you're so innocent, what're you doing hiding in this filthy alley?" the sergeant demanded, glancing at the rubbish piled six feet high.

"What would you do if you saw fifty men with guns following you? Stand there so they could use you for target practice?"

Both men stared at her for a time, weighing her story, but she knew they'd balk. She knew it as surely as she did that Shadrach's still-warm body lay dead in the ruined temple. Though she hadn't seen his murder, she'd heard faint cries before she'd grabbed Sybil to run. It had been his voice, an echoing rasping that would haunt her for the rest of her life. She'd made a horrifying choice: her baby over her husband. Why hadn't she gone back to see? Maybe he . . . But no, no, she couldn't let herself think that.

"Hey, Charlie," the blond whispered, licking his lips eagerly. "Let's have some fun before we turn her in, huh? Just fifteen minutes of play."

"Don't be an idiot. The Mashiah would cut you to pieces for something like that."

"Damn, Charlie, he won't know. Nobody'll ever find out. Less you spill your—"

"Shut up, damn you, Joe! I'm no informer!"

18

The two men dropped their voices to whispers. Rachel strained to hear. Was Charlie trying to talk him out of it? Something in that low interchange of words made her throat go tight, fear rising up like a chill, ever-swelling bubble to choke her.

"We'll have to kill her if we . . ."

In the long moment of waiting that ensued, Rachel studied a shaft of rose-amber light that crept down the gray stones to her right. At midday, the sun on Horeb gleamed like fire. She turned ever so slightly, desperately wanting to make certain her daughter couldn't see what was about to happen. Silently, she prayed. *Don't let her see, God. Please, I'll do anything you want!*

The blond smiled and leered at Rachel, stepping forward. "Come here, beauty. Don't make this difficult now. I won't take long and I get mean when women give me trouble."

"I—I'm not going to give you any trouble."

"That's the right idea." He pointed to a broad doorway with a thick mat. "Why don't you just go lie down over there and get comfortable."

She surveyed the doorway. It stood in the ruined cleft of an old bakery. The faint aroma of bread still clung to the stones, and it was only five feet from the corner to the street. If she ran, she might be able to distract them long enough for Sybil to get away. "I'm going," she murmured, preparing to run.

"Wait!" He grabbed her shoulder. Swinging her around, he prodded her belly so hard with his rifle, she doubled over. "Not so fast. You walk real easy, remembering I'm right here behind you."

Gasping in pain, she forced herself to shuffle to the mat. He followed so closely she could smell his stale sweat and the coppery odor of the blood that covered his uniform. *Shadrach's blood?* Or some other friend?

When they reached the mat, he brutally shoved her against the wall, ordering, "Put your hands against the door and spread. I'm going to have to search you first, honey. We've heard about you and your fancy training. So, you just be still if you plan on living to stand trial before the Mashiah."

He carefully leaned his rifle against the stone wall and reached for her. She stiffened as his grimy hands roamed her body, his smile widening.

"All right. Turn back around."

She made it halfway before he slammed a fist into

her temple, knocking her to the mat. Rachel stifled a moan. He unclipped his belt and pulled his pants to his knees before jerking up her robe and forcibly prying her legs wide. The sound of ripping fabric rang like thunder in her ears. She lay still as he dropped on top of her. Turning her head away, she concentrated on the feel of the cool mat against her cheek. *Hurry . . . Hurry . . .*

He fondled her breasts, then dropped his hands lower, thrusting his fingers brutally inside her. She shuddered, gritting her teeth.

"Okay, baby, the moment you been waiting all your life for," he whispered, laughing. Spreading her labia with his hands, he drove himself inside, grunting. "Oh, yes, that's sweet. You follow my rhythms now, match me."

She lay still, unable to will herself to comply.

"Do it!" He slapped her hard across the face.

A sob welled to catch in her throat. She forced her body to move beneath him.

"Good, that's good." In only a few moments, he panted, moving faster.

From near the street, the sergeant hissed suddenly, "God damn! Get up, Joe. There's somebody coming."

"Not yet. I'm almost *there*, man. Almost—"

"You bastard! It looks like the Mashiah's personal guards, for God's sake! They're dressed in gray. If they find us with you—"

"Ten seconds! That's all I need to . . ."

The sergeant stepped out of the alley and into the street, voice unusually loud as he talked blithely with another man only thirty feet away.

"Have you captured any of the rebels, sergeant?" an unknown man asked.

"No, sir. We haven't seen any of them. We've been patrolling since the raid this morning. Those that lived must have run off to the mountains."

Hope welled hotly in Rachel. One against one now. She glared at the blond. Sweat streaked his face, running down his neck. *Wait!* she commanded herself. Wait until he's the most vulnerable. Finally, he worked himself into a frenzy and started to gasp. When she felt his semen pulse into her vagina, Rachel lifted her right hand and drove her fingers into his closed eyes, crushing his lachrymals, blinding him. The soldier jerked back powerfully and started to scream. Rachel slammed a fist into his throat, rolled from beneath him, and with all the strength she could muster, kicked him in the head. He toppled backward, gasping, barely audible, "*Cha . . .*"

She lunged for the rifle and, gripping it in her fist, ran for her daughter.

The blinded marine finally managed to rasp, "God . . . God!"

"Joe?" The sergeant burst back into the alley. His eyes widened in horror at the blood streaming in rivulets down his friend's face.

Rachel aimed the pulse-rifle and fired, cutting him in half, then swept right, slicing off the blond's head. It rolled as though animate to rock against the bakery wall.

Where was the other man? The one the sergeant had been talking to? Had he gone to muster his forces? She felt the urge to run and check the street, but instead, shouted, "Sybil? Hurry, come to me!"

A thudding of knees and elbows against boxes sounded as the girl shoved through the rubbish to race to her mother. "Mommy! Mommy! I thought—"

"Take my hand, baby. Hurry!" Rachel slung her rifle and swiftly dragged the little girl up the alley. Turning down a worn horse path littered with dung, she ducked through a smashed doorway to pick her path swiftly across a floor covered with broken chairs and shattered colored vases. Glass squealed beneath her boots.

Sybil had begun to cry, a sharp suffocating series of sounds. "Stop it!" Rachel ordered sternly.

"I want to go home."

"I—I know you do. So do I, but we have to go away for a few days."

"Where?"

"To the mountains, if we can. They won't look for us in that maze of twisted rock."

"Will Daddy come, too?"

"Yes, he'll . . . he'll come."

Reaching the far side of the house, Rachel cautiously peered through a cracked window, examining the street outside. It led through the industrial part of town where empty factories loomed large. In the distance, she glimpsed the sandstone cliffs and a tendril of relief wound through her. Their jagged peaks pierced the pale blue skies like ruby lances. The Mashiah would never find them there. He hadn't the manpower to mount such a search.

21

"Hurry, Sybil. We have to go fast now."

"Okay, Mommy." Sybil lifted her arms to be taken.

Rachel picked her daughter up and braced her on her left hip. The girl buried her face in her mother's hair and sobbed silently. Rachel unslung the rifle, lowering it to firing position before she slipped out the doorway and ran onto the street, heading for the farm country that led to the mountains.

The sudden hissing of charged rifles exploded around her. She whirled to see six soldiers kneeling in gashed doorways, guns aimed. Beside the closest one stood Ornias, High Councilman of Horeb and intimate of the Mashiah. He served as Adom's brains, feeling the pulse of their religious movement and orchestrating events to encourage or discourage opinion. He'd come to Horeb only five years ago, claiming Gamant ancestry, but she doubted it. He had no knowledge of many of the most important ceremonies and cared even less to see them preserved. But he knew one facet of Gamant belief: Prophecies of the Deliverer. He knew it and had used it like a sword to slice out his own wealth and power. He'd taken a gangly man in rags who preached of a new god from the garbage dumps on the streets, and made him the glorious Mashiah promised in scripture. Adom Kemar Tartarus stood as Ornias' finest creation.

Her heart nearly stopped as she met his cold, lime green eyes. A tall, handsome man with light brown hair, his neatly braided beard vibrated as he laughed. "Put down the weapon, Rachel. You know it's hopeless."

She aimed the barrel at his stomach, knees so weak she could barely stand. "I'd rather die than—"

"Be realistic. Look at your beautiful little girl. Hmm? Do you want her dead, too?"

Rachel clutched Sybil closer, feeling her daughter's breath warm against her shoulder. Slowly, she backed away, steps grating on the loose gravel.

Ornias smiled maliciously. Wind whipped his white silk robe around his legs. "Sergeant? Please set your rifle on narrow beam and aim at the child."

"Mommy?" Sybil murmured tightly in her ear and Rachel felt her daughter's muscles go rigid, anticipating the shot.

"Come, come, Rachel. Will you kill everyone who loves you? First your father, then your mother—"

"My mother died in the plague!"

"Well, then, just your father, husband, and daughter. Isn't that too many for even your precious conscience?"

Tears of hatred blurred her eyes. Husband? So, it was true. Shadrach . . . Desperation and futility swept her. *Where are you, God!* Violently, she threw her rifle on the dusty red ground.

Ornias motioned for one of the soldiers to retrieve the weapon. Once it was out of the way, he chastised, "I told you a month ago you'd never get away with your treasonous rituals. Now, you've left me no choice."

"What are you going to do?"

"I'll have to take care of you and your rebel followers once and for all." He stroked his beard, smiling. "For the good of Horeb, you understand."

"You—you'd better make damn sure I'm dead, Ornias. Because if not, I'll find you and when I do—"

"A threat, dear?" The arrogance drained from his tanned face, replaced by anger. "Lieutenant Simon, march her to the square with the others. You know your duties?"

The dark-haired officer nodded. "I do, sir."

"Good." The councilman turned in a whirl of white and strode away.

Simon pointed with his rifle. "You heard the man. Move."

Rachel lowered Sybil to the ground and they walked, hand in hand down the windswept street. The stench struck her first. The air reeked of fear-sweat and death. Rachel clutched Sybil's hand tighter as they crested the ridge above the square. A public gathering place, it stretched six hundred by four hundred feet. Red and gray sandstone slabs had been arranged in geometric patterns to form the twelve-foot-high walls that completely encircled the area.

Rachel swallowed hard at the number of armed guards patrolling the walls. Each dressed in battle armor, their silver helmets gleaming in the sun.

The lieutenant stepped ahead of her, trotting to the gate and swinging it open. "Go on. Hurry up."

Rachel walked forward only to stop, stunned, when she saw inside. Hundreds of people packed the square, standing shoulder to shoulder. No one could sit. Children cried everywhere, mothers and fathers impotent to heal the wounds of thirst or hunger. And many of the people were plague victims. Oozing wounds gaped from their arms and faces, rotting flesh hanging in black strips from their torn clothing.

23

Lieutenant Simon prodded her with his rifle barrel. "I said, go!"

She turned on him, stuttering, "H–how long have these people been here?"

"That's no concern of yours."

"They can't even breathe in there!"

"You brought it on yourselves."

She stared in disbelief. *Is this some nightmare, God? What have we done to anger you so?* "Have you lost your humanity? These people are your relatives! Look over there—"

He turned his face away, deliberately shielding himself. "Anyone who turns against the promised Deliverer is no relative of mine. Get inside before I shoot you like a dog."

"Deliverer?" she scoffed, on the verge of hysteria. "Who has he saved? You? Your family?" She stabbed a shaking finger at the crowd in the square. *"Who?"*

"You haven't much time, Eloel." He shifted his aim to Sybil. "Inside!"

Rachel gazed hollowly at him, then gripped her daughter's hand and walked through the gate. Simon locked it behind her.

For two days they stood, tortured by thirst, the brutal sun searing their flesh. People went mad, screaming and lashing out at anyone who unknowingly pressed against them, trying to maintain their slim boundary of space. The sick and elderly, too feeble to stand, took turns sitting, heads braced on drawn-up knees.

Sybil clutched Rachel's leg like a life raft in a turbulent ocean. Her tiny lips had swollen so severely, she could barely speak. Rachel stroked her matted hair, wondering how much longer the Mashiah would force them to suffer. Many of the children and the old were already dead, their bodies hauled to a stinking pile against the east wall. Every time the burning wind changed direction to bring her the scent of rotting corpses, bile rose into her throat and she had to drape her sleeve over her nose.

Yet, for all her horror and despair, hate kept her standing, fired her soul with hope. Her mind worked in a flurry, planning the Mashiah's murder. It would be slow, agonizing—ten times worse than the anguish they now experienced.

Adom rarely appeared in public, and then only when thoroughly protected by guards. And always, *always*, with Ornias. But she'd find him vulnerable someday.

"Oh, God. Misha? Misha!" A withered old man moaned.

24

Tall and whip-thin, he stood only a few feet from Rachel, his eyes fixed intently on the ground. Sparse gray hair hung down over his ears. Rachel tried to pry her eyes away, but couldn't.

A young woman with cropped brown hair stood beside him, patting his hand. "There, there, Daddy. Misha went away to fight in the war with the Underground. It's all right.

"Did he?"

"Yes, Papa. Don't worry. It'll only make things worse. I'll move over a little. Why don't you try to sit down?"

But by late afternoon, the old man had gone out of his mind. He screamed, "Gamants, I see a sea of blood rolling down over us! A sea of burning blood! Don't you see it?" He lanced out an arm toward the mountains, wide eyes burning with hysteria. "Oh, dear God, dear God, we can't escape!"

A rumble of shouts and screams sounded as people staggered, pushing each other, straining to look where he pointed. When they discovered only mountains and sky, they turned sharply, staring.

"Can't you see it? What's the matter with you?" He fell to the ground, covering his head and writhing as though in the throes of an epileptic fit.

At first people only stood quietly, riveted by terror, but as his wailing grew to hideous shrieks, someone shouted, "Stop him! I can't stand it!"

"It's rolling down! See it fill the sky, the wave rises so high!"

His daughter dropped to the ground beside him, stroking his hair tenderly, "Daddy, please. Hush, it's all right. There's no sea of blood. You're just tired and—"

"Oh, my God! Pity! Have pity!"

"He'll drive us all mad!" an old crone wailed. "Don't let him talk!"

The young woman tried to calm her father, bringing his head to her lap and rocking him gently. "Papa, stop twisting, you'll use up your strength. You have to save your strength or you'll die like little Tommy. You—"

"Can't you see it?" he asked in an agonized whisper.

"The sky's empty, Daddy. Just a few clouds, that's all. There's nothing else there."

Still the old man screamed breathlessly. "What's the matter with you all? Gamants! The wave comes from the Magistrates. They've sent it to destroy us! To burn Horeb to a cinder and us with it! No! NO!"

25

"I don't care if you have to kill him," a straggly-bearded youth shouted. "Keep him quiet!"

A group of boys jerked the old man from his daughter's lap and clamped hands over his mouth, but he continued to shriek through their bruising fingers. Wordless cries of horror, his ancient eyes fixed on the silent blue sky.

"Make him stop! Make him stop!"

The boys slapped the old man until he sat quietly, knees pulled against his frail chest, eyes scouring the vacant heavens. His daughter gathered him in her arms protectively, sobbing, "Don't hurt him anymore! The Mashiah killed the rest of our family. He's crazy from the pain. He doesn't know what he's saying!"

Rachel glanced around the packed square. Terror lined every face, madness about to burst the very walls enclosing them. Trembling from fatigue and panic, people shifted uneasily, glaring at each other. Soon, they'd all be crazy enough to kill for a breath of silence, a slim boundary of space.

"We're losing our minds," a young man in a torn brown robe said uncomfortably to Rachel. "It . . . it must be the heat."

"Yes, the heat."

When nightfall came, fights broke out, people struggling to find sleeping positions. Rachel remained standing, letting Sybil sleep between her spread feet. In the distance, the jagged peaks of the mountains changed from red to indigo. She tried to imagine herself there, safe in one of the thousands of caves that honeycombed the hills. She dreamt of finding a spring where she could sit and let the cool water flow over her endlessly, of cupping her hands beneath it and letting Sybil drink as much as she could hold.

Then, in the middle of the night, when the stars gleamed like a sequined shawl thrown over the heavens, a wrenching scream set a jolt of shock through her. In the dim starglow, she saw the the old man stand up and stretch his arm toward the dark peaks. His hair jutted out at odd angles, making him look like a half-dead demon from the pit of darkness.

"Look! *The sea of blood!* It swallows our children! Oh, my God, my God, what have we done to deserve such punishment?"

Rachel stared at the starry sky, trying to force her thoughts from the horrifying prediction. The words pierced clear to her soul. A crack sounded in the darkness, followed by another and another. Boys grabbed him by the sleeves and threw him to the ground.

"Why can't you see it? It's the battle cruiser that caused it! And it's so close! Can't you—"

"For God's sake, shut him up! We've got to get some sleep!"

The sound of ripping fabric shredded the night and Rachel turned to see one of the boys tying the cloth into a knot and stuffing it in the old man's mouth, while another tied his hands. He struggled pitifully, choking.

His daughter stroked his shoulder in mute agony.

Rachel squeezed her eyes closed. Would the night never end? *"Lord of the Universe, why won't you have mercy on us?"* She put a hand over her mouth as silent, dry sobs choked her.

"Ma . . . Mommy," Sybil said, patting her mother's leg soothingly. "Don't cry. Why are you crying?"

Rachel slumped to the ground, squeezing tightly between two men and one woman, to hug her daughter.

"Get up, damn you! There's no room!" A man cursed and pounded her back, but she huddled against the beating, refusing to rise. Her legs were suddenly too weak to hold her.

"Don't hit my mommy!" Sybil shrieked, using her tiny fists to weakly flail at his leg.

In defeat, the man lifted his hands, muttering. "All right. For now."

Sybil crawled into Rachel's lap, slipping her arms around her neck. "Don't cry, Mommy. Here, I'll pat you to sleep." Her daughter extended a tired, dirty hand to pat her back. "It's all right, Mommy. Don't—"

"Shhh, sweetheart," she sobbed, stroking Sybil's tangles. "You're the one who must sleep. Tomorrow might be worse. We have to save our strength."

"But you have to sleep, too."

"All right, I'll try. Close your eyes now."

"Let's close them together," Sybil instructed, watching Rachel through one slitted eye until she closed her lids. Then her daughter relaxed into a tiny heap in her arms.

Rachel rocked Sybil back and forth as cold grew up around them. Outside the square, wind moaned like banshees roaming through the stone cold streets.

Her soul cried out as she watched a huge night bird land on the body of a child only six feet away and begin plucking

27

flesh from its stiff body. Flapping wings sent a chill breeze to brush her hair. She hadn't known the boy; still a fit of uncontrollable shuddering overtook her, as though the bestial wind were the last breath of one of her own loved ones.

Looking up, she noticed the guards on the walls. In the silver wash of starlight, their helmets shone a ghostly gray.

CHAPTER 2

A hunched figure in a worn black suit, Zadok Calas' boots pounded a steady cadence on the damp path. The leader of Gamant civilization, he was a very old man, his skin leathery and dark from centuries of enduring the tortuous winds of barely habitable planets. His fleshy nose hooked over broad lips, accenting the black eyes that constantly searched the trees. Cliffs towered like silent sentinels over the path. Torchlight, taunted by the cool night breeze, flickered from their jagged edges.

He gazed admiringly at the stars. On holy days they seemed to flare brighter. A warmth built in his bony chest, a warmth spawned by memories and the tiny hand tucked in his own. He patted the boy's fingers lovingly.

"Are you warm enough, Mikael? This wind has a chill—"

"Yes, grandfather. I'm always warm during Sighet." The seven-year-old looked up. His brown eyes glowed like full moons. Small and awkward for his age, the boy stepped carefully through the darkness, occasionally glancing at the torch-lit line of people weaving through the forested hills behind.

Zadok smiled as they crested a ridge, looking at the huge cave tucked into the side of the cliffs below. Soft golden light streamed from the entrance, dappling through the trees to throw patchwork shadows across the ground.

"Grandfather?"

"What is it, Mikael?"

"Can I touch the *Mea Shearim*?"

"Someday you can touch it. Not yet."

"But you said you'd give it to me when I got to be old enough. Why can't I just—"

28

"I've told you why. Don't you remember?" Zadok tugged his hand and they started down the hill.

Mikael lowered his gaze to stare at the moist earth passing beneath his feet. "I remember, but—"

"I thought you did."

"The *Mea* is like a thousand gates, isn't it, Grandfather?"

"That's what we think the old words mean," Zadok answered. "Because there are a thousand paths leading to the orchard of Truth. But each *Mea* is a single gate." He patted his chest where the object lay warm and comforting.

Darkness deepened around them, moonlight tarnishing the trunks of the trees and the curving branches overhead. Mikael edged closer to Zadok, childishly fingering the threadbare fabric of his black sleeve.

"Grandfather," he said very softly. "Grandfather?"

He gave the boy a searching look. Mikael was persistent. Once he asked something, he never let it go. "I'm listening."

"Maybe you could just let me look at it?"

"Later, all right?"

"Maybe now and then I wouldn't have to remember to ask again later."

"You think you might forget?"

"Sometimes it happens." Mikael stared morosely at him, eyes tight with longing.

Zadok suppressed a smile and tried to look stern, but relented after a few moments, pulling the chain out of his white shirt. Kneeling in the wet grass, he swung the globe for Mikael to look at. The tiny blue ball glowed of its own inner light. The line of people veered around them, other children pointing excitedly.

Mesmerized, Mikael unconsciously reached out. Violent swirls eddied across the surface of the *Mea Shearim*. Zadok gripped the tiny fingers firmly, keeping them away. "You want Epagael to find you so soon?"

"God already knows where I am, Grandfather. You told me so."

"Yes, but he'd want to talk to you if you touched this."

"I want to talk to God."

"You just think you do. He's not as friendly as most people imagine." He tucked the sacred object back into his shirt. Mikael watched intently.

"I know how to use the *Mea*, did you know that, Grandfather?"

"Do you?"

29

"Yes," Mikael blurted excitedly. "You have to find all of yourself *inside*—" he tapped his forehead, "—and then you have to put the *Mea* to your head and send yourself through."

"Usually, but sometimes God reaches out and grabs you when you least expect it. That's why you can't play with it. God always thinks you're serious when you pick the *Mea* up."

Mikael nodded, licking his lips. "Grandfather, tell me again about how the sky used to be filled with *Meas*? And how the Magistrates came and got them all and put them—"

"You have more important stories to think about tonight. Like Edom Middoth and the Exile."

"Did all the other *Meas* go to God, too?"

Zadok sighed. "The legends say that some did and some didn't. But since ours is the only one left, nobody really knows anymore. Now, you think about the Exile."

"But," Mikael halted, deciding, then gave in. "Okay, tell me about Middoth."

"You can't wait to hear it from Rev Bahir?"

"No, please tell me."

He smoothed the child's curly black hair and smiled. Rising, he took the boy's hand and started walking again. "All right, but only just a little. Otherwise, I'll spoil the Sighet celebration for you."

"Just a little." The boy beamed.

Zadok took a breath and his voice grew deeper. "Long, long ago, in the days of the Tranquillity, our people lived on one planet, a blue world of immense beauty. Then one day—"

"Edom Middoth came!"

"I thought you wanted me to tell this story?"

"Don't be difficult, Grandfather," Mikael mimed his mother Sarah's voice and it made Zadok laugh.

"I'm never difficult."

"But you know I want you to tell me about Jekutiel. About how she used her *Mea* to rescue us during the Exile. How she flew to God and He gave her ships out of a whirlwind and a huge pillar of fire led her to the planet where our people—"

"Ah, the *Mea* again. I think you know the old stories better than I do. Why don't you tell me what happened?"

"Oh, Grandpa. Please," Mikael pleaded, eyes lingering on the bump in Zadok's shirt. "You tell me. Like you do every year."

"I should be glad you want to know," Zadok said half to himself. "Not very many people do anymore." A sad reverie came over him. Most Gamant children were stolen away to be trained in Magisterial "Right Schools" before they could be taught the truths of the past. Mind probes turned children against their parents and friends, forced them to believe the facts of Gamant history and religion were false.

Zadok frowned, an ache invading his ancient chest. Though some thought the *Mea* was the real sacrament of Gamant religion, he knew it was "history." The *Mea* served as a sacrament only to the Gamant leader, leading him face to face with Epagael. But for the rest of the people, history took the place of the *Mea*. Through history the people saw the face of God and endured. All the words, deeds, thoughts and emotions of history were the bread and wine of the sacrament, which the touch of God—through the *Mea*—transformed into both the symbol and instrument of his Grace for all time. It was that Grace that the Magistrates stole from Gamant children by erasing the stories of history from their young minds.

Zadok looked tiredly around him, surveying the dark cliffs and starry sky. "That's why we live here in the caves, isn't it, Mikael? To protect you."

"You mean . . ." The boy asked in confusion, "You mean because Middoth made our people slaves and Jekutiel had to save them?"

"Oh, no, I was thinking something else, but you're right about that. That's another reason we live here, secluded from other citizens of the galaxy."

Zadok stopped as they rounded a corner. A deep baritone lifted powerfully from within the temple, drifting on the chill breeze to caress him like the hand of God. Squeezing Mikael's tiny fingers, he plodded forward.

People milled around outside the cavern, laughing and talking. Zadok's heart warmed. During great festivals, Gamants came from all over the galaxy to participate. Every year it seemed as though some long lost relative appeared out of nowhere.

"Papa?" Zadok's eldest daughter smiled and waved as she saw them approaching. A tall woman with long black hair and huge brown eyes, her silver robe fluttered in the wind. Her husband Mark and others stood clustered around her, smiling.

31

"My pride overflows," he praised, striding forward to gently stroke her cheek. Ezarin had risen through the ranks to the esteemed position of Rev, memorizing the precious ancient texts that had survived the holocausts of the past.

She lovingly kissed his bald head, then extended a hand to an old woman standing slightly behind her. "Papa, you remember Cousin Shoshi Mekilta?"

Zadok squinted at her. Hunched with age, the woman had straw colored hair pulled into a tight bun at the base of her skull. Her nose stuck out like a sharp dart point. "Elma's daughter?"

"Of course, you old fool," the woman growled.

"My Lord. I thought you were dead."

Shoshi's brittle cackle echoed from the cliffs. "You mean you hoped. I still haven't forgotten the time you cheated me out of my life's savings."

"You have a memory like the government. That was two hundred years ago."

She shook a crooked finger at him. "I don't forget easily. I'm a—"

"And thirty notes were your life's savings? You obviously didn't plan on living this long."

When Shoshi's face puckered hostilely, Ezarin quickly said, "Excuse me, Cousin Shoshi. Papa? You must sing tonight."

He grimaced at the interruption. He'd been enjoying bantering with Shoshi. "I'm too old to sing."

"He's too old to do *anything*," Shoshi added and snickered when Zadok's eyes narrowed.

"You're an old maid. How would know you what a man of my years is capable of!"

"Papa!" Ezarin blurted, suppressing a laugh. "Samual is ill. Someone must take his place."

"You have a lovely voice."

"You told me my voice sounded like cats screeching."

"And the last time you talked me into singing, half the congregation mysteriously went home early. I'm not going to embarrass myself—"

"I think I was at that ceremony," Shoshi sighed grimly. "Don't make him sing."

"I'm not going to sing!" he declared defensively. "Where's Hector?"

"His voice isn't as rich as yours."

"Ah, so he's here. He'll sing for Samual," Zadok declared and perfunctorily straightened the lapels of his black suit, ignoring her as though the discussion were closed.

Ezarin crossed her arms and squinted at him. "You're as hardheaded as a—"

"A rock," Shoshi said helpfully. "He has the brains of a rock."

"And you're a dictator just like your mother," Zadok spoke to Ezarin, ignoring his cousin. But at the mention of his beloved Nelda, his wrath and discomfort faded. *Nelda.* He squeezed his eyes closed, heart thudding dully in his chest. A brave and high-spirited woman, she'd been captured by galactic marines in the last Gamant Revolt, then raped and tortured for days before being thrown unceremoniously on his doorstep, her abdomen torn to reveal gangrenous intestines. He'd held her in his arms for four hours before she died.

"Papa," Ezarin comforted softly, seeing the path of his thoughts. "Mama wouldn't want you to—"

"Oh, I'm . . . I'm not, really."

They stood in awkward silence a moment, then Mikael wrapped an arm around Zadok's leg. "Let's go see Rev Bahir, Grandfather. I want to hear about Jekutiel."

"Yes, it's time, isn't it?"

Mikael nodded.

Turning back to Ezarin, he clarified, "You find Hector and tell him I said he's to sing for Samual."

"All right, Papa," Ezarin said and laughed. Her long hair danced in the cool wind sweeping down the canyon. "I'll find him. Go on, I'll meet you inside."

"I'm relieved," Shoshi exclaimed.

Zadok scowled at her, then winked warmly at Ezarin before leading his grandson through the rounded cave entrance. A hundred and forty-four candles glowed in the candelabras dotting the cinnamon walls of the temple. They cast flickering shadows over the fifty-foot-high ceiling. Lines of stone benches filled the huge room, creating a center aisle which led to a raised triangular altar two hundred feet ahead. The stone floors were strewn haphazardly with dozens of ancient rugs. Worn now with age, the brilliant colors had faded. People filed endlessly into the temple to take seats, their hushed conversations creating a pleasant hum.

Zadok guided Mikael to an aisle seat in the back. "Can you see?"

The boy leaned sideways to gaze up the aisle, then nodded vigorously. "Yes, this is a good seat."

"Wonderful. I want you to remember this day. This is the thousand year celebration of the freeing of our people." Mikael nodded and Zadok wrapped an arm lovingly over the boy's tiny shoulders and hugged him.

Ezarin entered and sat snugly beside them, face glowing.

A hush fell over the temple as Rev Bahir walked to take his place at the altar. Dressed in a long black robe adorned with silver fringes, he looked regal. A bowlegged, grizzled little man with a long kinky beard and raven hair, Bahir had a broad toothy smile. A huge golden triangle hung suspended from the chain around his neck. After clearing his throat several times to gain silence, he extended a hand to the worshipers.

"Good people, we come together this Shabbat night to celebrate the freeing of our People from the terrible tyranny of Edom Middoth who stole our forebears from their homes on distant Earth and carried them off to be slaves."

The crowd responded, "Let the name of the Lord be blessed this time forth and forever more."

"We come to praise the name of Jekutiel, the Cassopian queen who liberated our ancestors a thousand years ago, who gave them food and healed the terrible wounds inflicted by Middoth's brutal followers." Bahir's voice increased in volume to boom through the rocky temple.

"Let the name of Jekutiel be blessed forever and to all eternity."

"May her name be praised and extolled, exalted and honored as the great tool of Epagael. The tool that conquered wickedness." Bahir raised a fist and it cast a huge dark shadow against the wall behind him, wavering in the candlelight. "It was Jekutiel who destroyed Aktariel's evil emissary, Middoth."

A shiver played along Zadok's spine, a shiver of memories, of ancient stories, a longing that this feeling of community might last forever. He stole glances at the people around him. Their faces gleamed with faith and reverence, particularly Ezarin's.

"He who makes peace in the high places, may he make peace for us and for all Gamants. Amayne."

At the mention of Aktariel, Mikael's breathing quickened. Zadok patted him gently on the back. Leaning down, he asked, "What's wrong?"

"Aktariel's a wicked angel who fell from heaven."

"Yes, very wicked. He comes to deceive and destroy us."

34

Mikael shifted positions, getting on his knees so he could get closer to Zadok's face. "And he'll send another emissary, won't he, Grandfather? Like Middoth. He'll come and—"

"No." Zadok frowned. Where could the child have gotten such a notion? He'd have to check on those Shabbat Boker religious teachers and their lessons. "No, don't worry. Middoth was the last, Mikael. The old books tell us that now the true Mashiah will come to rescue us from the brutality of the Galactic Magistrates."

"But I think maybe Aktariel himself might come, Grandfather. What if—"

"Shhh." Zadok stroked his dark hair, but the boy's words wrought a pang from his heart. "Don't think such things, Mikael. God would not punish us so."

"But what if it's a final test?"

"We've had too many tests already, Grandson. Surely Epagael knows our faith by now."

Mikael dropped his gaze, confusion on his face. "But maybe not."

"Believe me. You don't have to worry. Remember, I've talked to Epagael and He never mentioned—"

"I had a dream last night, Grandfather. In it Aktariel swooped down and . . ."

A shuffling of feet came from the cave entrance outside and a man entered the temple. The gold stitching of his long robe reflected the light, glistening as if he were sprinkled with filaments of fire. His white hair and closely cropped beard accented his pointed nose. The stranger's eyes searched the temple meticulously, going over each candle-lit section of the crowded pews. As he turned, Zadok recognized him.

"Rathanial?" he called softly, waving a withered hand.

"Zadok, thank God." Sliding in beside Ezarin, Rathanial formed his hands into the sacred triangle of greeting, which Zadok matched.

"Old friend, how good to see you at this celebration. It's been so long—"

"Zadok, we must talk immediately." Fear stained his withered face, a hard glitter in his black eyes. "A new Mashiah has arisen on Horeb and we're—"

"Another false prophet?" Ezarin quipped sarcastically. "They always start wars. I think they should all be hanged." Standing up, she slid out in front of Rathanial. "Excuse me, I have a grand entrance to make."

Zadok smiled warmly, watching her leave. "Getting back to your subject, Rathanial. Do I take it things are not well on Horeb?"

Rathanial exhaled heavily. "Not well at all. The new Mashiah is gaining popularity. The planet is under siege from within. We've—".

"Under siege?"

"Yes, a rebel faction has arisen and—"

Rev Bahir's voice rose suddenly, repeating for the third time, "I will sing unto the Eternal for he hath manifested loving kindness unto me!"

Zadok held up a hand to halt Rathanial's recitation and looked toward the door. The words were Ezarin's cue to begin the Psalm of Thanksgiving. Where was she?

Bahir scratched his beard and leaned sideways to peer out the cave entrance. All eyes followed his, waiting. A din of whispering voices filled the temple.

"Excuse me," Zadok said, and slid out to the aisle.

"Zadok," Rathanial said tightly. "We must talk now, this can't wait—"

"In just a moment," he said apologetically, then called to Mikael's mother, "Sarah?" His youngest daughter stood near the front of the temple. She turned and Zadok prompted: "Jubilate unto the Eternal all regions of the galaxy. Serve the Eternal in gladness . . ." He motioned for her to continue the Psalm. A plump young woman with a round face and black hair, she instantly picked up Ezarin's part, "Come into his presence with joyous song. Know that the Eternal is God . . ."

Zadok strolled out of the temple. Above the peaks, the third moon rose through a layer of mist, casting a milky light on the tall pines. "Ezarin?" he called softly. "Ezarin?"

When no answer came, he walked farther out into the darkness. A bitter chill rode the wind, each gust like a knife through his thin suit. Where could she have gone? It wasn't like her to miss any part of a major ceremony. Even when sick, she'd pull herself out of bed just long enough to say or sing her part. She was a good girl, more like her mother than Sarah, with those slanting brown eyes and crooked smile.

Zadok stopped. A dark patch marred the dirt trail, glowing blackly in the moonlight. For one short instant it was as though the moon had ducked behind a cloud, leaving the world in pitch blackness. The fresh green grass looked sickly, the new leaves of spring dotting the trees like autumn's final fading remnants.

He knelt to touch it. His fingers came back warm and red.

"Ezarin!"

He clamped hands over his eyes as images of another Sighet day overwhelmed him—his mother's funeral. He stood once more at the graveside, fingers twined securely with his father's. The old man's tears dripped in a steady silent stream down his chin to trickle coolly onto Zadok's arm. "Blessed art thou the Eternal," he kept sobbing.

Yosef, Zadok's brother, pushed closer to him, whispering, "Aunt Selah says Grandmother died the same way." But Zadok had been too young to understand. Though he'd gone with the search party, he'd been too far back to see his mother when they'd found her. And no one had told him how she'd died, only that she had and he needed to lay out his finest suit and fast. He'd spent three agonizing days learning the Mourner's Kedis. The words were difficult for him: "Magnified and sanctified be his great name in the world."

A night bird cawed in the forest. He jerked to look and saw a gray weabit hop beneath a bush, fur shimmering in the ghostly light. He stood starkly still for a moment, then the muscles of his withered jaw quivered and he began running back down the path toward the habitation caves.

"Ezarin? *Ezarin, answer me!*"

CHAPTER 3

. . . when a widow reigns over the whole world and throws gold and silver into the wondrous brine and casts the bronze and iron of ephemeral men into the sea, then all the elements of the universe will be bereft. When God who dwells in the sky rolls up the heaven as a scroll . . . an undying cataract of raging fire will flow, and burn earth, burn sea, and melt the heavenly vault . . .

The Sibylline Oracles: Book III
Date: 163 B.C. Old Earth Standard

37

Rachel leaned her head tiredly against the stone wall and stared vacantly at a bird soaring on the wind currents overhead. Beneath her drawn up knees, hidden and shaded by her sweat-stained blue robe, Sybil lay in a deep sleep. Rachel let her leaden arm drop to gently pat the little girl's exposed toes. The furnace temperatures of the afternoon, rather than lessening with the coming of evening, changed to a stagnant smothering heat that sapped what little strength they had left.

A gust of wind whipped across the walls, peppering Rachel's face with coarse grains of sand. No one moaned, no one moved. A deadly hush had fallen over the square, as though every prisoner held his breath. When would He come? When?

She let her thoughts drift blissfully to Shadrach and the pleasant days of their youth. They'd met in a secret history course taught by the Gamant Underground. Nonapproved classes were condemned by the Magistrates. Teachers and students sentenced to death. From their first argument over the role of revolution in everyday life, he'd drawn her to him like a moth to flame. His sharp mind and gentle touch were balms on her soul. She'd loved that tall man with the sparse beard and amused eyes.

Her thoughts jumped to three days ago in the temple. Her last image of him was standing at the altar, conducting the Sighet celebration. His bronze hair glinted in the light filtering through the shattered walls. There'd been no amusement in his eyes that day. Worry shadowed his face like a deadly shroud.

She shook her head violently, refusing to see the next few moments of the memory.

From outside the high walls came the monotonous churning of cart wheels on stone and the jingle of a harness.

"Do you think they know we're here?"

She turned weakly to look at the old man. He'd told her his name several times, but still she had to struggle to remember. Talo? Yes, Talo. A big, rawboned man, hairy chested and hard-bitten, his stubble of white beard was reddened with dust. He looked at her through blood-shot sleepless eyes. Beside him, his niece—Myra was her name—stood numbly. Rachel hadn't heard her murmur a single word in two days. All her hope seemed to have died.

"The people outside, I mean," he clarified.

"Of course, they know."

He rubbed a grimy hand over his face. "I can't believe I'm awake. How can our own people allow us to be tortured this way?" He pinched his cheek so hard a white splotch appeared beneath the sunburn. "This must be a terrible nightmare."

"So long as they can turn their heads and no one bothers them, they don't care."

"For three years we've been fighting to keep the old ways, the ways of kindness. And now no one cares what happens to us? Those are our relatives out there!"

As if to reinforce his words, echoes of shod hooves and soft religious singing carried on the wind. Somewhere, a man laughed gaily.

"Are they?"

His eyes roamed her face. "How can you ask such a thing? Of course, they are. Horeb is a Gamant planet. We're all brothers and sisters."

"The world has changed since the coming of the Mashiah. The word 'family' now only applies to those who follow him."

"Being here is evidence of that, but—"

"Today, Talo, even cousins turn their heads."

He fumbled with the tattered hem of his gray sleeve. A stone dove called from somewhere in the burned section of the city. In her mind, Rachel pictured the pearl-colored creature perched precariously on the jagged walls of a ruined building, wind blowing its feathers the wrong way. The bird called again and its lilting mourning cry penetrated clear to her soul.

"Yes, it's the Mashiah," Talo agreed. "He ruins their minds. He has some kind of magic that—"

"He's not a magician. People flock to him because he promises salvation through a new god. Few believe in the old God anymore. He's abandoned us too many times."

"That makes me sad. The only thing we have left is Epagael."

"You still believe? *After this?*"

"Of course. Don't you see? God has to know if we have the faith to conquer the spark of Aktariel within us. It's a test. We've no right to hate God. Like a father punishing his child, every instant of pain has a reason, to teach us something. It's a sign of love. It hurts God as much as it does us."

"God is dead!" she spat bitterly. "The God of love, of Avram, Yeshwah and Sinlayzan has been murdered! *Here, this very day!* If He ever existed." Her heart pounded, listening to herself. Did she believe that? Had the past seventy-two hours trampled her faith to nothingness?

Tears welled in the old man's hard eyes. "Do you know that this torture isn't the greatest horror to the old people who still believe?" He waved a hand at the sweltering square scented with carnage. "No, this passes. The greatest horror is the death of God in the souls of the young. I can endure holocaust, but you losing your faith breaks my heart." He clutched the fabric over his chest.

Rachel didn't answer. Ten feet away, a young girl, perhaps ten, wailed, a pathetically soft and shrill sound. She stood and gripped the feet of her dead brother, trying to drag him to the growing pile of corpses in the far corner of the square. The poor child must have died sometime that morning, for his body had begun to swell miserably in the searing heat. "Move?" the girl begged a cluster of people blocking the way. "Please! I'm not very strong and I have to—"

"Go the other way round. We're too tired to move." A big man waved a weak hand.

She struggled to comply, dragging her brother three feet in the opposite direction. But no one there would move either. All paths stood closed. Finally, in defeat, she dropped back to the ground and buried her face in her brother's dirty shirt to muffle her sobs.

"Yis . . . yisgadal ve'yiskadash sh'mey rabbo," Rachel murmured the beginning of the prayer of death. No one really knew for certain what the ancient words meant anymore. Yet still, they comforted.

Beside her, Talo bowed his head. Tears dripped from his long nose to glisten in his gray beard. "Do you . . . do you say it for the boy? Or for all of us?"

Rachel stared absently. How could he have so much water left after so many days of thirst? It didn't seem possible. Her own tears had dried up long ago.

"They're going to slaughter us," he cried. "You know it too, don't you?"

"Everyone knows it."

"We must *do* something. We can't just let them kill us. What can we do?"

"I don't know."

"We have to do *something*!"

"Like what? Do you want to try and climb the walls? In our weakened condition and against armed guards who can kill a hundred with a single sweep of their guns?"

"I won't just sit here and let them . . ." He blinked back his tears, clamping his jaw to steady it. "I'm going to try. It's better to die from a rifle than endure this slow agony. We're not . . ."

His words were cut short by the hiss of a *samael*, one of the ships of the planetary marines. The black ovoid shape swooped out of the heavens to float ominously over the square, watching. Against the deepening blue of the sky, it seemed a gigantic hovering turtle. Hatred smothered Rachel. Such a strange contrast: The herders and their rickety carts in the streets and this monstrous device of technology. Horeb had never known such science until the coming of the Mashiah. It remained his private reserve.

"Do you think he's in there?" Talo asked, hope widening his eyes. "The Mashiah. Do you—"

"What does it matter?"

"Maybe he thinks we've suffered enough and will let us go. Maybe he's come to—"

Rachel laughed bitterly. "You think God's sent him to save us?"

"Yes . . . yes, that's it. God has finally seen our agony and—"

"Even God turns his head today, Talo. *Even God*. You'll see."

"It's not true!" he shouted angrily, leaning menacingly close. "We're his children. He loves us!" But he sounded like he struggled to convince himself more than her.

Rachel's attention shifted. She squinted at the guards. They'd changed positions. Instead of walking the walls, they stood massed at the far corner. Receiving orders to do what? Behind them, the spires of the mountains shimmered in the heat, the fires of sunset turning them a brilliant maroon.

She closed her eyes. "Be'ol'mo deevro chiroosey—"

"We're not going to die. You'll see. He's come to forgive us."

Rachel shook her head.

"Rebels?" a voice boomed from the *samael*. "Greetings from the Mashiah."

"Dear God, let us go!" Talo shrieked.

A din rose in the square, people screaming for mercy, striking those next to them to drive them far enough away that the Mashiah could see their waving arms and repentant faces. But Rachel knew the voice belonged not to Adom, but to Ornias. She'd heard that breathy coo a thousand times. The *samael* dropped lower, gliding slowly over the mob.

"I'll convert!" a man screamed. "Let me convert to the religion of Milcom!"

"I've seen the Truth! I know the Mashiah is the promised Deliverer. Let me . . ."

Similar wails swelled throughout the prison, people weeping and promising allegiance to Adom Kemar Tartarus if only he would let their children live.

Rachel gazed down at the soft outline of Sybil's legs betrayed beneath the hem of her robe. Was her baby dead? Is that why she didn't move even though a cacophony of shrieks and shouts filled the air? Horrifyingly, she hoped it was so. She didn't want to see what they might do to her only child. "Better dead than made an example of by the Mashiah."

"No," Talo insisted, eyes glistening with tears of hope. "He's going to save us. I feel it. Don't you feel it? God has sent him to release—"

"Witness," Ornias crooned from the black ship, "the power of the Mashiah you have each turned against."

A blinding flash of violet slashed a six foot wide trench into the red soil by the far wall. The human beings who'd been standing there vanished in a crimson splash. Rachel shielded her eyes as dust and debris blasted into the air. *Thank God . . . thank God he's using the ship's weapons rather than letting the marines use their rifles.* Death under the cannons came quickly, painlessly.

Screams eddied through the square, people shoving to get as far from the deadly beams as possible. A thick, choking veil of dust rose. Rachel didn't move, afraid that if she reached down to pick up Sybil the child would be dead and she couldn't bear it. Frightened men and women pushed around her, crowding desperately against the back wall.

In the space created, Rachel saw a boy sitting on the ground next to his dead mother. His eyes stared absently at nothing as he tenderly stroked her stiff hand, murmuring soft words. In the background, guards trotted around the walls, resuming their former positions. Except that this time, their rifles hummed, a slash of sound beneath the wails of terror.

She closed her eyes, every muscle in her body going tense with her last ounce of strength. "Ve'yamlich malchoosy—"

And then the firing began.

The masses panicked, running headlong to avoid the lashing beams of death that panned the square. Several people struck Rachel at once. She threw herself on top of Sybil. People toppled over them and, in horror, Rachel realized the hot liquid drenching her was blood.

The shrill squeals of the rifles continued endlessly, like wails filtering from a half-open door leading to the pit of darkness. After about ten minutes, the bursts of fire went from constant to sporadic. As though anyone living who raised his head became the next target.

Very quietly, Rachel heard Sybil moan, and a wave of relief and despair vied inside her. Alive? Oh, dear God, alive for what purpose? To suffer another two days until the thirst killed them?

"Mom?"

"Lie still."

"Thirsty . . . Mommy."

"You sleep, baby. When you wake up again. I promise, we'll find water." *Yes, we'll find water, if we're alive to crawl.* Surreptitiously, she patted her daughter's arm and gazed upward, through the tangled mass of bodies, to the sky.

A few stars poked through the blanket of the heavens. Brilliant suns floating in a vast void of cold. Rachel laid her head on the warm red earth and tried to sleep.

In the darkness before morning, she awoke, her strength partly renewed, and eased her head up to peer around a corpse's arm at the walls. The desert-scented winds carried the pungency of blood as they brushed her face. In the distance, the moon rose through a dusty haze, a luminous fagot of orange that cast a foreboding light across the peaks. No guards seemed to be present. Perhaps they'd massed somewhere else. Gently, she shook her daughter.

"Sybil? Can you crawl, baby?"

The girl nodded weakly. "Yes, where are we going?"

"To the gate."

Rachel wove her arms between bodies and thrust upward, creating an opening in the black blanket of dead, then quietly, slowly, edged out and pulled Sybil up. The coolness of the night bathed her.

Sybil trembled as she looked around. Her voice came out a hoarse and dreadful whisper. "*I—I can't!* I don't want to touch any . . . anybody—"

"You have to, sweetheart. If we don't get out of here, they'll be back to kill us."

"*No, Mommy! NO!*" she screamed wildly, scratching to get in her mother's lap. Her frantic fingernails tore Rachel's neck and shoulders as she climbed up to hug her neck frantically.

"Listen to me," Rachel said sternly, hugging her close. "Listen to me! Do you want to wait for the guards to come back with their rifles?"

"Mommy, don't make me. *Please!* I—I can't touch . . . *them.*"

Rachel followed Sybil's gaze to the terrified faces frozen in death. Mouths gaped hideously, arms and legs twisting in pleading gestures from the butchery. She patted Sybil's back, trying to soothe her fears. Dear God, had she forgotten what her daughter had been through? "I'm sorry, baby. Mommy's sorry. I'll try to carry you while I crawl. Can you climb on my back and close your eyes?"

"Yes," Sybil whimpered. "Hurry, let's go."

Rachel got to her hands and knees and Sybil scrambled on top, wrapping her arms tightly around Rachel's shoulders. Other people moved in the tangled mass of dead, all heading in the same direction. Feebly, Rachel crawled after them, knees squishing in the bloody clothing she crossed.

Sybil sobbed over and over into her hair, "Mommy, Mommy, Mommy . . ."

"Don't cry, Sybil," she tried to soothe, but her voice came out harsh, gravelly. "We're all right."

"What about Daddy? I saw other people from the temple here. Maybe he's home waiting for us?"

Rachel felt as though her heart would burst. Cold sorrow drowned her. "Maybe, sweetheart."

She braced one hand against the grisly leg of a dead woman who'd been cut in half by the beams, and scanned the square. Why were the guards gone? Had the Mashiah decided to let those still alive escape? To tell the story? To frighten others into submitting to his demonic rule?

Hatred welled up to choke her. She concentrated on it—encouraged it—hoping it would mask her terrible grief. Adom was a mad genius. An actor playing a role to perfection. She'd stood before him a dozen times to receive his soft words of castigation regarding her rebel activities. He'd always been kind, so kind, and gentle, forgiving. Or so it seemed, until the next day when he ordered the murder of hundreds of her followers. Punishing her . . . yes, he knew how to punish. Just as he did now. What would he do? Let them mass at the gate before he opened fire again?

Rachel's weak arms gave out suddenly and she slumped down onto the blasted chest of a young girl. Maybe twelve, the dead child's horrified expression seemed to beg her for mercy.

Sybil choked, "Don't stop, Mommy. *Don't stop!*"

Rachel pushed painfully up, forcing her trembling body to move. "Shhh, sweetheart. I'm not."

CHAPTER 4

Mist rolled down the tree-covered slopes of Kayan in visible undulating waves, sticking to the pea green leaves of spring like diamonds. Dark clouds billowed on the horizon, roiling over the jagged peaks. The cool air smelled richly of earth and pine.

Zadok twined through the underbrush, heart pounding. His brown woolen robe clung to his body in clammy folds, making it difficult to walk, yet still he forced his ancient legs forward.

"Where are you, Daughter? Ezarin?" The entire village had joined the search. Around him, the slopes crawled with movement.

"Zadok?" Rathanial called from somewhere through the trees to his side.

"Over here!"

"Macus thinks he's found something."

"Where?"

"In the meadow up ahead."

"I'm coming!"

He shoved a berry bush aside and worked toward the

meadow. It seemed to take forever to wind around the thorny bramble. He stepped over a rotting log and broke into the meadow. Shreds of mist curled through the tops of the trees. People huddled close against the chill, milling nervously in the thick wet grass. All eyes were upon him, and the knowledge that had been swelling in his breast for twenty hours grew larger until it became a certainty. A terrible certainty. Yet, still, he forced himself to ask, "What did you find?"

Macus lowered his eyes, staring at the ground, but not before Zadok caught the glimmer of tears. Over a hundred with a shock of red hair, he'd grown up with Ezarin, played with her in his own backyard for a dozen years. They'd been as close as brother and sister. Zadok's heart thumped so loudly he thought it might burst through his chest.

"What is it?" he demanded, but his voice had weakened; it sounded more like a plea.

Before he could call again, Rathanial pushed through the crowd, hurrying toward him. He looked like an elegant Angel of Death in his shimmering silver robe and carefully trimmed white hair. A hush filled the meadow.

Rathanial blocked his path. "Abba, it might not be a good idea to—"

"Tell me." He gazed into the man's pained eyes. "Tell me!"

"It's only a . . . It's not a sight you should see. Let me take care—"

"If you're not going to tell me, get out of my way, you fool!"

Zadok pushed him aside and forced his trembling knees to work toward Macus. As he approached, people cleared a path and he glimpsed the blood trickling down the small earthen channel, pushed and diluted by rain. His steps faltered. People shifted uncomfortably, some shaking their heads in disbelief, others grimacing in anguish and fear. He clenched his fists.

"I knew," he murmured unsteadily.

"Grandfather," Mikael called, "It's not Aunt Ezarin. I know it's not. She never wore a ring like that—"

"Shhh." A ring? Her Jekutiel ring? She only wore it at festival. Mikael must not have noticed. Tramping slowly forward, Zadok smoothed the boy's wet black hair, then bent to kiss him on the top of the head. His grandson stared up with wide eyes, hugging his mother's leg. Sarah stood stiffly, eyes set imploringly on Zadok. The storm had drenched her long hair, turning it into a stringy black mass that clung in clumps to her face.

"Papa . . . . ?"

He laid a hand comfortingly on her shoulder and smiled weakly, reassuringly, into her round face. "I know. I've feared it for hours. I should have guessed long ago."

"What do you mean?"

He met her eyes and saw the sparkle of terror there. Reaching up, he wiped the rain from her face and patted her cheek gently. "Let's talk about it tomorrow, hmm?"

"You don't think the Magistrates—"

"Later," Zadok said grimly, noticing fear brighten in the eyes of those huddling around them. A hushed murmur grew. "Don't worry. I'll figure some way of stopping the madness."

Turning, he stepped into the brush to examine the place from which the blood flowed. It wasn't a body; only an arm. A woman's arm, ripped from the shoulder and thrown carelessly into the deadfall of the forest. Zadok forced a swallow down his tight throat.

"Hurry," he said, waving a hand at the woods. "We must find her. Maybe she's still—"

"Fan out," Rathanial ordered. *"Go!"*

People raced away, snapping twigs and branches in their haste. Mikael's muffled sobs carried on the cool wind. Zadok stood still, gazing absently at the tall pines covering the slopes. The trees highest on the mountains flailed wildly in the wind.

"You, too, Rathanial. Go."

"Are you sure you don't need—"

"I don't."

The white-haired man nodded in slow deliberateness and tramped away through the underbrush. Zadok sucked in a deep breath of the pine-sharp air and bent to remove the ring. Six hundred years old, it had belonged to his great-grandmother. A sacred gift from one of the Zaddiks, holy men, of old Earth. The sapphires and emeralds forming the triangle within a triangle sparkled in the dim light of the cloudy day.

He winced at the still warm feel of his daughter's flesh, recoiling involuntarily. She couldn't have been—dead—for more than an hour. He felt suddenly sick and dazed, heart stricken too sore for tears. Memories welled up like a flock of frightened birds, darkening the sky of his soul. He remembered playing dolls with her when she was five, and teaching her the ancient songs, her tinny seven-year-old voice screeching in his ears, holding her close when she woke up from nightmares in the darkness. She'd suffered so many bad dreams all her life. A portent? "Ezarin. My Ezarin."

Forcing himself, he reached out again and gently removed the ring, then slipped it in his robe pocket.

"Who would do this?" With quivering fingers he tenderly stroked her arm one last time. "You know how much I loved you. Epagael will keep you until I get to Arabot."

Shouts came from the forest ahead, echoing around the steep slopes. Zadok rose tiredly and looked up into the dark clouds roiling over the peaks. Cold mist sheeted his face.

"God?"

A roll of distant thunder answered.

"Is it me? Have I done something to anger you?"

Another shout twined through the forest, louder, insistent. As he tramped through the brush, he slipped into deep thought. Oh, there were endless possibilities of who the . . . the murderer might be. The Board of Galactic Magistrates hated Gamants. His people had always been fighters. No matter how hard the various galactic governments had tried to obliterate Gamant culture, the people remained fiercely loyal. And it forced the Magistrates to make examples of them, burning their planets to cinders, stealing their children, cutting off their trade routes.

"Our goal," Zadok mouthed the Magisterial hard-line, "is to cleanse social wounds by breaking down the walls of cultural separation." They meant, of course, destroying Gamant religion and lifeways.

"Fools." Gamants would never willingly give up their heritage. Though, he admitted woefully, many had under threats of starvation or death. But that was different, unavoidable.

And there were other enemies, hundreds of them.

Movement caught his eye. He turned, searching the lacing maze of pines. "Macus?"

Like an echo in his soul, he seemed to hear the faint strike of glass against wood. A Darkness moved through the trees, casting a long cold shadow over him. He jerked around, searching.

"Rathanial? . . . Who's there!"

Seconds later, a heavy thud sounded, and a faint cry climbed the slope on the wind, someone screaming, "A leg . . . dear God."

Zadok clutched the brown fabric over his heart and squeezed his eyes closed. "Part of a pattern," he murmured in anguish to himself. When he'd reached the age of thirteen and learned the truth about his mother's and grandmother's deaths, he'd thought they formed part of a terrible plot. But his father had sternly assured him his thoughts were fantasy.

"Abba?" Macus' thin voice called. "We've . . . we've found her."

Zadok stood paralyzed, tears welling in dreadful knowledge. He couldn't force himself to move. His weak legs remained rooted to the wet earth.

"Grandfather!"

He started at Mikael's shrill voice, turning an ear toward the origin point. Sarah's wordless comforting of her son twined with the rising wails of agony. How could she sound so calm? Hadn't she realized she stood *next* in line?

Zadok's boots whispered through the rain-soaked weeds as he staggered down the slope. Stepping into the circle of people, he gasped. Ezarin's head lay propped on a wet log, eyes staring vacantly at the interlacing branches overhead. Her torso rested a short distance away in a clump of weeds.

"Dear . . . God," Rathanial murmured unsteadily, clamping his head between his hands. "They'll kill us all! Don't you see?" He swung around to Zadok, staring wide-eyed and near hysteria. Rain stood out in beads across his wrinkled face, soaking his white hair. "They've come for you!"

Zadok shook his head vaguely. "For my oldest daughter."

"It's beginning! Can't you—"

"It began centuries ago."

"What?"

Darkness seemed to spring from the forest, its shadow covering Zadok again, blotting the gray sky as it bent low to stare at Ezarin. He stiffened, eyes frantically searching the woods. Who or what could cast such a shape? Did no one else see it? He glanced around the group; no one saw anything but the gruesome sight before them. Zadok stepped involuntarily backward. The wrenching ache of his throat returned as he remembered his father struggling breathlessly under that same looming darkness to break through the mass of screaming relatives who milled around the remains

49

of his mother. Even then he could see the shadow. The coppery odor of blood again made his mouth water with the urge to vomit. His brother Yosef's wailing filled his ears, mixing eerily with Mikael's.

Frantically, he searched the trees and the cloudy sky, feeling as though an ancient terror lurked only an arm's length away, waiting.

"Who are you?" he shouted into the misty heavens.

People around him shifted uncomfortably, following his gaze. A soft murmuring of frightened voices eddied through the wet woods: "He's sick with grief. No wonder . . ." "You can't expect sanity when something like this happens!"

"Who, Papa?"

"I don't . . ." Then it was gone. Zadok's voice drifted into nothingness.

"Abba?" Rathanial rasped. "Hurry, let's take—her—back. We must talk. The Mashiah has gone too far this time."

"The Mashiah?"

"Yes! This is surely his handiwork. Just like the drought."

"Let's discuss it later." Zadok held up a hand to halt the tirade. He was too bitterly numb to endure it. Slowly, he walked forward and gently picked up Ezarin's head, cradling it in his arms like he'd done when she was a child. A soft lullaby came to mind and he sang it hoarsely, stroking the long black hair that formed a web over his eldest's blood-spattered face.

"Papa," Sarah whispered, extending trembling hands. "Let me? You don't need to—"

"No—it's my last chance."

He led the way slowly down the drenched slope, winding around deadfall and thick briars. They followed in single file behind him, fragments of the Mourner's Kedis echoing eerily from the mountains. By the time they reached the caves, the sun hung like a crimson ball over the peaks, the blaze of sunset lingering on the swirls and hollows of the cliffs.

* * * * *

Ornias leisurely paced before the fireplace in his bedchamber, listening to the wind hurl itself out of the night, whistling through the cracks around his windows. The fire in his stone hearth crackled and sizzled, throwing wavering light over the rounded arches along the walls and reflecting eerily in the vaulted ceiling.

"Will that be all, Councilman?" Shassy asked, glancing longingly at the door. She wanted to leave, and badly.

Swirling a glass of fine Kayan sherry in his hand, he glanced admiringly at her. A beautiful black woman, she had broad cheekbones and an aquiline nose. Her thin lips were pursed tightly with disdain as she met his eyes.

"No, let's talk for a while, shall we?"

"I really must be going." The silken fabric of her periwinkle robe shimmered in the golden flickers of the fire as she moved to collect his dinner dishes. Glass clinked against metal as the silence stretched. A tall woman, she had a lithe body and full breasts. Thick raven curls fluffed to her shoulders. But her eyes fascinated him most, drawing him to her like a wolf to a wounded rabbit. Black as night, those eyes glimmered with hatred for him and fear. Though she seemed defiant just now, standing rigidly next to his bed beneath the high vault of the ceiling. He smiled, finding it both enticing and amusing.

"You said you thought the rebels would fight back. I'm curious to know why?"

"I didn't say that, Councilman," she defended, eyes evading his.

"Isn't that what you meant by 'they have a right to protect themselves'?"

"No."

"Well, what did you mean?" he pressed, knowing she despised talking to him, enjoying it all the more because of that fact. Leaning a broad shoulder against the corner of the hearth, he sipped his sherry.

"I—I simply meant it's the nature of humanity to mass together when threatened."

"Ah, you think they're massing to attack us. Well, I wouldn't doubt it. They're remarkably suicidal. I just hope they—"

"Suicidal?" she asked disbelievingly, beautiful face tensing. She braced a half-full wine glass on the tray. "They're desperate. You've hit them so hard this time, their minds can't accept the truth. And those who understand are terrified of what might come next."

"I certainly hope you're right. Maybe they'll knuckle under and accept their fates as citizens of Milcom's regime."

"They'll never accept it! All their lives, Epagael has been the center of their faith. You can't expect them to abandon Him in three short years."

51

He laughed softly, gazing at the amber waves washing his glass as he swirled the sherry. "Not only do I expect it, I demand it."

"And what does the Mashiah demand?"

Ornias blinked contemplatively, disturbed by her haughty tone. Not only that, discussing Adom gave him a stomach-ache. "He demands whatever I tell him to."

"Where is he?"

Ornias glanced across the room at her, seeing her shoulders tighten, her beautiful face alight with hope. She looked like a proud black goddess against the background of gray stone wall.

"Does it matter? He's a weak man, Shassy. I assure you Adom could care less how I run the domestic affairs of Horeb. Did you think he might order the rebels saved?"

"I just hadn't seen him in a few days and I wondered where he was. That's all." She stared hard at the floor, hopes dashed.

"Adom is indisposed and will be for another week, I suspect. Milcom called him suddenly." He burst into laughter, throwing his head back and letting the mirth shake his shoulders. Adom—such a prize.

"You make fun of his God?"

"Fun? No. I take Milcom very seriously. Just like I do every other god that influences the behavior of people. The human mind is a remarkably malleable thing. Contour a perspective here, twist an arm there, and you can build an empire based on the right kind of god. History proves that and I'm an ardent student of history."

"You don't believe in Milcom?"

"I believe in Milcom's *power*. And I deeply appreciate what it's done for me." He motioned to the magnificent bedchamber with its rich satins and velvets, then let his gaze linger on the way her robe clung to her flat belly and accented the swell of her breasts. Yes, she understood. He saw it in her suddenly downcast eyes. Shassy was as much a spoil of his ever-increasing power as were the *things* of his reign.

"That's blasphemous."

"Yes, it is."

"I hope God strikes you dead for it."

He took another long sip of his sherry, watching her over the rim of his faceted goblet. "And for lots of other things, I

52

imagine. Well, I sincerely doubt it will happen, so don't get your hopes up."

"My hopes are all I have left."

"Oh, Shassy," he chastised irritably. Finishing his sherry, he set the goblet on the mantle and eyed her askance. "You, of all people, know what I mean. Admit it, you'd love to have my power. With it, you could make enough money to bribe whoever you'd like. Then your husband wouldn't have to sell you for—"

"I'd—*we'd* never use power the way you do, to torture and starve. We'd use it for good things." She turned away from him to stare at the elegant red velvet and pearl satin spread over his bed.

He laughed shortly, demanding, "Look at me, Shassy."

When she refused, anger rose in him. He strode quickly across the room, put a hand beneath her chin and twisted so he could see her face. Her dark eyes flamed. "I can tell you don't want to talk about your husband, but let me remind you of one thing before we close this discussion. I didn't kill him, did I? And I very well could have. Instead, I made a bargain. A harsh one, I agree, but necessary if I'm ever to get off this barren rock and establish the religion of Milcom—"

"Don't be a hypocrite!" She shoved his hand away, pacing with the lithe grace of a tiger. Her blue robe shimmered in the firelight. "You don't care any more about Milcom than we do. All you care about is profit. *We're* interested in the survival of Gamant culture. And we've had to bargain with the likes of you to secure it."

"Ah, careful," he said, waggling a finger. "You're not interested in Gamant survival. You're interested in preserving a series of useless rituals and preposterous beliefs. There's a *big* difference. Your attempts at preservation may well be counterproductive to survival."

"You're a beast. Using torture and starvation—"

"Torture and starvation are powerful keys to shaping civilization. Never underestimate their value in the right hands. Besides, my punitive actions are reluctantly taken and then only out of massive pressure from the majority of our populace who hate the rebels' blaspheming." He gave her an endearing smile. "I simply hearken to the will of the flock."

"How can you value human life so little? Have you no conscience?"

"Not if I can help it. It cuts into the profits."

Her nostrils flared with disgust. *"Mercenary!"*

"I've been called worse. I—"

"I'm sure you have."

He laughed uproariously and moved to stand so close beside her that he could smell the floral scent that clung to her clothing. His gaze drifted with satisfaction over her suddenly trembling hands. She tried to lift the tray, but a wine goblet tumbled to the floor, thudding dully on the red rug. She set the tray back on his bedside table and knelt to retrieve the glass.

"Don't be nervous. You know I can't stand weakness. Have I ever hurt you?"

She shook her head and straightened with the glass in her hand, tucking it back on the tray, evading his eyes.

"Nor will I. You're a valuable woman." He softly caressed her hair, studying the way the curls caught the firelight. "Shassy, I made you my *personal* servant. Remember that. Things could be a lot worse. I could have you assigned to the prison work colony, or thrown you into one of the subterranean cells for murderers and rapists. You'd be just as well-guarded there as you are here." He gave her a broad smile. "And not nearly so pampered."

"Pampered," she spat, clenching her fists.

"I treat you better than the rebels, don't I?"

"I suppose I should be grateful for that."

"You certainly should, considering you and your family are of their ranks."

A swallow bobbed in her throat. "I'd better be going, Councilman," she said stiffly, recoiling from his touch.

"Do you still have sympathies for the rebels?" he asked in mock curiosity. Of course, she did, but he wanted to hear her say it. "Is that why you're so touchy tonight? I suppose, given your husband's political philosophies, that you—"

"I have no sympathy for them."

"Don't you? Good. It's always nice to discover unsuspected things about confidantes." He lifted a hand to her hair again, stroking it seductively. "And you are my confidante, you know?"

"I'm your prisoner!"

"Yes, but I've been trying very hard to make your stay here pleasant. You have privileges no one else does, don't you? Who else in the palace sees me so vulnerable?" Of course, that was a lie. No one, *ever*, saw him vulnerable. In fact, he couldn't remember the last time he'd felt that

54

way. Perhaps four or five years ago, before coming into his proper station as master of everything important on Horeb.

Shassy picked up the tray again, clutching it to her chest to stabilize it, and tried to push past him to go to the door. "Excuse me, Councilman, I have to—"

He steadfastly blocked her path, smiling. "I don't think you'll be going tonight, Shassy."

"I—I must." A spark of panic touched her voice. "The palace librarian wanted me to—"

"I'll send word to him you won't be coming. He'll find someone else to do the Mashiah's research on ancient texts and—" he waved a hand distastefully "—whatever else Adom ordered you to trifle with before he went into his blasted prayer room."

Tears welled in Shassy's eyes. "Not tonight, Ornias, please. I can't bear—"

"Don't plead, Shassy. It's beneath a woman of your status in life. Secret though that status might be." He took the tray from her hands and set it on the floor. As he rose, he stopped to nibble her breasts, letting his hands caress her thighs. Every muscle in her body went rigid. "Do be more polite this evening, though, will you, darling? It took me nearly a month to heal from your stab wound last time. While I've had everything sharp and heavy removed from the room, I suspect you could use a pillow to try and smother me—and I wouldn't take kindly to that." He straightened and met her eyes, smiling cruelly. "I might have to break your sweet neck for it." His hand slid suggestively down her mahogany throat.

"Kill me and you lose everything."

"Quite true. So, maybe I'll just—hurt you? Eh?"

Defiantly, she insisted, "I won't stay. You've no right to force me to."

"Oh, but I've every right. I'm the master of Horeb and you are but a tool—"

"The Mashiah is the master of Horeb! He rules, not you."

"Don't be a dimwit. The only thing Adom rules is his own bodily functions . . . and I worry about those sometimes. Besides, where is he now, when all the rebels are crying for him. Hmm? He's locked away in his prayer room having delusions of the great and mighty Milcom."

Shassy kicked the tray. Splintering glass exploded. Ornias

stepped sideways to avoid the splash of liquids, and Shassy slipped by him, running for the door.

He waited patiently until she'd flung it open, then remarked conversationally, "I'll just have the guards bring you back, my dear. Would you rather I do that? Shall I offer them a reward for your return? Say—an hour alone with you?"

Hearing her steps stilled, he turned, frowning sympathetically. "Do be sensible. We're in this together. My goal is inextricably tied with yours. *Freedom* comes at a price."

She squeezed her eyes closed, lips trembling as she bowed her head. After an eternity of silence, she braced a hand against the door and slowly pushed it closed.

CHAPTER 5

The caves of Kayan formed an intricate labyrinth beneath the lush surface of the planet. Narrow passageways wound for thousands of miles through the hard cinnamon-colored rock. In the darkest depths of the maze existed rooms known only to Zadok.

As he hobbled down the tunnel, he counted the turns. "A hundred and twenty-one." Rounding it, his lamp lit an even narrower shaft.

If Rathanial had followed his instructions exactly, he should be waiting in the tiny niche Zadok lovingly called the Sanctum. If not, they'd hopefully find him in the next few days, wandering lost and terrified on an upper level. He'd only misplaced one visitor in the past two hundred years. And when he came right down to it that had been good riddance. He'd strongly suspected the man of being a spy from the Magistrates sent to assassinate him, though the fellow had the finest references, of course.

Zadok rounded the final turn, "One hundred and twenty-two," and proceeded down the spiral staircase cut into the rock.

In this deep part of the caverns, the rock smelled dry and the air was touched with a hint of spice. Each footfall echoed from the walls. Even breathing magnified in the narrow corridor until it seemed to come from every pore of the rock. No stranger could approach the Sanctum without being heard.

Zadok stepped into the inner cave and let his eyes rove the room. He hadn't used it in years. A rounded cave measuring ten by ten feet, the ceiling hung so low tall visitors had to stand hunched. Candlelight played over the stark walls and drawn face of Rathanial.

"You said you wanted a secluded place, old friend. I hope this meets your needs."

"I hope so, too," Rathanial muttered uncertainly.

Zadok examined his friend closely. What could he fear so terribly in this isolated chamber shielded by billions of tons of rock? "I'm sorry I'm late. I had to—"

"Don't explain," Rathanial said quickly, rising. The gold bullion of his embroidered robe caught the light and shimmered.

"Funerals take such preparation," Zadok said anyway. "All the relatives have to be notified. My brother Yosef and his friend Ari Funk are coming."

"From Tikkun?"

"Yes. It's a great distance, but he's promised to grab a fast transport to be here by day after tomorrow."

"I'm grateful that in this time of sorrow you agreed to see me."

Zadok forced himself to smile with as much warmth as he could muster. "Let me get us some wine. You've had a long journey and stayed, I know, far past the time you'd intended."

Rathanial nodded respectfully and took his chair again. Zadok went about gathering pewter goblets and a bottle of Cassopian Alizarin from a shelf carved into the rock. He unceremoniously blew the dust from the goblets.

When he turned to walk to the small table, the sparseness of the room struck him. Only one table and two chairs adorned the cave, sitting atop an ancient homespun brown rug. He remembered when orange and tan designs had graced the fabric, but they were long gone. Had everything in the world faded to brown? Had the entire universe decided to fold back in upon itself? Though he'd bathed and changed, the scent of blood still haunted his nostrils. *Ezarin* . . . A sharp pain pounded in his breast.

He set the goblets on the table and poured each full, then dropped into the hard chair and looked tiredly at his visitor. Rathanial's white hair and beard gleamed in the soft light. He met Zadok's eyes anxiously.

"Tell me about your new Mashiah. You wouldn't have come to me if you didn't think there was a possibility he—"

"I'm not sure, Abba. We need you to test him."

"To test him," Zadok repeated and leaned back in his chair. It meant leaving Kayan, his family. It was hardly the time to be gallivanting off to other worlds. Not only that, he'd grown so tired of the parade of charlatans, he didn't think he could endure another testing.

"I don't—"

"You're the only one who knows the secret path to the Veil of God!"

Zadok heaved a disgruntled breath. "Of course." The route through the seven heavens to the Veil where the acts of all generations, and the true Mashiah, were written was a secret he could pass on only at his death—which he feared might not be too far distant.

"Abba, I fear we can't survive without your help. We need . . ." He stopped suddenly and looked around the room, eyes widening. Breathlessly, he leaned across the table, coming so close Zadok could smell his stale perfume and dank sweat.

"Tell me what you need?"

Fear gleamed in Rathanial's dark eyes. "Terrible things are happening."

"For example?"

Rathanial drew a deep breath and a brief shiver played over him. "Abba, I swear, I did everything I could. I distributed pamphlets about the Mashiah's wickedness. I held secret desert meetings with the political leaders of Seir . . ." He swallowed. "But—but no one listened. It's that Adom is so charismatic! No one sees him for what he truly is! He seems so innocent and pure that people are fooled! And I've tried—"

"Rathanial, *give me specifics!*"

The man stood and paced a few steps, robe glittering like cornsilk at dawn. Zadok saw his mouth tremble. Then, as if embarrassed, Rathanial pressed fingers firmly to his lips to steady them. "We have . . . eavesdroppers in all our meetings, Abba."

"Eavesdroppers? You mean traitors?"

"No. No, I mean . . ." He waved a hand tensely. "Otherworld 'listeners.' "

Zadok sat unmoving, tawny light playing across his withered features. "Explain."

58

"I wish I could, Abba. Truly, if I knew—"

"Try."

"Some in our community think the listeners are Adom's guardian angels. The Mashiah claims, and has witnesses, to verify his miraculous birth."

"Don't they all?" Zadok squeezed the bridge of his nose, smiling faintly. "Saviors arise constantly, Rathanial, like weeds in a garden. Our duty is to pluck them up and get on with our lives."

"This savior is different."

"Oh?"

Nervously, Rathanial ran a hand through his white hair and sat down again. "It's said that a man of shining white appeared at his cradle. The man wrapped Adom Kemar Tartarus in a swaddling cloth of fire and gave him flames to eat."

"So he knows the ancient stories of Elijah's birth. He's more sophisticated than most charlatans."

"Since he's been in power, the grass has failed."

"Horeb is a desert planet. There's little grass anyway. A quarter inch of rain either way and—"

"It's not a natural phenomenon. Even in bad years we've always had enough grass to feed the stock."

"Uh-huh." Zadok skeptically raised his bushy gray brows. Everyone wanted to believe their savior was either the true redeemer, or the promised Antimashiah who'd precede Him. No one wanted to believe in the capriciousness of nature.

"What's your answer," Rathanial inquired sharply, "for the plague that's wiped out seventy percent of our population?"

"What plague?"

"The mountain valleys are filled with our dead! We'd no place to bury the vast numbers—"

"Why didn't the Council on Horeb write me of this?"

"Zadok," Rathanial murmured tightly, eyes scanning the room as though for "eavesdroppers." "We did. Many times. You never responded. That's why I risked my life to come to see you myself."

"I never received—"

"I know that now. At first I thought . . . Well, you know how far out Horeb is and we have few of the governmental problems of other Gamant planets. There's no interference with our schools or politics."

Zadok glowered at his goblet, studying the way the light shimmered in the maroon wine. Something about this whole affair stank. Why hadn't his own secret sources in Rathanial's community been able to get the information out? Were they still alive? If not, why? *Who* was the traitor? "Tell me about the plague?"

"Hideous wounds maim and kill. It's said . . . said that invisible demons gnaw the flesh of our people. Though, God knows, I don't believe that and, anyway, it's almost over now that everyone born under the House of Ephraim is dead."

"The branch from which the final Mashiah is to come?" Zadok ran the ancient prophecies through his mind as his gaze drifted over the dusty wine bottles on the far shelf. The first Mashiah had come from the House of Yosef, the second from David. Those, the people knew from history, had died fighting for Gamant survival. And the third Mashiah was to come from the House of Ephraim. This redeemer, legend foretold, would finally free the People. Zadok let his tired mind ramble over what Rathanial had told him. Some element of the story rang ominously in the back of his thoughts. "What'd you say this Mashiah's full name is?"

"Adom Kemar Tartarus."

"Something about the first letters," Zadok mused. "Do you perchance—"

"A-K-T? He also has them burned into his forehead. Theoretically the man of fire put them there at his birth."

"Hmmm." Where had he heard the letters mentioned before? The vast majority of ancient texts had been burned by the Magistrates in the last Gamant Revolt—a revolt he'd led. But the letters touched some deep fear inside him. "Do you, perchance, have a copy of the Apocalypse of Daniel . . . or maybe it was the Apocalypse of Ezra?"

Rathanial shook his head. "Neither, I'm afraid. The Magistrates purged our library a hundred years ago. Why?"

"Oh, it's probably nothing, just a failing memory."

"They might have a copy on Tikkun. You could ask your brother to check the archives."

"I checked there myself, several years ago. Perhaps there are no copies of those books left any place. A shame, they tell a great deal of the coming of the true Mashiah and his travails." He paused, sipping his wine. "Tell me more about Tartarus? Where did he come from? What's he like?"

"He's a curious character . . . born on Horeb. Fourteen years ago, when he was fifteen, his parents died in a freak accident in the mountains. The family had gone out for a picnic and, somehow, the rocks above his parents loosened and a landslide came roiling down on top of them."

"But the boy survived?"

"Yes. He claims Milcom, his god, came to him just before the landslide and led him away into the hills to give him a series of visions."

"And the content of the visions?"

Rathanial shrugged. "No one really knows, but he came down from the mountains weeks later, preaching that Epagael was wicked and Milcom was good. He says the two are locked in a constant battle over the existence of the universe."

"He's been preaching ever since the accident?"

"Yes, but only recently has he gained any followers. You see, Adom used to be the equivalent of our 'town drunk.' He stumbled through the streets in stinking rags, pathetically preaching his message of salvation while he dug through the garbage dumps for food."

"How sad," Zadok murmured. What had happened to Gamant charity on Horeb? The boy should have been taken in by someone and protected from himself. He squirmed uncomfortably in his chair. "Is his mind gone?"

"Sometimes it seems so. The servants in his palace report that after Milcom talks with him, he wanders for hours, mumbling to himself, waving his arms like a madman. But at other times, he seems perfectly normal. And it's at those times, Zadok, that he addresses the masses."

"And sways them to his bidding? Interesting. His madness must lend him some magnetic charm. I've seen it before in the mentally ill. The delusions spawn such confidence they seem invincible and charismatic."

"Yes, but Adom has no understanding of the needs of his ever-increasing flock. He—"

"None of them do. Each exists somewhere in a dark corner of his own mind, separated from reality. It's a tragic ailment."

Rathanial nodded curtly, staring hard at the scarred surface of the table. "Madness isn't a debility, however, when you have an evil genius around to orchestrate the religious movement."

"Tartarus has such a genius?"

"Yes, an off-worlder named Ornias." His voice lowered to a whisper as his eyes cautiously examined the shadows in the room.

"Off-worlder? From where?"

"I've been investigating for four years, Zadok, and can find almost no records about him. I'm fairly certain he was born on Palaia Station, but—"

"Palaia?" Adrenaline flooded Zadok's veins in a rush. "The home of the Galactic Magistrates?" The implications staggered him. A plant? A spy sent to undermine Gamant culture and religion?

"Yes, but I'm not even positive of that. He must've changed his name several times and flitted around the galaxy like a firefly, because, except for a few scraps of data, he seems to have been born a few years ago when he appeared on Horeb."

"I see. And what happened when he arrived?"

"Almost instantly, he plucked Adom from the streets, buying him clothing and taking care of him. He kept Adom out of sight for months, then began a massive publicity campaign announcing the arrival of the 'Promised Mashiah.' He set up a preaching tour all over Horeb, even hitting the small nomadic villages of the vast desert regions."

"Selling him, eh?"

"Yes."

"It seems to have worked."

"Obviously," Rathanial responded bitterly. "Now Ornias is running a campaign to destroy all the Old Believers, calling them traitors or demons sent to deceive the faithful."

"What if my testing reveals Tartarus as a fraud and his followers still don't believe? Fanatics are notoriously stubborn. What do you plan on doing then?"

Rathanial held his breath a moment before blurting, "I've been meaning to tell you." He twisted his hands anxiously.

"What?"

"I've summoned Jeremiel Baruch. He's to report to you before—"

"Why?" Zadok sat forward so suddenly, he knocked his goblet over. Wine splashed the table, running in a stream onto the stone floor. Quickly, he pulled a handkerchief from his pocket and sopped it up, leaving the stained rag pushed against the wall near the candle. "Baruch has enough problems without our making demands on him! Why can't you organize your own forces?"

"Adom and Ornias are too powerful! We've got to have help!"

"You did that without asking me?"

Rathanial's mouth quivered. "I thought we'd already established I couldn't get *any* messages to you, Zadok. Baruch was the only one who responded to my pleas for help."

"I thought your order was nonviolent?"

"Sometimes violence is the only way to salvation."

Zadok pursed his lips and gazed long at the stone floor. Baruch was wanted by every galactic official in the sector for his subversive activities. Rumor had it that the Magistrates had him bottled up tight in the Akiba system. He'd be risking not just himself but his entire army if he came. If the Magistrates found he'd left his troops alone, without his brilliant guidance, they'd surely attack, figuring his forces were critically weakened.

"Your daughter," Rathanial said hesitantly, bringing the subject back, "was in the line of Ephraim."

"Of course."

Silence hung heavy in the dry cave air. Rathanial studied his wine, waiting. When Zadok said no more, he asked darkly, "How many women from the House of Ephraim are left in Gamant civilization?"

Still angry about Rathanial's tugging Baruch away from his forces, he answered sharply, "My daughter, Sarah, and a sixth or seventh cousin, three times removed. There may be more, I don't know."

"A cousin?"

"Yes, I think she's still on Horeb as a matter of fact. But I'm not—"

"What's her name?"

Zadok shrugged. "I haven't the vaguest idea. My father didn't like that side of the family. He wouldn't even let us write to them. 'Savages and hoodlums,' he called them."

Rathanial's gaze darted over the room as though running every name he could think of through his head. "Could it be—"

"Don't even try. I wouldn't recognize it if you said it."

They held each other's eyes pensively, Rathanial clearly worried and trying suddenly to hide it.

"Abba, I know I've angered you, and I'm sorry. But surely you can see I had no choice."

"You should have come here before you contacted Baruch. You've placed all of us in a dangerous position. Without the Underground, we're surely lost. And the best way to destroy the Underground is to get its leader killed."

Rathanial nodded tensely, shame on his face. "I just couldn't see any other way."

"What's done is done. However," Zadok warned, leaning forward to point a stern finger, "you'd better protect him with every resource you've got. If I find you've left him open for assassination—"

"I—I won't. I've guaranteed him the best security I can provide."

Zadok slouched roughly in his chair and crossed his legs at the ankles, glaring at the far wall to relieve some of his frustration. "Is there anything else you need?"

"Just one thing."

"What is it?"

"I know it's a bad time. I know you're needed here, but you must come and test Tartarus immediately. Before it's too late and we find he's the Antimashiah of prophecy. We can't allow—"

"That's another thing. What makes you think he'll submit to my testing?"

"Because he must to maintain the faith of his followers. You're the leader of Gamant civilization and if you challenge him to undergo it, he'll have to."

"Yes, yes," Zadok murmured exhaustedly. "Pressure might work." He poured himself another glass of wine and gulped a mouthful, wiping his lips with the cuff of his sleeve. The drink had a strong resinous flavor. "Let me get things settled here. I have to meet Yosef at the spaceport and take care of . . . the funeral. Plus we'll need to wait for Baruch. Then I'll go back to Horeb with you."

"Thank you," Rathanial said in desperate gratitude, closing his eyes for a moment. "Thank you, Abba." He finished his wine quickly and stood, uneasily bending to give Zadok's cheek a quick kiss before he strode to the door. "I'll pack my things in preparation for our journey."

Zadok nodded tiredly and listened to his heavy steps thudding down the winding maze of corridors.

Lifting his goblet, he swirled the liquid, watching the delicate maroon waves that washed the pewter. An ache expanded in his chest, as though the strands of destiny tugged tightly around him. He'd known Rathanial for a hundred years, yet he'd never seen him so frightened, so out of control. Perhaps things were worse on Horeb than he'd said. Maybe that's why he'd desperately summoned Baruch. Still, it enraged Zadok. He puffed a hostile breath and pounded a fist against his leg, trying to analyze the disturbing sequence of events: Horeb had flared into civil war under a new Mashiah who claimed to be the promised Deliverer; Rathanial had been unable to get any messages to him about it; Baruch was risking his neck to try and resolve the planet's problems; and . . . Ezarin had been brutally murdered. Were the events connected?

Images of the terrible shadow returned. Zadok straightened in his chair, skin prickling. "An otherworld eavesdropper? Or maybe just your imagination, you old fool."

He leaned his bald head against the gritty surface of the wall and stared longingly at the cinnamon ceiling. He felt as hollow and cold as the cave itself. "Think. The People need you to think."

He ran memories through his head trying to correlate disparate events. Gamants had always been in trouble. Legends held that the talent for making enemies went as far back as ancient Earth where their distant ancestors had protected the Old Ways by going into hiding and killing anyone who threatened to expose them. The secret sect that resulted had flourished in ancient Abyssinia and Shoa. But the sect's safety had dissolved during the first extraterrestrial invasion of Earth. Giclasian military governors had outlawed all "mystery cults," as they called them, believing the sacred meetings to be treasonous strategy sessions. Different cultures and religions had been thrown together to increase internal human conflicts, and discourage alliances. Then they were forced to work exploiting the planet's rich resources. Some were shipped off-world, families wantonly destroyed. War after war resulted and the Great Night of Glass ensued. Gamants began to forget the old teachings. Slowly, but surely, other philosophies tainted the original—or strengthened—depending on the way you looked at it. A thousand years later, when Edom Middoth raided Earth for his army of slaves, the Exile ripped the tradition asunder. After Jekutiel's triumph, the people drifted apart, searching out other planets. Exiled factions remembered the myths, legends, and rituals differently—many only partly. They groped to pull the threads of their identity together and, in the process, blended with their neighbors, picking and choosing things from foreign traditions that sounded comfortingly familiar. No one knew anymore how much the current rituals resembled the originals. Not that it mattered to Zadok. Gamant culture may have mutated—*but it had survived*.

His mind wandered, pausing here and there indiscriminantly until he lost his train of thought. Perhaps he was just too tired to think tonight. But how much time did he have? He shook his head wearily, lowering his chin to rest on his chest.

He sat in the cave long into the night, staring vacantly at the floor.

CHAPTER 6

Jeremiel crouched in the wet grass beneath a towering pine. The ice-bitten wind lanced his suit. He watched the lavender light of morning blush color into the dew drops sparkling on the brush around him, then turned his gaze to the caves below.

The right caves? Pulling the map from his pocket, he checked it over and compared it with the surrounding terrain, pinpointing his location as best he could through the clutter of trees and peaks. *These must be Zadok's caves.*

But still he wasn't certain, and to walk into an unknown camp would be suicidal. Puffing an exhausted breath, he let himself slump backward, sitting down in the wet vegetation so he could think. The pungent scent of damp pine duff tantalized his nose and he pulled in a deep breath.

"I have to be close."

Rudy had dropped him three days' journey from the caves, far enough away that hopefully no one would think it suspicious even if they noticed his descending jetpack. But the distance made following the map confusing. Kayan burst with deep valleys and high ridges, thick forests and dense underbrush. For the past day, he'd felt like he was playing a game of wits with mountain peaks.

Movement caught his eye and he leaned forward cautiously. Two men stepped out of the caves and into a small meadow. In the dim gray of dawn, he couldn't make out their faces. Slipping his small pack from his shoulders, he pulled his noculars and focused in on the shorter man. His heart skipped a beat. *Zadok.* But who was the other? He could be a damned Magisterial ambassador for all Jeremiel knew. He couldn't take the chance of exposing himself yet.

Zadok started off, leading the stranger down a grassy path which wound around the base of the mountain toward the capital city below. Quietly getting to his feet, Jeremiel weaved through the trees, following.

As he shadowed them, the wind brought him fragments of conversation. Discussions about Gamant politics, ethics, and history passed between the two. The tall white-haired man nodded obediently each time Zadok pointed his finger sharply.

When they reached the street leading into the city, Jeremiel waited, huddling in a thickly wooded area above the spaceport. He watched Zadok hesitate at the door outside, waving his ancient arms wildly.

"Damn it, Zadok," he whispered. "Don't go inside. You'll be a sitting duck if anyone wants to murder you."

Jeremiel's tension grew as he studied Zadok's pacing and the white-haired man's pleading gestures. "Don't do it!"

Finally, Zadok threw up his hands and entered the port, followed by the stranger. Jeremiel shook his head. Zadok, the old war-horse, had let himself be talked into going into a crowded government center where he couldn't run easily? It didn't make any sense. What's more, it set an alarm to ringing inside Jeremiel's stomach. The Magistrates were very clever. They could be using Zadok as bait—to lure *him* into that damned building.

He crouched in the brush and surveyed the building thoroughly. Soldiers lurked at every entrance, but they didn't seem to be part of the specialty squads. They strolled around carelessly, talking loudly to each other. "Poorly trained. They're probably part of the planetary personnel." Everyone knew Kayan's military installations were largely filled with clerks and accountants.

But you could never be sure with the Magistrates. They might have moved in a clandestine services branch within the past week. Hell, for all he knew there could be a cruiser in orbit right now.

He glanced uneasily at the cerulean sky and backed deeper into the wet brush.

The Magistrates were an enigma to most species in the galaxy. All four were Giclasian and possessed extraordinary skills at manipulation and organization. Their violent natures were legendary. Over two millennia before, boasting that they sought to unite the galaxy by establishing a communal economic structure, Giclas had swept planetary systems in huge fleets, killing anyone who didn't agree. Then they'd forcibly formed the Union of Solar Systems and set themselves up as rulers, protecting the citizens, seeing to the exploitation and redistribution of the Union's resources. It turned out they were so good at it, most planets didn't even mind being bilked for all they were worth. Gamants, however, were different. In the early days, before the Magistrates perfected their methods of exploitation, they'd watched their rich planet raped to the point of devastation. Revolt had stirred. Gamants demanded the right to manage their own resources. The Magistrates refused and Gamants had organized a secret military to penetrate and sabotage Magisterial installations. After the Exile, they'd been crushed several times on dozens of different worlds. It had taken centuries, but Gamants had finally won on the plains of Lysomia—and effectively been cast out of the Union. Though the treaty stated that Gamants were still "Citizens of the Galaxy" and subject to certain governmental laws and policies, they were left largely alone. Or deliberately isolated, depending on your perspective. Trade routes were cut off, trading partners threatened or mentally "corrected," until Gamant planets stood as lonely isles in the Union. The situation had heated up recently when the government exercised its right to establish "peaceful" military installations on Gamant planets and to negotiate for the right to "school" Gamant children.

Everyone knew what happened in the schools. The Magistrates had begun a devastating program to kill Gamant culture from within the brain. And the military bases protected the process if anyone objected.

Jeremiel shifted position, leaning forward to watch the guards who had left the front doors to gather on the landing field. "God damn, if we could just kill their power base."

Palaia Station was the key. It had been established to house government personnel and energy resources, but no outsider had ever been able to penetrate its veil of secrecy. Formed of an infinite series of electromagnetic shells, the place was an impregnable fortress. Jeremiel had tried to break in a hundred times, but to no avail. The man who could crack Palaia's secret would rule the galaxy.

Anxiously examining the port, he got to his feet and moved closer, to the very edge of the forest. His skin prickled with a feeling of danger.

"Damn it," he cursed to himself. The overwhelming urge to go into the port and drag Zadok out rose in him.

"Don't be a fool. It's too risky. He's probably just meeting someone and will be out in no time."

Settling himself uneasily in the midst of an overgrown mahogany bush, he waited, eyes glued to the doors.

* * * * *

Yosef Calas adjusted his round spectacles and pressed close to the portal of the ship, peering at the emerald world below. The wedge-shaped continent of Taxo shone opalescent amid clinging fogs. A rainbow of colors eddied with the changing slant of sunlight as the ship descended. Deep green valleys and jagged granite peaks loomed out at them as they approached.

"Ari? Come look at this. Beautiful, isn't it?"

His friend didn't move from his chair. "They all look alike to me. Planets are planets. Balls of dust."

Yosef scowled. Ari sat with his long legs propped on the control console of the tiny ship, slowly sipping a beer. An extremely tall old man, his thick gray hair hung in a rumpled uncombed mass over his ears. He had a withered triangular face with hollow cheeks and a crooked nose—from provoking one too many fights in the gin mills. Yosef wondered at times of any part of his friend's thin body were actually connected to his head.

"You lunatic," Yosef charged, disgruntled. He waddled over and roughly shoved Ari's boots off the white console. "How many times does the captain have to tell you you could blow us up doing that?"

"He doesn't mind anymore!" He thrust a hand at the middle-aged man in the gray space suit, helmet clamped down, whose hand rested suspiciously near the eject button.

"Sure, and your mother really knew your father. The poor man is just tired of telling you, you simpleminded—"

"Bah!" Ari gave him a broad smile. "Hey, come'ere. You want to know what this switch does?" He wiggled a red lever marked "AutoDes."

Don't touch that! the captain yelled, rising half out of his seat.

Yosef jumped, staring. The man's voice sounded scratchy through the helmet speaker. "Get over there and sit down in the passenger seat! Damn! I don't know why I take assignments like this."

Ari punched Yosef in the side, winking. "He's the simpleminded one. We paid him a planet's ransom and he doesn't know why—"

"You have to pay for speed, *you old bozon*. This is one of the fastest ships in the sector," the captain defended.

Yosef threw up his hands and sat down in one of the lavender passengers' seats, hitting the button to secure the lifesystems field around him.

Ari eyed him condescendingly. "You're not scared, are you?"

"Not so long as I'm protected from vacuum." Yosef punched the arm button for music and turned it loud enough that he couldn't hear Ari's continuing remarks. Unfortunately, he could still see him waving his arms.

The *Seros* was a very small ship. Built for speed, it seated only four. Dials with wavering colored lines covered the forward panel, while levers, buttons, and computer screens filled the control console beneath. A simple round viewing portal adorned each side of the vessel. As Yosef looked around, he caught his reflection in the silver shielding over his head. Short and pudgy, the circle of white hair around his otherwise bald head lay neatly against his freckled scalp, but just to make sure, he licked his palm and slicked it down. His round face had sagged a good bit in the past fifty years. Deep wrinkles wove a pattern of harsh years across his sun-bronzed skin, but his brown eyes were still dark and sharp over his blunt nose. Straightening the high collar of his pale green suit, he looked back at Ari.

His lifelong friend stood over the captain, trying to push buttons while the suited man repeatedly shoved his hand away from the controls. Red-faced, the captain's mouth formed a series of unmistakable profanities. Yosef shook his head and closed his eyes, feeling that familiar sense of weightlessness just before touchdown.

The ship wobbled a little before easing onto the landing pad. Yosef opened his eyes in time to see the captain shake a fist at Ari, then grab his flight bag and disappear through the open hatch. Yosef turned off the shield and sat forward.

"What a quark," Ari accused, flailing an arm at the hatch. "He wouldn't even let me try to land the ship."

Yosef sighed in exasperation and went to the luggage compartment to retrieve his single bag. "Come on. Zadok's probably been waiting for hours."

"We pay two thousand lirot and still we're late. We should have—"

"If you hadn't jammed the acceleration lever just after

70

takeoff, we'd probably have been on time," Yosef pointed out as he exited the hatch into the bright sunlight of Kayan.

The chill wind stung his face, carrying with it the moist promise of rain. A bank of blue-black clouds loomed on the horizon, pushing toward the city. The spaceport sat in a bowl in the land surrounded by thickly forested hills. Ahead of him, a complex of single-story gray buildings formed a semicircle. People in multicolored clothing from a variety of planets crowded around one area. Yosef waddled toward them, assuming the main door must be close.

"Wait a minute," Ari said from behind him.

Yosef stopped and gave his friend a hard glare. Ari's blue suit looked like he'd slept in it. "What is it now?"

"Look at that." His friend pointed.

Adjusting his spectacles, Yosef squinted at the purple-suited men frisking people. "They're marines. What's wrong with that?"

"Marines don't guard spaceports unless—"

"Have you ever been to Kayan?"

"That doesn't matter, marines don't—"

"They won't bother you. Now, come on!"

"Bother me? Of course not. I'm not going to stand in line so they can feel me." Ari pushed past him. Yosef narrowed his eyes and sighed. No telling what Ari had planned. Reluctantly, he followed.

When they neared the building, the soldiers were busy questioning someone else and Ari took the opportunity to hit the button to open the door marked: "Arrivals—Customs." He'd made it halfway through the door, when a harsh command stopped him.

"Hey!" one of the guards shouted, stabbing out a finger. "Halt."

Ari looked around himself as though wondering who the guard meant.

Yosef pursed his lips in embarrassed dismay, murmuring, "You idiot. They'll probably arrest us now."

"You two," the guard ordered. "Come over here. We have to check your papers before you get inside."

Ari tilted his head quizzically, like he didn't understand intergalactic lingua. Yosef quickly trudged to the guard, explaining, "He's senile. You have to use hand signals with him." In an elaborate gesture, he waved his friend toward the soldier's check station. "Just like calling a dog, see?"

Ari squinted, perturbed, but complied. When he got close

71

enough, he growled in Yosef's ear. "As usual, you ruined it. We could have gotten through easy if you hadn't—"

"Excuse me," the guard interrupted, repeating Yosef's elaborate waving to instruct Ari to come closer. "Come."

Ari gave Yosef a scathing sideways glance. "What do you want?"

Politely, the guard explained, "I need to search you, sir. Please put your hands behind your head and spread your legs."

Ari reluctantly did as he'd been told. The guard retrieved a long wand from his belt and ran it up and down Ari's legs, checking the readings on the dials for any of a number of hidden substances. "Well," the soldier commented, "you look all right."

"Of course, I'm all right."

"One last thing," he said, and knelt to physically examine Funk's legs with his hands.

Ari jumped. "Wait a minute—"

"It's standard procedure, sir."

"I don't care, I—"

"Hold still!" the guard demanded as Ari squirmed like a fish on a hook.

Funk clamped his teeth and scowled, giving Yosef an evil glare, as though he were responsible. Yosef yawned, ignoring him.

When the guard's hands rose to Ari's crotch, the old man smiled broadly. "Pretty nice, aren't they?"

The guard halted, face growing red. *"I beg your pardon?"*

Yosef gritted his teeth and closed his eyes, knowing prison waited just inside the terminal. Ari jumped on any opportunity to antagonize government personnel.

The guard stood up and thrust out a hand. "Let me see your papers."

Yosef dug inside his coat pocket and handed his over, waiting for Ari to do the same. Then he jabbed his friend in the kidney and whispered, "I want to talk to you!"

"What for?

He gripped Ari's sleeve and dragged him a short distance away while the soldier examined their travel authorizations.

"What'd you do that for? They're going to run us through the mill now."

"Bah!" Ari waved a withered hand. "I didn't do it, he did."

"You imbecile. You're the one who resisted."

"Did you see him run his hand around that other man's jewels?"

72

Yosef shifted positions, thinking. "No, but—"

"These Philistines are all alike: jealous. They have to make sure the stories about Gamants are true."

"I knew I shouldn't have brought you. You're nothing but trouble. Insulting people—"

"Have you ever seen Philistine testicles?" Ari pressed, propping his hands on his bony hips.

"I've never made a study."

His friend formed a tiny circle with his thumb and forefinger. "Pathetic things."

"What do you do? Spend all your time in latrines examining people?"

"You don't have to be scientific about it. You see one or two sets and you can tell the difference."

"Calas! Funk!" the guard called sharply. "Here's your papers."

They walked back and retrieved them. "Thank you," Yosef said politely and headed for the door.

"Wait a minute," the guard protested, thrusting an arm roughly at the Seros. "Get back on that ship. No Gamants are allowed on the planet's surface today."

Yosef cast a sideways glance at Ari and cringed as he saw his friend's mouth tighten until it looked like a withered prune. "What do you mean? We're just as good as—"

"Cut it! I don't care one whit about your mother's mother. My orders are that *no* Gamants are allowed in today. I'll let you know when the situation relaxes."

"What's tense about Gamants?" Ari insisted, his chin thrust out indignantly.

"I don't have access to that information, sir."

"Well, go find out!"

A hot gleam filled the guard's eyes and Yosef grabbed Ari by the tail of his coat, pulling him backward. "Forgive him, Private," he whispered conspiratorially. "His doctors have been working day and night to find out what's wrong with his brain, but to no avail yet."

The youth frowned suspiciously. "I suggest, then, that you take him back to the ship so he can't get in any trouble."

"I'll do that."

Yosef forcibly dragged his friend away. But when they'd gone no more than ten paces Ari blurted, "I'm not going! They can't treat us like this. We're citizens of the galaxy, too."

Yosef opened his mouth to respond, but pain flashed so

73

powerfully in his head, he staggered. The world spun around him. What was it? Something was wrong somewhere. Something was very wrong. The pain grew until he thought it would burst his skull. He clasped his head between his hands, trying to press the agony away.

"I refuse to—"

"Shut up."

Ari blinked at the harsh tone and his expression changed from defiance to concern. "You all right?" he whispered, grabbing Yosef's arm to steady him as he stumbled backward. "What is it?"

"My head . . . I . . ."

"Come on, let's go sit down."

"I *have* to get to my niece's funeral, Ari. If I land in prison because of something you—"

"All right, all right," Ari conceded guiltily. "I didn't mean to mess things up." Gently supporting Yosef's arm, he led him back toward the *Seros*.

"Is it just a headache or something more?"

"I don't know." Yosef blinked as the pain began to fade as quickly as it had come. "But I feel a little better now."

They climbed the steps to the ship in silence. Yosef, in aggravation, threw his bag into the compartment. It bounced from the wall to land on the floor near the control console. He waddled to a chair and flopped down.

Ari exhaled and went to the tiny galley. Slapping the button to the cooling unit, he pulled out two bottles of beer and came back to sit beside Yosef.

"Here," he said softly, handing over the brew. "You need this more than I do."

"Thanks."

Ari frowned, looking Yosef over in painstaking detail. Concern was plain on his withered face. "Are you feeling better? You look pale."

"I'm better. The pain went away as suddenly as it came."

"Probably just the sun. Don't worry about it. A cool drink will make you feel better."

They sat in silence for a while, sipping at the cold beer. The frosty bottle felt soothing in Yosef's hot hand. Absently, he scanned the rows of blank computer screens on the control console.

"So," Ari said softly. "What do you think? They have quotas on Gamants today or something?"

"Maybe."

74

"I think it's because someone's scared witless. I'm telling you marines don't guard spaceports unless they're expecting big trouble."

"From Gamants on the planet?"

Ari shook his head and tipped his bottle high, taking a long swallow before snuggling back in his chair. "From somebody coming in."

"That makes sense."

"Who do you think they're trying to nab?"

Yosef shrugged uneasily. At this moment, he could have cared less. He struggled to analyze the emotions that roiled inside him. His grandmother had suffered the same types of attacks he'd just experienced—always just before something terrible happened. He squinted out the portal. Afternoon sunlight lay in glimmering pools of amber on the needles of the pines clustering around the landing field. He took a deep breath and let it hiss out his nostrils. "All I care about is getting to my brother. I don't know what it is, Ari, but I got a bad feeling standing out there."

"You're going to a funeral. Of course, you feel bad."

"It's not that. I never even knew Ezarin. I feel nothing for her except pity. But Zadok—"

"Don't worry. You'll see him soon."

Yosef nodded, but his fingers tightened around his beer bottle until the nails gleamed white. He knew that blinding pain, had experienced it twice before in his life. Unwillingly, he let his mind drift back to his childhood and the days before his mother's horrifying death.

A weight pressed down on his chest with such terrible force he could barely breathe.

CHAPTER 7

Cole Tahn paced the oval bridge of the *Hoyer*, arms crossed over his broad chest. His formfitting purple uniform looked crisp. The gold braid on his shoulders shimmered in the harsh light. A tall man with brown hair and blue-violet eyes, he moved with the controlled strength of a hunting lion.

"Halloway, how long until we exit light vault?"

She flipped auburn hair over her shoulder, reading the monitors on the navigation console. "Approximately three minutes, sir."

"Macey?" he called to his redheaded communications officer. "As soon as we sight Kayan, I want you on com to every colonel manning our six military installations."

"Aye, sir. Message?"

"Tell them we're coming in under section twenty-one of the Treaty of Lysomia. I want a state of emergency declared immediately: curfews, house searches, and the suspension of the writ of *habeas corpus*." He pointed a finger harshly. "You tell those people, we know Baruch is down there and, by God, we're going to get him this time. Anyone found to have offered refuge to this criminal will be subject to immediate execution. Got it?"

"Yes, sir."

The entire spectrum splashed his forward screen as they exited the vault, waves of purple and yellow eddying around the edges. Kayan swam into view, lush, blue, with clouds forming a lacy pattern over the vast oceans.

Tahn's shoulder muscles went rigid, and a queasy anxiety invaded his stomach. He stepped down to the second level, walking over to stand before the broad screen and stare hard at the planet.

"Baruch," he whispered. "Damn you, *I know* you're there. This time, we meet. This time *it ends!*"

* * * * *

Zadok and Rathanial stood uncomfortably in the huge spaceport. Over a thousand people packed the vast rectangular room, unhappily enduring the delays and canceled flights. Hostile bickering sounded all around them.

"I hate these places," Zadok grumbled, wiping sweaty hands on his tan robe.

"Government places?"

"Any crowded place." He leaned a shoulder against the grimy white wall. How long had it been since he'd voluntarily placed himself in such a vulnerable situation? Crowds affected him like cages; a man couldn't move if danger threatened, except to stumble over bystanders. Silently, he resented allowing Rathanial to talk him into coming inside.

"It looked like it might rain earlier, but the clouds have gone. Do you want to wait outside?" Dressed in an iridescent silver robe shot through with amethyst stitching, Rathanial looked like royalty in exile.

Zadok puffed an exhale and examined the route to the door, which would force them to weave around at least a hundred sweating, perfumed bodies. "No, I don't think I could endure it."

"We could go slowly, skirt the wall."

"Where could Yosef's transport be? He said he'd be on a direct flight."

"Perhaps they got started late."

"Perhaps."

"You know how unreliable some of those fast transports are. For the most part, they're manned by opportunistic incompetents."

"Ummm."

"I'll be happy to wait outside with you if you want," he offered again. "Though, truthfully, I think it's safe in here. When you're—"

"Do you?"

Zadok ran a hand over his moist scalp, cocking his head inquisitively. Somewhere in his mind the pungent scent of Orillian pines rose and he saw again the spaceport they'd taken a hundred years ago, crowded with captives, stinking with fear-sweat.

"Zadok?" a voice echoed in his mind. The young golden-haired lieutenant, Rulinsi, waved a hand. "What do you want me to do with these?"

Civilians were being herded in so quickly and in such large numbers, no one could keep count. This group consisted mostly of children. He'd started shouldering through the crowd when the explosion hit. It blasted from the edge of his forces, sending blood and bits of flesh flying. He dove for the floor as the captives stormed the doors. *What had happened? Had his people failed to search someone in the foray?*

Mistakes happened in crowds. There were always too many enemies and too few allies.

"On second thought, I am going outside," Zadok decided suddenly and headed toward the door, pushing between people.

Rathanial frowned, following hurriedly. "Abba, do you want to ask about your brother's flight before we go? Maybe it's been delayed for hours. In that case, there's no reason for us to stay in the city. We can return to the caves."

Zadok halted in mid-step. He felt abruptly as though the walls were pressing in around him. An inner urgency told him to get out of the building as quickly as he could. Licking his lips nervously, he gazed around. A small man with fuzzy black hair stared hotly at him, then turned away.

"I don't . . ." Of course, what Rathanial said made sense, but he couldn't bear the thought. "No. I'm leaving. If they're not here in another hour, we'll . . ."

His attention jerked to a tall blond man who weaved slowly through the crowd toward him. He was dressed in a black jumpsuit and had a heavy reddish-blond beard. Zadok squinted, searching the strong chiseled features and piercing blue eyes. Was it? He hadn't seen him in years and the hair color was wrong, plus the beard obscured much of the face, but—

"I think," Zadok whispered, turning to Rathanial, "that our plans have changed."

"Whatever you say, Abba. Just tell me what we're—"

Suddenly a small man with black fuzzy hair thrust his way through the crowd behind Zadok and blurted, "Traitor! We'll stop you! *For the Mashiah!*"

The air crackled and a searing pain blasted Zadok's chest. His legs went out from under him; he slammed the floor hard.

The blond shouted, "No!" and flung himself on top of Zadok to shield him.

In an instant the building burst into hideous screams and rampaging feet. Zadok lay quietly, watching the red stream from his mouth. He knew what the dark color meant. He'd seen far too many people dead or dying to delude himself. Weakly, he tugged the black sleeve of his protector.

"Jeremiel . . . I wasn't sure it was you at first."

"Save your strength, Abba," the man ordered, pulling his pulse-pistol and pointing it around the room. "I'll get you out of here somehow."

"Rathanial?" he coughed, then choked on the clotted blood that bubbled up his throat.

"Who?"

"He . . . he sent for you. He's—"

"The Desert Father from Horeb?"

Zadok nodded feebly.

"I don't know what he looks like, but . . ."

Zadok fell into another fit of coughing and Jeremiel gently rolled him to his side to allow the fluid to flow unimpeded from his mouth.

"Listen," Zadok breathed desperately. "The Veil . . . you must know the ancient texts . . . to get through the heavens."

"Hurry!" Rathanial shouted from nearby.

Through a gray haze Zadok saw him shove a man aside and race to Jeremiel's side. A short distance away, the small fuzzy-haired man lay dead, his throat slit.

"Let's go, *now!*"

Jeremiel picked Zadok up in strong arms and ran through the room, following Rathanial. People cleared a wide path, staring in horror at the blood trail splotching the floor.

"Jeremiel . . . the *Mea Shearim* . . . give it . . . give it to my grandson. Tell Mikael to study . . ."

"I will, Abba."

With his last strength, Zadok reached up and gripped the sacred object, placing it against his forehead and concentrating. "Baruch . . . atta Epagael."

"Say again, Abba. I couldn't hear."

Zadok's vision faded and he heard a deep soothing voice calling his name over and over. It took only a moment before he ceased to feel Jeremiel's arms and the bouncing ride, the screams in the room and Rathanial's frantic instructions, giving directions back to the caves.

He felt himself moving, being pulled away. He flew effortlessly through a vast ocean of emptiness; not even starlight illumined his journey.

* * * * *

The moon hung like a silver coin over the square, casting an eerie glow across the twisted bodies within and lighting the gate and the empty street beyond. Boulders which thrust up here and there before buildings in the merchant's section of town seemed huge hunching beasts, their shadows stretching across the square in dark ominous patterns. Wind whispered between the shops, bringing the scents of baking bread and sweet spices. A few lights glimmered from homes.

Rachel's soul shriveled. Horeb woke and turned her head.

"Are they waiting out there to finish the rest of us?" a woman whimpered from somewhere near the gate. "Dear God, what shall we do?"

"We can't stay," an unknown man responded. "We've no choice."

The living massed by the gate, dark shapes moving like ghosts in the luminous night, tired gestures casting monstrous shadows across the red and gray patterns of the back wall.

"We're going to go faster, baby. Can you hold on?" Rachel asked the child clinging to her back.

"I'm very tired, Mommy."

"Just a little farther and we'll rest, all right?"

Sybil dropped her head in what Rachel assumed to be a nod, and clutched her mother more securely around the shoulders. Rachel pushed her dehydrated body to its limits, struggling to find steady places to brace her hands and knees. Many of the bodies had grown stiff, making the task easier. When they arrived near the gate, Rachel saw that the numbers of living were far greater than she'd have believed possible. There must have been two hundred. The wounded, old people, and children pressed tightly against the stone wall, while the younger people huddled in a knot a few feet from the gate. A small slice of empty ground spread near the walls. Apparently, people had run toward the center of the square when the guards began shooting. Now that space formed a blessed buffer zone between the living and dead. Reaching the edge of the tangled mound of bodies, Rachel pulled her daughter from her back, and set her on the ground. Sybil stumbled, falling, her legs too weak to hold her.

"Are you all right?"

"Yes." Sybil sniffled, rubbing an arm beneath her nose as she stared wide-eyed at the gruesome path they'd just taken.

"Stay right beside me. Don't leave me for a second. Understand?"

Sybil nodded, twining a hand in Rachel's blood-drenched robe to pull herself up. Together they shuffled to join the group near the gate. Composed of about twenty of the heartiest survivors, they turned to stare at her.

"I . . . I think we should try to sneak out one by one," a tall man with light brown hair and a pointed face said. "If they are out there, they won't notice just one person slipping by in the darkness."

"Don't be a fool," Rachel said.

He turned sharply, glaring. "Who are you?"

"Rachel."

"I'm Colin and I don't like you calling me a fool. We can't just—"

"The soldiers have heat and light sensitive scopes on their rifles," Rachel explained. These peasants knew very little about the high technology that had invaded Horeb in the past year. "If they've set up an ambush, they'll be grateful for one target at a time. We have to go in a flood."

"All at once? But they're sure to see—"

"Yes, but a mass exodus will startle them for a moment and with all of us running closely together, some are bound to survive."

"I won't sacrifice myself to shield someone else from the fire!" a pudgy little woman to Rachel's right exclaimed. Her red hair blazed even in the darkness.

"It has to be a unified effort or we'll all be killed."

"It's better," a deep, fatigued voice whispered from behind them. "For some of us to survive than none of us."

Rachel turned, knowing that voice, to see Talo. He staggered forward, his niece Myra supporting him. He had an arm missing. The stub protruded at a hideous angle, wrapped in filthy rags. His gray beard blended so well with the dove-colored light, it was difficult to make out his face.

"Talo," Rachel greeted, heart going out to him. "I'm glad you made it."

"God has something in mind for me."

"Living, hopefully," Myra gasped, breathing hard as they came to a stop beside Rachel and Sybil. Myra's pretty face shone darkly with bruises, one eye swollen almost shut. Her dark hair hung in a straggly mass over her shoulders.

"Not if we listen to this idiot," Rachel said, pointing tiredly at Colin. He stiffened.

"You arrogant—"

"You think we should storm the gate together, eh?" Talo asked Rachel, glancing sideways at Colin. "I agree. When do we go?"

A soft buzz of dissenting voices rose. "Ridiculous! They'll kill us like schools of fish in a net. Stealth is the only way to survive!" "I won't throw my own life away for the rest of you!"

"Wait," Rachel said. "Don't you see? We don't know where the guards might be stationed, but surely the majority are hiding around the gate. Our best chance is to—"

"Then maybe some of us should climb the walls on the far side," Colin said hopefully, nodding at the people around him, trying to gain support. "They'll have fewer guards there."

Talo shook his head. "You go if you want. I'll take my chances with the group going out the gate."

The red-haired woman wrung her hands, sobbing, "I'm too tired to cross the square again. I can't make it." She pressed trembling fingers to her lips.

"What will we do with the wounded?" Colin asked harshly. "If we storm the gate, we'll never be able to drag them with us. But if we sneak out one at a time, we can each carry a child."

"We have to leave the wounded who can't run by themselves," Rachel said coldly, meeting each set of condemning eyes in turn. Hate poured from the assembled faces, but she felt only an irritation at their impracticality. Gazing up at the sky, she could tell from the turning of the constellations that dawn loomed less than two hours away. Lancer, the spear thrower, had a foot touching the tallest peaks in the distance.

A gust of wind whistled around the square, whipping the hem of her bloody robe until it cracked. The stench of death and decay nearly overwhelmed her. Her empty stomach cramped. Sybil clutched Rachel's leg and closed her eyes. Gently, she patted her daughter's hair.

"Would you leave your mother?" the redhead raged. "You're as bad as the Mashiah!"

"My mother died in the plague," Rachel responded softly. "But if she were here and I knew that carrying her might mean death for four or five of you, I'd leave her."

"Four or five? What are you talking about?"

"Many of us who are healthy will stumble and fall anyway, tripping others. But think how much more slowly you'll have to go and how much more likely you'll be to fall if you're carrying someone else. Then there'll be two bodies on the ground to trip others. If an ambush awaits us, falling means death."

"But maybe there is no ambush!"

"Then we can come back for the wounded without fear."

"And," Colin said in a low savage voice. "If we leave the wounded and there *is* an ambush, they're sure to die."

"Yes. Undoubtedly."

"What about the people still alive out there?" The redhead turned around and gazed in horror at the swelling bodies filling the square. The dead moved in a constant writhing, or so it seemed, until one realized it was the hungry night animals at work. "Some are certainly still alive, but buried and too weak to climb out. We should go over the square, calling to see if anyone answers."

Rachel and Talo glanced at each other then lowered their gazes. No one supported the little woman, knowing instinctively that such a long search would mean death for all of them.

"I'm—I'm . . ." the redhead said unsteadily, "at least helping my mother. I don't . . . don't care about the rest of you. You can go around us!" She sliced the air with a fist and staggered wearily toward the wounded. When she reached the wall, a thin elderly woman embraced her and their combined sobs rode the wind like the mournful strains of a violin.

Rachel's gaze drifted over the group. Fear and hope stained frail faces.

A heavy silence descended. The ravening calls of the birds feasting on the flesh in the square grew to a ghastly cacophony of caws and shrieks. The moon cast a ghostly silver sheen over flapping wings and tearing beaks and Rachel thought she caught sight of a wild dog bounding near the far corner. He must have slithered beneath the gate on his belly.

"I'm . . . I'm going to carry my uncle," a boy of perhaps sixteen said. He turned and left. Many others followed.

Talo exhaled through his nostrils. "Rachel, you know the Mashiah better than any of the rest of us. Is there an ambush set up out there?"

"I don't know."

"Is it likely that he wants us to get away? Maybe to tell the story of the massacre to frighten others?"

"Yes," Colin said in relief. "That's probably it! That's why the gate is open. He wants us to—"

"It's *open*?" Rachel demanded. Fear made her voice as sharp as a knife. "You've tried it?"

"Yes, immediately when I got here. It's closed, but it's unlocked."

Rachel stood paralyzed, gripped by a stillness that was part evening chill and part terrible premonition. The frail tendrils of hope that had risen in her died. "Then it's surely a trap. He knew some would survive and . . . We haven't much time. Let's get organized."

"But perhaps we have a friend on the outside and that's why the gate is open?" Colin pointed out.

Desperate smiles touched the remaining faces in the circle. Everyone wanted to believe. Cries of, "Yes, a friend wants to help us," and "Of course, they couldn't have rounded up all of the Old Believers. It's one of our relatives out there!" tore the night. People turned desperately hopeful eyes to the empty moonlit street beyond the gate.

Rachel murmured, "Don't be fools! We can't take that chance."

"God," Talo whispered miserably, "is the only friend we can rely on."

Rachel gazed curiously at him. After all this, faith still gleamed in his dark eyes. In the depths of her being, in the recesses of her weakened consciousness, a hatred rose up, not for Talo so much as anyone who could still believe. She felt like leaping for his throat and shouting, *"You stupid, stupid fool! What has God done for you this day?"* But she hadn't the strength.

Strings of people came to surround the circle, some too old and feeble to stand; they dropped at the edges of the decision-makers. Many supported wounded, some hobbling themselves, all so weak they panted and trembled. All of them stared through wide, afflicted eyes, listening anxiously.

"Are we agreed we'll storm the gate?"

"I agree," Talo said.

"So do I," Myra added.

Reluctantly, people around the circle threw in with them, even Colin. Yet still, it took nearly an hour to work out disagreements of who would stand where and who would go first. Then they steeled themselves in anticipation. As dawn faintly grayed the horizon, Rachel led Sybil to the front to stand next to Talo. The old man gazed calmly out onto the street, a hint of a smile curling his lips.

"Any movement?" she whispered, eyes darting over the lightening buildings.

He shook his head. "Nothing suspicious. See there? Look at the stone doves gathered outside the bakery waiting for their daily tidbits."

Rachel looked. The yellow shop with the huge front windows had a dim light on. A long golden rectangle illuminated the birds strutting outside the door.

"Pretty."

"Yes, they're good birds, friends. I used to feed them. Every morning. I came down with bread I'd saved from dinner and I'd sit on that rock there for an hour and throw them pieces. They know me."

He smiled, as though he knew he'd do it again soon. Cold sorrow drowned her heart. None of them would ever enjoy the freedom they had once had. *If* they escaped, they'd be in hiding until they could overthrow the Mashiah and his wicked rule. And how long would that take? How many years of violence?

"The true Mashiah," Talo said, turning to her with hope glowing in his eyes. "He's coming, you know? Last night, I remembered a verse in the Tahrea. When the numbers are added up right, it predicts he'll be here within weeks." He smiled, a frail, uncertain gesture.

"I pray you're right, Talo."

"I am. You'll see."

Rachel stood silently, watching for a few minutes as the night changed from a deep gray to a seashell opalescence that dimmed the stars. Lancer dipped below the horizon.

"We're ready," Colin called. "Dawn is almost here. We'd better hurry."

Rachel swallowed hard and nodded. "I'll shove the gate open. As soon as it's wide enough, we'll flood out. Does everyone understand?"

She took one last look at the people. Eroded faces with inflamed eyes gazed back, heads nodding. Their greasy mops of hair and bloodstained clothes made them look like ghouls from the darkness of Aktariel's pit. Yet, a severe courage filled their terrified eyes. With the last ounce of strength, she knew, these people would fight to endure.

Though the gesture came from a nationalistic feeling of pride rather than a religious one, she formed her hands into the sacred triangle. "I pray we all make it, brothers and sisters." The symbol was repeated throughout the crowd. People bowed their heads in prayer before crouching, ready to run.

Rachel lifted Sybil to her hip.

"I'm scared, Mom."

"So am I, sweetheart. Can you hold me tight?"

Sybil nodded and wrapped her arms around Rachel's neck. "Run fast, Mommy."

"I will." Rachel kissed her daughter's cold cheek and squeezed her own eyes closed momentarily before taking a deep breath. Mustering her courage, she raced for the gate, swinging it wide and bursting out into the red sandstone street. Like a shot, she headed straight for the flat-roofed houses of the residential section. She knew the sewers and secret cellars so well, she could lose any pursuer there. Talo sprinted at her right, people spilling in a flood around them.

For a brief moment, it seemed everything would be all right. The stone doves burst into flight, circling lazily above them. Smoke rising from chimneys twisted heavenward, reflecting the lavender rays of morning before vanishing in the wind. Sweet scents of fresh baked muffins and pastries filled her nostrils.

"Now!" a harsh voice shouted from somewhere faraway.

And violet light streamed out, slashing the fleeing, ripping off arms and legs. The crackle of the pulse rifles rose to a shrill constant wail, drowning the screams of terror.

"Dear God!" someone shrieked. "They did it. Dear . . ."

"My baby! Don't kill my baby!"

Just before Rachel and Sybil reached the safety of the residential section, she heard Talo cry out in pain and saw him fall. Still alive, he writhed on the ground. Rachel gripped Sybil tighter, running with all her might, heart pounding in her chest.

The dawn air, sparkling with sunlit red dust, rose over a widening pool of blood trickling through the streets of Seir.

Rounding a corner, she sprinted up a narrow alley where tall buildings towered over them, leaving her path in complete darkness. Finding the rectangular opening she'd used a hundred times, she kicked off the sewer cover and shoved Sybil into the wet blackness. On her stomach, she slithered in behind and jerked the cover back into place with a ringing clang.

CHAPTER 8

Ornias hummed to himself as he strolled the magnificent marble halls of the palace, eyes routinely appreciating the breathtaking coral arches and rich paisley rugs. Brilliant sunlight shone through the lace curtains covering the windows high above him, sprinkling his path with dapples of gold. He playfully tapped each of the rose agate statues of the saints as he passed them, smiling disdainfully.

How could any thinking human being possibly believe such foolishness? Saints and angels, demons and gods. Pure bunk. But oh, how very lucrative.

He laughed softly, delight filling him, as he rounded a corner and headed down a long hallway toward Adom's personal office. A servant girl dressed in the gray robes of the palace staff raced toward him at a trot.

"Good morning, Councilman."

"Good morning, Amelia."

She smiled gratefully that he'd spoken, and lowered her gaze respectfully as she passed. Respect? Or fear? He caressed his braided beard, hoping it was the latter. Fear wrought far more obedience than respect. And things seemed to be developing wildly on Horeb. He needed obedience, not reverence—though that didn't hurt things, of course.

When he arrived at Adom's ornately carved door, he straightened his damson colored robe and ran a hand through his light brown hair. Knocking, he called softly, "Adom? It's Ornias. I got your message that you wanted to see me."

He listened, pressing his ear close to the wood. No sound came from within. "Blast it," he cursed under his breath. "You haven't gone back to that godforsaken prayer room again, have you?"

Irritated, he knocked louder, this time shouting, "Adom? Are you in there?"

"Oh!" a soft confused voice answered from within. "Yes, Ornias. I'm coming."

He squeezed the bridge of his nose, heaving an annoyed sigh and muttering, "I'm so glad, Mashiah. I feared you'd vanished into the Pit again."

The door opened and Adom stared questioningly at him. "I . . . Did I call for you?"

"Yes, Adom. Shassy brought me the message that you were out of conference with Milcom and wanted to see me." He narrowed his eyes, irritated, though he didn't know why. Adom did this to him constantly.

"Oh, well, come in." The Mashiah pulled the door wide and left it ajar as he strolled contemplatively across the floor, a hand rubbing his smooth chin. "I wonder why I . . ."

Ornias entered and closed the door behind him, scrutinizing Adom. The man looked bitterly tired. Dark circles glowed beneath his vulnerable eyes, and his pale blond hair hung in greasy strands that draped across his chest. His green robe seemed the only thing about him that was fresh. He usually looked like he'd been worked over by a boxer when he finished "talking" with Milcom, but this time appeared worse than before.

"Are you all right?"

"Hmmm?" Adom turned halfway around, staring at him quizzically. "What did you say?"

Ornias exhaled heavily, striding across the room to put a hand at the Mashiah's back and guide him to the plush crimson velvet chairs positioned in front of the window. "Sit down, Adom. I'll get you some brandy."

"Oh, all right. Thank you."

Ornias strolled to the liquor cabinet and peered through the glass doors at the bottles inside. Making his selection of a hundred-year-old cognac from Orillas Seven, he pulled at the latch and retrieved it, then scooped up two glasses on his way back to drop into the chair across from Adom.

"How is Milcom?" he asked idly as he unwrapped the stopper and blew the dust from the bottle.

"God is worried."

"Is He? About what? Something we've done?" Ornias smelled the rich aroma of the liquor before pouring the glasses full of the copper colored ambrosia.

"No, it's not us. It's the universe. The fabric is torn somewhere."

Ornias gave him an annoyed look. *Please God, not more of this drivel. Spare me!* "Indeed? I assume that's bad?"

"Yes . . . I—I think so."

With his boot, Ornias pulled out another chair and propped his feet on the seat, leaning back and sipping his drink. Discussing Adom's delusions always bored him, but it kept the Mashiah happy and, consequently, couldn't be helped. But worst of all, he hated the conversations about the new "tears" in the universe. They seemed to come so frequently of late, he felt an almost uncontrollable urge to slit his own wrists.

"What does that mean? A 'tear' in the fabric?" he inquired for the thousandth time.

"Oh, it—it refers to the growing singularity patterns. Though I'm not sure I understand it, really. Milcom says that as more appear, the vortices are stretching further, like huge tornadoes, sucking up everything in their paths."

"Really? How interesting." Ornias sighed gruffly and gazed out the window. From where he lounged, he could see the merchants' district of Seir. People stood before shop displays, peering in at new clothing, baked goods, or furniture. He smiled. Without him, Horeb would have none of those things. It'd still be a backward wasteland without trading partners. Still, he despised the place. The ignorance of the people and squalor of the planet had begun to soil his self-image. But things were shaping up. It wouldn't be long now until the Magistrates gave him whatever he desired.

"How have things been going here?" Adom asked, blinking owlishly.

"Oh, nothing you need to worry about. I had to issue some more proclamations against violence and—um—discipline a few recalcitrants. Nothing important."

"Ah . . . good."

"I've been worried about you. Milcom kept you for over a week. Did you realize that?"

Adom nodded, brow furrowing. He picked up his cognac and tasted it pensively. "He needed to talk to me. We're going to have severe problems in the near future."

"Because of the singularity patterns?"

"Partly. But mostly because the rebels here are mounting a major attack against us."

Ornias set his glass down on the carved table with a sharp clink. Not that he believed this Milcom business, but Adom had been surprisingly correct in his predictions over the past three years. "Like what?"

Adom gazed up at him through sober blue eyes. "He wouldn't tell me for certain. Only that we have to double the number of guards around the new temple and palace. Milcom says there will be attempts to destroy both. We have to be prepared."

Ornias swallowed nervously, taking a potent swig from his glass. "I'll take care of it immediately."

"And God said you must stop giving the marines so much power, Ornias. They're abusing it."

He glanced up, disconcerted. A small spot of anxiety swelled in his chest. Adom knew nothing about his attempts to squelch the rebellion that threatened to burst the planet at its seams. "To what are you referring?"

"Well . . . I don't know for sure. But Milcom said to tell you you're being an asinine idiot."

"Did he?" He drummed his fingers on his leg. "Well."

"Oh, don't feel bad. God wasn't being mean. He thought you needed some guidance."

"I see."

Adom smiled. "I knew you would." Then with manic briskness, he leapt from his chair and cocked his head as though listening to someone. Running across the room for the door, he called over his shoulder, "Well, I need to go and check on the flowers in the gardens. So if you'll excuse me—"

"Adom! Sit down! Finish telling me about the rebels and their plots!"

"The rebels?" He stopped, walking backward a few paces. Ornias squeezed his eyes closed, asking through gritted teeth, "You said Milcom wanted us to double the guards. Did he also tell you when we might expect the first attack?"

Adom blinked as though he hadn't the vaguest idea what Ornias was talking about. "Attack? Oh! . . . Oh, no . . . He didn't." He whirled and headed for the door again.

"Have a nice trip to the garden, Adom."

"Thank you. Don't you want to come? The Silmar hyacinths are *lovely* this time of year."

"Yes, I know. But I have things to do."

Adom smiled broadly. "All right. I'll see you later, then." He opened the door and exited into the hall, leaving it so wide that Ornias could see out the hall windows to the vast red desert beyond. Whirlwinds of dust bobbed across the plain, partially obscuring the rocky plateaus in the distance.

Finishing his glass of cognac, he shook his head and poured himself another. Adom always acted a little "strange" after visiting with God, disoriented and aloof, but he usually came back to normal—at least normal for Adom—in a few hours. This period of lunacy was lasting much longer than usual. But then Adom's sojourn with Milcom had lasted longer than usual, too. Perhaps he should have expected this.

Downing his second glass, Ornias stood and perfunctorily smoothed the wrinkles from his damson silk sleeves. "Still, I swear he's getting worse every day."

* * * * *

Dust whirled in ruddy plumes throughout Seir, sizzling against the windowpanes of the tiny boxlike houses that lined the dirt streets near the Mashiah's magnificent palace. On the horizon, drifting clouds glowed a polished carnelian.

Rachel, Sybil, Talo, and Colin stood hidden, watching the long lines of worshipers file into the new Temple of Milcom. Set on a hillside in the center of Seir, the hexagonal structure rose two hundred feet into the dry air, gleaming golden in the dusty haze of sunset. The building's main feature, an enormous glass dome which the architects called the Vault of Heaven, reflected the sun's blaze, creating a great bloody smear against the sky.

Her heart tightened as she logged the number of guards. "They must have tripled their forces around the temple."

"Doesn't matter. Talo and I, we set everything up night before last."

Rachel nodded, noting the faithful who crowded to get inside. Friends. Relatives. "Enemies. Traitors who stood by and watched us slaughtered."

"Tonight," Colin whispered savagely, his pointed face twisted by a cruel smile, "they initiate the structure, consecrate it to Milcom." Wind whistled through the alley, stirring the gray rags he wore.

"Shoah . . . shoah . . . the end of all," Talo moaned and put his hand over his withered face.

Rachel bowed her head. She felt a fatigue so deep consciousness could not probe it. Time and events had telescoped, jumbled like a nightmare that had no reality or reason.

"We fight for what is rightly ours," Colin spat.

"But can't we wait until it's empty? Then—"

"Go home, Talo," Rachel murmured, studying the thick bandage around his waist. It bulged from beneath his brown robe. He was lucky to be alive. The marine's shot had just missed his kidney. Still weak, his abilities and endurance were unreliable. "The finale is already staged. We can do this without you."

"No. I—I fight for Epagael, too. Blessed be the name of the True God."

As the sun dipped lower, light penetrated between the narrow bungalows to land on their faces in slashes of dusty coral. Rachel shuddered. The twilight breeze wore the frosty cloak of winter.

"Mommy," Sybil murmured fearfully, looking from one adult to the next. "I'm cold. Let's go home. Can't we just go home? I don't want to go into the Mashiah's temple."

Rachel straightened her borrowed peach-colored robe. The Kayan silk glistened in the fading light, the beads around her hem and collar shimmering like tiny crystal tears. Lifting her veil and fixing it to cover her face, she knelt and did the same with Sybil's sky blue veil. Her daughter looked at her in utter terror.

"Mom, why do we have to do this? If everything is

already set up, why do we have to go inside?" She gripped Rachel's shoulders frantically.

"We just do. We won't be there for long. I promise. You remember what I told you?"

"You mean that I can't talk?"

"That's right. You just pretend to be shy, all right?"

"But . . . Mom . . . Please, we can kill him from out here. We don't have to—"

"Hush, darling. We're going in."

As she rose, Talo gripped her arm tightly. His withered face was pinched with worry. "Why are you doing this? It's dangerous for you to be inside."

Rachel shook off his hand, holding his eyes with her own. *"I want to see his face."*

"If not for yourself, think of your little girl. What if you get caught in the stampeding crowd?"

"We'll be all right."

"What's that word mean, Mommy?" Sybil whispered. Brown curls peeked from beneath her veil. "Stampede?"

"It means people will run."

"Over us?"

"No, don't worry, baby. We'll be standing in the very back of the temple, so we can get out first if people panic."

Sybil shoved trembling hands into the pockets of her robe and stared at the ground.

Talo clenched his hand into a hard fist. "But you can't always be certain—"

"Nothing is ever certain."

He regarded her in strained silence. The moment stretched uneasily and it took all of Rachel's strength to control the sick sense of foreboding that gnawed at her vitals.

"Are you ready, Sybil?"

"I guess so, Mom." She heaved a halting exhale and squared her tiny shoulders in anticipation.

"That's my brave girl." Rachel squeezed her hand and looked a final time at Colin. "You know what you have to do?"

His eyes gleamed savagely "Yes. Talo and me, we can do it."

"Good. When it's over, I'll meet you at the old burned-out bakery."

Both men nodded, Talo licking his lips and glancing anxiously at Sybil. His gray beard quaked as he formed his hands into the sacred triangle. "May Epagael protect you."

"And you," Rachel responded mechanically.

She led Sybil down the street, carefully selecting a point in the line of worshipers where she recognized no one. They casually blended in and Rachel pulled her daughter closer. Robes of fuchsia and maroon, saffron and emerald dotted the line. When the wind changed directions, the scent of exotic perfume nearly overwhelmed them. A sign of tremendous wealth, the excess labeled the wearer part of the Mashiah's inner circle. Hatred swelled so suddenly her eyes filled with tears. She clenched her hands into fists to still the rising tide of insane emotion. Her glance darted hawkishly through the crowd searching for the wearer.

As they slowly moved toward the huge wooden doors, strains of music wafted out to them. Sweet and high, the notes touched some deep part of Rachel's tormented soul, soothing it, stroking like the tender hand of a lover.

Sybil's young body went rigid as the interior of the temple became visible. In a sudden motion, she stopped, stared up pleadingly and lunged backward, trying to get away. Rachel gripped her hand tighter, struggling to keep Sybil in line.

"Stop it!" she whispered. "Stop it, *now*!"

"Mom . . . *I—I can't go in there*! What if he—"

Rachel pulled Sybil out of line and knelt beside her. Pressing her mouth against Sybil's ear, she whispered, "I know this is hard. Do you want to wait for me out here?"

"*No*! No, I want to be with you, but—"

"Then hurry, before people get suspicious."

"Mom, hold me tight, just for a minute? I'm afraid."

Rachel complied, stroking her daughter's back comfortingly. "It's all right. We're just going to be inside for ten minutes. Then we'll run and we won't ever come back here again. You understand?" Sybil nodded. "Are you going to be all right?"

Eyes had turned to them, watching curiously. Sybil watched them back. Swallowing hard, she whispered. "Yes, I'm sorry. Let's hurry."

Standing again, she put a hand on Sybil's shoulder and they drifted with the flow. Once inside, Rachel dragged Sybil along the back wall while the other worshipers went forward to search for seats. Though the temple stretched three hundred feet in front of her, so many people pressed into the room, that few seats were left. A horde of worshipers began lining the walls.

In awe, Rachel's mouth parted slightly. The last rays

of sunlight streamed through the glass dome, burning over the gold inlay of the walls and altar. Interlocking inverted triangles gleamed wherever she looked. The pews, arranged in chevrons, fit neatly into each hexagonal niche.

Unease crept up around her like a cold winter mist. If she'd only known the location of the altar, she could have entered by a different door, but now it was too late. She stood no more than fifty feet from the blasphemous platform and trying to get farther away would arouse too much suspicion.

"Stand a little behind me, Sybil," she whispered. The girl nodded and pressed back against the wall, bracing her trembling knees against Rachel's left leg. She reached around to gently pat Sybil's cheek.

People continued to file in, though the temple threatened to burst at the seams. Before Rachel knew it, at least fifteen worshipers littered the path between her and the door. Big men, most of them, she'd have to force her way out when the time came.

As the sky darkened, lamps glowed to life in the temple. The soft light shimmered from silks of violet and ivory, sparkling off jeweled hands and hair nets.

Of a sudden the musicians on the other side of the building stopped playing and began a new song, louder, the notes clashing violently.

Ornias strode gracefully into the room, smiling beneficently as he made his way down the center aisle toward the altar. Dressed in rose-colored satin, his light brown hair and braided beard seemed to glow in the ocher lamplight.

Rachel clutched up inside. A tremor shook her so cruelly she had to force herself to close her eyes and go deep inside to find the source and halt it. When she opened them again, the High Councilman stood majestically at the altar, opening the thick book that lay on the podium.

A hush fell over the room.

"My people," he cooed. "We come together this Shabbat night to give thanks to Milcom for this magnificent temple."

In rumbling unison, the faithful murmured, "May the name of the Eternal be blessed now and forever more."

Ornias lifted a fist over his head and his hand cast cobalt shadows on the wall at his back. "With love abounding hast thou loved us, O Lord our God. With great and exuberant mercy hast thou had compassion on us."

"Blessed be the name of Milcom."

Rachel stared numbly. *Compassion?* Was there any left in the universe? Yet, for all the terror of the past few days, the religious ceremony touched a place inside her that needed comforting, cried out for the former peace she'd felt at such rituals. *Oh, Epagael, why did you forsake us?*

"Our Father, Our King! Enlighten our eyes in the Law. Teach us to follow the path of your anointed Deliverer . . ." Ornias closed his eyes and bowed his head. Lamplight winked from the jewels in his hair. "Adom Kemar Tartarus. Let His name be graven in our hearts so that we might proclaim your glory to the universe." Slowly, his upraised fist lowered to rest on the podium and he looked toward the rear of the temple.

A tall shadow appeared on the far wall, wavering in the dim light. All heads turned, reverence washing across faces. Adom stepped into the temple, chin tipped heavenward, hands spread wide. Pale blond hair cascaded in waves over his chest. He had deeply set blue eyes, riding atop high cheekbones and a straight patrician nose. A God incarnate, the flashing silver of his robe made him seem a pillar of embodied starlight.

He floated across the floor like a dandelion seed wafting on gentle morning winds. He lightly touched the heads of the children he passed, smiling gently. When he neared Rachel, her heart thundered. She bowed her head to stare at the floor.

He passed silently, mounting the platform to take his place behind the podium. Ornias stepped down to stand no more than ten feet away from her.

A look of deep and abiding love filled Adom's eyes as he gazed out over the congregation. "Baruch atta Milcom," he praised and his deep voice seemed to caress the very walls.

"Blessed be his Deliverer," the temple responded.

Rachel counted off the minutes. How long? Should she start moving toward the door? No, let him get into his sermon, then she'd go, when he'd captured people's attention completely. But as she looked around the temple, she knew he already had, no one so much as moved while he readied himself. Worshipers' faces brimmed with adoration.

"Believers," he said softly. "No one can deny the awesome beauty of your labors. This temple will remain for millennia as a light unto heathen civilizations. The first temple to the Great and Glorious Milcom."

"We beseech thee, O Eternal, save us."

"We promised, O Mighty One of Sinlayzan, to find you a dwelling place. Lo, we have found it in the deserts of Horeb. And here . . . here we will set up the fountain of your Truth. Here, we will begin the battle to wipe your enemies from the face of the universe. To establish righteousness and fear in the hearts of human beings."

Fear. Rachel's stomach fluttered, memories of the past week rising up to slap her again and again. She turned fever-brilliant eyes on Adom, hatred pouring from her face. For a brief instant his gaze touched hers, and she trembled. What was it about him that set the soul to yearning? Some magnetic aura of confidence and innocence surrounded him. Even she . . . even Rachel Eloel . . . felt it.

"My Beloved People," Adom said. Pain tinged his voice. "The past few days have been difficult for all of us. There are those in the fold who seek to destroy all we have built."

A buzz of hostility echoed through the temple.

He looked up pleadingly, lips quivering. "I have prayed for days without end that the rebels would come to me, but . . ."

"Don't try to talk to the filthy demon worshipers!" someone shouted.

Adom squeezed his eyes closed a moment. "I want only to end the hate." He dropped his voice to a whisper. "Tell me how? Tell me, my people?"

Then, as though God himself had told him, he cocked his head and looked piercingly at Rachel. Tears filled his eyes. "Tell me how?" he repeated, but this time the question was asked of no one but her.

A flood of adrenaline raced like fire through her veins. *Dear God, he knew!*

Roughly, she gripped Sybil's sleeve and shoved her along the wall as she backed toward the door, forcing men out of her way.

Throughout the temple, people responded to Adom's question. "Imprison the dissidents!" "Punish them!" "Kill them!" Kill them . . . kill them . . . *kill them . . .!*

Rachel bumped into a burly man who refused to move. He was in the midst of waving a fist and shouting, "Give them to us. We'll take care of them!"

She tried to shove around him and he stopped to glare. "What's your hurry?" he demanded. "The ceremony isn't over."

"My little girl is ill," she whispered imploringly. "She has to get out to the fresh air before she—"

"She doesn't look sick to me," He frowned at Sybil. "You sick, kid?"

"Yes, sir."

"I think you're playacting. You babes are all alike. You get a little tired of standing and you want to go home. But you *need* to hear the Mashiah for your own good. Understand, girl?"

"Get out of my way!" Rachel ordered, slamming a fist into his chest. "I didn't ask for your advice on raising my child!"

"Well somebody needs to give you some!"

"Get out of our way before I . . ."

The first explosion rocked the temple and a rumble like the ground ripping asunder shook them. The glass dome shattered; splinters flew high into the slate blue sky to hover like the stars themselves before crashing down.

A roar of horror laced the temple. People ran.

"Stampede, Mommy!" Sybil yelled. "Come on, let's go!"

Rachel grabbed her hand and tried to shoulder through the onslaught of terrified people who raced for the door nearest her. But in the wave after wave of bodies, she was shoved back against the wall and knocked to the floor.

"Mom!" Sybil wailed as the second explosion blasted the far wall. It toppled down, smashing pews and people beneath its weight. Tortured shouts and squeals rolled through the tumbling structure.

Rachel pulled Sybil to her chest, shielding her from the flailing arms and legs as people stormed the doors. Flames burst to life engulfing pews, stealing toward the altar.

"Adom?" she heard Ornias scream. "Hurry, we must leave! Adom!"

Rachel glimpsed the Mashiah's pale face. He stood like a statue on the altar, eyes still fixed on her.

"Tell me why?" he shouted again.

Rachel fought against the magnetism of his vulnerable eyes, screaming, *"You slaughtered my people!"*

He blinked, face slackening. "What?"

"Adom! For God's sake!" Ornias yelled at the top of his lungs, gripping the Mashiah's sleeve and dragging him from the altar. "She's trying to *kill* us!"

Adom shook off the councilman's strong hand and lunged for the side door.

Rachel got to her feet and ran, stumbling, through the shattered pews and broken stones to get outside. Worshipers stood paralyzed in the night air, the flames of devastation flickering across their horrified faces. When the cold wind struck her, she inhaled sharply and swung Sybil to her hip, dashing headlong up the steep street.

A terrified group of women and children passed her, tears soaking their cheeks. One woman wailed, "The filthy rebels did this. I know it! I hope Milcom wipes them from the face of the world!"

Rage pierced Rachel's breast. Did none of them care that a thousand of their relatives had been brutally murdered only a few days ago? As she reached the crest of the hill and prepared to round the corner, she heard a hoarse scream surge over the roar of the final blast. From nowhere it came, everywhere. She whirled around and her heart almost stopped beating.

Below, on the temple grounds, Colin stood surrounded by a ring of howling worshipers. Ornias, rose-colored robe shading crimson in the light of the fire, shouted orders she could not hear, but in agony she realized their intent when a young man took a truncheon and began brutally beating Colin over the head. He dropped to his knees, covering his bloody skull with his arms.

Adom, where was Adom? In vain she searched the crowd for him. Had he died in the final tumbling of walls? Silently, she prayed for it to be so. And Talo? Had he escaped?

Rachel watched Colin sprawl across the firelit ground. The crowd surged over the rebel until she lost sight of him. Then, suddenly, Ornias turned in her direction and his arm lashed out. Through the roar of the fire, she faintly heard him shout, "There! There's the culprit. Rachel Eloel is responsible for this destruction!"

Faces turned her way and an angry mob coalesced before her eyes, grabbing stones and sticks, racing up the street toward her, screaming curses.

"Mommy! Come on!" Sybil shrieked, tugging Rachel's hand with all her might. "We have to go to the old burned-out bakery, Mommy! Come on!"

Rachel gripped Sybil's hand and they ran wildly through the streets.

CHAPTER 9

Jeremiel had to bend low to follow Rathanial and Sarah through the narrow tunnel that led into the dark depths of the mountain. The protective fabric of his black jumpsuit scraped shrilly against the stone. In the dry coolness, the smell of the fresh-baked bread Sarah carried in her basket struck him painfully. It had been three days since he'd eaten anything substantial. Since he'd been forced to make his way on foot through the tangles of vine and wet forests, energy bars had been his only sustenance and they were a damn poor substitute for real food.

Rathanial stopped, blinking quizzically at yet another of the many smaller tunnels that jutted off from the main one they trod. "Sarah? Isn't this the turn? I thought I remembered—"

She shook her head and long black hair fell over her shoulders. A pudgy woman with a face too round and eyes too large, she reminded Jeremiel of a timid owl, the type that stuck to the high cliffs of old Earth, refusing to be seen until the cover of night crept over the land.

"No, no, it's farther." But her voice cracked with such doubt that Rathanial shot a worried glance at Jeremiel.

"Are you sure?" Rathanial asked softly. The lamp in his hand wobbled, throwing uncertain shadows on the brown walls.

"No. We may have . . ."

Jeremiel leaned a shoulder against the stone and massaged his forehead, listening absently as the two continued to quietly discuss whether they'd already missed the turn or not. The pungent scent of pine duff still clung to his jumpsuit, rising pleasantly in the confines of the quiet tunnel. They'd passed a number of workers in the halls above, but none appeared here, though tracks marred the dark brown sand.

"But, my dear Sarah, I was down this way only . . ."

Jeremiel closed his eyes. He felt devastatingly lonely and tired. The chasm of dread in his chest yawned wider, until it seemed a somber, frightening darkness pervaded everything like a midnight wind. Zadok's death formed part of it. He silently wondered what the future held with that old stalwart of strength and tenderness gone. His thoughts roamed briefly over the past fifteen years. No matter how risky his ideas for antagonizing the Magistrates, Zadok had always offered support, both financial and moral. But with him dead, there'd be an internal struggle for power, upsetting the applecart for a time. Power-mongers within his own ranks would scratch to the surface and certainly the government would now consider him vulnerable. His forces could expect repeated attacks for the next few months. Maybe Rudy had been right. He should have forgotten the entire Horeb affair.

He hugged himself and frowned, watching the lamplight flicker over the cinnamon walls. He seemed to make the wrong choices so damned often lately. Syene . . . Syene. Her sweet name tormented him.

"Just a little farther," Sarah was saying. "If we haven't found it in another fifteen minutes, we'll turn back."

"That's agreeable." Rathanial nodded and shrugged apologetically to Jeremiel. He matched the shrug, smiling his understanding.

They started off again, footsteps echoing eerily down the tunnel. In only a few moments they came to a staircase carved into the rock which led downward.

"Ah, you were right, Sarah," Rathanial said in embarrassment and patted her shoulder. "I shouldn't have argued."

"It's all right. I wasn't sure myself." She led the way expertly now. Down, down, until finally they stepped into a small rounded room with a single table and two chairs. Jeremiel ducked his head in defense against the low ceiling, gaze roving the dusty bottles of wine sitting in the wall niche.

"What is this place?" he asked, dusting off his black pants. It smelled of old wax and dry paper.

Sarah walked shakily forward, the soft light catching in her yellow sleeve bows. "It was Papa's Sanctum. He came here to read and study. It was the only place he believed truly s–safe." Her voice broke and she put a trembling hand to her mouth.

Jeremiel sympathetically dropped his gaze. The double funeral in the pouring rain that morning had left all their emotions raw.

"Sarah," Rathanial whispered. "Come and sit down. You'll feel better."

She smoothed her skirts and did as instructed, sinking into one of the chairs and placing the basket on the table. Jeremiel sat on the floor, stretching his long legs out and leaning back against the cold stone. A chill seeped through the wall to touch his shoulders.

Rathanial paced nervously, a hand propped beneath his white-bearded jaw, ancient eyes filled with a worry so deep it felt palpable in the still room. The ruby threads in his silver robe gleamed darkly in the candlelight.

"If you don't mind," Jeremiel asked, a penitent look on his face. "Before we begin this in depth, Sarah, could I trouble you for a piece of that wonderful smelling bread? You see, I haven't—"

"Oh, of course," she answered guiltily, thrusting the entire basket at him. "I'd forgotten I'd even brought it."

He took a thick slice and offered the basket to Rathanial who shook his head. Setting the loaf by his side, Jeremiel took a huge bite out of his slice, gratefully sinking back against the wall. A sweet bread, it tasted of nuts and Kayan oranges.

"Well," Rathanial sighed, "I suppose we should get down to business. None of us expected the sort of travesties we've witnessed in the past several days, but they certainly have a grave bearing on the future of Gamant civilization." He looked from Jeremiel to Sarah and back again.

Sarah watched him through wide, pained eyes, twisting the fabric of her skirt in her fingers. "What business?"

"The business of protecting Gamant interests throughout the galaxy, my dear."

"For example?"

"Many things," Rathanial said, slightly irritated. "Like what to do with the Mashiah on Horeb. How to best approach the Magistrates from here on out. How we can mend broken fences among our own people."

Jeremiel frowned. Had Zadok kept her so much in the dark about his leadership that she didn't realize the severe challenges ahead? He wondered what that said about the old man's confidence in his youngest daughter?

"Rathanial," he interjected, chewing and swallowing a mouthful of bread, "before we get into 'business,' let's discuss the past few days. Who was the man you killed at the spaceport?"

"I don't know. I've never seen him before."

"But you have suspicions?"

"He's probably one of the Mashiah's hired assassins."

"The Mashiah you wrote me about?"

"The same."

"Why would he want to kill Zadok?"

Rathanial waved a hand anxiously, then wiped his sweating palms on his silver robe. "I . . . It clears the way for him to declare himself the leader of Gamant civilization. I think that's been his plan for months."

"But I thought that burden fell on Zadok's younger brother?"

"Yes, except we've been trying to contact Yosef for hours. He seems to have disappeared between Tikkun and here."

"Disappeared?"

"Apparently. He left Kayan a few days ago and hasn't been heard from since. I think we must presume he's dead."

Jeremiel nodded. "Given the past few days, I'd say that makes sense. So the leadership goes to Sarah now?"

"Legally, yes."

"Only legally—not rightfully?"

Rathanial cast a glance at Sarah who gazed up timorously. She looked like a frightened child. "Yes, rightfully, too. But powerful men rarely hesitate over a few flimsy moral issues. Adom cares nothing for our tradition. He seeks to begin a new branch of Gamant civilization."

"Then we must immediately organize a contingent of guards for Sarah."

"Oh," Rathanial said tightly. "Sarah will be well protected here."

Jeremiel's' brows drew together. "After what just happened to Zadok and Ezarin, how you can be certain of that?"

"Oh, all right," Rathanial conceded with obvious reluctance. "We'll arrange for more bodyguards. How does that sound, my dear? Will it make you feel better?"

Jeremiel's hackles rose at the vaguely resentful tone. The woman had just witnessed the deaths of two members of her family and a third had probably shared their fate. *Of course* a heavier guard would make her feel better, and she had every right to it.

"But I don't understand," Sarah said quietly. "If Horeb's Mashiah knows he's not next in line, killing Papa, Ezarin, and Uncle Yosef would serve no purpose."

Jeremiel blinked in disbelief. "I'd suggest he plans on killing you and your son next."

She glanced at him so fearfully, he dropped his gaze. "Papa mentioned something like that the day we found Ezarin."

"Then again, perhaps Ezarin's death and Zadok's are two unconnected events. It might be that—"

'It might be,' Rathanial said tiredly, pacing the small room, "that Zadok was killed because the Mashiah discovered I'd come to Kayan to ask him to test Adom's authenticity."

"*Is* that why you came?" Sarah asked.

Rathanial wet his lips and his glance darted nervously around the cave, as though he feared the faraway prophet could hear. "We must be careful. There are 'ears' everywhere in these troubled times."

"Are you saying that the Mashiah might have had Papa killed to keep him from doing the testing?"

"He's a very cruel man and he fears being exposed for the fraud he is."

"But it still doesn't—"

"I'm not certain, Sarah. Zadok, as you well know, had a thousand enemies. It may have been a Magisterial plot, or possibly some of the energy merchants finally discovered—"

"But you believe the Mashiah did it." She leaned forward pensively and the light played through her tangled web of black hair, stitching her round cheeks with a lacy pattern of shadow. "You said the day we found Ezarin that he was responsible."

"Yes, but I may very well be wrong. My own perceptions are limited these days. I see Adom as responsible for everything evil."

"From your letters," Jeremiel said and took a deep breath, "I'd say that response is natural." He took another bite of the flavorful bread and chewed it while contemplating the toes of his black boots.

"Yes, but it terrifies me."

"Then someone must test him," Sarah said.

Rathanial blinked. "Do you know how?"

She reached into her skirt pocket and drew out the *Mea Shearim*, holding it by the chain at arm's length. A quaver came into her voice. "Papa died before he could tell me."

"I suspected as much. That means the way to the Veil is lost forever. We must figure out other—"

"Maybe."

The old man turned sharply, fixing her with a breathless

look. "What do you mean? I thought Zadok was the only one who knew the—"

"He was. But he always said anyone could find out if they searched the ancient books long enough."

"Which ancient books?"

Her thin black brows drew together over her nose and she opened her mouth as though to speak, then hesitated. Jeremiel's eyes went from her to Rathanial. It seemed to him as though neither wanted the other to know—as though they doubted each other's trustworthiness. That provided food for thought. What did Sarah see in Rathanial that left her dubious? And vice versa?

"Sarah!" Rathanial snapped. "Tell me!"

"He—he never specified," she said, but shifted her eyes in such a way that Jeremiel found it as hard to believe as Rathanial apparently did. A cold mask dropped over the old man's features.

"I see. Well, we'll have to put our scholars to work immediately." He paced, drumming his fingers on his forearms.

Watching the two of them, a sapping feeling of hopelessness dragged at Jeremiel, as though the hard stone beneath him might turn to quicksand at any moment. Gamants suspicious of Gamants—when all they had left in the galaxy was each other. A soft clink sounded from the corridor outside. Jeremiel pushed back against the wall, straightening, ears instinctively trained on the silence.

"What is it?" Rathanial asked, horror sparkling in his eyes. He took a step forward. "Did you hear—"

"Just a . . . No, nothing. I'm . . . just tired, I guess." He forced a smile, but the sense of danger persisted.

Rathanial's eyes examined the doorway steadily, then he turned to Zadok's daughter. "It was very kind of you to show us the way here, Sarah. But could you, that is, would you mind if I spoke alone with Jeremiel for a time?"

"Not at all," she said as though relieved. She got to her feet in a rustle of skirts. "I'll meet you in the main gallery when you've finished discussing . . . when you've finished."

"Yes, that's fine. We won't be long. Perhaps an hour."

"Good, I'll see you there." She smiled feebly and rushed toward the stairs.

"Uh . . . dear," Rathanial called softly, "would you mind leaving the *Mea Shearim*? We promise to take good care of it."

She glanced at the blue ball on the end of the chain, then clutched it to her ample breasts. "I'm not sure that's wise."

"Please, Sarah, I don't know how to use it anyway. We both know that. I want it only because Jeremiel is knowledgeable on the ancient texts and I'm hoping that with it here in *his* hands, he might able to remember some passages from the magical papyri. It is, after all, a possession of all Gamants, isn't it?"

Her dark gaze sought Jeremiel's and she held it for a long moment, probing. He shifted uneasily, feeling a keen mind behind those black orbs, keen and fearful. Finally, she handed it to him reluctantly, whispering, "You mustn't touch the globe. Hold it only by the chain."

He took the object, surprised by how warm the gold felt in his fingers. "I will."

She cast a quick glance at Rathanial, then darted into the hallway. The white-haired elder stood for what seemed an eternity, listening until her footsteps faded to nothingness.

"Dear Lord," he finally whispered, slumping into one of the chairs. "What's happening to us? She doesn't trust me, *me*! with the secrets of Gamant civilization."

Jeremiel lifted his brows, nodding. "That was rather obvious. And what's this about my being 'knowledgeable'? You know I haven't studied the texts since I was a boy. I haven't had the time."

"Oh, it was just a ploy. I thought if she wouldn't leave the device with me, she might with you."

"Hmm."

"I had a bad feeling about her taking it out of this room. I don't know why, I just did. She seems so—frail."

Jeremiel gave him a sideways glance. Frail translated to incompetent, but he didn't challenge the surreptitious assertion. Instead, he lifted the *Mea Shearim* until the globe swung before his eyes. Blue swirls eddied across the surface. "All my life I've heard about this sacred object. I know that it supposedly serves as a gateway to God. But what is it? I mean really?"

Rathanial stiffened, glaring. "What do you mean, *really*?"

"I mean scientifically. What does it do?"

"It opens the path to God," Rathanial insisted stubbornly. Then, changing the subject, he interjected, "I'm opening a bottle of wine, would you like a glass?"

"I would love a glass, thank you." Quietly, he scrutinized Rathanial as the old man went about blowing the dust from a bottle and opening it, then pouring two pewter goblets full and handing one to Jeremiel. In a series of gulps, he emptied the glass and held it out for more. Rathanial eyed him curiously, but refilled it. His manner had grown terse, disinclined to discuss the necklace at all.

In a clear delaying tactic, the old man said, "Jeremiel, thank you for coming. Especially now, after Zadok's . . . death. The people will feel lost for a time. They'll be ripe for the picking by any false prophet who claims divine right."

"Your message left me little choice, Father. Your exact wording was: 'The very survival of Gamant civilization hangs in the balance. We desperately need your presence here.' "

Rathanial pursed his lips and stared into the dark wine. "And I meant every word. You've no idea what Adom is doing. He's brutally murdering anyone who still holds to the old faith. He's even set up a torture chamber, I've heard, to force unwilling prisoners to name their fellow 'demon worshipers.' "

"Demon worshipers?"

"Oh, yes, he considers anyone who believes in Epagael to be a cohort of Aktariel's."

"He proposes a different God, I assume?"

"Milcom. A bastard God taken from some obscure ancient text."

"After hearing about your plague and drought, I find it hard to swallow that people are buying this Milcom business. Can't they see that since the Mashiah has come to power, their society and safety have crumbled?"

Rathanial took a long drink of his wine and, frowning, went back to drop into his chair. His brow furrowed deeply before he looked up. "I don't understand it either, except that Adom has such a magnetic personality people can't resist believing his explanations for Horeb's destruction."

Jeremiel took long drinks of his wine, wishing it were a strong Ngmora whiskey that would quickly soften the edges of his inner pain and anxiety. "And his explanations are?"

"Some preposterous notion that the plague and other scourges mean that Epagael has abandoned us to the pit of darkness. He says a more powerful deity has arrived to offer salvation."

"Milcom."

"Of course."

"So people are supposed to convert and live happily ever after, is that it?"

"Yes." Rathanial closed his eyes for a moment before saying with a quaver in his voice, "And those who convert do."

"What do you mean, they do?"

Rathanial hunched forward, eyes pleading. "It's . . . it's frightening, Jeremiel. As soon as Adom immerses people in his consecrated water, they . . . they don't get the disease and—"

"So maybe he generated the plague himself and has the only antidote? Given in the waters of his mysterious baptism? From your reports I'd expect as much."

"I thank God you received my messages. Zadok never received any that I sent him. He knew nothing of our dilemma until I—"

"He never received *any* of your messages?"

"No."

"Who did you send them by?"

"Our best couriers. Loyal Gamants. None of whom ever returned from their missions." A brittle look of old sorrow touched his face and the goblet in his hands trembled slightly. He carefully set it on the table. "We sent out search parties, of course, but no remains were ever found."

Jeremiel forced his face to remain bland, but his mind whirled. *Then how, my friend, did you get here so easily? Did they let you go? Why?*

"Did you have any problems getting to Kayan?"

"No. But I took extraordinary precautions. You can't imagine—"

"Uh-huh." Jeremiel exhaled wearily and laid the *Mea Shearim* in his lap. Draining his wine, he offered the cup to Rathanial for refilling. The old man obliged, pouring it full. A slight glow touched him, the liquor blessedly soaking through his empty stomach. Too bad he hadn't more time. If he'd had the luxury, he'd have found a quiet place alone and gotten reeling drunk while he screamed curses at himself.

"And after you arrived on Kayan, first Ezarin was killed, then Zadok?"

"Yes, but I—I don't know if there's a connection. I was very careful on Horeb. Only one other person knew of my departure, a trusted monk who's been with me for a hundred years."

"But clearly the information leaked. Who is this *trusted* monk?"

"He couldn't be responsible!" Rathanial insisted violently.

"I trust Father Harper more than I do myself! I swear to you, he never would have told anyone."

"But the facts can't be denied. Ezarin and—"

Rathanial whirled to slam a fist into the table. "You said yourself, the events could be unconnected! We don't know for certain that my people on Horeb are to blame!"

"Certainty," Jeremiel said and raised bushy blond brows, "is hardly something we can wait for. We must make decisions based on the best information we have. And, at this moment, that points to treachery."

"Oh, all right," Rathanial put hands on either side of his head and pressed hard, as though to force such a thought from his brain. "But it isn't my people who are betraying me! Though . . . yes, I think I knew from the beginning, when Ezarin first disappeared that somehow the Mashiah had found out, but it couldn't have been Father Harper. It's . . . it's the 'listeners.' They're everywhere."

The eerie glow that touched the old man's eyes set Jeremiel on edge. "Listeners?"

"Yes. Terrible things, they come in the night and cluster in the shadows."

"What are they?"

"We don't know. They won't speak with us, and we can rarely speak without one of them appearing."

"Human?"

"No . . . no, I don't think so."

Jeremiel frowned, fervently praying the old monk wasn't going to tell him real demons existed. He could bear anything except a retreat to the supernatural. "Then what?"

Rathanial swirled his wine uncomfortably, as if guessing Jeremiel's thoughts. "Perhaps some sort of spectrum-projection with sensing abilities."

"Projection?" A tingle of cold went down his back as he glanced frantically around the room. The Magistrates had very sophisticated devices and it was rumored they had a special project to work them into the religious frameworks of the people they wished to spy upon. "Have you seen them here?"

"No, no, I'm sorry, I didn't mean to frighten you. I haven't, not on Kayan."

"So the projector, if that's what it is, has distance limitations."

"I suppose. Regardless, they're certainly the Mashiah's tools or . . . or emissaries, sent to report on our activities."

Jeremiel gave the old man a sidelong look, finishing his wine and retrieving the *Mea Shearim* again. The closer he brought it to his face, the brighter the globe beamed. "Is this 'gate' the only one in existence?"

"Yes, so far as we know. Though the ancient texts say there were thousands in the old days, the days of Exile."

"*How* does the *Mea Shearim* open the path to God?" He returned to the question he'd asked earlier. Rathanial's face paled and he ran a wrinkled hand through his white hair.

"No one knows. It's part of the mystery of Epagael."

"Uh-huh," Jeremiel grunted. Wiping the crumbs from his hand on his pants, he reached down and unclipped his belt buckle, then hit the button on the back. A soft hum sounded, two hidden panels sliding back on the top. He circled the *Mea Shearim* with the buckle.

"What's that?" Rathanial demanded, appalled.

"Hmm? Oh, a hand-corder. It's—"

"It's sacrilegious to subject a holy object to such things!"

"Yes, but fascinating. Look at these readings." He tipped the corder so the father could read them, then smiled indulgently, realizing the man hadn't the slightest understanding of the symbols and, in fact, despised his own curiosity about them. "Shall I interpret for you?"

Rathanial's eyes narrowed with emotion. "What's it say?"

Jeremiel smiled. At least the question marked a step in the right direction. "The outer containment vessel, the globe itself, consists of cooled beryllium ions. They seem to form some sort of magnetic trap."

"Trap?"

"Yes, the ions are organized into a series of concentric spherical shells. They slip around the shells in a liquidlike phase, but rarely diffuse from one to another." He blinked contemplatively. "Reminds me of Palaia Station."

He hesitated, waiting for Rathanial to say something, but the old man's jaws were clamped as tight as a clam's shell. Jeremiel sighed and continued. "I think we—"

"Shells around what?"

"That's certainly the brass ring question. I can't tell with this small hand-corder. But I can say that whatever's inside emits particles at a rather astounding rate."

"What kind of particles?"

"All kinds."

"Are you trying to be funny?"

"Not even inadequately." He threw the Desert Father a

tired smile. "As well, the core of the object is extremely heavy."

"How heavy?"

"About," he murmured, checking the dial again, "four billion tons."

Rathanial's face puckered in disdain. "That's ridiculous! I've held the *Mea Shearim* and it's as light as a feather."

"Yes . . . curious, isn't it?" Jeremiel frowned at the blue ball. "I wonder if the ions are cooled by the same source that counteracts gravity. Or maybe the object itself isn't actually in our space. Perhaps the mass exists in another universe and we see it through the 'gate'?"

"Let me have it!" Rathanial demanded, rising from his chair and extending a hand. "With your reverence for it, you might break it."

"I certainly would not want to break it," Jeremiel said and handed it over. "Even with limited information, I'm fairly certain that could prove disastrous. Incidentally, Zadok said I was to give it to Mikael, his grandson. So don't think you're going to run off to Horeb—"

"I know how the tradition works."

"Do you also know the history of the object? I'd be interested to know when it came into being?"

Rathanial returned to his seat and reverently put the *Mea* in his pocket. "The webs of mythology woven around the *Mea* are intricate. Some scholars say it can be traced to the ancient, and now lost, books of Exodus and Deuteronomy. Those works discussed two sacred stones, the *Urim* and *Thummim*, which were placed in a priest's breastplate. *Urim* and *Thummim*, it's said, meant *lights and perfections*. Even then they were connected with ascertainment of the divine will. The only surviving quote about them goes something like, 'And thou shalt put in the breastplate of judgment the *Urim* and the *Thummim*, and they shall be upon Aaron's heart when he goeth in before the Lord.'"

"Who was Aaron?"

"Nobody knows anymore. Some priest apparently."

"Curious," Jeremiel said softly, "that the chain is long enough to insure the object still rests over the heart. What other myths discuss it?"

"Oh, there are hundreds. Sinlayzan's people called them 'thunder stones,' and believed they were related to the gate of the world, the *loka-dvara*, through which a soul might pass to the beyond, wherever that is. There are even stories

110

that Yacob, the Father of the people, went to sleep on a stone at the place where heaven and earth opened on to each other and God came to talk to him." He lifted a hand and shrugged. "But who knows. There are other scholars who maintain the origin of the *Mea* goes no farther back than the Great Night of Glass."

"Somewhere in the back of my mind, I remember stories about the *Meas* being related to Indra's Net. Do you know any of those stories?"

"No, though I'm sure Zadok did. I even heard him discuss fragments of that myth only last . . ."

A frigid wind gushed through the door of the small cave, snuffing the candle. A blanket of darkness descended. Jeremiel was halfway to his feet when a scream rent the air from the corridor, a scream of such wrenching agony that he felt his heart jump.

"Dear God," Rathanial whispered tightly. "What . . ."

Jeremiel's hand went to the pistol dangling from his belt. Pulling it, he slipped out to the spiral staircase and eased up the steps.

A second scream followed, a woman crying out in horror, and footfalls thundered, as though someone stumbled frantically through the blackness.

"Sarah?" Jeremiel shouted and his voice echoed a hundred times as he ran, one hand braced against the wall to guide him through the pitch blackness. "Sarah!" He took a remembered right, then a left.

Other voices stirred in the corridors. The rattle of booted feet striking stone erupted from somewhere up above.

"*Sarah?*"

"Here," a weak voice answered and Jeremiel whirled.

"Where?"

"Over here, against the wall."

Jeremiel followed her voice, one hand extended in front of him, bumping stone after stone. Finally, he heard her hard breathing and knelt. Reaching, he searched the cool air until his fingers landed on her face and she jumped. Gently, comfortingly, he stroked her cheek. "It's all right, Sarah." Her skin felt cold, bitterly cold, beneath his fingers. "Was it you who cried out?"

"Yes."

"Why? Did you—"

"There's something terrible in this corridor. I've never seen anything like it. And it came at me!"

"What? What was it? Could you . . ."

He stopped as the glare from a dozen candles blazed farther up the corridor. A buzz of voices drifted to them. People in multicolored robes crowded the narrow space, questioning looks on their taut faces. In the renewed light, he could make out Sarah's horror-widened eyes fixed on the corner, and he followed her gaze.

It stood there, a terrible darkness in the shape of a man, watching.

"Blessed Epagael," Jeremiel whispered, barely audible. He turned his pistol on the "listener." So much for his distance limitation theory. "Who are you? What do you want?"

People gasped, suddenly unsteady lamps flickering wildly over the room. The shape disappeared, or blended into the other shadows. Jeremiel wasn't certain. Reaching over, he gripped Sarah's arm and helped her to her feet.

"Come on," he said. "Let's get to the surface where there's light."

"Yes, let's hurry." She ripped away from him and shouldered through the crowd, running back up the corridor. He followed, keeping pace, listening to the hushed voices echoing behind them. A minute later, it occurred to him he hadn't seen Rathanial in that crowd and the knowledge slapped him brutally. He spun, grabbing a lamp from one of those following, and raced back toward Zadok's private sanctum, calling, "Rathanial? Rathanial!"

As he lunged down the spiral staircase, he heard a soft clink. A vague sound like glass against stone, and he stopped dead midway down. "Rathanial?"

No voice answered. Swallowing convulsively, he descended the final steps and walked into the small cave. Lifting his lamp high, he saw the old man lying beneath the niche in the wall where the wine bottles sat. Now, though, those bottles lay in a broken array, glass and pewter goblets scattered clear across the room. Jeremiel could see no injuries, but one of Rathanial's hands stretched out and scratches marred the sandy floor as if he'd been groping to find something.

"Father?" He quickly went to Rathanial and knelt, turning the old man over. A weak groan came from his lips and his eyelids fluttered. "What happened?"

"The *Mea Shearim*," Rathanial rasped. "He . . . took it."

"Who?"

"Something that came . . . out of the darkness." Rathanial tried to sit up, but fell weakly back to the floor, a hand to his head.

Jeremiel fearfully examined the shadows as he fingered the smooth trigger of his pistol. Had the "listener" descended the stairs to the Sanctum? Standing, he moved slowly, carrying the light around the cave, vanquishing each shadow. He started to suck in a relieved breath as he neared the door, but a subtle movement caught his eye. The darkness near the door seemed to ripple for an instant. He jerked up his lamp, throwing a glare across the entryway. Fear struck him like a fist and he stepped backward. Behind him, Rathanial gasped.

The velvet blackness hugged the walls as it silently slithered away.

CHAPTER 10

A dark whirlwind swirled around Zadok. Being in the "eye" had always prickled the hair on the back of his neck, but this time it seemed especially frightening, as though an evil force lurked close by, watching, hoping he'd fail. Soft, indistinct voices bombarded him from all sides, their clarity muffled as though originating from a great distance. He took a deep breath and trudged blindly up the tunnel toward the faint graying that wavered in the distance.

"Curious," he mumbled to himself, feeling a little like a lost wayfarer. "Always before, the glow of the *Mea* lit my path. Now I've got nothing."

A face flashed in the whirling darkness; he stumbled backward, breathing hard. The blonde woman shook a fist, raging in an unknown voice, eyes sparkling like amber jewels. Zadok clutched the rough wool fabric over his breast and forced a swallow down his throat. He'd seen a thousand different faces in his trips to Epagael. Why did they frighten him so this time?

"Because you've nothing but their light to guide your steps, you old fool." A tremor of tormented regret touched him and he lowered his eyes to the gyrating blackness beneath his feet. "Well," he sighed. "This will be the last trip, so use whatever's available to get where you're going." He lifted his face to squint at the grayness in the distance. "Sedriel?" he shouted the name of the angel who guarded the gate to the first heaven. "You arrogant handmaiden of Aktariel, it's me. Zadok! I'm coming to see you again. Get ready to open that gate!"

No answer came, but Zadok knew the giant beast heard. He and Sedriel had played this game over a hundred times, baiting each other, bantering unmercifully. Of all the gate-keepers, Sedriel was the most unabashedly haughty, like a field hand suddenly elevated to the position of crew fore-man. Zadok always wanted to slap the superior expression off the winged creature's face, but wisely relented when he reconsidered the beast's enormous size and power.

To his right, the figure of a woman with long black hair appeared. She scrambled on her hands and knees, tears streaking her face. "Epagael!" she screamed. "Milcom! Let me go home? Please, I beg you. My little girl needs me. Don't take me away yet!"

Sedriel faded to the back of Zadok's mind as an iron band constricted around his heart, memories of his first trip through the timeless tunnel coming back. He'd raced around in circles, screaming his head off, terrified. Then he'd noticed the light ahead, and followed it.

"Epagael!" the woman sobbed. "I believe . . . *I believe*! I'm sorry I ever doubted." She covered her face with her hands. "Let me go home."

"Follow the light," Zadok urged softly, pointing ahead. "That's the way to God."

She seemed to hear, cocking her head and searching the blackness blindly for him. "Who are you?"

"An experienced friend." Zadok reached out a hand to stroke her dark hair comfortingly, but she vanished into the void. Only a deeper swirl of darkness marked where she'd stood. He closed his hand on air, then jerked his gaze ahead as another figure glowed to life, a tall man swinging a sword. Zadok watched in silence for a few moments as the warrior carved the darkness.

"Stop wasting time, you spineless old numbskull," Zadok chastised himself. "The whole galaxy needs to know the will of Epagael. Why are you standing here like a coward? The only way to get to the Veil is to keep walking." He ran a tired hand over his bald head and pursed his lips anxiously, talking intimately to himself. "Course, we both know why you're delaying. The worst is yet to come."

Heaving a halting sigh, he looked sideways at the gray patch. It slid closer, bearing down on him. "I'm coming," he muttered. "Don't rush me, Sedriel! I'm—"

"Zadok?" a beautiful heavenly voice chimed. "Is that you?"

Zadok scowled, putting hands on his bony hips. "I told you it was me. Have you gone deaf in the past three years? Or just senile?"

"Ah, Zadok," Sedriel's laughter boomed through the black tunnel. "How I've missed you. Come. Come, you pusillanimous mortal. You insignificant wretch born from a putrid white drop. Come and let me—"

"I'm coming! Blast you, you flaming beast." Zadok plodded up the tunnel, watching as the grayness brightened into a brilliant spot of gold.

* * * * *

Stark moonlight streamed through the loft window to frost Sybil's mahogany hair with silver. Standing on her knees in the dry golden straw, she anxiously crushed the hem of her blue robe with tiny fingers. Around them, a dilapidated plank barn spread, beams dangling by a thread from the wounded roof. Starlight fell through foot-wide gaps, lighting the pitchforks and horse tack still littering the stalls below. The scents of animal dung and aged leather clung to the air.

"Mommy, what do you see? Are they coming after us?"

"I don't see them yet." Rachel edged closer to the window, gazing over the dead fields that bordered the derelict farm. In the distance, Seir sparkled like an overturned chest of pirate plunder. Gold and white diamonds twinkled on the edges of the brilliant ruby blaze that lit the center of the city. At the sight of the roaring flames, her heart soared . . . and ached. How many had died? Had she killed the friends who'd played with her in her yard when she was a child? The cousins who'd vehemently cautioned her against falling in love with Shadrach, a known "rabble-rouser?" The old people who'd glared hatefully and spat at her when she'd dared suggest the Mashiah was not the promised Redeemer they'd awaited all their lives? Rachel clenched a fist tightly.

115

She'd never intended to kill anyone . . . never. But sometimes, death couldn't be avoided.

"Who used to live at this farm, Mommy?"

Rachel pushed the thoughts of the dead from her mind. "I think their names were Mahn."

"Where did they go?"

"They probably left when the drought killed all their animals. Or maybe they were plague victims."

Sybil hesitated, staring up forlornly. "Or maybe the Mashiah came to kill them because they still believed in Epagael?"

Rachel turned to meet her daughter's anguished gaze. She hadn't the energy or inclination to make up a quaint comforting story. Besides, Sybil's stern face said she wouldn't believe it anyway. "Maybe."

Sybil contemplatively picked a piece of straw out of her brown curls before asking, "Mommy? The Mashiah will try harder to kill us now, won't he?"

Hearing the fear in that frail voice, Rachel rolled over and reached out for her daughter. Sybil quickly crawled into the circle of her mother's arms. "Won't he, Mommy?"

Rachel smoothed the tangles from Sybil's pretty face. "I'm going to treat you like a big girl, okay?"

Sybil nodded, a swallow bobbing in her throat. "That means yes, doesn't it?"

"Yes. I think we've got another hour, maybe, before the Mashiah sends out the *samaels* to find us." Just the thought of the horrifying black ships sent a chill up her spine. She'd only the most basic idea what the devices could do. Shadrach had patiently explained as much as he knew to her, but no one knew very much. Could they track them even in the caves? She glanced at Sybil's hopeful face, praying her daughter wouldn't ask that question.

"Can't we go away and hide in the mountains? You said before that he couldn't find us if we—"

"We're going to try, baby." Rachel kissed Sybil's forehead and hugged her close. The feel of the tiny hands patting her back comforted like a warm blanket on a cold winter's night. She let herself drown in the feeling for a few moments before saying, "Sybil, I want you to do something for me. Can you try?"

"What is it?"

"Remember your grandmother's middle name?"

116

Sybil frowned, gaze darting over the rotting boards of the barn. "No, I—"

"Mekilta. Can you say it?"

"Mekilta."

Rachel took a deep breath of the grass-scented air and let her eyes rest on the splinters of moonlight piercing the broken roof over her head. "If anything happens, Sybil, and we're separated, I want you to—"

"But we won't get separated, Mommy," she whispered imploringly. "You won't let them get me!"

"No, no, sweetheart, I won't. But if something happens. Say . . . the Mashiah captures me. I want you to run back into town and stop at the first house you see and pound on the door. When the people answer, you tell them you're Sybil *Mekilta*, all right? Can you remember not to say Eloel?"

"I can remember, but I want to be with you. Even if the Mashiah—"

"After you tell the people you're Sybil Mekilta, you say your mommy and daddy died in the plague and you need a new home, you understand?"

Tears glimmered in her daughter's eyes and her mouth trembled. She twined fingers in Rachel's hair and tugged absently. "Mommy, I don't—"

"Do you understand?"

Sybil put both hands over her mouth and started to cry, the soft sobs like a mewing kitten. "Mommy . . ." she said in a choking voice. "Where's Daddy? Why can't I go and live with Daddy if the Mashiah gets you?"

Rachel squeezed her eyes closed and felt a single tear roll down her cheek. Somewhere in the past few days her own unbearable anguish had faded to resigned acceptance. She'd forgotten her daughter didn't know the truth. But even if she'd remembered, she soothed herself, there'd been no time to discuss Shadrach's death. And now . . . now it seemed the most difficult thing she'd ever had to do in her life.

"Mommy? Mommy, it's okay." Rachel felt the girl's hand brush away the tear on her cheek, then arms went around her neck. "Daddy's hiding somewhere. I know he is. I had a dream that Daddy was in an old basement eating soup. He couldn't come to us because he was sick, but he'll get well, Mommy. And then he'll—"

"Sybil," Rachel whispered unsteadily. "Mommy needs you to be brave. Can you?"

117

Moonlight washed Sybil's face as she looked up and swallowed hard. "Yes."

Rachel steeled herself, trying not to let memories overwhelm her. "You remember when the bad men came into the temple during the Sighet celebration?"

Sybil shuddered involuntarily and silence draped like a shroud around them. Rachel fought to keep her composure while she gathered the right words.

"Is . . . is Daddy all right? Mommy . . . ?"

Rachel sat up and her arms went around Sybil blindly, her own grief choking her. "No."

"Did the Mashiah's soldiers hurt Daddy?"

"Daddy's dead, baby." Pain struck her anew and she wept. Shoulders heaving, tears dropped to soak her daughter's hair.

"No, Mommy," Sybil insisted, wiping a hand beneath her running nose. Dirt streaked her face like soot. "He's alive. I saw him in my dream. He's—"

"He's *dead*, baby!"

"You'll see, Mommy," Sybil whispered calmly. "Really—"

"Don't," Rachel gritted through her tears. "I don't know how I know, Sybil. But I know. I feel a hollow space in my soul where he used to be. He's gone." *And Ornias said so.*

"Don't cry, Mommy." Sybil tiptoed to bring her cheek comfortingly against her mother's and with one hand stroked the back of Rachel's hair. "Don't cry. Even if Daddy were dead, we see him again in heaven."

Rachel held the girl in a grip that made breathing difficult, her mind examining the long years ahead. She could tell Sybil was humoring her. The little girl didn't believe. Was her young mind experiencing wound shock? Dear God, when the gates burst wide and the truth dawned, how would the child react? How could she herself survive without Shadrach's strength and tenderness? When he'd gone, he'd taken the joy from her life. And heaven? God had turned all her dreams to dust. If she lived as long as God himself, she would never forget those days in the square when the violet lances murdered her faith forever.

Rachel opened her eyes, pulling back to look reassuringly at her daughter. "You're right, baby. Daddy will be waiting for us in heaven."

Sybil nodded and squared her tiny shoulders as though single-handedly ready to carry the unbearable burden. Kissing Rachel's wet cheeks, she whispered, "Come on, Mommy.

Let's go hide in the mountains. They won't find us. We can kill grass hens with rocks, like Daddy showed us, 'member?"

"I remember." Spring days and picnics in the mountains floated through her mind, making her ache so terribly she worried that she couldn't bear it.

"And we can gather the radi roots that grow around the waterholes, that way we'll get our vegetables. Okay, Mommy?"

"Yes . . . okay."

"Let's go now. Can we? We have to go soon, before the Mashiah sends out the black ships to find us."

Rachel gazed longingly out the window. Wisps of cloud drifted through the leaden sky above the jagged peaks, glowing like polished pewter. As the moon slowly sank, the black shadow of the mountains wandered prodigally across the desert, snuffing the glimmer of sage and thorny radi bushes. From this vantage the peaks seemed so close she could reach out and touch the cold stone. But she knew the foothills were five miles away and the safety of the caves at least ten.

"First we'll go down to the farmhouse and see if the people who used to live here left any food in the cupboards. Then we'll—"

"I'll help, Mommy. We can make baskets out of our hems to carry things." Sybil scrambled on hands and knees over the tawny straw, heading for the ladder.

Rachel followed sluggishly, heart thudding dully in her chest.

* * * * *

Dawn's pearlescent gleam reflected from the mist twining through the vines and trees, spawning a shimmering veil in the icy cold.

Jeremiel shivered slightly as he stepped to the mouth of the cave and braced a shoulder against the gritty stone. The sky shone a dull putty color, rain gently sprinkling the forest. Pine boughs rustled in the cool breeze, their pungent fragrance mixing with the scent of damp earth.

His dread had lightened some, replaced by a terrible weariness that made all things seem blessedly unreal. "A relic of the damned," he murmured lest he delude himself. "Not a reprieve."

Or maybe his exhaustion prevented him from seeing any-

119

thing that didn't wear the brand of despair. For two months he'd been living out a precarious charade, laying battle plans for his troops, speaking to people only when absolutely necessary, retreating tensely to his cabin at night, knowing in an hour he'd jerk awake in the darkness, sweat pouring from his body. His officers knew enough to leave him alone, thank God. He could not have borne any attempts at sympathy, not and maintained the hard practical exterior his forces needed. Perhaps this new lassitude heralded an easing of the pain, an understanding and acceptance of what had happened?

"Acceptance?" he whispered to himself. Even if the brutal anguish eased, would that ever come?

"From the look on your face," Rathanial said softly from somewhere behind him, "I'd say you're deeply worried. Is your concern for Horeb?"

Jeremiel took a breath and said through a long exhalation, "No, just thinking in general."

"About what?" The old man strolled forward to stand next to him in the cave entry. His tan robe looked freshly washed and smelled of smoke, as though it had been dried over an open fire. His white hair and beard were transformed to a slate gray in the sullen light. "Forgive me, but you looked as though you were having a serious conversation with death."

"Umm, did I?"

"Yes, I've seen that same look from soldiers on the battlefield, weary to the point of having lost hope." He turned sharp eyes on Jeremiel. "You're not feeling that way, are you? I know you've fought many hard battles in recent months."

"I'm fine." He held the old man's gaze, his own face dark and impassive. Rathanial's narrow shoulders stiffened, as though sensing more than he should have. Silently, he cursed himself. Was his fragility so obvious?

"Jeremiel, the road ahead is a very difficult one. If you're not feeling—up to it—then I think perhaps we should wait until—"

"I'm more than capable of doing anything that needs to be done to save our people on Horeb."

Rathanial folded his arms and jerked a disbelieving nod. "I know you've always been reliable in the past, Jeremiel. But each of us goes through periods of disorientation. I'd understand if you wanted to wait."

"Don't push me, Rathanial. I said I'm all right." He heard the chilling tone invade his voice, but didn't care. Why was the old man so persistent? Damn it! Did he know about Syene? The questioning of his abilities only made him more determined to get to Horeb. *Did Rathanial know that?*

"All right. Well, let's discuss our plans."

"We'll take separate ships." Jeremiel said, glad to be discussing something safe like strategy.

Rathanial shook his head. "What? Why? I'd anticipated we'd go together."

"Separate ships will increase our chances that at least one of us will get through. Have you made arrangements?"

"Yes, a small shuttle will pick me up tomorrow. It's all arranged. I'd—I'd thought you'd be coming with me?"

"No."

"Do you have transportation?"

"Not arranged."

"Jeremiel," Rathanial said hesitantly. "I don't want you taking unnecessary risks. Especially when you're not . . ." At Jeremiel's hard look, the old man stopped. "Perhaps I should contact my people and get them to send another ship? It will only take a few days."

"That would arouse suspicion. Don't be concerned about me. I will, in all probability, get to Horeb before you do." An ironic smile touched his face.

Rathanial's withered lips pursed. He shifted his gaze to the opal mist twining among the trees. The clouds on the northern horizon glowed with a lining of fallow gold from the rising sun. "Well, if you say so. I'll meet you there, then."

"Tell me how to find your secret caves?"

As Rathanial related the instructions, pain lanced Jeremiel's breast. Another battle would be waged for the good of the people, more lives wasted in what increasingly seemed a futile war to preserve Gamant heritage.

". . . and you must remember, the panel is beneath an overhanging ridge of tan sandstone."

"I'll remember."

"You may have to get down on your back and reach to find it. It's not obvious if you've never . . ."

Was culture worth the blood it cost? There'd been a time in his life when such a question would have enraged him. He'd believed then they should fight to their last breath to preserve the Old Ways, but now . . . ? Especially on Horeb, where Gamants would die on both sides of the war? "Culture" spread talons like an amorphous, bloodthirsty monster. A caged beast, it demanded more and more from its feeders. And just now, he felt as though the beast's grasping claws were tightening around his throat. He wanted to bolt and run.

From the deepest corners of his mind, he heard his father calling and saw again the snow swirling around the man as he stamped his feet and entered their house on Tikkun. A thirteen-year-old Jeremiel ran barefooted across the floor to hug him around the waist. "How was it, Papa?" The meeting had been critical.

Patting him gently, Menachem Baruch unwrapped the blue and white prayer shawl from his shoulders and folded it, kissing the fabric softly. "Not good, my son," he said weakly.

"Why? What happened?"

"We . . . we haven't any strength left. There's no money. There's no hope. Everyone is confused about the future." Placidly, he walked over to deposit his shawl into its special box in the closet. Turning back, he whispered, "Old Ruth is sick. We didn't have enough people to make decisions."

"Papa! You couldn't form a minyan? Not even ten came? Not even *ten*?"

His father appeared preoccupied, concentrating on straightening his threadbare black suit, tearful eyes shielded by drooping lids. "In the old days there were so many Gamants on Tikkun you couldn't count them." He raised a strong hand, a carpenter's hand, and waved it through the air. "When you walked down the streets, people patted each other affectionately. And on Shabbat, the whole planet grew still. Not even the wind stirred outside the houses. Candles glowed up and down the streets. Sacred singing rose like the blessing hand of God, winding between buildings, climbing through every window." He focused hollowly on the floor. "Not even ten. I—I guess it won't be long now until there's no use going at all."

"No use? Papa, don't talk like that! Don't ever—"

"*Jeremiel? Jere—*"

"I'm listening, Rathanial." He squeezed the bridge of his nose, blocking the memory. Turning, he leaned his back against the cold stone and met the old man's gaze squarely.

"I expect to be there by the end of the week. Will that be soon enough?"

Rathanial eyed him uncomfortably. "Sooner than I'd expect from anyone else. Anyone human at least. But your inhuman feats are legendary."

Jeremiel felt no confidence at the praise. "Will you notify your people that I may arrive before you do?"

"Yes, they'll be waiting."

"Good."

Rathanial's brows drew together and he paused awkwardly. "Uh, Jeremiel, can I ask . . . I don't mean to pry, but you're not planning on doing anything illegal to get to Horeb, are you? I mean, you wouldn't take chances like stealing—"

"Depends."

The old man glanced up, distressed. "Well, it's your business, of course. But if you choose that 'method,' be aware that galactic marines are swarming all over Kayan. They've declared a state of emergency in Capitol. We assume you're the target. The spaceport is heavily guarded."

"I appreciate that news. Is there anything else?"

"No. I thought that would be enough."

"Have a safe trip, Rathanial."

The religious elder bowed. "May the blessings of Epagael accompany you."

"Thank you, Father."

Rathanial briefly embraced Jeremiel before turning to stride into the darkness of the cavern. Jeremiel listened to his retreating footfalls before gazing back to the watery forests of Kayan. The clouds had parted, leaving a peephole for the sun. A bar of gold shot through the heavens, flashing from the wings of soaring birds.

Unrolling the hood from his collar, he flipped it over his head and stepped out of the cave. He'd have to be on his way soon. But first he wanted to walk in the mist until it soaked him through, lanced his bones. Maybe when his flesh felt as cold as his soul, he'd be able to think straight again. *He damned well had to have his abilities back by the time he got to Horeb.*

He strolled along the base of the high cliffs, inhaling deeply of the damp stone and pine.

CHAPTER 11

Around Capitol, the high mountains glimmered in the starlight. The rain had stopped, leaving dark clouds clustered over the peaks. Pines pierced the sky like dark spears. Mist huddled around their trunks, swirling in the breeze.

Jeremiel crouched on a forested hill overlooking the city. Towering triangular buildings clotted downtown Capitol. Reflective-paned windows gleamed ghostly in the murky light. The streets lay empty to the fog, though the landing field's main gate swung wide open.

He shook his head, heaving a disgusted breath. What did they expect? That he'd take the bait and waltz right into their arms? "Surely you don't think me that much of a fool?" he whispered to the cool damp wind. "Then again, maybe you do. You brave boys in purple aren't known for being particularly bright."

A frigid gust flattened his suit against his ribs as he stepped out to get a look at the corner of the spaceport. The twelve foot fence and a single gray building were visible. Six transport vessels dotted the landing field, but only one sat close enough to the fence that he might be able to get to it. From what he could tell, he'd have to walk down one street and up another to gain enough elevation to make his leap viable.

Where would they be waiting? On the field, in the buildings or hiding in the highlands around the perimeter?

He uneasily surveyed the forested hills, then pulled his pulse-pistol and set it on wide-field before tucking it back in the slanting pocket at his side. Silently, he strolled down onto Tenth Avenue. Around him, brick apartment buildings squatted. The narrow slitted windows threw irregular patches of light across his path. From somewhere singing and laughter rose, wafting down the cold empty streets.

The sounds warmed him. He hadn't had a family since his father died when he'd turned fourteen, but he craved such togetherness. Loneliness stood as the single greatest debility of command. Soldiers feared getting too close to their generals, lest they discover the man's or woman's weaknesses. The only reliable general was an invincible one. Frail humans couldn't be trusted.

He clenched his hands into fists, straining against his own impotence. Syene had understood. For three years she'd been his shield, a thin, shining blade that had flashed between him and the world, screening callers, never letting anyone see him unless he were in stern control of himself. No one but she knew the times he'd wept after losing soldiers to a poorly executed battle plan. No one but she knew the bouts of self-doubt that plagued his soul. Painful memories of her tinkly little-girl laugh haunted him. The sound rose so clearly in his mind that he thought he'd heard it. He jerked, starting to turn, hope bursting in his breast, before he physically stopped himself. Dead. *She was dead.*

Steps faltering, he leaned a shoulder against a wall and stared sightlessly at the fog. His heart pounded painfully. The mist shifted, forming strange haunting shapes, almost faces, which melted instantly. He licked his lips and shook aside the perspiration-soaked ends of his blond hair where they glued themselves to his face.

He'd taken two steps forward when the scratchy sound of petrolon against fabric made him halt in his tracks.

"Real easy, mister," the soft voice said from behind. "Get your hands up. . . . That's real good. Now turn around. I want to see your face."

Fool! Were you wallowing in your own sorrow and missed their approach? Swallowing the lump in his throat, Jeremiel turned.

The marine held a rifle pointed at his stomach. Young with raven hair and hard green eyes, he looked like a combat veteran. His purple uniform showed dirt and worn sleeves. Not the gear of a martinet. He stepped forward and Jeremiel stifled a frantic urge to pull his pistol and kill the man. But the sound of fire would attract attention from all over Capitol. He'd spend the next two months in hiding and the Magistrates would tighten security around the spaceport. He'd never get off Kayan.

Smiling nervously, he spread his arms wide and walked to meet the marine. "What's this all about, Lieutenant? I'm on my way home from work."

"We've notified every business and every home. Don't pretend you don't know about the curfew. What's your name?"

"Michael Schacter. I own my own equipment business on the other side of town. I've been working in my shop most of the day. I got no messages from the police."

The marine scrutinized Jeremiel, examining every facial feature. Recognition dawned in his eyes. "You're going to have to come with me to headquarters. We're—"

"What?" Jeremiel demanded, stepping closer, readying himself. "I have a family waiting for me at home. How long is this nonsense going to take?"

The marine's finger tightened on the trigger of his rifle and a prickle climbed Jeremiel's spine. *"If you don't back up, mister, you may never get home."*

"I'm backing."

"Turn around and head for the spaceport." He pointed up the street with his rifle. "I'll be right here behind you."

Jeremiel nodded hurriedly and walked into the silver veils of mist that eddied up the street. Gaunt pines clustered in the distance, towering somberly over the dark gray building.

"I don't see any lustreglobes on in the terminal. Which building are we—"

"Just keep walking."

"I'm going. Don't get nervous."

"Nerves aren't one of my problems."

"I'm glad to hear that."

As they neared the government installation, glossy-leafed ivy and wild grape appeared in planters along the streets. Wind whistled through the trees surrounding the landing field. Close . . . they were close.

"Take this left up here," the lieutenant ordered.

Jeremiel complied and ducked beneath the overhanging branches of a Kayan oak. Thick berry brambles formed a jade wall on his right.

As the marine ducked to follow, he dropped his gaze for a split second. Jeremiel whirled and kicked out with all his might, knocking the lieutenant backward. The man reeled, tumbling into the berry bramble as he snapped a wild shot from his rifle. A violet beam lanced the fog, the shrill whine echoing from the buildings.

Damn it! The entire sector will be grabbing rifles and heading in this direction! Jeremiel jerked his pistol from his pocket and leaped, trying to reach the soldier before he could get off another shot. "Hold it!" he shouted.

The lieutenant brought up the rifle again just as Jeremiel reached him. Instinctively, Jeremiel slammed the barrel away with his fist, sending the gun flying onto the wet street. The marine lunged desperately, knocking Jeremiel's feet out from under him, trying to wrench the pistol from his strong grip.

"You . . . can't make it, Baruch," the marine panted, slamming a knee into Jeremiel's side as he fought for the pistol. "We've got . . . people everywhere."

Panic rushed like fire through Jeremiel's veins. He heaved the marine aside and rolled on top of him, struggling to twist the pistol so the barrel aimed at his enemy's head. If the boys in purple in the buildings had been unable to triangulate from the echoes of the first shot, another would make it easy. And bring the weight of Kayan's military might down on him, but it didn't look like he had a choice.

"Don't be a fool . . . Baruch," the marine gasped, gripping his forearm in iron hands and shaking, trying to dislodge the pistol. "Surrender. The Magistrates—"

"Will hang me from the highest tree."

"You'll get a trial."

The marine thrust up violently, bashing an elbow repeatedly into Jeremiel's temple. A light flashed in his head, momentarily stunning him. The marine wrenched the pistol from his hand and pushed from beneath him, in one move rolling away and lurching unsteadily to his feet.

"You damned bastard," the marine accused, aiming the pistol at Jeremiel's middle. "You just signed your death warrant."

Jeremiel sat up, noticing absently the blood streaking his face in hot rivulets as he tensed, waiting for the shot. When it didn't come, he gazed questioningly at the marine. The man stood, breast heaving, green eyes hard.

"Planning on collecting the reward?" Jeremiel said through a long exhalation. That seemed the only explanation for why he wasn't already dead. Some strange part of his soul, deep down, felt a vague sense of relief at the thought of death, while the rest of him screamed for him to get up and do something.

The marine's jaw moved with grinding teeth. In the background, fog wavered before the gray buildings. "Can't. Government employees are prohibited."

"I'll remember that."

"Don't hardly think you'll need to, friend. We'll ship you directly to the neurophysiology department." He smiled grimly. "After 'chatting' with them, you won't need to remember anything ever again."

127

"Something to look forward to," Jeremiel groaned as he struggled to get his feet under him, falling back to the ground.

"Get up."

"Just give me a second to—"

"I said *get up!*" the marine shouted, taking a threatening step forward.

Jeremiel swung around with lightning speed, kicking the marine behind the knees, sending him tumbling in the general vicinity of the rifle. Jeremiel leapt for him, shoving the pistol out of alignment as he reached for the rifle. He gripped the stock as the marine slammed a stunning right into his solar plexus. They rolled, grunting and gasping, until Jeremiel found himself on top. He jammed the rifle down across the soldier's throat, throwing his entire two hundred pounds across the barrel. The lieutenant writhed, kicking wildly.

When the marine's eyes rolled back in his head and his wild arms went slack, Jeremiel drew the knife from his boot and quickly slit the man's throat. Wiping the bloody blade on his victim's purple jacket, he dragged him into the dense green brambles. The wan light glistened from a pool of blood on the sidewalk, but at least the body lay hidden.

Pulling up his hood to hide his blond hair, Jeremiel slithered through the vines to get to the other side, then crawled quietly along the black shadow of the jade wall, wondering where in the hell the other marines were? Why hadn't they come? Had they expected a diversionary maneuver and told their ambush team to stick tight? Or were they watching him even now, waiting for the best shot?

He shoved the rising alarm from his mind, quickening his pace through the bramble. When he reached the end, he lay on his stomach searching the darkness ahead. He'd passed the edge of the building complex. His hill rose only fifty yards away, but it would be a dash across a nearly treeless expanse of wet grass.

He wiped sweat from his eyes and squinted at the compound. Fog obscured much of the pad, rippling in the single bluish lustreglobe lighting the field. Nothing stirred.

But he could sense the ambush in his tightening gut. "You're out there, goddamn you. I know it."

Rolling to his side, he pulled his pistol and braced it on a thick vine, slowly scanning through the scope. Red glows dotted the field: Twenty-eight in all.

"Too many. *Too damned many.* "

Blood surged in his ears as he sucked in a halting breath. They really planned to stop him this time.

He turned his scope on the ship just over the fence. A small transport, it looked well-kept, but he couldn't tell from this angle what sort of engines or weapons it possessed. Fear crawled in his gut.

"Just be fast, baby," he whispered. If it had legs, he might be able to get the shields up and lift off before . . .

A crunch sounded in the bramble.

Jeremiel stiffened, holding his breath. An animal? The plop-plop of mist dripping from the vines seemed immensely louder in the silence. He lay still for a full five minutes, listening, then let out a relieved breath and squinted through his scope at the ship again. Crates filled the area in front of the doors marked "Customs," stacked ten feet high in places. And a series of square-bodied loaders hugged the sides of the buildings.

Another crunch. Closer.

"Jeremiel?"

Rolling to his back, he slowly brought his pistol scope to bear on the tangled briar. The man crouched not more than thirty feet away, ugly with missing teeth and a square head. But he wasn't dressed in purple.

God damn, how had he gotten so close? Silently, he cursed himself for being exhausted, negligent, for calling attention to himself.

"Baruch! I'm a friend. I've come to help you."

Possible? *Yes.* Gamants from all over the galaxy often risked their lives to aid him or his forces. But more likely this fellow was one of the many bounty hunters who dogged his trail. In any case, he couldn't take the risk.

Jeremiel scanned the vines thoroughly, discovering two more men moving quietly toward him. They didn't have a shot yet, but would shortly.

Heaving an anxious sigh, he shoved to his feet and charged the hill. Mist fluttered around him as he sprinted toward the fence.

* * * * *

Yosef reclined in one of the lavender passenger seats of *Seros*, staring distractedly around the cramped cabin. Refuse scattered the ship, a can here, a wadded sheet of crystal

129

paper there. Beer bottles and candy wrappers created a growing mound in the corner. How many days had they been here now? His heart ached a little knowing he'd missed Ezarin's funeral. Would he ever get to see his brother?

"You know, I hate these colors," Ari growled, waving a hand at the ship. "Putrid purple and gruesome gray. What idiot do you think designed this thing?"

Yosef pulled his spectacles low on his nose and turned down the pleasant music he'd been listening to so he could examine his friend. Ari slumped in the commander's chair, long legs sprawled like tentacles across the carpet. His white hair stuck out at odd angles. A beer sat propped precariously against one of the red levers on the control console.

"Huh? Who do you think? That worm-brained captain?"

"*What's* the matter with you?" Yosef growled, waving a hand.

"What?"

Yosef's eyes narrowed. "Here we are, *prisoners*, and you talk about colors! I thought you were working on an escape plan?"

Ari belched and leaned back in his chair, smiling conspiratorially. "I've already got it figured out."

"Well?"

"You told me you didn't want to hear it again."

"You imbecile! Were you going to tell me that same stupid idea?"

"You haven't heard the latest amendment."

"The only thing I want to know is if you've figured out how to keep us from getting killed *after* we blow up the spaceport and *before* we crash-land at Zadok's?"

Ari worked his brows up and down, grinning. "Sure."

"No!" Yosef threw out his hands. "Don't tell me. I can't bear to listen to another one of your harebrained—"

"You're just jealous because you haven't thought of anything," Ari pointed out smugly, crossing his arms in defiance.

"You know what happens when both of us think at once? We end up in trouble."

Ari snickered, then swigged down his last drops of beer, making a ghastly sucking sound at the end. He tossed the bottle into the pile. Yosef gave him an irritated glance, then pushed up from his seat to hobble back and forth across the tiny cabin.

"I can't figure out why they're keeping us so long. All our papers are in order and we're—"

"They haven't caught that Underground leader they're looking for."

Yosef squinted. "What Underground leader? Where'd you hear that?"

"From that ugly little marine who came up this morning."

"The one you threw out?"

Ari waved both hands emphatically. "He was a bozon. He tried to tell me I couldn't sing Gamant religious songs over the ship's loudspeaker to greet incoming ships. The twerp. He's lucky I didn't—"

"Ari, blast it! What did he say about the Underground leader?"

"Oh . . . he said they hadn't caught him yet."

Yosef squeezed the bridge of his nose in exasperation, then whispered, "What was the leader's name?"

His friend lifted a bony shoulder in a shrug and said through a yawn, "I don't think he trusted me enough to tell me."

Yosef stared.

"Besides, he didn't actually call the man an Underground leader. You know how these Philistines are. They get things mixed up. Let me see?" Ari rubbed his wrinkled chin. "I think he said 'a Gamant agitator.' "

Yosef waddled to sit in the chair next to Ari. "I wonder who it is? It could be somebody we know."

"Like who?"

"Like maybe Sariel Loman or Ruth Wilo. Both of them were born on Tikkun, remember? I used to sing with Ruth's father, old—"

"What does it matter?"

"It could matter a lot, you dolt. You know how the Underground goes around rescuing children from those horrible schools the Magistrates put them in, and brings food and supplies to developing planets the government has embargoed because they stick to the Old Ways."

"Sure. So what?"

"What if the Underground is planning a raid here on Kayan?"

"There aren't any Magisterial schools on Kayan. Are there?"

"Not that I know of . . . but how would I know? Zadok is too busy to write much and—"

"Hey!" Ari's eyes gleamed suddenly. "You think maybe we're going to be in the middle of a fight? Eh, you think so?" He spun in his chair and started jiggling several levers and pretending to punch buttons. "I know just the switches to hit! See this green one?"

Yosef read the label and puckered his mouth in disdain. "Quit slapping at that! You want to blow us up?"

Ari sat forward, straightening the lapels of his blue suit. He cocked his head cleverly. "You just think I don't know how to run this ship. I've been making a study of all these dials and . . ." He stopped, blinking at the ship's portal as he leaned slightly out of his seat.

"What's the matter?" Yosef turned to follow his gaze.

"Did you see that?" Ari got up and peered out the circular window into the growing fog. "Look! There he is again."

Yosef trotted to crowd next to him, pushing his spectacles up and squinting into the fog. "Who?"

"I don't know his name!" Ari blurted and pointed. "But it's one of those ugly marines. He just ran from that ship over there to hide behind that big crate. Wait and you'll see him move again."

"Bah!" Yosef spat, seeing nothing but wavering mist. "Your eyes are just another part of you that's stopped working."

"What do you mean, another *part*? At least when I take Agnes out on a date she's got something to think about. *All* of me works enough to scare the bejeezus out of—"

"Everything except your brain."

A shrill explosion of rifle fire buffeted the landing field. Brilliant violet beams split the fog, forming a deadly luminescent web around *Seros*. Yosef stumbled back, hands sliding off seats, to fall to the floor.

"My God!" Ari shrieked. "They're shooting at us!"

* * * * *

As Jeremiel hit the fence, the pad came alive with running soldiers. The ground in front of him jumped, a furrow slashing the wet soil. Screams of "There he is!" and "It's Baruch!" tore the air.

Throwing himself over the barrier, he landed hard on the wet surface. As he ran, he spied a marine leaning from behind a crate, rifle leveled. Panicked, Jeremiel jerked the trigger of his pistol. The shot went wild, exploding the crate, sending boards flying. He fired again and this time, the stench of burning flesh met his nostrils.

God damn, there're so many.

He dove for the ground as a beam crackled by his leg. Rolling frantically, he leaped to his feet to run. But he couldn't avoid the next shot. It took him from behind, slamming his thigh and hurling him back to the ground. Blood flowed hotly down his leg, the wound gaping.

"Oh, my God, my God," he groaned, stunned. He slithered on his stomach, struggling to reach the transport that stood no more than ten feet away now.

Fear knotted in his stomach. The shot had deliberately wounded, not killed. They had orders to take him alive. *That's why the marine on the street didn't kill me when he had the chance.*

Another shot struck the landing gear of the transport. The ship listed sideways, suspended for a moment, before it crashed down.

A swarm of marines rose and rushed and in that instant, he knew it was over. He couldn't reach the ship. They had him surrounded. He licked his lips, futility sweeping him, but he kept crawling out of habit. "Never give up. Never." The possibility of capture by the Magistrates terrified every Gamant rebel. The mind probes wrenched information from a person's memories at horrifying cost to the personality centers of the brain. He'd raided the Retraining Centers for such vegetables. But his own life mattered little. What he knew mattered greatly. Ten minutes beneath the probes and he could jeopardize the entire Underground movement.

As the marines neared, he lifted his pistol and laid the barrel against his temple. An eerie calm came over him. He saw the marines' eyes widen, their steps falter, and vaguely heard someone shout, *"Stop him!"*

Then, as though in a dream, the ground trembled and a violet beam shot from the transport vessel. The shot blasted the terminal, shattering the building. A roar erupted as flames lanced the fog.

Marines screamed and ran for cover as the second shot exploded a nearby ship, then panned erratically to the right, bursting crates and shattering another building. The landing field writhed with shouts and pounding boots.

An instant latter, all sounds stopped as a shimmering wall snapped on around him. He shook his head violently, staring in disbelief.

133

"Shields. Blessed Epagael," he murmured in awe. "Somebody in that ship is on my side." With all his dwindling strength Jeremiel pulled himself toward the vessel, watching idly as the marines' fire splashed the shields in purple waves.

When he reached the entry, it magically opened and an old man with spectacles low on his nose gingerly came down the lopsided steps, clinging to the railing. Suspiciously the elder demanded, "What's your name?"

"I . . . Jeremiel Baruch."

"Ah, of course," the man shouted gleefully and smiled. "I knew your father, too! Hurry, son, we haven't much time." The old man helped him to his feet, supporting him as they climbed into the ship. As the hatch snapped shut, the elder turned suddenly, eyes going wide, and blurted, "You do know how to fly this thing, don't you?"

Jeremiel started to nod, but another old man, tall and lanky and with a mop of gray hair, yelled. "I know how to fly it, you old fool! I figured out the weapons and the shields, didn't I?"

"You couldn't fly . . . !"

Jeremiel ignored them, blinking at the brilliant lights in the ship. When the soldier's shot took out part of the landing gear, everything loose had tumbled into a pile at the far side. Garbage stood heaped two feet high. Hanging onto seats and consoles, Jeremiel slid, dragging his injured leg, to drop into the command chair. "Do be seated, gentlemen. We haven't time to discuss this."

"Wait a minute! I'm the captain! I'm going to . . ."

Jeremiel hit the acceleration switches and the ship lifted through the mist, then shot away across the dark, starstrewn skies of Kayan.

CHAPTER 12

Ornias poured himself a glass of Cassopian sherry and leaned gracefully against the ten-foot-long ebony table. In the harsh light of the lustreglobes, the silver threads of his sapphire robe glittered. Running a hand through his neatly parted brown hair, he smiled and drank, relishing the honeylike sweetness as he looked idly around the stone room. Crimson slabs of sandstone extended twenty feet long and fifteen wide, stretching twelve feet high to touch the ceiling. The coppery scent of blood and the sickly sweet odor of vomit penetrated the room.

"Have you ever tried this sherry? Marvelous stuff."

Only an echoing silence greeted his query which made him smile. He blinked contemplatively at the colorful array of torture devices from around the galaxy. They lined the walls like irregularly hung pictures. He preferred the terrors of the Old Ways, believed them more persuasive. As a result, most of his utensils sent his captives' imaginations whirling back to the Dark Ages of old Earth. Battle axes, maces, thumbscrews, and a variety of knives adorned his collection, scattered among more recent technological innovations.

"Silence is death in your case. You know that, don't you?"

Chains jingled and Ornias took another leisurely sip of his sherry, before shifting his gaze to his captive. The rebel hung a foot off the ground, shackles biting into his wrists and ankles. The white bindings of his wounds hung in tattered filthy rags, dark umber flesh protruding from beneath. A sheen of sweat covered his handsome face. His once bronze hair draped in a greasy matted mass about his face. Yet his green eyes gleamed, hatred pouring out.

Ornias sighed and strolled across the floor to stand before the rebel. "Shadrach, please, be reasonable? This is getting you nowhere. Tell me only—"

"Go to hell."

Ornias smiled condescendingly. Did these rebels never learn? Their stubbornness forced him to dole out more and more punishment. Even though it seemed to have no effect, their suffering made him feel better, provided him vengeance for the pain and irritation they caused him. "There isn't any supernatural hell. Or don't you know the teachings of Milcom?"

Shadrach braced his head against the wall and stared at the ceiling. His sparse brown beard shook with the strength of his emotion. "Milcom is a bastard god."

Ornias moved closer. Despite the man's remarkable endurance, he did have weaknesses. Like all of his kind, he had a menial hive mentality. "Don't you want your other comrades in arms to survive?"

Shadrach squeezed his eyes closed, obviously running faces

135

and memories through his mind. Ornias watched the tortured twitches of the muscles around his lips with satisfaction.

"My guards have captured Samual Linstrom."

"Samual?" Shadrach inquired weakly, squeezing his lids tighter as though against pain. "He's barely fifteen. He knows nothing of the depth of our movement. Let him go. What can you possibly—"

"But he's such a *good* boy, don't you agree? Kind to a fault, he's worked his way into the heart of every rebel in your organization."

"What does that have to do with anything?"

"I'm sure if you don't care about the horrifying days that await him, some of your filthy coconspirators will. Surely someone must want him saved. Don't you think so?"

"I don't care."

"Really?" Ornias stroked his braided beard, cocking his head inquisitively. "I think perhaps I'll put Linstrom's screams on the loudspeakers throughout your section of the city. That way all your coconspirators can hear the final fate that awaits their treasonous actions."

"Have you no humanity left?" Shadrach pleaded, opening his moist eyes. "Samual's parents are nearly two hundred and nothing but skin and bones since the drought killed all their crops. He's the son they prayed for for over a century. That would kill them."

"That's the point, isn't it? We have to make a few examples to demonstrate we won't tolerate further disruptions of our sublime . . ." he chuckled, squeezing the bridge of his nose at the absurdity, "our sublime religious faith."

"No one will help you. No matter what threats you make."

"Well, then I'll be forced to blast your entire section of the city. That will certainly rid me of my problems."

Shadrach fought against the chains so violently, Ornias took two quick steps back in shock. "*Bastard*! Those are innocent people! How can you—"

"Oh, far from innocent. They've shielded you and your rabble for years. They've provided homes for meeting places and stripped their own cupboards bare to give you supplies to kill the Mashiah's forces—*my forces*. I'd hardly call that innocent."

"A thousand children live in that part of the city!"

"Children grow up to be warriors. For every one we kill, we can rest easier at night."

"Dear . . . Lord . . ." Shadrach whimpered, bowing his

136

head as silent sobs wracked his wounded body. "You're inhuman."

"Come, Shadrach. You've fought for three years to protect those people. I know how much you care about them." He dropped his voice to a conspiratorial coo. "Come . . . surely you had an escape plan. Just tell me where Rachel might have headed. That's all, just . . ."

Shadrach jerked forward to spit in his face and Ornias gasped, rage welling as the spittle ran in slimy streams down his cheeks. Taking a pale blue silk kerchief from his pocket, he wiped his tanned face, fighting to control his breathing. One should never let an enemy know he'd triggered a reaction; it weakened the status of the power-holder. With a concentrated nonchalance, Ornias slowly paced before the rebel, noting with outrage that a faint smile twisted the man's lips.

"I'm so sorry you did that," Ornias murmured. "The only reason I had doctors tend your wounds and keep you alive was because I trusted you'd come to your senses. But now I see I was terribly wrong."

"Then kill me!" Shadrach demanded through clenched teeth, struggling against his bonds. The shackles jingled, fresh blood spotting the bandage over his stomach.

"Oh, I don't think that's the best course of action yet." Then, with the patience of an executioner, Ornias meandered to the wall of colorful devices. Placing a hand to his chin, he gently caressed his braided beard as he looked over the selection. From the corner of his eye, he saw Shadrach's face go slack, the haughty look vanishing to be replaced by one of abject terror. Ornias took his time, lifting first a mace, then a cat-o'-nine-tails, before reaching for another device.

"Ah, this should do." He retrieved a small black box and stroked it with loving fingers. "Yes. Simple. Clean."

As he walked back, Shadrach tensed, setting the chains to jangling again. Resigned horror filled the man's eyes.

"Do you know what this is?" Ornias asked conversationally, holding up the box.

No answer came, but sweat beaded on the rebel's face.

"It's called a 'flayer.' A quaint and effective device originated during the last rebellion on Ganor. Legend has it that victims survived for days after it did its work, flies and insects swarming over bared muscles. I've always thought the concept very interesting."

137

Shadrach's breathing quickened, chest rising and falling as though he'd run a hundred miles.

Ornias needlessly straightened his sapphire robe. Reaching for his sherry again, he sipped patiently. "One last time, Shadrach. Hmm? Let's talk. Don't force me to hurt you like this. You need only—"

"Get it over with!"

"You refuse to discuss where your beautiful wife might have gone? Just tell me who could have given her shelter?"

"I'll never tell you! *Kill me!*" Shadrach screamed, tears glistening on his lashes. His muscles suddenly went weak. "Just . . . just kill me."

Ornias pondered the man's imploring eyes, then shook his head. "Perhaps later."

A soft hum filled the room as he flicked the flayer on.

* * * * *

Jeremiel reached across the console to hit the fuel monitor, then checked a series of different gauges for atmosphere, food and water reserves and weapons charge. Gradually, he worked the vessel up to maximum acceleration, carefully watching the two old men reclining in the passenger seats. How many gravities could their hearts take? Despite the compensators, fluctuations occurred. They looked fairly fit, but at their ages, who could tell? They had to be pushing three hundred and fifty. Frowning, he input the course correction for Horeb and finally swung around. The elders occupied the lavender seats, eyes glued to him.

"Are you two gentlemen feeling all right?"

The tall skinny old man frowned menacingly. His wealth of gray hair hung in thick unruly strands. "Of course, we're all right."

"Good. Let me know if you suffer from any dizziness or—"

"Don't worry about us. We're healthy as leeches."

"Uh—all right. Then let me thank you for saving my life."

"Bah! We didn't save you," the grumpy patriarch informed him. "We blasted those fool marines who'd kept us prisoners for days! Saving you was an accident."

Jeremiel lifted his brows, but nodded amiably. "Well, that doesn't change the fact that you accidentally—"

"Wasn't your father Menachem Baruch?" the pudgy elder who'd helped Jeremiel into the ship asked, leaning forward

138

eagerly. His pale green suit accented his freckled face and nearly bald head. "From Tikkun? Wasn't he?"

A small warning bell rang inside Jeremiel. Who would know his family? Was this some trick? A trap laid by the Magistrates? He scrutinized the old man severely, probing his warm, beaming eyes. He detected no guile there, but responded guardedly, "You knew him, you said?"

"Oh, yes. A wonderful man. And weren't you studying with Rev Ishmael for a while? The Cabala and Merkabah as I recall?"

Jeremiel blinked in surprise. Only the deepest intelligence personnel of the Magistrates would know such data. Were these old men plants? He looked both of them up and down and decided he'd have to be crazy to think them competent at anything, especially deep intelligence work. They appeared nothing more than aged retirees on the brink of senility.

"Yes," he said tersely. "I've studied the ancient mystical books." Reaching beneath the console, he pulled out the ship's mini-med unit. Wound shock had worn off and his leg throbbed agonizingly. Arranging the unit over his wound, he switched it on.

"Lord!" he groaned, wincing as the machine probed and prodded, swabbed and medicated. The pain finally seeped into nothingness and he let out a relieved breath.

"I knew your mother, too," the old man blurted suddenly, a look of serene happiness on his face.

"It's been a long time since I met anyone who knew my family. Especially my mother. I barely recall her. She died when I was four."

"Yes, yes! Mira had a beautiful voice. We used to sing in temple together! Oh, it was years ago, but I remember. She was the best cantor I ever knew."

Jeremiel leaned back in his chair, letting the mini-med finish its work as he considered the old men. The bespectacled passenger sat on the edge of his seat, an almost loving look on his withered face, while the other eyed Jeremiel as though he were a Giclasian garbage snake. A curious duo, these two. "Forgive me, do I know either of you?"

"You don't remember?" the eager elder asked in a pained voice. "No, you were very young, I guess not. I'm Yosef Calas and this is my friend, Ari Funk. We're from Tikkun, too."

The name struck Jeremiel like the blow of a fist, taking his breath away. For the first time, he noticed the clear similarity of features and tone of voice. "Calas? Zadok's brother?"

"Yes! You know Zadok? We came to Kayan to see him. Well, actually, to attend the funeral of his daughter, Ezarin. Did you see him? How is he?" A desperately hopeful look suffused the wrinkled face and Jeremiel lowered his eyes to stare at the gray floor. He should get the news from a family member, not a stranger who'd practically kidnapped him from Kayan.

Yosef cast a worried glance at Ari, then asked, "Is . . . is Zadok all right?"

"Mr. Calas, I'm so sorry to be the one to have to tell you . . ."

"Tell me what?"

"I was . . ." He halted, pursing his lips tightly at the unfairness. "I was with him when he was killed," Jeremiel finished softly. "It was at the spaceport a few days ago."

Tears welled in Yosef's brown eyes and he sank back into his chair, fiddling aimlessly with the control panel on the arm. "A few days ago?"

"Yes. His funeral was held the same day as Ezarin's. The line of people who came to grieve stretched for miles. He was a good man. Everyone loved him." The words sounded so lame he clenched his fists at his ineptness. He'd traveled across the galaxy relaying messages of death and sorrow to the families of people in his forces, but he'd never grown good at it. Something inside him rebelled at the absurdity. Why was it that the best always died the worst? He bitterly resented the injustice of it.

"Not everyone," Yosef murmured, blinking back tears. "Who killed my brother?"

"I wish I knew. Supposedly someone from Horeb. An assassin sent by the new Mashiah who's arisen there. But no one's sure."

"Why?"

"Zadok was about to go to 'test' the Mashiah's authenticity. Apparently the false prophet wasn't ready to be revealed for the fraud he is yet."

"Oh . . ."

Ari reached over and gently patted Yosef's wrinkled hand. The willowy old man's face had puckered with sympathetic despair. Jeremiel frowned; so the ancient patriarch wasn't senile. "It must have been when the headache hit you."

Yosef nodded.

"There's nothing you could have done," Ari whispered tenderly. "A man with as much power as Zadok has lots of enemies."

Yosef wiped his nose on his green sleeve. Jeremiel started to turn back to the control console, but Yosef's frail voice stopped him.

"Did he—suffer?"

"No, no, not at all. It was a clean chest shot. He barely knew what was happening to him."

"I see," Yosef murmured.

"Mister Calas, do you realize you're the rightful leader of Gamant civilization? Sarah is—"

"Oh," he whispered, waving a trembling hand. "Zadok and I talked about it once. I told him if the time ever came, I'd yield to someone else. I'm glad Sarah has taken the responsibility. She'll get no challenges from me."

"I understand."

Yosef leaned back in his chair and closed his eyes. His lips trembled, a single tear glistening like a diamond on his cheek.

Ari reached over and set the selector on Yosef's chair for some pleasant music, then got up and took the copilot's chair next to Jeremiel.

"He'll be all right," he muttered. "He just needs time to get used to the shock."

Jeremiel nodded, heaving a disturbed breath. Absently, he studied the med unit which now felt warm and soothing against his flesh. "Of course. I'm sorry I had to be the one to tell him."

"Oh, it's better that he learned of it now. The sooner one knows such things, the sooner one can get over them."

"I hope you're right. To be honest, I'm not sure Gamant civilization will ever recover. Zadok was a single beacon of strength in a very dark, very hostile galaxy."

"Don't worry about Gamants," Ari grumped, slicing the air with a fist. "We always bounce back."

"In the past, that's been true. But our people have never faced the kind of threat we now face. The Galactic Magistrates have the best technological minds in history. Their latest weapons are dazzling, utilizing knowledge we can only guess at. And they're hell-bent on destroying us and our 'damaging, separationist philosophies.' Right now I'm worried sick they might . . ." He halted abruptly, squinting at the console monitors. A blip caught his eye. He leaned forward, frowning. "Damn it."

141

"What do you see?" Ari hunched over his shoulder, trying to observe every screen in the general vicinity.

"They're after us. I thought I'd covered the ionic—"

"Can we outrun them?"

"Yes, I think so. We've got a good head start. But they'll be tracking us. When we land on Horeb, they'll be all over us, like—as a friend of mine says—ducks on a june bug."

"June bug? What's that?"

"I haven't the vaguest idea, but ducks apparently like to eat them as much as the Magistrates would like to eat me and every Gamant alive."

"They won't get you."

"You're a hell of an optimist," he said, glancing sideways at the frizzy haired old man. Ari had a cheshire cat smile.

"I'm a realist."

"Are you? That's good," Jeremiel responded irritably, wishing he had about four battle cruisers at his back. "I need realists around me just now. I like company in times of travail."

"You're too sensitive. Me and Yosef, we'll get you out of this."

Jeremiel turned up the resolution on the screen to see if he could make out what sort of ships pursued them. *God damn. It wasn't Tahn, was it?* His shoulder muscles tensed. "And how do you plan on doing that?"

"We'll drop you off somewhere over the planet and me and Yosef will fly this baby to the nearest city. When those stupid marines catch us, we'll just say you held a gun to our heads and forced us to fly with you as hostages. Then we'll tell them you jumped ship and we don't know where you are. And that'll be true."

"But risky, friend, very risky. They probably won't believe you. And if they take you in for questioning and decide to use the mind probes—"

"What could they find out? That Yosef forgets lots of things or that I fart all day long? They won't have to use mind probes to find that out." Ari smiled sardonically.

"Uh . . . yes, you've got a point there. But I'm not worried about you revealing information. The probes destroy critical centers of the brain."

Ari snickered. "Bah! Those centers were gone long ago! We're not worried."

"It's kind of you to offer, but—"

"Somebody has to help the Underground before the Magistrates kill us all. And they will, you know."

Jeremiel looked up, expression softening. This old man knew more about life than it appeared. Ari met his gaze with the stern determination of a seasoned war veteran. Of course, maybe he was. He was old enough to have been involved in the last Gamant Revolt. "Yes, I know. I fear that's precisely what the Magistrates have in mind."

"So, we'll drop you off somewhere and land in the nearest city and find a good restaurant for dinner."

"Horeb has a poor reputation for restaurants." Jeremiel stalled while he thought over the offer. Maybe the Magistrates wouldn't hurt these old men? Maybe it was naive to assume, but who in his right mind would think they knew more than what they'd eaten for breakfast? And it appeared his best chance—unfortunately. Silently, he railed at himself for needing to accept.

"You're going to have trouble landing," he said sharply. "With the gear damaged you'll have to set her down real easy and expect to tumble sideways. Strap in good and use the attitude jets for all they're worth." He pointed to the appropriate levers on the console. "You said you knew how to fly this thing. Do you?"

Ari smiled wryly, bushy gray brows arching. "God, no. But I could have anyway."

"Uh-huh." Jeremiel filled his cheeks with air and spewed an anxious breath. "Well, I've got four days to teach you everything I know. Are you ready?"

Ari leaned back in his chair like a professional patiently awaiting his latest instructions for a spy mission. "I'm *always* ready."

Jeremiel massaged his forehead.

CHAPTER 13

Adom glanced around as he paced his luxurious red and gold bedchamber. Cups of stone cold tea littered the dresser and table, and hid on the floor beneath piles of tossed clothing. Books formed a precarious stack on his desk, gold bindings luminescent in the light streaming through the broad windows. Satin sheets twisted in a rumpled mass against the ornate brass posts of his bed. His blankets draped carelessly into the untouched breakfast tray on the floor. Sleep had eluded him; his memories continually replayed the horrifying destruction of the temple.

"Rebels!" he whispered in anguish, slamming a fist into the wall.

He glanced out the open window. Whirlwinds of red dust wound through the fire-gutted streets of Seir, tormenting charred roof timbers until they banged and creaked mournfully. In the sky, a dust-spawned halo encircled the flaming ball of the sun. Eerie light penetrated the haze, turning the shadows from gray to a smoky azure. In the distance, he could see what remained of his holy structure: a scorched and gaping maw. Burned out buildings stood like lone sentinels around it. Though fire crews had worked through the night, smoke still curled from the rubble to twist away in the wind.

"Dear God, what should I do? *Tell me*?"

He spread his arms and pleadingly stared at the thousand-year-old image of Milcom painted lovingly into the dome of his ceiling. "Tell me . . . Lord? Lord!" Guilt plagued him. Wave after wave of cries penetrated his sanctuary, floating up from the gardens outside. The fetid odors of death and filth drifted to him on each gust.

"Adom! Adom! Adom!" the cries continued until he thought he'd go mad.

He clamped hands over his ears, shouting, "I can't stand this! Help me, God!"

Finally, the agony in his breast became so unbearable, he threw open his door and raced down the magnificent marble hall. Winding through the rich corridors lined with brooding statues of the saints, his feet pounded in a dull staccato. They watched him, those disapproving deities, angry with his incompetence. He took the stairs down three at a time, avoiding their gazes, to burst through the palace doors and out onto the top step of the pink fan-shaped entry stairs.

A roar of adulation and anxiety rose. For a full minute, no sound existed except a rumble like that of the sea. His heart thundered fearfully as he gazed over the enormous hexagonal garden filled with rock sculptures, peak-roofed gazebos and panic-stricken men and women who shoved each other, shouting as if crazed.

A hot northerly wind blew, flapping the hem of his maroon robe as he gingerly stepped down the marble stairs.

Behind him, the massive bronze doors pinged with the peppering of wind-blown sand. Women sobbed and screeched near the bottom steps. Behind them, hard-eyed men shouted, daggers hanging menacingly from belts. To the side, a special section had been cleared where the injured lay in irregular rows, flies swarming in a black hungry cloud over their wounds.

"All this," he whispered miserably, a sob rising in his throat, "because they wanted to kill *me*?"

Gray-robed palace guards stared at him anxiously, unsure whether to stay in their assigned positions or move to protect him. He shook his head at them, then turned and raised his arms in a reassuring gesture to the throng. "I'm sorry. I'm so very sorry."

Hope laced the sweating people. They jostled relentlessly to get closer, toppling sculptures, screaming at each other and at him. Tears welled in his blue eyes, blurring the images of uncombed hair and unwashed bodies, of pain and desperation.

"I'm . . . I'm so sorry," he sobbed.

A weeping woman in a torn, bloodstained tan robe ran up the stairs carrying an injured child. "Mashiah, I beg you! He's a good boy and he's only five. One of the stones in the temple fell on him. Be merciful. Heal him. *Please!*"

Adom stared impotently at the dried blood spattering the boy's crushed chest. Could Milcom work such a miracle? The child already seemed beyond hope.

He extended trembling arms. "Let me have him."

The woman started to thrust the child into his arms, but from behind, an old man jerked the hem of Adom's robe so forcefully, he stumbled backward.

"Mashiah!" the man cried. He sat hunched on the step, clutching his dead wife to his breast. "Could you bring her back to life, Mashiah? I can't live without her!"

"I . . . I can't make the dead live again. Forgive me."

The old man's face puckered and he wept miserably, rocking his wife's corpse back and forth. "Why can't you . . . why can't you . . . why can't you?" the man repeated over and over.

Everywhere the faithful looked at Adom through eyes of madness, imploring him to ease their suffering, and he felt so helpless, so frail beneath the weight of their despair.

And there were so many. . . .

"Milcom?" he called into the eddying crowd. "Milcom, I beg you. Help us?"

He took another timid step down the stairs, reaching out to touch the dying boy. The mother gripped his maroon sleeve and buried her face in the silk. "Bless you, Mashiah. Bless you!"

Adom took the boy in his arms and sat hard on the warm stone step. "It's all right. Milcom sees his injuries." He smiled weakly, placing a hand on the boy's fevered brow and offering a soft prayer. "Please, God, do you see us here? Please . . ."

"He's healing!" someone shrieked and the crowd surged up, a massive, foul-smelling wave of screaming bodies. For an instant, he felt their cries like a gripping hand at his throat, malevolent and suffocating. He swallowed hard and closed his eyes, clutching the boy tightly to his chest. After several minutes, he felt a tingling heat course through his veins and sensed the boy's breathing had grown easier.

The child stirred.

"Oh, Mashiah," the boy's mother sobbed, "thank you. God bless you." She knelt and took her son in her arms.

"Mashiah!" a filthy woman in gray rags shrieked, shoving against him. She fairly threw her child into his lap. "Mashiah, cure my little girl next. Please, she's—"

"No, my son is sicker and we've been waiting all night!" A dark-haired crone crowded into the circle.

From every corner, every crevice, they came, shouting, pleading, shoving him. A smothering fear welled inside him.

His guards murmured among themselves, tension spreading down the line. They, too, feared the crowd . . . feared they couldn't protect him if someone in the mob decided to commit murder.

He looked down at the girl. Her battered head lolled limply over his leg, tangled black hair forming a web over her bloody face. An ache built inside him. "Milcom?" he prayed softly and placed his hand behind her frail neck. "Heal this child?"

Behind him, a clamor of voices rose up, fiery and indignant. He didn't understand the sudden enmity until he heard Ornias' voice penetrate the outrage, "Adom? Adom!"

"Don't take him from us!" "He's our only savior!" "Let me touch the hem of his robe!"

Adom concentrated. Finally, the little girl shuddered and opened her eyes, croaking, "Mama?"

"Blessed Lord!" the mother shouted reverently. "I believe in Milcom, Mashiah. *I believe in you.*" She kissed his hand and picked up her daughter before shouldering through the crowd.

"Adom!"

He didn't want to turn, but reluctantly did so anyway. Standing tall, the Councilman's ebony robe billowed like a bat's wings as he waved for Adom to come to the palace.

"No," he murmured stubbornly, gritting his teeth as he looked back to the faithful. "I can't leave them." Quickly, he stood and pushed farther down into the masses, touching anyone within reach. People pressed against him in a smothering tide, faces beaming with adoration and hope.

"Mashiah, I love you," a one-legged beggar implored, stroking Adom's arm. "Don't let him take you from us."

"Guards!" Ornias shouted harshly. The gray-robed troops immediately began closing ranks, tightening their circle, thrusting the beggar and other worshipers aside until finally they'd separated the people from Adom like chaff from wheat. Two guards gripped his arms hurtfully hard and quickly hustled him up the marble steps. He heard the shrill wails of those still desperately pleading for his attention.

"Mercy, Mashiah! Have mercy!"

He tried to turn, but the restraining arms of the guards prevented him. Before he knew it, the mauve velvet shadows of the palace enfolded him. Ornias slammed the bronze doors with an echoing clang and locked them. He smoothed his light brown hair which the wind had tousled and eyed Adom reproachfully.

"For God's sake, Adom, were you trying to get yourself killed?"

"No, I—I . . ." He jammed his hands in his pockets, straining at his own inability to challenge the man. He only wanted peace and tranquillity around him. "The people came in droves throughout the night and I couldn't bear to hear them call my name any more. So I—"

"Well, you mustn't do that again. I know you trust everyone, but not everyone *deserves* your trust. Human beings are a scurrilous lot. You—"

"I know my flock. They're good people."

Ornias sniffed condescendingly. "Yes, well . . . Please notify me the next time you want to wade amongst them? That's all I ask."

"If . . . if you're near."

Ornias scowled. "I apologize for being gone these past few hours. I know they've been difficult for you, but we captured one of the rebels this week and I've been questioning him."

Hope flared in Adom's wounded soul. He took a step toward the Councilman. "Where's Rachel Eloel? Have you discovered—"

"Not yet, but I will."

"I hope it's soon."

"I'm working as hard as I can, Adom. But I need more time."

Anxiety burned so brilliantly in Adom's chest he felt sick. "We must find her. Anyone who could kill so thoughtlessly is a danger to herself and everyone else. We can't let her stay free."

"Of course not. We'll find her. Don't worry." Ornias came up beside him, putting a hand at his back and guiding him deeper into the protective womb of the palace. The structure formed a gigantic triangle in the heart of the city. Gothic arches stretched fifty feet high throughout, the pink marble darkening to magenta at the peaks. Fringed tapestries covered the walls, accenting the plush paisley carpets of turquoise and indigo, pearl and apricot. Pieces of intricately craved furniture stood between the pillars: high-backed chairs, tables with vases of dried desert flowers, locked bookcases containing rare volumes of religious literature . . . and the disapproving saints.

"I must talk to her, Ornias. She's not sane. She needs help."

"You'll have your chance, Adom. I promise. But you mustn't let it worry you. You've far more important things to think about."

Adom shivered, remembering the blood-spattered stones of the temple, the charred limbs twisting from beds of ash. "What could be more important?"

"For one thing, we must find a way to feed the homeless multitudes. After the drought, our storerooms are nearly empty. We've little food to spare. I was thinking maybe we should contact the Magistrates. They're always willing to—"

Adom turned sharply, meeting the Councilman's cold, lime green eyes. Why did Ornias always look so perfect, so utterly confident and untouched by any and all tragedies? It angered him a little. "Have you lost your mind?" he whispered urgently. "For every loaf of bread the government brings, they demand a pound of flesh. Namely our children. They'll want to establish a Right School on Horeb. I won't have it!"

"You always get carried away with emotions, Adom. I'm trying to do something practical."

"You won't contact the Magistrates!"

"All right," Ornias agreed reluctantly, throwing up his manicured hands. "You know I'll obey your wishes, but what do you suggest to keep the wolves away from our door? Starvation is unquestionably the greatest impetus for apostasy that's ever been devised. We can't just let—"

"I'll . . . I'll ask Milcom. He'll tell us what to do."

"Adom, *really*. God has other things to do than hear our petty cries every day. We need to handle this ourselves. What if I contact Kayan or Tikkun? Other Gamant planets will surely want to donate supplies."

"What are you saying? That you don't believe Milcom will help?"

"No, no, of course not. It's just that I don't want to 'wear out our welcome' in heaven, if you get my meaning? Too many requests over insignificant—"

"*Insignificant*? We have a thousand desperate people standing in our gardens." His voice dropped to a frail murmur. "Some are dying."

"I'm well aware of that and if we don't provide them with some bread and milk they're liable to take out their frustrations on us. You don't want to see the palace burned by such vermin, do you? That's why we must take some concrete action, before they get out of hand and storm the doors."

"Milcom will feed them."

Ornias lifted his thin graceful brows and roasted Adom with his gaze. "You mustn't expect—"

"He's never come to you! That's why you doubt. *But he has come to me*."

"Of course, Adom. Don't get upset."

"You will take no action until you hear from me tomorrow. And I don't want to be disturbed unless it's an emergency. I'll be in my prayer room."

"Very well, but . . ."

Adom veered sharply right at the next hall, leaving Ornias behind, his mouth still open.

His heart thudded so loudly he could barely breathe. Who did Ornias think he was? He had no right to treat him like a

149

child. His stomach muscles clenched tight every time he had to deal with the councilman over any serious subject. He felt oddly as though they gazed at each over the sights of pistols, each waiting for the other to make a mistake. Yet it was a silly feeling, he knew that. Ornias was no different than any Gamant. They were all a little violent underneath their pleasant ways. Still, Ornias made him shudder deep inside.

"You're . . . you're just careworn lately," he crooned to himself, hoping to soothe the frantic pounding of his heart. "It's all right. Milcom will guide you. Don't . . . don't panic."

A chill crept from the salmon-colored walls to taunt his bare feet. He hurried, obliviously passing the rich brocaded drapes and thousand-year-old Elnat mahogany statues of the martyrs. Taking the stairs that plunged into the bowels of the palace, he soon found himself panting in a pool of darkness at the bottom. Tendrils of cold breathed from the stones.

"Milcom? It's me. I'm coming to you."

Before him stretched a long corridor, bare of all furnishings except lamps in wall niches. The servants kept them lit, but they were so widely spaced they cast scant patchy light on the towering rough-hewn walls. Like a huge stone coffin, the hall reeked of damp and decay. Adom blinked to help his eyes adjust to the dimness, then quickly strode to the door at the far end, his maroon robe fluttering behind him.

Quietly, he entered his small sanctuary. The sweet scent of sandalwood caressed him. Lamps glowed here, too, one on each of the four walls. A mantle of gold glimmered from the blue and ivory geometric designs of his round prayer rug, flashing from the inverted triangle hanging on the gray wall directly in front of him. A pile of tapestried pillows tumbled over each other in the corner.

He went to the rug and knelt, bowing his head and forming his hands into the sacred triangle. "Milcom, your people need you. I need you." His voice sounded immensely deeper in the candlelit stillness. "Please, Lord?"

When no answer came, desperation touched him.

Determined, he cleared his mind and concentrated, focusing all his anxieties into a single cry for help. Standing amongst the homeless, he'd felt barren and lost, groping for guidance that only God could give.

"Milcom, I beseech you. We can't survive without your . . ."

A form passed before the lamp to his left, casting a long cool shadow over him. He exhaled in sudden relief. Taking a deep breath of the scented air, he turned. Milcom stood regally. A god in the shape of a man, his muscular body shimmered like cut crystal in the soft light. Dressed in a hooded cloak of viridian velvet, the celestial being smiled and to Adom it felt like the coming of the sun. Joy leapt in his soul.

"I knew you'd come, Lord."

"Of course, Adom. You're never alone. I'll always be here when you truly need me."

"Since that day in the mountains when you saved me, I've known you watch over Horeb."

Milcom gracefully threw back his hood and walked to stand only two feet from Adom, gazing down concernedly. His wide amber eyes shone brightly, singularly gentle. "I've sensed a stir in this universe. What's wrong?"

"A stir?"

"Yes," he said and frowned. Tiny lines of light appeared around his eyes. "Your voice formed only part of it."

Adom blinked in confusion. "Does it have to do with Horeb?"

"I'm not sure. What's happening here?"

"The rebels destroyed our new temple and hundreds were killed or injured. But worse than that, the fire consumed a fourth of the city, leaving thousands homeless and hungry. Even now, they cry for bread in the streets. I—"

"Yes," Milcom said, closing his eyes and cocking his head. A pinched look of sadness came over his brilliant face. "I hear them."

"Lord, can you—"

"They'll have bread. Even if I have to tug it from another universe. Michael's coffers are overfull, after all." A remorseful smile touched his lips. "Don't concern yourself about it, Adom."

Gratitude flooded his fevered body like cool water. "Thank you, Lord."

"Tell me what else is happening. I sense a deep worry in you that goes beyond the temple disaster." Milcom scrutinized Adom with a piercing look.

Adom lowered his gaze to trace the entwining swirls of blue and ivory in his rug. The lamps flickered as though

151

touched by a breeze. "You've always known my soul. I'm terribly worried about the rebels. Rachel Eloel has escaped. Yet I know if I could only talk with her, preach to her for a few days, she'd understand your will and come around to our side. But we can't find her."

"Indeed? You want to preach to her after what she's done to Seir?"

"Yes, Lord. She needs preaching badly."

Milcom laughed softly, though why Adom didn't know. "And what would you tell her?"

He blinked, gazing into Milcom's warm, crystalline features. The angles of his perfect face were as sharp as though chiseled from glass. "I'd tell her of your goodness and power. I'd explain to her the wickedness of Epagael. I'd show her—"

"She won't believe you."

Adom frowned, mouth ajar. "But why, Lord? Surely any thinking person can see the Truth?"

"Thinking has very little to do with religion. I thought I told you that?"

"You did. But I—"

"Never believed it?" Milcom smiled and gently laid a hand on Adom's shoulder. The warmth sent a tingle through him, making him feel better, for it had occurred to him that his disbelief might have constituted disobedience. A thing he never wished to be guilty of. Milcom had saved his life and continued to fight to save the life of the entire universe. He owed him obedience and faith.

"Heart is the key, Adom. If people want to believe something, they'll bend logic into a fine container."

"Yes, I've seen it. I'm sure that's why so many still hold to Epagael."

"Partly. It's also their heritage. Old ways die hard. Especially old gods. That's why I've always told you that gentle means of conversion are best."

Adom looked up imploringly. "We've been trying, Lord. But the rebels refuse to listen to us. How can I lead them to the salvation you offer if all they want to do is kill us?"

"Well, there are some things you're doing wrong. I'm sorry I've been too busy to return here to guide you recently."

Milcom paced slowly to stand before the huge triangle which glistened in the candlelight. His velvet robe swayed as he put a hand on his golden chin. "Look at this sacred symbol. Which is right? Should the apex be up or down? Or maybe sideways?"

Adom frowned. "Down, Lord. You've taught us the world is the source of all that's good."

"And what is the world?"

"The . . . the soil, the trees, the animals, the people."

Milcom nodded thoughtfully, but kept silent. As the hush continued, Adom shifted uncomfortably.

"Lord? Did I say something wrong?"

"What makes you think the world doesn't include the sky? The stars? The entire universe?" He waved a hand around his head as though casting a lasso.

"I don't understand? I thought—"

"Forgive me. When I said 'world,' I was thinking of an ancient Greek word, *cosmos,* which refers to everything that is not god. The cosmos is the ground of our being, not Horeb. You following me?"

"Not exactly, Lord." Red crept into Adom's cheeks. He always felt so dimwitted during this type of discussion. God had knowledge of the entire breadth of the multiple universes and Adom had difficulty even conceiving that other planets existed. He'd never been off Horeb, though he'd read extensively about galactic exploration when he'd been younger—before Milcom found him.

"Hmm . . ." God lifted amber brows. "Well, suffice it to say that the entirety of creation should be considered 'world.' "

"So the triangle can point in any direction?"

"The creation lies in all directions, doesn't it?" Under his breath, Milcom added, "And no direction."

"What was that last, Lord. I didn't—"

"Never mind. Embrace the creation. *Understand it, in all its horrifying facets.* That's the essence of salvation and that's what you must teach to bring people to our way of thinking. Don't tell them they're damned because their holy triangle points in the wrong direction. Understand?"

"I think so."

"You *think* so?"

"No, I—I do . . . understand."

"Good. Can you teach *Rachel Eloel* about the creation?"

Adom steeled himself. He felt a strange attraction toward the woman. She was very beautiful. Just thinking about her sent a warm flush through him, even though a part of him hated her for the suffering she'd caused. "I don't know, Lord. She'll be difficult. But I'd like to try."

Milcom nodded contemplatively, rubbing his golden chin. "Well . . . all right. I'd planned on doing it myself, but perhaps your gentle innocence will be a better tool."

"What do you mean, Lord?"

God ignored his question, responding instead, "I'm going to help you with this one." Striding forward, Milcom reached into the pocket of his cloak and drew out a necklace. The blue globe dangling from the chain emitted a blinding cerulean halo in the god's hand. "You must never touch the globe. You understand?"

"Yes." Adom extended fingers and Milcom laid the chain in them. Immediately, the brilliant halo vanished, the globe becoming a simple blue ball. Adom's mouth fell open slightly in awe. "What's it for?"

"It's for Rachel."

"But I don't under—"

"*For her and no one else.* Clear?"

"Yes, Lord."

"Give it to her as a gift. Uh . . . and you might not want to mention it's from me. That might, shall we say, *taint* her appreciation."

Adom grimaced, appraising the thick chain and azure globe. He frequently failed to understand Milcom's intentions, though he tried very hard. "All right, Lord. Will you bring her to me?"

Milcom dropped his gaze and smiled faintly. "Not exactly. But she'll be back."

"Thank you, Lord."

"Adom?"

"Yes?"

"Don't tell the councilman the content of this visit. He's not exactly the type I'd want aware of the *Mea*'s existence."

"The *Mea*?" Milcom pointed to the blue ball. "Oh, very well, Lord."

Milcom turned to go, strolling back to the place from which he'd appeared. Candlelight glistened brilliantly from his body as he neared the lamp, throwing prismatic reflections across the ceiling.

"Lord?" Adom said in a voice smaller than he'd intended. "Am I doing all right? I try so hard to do your will, but sometimes I feel so stupid and inadequate."

"You're doing fine." Milcom watched him through bittersweet amber eyes, and Adom felt as though that look hid a wealth of pain. "Just keep being yourself. Never forget that the light of salvation shines through the hurt eyes of everyone around you. Love everyone, teach everyone, and remember God."

"And you'll take care of us?"

Milcom nodded seriously. "I'll do my best, Adom." Bringing the hood of his viridian velvet cloak back over his head, he held up his crystalline hands and mumbled something soft, inaudible. A whirling blackness appeared in the stone wall, like a gaping hole in time and space, and he stepped through into the roiling darkness beyond.

CHAPTER 14

Woe, Woe, good people . . . He has upon his forehead three letters: A K T. And he will reign for three years. And in his first year, all the grass upon the earth will fail. Then there will be a mighty plague. . . . People will be calling upon death and digging up tombs and saying, "Blessed and thrice blessed are you who have already died, because you did not reach these days."

The Greek Apocalypse of Daniel
Date: 800 A.D. Old Earth Standard

Rachel and Sybil struggled up the steep path weaving the dark mountainside. Huge boulders were scattered along the slope in an avalanche of monstrous wind-sculpted statues. Frosted by starlight, the slope seemed a ruined garden of the gods; upraised fists and angry Promethean faces threatened in muted defiance, their raging expressions long quieted by the sand storms of Horeb.

"Mommy?" Sybil panted. "Help me?"

Rachel turned to see her daughter tugging futilely at the tattered hem of her blue robe. Seized in the stubborn arms of a thornbush, the fabric refused to come loose. A dense tangle of underbrush sprouted from every crack in the rocks. Darkness made avoiding the prickly traps nearly impossible.

"I'm coming, baby." Tiredly, she worked her way back down the steep path. She gripped her daughter's hem and jerked hard. The sound of shredding fabric seemed to shriek in the silence. A fluttering ribbon of blue clung to the branch.

Sybil brushed tangled brown curls from her eyes, and looked up, dirty face drawn with exhaustion. "Thank you, Mommy. Let's go, I'm sorry I—"

"Sybil?" Knees shaking from weariness, Rachel braced a hand against a rock face and let the desert winds caress her. "Let's just stand here for a minute."

"Are you okay, Mom?"

"Yes, I just need to rest."

"Maybe I could go a little farther up the path? I can climb some more."

Her daughter wiped a sleeve under her running nose and straightened her back. In the starlight, her eyes shone gray-blue as though frosted with steel dust. The small pack of food on her back jiggled with each sluggish move. *My poor baby. You want to keep climbing because the terror inside won't let you stop until we're safe. Dear God, the horror you've suffered. Will you ever be able to live normally again after this? Will the scars in your mind ever heal?*

"Just go a little farther, Sybil. Don't get out of my sight."

"I won't." The girl plodded upward, patting Rachel's leg as she passed.

Rachel fell tiredly against the boulder. Her own small pack pulled miserably at her shoulders. Her gaze drifted back toward Seir. Only a tiny slice of the city stood visible beyond the towering boulders, lights glimmering through a haze of dust.

"Mashiah, are you coming?" she demanded quietly, fear tightening her breast.

Overhead, a meteor streaked the night skies, leaving a luminous trail of silver above the mountain peaks. She blinked, shaking her head, sure she'd seen it veer erratically. A ship? But it vanished before she could look again. In the brush, a bushbob sawed, the insect's song like a rusty hinge in the breeze. She listened for a time, letting the sound sink into her tormented soul.

"Adom . . . damn you. Just let us go." But she knew he wouldn't. She *had* to keep moving. Even now the *samaels* might be leaving Seir in search of them—if they hadn't already. She turned and started up the path again, feet thudding heavily against the stone.

"Sybil? Where are you?"

"I'm right here. On this rock."

"Where? I can't see you."

"Over here."

Rachel squinted through the darkness, but couldn't spot her. Digging fingers into crevices in the rocks, she used the stones to help lever her weary body up the slope. When she came to the curve, she found Sybil lying curled in a ball on a flat slab of red sandstone. She lifted her head weakly, looking bitterly fatigued. Rachel's soul shriveled at the sight. How much longer could the child keep going at this pace?

"Where are the caves, Mommy?"

"Not very far. Maybe another mile."

"Is that path straight up, too?"

"Yes, baby, I'm afraid so. Do you . . ." Rachel vacillated, tormenting herself inside. Sybil desperately needed sleep, and so did she, but could they afford it? "Do you want to nap a little while?"

"No, Mommy. We can't rest. The Mashiah might find us and kill us." Sybil started to slide down off the rock, her legs trembling.

"Stay there, sweetheart. We'll take just a few minutes to catch our breath. I think we'll be safe."

"I don't think that's a good idea. Why don't—"

"Let me do the thinking. I'm four times as old as you."

"Sometimes that doesn't matter," her daughter said skeptically, cocking her young head in a birdlike gesture that made Rachel smile.

"Trust me this time."

Sybil bit her lower lip, dropping her gaze to stare uncomfortably at the red sandstone beneath her legs. "You won't go anywhere?"

"No, I'll stay right here beside you."

"You won't let the Mashiah get me?" A tremor shook her voice.

"Never. You rest, Sybil."

"Maybe . . . maybe I'll just close my eyes for a little while."

"You do that. I'll keep watch."

Rachel slumped to sit on the edge of the slab and folded her dirty hands in her lap. Her peach robe hung in rags, the remaining opal beads reflecting the starglow in irregular patterns. Her waist-length hair draped over her shoulders in matted tangles.

She let her eyes rest on Sybil. The silver light etched a soft line around the child's pointed chin. Rachel wanted to reach out and touch her lovingly, but feared disturbing her desperately needed respite.

"Shadrach, Shadrach . . ." she whispered barely audibly, drawing strength from his name, as though he could still hear the plea and sense her love and need for him. "We tried, didn't we? But we failed. The old ways we cherished are gone forever. No one cares anymore. Forgive me . . . forgive me for not going back to look for you. I was afraid Sybil might be caught in the fire."

A brisk gust whistled up the path and she closed her blurred eyes, feeling the sting of wind-whipped sand against her face. In her mind, she heard Shadrach telling her she'd done the right thing, the only thing she could. She'd saved their child. Faintly, overhead, she thought she heard the whoosh of wings in the darkness. Night birds?

Absently, she looked up and froze.

Flying slowly over the path, the ship mocked a creeping beetle. Blacker than the darkness itself, the *samael* edged forward, blotting the stars as it came.

Fear choked her. She reached out a quaking hand to gently shake her daughter.

"Is it time, Mom—"

"Shh!"

"What?" Sybil whispered in terror, lying rigidly still.

"They've come." With her chin, Rachel pointed to the hovering craft. Sybil remained motionless. As the *samael* closed, they heard its hiss over the murmur of the wind. The marines must have been examining every crevice, heat and movement sensors on narrow beam, otherwise they'd have already spied them.

"We still have a chance," she muttered frantically. "Sybil, very slowly, I want you to slide down this slab and find a hollow in the rocks. Like a small cave beneath a boulder. If they catch me, you run so hard you can't breathe!"

"No, Mommy, I want you to—"

"Don't sass me now. Go!"

She heard sand scritch as Sybil slipped down the other side. A soft patter of feet sounded as the little girl retreated.

Rachel sat perfectly still, giving Sybil time to conceal herself before she tried escaping in the opposite direction. If she could draw them far enough away, Sybil might escape.

Rachel licked dry lips, watching the craft for a few moments longer, trying to force her stunned mind to think. The first moon rose in the distance. A timid sliver of white, it silhouetted the dark jagged peaks and splashed the land with a watery carpet of silver. The shadows of towering boulders stretched long fingers to chill her. Frantically, she searched the rocky terrain with her eyes, jumping when a large rock flew out of nowhere to slam a boulder fifty feet away. The *samael* changed direction suddenly, one side gleaming like polished pewter in the moonlight as it turned, veering off the path to check the movement it had sensed.

Rachel heard a faint whisper behind her, a deep masculine voice ordering, "Quickly, swing your legs over the edge and drop down to the path. There's a narrow crawl space between the rocks that leads to the left. Take it."

"Who—"

"*Do it!*"

Fear knotted in her stomach. *One of the Mashiah's men?* She hadn't the time to wonder about it. She slid to the ground, found the tiny tunnel beneath the cascade of rocks and slithered through on her stomach. Scents of dried grass and rodent dung stung her nostrils. Middens of twigs, dried berries and oddly shaped rocks formed nests at the bases of the boulders. Dust swirled, lodging in her lungs as she scrambled. The overwhelming urge to cough struck her. She forced it down, feeling like her chest would explode. When she slid out the other side, she saw Sybil crouched next to a tall blond with a reddish beard. Moonshine penetrated the shelter, flashing from their faces. The man had a straight nose and delicate cheekbones. His eyes caught and held hers. Piercing, they were unsettlingly blue. His black suit accented broad shoulders, narrowing to a trim muscular waist. He expertly pointed a pistol at her head.

"If you don't mind me asking, whose side are you on? I assume you're fleeing the Mashiah?" he whispered as his eyes searched the starry sky visible through a slender crack above.

She nodded, afraid to talk lest the cough burst out.

"Good, follow me." He lowered the pistol and got down on hands and knees, leading them through a series of narrow tunnels which widened into a tiny rounded cave. Complete darkness enveloped them and she buried her face in the folds of her robe and coughed desperately. Rachel heard the stranger lean back and she gripped Sybil's arm, pulling her against the cool wall with her.

They sat in silence for over an hour, listening to each other's breathing, before he finally spoke. "Stay here. I'll be back shortly." A scuffling of boots sounded as he crawled over the stone floor.

"It's all right, baby." Rachel pulled Sybil closer, stroking her dirty hair.

"Who's he, Mommy?"

"I don't know, but let's be quiet for a little while longer, all right."

Sybil nodded and stretched out on the floor, putting her head in Rachel's lap. It seemed only seconds before her daughter's breathing changed to the deep rhythms of sleep. Exhausted herself, she leaned her head back against the gritty surface of the wall and tenderly patted Sybil's leg, letting her thoughts drift. Who could he be? From his single question and the way he'd pointed the gun at her head until she'd answered correctly, he *apparently* wasn't part of the Mashiah's forces. She'd never seen him in Seir. A man of his good looks and obvious competence drew attention. Could he be from another part of Horeb? Tiny villages scattered the deserts but such nomadic groups usually scorned the city. And he didn't seem the type to be an average herder. An off-worlder? Why would someone from another planet who knew of the Mashiah and *opposed* him come here? Many who supported Adom had flocked to Horeb over the past three years, but their reasons were obvious: they longed to be near the blessed Redeemer. In these troubled times, everyone sought salvation. But this man was different, his presence a mystery, and all mysteries frightened Rachel. She bounced so many possibilities around her head that by the time he returned, perhaps a half hour later, a deep mistrust filled her breast.

"I think we're safe for now," he whispered. A rasping sounded as he dragged something across the floor and in a few seconds light flared. Rachel jerked as the palm-sized lustreglobe cast a stark white glow over the ceiling and walls. A velvet thick layer of soot covered the roof, proving they weren't the first people to take refuge here. In the center of the floor, a tiny pile of rocks marked the spot of dozens of fires.

"Who are you?" the stranger asked warily, fiddling with his pack to draw out two bottles of amber liquid. He handed one to her, explaining, "High energy concentrate. It's sticky, but good for you. Drink it."

They locked eyes for a long moment before she glanced at the pistol clipped on his belt and murmured, "Do you know how to communicate without giving orders?"

He dropped his gaze. "Not very well. Let me try again. I'm the man who just saved your life. And who might you be?"

"What's your name?"

He hesitated, then took a long swallow of his drink and wiped his mouth on his sleeve. "Since *I* saved *you*, I think I'm entitled to know who you are first."

Anger burned suddenly in her breast, and she pounded a fist into the floor. "I've been running for a week, trying to escape the certain torture and death the Mashiah has in store for me. I won't tell you who I am until I know you're not one of his men in disguise! Now who are you?"

He lifted his brows and heaved a disgruntled breath. "Jeremiel."

"Jeremiel . . . ?"

"*Jeremiel*. And you are?"

"Rachel."

He glanced knowingly at her. "Pleased to have been of service . . . Rachel." He pointed at Sybil who shifted in her lap. "And who's that?"

"My daughter, Sybil."

"Quite a little girl. She bit me when I tried to drag her deeper into the rocks." He pulled up his sleeve, showing a red crescent of teeth marks.

"She didn't mean it. She was just—"

"Oh, yes she did. You didn't see the satisfied gleam in her eyes at the sight of my blood."

"She was frightened."

"So was I." He snuggled his broad shoulders against the red wall and nodded with certainty. "That ship didn't exactly look friendly to me either. Why does the Mashiah want to kill you? I assume that ship was one of his?"

She nodded tensely. "Yes, a *samael*. He uses them to terrorize the populace."

"*Samael*? That's what he calls his ships?"

"Yes, I don't know what it means."

"Doesn't matter, it just rang some fuzzy bell in my memories. Why was it pursuing you?"

At the predatory look on his face, she folded protectively

161

in upon herself, suspicions running rampant through her tired mind. "You're obviously not from Horeb. What are you doing here?"

"Let's take one question at a time. Mine first, hmm?"

Sybil shifted in her lap, lifting her head hostilely. "I don't like him, Mommy. He doesn't trust you."

"It's all right, baby. I feel the same way about him. You sleep now. We might have to run again soon."

Sybil threw Jeremiel a distinctly unflattering look, then buried her face in Rachel's shredded robe. Anxiety tormented Rachel, but as she looked up, she saw the corners of his mouth tuck in a suppressed smile and some of her tension eased. He seemed human at least.

"She's perceptive," he whispered.

"Very."

"Does the Mashiah want to kill her, too? Or is he just—"

"Yes."

"And your husband. Where's he?"

"He . . ." Rachel's heart pounded sickeningly. She tried to lift the bottle for a drink, but her hand shook so violently she sloshed the liquid all over her robe before it could touch her lips. Gripping it in both hands, she lowered it to rest on the firm stone floor. "D–Dead."

"The Mashiah's work?"

She nodded.

He frowned and methodically wiped beads of moisture from the sides of his bottle. When his voice came, it sounded gentle, reassuring. "I'm sorry. I pray Epagael keeps him well."

"Don't talk to me of prayers," she spat vehemently. "If God sees fit to punish us so terribly, he can damn well do without prayers. Or anything else for that matter."

"You're a nonbeliever?"

"Only a fool would believe in a beneficent God after what he's done to us."

"Yes, but I like fools. As a loyal member of their ranks, I don't think we could have survived without them."

"Imbeciles who'll be the doom of all of us."

"More likely they'll be our salvation. Them and their stubborn senses of righteousness—fighting to the last breath in defense of God and their people."

Rachel gave him a scorching examination. "So, you're a fool, too?"

He raised bushy brows, reddish beard wiggling slightly

with his grinding jaw. A hollow look of old pain invaded his eyes. "If you mean by that do I believe in a God who watches over us and loves us? No. I think the only shields Gamants have are the sophistication of their weapons, the strength of their bodies, and the skill of their brains." He met her hard look and gave her stare for stare. "But just because I've lost my faith, doesn't mean I scorn it in others. Anyone who feels they owe God a few moments each day is—"

"God's job is to protect us. *He promised* in His covenant with our ancestors. Yet, He's broken the bargain time and again. We owe Him nothing!" The passion and hatred ringing in her hushed voice surprised her a little, but he seemed to accept it calmly. He looked at her without surprise.

"Well, that's your business, of course. Let's get back to our original subject. Why does the Mashiah hate you?"

She countered, "What are you doing here on Horeb?"

"Are you alone, or were you coming here to meet someone?"

"Who are you?"

He squeezed the bridge of his nose in irritation. "Does this bantering have a purpose?"

"Yes."

"Well, we seem to be at a stand-off."

"Try answering my questions. That should break it."

Sitting up cross-legged, he absently dusted some of the red dirt from his black suit. "Let's try talking of a neutral subject. Tell me what's going on here?"

"You don't know? Then why are you here?"

He regarded her for a moment, eyes oddly intent, as though probing her soul. Then he whispered, "I'm here to organize and lead a faction who will overthrow your blasted Mashiah."

"Why? Horeb is a barren planet. We have no desirable resources. What business is it of yours what goes on here on this insignificant waystation between—"

"Look, Rachel." He leaned forward menacingly. "I spend the vast majority of my time wandering around the galaxy trying to protect Gamant lives. So it's rather annoying when I discover Horebians are gleefully killing each other. I'd much prefer to fight the Magistrates—the true threat to our existence—but you and your comrades have given me no choice."

"The Mashiah isn't a comrade of mine."

"No? Why not?"

"So you're here to stop Gamants from killing Gamants."

"Something like that." He cocked his head like a hawk spotting a mouse. "Why does the Mashiah want to kill you?"

Bitterness throbbed in her, and she suddenly felt every weary ache in her body. His name haunted her. Jeremiel . . . ? Who protects Gamants? She stopped breathing. "Jeremiel *Baruch*?"

His bushy brows lifted. "The last time a woman said my name like that, I had to dive for cover. And I hate running battles."

"Jeremiel Baruch—the leader of our Underground forces?"

"Why does the Mashiah want to kill you?"

She patted Sybil's warm leg to reassure herself. "I—he built a new temple to Milcom and I blew it up on the day of its initiation."

He leaned back against the wall, a new respect in his eyes. "I bet he found that annoying."

"He did."

"Since the *samaels* still have direction, I assume he survived?"

"Unfortunately."

"Well, nobody's perfect. We'll get him next time."

"We?"

"You haven't lost your fervor for battle, have you?"

"I've never had any fervor. I just did what was necessary to survive."

"You don't want to join the fight?"

Tendrils of terror wound through her, Adom's serene face overlaying her memories of the square like a ghostly executioner. "I—I want him dead, but . . . I just want to find a place where my little girl and I can live together without worrying about being killed in our sleep."

His stern gaze softened. He blinked and looked at the dusty stone floor. "I see. Well, we'll do it without you."

Rachel miserably examined his handsome face and noticed for the first time the dark circles beneath his eyes and the deep lines etching his forehead. A curious wistfulness brushed his gaze.

"Maybe I can . . ." she began, trying to think of something she could do to help without becoming directly involved. "No, then he'd . . ." In a sudden wash, all her fear, stress and weariness flooded to the surface and a sob rose in her throat. She drew up one knee and braced her forehead on it.

"What would he do if you helped?"

Kill thousands! she silently thought, unable to utter the horrifying words. She couldn't bear the thought, just now, of even speaking of Adom or Ornias. The hatred that welled smothered her strength.

"What's been happening on Horeb?" Jeremiel pressed softly. "Obviously you didn't blow up his temple alone. Did you have an organized resistance effort?"

She mustered enough strength to nod.

"How many?"

"Damn it!" she blurted. "Can't you see how . . . how tired and beaten I am? Stop trying to wring information from me! I need a few hours of sleep and peace."

"We all do. But how long do you think your comrades in the city will last without you? Do they have other leaders or were you and your husband the only—"

"We were the only two, but others will rise. I'm sure of it." Hearing the uncertainty in her own voice, a curious feeling, stronger than grief, stronger than hatred began to beat in her chest. The Mashiah wanted to kill them all, wipe the old Gamants from the face of Horeb. What was she doing, thinking of herself? Her mind recalled the faces of friends and family, the faithful believers, who still huddled in burned-out buildings throughout Seir and her heart went cold and dead.

"Better?" he asked.

"I'll never be better."

"How many?"

She lifted her head angrily, meeting his eyes. *"Before or after the holocaust?"*

"What do you mean, 'holocaust'?"

"He rounded up about a thousand of the Old Believers earlier this week, locked us in the square, then . . ." Her voiced failed as memories flooded back: The little girl dragging her brother, the boy stroking his dead mother's hand. "Then," she blurted, "he . . . he positioned the marines around the walls and they began firing, and kept firing, until nothing moved. Except . . . the night birds . . . looking for food."

Through tear-blurred eyes she saw he sat stone still, hatred and grief flickering over his face.

He picked up his bottle, draining the liquid dry. But Rachel noticed how tight his grip was, how white his fingernails. "I promise you, Rachel, he'll pay with his life."

"Don't make promises you can't keep. I've been trying for three years to kill him and haven't—"

"We'll discuss my abilities to keep promises later. Since we'll have to be up long before dawn, maybe we'd both better try and sleep." He turned away from her to reach for the lustreglobe.

"Yes, all right." Without a word more, Rachel rearranged Sybil and stretched out on the cave floor between her daughter and Jeremiel. The light went out and, after a time, she heard Baruch lie down a short distance away.

Rachel's mind raced over what he'd said, and what she'd revealed. The more she thought, the more unsure and panicked she grew. Why had she told him those things? She didn't *know* he was Baruch! Confiding in anyone was dangerous, but a complete stranger? Terror rose to overwhelm her. She tried to force herself to believe he really had come to rescue them—but she couldn't. It made no sense. Horeb hung at the very edge of inhabited space, but even so they heard news of other worlds. Rumors said Baruch waged a great battle against the Magistrates in the Akiba system— months away. Fear reared like a wild stallion in her soul, trampling her hopes to dust.

Dear God, what have I done?

She buried her face against her sleeve suppressing the sob that roiled in her throat. *Do something!* she shouted at herself, feeling to tired to move; knowing she must. She waited until his breathing slowed to deep rhythmic patterns. Then, with the silence of river mist, she moved closer to him, so close that she could feel the warmth rising from his body and smell his masculine scent. She found comfort in that, but her weary mind quickly denied it. If she thought about Shadrach now, the floodgates of her grief would burst wide. Stretching out her hand, she searched the floor at his side for his pistol, but touched only cold sand and gravel. Would he sleep with it clipped to his belt? Finding nothing, she steeled her nerves and moved closer still, hovering over him. Silently she dropped a hand to his waist.

A grip like iron encircled her wrist. "I do hope you're making pleasant advances, Rachel," he whispered. "Otherwise, I might be tempted to shoot you."

166

She tried to jerk her arm away, but he held it fast, fingers biting into her flesh.

"You're hurting me!"

"I hope so. Don't you consider it bad manners to steal from a man who saved your life? It's a little ungrateful, it seems to me."

"Let me go!"

He sat up in the darkness. "Rachel, I haven't had a decent night's sleep in weeks. I sincerely need one tonight since I suspect tomorrow will be a very long day. But I can see that in order to achieve it, you and I will have to be close."

"What are you talking about?"

"I'm talking about a compromise." He wrapped muscular arms around her and dragged her to the floor with him. She struggled vainly for a few moments, fear and indignation tormenting her. "Release me, you—"

"Listen carefully," he murmured. In the darkness she felt him lean over and heard a soft clatter as the pistol touched the floor behind him. "Neither one of us can get to it now, without the other being awakened by the movement."

"Why don't you just let me sleep with it? I won't harm you," she suggested truthfully. "Then we'll both feel comfortable."

"Maybe you will, but it won't do a thing for me. Thieves raise my hackles."

"My word is good."

"Yes, I suspect it is, but I can't be certain, can I? I can't afford to trust you any further than you can me. This is a much better arrangement, I think. This way—"

"You can still reach it," she argued vehemently, seeing the logic of his suggestion, fearing him anyway.

"All right," he sighed. "It's suicidal, but back up a few feet and I'll follow you."

She complied, leading him a good arm's length from the weapon. Her heart thundered as he pulled her gruffly against him and lay down. Cold seeped from the floor to make her shiver.

"Let's try to get some sleep now, shall we?"

"I can't sleep with you pressing the air out of my lungs."

He shifted to give her more room, but continued holding her hands in a deadly grip. "Now?"

Grudgingly, she murmured, "All right." But resting her head on his arm, she fought sleep, afraid to succumb. Afraid that her exhaustion might overpower her and she wouldn't awaken if he reached for the pistol. As well, pressed this close, she could tell just how big a man he was, twice her size, and she knew he didn't need to use the pistol to kill her. An arm across her throat would be enough.

Yet he made no moves to hurt her and she found herself drifting off to sleep.

Throughout the night, she wavered between horrifying dreams and bitter wakefulness where she felt his heavy arm against her side. Once, she found herself back in the square, the dark form of the *samael* blotting the sky as it circled. Ornias' pleasant coo blared across the screaming mob: "Witness the power of the Mashiah you have each turned against." The sickening pounding of her heart came back as she saw the guards lift their rifles and the crowd was suddenly awash in a sea of blood.

She jerked awake, panting into the blackness. Terror and futility swept through her and silently she wept. Tears trickled down her face to soak his sleeve.

She felt Baruch tense, then he paused, hesitantly lifting a hand and letting it hover silently in the darkness for a moment before lowering it to gently stroke her hair.

Sybil scanned the black cave ceiling, pretending to be asleep. Her mother's cries had awakened her often in the past week. But tonight the soft whimpers twisted oddly in her stomach, making her feel like she had to throw up. She'd been in the middle of a dream. The last picture still lingered in her mind. She'd been a lot older, standing on top of a grass-covered hill looking down on a bloody battle. Men and women screamed in agony, writhing as they died. Beside her, a young man stood, holding her hand so tightly it ached. His black curly hair fluttered in the chill wind. He gazed at her with love and desperation in his eyes. "Sybil," he'd said over the roar of cannons, "I can't find Jeremiel and I—I don't know how to stop this by myself. You know the filthy Magistrates better than I do. Where are they vulnerable?"

"Indra's Net," she'd whispered. "we must cast it back into the sky."

He'd turned glowing eyes on her, and then her mother's soft cries had interrupted and she'd been drawn back to Horeb. She didn't know what Indra's Net was, but sometimes she had funny dreams. Her daddy had told her people's brains just did that, talked to them at night without making much sense. But she thought it was more. The dreams felt *so real.* And this one scared her more than all the others she'd ever had. The sharp scent of blood still clung in her nose.

She slid a hand down to rub her cramping stomach and stared worriedly at the big man who held her mother.

CHAPTER 15

Echoes of unknown voices moved across Zadok's path as he trudged into the gray haze at the end of the tunnel. The sweetness of spring grasses met his nostrils, carried on the faint breath of wind caressing his wrinkled face.

"Zadok?" the majestic heavenly voice of Sedriel called. "Stop dallying. Things in your universe are growing dramatically worse by the second."

"I know. I feel it in my heart," he responded, clutching the brown fabric over his chest. For the past hour, he'd felt dread building to an incapacitating crescendo. *What's wrong, Yosef? Did I leave you too unprepared for this madness? My fault . . . my fault.*

Taking a deep breath, he stepped out of the tunnel into a wildflower strewn meadow. A swarm of flies glittered over the enormous rapier-thin arch forming the first gate to the seven heavens of God. Against the arch, Sedriel leaned lazily, arms folded. Brilliant white wings fluttered to keep the flies at bay. His cut crystal features gleamed in the warm sunlight.

"It's about time. I've been waiting for days."

Panic rose in Zadok's mind. Time always seemed to waver in the tunnel. Once, he remembered, he'd spent a week talking with Epagael and returned to Kayan before he'd left. "Did it take me that long to get here?"

"You're getting slothful in your old age."

"Don't antagonize me, Sedriel. I'm in a hurry."

"I don't blame you. But I doubt there's anything you can do to stop the whirlwind set in motion by Aktariel. He's been very clever this time."

Zadok's breaking quickened. "What do you mean? What's that wicked angel done?"

Sedriel smiled and nonchalantly straightened the sleeves of his shimmering golden robe. "Oh, he's selected the perfect dupes. Disenchanted boobs who can't see beyond the end of their own noses."

"Are you going to tell me what he's done? Or do I have to ask Epagael myself?"

"Don't be hasty, Zadok." He bowed his glowing head and laughed softly. "We've all the time ever created."

"Get out of my way!" Zadok trudged forward in a rush, trying to get through the gate before the keeper could stop him.

Sedriel hurriedly thrust out a crystal arm, blocking his path. "Not so fast, patriarch. You've a few questions to answer first."

"*What?* I thought we'd passed that years ago? I've repeatedly demonstrated I'm well-versed in the secrets of the Gamant zaddiks. Why—"

"Because I just decided I'm no longer certain you're worthy to view the Veil."

Zadok's mouth dropped open. "Blast you! You arrogant beast! You play games while Gamant survival hangs in the balance? Have you lost your alleged mind? I've been before you one-hundred and forty times—"

"A hundred and forty-two."

"What question could you possibly have to ask that I haven't already answered?"

Sedriel calmly shook his golden hair out of his eyes and smiled down smugly. "Let's see. Have I ever asked you about Avram's escape from Ur?"

"Yes! About his escape and the building of the tower of Babel. Both are unique to the ancient book of Pseudo-Philo. What does that have to do with my seeing the Veil this time?"

Sedriel smiled craftily. Behind him, in the pale blue sky, a circle of round-faced cherubim flew, chasing each other childishly. "Oh, a great deal, Zadok. Yes, a very great deal. You know the meaning of that ancient word?"

"Which word?"

"Ur."

Zadok searched his mind. "No . . . I—I can't—"

"You silly old fool. Is your memory that far gone?"

Anger rallied Zadok and the translation flooded to his lips, "Fire! I remember, it's—"

"Very good. Avram was the Father of the people. And who was the Mother?"

"Rachel. She—"

"Avram escaped from the fiery furnace. Do you think she will?"

"What are you talking about?" Zadok demanded in rage. "You're playing games with me again! If Aktariel is deceiving the people, I have to get to the Veil to find out what we have to do to save ourselves! Let me pass through the gate!" He waved both arms in wild fury.

Sedriel floated upward, flapping his eiderdown wings so furiously the wind pushed Zadok back several paces. He shielded his face with his hands.

"Be glad your outbursts entertain me, Zadok, else I might throw you back into the void before it's time."

Zadok lowered his arms. What sort of cryptological amusement was the angel perpetrating? It angered him that he couldn't grasp the hidden meaning, and with Sedriel the meaning was always hidden. "Lord," Zadok blurted in irritation, "if I must answer another question to prove my worthiness to pass the gate, please ask it quickly."

Sedriel yawned and stared out across the blue and yellow wildflowers sprouting from the meadow. "I don't really want to. The longer I delay you here the more interesting the permutations of Aktariel's plan become. And the more thoroughly I'm entertained."

"Ask!"

"Oh, very well. Hmm . . . Recite the seven hundred and twenty-two secret names of God."

"That'll take an eternity!"

"Then the sooner you get started, the sooner you'll be on your way." Sedriel gave him a smile of mock sympathy that enraged Zadok. The angel leaned slightly forward as though hanging breathlessly on his every word.

"All right, listen. You might learn something." Sucking in a deep breath, Zadok spewed, "Iao, Louel, Sabaoth, Eheieh, Elohim Gibor, Eloah Vadaath, Hadiriron, Meromiron, Beroradin . . ."

* * * * *

"Rachel!" Jeremiel's hushed voice intruded urgently through her slumber. "Rachel, wake up. Hurry!"

She scrambled up in a daze, instinctively grabbing Sybil

and clamping a hand over her mouth as she stared wide-eyed at Jeremiel. He hunched on one knee before the cave entrance. *When had he moved from her side?* The gray rays of false dawn filtered into their rocky shelter to touch his blond hair and dusty black suit. He gripped his pistol in a tight fist. Turning quickly, he hissed, "Go! Crawl through that hole over there!"

She jerked around and spied the small crevice. "But why, what's—"

"Get out! Do you want the Mashiah to find us?"

Adrenaline flooded her brain. She grabbed her daughter like a sack of potatoes and threw her through the opening, then squirmed in behind her. They both crawled as though Aktariel himself were after them. Jeremiel scrambled in almost immediately. As they fled, her foot occasionally touched his shoulder. Several minutes later, they emerged into the slate-colored light of pre-dawn.

Pitching unsteadily to her feet, she grabbed Sybil's tiny hand. They stood in a jumbled plain of red sandstone, boulders thrusting up like ancient pillars around them. Jeremiel slithered out of the crevice, wiping blood from his torn arm. His tension was palpable as he scanned the lightening heavens and fingered the trigger of his pistol.

On the cool morning wind, she heard faint shouts and the sounds of a dozen or more men struggling up the distant rocky slope she and Sybil had climbed the night before. Her spine went rigid.

"They must have found our tracks," she explained in dreadful penance. "I didn't think to cover—"

"Of course not. Forget it," Jeremiel urged. "Move!" The sandstone shone like old blood in the dim light. Wind and water swept the rock so thoroughly, not a speck of sand or gravel grated beneath their pounding feet.

An excited shout echoed from above and Jeremiel turned sharply. Rachel felt ill, knowing they'd be captured. "They're coming," she whispered huskily. "Ornias will take us—"

"No, he won't!" Jeremiel trotted forward with the silent grace of a dancer and slipped an arm around her waist, dragging her hurriedly into a steep-sided ravine.

Cool morning shadows clung to the rocks. A faint breeze stirred the dust, sending sand puffing up before them. And the shouts of the men came again. This time much closer than before. Wretched terror choked Rachel.

Sybil charged ahead, tiny legs pumping. Rachel had no idea how long they dashed down the ravine, but by the time they reached bottom, she was staggering, gasping for breath.

In a sudden violent movement, Jeremiel pushed her aside and leapt for a huge shell-shaped rock, frantically running his hand along beneath the shelf. "It's here. I couldn't find it last night, but now I know this is it."

"What?"

Rather than answering, he hit the ground on his stomach and rolled to his back, sliding half-beneath the precariously tilted boulder.

Nearby, a hiss rose, closing quickly. Panic blurred Rachel's senses. Sybil made a small cry of terror and ran to hug her mother's leg, eyes like saucers.

"Let's run, Mommy! Hurry!" Desperately, she tugged her mother's arm. "Hurry!"

"Stay here!" Jeremiel commanded, wiggling farther along the underside of the stone shelf, hand searching.

Rachel cast a terrified look over her shoulder, wondering why she trusted this stranger enough to obey. The wind increased until it whipped her hair into stinging threads. As the hiss grew, fear and hope drained from her until she suffered only numbness, knowing the *samael* would loom over the high rocks any moment. All the struggling, all the deaths would have been for nothing.

"There!" Jeremiel grunted and a gravelly sound of rock sliding split the air. "Sybil! *Come on!*"

Rachel watched her daughter dive through a rectangular opening barely large enough for human entry. Jeremiel waved ferociously and Rachel dropped to her stomach to slither through the opening, feeling him brutally shove her forward as the entrance grated closed. Darkness fell like a black velvet blanket around them.

"Mommy, where are you?" Sybil whimpered and slapped floor and walls with her hands, hunting.

"Here, baby. Follow my voice. Follow my . . . There." She pulled her daughter to her lap.

"They almost got us."

"But we're all right."

"For now," Sybil murmured, breathing raggedly in Rachel's ear.

After a few moments of listening intently to the darkness, Rachel whispered, "Jeremiel, what is this place?"

"The antechamber to the caves of the Desert Fathers.

173

Someone should come to meet us fairly shortly. But I don't know how long—"

"The *who?*"

"Desert Fathers. They're a secret organization. They've lived on Horeb for almost a thousand years now."

In the blackness, she heard him move, as though he reached over his head and to either side to test the size of the cave. A swish of air from his waving hands caressed her cheek.

"I've been here all my life and never heard of them."

"Of course not. If you had, they wouldn't be very secret, would they?"

A difficult swallow bobbed in Rachel's throat. At least outside she'd known what she faced, but here, who knew? A secret organization that hid in the mountains? Who could they be and why did they hide? Nausea roiled in her stomach. Unseen horrors might lurk just beyond her reach and she wouldn't realize it until too late. "Jeremiel, I don't like this. Isn't there somewhere else we could wait? I feel claustrophobic here."

"Right now, I'd say this is the safest place on all of Horeb, Rachel. Trust me."

"You trust too many people and you end up dead."

"Yes," he said blandly. "I certainly understand those fears. Dead—or at least weaponless."

A defense bubbled to her lips, but she never had a chance to use it. The darkness stirred. A chill wind touched her hair and a flood of fetid odors sent terror through her. She got her feet under her, preparing to run. *"Jeremiel . . . ?"*

"It's all right." His muscular arm went around her and he unthinkingly drew her against him. Soft scratching sounds came from the side of the cave that led deeper into the mountain. "Curtain time."

"What?"

"It's an old expression. It means we're about to be granted an audience with the great and wise Desert Fathers. Let's go." He released her.

"Wait!"

She felt more than saw him turn. "What?"

"How do we know that's who it is? We could be walking into a trap."

"Could be, but I doubt it. The Most Reverend Father himself told me how to find this chamber. I'm relatively certain he's not a spy for the Mashiah."

"How can you know that?"

"Tell you what, I'll go first. If you hear me cry out, make a run for it." The sounds of his boots scraping against the stone floor retreated. A short time later, he softly called, "Rathanial?"

Flickers of gold illuminated an adjoining cave, throwing the long shadows of two men across the floor at her feet. In the light, she saw that the cave stretched about thirty feet upward, forming a rounded red dome. Through the broad opening to the next chamber, she occasionally glimpsed one of Jeremiel's hands flashing in some gesture. Rachel trained her ears on the hushed voices.

An unknown man whispered angrily, "How could you have brought her *here*?"

"I thought our goal was to save Gamant lives. I *didn't* think letting the Mashiah get his hands on her would advance that cause." Jeremiel's voice carried traces of irritation and disbelief.

"All right, but they're your responsibility. I'll have none of it!"

A lengthy silence ensued, where Rachel heard the grating of boots on sand as someone shifted positions.

"I'll accept that."

The crack of hands slapping sides or perhaps a fist hitting a palm echoed through the caves. "All right, hurry. There's nothing we can do about it now. Things here have gotten considerably worse in the last twenty-four hours."

Sybil frowned up at her, pretty face streaked with dirt and black smudges of soot. "Mommy, I don't like that man." She mouthed the words so no one would hear.

Rachel patted her hair. The Desert Fathers didn't want them here. What sort of monsters would refuse sanctuary to a woman and child who fled the horrors of the Mashiah?

"Rachel?" Jeremiel's deep voice echoed. "It's safe. Why don't you and Sybil grab my pack and come in."

She snatched his pack from the ground and grabbed Sybil's hand, quickly striding forward, ready to do battle with the devil. Only the devil turned out to be a small white-haired man with a silver beard. His dark eyes appraised her resentfully, but a resigned acceptance lay beneath it.

"My dear Miss Eloel," he greeted, walking forward with his hands formed in the sacred triangle. His swaying amber robe seemed almost to blend with the candlelight. *How did he know her last name?* "I'm sorry you're here. There are great

175

dangers in the future. But since you are, we'll make the best of it to protect you. I'm Rathanial, Most Reverend Father, hereabouts."

Rachel returned the mudra of greeting and glanced at Jeremiel. He stood stiffly, arms folded across his broad chest, studying Rathanial with a curious gleam in his eyes. When he noticed her attention, he uneasily lowered his gaze to the red stone floor.

"Reverend Father, we'll try not to cause you any trouble," Rachel responded gratefully. "Thank you for giving us refuge."

Rathanial bowed slightly in acknowledgment and turned to Jeremiel. "Come. I'm sure you're all hungry and tired. We've hot food waiting."

In a flourish of swirling robe, he turned and fairly stalked from the chamber, heading down a long diamond-shaped hall cut through the stone. The candle in his palm sent wavering flashes of burnished copper over the walls.

As Jeremiel started to follow, Rachel caught his black sleeve and gave him a questioning look. He lifted a shoulder and shook his head slightly. Honest bewilderment and something deeper glimmered in his eyes. Suspicion?

"You go first," he said with calm confidence, then placed a hand at her back and gently pushed her forward.

* * * * *

Yosef pressed his nose to the portal of the ship and watched the world below spin from dark to light. Horeb was a rough-hewn planet of spiny red and gray ridges, separated by vast expanses of desert. Only rare patches of trees dotted the highest peaks. Toward the north pole, a small sea splashed the land, but no towns clung to the shores. A curious fact, Yosef thought, since on his own homeworld of Tikkun, ninety percent of the population clustered around the vast blue oceans. Perhaps the waters here were poisonous? Or dangerous creatures roamed the shores?

"Hey! Look at that!" Ari blurted, thrusting a lanky arm toward the opposite portal.

Yosef adjusted his spectacles and waited for the terrain to spin around to him. When it did, his eyes narrowed. "How many orbits have you made?" he demanded, seeing the same spindly band of star-shaped ridges flash by for at least the fourth time.

176

"I'm just getting my bearings." Ari defended, pushing first one lever, then another. He looked like a child in a toy shop, a broad grin lighting his thin, lined face.

"You're playing!"

"I'm studying."

"When are we going to land?"

"Pretty soon," Ari said and chuckled. "As soon as I remember how to work the attitude jets."

Yosef's bushy gray brows drew together. "Attitude jets? What do those do?"

"When we're landing, they keep us from tumbling around like a thrown rock."

Yosef blinked, then staggered away to drop into a chair. He pulled a handkerchief from the pocket of his green suit and mopped his freckled brow. "Oh, my God."

"Don't worry." Ari sliced the air with an unconcerned hand. "If I can't remember, I'll just make sure we crash into something soft."

"Soft?"

"Sure."

"Have you seen *anything* soft on this planet? The whole place is a huge spiny rock!" He flailed his arms.

"Around that big city, there's a field of dead grass."

Yosef sat forward, wetting his lips. "Wait a minute. Isn't that the tiny field that's surrounded by those rugged mountains?"

"That's the one."

"We'll bounce around like a pong ball, for God's sake!"

Ari turned in the captain's chair. He'd taken off his blue jacket and draped it over the pile of cans in the corner. His white shirt was unfastened to the middle of his bony chest, showing straggly gray hair. "Hey, it's hot in here, don't you think? I wonder if we can figure out—"

"You're just feeling the fires of hell breathing down your neck! How come you don't remember what Jeremiel told you about those jets?"

Ari shrugged, looking like a kicked puppy. He scuffed the toe of his boot against the lavender carpet. "There were so many things to remember and I was thinking about you. You weren't doing too well just then."

Yosef felt red rise in his cheeks, remembering the bouts of loneliness and pain he'd felt over Zadok's death. He *hadn't* been doing too well, though no one would have noticed but Ari. He got up to lay an apologetic hand on his friend's shoulder. "We've been together for three hundred years, you know that?"

"Sure. I know that."

"Ari?"

"Hmm?" The old man looked up through hurt eyes.

"I guess it's all right if we have to crash into something. You just do the best you can."

Ari hung his head and nodded.

"I shouldn't have said anything. I'm sorry. I couldn't have done any better. You go ahead and . . ."

From the control console a shrill beep sounded, a red light flashing. Ari jerked up his head, squinting at a series of dials. At the same time Yosef caught a glimpse of something swooping by the portal. He raced to the window to peer out. A needle-nosed ship slid effortlessly alongside them, the shield-shaped insignia of the Galactic Magistrates marking the tail section.

"Oh–Oh."

Yosef waddled across the now filthy carpet to the other portal. A similar ship hung visible a short distance away. "We're surrounded!"

"There's one on top of us, too, and he's descending."

"They're trying to force us down?"

"Looks like it."

A green light flared on the control console and Yosef gasped, "What's that?"

"They want to talk to us."

"Do you know how?"

"Sure, but I'm not going to."

"Why not?"

"What do we care what they think?"

"*What do you mean what do we care?* Maybe they're under orders to shoot us down if we don't respond. Huh? Think of that?"

"Not if they think Baruch is still in here. He said he was sure they were supposed to take him alive. That's why we don't want to talk to them. Maybe they have his voice print or something. And when they run ours through and it doesn't match up, they might figure it's okay to flare us."

"Dear Lord." Bracing a hand on the back of the copilot's seat, he swung it around and dropped unsteadily. Punching the waistband restraints to "on," he laced his fingers over his stomach and leaned back. "Okay, run us into something soft."

"You're sure you don't want to argue about it some more?"

"No, go ahead."

Ari grinned, slapped two switches and the *Seros* plunged, diving toward the planet's surface. The g force threw Yosef back in his seat, but from the corner of his eyes he caught a glimpse of a bolt of violet and whirled to see the government ship fire again. The shot crackled off their bow.

"They're trying to kill us!"

"If they were, we'd be dead. They're trying to scare us into following them down."

"Why don't we let them? What could they do to us?"

"I'm not going to give them the satisfaction of thinking they have the upper hand."

"*Satisfaction?!*"

Ari jammed another lever forward and they whipped sideways, forcing the ship on their right to lunge away. Snickering, he then hit two buttons to send them plummeting into a narrow canyon where the red walls undulated like a serpent. The *Seros* weaved drunkenly to avoid protruding rocks and Yosef felt his stomach rise in his throat, terror raking his gut. The two ships that had been flying alongside vanished as Ari dove deeper into the canyon where the walls narrowed to a thin ribbon of passage.

Searching the portals on each side, Yosef gasped, "Where'd they go?"

Ari glanced at a monitor and grinned. "Cowards! They're afraid to come down here with us. They're flying up over the mountains."

"But we have to break out of here sometime, then they'll catch us, won't they?"

"Who cares? This is fun, isn't it?"

"No, it's *not* fun! It's *insane!* We have to find a place to land!"

"I've got this all planned," Ari informed.

"You do?"

"Sure. Watch this."

Yosef looked up to see the red walls suddenly widen into that grassy field Ari had spoken of earlier and realized the old coot really must have had this planned. Two- and three-story buildings lined one side of the meadow. Outside, donkeys stood hitched to rickety carts. They pranced nervously, watching the ship approach. And in an instant, the government ships were back, sliding alongside them, the green button on the console flaring demandingly.

"What are we going to do?"

Ari glanced at him and smiled. "Go some place they won't."

"Like where?"

In answer, Ari squinted contemplatively at the controls, shrugged and shoved three levers simultaneously. The *Seros* wobbled violently, slowed and lunged sideways, sailing heedlessly toward one of the buildings with the donkeys outside.

"Ahhh!" Yosef screamed as the ship clipped the corner of the building, spun like a crazed top and crashed through a warehouse. Crates, boxes, and huge petrolon barrels tumbled around them, blocking the portals.

The ship came to rest at an angle so steep Yosef dangled half out of his chair, held there only by the waist restraint. Ari hung over him, arms waving wildly. Slapping Yosef on the shoulder, he called, "Come on. Let's go find out who lives here." Releasing his own restraints, he fell out of the chair and slid toward the door. Yosef grunted, trying to follow with some dignity.

"Hurry it up! Open that door."

Ari reached up from where he sat and pushed the button. The door slid back and a hundred cans of food cascaded over him. Grumbling, he shoved some away, then slithered over the rest on his belly. Yosef took a deep breath and followed.

Ari helped him down off the pile of cans and together they trudged through the mangled warehouse.

"Hey," Ari said, bending to retrieve a can. "Look at this. They have red beets here. Where do you think they get red beets? We can't get them on Tikkun. I'll bet they—"

"Would you hush! We have to get out of here before those marines land and lock us up."

Ari tucked the can in his pants pocket and kicked a box out of the way. Yosef shoved futilely at a crate, then decided to go around it, following Ari through an avalanche of bottles. They moved toward a door that had been knocked off its hinges; it banged loudly in the wind. Pushing out into the bright sunlight of midday, they covered their eyes.

"Hum . . ." Ari muttered.

"What?" Yosef blinked to let his eyes adjust and then saw the mass of people crowding around them. One man, with light brown hair and an elaborately braided beard, shouted commands to uniformed men and women. His white robe flapped in the searing wind. The police circled them, weapons drawn and aimed unambiguously at Yosef's and Ari's chests.

"Hey!" Ari shouted angrily, his chin stuck out. "Quit that! We're Gamants, too. We came to see the Mashiah."

Yosef jerked to stare openmouthed at his friend. When did Ari's brain start working again?

The man in the white robe glared, eyes narrowing as the Galactic Magistrates' ships landed in a burst of dust and flying gravel. People gasped, babbling excitedly.

"This might get sticky," Ari murmured.

As marines with rifles poured out of the ships, racing to surround the battered warehouse where the *Seros* rested in a lopsided heap, Yosef's mouth puckered. *"Might?"*

CHAPTER 16

Yosef took a deep breath of the pungent frangipani incense and let his gaze roam the room, pretending to ignore the hushed conversation of the men weighing his fate in the far corner. A vaulted ceiling of coral marble stretched over his head. Against the walls, furniture of carved dark wood sat atop a rose strewn carpet. Crimson brocaded draperies hung in shimmering elegance over the windows which looked out upon the vast wilderness of Horeb's rocky plateaus. His eyes lingered on the ridges. From this angle, they looked like the huge vertebrae of some long dead monster of the sands.

Ari nudged him in the ribs, whispering hoarsely, "Pretty tacky, isn't it?"

"You've never had any taste."

"Selling religion must pay pretty good, eh?"

Yosef eyed his friend askance. Ari's long face twisted in a perpetual scowl as he took note of everything in the opulent room. He understood the feelings. They'd seen the starved faces of the children, the rags the common people dressed in, when they'd landed. And the Mashiah lived like this? It deeply offended Yosef's sense of righteousness.

"Religion always pays good."

"I bet if he sold this antique rug he could feed half the city."

"Probably."

Ari exhaled disgustedly and, as though testing the stability of his chair, gripped the ornately carved arms and shook them. Apparently reassured that they were well-made, he leaned back and extended his legs, letting them sprawl across the carpet as he patiently picked lint from his blue pants. "What do you think they're going to do to us?"

"I don't know."

"They'll probably kill us."

"After what you did to that warehouse, I wouldn't blame them."

"Let's just hope the Mashiah kills us. If they give us to that ugly captain, we're in big trouble."

Their heads turned toward the far corner of the room. In front of the windows, the tall slim captain of the Magisterial ship, called the *Hoyer*, paced anxiously before the High Councilman. Both were young, perhaps thirty-five, but each appeared quite different in his manner. Cole Tahn, the captain, stood stiffly erect, his handsome face pinched in irritation. He had dark brown hair, neatly cropped over his ears, with large blue-violet eyes and thin lips. He moved in the quick deliberate patterns of a man accustomed to immediate compliance with his orders, annoyed by any deviation. Ornias, however, strolled through the bars of golden light penetrating the window like a cat stretching in the sun: lazy, graceful, and ever vigilant. His tanned face and arms shone in stark contrast to the shimmering white of his robe.

"Councilman," Tahn said sharply. "I tell you, they are not innocent. They came in here in the company of Jeremiel Baruch and must be in collusion with him."

Ornias stroked his braided beard, noting distastefully the dirt clinging to the cuffs of Tahn's purple pants. "If Baruch was with them, where is he now?"

"Obviously, he jetted or chuted, and is still on your planet."

"I'm not convinced of that, Captain. Perhaps your men were mistaken and he boarded another ship. In the heat of battle things often get confused. One ship looks like another and one man in black like—"

The captain clamped his jaw tightly. "We know for a fact that's the ship he stole on Kayan."

182

"Did you see him evacuate over Horeb?"

"No, but—"

"Then you have no evidence he's here."

"With your permission, Councilman, I'd like to question the two suspects. I'm sure they can answer your questions better than I."

Ornias sighed deeply, waving a hand toward Ari and Yosef. They sat up straighter, shooting each other a wary look.

"Don't tell him anything!" Ari hissed from beneath his hand.

Yosef puckered his lips disdainfully. Did Ari think him stupid? He wouldn't tell Tahn anything that wasn't already obvious. Wherever Jeremiel hid, he didn't need anyone blabbering possibilities.

The captain strode over and spread his legs, staring down menacingly. "Who are you?"

"Ari Funk. This is Yosef Calas. We're from Tikkun. We came to worship the Mashiah."

"Calas?" The captain grimaced distastefully and Yosef noticed that Ornias turned quickly, eyes narrowing. "Any relation to Zadok Calas?"

"My brother."

"You know he's dead?"

"I know," Yosef dropped his eyes to one of the beautiful roses adorning the carpet. Ari's bony hand sneaked out to pat him gently on the arm. While grief stirred in his breast, he also noted the concern both his possible executioners expressed over Zadok. Why? What had his brother done recently to excite such interest?

"A tragedy. When did it happen?" Ornias inquired silkily. In the light streaming through the windows, the man's brown hair glistened like Cassopian satin. The smug look on his face told Yosef far more than his words; he grew anxious to be off Horeb forever.

Tahn responded, "About a week ago."

An odd gleam of triumph lit the Councilman's eyes and a sudden tendril of hatred replaced Yosef's apprehension.

"What were you doing on Kayan?"

Yosef pushed his spectacles up on his nose and answered forlornly, "We went there to attend my niece's funeral. But your people declared a state of emergency and Mr. Funk and I never got to leave our ship."

"Where's Jeremiel Baruch?"

"Who?" Ari asked.

"Don't act innocent. We found his prints all over the *Seros*. We know he was with you when you left Kayan."

"Yes, but you boys in purple are known for being block-heads," Ari remarked. "Though, I don't know, maybe he was in the ship before we got there. What does he look like? Maybe we passed him—"

"Old man," Tahn said disbelievingly, putting hands on his hips and leaning forward to stare Ari in the eyes. "Do you know I could hang you from the highest tree?"

"Come now, Captain," Ornias reproved. "He may be under Magisterial suspicion, but he is a Gamant on a Gamant planet. You have no authority other than what we *lend* you to complete your investigations."

"Once I complete my investigations, Councilman, I antic-ipate interdicting your entire planet."

"Indeed? Well, let's hope it doesn't go that far."

Deep blue glints shone in Tahn's violet eyes as they bored into Ornias. Straightening slowly, he asked, "You know the penalties for harboring a criminal sought by the government?"

"We are harboring no one, Captain. Please hurry and finish interrogating these worshipers. I'm sure they're impa-tient to get to the baptismal waters in the Hall of Converts."

The captain turned back to where Ari sat patiently pick-ing lint from his pants, rolling it into balls and dropping them on the carpet. A fuzzy blue mound had grown.

"Funk, given your landing here, there's no way you could have piloted the *Seros* through the light vault from Kayan." Tahn stopped to eye Ari severely, but when the old man merely blinked mildly, he continued, "Be reasonable. Why would Baruch come to Horeb?"

Yosef held his breath, looking sideways at his friend. Ari wasn't going to start an argument, was he? Bragging that he'd flown the ship? It would be just like him and that would only make their predicament worse. On the other hand, he wondered what his friend could answer that wouldn't increase Tahn's suspicions about what they knew. Blessed gods, it looked like they might end up with the Magistrates even over the councilman's objections.

"Why would Baruch come to Horeb?"

Ari cocked his head and blinked contemplatively at the far wall for several seconds before responding, "That's a good question, but I'm afraid you're asking the wrong person. Yosef is much better at guessing games than I am. Yosef . . . ?"

Exasperated, the captain shouted, "Did Baruch come here to recruit more Gamants for his forces?"

Ari shoved Yosef's shoulder. "Well, Calas, what do you think? Answer the captain!"

"Blast it, old man!" Tahn bent low to glare into Ari's startled gray eyes. "Despite what the councilman says, if I discover you're in collusion with Baruch and his band of murderers, I'll lock you up for a thousand years."

Ari laughed condescendingly. "Do you have some new medical techniques we don't know about? It might be worth it for us to surrender."

Seeing the captain's nostrils flare, Yosef squeezed his eyes closed. Twenty would probably do. And if they used the mind probes, their abilities to appreciate the last score would be questionable at best.

"*Why,*" Tahn enunciated the word harshly, "did Jeremiel Baruch come to Horeb?"

"Maybe he came to worship? Huh, did that occur to you?" Ari spat hostilely.

"He's not religious. His only faith is in his fellow criminals and the weapons he can steal from us."

"How do you know that?" Ari challenged indignantly as he brushed irritably at the mass of white hair which hung about his thin face.

"I've fought against him a dozen times. I understand the way his mind works damn near as well as I do my own. Now why don't you tell me why he's here?"

"I don't know."

"So you admit he's here?"

"Did I?" Ari cocked his head as though he might have forgotten.

Tahn's brow creased and he briskly rubbed the back of his neck. Yosef figured the muscles must have tensed up. "I don't like games, Funk," Tahn growled.

"Say," Ari looked up at him inquiringly. "Why do *you* think he'd come to Horeb. It's a despicably barren planet. Now that I think about it, I must admit I'm curious about his whereabouts myself. Maybe he's—"

"You're a liar."

Ari blinked, looking like a demented owl. "I'm not a liar. Yosef is. But that's only because he's senile. He can't help it."

185

Yosef smiled at Tahn, lifting his shoulders apologetically—and silently promising himself he'd kill Ari later.

As though it had bearing on the subject, Ari pulled the can of beets from his pocket and looked at it seriously. "Did you know that beets were an ancient gift of the gods? They're good for colds and certain types of epigluton viruses. But they're getting very rare now and—"

"Councilman," Tahn said through gritted teeth. "Allow me to take these two actors to my ship? If they're truly innocent, I'll return them."

"Captain, surely you can see these two elderly worshipers are no threat to you or Horeb. And they know even less about Baruch than you do." Ornias came over to stand near them. "We have many worshipers from all over the galaxy coming to Horeb. These two gentlemen's intentions are clearly godly. Why are you persecuting them?"

A hard glint of anger flickered in Tahn's eyes. "My purpose is to find and apprehend Jeremiel Baruch. He's a murderer and a thief and wanted in every sector of human space for his depredations against innocent citizens of the galaxy. I follow orders, I don't persecute!"

"Baruch is not here, Captain. I thought we'd established that?"

"I don't believe we've established anything."

"What further evidence do you need?"

"If you won't allow me to question Funk and Calas, I'd like permission to initiate a massive search on Horeb."

"No."

"Why not? If you have nothing to hide?"

"Because," Ornias said, smiling. "It's against our planetary laws, which are founded on the Treaty of Lysomia. That treaty, I'm sure you realize, clearly states that independent Gamant planets have the right to establish and mete out systems of justice according to their own moral standards unless a state of anarchy exists, government property is endangered, or the populace is committing acts which threaten the security of the galaxy. Correct, Captain?"

"Hiding Baruch would be such an action, Councilman."

"*He's not here.* As well, there are no government properties on Horeb and we are at peace. Therefore, our laws are in effect and they prohibit external military forces from interfering with our normal lives. So you see," he said pleasantly, spreading his arms, "my hands are tied. I've already 'bent' the laws by allowing *you* here. We certainly cannot consider letting your forces carry out a search. However, I guarantee that if we discover Baruch is on Horeb, we will do everything in our power to apprehend him and turn him over to you."

Tahn's blue-violet eyes narrowed. "Uh-huh. Well, I'd like to speak with the Mashiah about the search, if you don't mind. He's the final decision maker on Horeb, isn't he?"

"Yes, of course, but he'll tell you the same—"

"I'd like to ask him myself."

Ornias regarded the captain for a moment, then smiled pleasantly and moved to a brass gong near the double doors. Tapping it softly, he waited until a beautiful black servant woman in fine lilac faille appeared. Stroking her cheek seductively, he cooed, "Shassy, dear, please see if the Mashiah has a moment to spare? Captain Tahn from the Magisterial ship, *Hoyer*, would like to speak with him."

She pulled back from his hand, but the movement was performed so subtly Yosef doubted anyone else had noticed. Lifting a brow, she appraised the captain as though *he* were the servant, and one deserving an exceedingly slow execution. Yosef frowned. Her demeanor shouted of royalty in captivity. She certainly didn't consider herself a common laborer in the house of the Mashiah. Who was she? And why did she endure the role of whore to the High Councilman?

"I'll see if Adom is free," she stated, turning and exiting the room.

Ari leaned forward, eyes wide. "He's our new savior, you know? He's going to kill all you ugly Magistrate types and free us."

Ornias cringed, closing his eyes, then opened one to glance at Tahn. The captain merely pursed his lips and exhaled violently through his nose. "I'm aware of your quaint religious beliefs, Mr. Funk."

In a few minutes, a patter of soft steps echoed from the corridor outside and a young man with long blond hair and large blue eyes sprinted into the room, stopping abruptly when he saw Tahn's purple uniform. He looked at the captain breathlessly. Yosef frowned. Except for his regal scarlet robe, the famed Mashiah seemed nothing more than a gangly good-looking boy.

"Captain Cole Tahn," Ornias introduced, "this is Adom Kemar Tartarus." He stepped protectively closer to the Mashiah.

Tahn extended a hand only to uncomfortably drop it as Tartarus formed his fingers into the sacred Gamant triangle.

"May the blessing of Milcom be with you, Captain," the Mashiah greeted in a surprisingly beautiful voice. Almost frail, it rang with childish innocence.

Glancing at Ari, Yosef saw his friend's bushy brows draw together inquisitively. *This* was the man who worried Jeremiel? Tartarus looked as though he'd crumble if anyone shouted "boo!" at him. But appearances often deceived. Perhaps the boy played a role of naïveté for the captain's benefit.

"Mashiah," Tahn said sternly. "We suspect that these two men," he leveled a hand at Ari and Yosef, "arrived here in the company of Jeremiel Baruch. As I'm sure you're aware, Baruch—"

"Jeremiel Baruch?" Adom asked curiously, head tilted so that his blond hair shimmered in the sunlit dust floating through the room. "Who's that?"

Ornias put a hand on his broad shoulder, softly explaining, "He's a rebel."

"A rebel?"

Tahn gritted, "A Gamant rebel. He crisscrosses the galaxy sowing discord. I have a warrant for his arrest."

"The captain wants to initiate a *massive* search for Baruch across the face of Horeb," Ornias supplied. "I've informed him that Horebian laws forbid outside military forces from—"

"But," Adom interrupted mildly. "How do we know he's here?"

"We know," Tahn stated flatly. "The ship Funk and Calas landed in reeks of him."

"Er—crashed in," Ornias clarified. "They demolished our food warehouse, Adom. I was there with the planetary marines distributing food to the hungry multitudes when they arrived."

Adom whirled to stare at Yosef and Ari, brow furrowed deeply. "Are you two all right?"

They nodded in unison and Adom's smile warmed a little. He walked over to stand in front of them. The pungent scent of sandalwood clung to his dancing scarlet robe. "Did Jeremiel Baruch come here with you?"

Ari shook his head. "No, Mashiah. We came here alone . . . to seek you out."

"You're new worshipers?"

"Yes."

A heartwarming smile lit the youth's face. Like a child receiving a puppy at Chanukah, Yosef thought. He watched intently as tears welled in Adom's eyes and he bent to first pat Ari's sprawled leg, then touch Yosef's shoulder soothingly. *A peculiar boy. His emotions seem pure and utterly honest.*

"Don't worry," the Mashiah assured. "You're safe now."

Turning back to Tahn, he said, "I'm sorry, Captain, but I'm afraid the Councilman informed you correctly. We don't allow foreign—"

"But Mashiah!" Tahn insisted. "Baruch is a known murderer."

"He's not here."

"We don't know that! These men, in all probability, are his cohorts and are protecting him."

Adom turned halfway round to glance trustingly at his new converts. "They say Baruch wasn't with them. If he wasn't with them, then he isn't here, Captain. Or . . ." He blinked. "Do you suspect he might have arrived in another ship?"

Tahn shoved his hands deep in his pockets. "No."

"Then—"

"If you refuse me the right to search, Mashiah, at least let me take these men back to my ship for further interrogation. We have a small neurophysiology section on the *Hoyer* that—"

Yosef sucked in a sudden breath, heart pounding. Everyone turned in his direction. "Mashiah," he softly pleaded. "We want only to experience the peace of . . . Milcom. If it is your wish, we'll go with Captain Tahn, but I assure you, we know nothing of this Baruch."

"I believe you," Adom said, eyes welling with concern. Like a mother cat protecting her litter, he lunged at Tahn, speaking as sharply as Yosef guessed he ever did. "Captain, please leave us now. Baruch is not on Horeb and these men are under our jurisdiction. As a result, I see no further need to waste your time or that of the Magistrates."

"I'll go," Tahn replied begrudgingly. "But be aware the Magistrates are growing tired of your insolent and uncooperative attitudes. We already have an uprising on Kayan to subdue after Calas' death, I won't have one starting here. The *Hoyer* will remain in Horebian space until we have convinced *ourselves* that Baruch is not here." Bowing stiffly, he stalked out the doors.

His bootsteps echoed stabbingly down the marble halls.

Ornias gave the Mashiah an oily smile. "Very good, Adom. Though I suspect we haven't seen the last of him. He's rather persistent."

"It doesn't matter. The Magistrates are always . . ." His voice drifted off as his eyes went suddenly vacant. He cocked his head as though listening and Yosef stared unabashedly. The youth seemed swept away in some ecstasy.

"Adom?" Ornias called softly, glancing nervously at Yosef and Ari. "'Adom!"

A black shadow descended, creeping up the walls. The windows banged as a chilling wind whistled through the room. Yosef whirled at the sound. A bank of clouds blocked the sun, dark and roiling.

"Or . . . Ornias," Adom managed at last. "Milcom calls me. Please see to the needs of our guests." Without further farewell he hastily turned and left.

Ari lifted his brows expressively and mouthed the word, "addled," to Yosef.

The councilman glared at the last place Adom had stood. "Uh . . . as you can see," he patiently explained, "God overtakes him without warning sometimes. Please, Mister Funk and Mister Calas, if you'll follow me, I'll show you to the Hall of Converts. It's on the far end of the palace."

They rose, bumping each other in their hurry to follow the white-robed leader down the towering coral halls.

"Mr. Calas," the councilman crooned as he led them around a corner. "Please accept our deepest regrets at the death of your brother. We had sincerely hoped Zadok would come here soon to test Adom."

"Test him?" Ari asked.

"Yes, to assure his authenticity as the true Mashiah promised in scripture." Halting abruptly, Ornias smiled. "Mr. Calas . . . Yosef . . . do you perchance know what happened to the *Mea Shearim*? Surely your brother had it when he died. Did he give it to someone else, or—"

"*Mea*? What's that?" Ari interrupted rudely, looking from one man to the other.

"You don't know?" Ornias inquired.

They both shook their aged heads.

"Forget I mentioned it, then. It isn't important anyway." Ornias laughed softly and began striding down the hall so quickly Yosef had to run to keep up.

As they rounded another corner and entered a long rec-

tangular room filled with fountains and rose agate statues of
the saints, Yosef slowed his pace, falling behind. The sound
of his steps were muffled in the black and gold tufted
carpets. One entire wall opened onto a vista of the distant
mountains. Jagged red peaks thrust up to pierce the turquoise sky.

What, he wondered as he walked, *would a councilman on
Horeb want with the sacred gate to a god he did not even
worship?* And what trouble had arisen on Kayan after Zadok's
death?

* * * * *

Zadok leaned wearily against the rapier arch of the first
heaven, glaring at Sedriel who floated in the azure sky,
wings lazily stroking the air. The despicable angel had a
cocky smile on his face.

"Well?" Zadok asked gruffly.

"That's not seven hundred and twenty-two."

"You don't know how to add, you blasted imbecile!"

"Don't taunt me, Calas. Shall I cast you back to the
Void?"

"Do you know *any* of these names, Sedriel? Or did someone just tell you how many fingers to put down?"

The celestial being smiled smugly. "You're the most bom-
bastically ignorant human in creation, did you know that,
Zadok? I don't know why Epagael endures your existence."

"You dimwitted—"

"I thought it was imperative you get to the Veil as soon as
possible? Will you let your anger prevent it? Hmm? Insult
me just one more time and—"

"All right, all right." Zadok's indignation drained away.
For once, Sedriel was right. Though his throat had grown
raw, he took a deep breath, exhaling, "Kebiriron, Dorriron,
Sebiroron, Zahiroron, Webidriron . . ."

* * * * *

In the candlelit prayer room, Adom listened carefully,
trying very hard to understand. God stood only a few feet
away, his blue cloak fluttering as he moved.

"Yosef Calas can be a great aid to you, Adom. Treat him
well. Bring him into the fold."

"I try to treat all my people well, Milcom. I love my—"

191

"Yes, yes." The cut crystal god sighed and massaged his forehead. "I know you do. And I want you to."

Adom cringed at the irritated look on Milcom's glowing golden face. "I'm . . . I'm sorry, Lord. Did I say something wrong?"

"No, Adom. Forgive me. I'm in a hurry today, that's all. I think every blasted angel in heaven is placing bets against us. The traitorous . . ." He threw back his blue satin cloak to prop hands on his hips as he paced before the huge inverted triangle on the wall. Candlelight flickered wildly off his taut face. "I sense the buildup of power. I don't know if we can counter it."

"I don't understand, Lord. Why would the angels want to stop us? Don't they know you're trying to save us all from the wicked Epagael?"

God stopped pacing abruptly and pursed his lips against some pain or irritation Adom couldn't grasp. Tersely, he responded, "Their universe is directly tied to Epagael's. They know little of our fate here."

"I see."

"Did you understand what I said about Calas?"

"Yes, I'm—I'm to take special care of him."

"Correct. Let me briefly tell you why, then I must be going." He began pacing again, this time furiously. His body threw an iridescent kaleidoscope across the blue and cream rugs. "By virtue of his name, Calas can influence your ascent to power in Gamant civilization."

"Will that further our message of salvation, Lord?"

"Yes. *And we haven't much time now. It's* very *important you follow my instructions exactly.*"

"I will, Lord. Please tell me what I must do?"

"Rachel's the key. When she arrives, you must—"

"She's coming?" he asked breathlessly, feeling his heart start to pound. He longed to have her close where he could teach her, preach Milcom's message of redemption, and . . . and just talk to her. He knew his tender emotions for her rose from a childish part of his heart, but he couldn't help it.

"When she arrives, make sure she meets Ari Funk. *Do your best to insure they like each other.*" Milcom heaved an uncertain breath. "Which will be no easy task."

"I'll do everything I can."

"One last thing, Adom. Funk and Calas aren't as naive as they seem. Remember that."

"What do you mean?"

192

Milcom pinned him with glittering amber eyes. "I mean you should watch them closely. They can be a great aid, or send this whole thing tumbling down around our ears, depending upon whose side they choose in the end." He flicked a hand irritably. "Set your watchdog, Ornias, to keeping track of their movements."

Adom nodded obediently. "If you think it's necessary. Is there a reason, Lord? Are they dangerous?"

"Let's just say they're crucial enough to warrant attention. But they won't hurt you, Adom. Don't worry about that."

"I'm not worried. I know you protect me, Lord," he murmured lovingly, turning adoring eyes on Milcom. "I fear nothing so long as you still care."

The crystal god bowed his head. He stood silent for so long that Adom began to feel anxious. Had he said something wrong again? He clenched his teeth, wordlessly chastising himself for being so stupid and inept. "Lord," he muttered softly, "I know I'm not very smart. Punish me if I've offended you."

"You never offend me, Adom," Milcom breathed unsteadily and when he looked up, Adom could have sworn he had tears in his gleaming eyes. God strode quickly to him and placed a comforting hand on his shoulder. The warmth sent a tremor up Adom's spine. "It's not you. I'm feeling . . . betrayed. People who once clandestinely voted with me for destruction are now—"

"Who, Lord?"

Milcom gazed down, an urgency creasing his face. "Never mind. You wouldn't understand." He dropped his hand and strode quickly to the far wall. Lifting his hands, the black vortex spun outward, seemingly swallowing the stone wall from which it sprang. "I'll try to give you advance warning before Rachel arrives."

Clenching his upraised hands into fists, he vanished into the cyclone of darkness and it spun closed behind him.

Adom blinked weakly at the stone wall with its flickers of candlelight, responding meekly, "Thank you, Lord."

CHAPTER 17

Talo bowed his head over the Shabbat meal, idly studying the hard biscuits and thin porridge as he listened to his niece, Myra, murmur the holy prayers.

"Blessed art thou, O Eternal, King of the Universe, at whose behest the evening darkens, who in wisdom opens the gates of heaven and whose understanding varies the seasons and arrays the stars in their watches in the firmament according to His will. He creates day and night, causes the light to vanish . . ."

Gray strands of hair fell over Talo's eyes. Through their web, he gazed at the tiny room. Though it was a burned-out husk, they'd done their best to make it livable. The only room in the house that could be repaired, they'd shoveled for days to rid it of ash and charred board from the collapsed roof. Then they'd stolen . . . *No*, he told himself— *they hadn't stolen the boards for the roof. They'd gathered the least burned remnants from the homes of friends. Dead friends. People who wouldn't have wanted them to be cold at night just to fulfill some ancient code of honor.* After patching the roof, Myra had hung faded pictures of the saints in an irregular fashion along the soot-licked, blistered yellow walls. A good girl, she lacked the artistic sense of his beloved Drala, buried now for fourteen years. And he had no right to complain about the arrangement of the pictures, or anything else. He hadn't been much good to anyone since the holocaust in the square. The pain in his shoulder seemed unceasing and he constantly reached for things with his missing arm, feeling the flesh still warmly present in his mind. At least Myra had done her best to make the shanty a home and he felt a deep affection for her putting out the effort. He peered at her lovingly. She sat on the opposite side of the table, head bowed as she murmured softly. Dressed in a tattered tan robe, brown hair hung in a stringy mass over her shoulders. Her gaunt face had a haunted look, cheekbones protruding cadaverously—but they all looked like that now, those who'd survived.

". . . With ever-enduring compassion you have loved the people of the house of Horeb. And, O! do not withdraw your love from us. Blessed art thou, the Eternal who cherishes the Gamant people."

Talo closed his eyes, responding fervently, "Hear, O Horeb, the Eternal our God, the Eternal is One."

Myra paused for a short time and his passionate words seemed to ring in the candelit silence. When she continued, her voice sounded strained. "Take heed, lest your heart be given up to folly and you turn aside and serve strange gods and prostrate yourselves before them. For then the wrath of the Eternal will be enkindled against you and he will restrain the heavens, so that there shall be no rain, and the soil shall not yield its produce and you shall perish speedily from off the goodly land which the Eternal gave you. Blessed art thou . . ."

That's what has happened over the past three years, Talo nodded harshly to himself. The Gamants on Horeb had turned to the Mashiah and the foreign god, Milcom, and drought had ravaged the land. Epagael, in His wisdom, punished them for straying. Punished, like a father punishes a son, in love, so that the child might see the error of its ways and return to the path of truth and righteousness.

"It is He," Myra prayed, softer still, a quaver in her voice, "who freed us from the hand of kings: Himself our King who delivered us out of the power of all Tyrants."

The words, of course, referred to the liberation of Gamants from the wicked Edom Middoth, but there were those these terrible days, who turned to Milcom because of them. Many saw the Magistrates as tyrants in whose power Gamants remained. Therefore, they believed Epagael had betrayed them. But Talo knew better. The words eddied out of the darkness of history. They had nothing to do with the present. Except, in a way, they did. The true Mashiah's arrival stood only a breath away; he knew it, could feel it in the depths of his tortured soul. And *He* would free them for all eternity by establishing the millennial kingdom in this galaxy.

"Blessed art thou, O Eternal, who blessed the Gamant People with peace."

"Amayne," Talo whispered passionately, vaguely hearing Myra echo the word.

"Uncle? Please pass the bread."

Talo retrieved the wooden basket of hard biscuits and handed them to her. After thinking of the coming of the

Redeemer, the candles on either end of the table seemed to glow brighter, the chilly house to feel warmer. "Niece, what news did you hear when you were out visiting today?" he asked, taking a biscuit and dipping it in his bowl of porridge to soak it soft.

Myra exhaled irritably. "Sholmo says the Mashiah is planning on attacking us again. I don't believe it, but—"

"It's probably true. He won't leave us alone until we're all dead. True Believers are a threat to him."

"But why?" Myra cried, pounding a fist into the table. "We're only a handful now. How can we be a threat?"

Talo pursed his lips, not wanting to reveal the secret thoughts he'd been having lately. He'd been adding up different passages in the Micha and was sure he'd determined —finally—the true nature of Adom Kemar Tartarus.

"I think we should leave here. Maybe we can buy passage on one of the merchant ships that docks every six months. If they'll take us to New Payestine, we can—"

"I'm too old to start a new life. Too old to scratch a living from a planet far away. Besides, those Gamants on New Payestine are fools. Living in the heart of Magisterial power? Insanity."

"How do we know? Maybe the Magistrates will be kinder to us than the Mashiah? Huh? Did you think of that? The Mashiah—"

"Impossible."

"How do you know?"

"You wouldn't believe me," he reprimanded softly, looking at her affectionately. "I know you don't hold with the old system of numerological—"

"Oh, Uncle," she said in exasperation, "you haven't been wasting time adding up sentences again, have you?"

"It's not a waste. God hides things in the books, He—"

"If He hides things it's because He doesn't want us to know them."

"No. It's because he doesn't want casual readers to discover them. But if you're serious, and you read enough, you can see the way He engineered the passages so that those who really *need* to know can decipher the messages."

Myra shifted uncomfortably and Talo wilted, retreating inside himself where he felt safe. The expression on her face reeked of near anger at his squandering of precious hours on useless things.

"Did you finish mending the hole in the wall?"

"No, I—I forgot," he defended weakly. "I'll get it done tomorrow."

"I asked you to do it a week ago, Uncle. You know mice come through that hole and no matter how hard I try to hide the flour they always get into it."

"I know. I forgot. I'll fix it tomorrow."

Myra scrutinized him disbelievingly. In defense, he picked up his spoon and dipped it in the porridge, avoiding her condemning eyes. The soup tasted like pure water, the few radi roots too weak to add flavor. "I'm sorry, niece."

She nodded, squeezing her eyes closed. "No, I'm sorry. It's just that I've been racing around the burned-out sections of the city, trying to trade for food with the few survivors, but there's so little here. I'm frightened. I don't know where else to look without going into the heart of the city and trading there."

"You can't do that! If someone recognizes you—"

"What choice do I have? Rumors say the believers in Milcom have plenty of bread and milk—that their god conjured it from the air. Maybe if I wear a veil and—"

"I won't eat tainted food," Talo whispered miserably. Leaning forward, he cast caution to the winds, blurting: "You won't believe, but I'm going to tell you anyway. Epagael has revealed to me, through the numbers in the Sibylline Oracles, that Tartarus is *the Antimashiah foretold by scriptures!* I won't eat food magically created by his demon assistants. It would probably strike us dead in our beds!"

"Uncle . . ."

"It's true. I don't care if you believe," he murmured, turning away to gaze blindly at the mouse hole in the wall. A dark cavity, it gaped four inches wide. A hollow chasm throbbed in his chest at his lie. He did care if she believed. How could they fight Tartarus if no one knew his true nature?

"I'm sorry, Uncle. I just . . ." She jerked up her head, listening as steps thudded outside. "Quickly! Blow out the candles." She lunged for one while he snuffed the other. They stood, hearts pounding sickeningly, waiting. A friend? Coming to greet them on Shabbat eve?

A soft knock sounded at their door. "Myra, let me in!"

"Sholmo? I'm coming."

Talo heard her steps whisper across the floor and moonlight splashed the room as she flung the door wide. Sholmo leaned heavily against the house, a look of horror on his dark face, eyes wide. "I warned you," he cried. "Get out, quickly!"

Without awaiting a reply, he lunged into the darkness, and Myra closed the door. "Hurry! Grab the biscuits and your coat. We have to run!"

Harsh voices issued from outside and Talo shuddered as a piercing shot whined. Then a boot slammed into a door across the street. "They're here! Fan out. Find them!"

"Oh, dear God, dear God! Please let him get away!" Myra whispered, tripping over a chair as she fled in the darkness, heading for the door that had once led to the bedroom, but now led through a jumbled mass of charred timbers to open onto the street behind them. "Uncle, don't stand there. They've come for us!"

"Let me get my books. I can't leave them!"

With a wrenching bang, the front door flew back. Guards poured into the tiny room, rifles aimed. In the sudden light spouting from their helmets, Talo saw Myra standing in the bedroom doorway, her face a bluish mask of terror.

"Get your hands up!" a blond sergeant ordered, spitting at Talo.

"I . . . we want no trouble," he moaned softly, lifting a trembling hand over his head. "What do you need from us?"

How deeply Talo wanted to hear some words of confidence. Maybe they'd tell him they only came to confiscate the food, or search for any uroplatinum or titanium they might be hiding. The Mashiah had ordered all precious metals confiscated. Perhaps the guards' visit was simply routine, a question of sanitation or who owned the mule out back?

But the cruel smile on the sergeant's face told him the firmament itself was about to open up and swallow up everything he held dear.

"You filthy peasants," the guard accused, glancing speculatively from him to Myra. "You'll each be allowed to take one pack on your backs. Fill it with food, maybe a few warm clothes. That's all."

"Where are you taking us?"

"To heaven," he said with mock sweetness. "To heaven to rebuild Epagael's pearly gates."

"What does that mean?"

When the guard in gray didn't answer, Talo looked at his

niece. Myra met his gaze with terror-stricken eyes, as though she thought him mad for asking any questions at all. His knees went suddenly weak and he gripped the table to steady himself. Perhaps he *had* lost his mind. What new horror awaited them—what new gift had the Mashiah wrapped for them?

Outside, he could hear other guards shouting, "All Epagael worshipers, into the streets! Hurry!" A group of three passed by his door and he saw them herding friends away into the darkness, striking with truncheons when anyone resisted or fell to the ground. Their blows landed indiscriminately, bashing until the cries of men, women, and little children mixed in an eerie symphony of misery.

Talo shuddered as the blond sergeant's eyes narrowed. The man took another step into the room, commanding, "I said hurry!"

"Yes, yes, all right," Talo agreed, disoriented. "One pack? What should I take?"

"Uncle?" Myra hurried to him, keeping her eyes down in the presence of the guard. "Let me help you."

"Nobody helps anybody," the sergeant growled. "Get your *own* things ready. If this old man doesn't have the strength to meet the schedule, we'll leave him behind."

Behind? Talo wondered. Did the soldier mean he could stay home if he wasn't strong enough for the work ahead? Maybe he should throw himself on the man's mercy? Then he could spend day and night studying the ancient books, deciphering the cryptic words of God. A small glow warmed him. Yes, that would be a welcome fate. Even if he had to starve while he did it.

"Sir?" he inquired gently, turning sideways to reveal the ragged stump at his shoulder. "I'm not a good choice for hard work. I won't be of any use to you. Let me stay here where I can—"

The guard burst out laughing, throwing his head back and cackling until he had to hold his stomach. "You're *asking* for it?"

Talo looked at Myra. She stood there frozen, eyes wide with terror.

"He doesn't know what he's saying," she pleaded, wringing her hands. "He's so old he doesn't—"

"Shut up!" the guard raged, slapping her hard across the face. "I don't need any stupid peasant to tell me anything!"

"Don't hurt her!" Talo blurted, instinctively racing forward and shoving the man away.

He knew immediately the action had been wrong. A swell of gray-suited men closed around him, truncheons and rifle butts raised.

"Don't!" he heard Myra scream jaggedly as the first blow smashed into his temple. "Leave him alone! He can work!"

He fell to the floor, crouching against the blows, feeling blood spurt from his head and throat. One man repeatedly bashed the back of his skull. Unbearable agony lanced him. Is that what the sergeant had meant? Leaving him "behind" meant killing him?

Myra stood with her arms folded, fearfully examining the street. The guards had dragged her uncle out and thrown him into the massing crowd. He sprawled at her feet, blood still flowing from his head and back. The wound from his missing arm gushed red, sending rivulets slithering across the soil.

In the silver gleam of moonlight, she gazed upon the people sitting among bundles in the middle of the road. Children weaved through the mob, crying, some shouting names of parents who could no longer answer. A few people tried to comfort them, laughing and promising they'd find their families when they got to where they were going. Adults huddled together for the most part, candlesticks protruding from some packs, golden goblets gleaming in others. Many had prayer books pressed protectively to their chests. Had they all lost their minds? These guards were taking them to their deaths, and they clutched trinkets? Insane rage welled in Myra's chest. Had all sense vanished from the universe?

She tipped her chin to stare imploringly at the stars sparkling around the crescent moon. Cold wind whipped up the street.

"Epagael, where are you?"

CHAPTER 18

Sarah sat uncomfortably in the long white hall of the temporary government building in Capitol. Established to house the military troops sent to quell the riots that tormented Kayan, it was full of soldiers in crisp purple uniforms, who wandered the corridors throwing her spiteful looks as they passed. Did they hold her responsible for their transfers to the "cultural wasteland" of Kayan? She'd heard them murmur things to that effect. Straightening her black robe, she fiddled with her single braid, letting worried eyes flash darkly over the foreboding whiteness.

To her right, a door snicked open and a tall gray-haired man in a purple uniform stepped out. He had a pug nose and black bushy brows that formed a solid line across his wrinkled forehead. The gold braid on his shoulders marked him as a high-level administrator.

"Miss Calas?"

"Yes," Sarah said and stood.

He awkwardly formed his hands into the sacred Gamant triangle and bowed slightly. Surprised, she hesitated a moment before returning the gesture. Did he think the greeting would ease tensions between them? Absolve the Magistrates of responsibility for invading an independent planet?

"I'm First Colonel Silbersay, current military governor of Kayan. Thank you for heeding my call so quickly. Please, come into my office." He gestured through the door and Sarah swept past him, anxious to have the meeting over.

A windowless cubbyhole of no more than eight-by-ten feet, it contained a simple metal desk and two chairs. Crystal sheets were scattered around the room, most stacked in precarious piles leaning against one wall. Sarah took the chair in front of the desk and folded her hands nervously in her lap, waiting for him to make the first move.

Silbersay closed the door and dropped into the remaining chair, asking, "May I get you a cup of Taza or perhaps some—"

"No. Thank you."

"Well, then, perhaps some Orillian tea or—"

"Colonel, I'm sure you didn't call me here for pleasant inanities. What did you want to discuss?"

Silbersay's mouth pursed and he stared down at his cluttered desk, eyes on one particular sheet. Sarah could see the purple shield insignia of the Galactic Magistrates shining in the glare of the lustreglobe overhead.

"What do the Magistrates want?" she asked.

"They've authorized me to open new talks with you."

"We're not interested in new talks. We're interested in having you leave our planet immediately."

The Colonel laced his fingers and spoke gravely. "I'm sorry you're uninterested, as well, in even getting to know me. I can be a great help to you. I'm not your enemy."

"Any military official from the Magistrates is our enemy."

"I see. Well, I suppose I should get on with it, then. Miss Calas, we understand that since your father's death, you are now in charge of Gamant civilization, is that correct?"

"It is."

"Then, may I ask, do you plan on continuing his path of obstinacy in relation to the government?"

A chill crawled her spine, but she gave no evidence of it. What would he do if she answered "Yes"? What the Magistrates considered "obstinacy," Gamants considered a technique of survival. "Please be more specific. To what are you referring?"

Silbersay drew a breath and leaned back in his chair. "I'm referring to Kayan's—and other Gamant planets'—refusal to accept any government aid."

"We don't need your aid."

"Perhaps you are uninformed about our vast technological knowledge."

"I know you can provide us with wealth beyond our wildest dreams, but we're not interested."

"Wealth aside. Do you realize that, for the asking, we could bring your communities from the Dark Ages to the present? Our technological advances can rid Gamant society of the scourges of diseases like arthritis and cancer. And simple eye disorders or birth defects, which are practically unknown in the rest of the galaxy, can be cured almost instantaneously. You need never again worry about food supplies or—"

"You'll just ship in medical specialists and tons of food, is that right?"

"Yes. The Magistrates are very efficient at the redistribution of goods and personnel."

Sarah stared at her hands. Unconsciously, she formed the fabric of her black robe into peaks, then smoothed them away.

"Miss Calas, forgive me for being so blunt, but your people have suffered for centuries because of the stubbornness of your father. We have so much to offer. Let us help you?"

A grim smile curled her lips. Every time in the past that the Magistrates had brought help, they'd taken children in return. Claiming that education was their primary goal and Gamants were too backward to understand how to properly school their own offspring. They'd "trained" the children for them—and Gamant civilization had lost a generation of fine minds. She cocked her head and glared hotly at him. "And the cost?"

"I beg your pardon?"

"The cost." She leaned forward to prop a fist on his desk. *What's your price?*"

"Well . . ." He waved a negligent hand. "We customarily require a few minor changes in social structure. For example, we'd want to establish a Right School on Kayan and—"

"And all children would be required to attend under penalty of parental imprisonment? Isn't that the way it works elsewhere?"

"It varies. The practice is generally tailored to the society, but, of course, we'd expect cooperation with our policies in exchange for the goods and service we offer."

"Cooperation?" she spat. Her dark eyes had, unbeknownst to her, taken on a violent gleam, as though she might spring over the desk at any moment and attack him. "I call that blackmail."

Silbersay nonchalantly straightened the gold braids on his uniform, keeping silent. What did he think she was? Stupid? Weak?

"Colonel, what you ask is impossible for us to agree to. Magisterial programs are designed to destroy cultural uniqueness, particularly religion, and we will not allow it!"

"Religion," he responded condescendingly, "oppresses technological and intellectual development. The government is merely attempting to circumvent your superstitions, not destroy them, so that the health and welfare of developing planets on the outskirts of the galaxy might be enhanced."

Sarah stood, shoving her chair back so savagely it squealed across the tiles. "Thank you, Colonel, for having this chat with me. But I assure you, we do not now, nor will we *ever* need your assistance." She started for the door, but his commanding voice stopped her.

"Miss Calas . . ." He waited until she turned to meet his hard gaze. He had his fingers steepled below his chin, brow furrowed deeply. "The few scattered government installations on Kayan have been under considerable attack since your father's death. I hope you're aware that if such violence continues, we will be forced to take defensive action to subdue your planet."

"Defensive action?"

"We will fight back."

"I don't—"

"I've refrained so far, assuming the riots a temporary expression of grief, but if it appears they've become a pattern of terrorism, you'll leave me no choice."

Sarah stood numbly, picturing the devastation of beam cannon fire to the small Gamant villages strewn over the lush surface of the planet. "Colonel Silbersay . . . did the government assassinate my father?"

He blinked, startled. "I know the rioters are convinced we did, but I assure you, we had nothing to do with it. Your father was a known rabble-rouser, but had *we* wanted him out of the way, we'd have accomplished it years ago by covert means. Public murders are rarely advantageous."

Sarah's eyes pinned him, searching. Was it truth? Or a clever lie? His face remained stony, black brow lowering over his nose.

"Miss Calas," he continued, "we've studied Gamant personality characteristics in depth. Your people, if you'll excuse the term, are 'barbarians.' We know that you react to perceived injustices by violent, irrational behavior. We'd just as soon avoid another Gamant Revolt. And surely murdering your patriarch would rouse such a response."

"Yet you continue to coerce Gamant planets into adopting Magisterial policy by bribing trading partners away, embargoing recalcitrant communities, attacking—"

"That," Silbersay said and nodded politely, "is a matter of political strategy and not my jurisdiction."

"Yes, we've noticed it becomes increasingly difficult to find someone whose jurisdiction it *is*."

He gave her a sharp look as she slammed a fist against the

button to open the door. When it snicked back, she left and walked briskly down the long white hall, heart thudding dully in her chest.

The riots wouldn't stop and she could do nothing about it. Oh, she'd send word, relaying the Magistrates' threat, but that would only *convince* the guerrillas the government had killed her father. The damned martinets understood nothing of Gamant culture. The "Leader" was merely a preserver of culture, an intermediary between groups, an adviser on social adaptations, not a king or president. She, and her father before her, governed by virtue of the respect their people granted them, not by any absolute authority resulting from their title.

And she, as a new Leader, hadn't yet gained the respect necessary to quell the riots. Oh, some of her father's influence shrouded her, so some villagers would listen, but for how long? And how far could she push it?

"Papa," she murmured forlornly. "How did you stand those first few years?"

But deep in her heart she knew. Her father had opposed every government overture, had organized and led battles when the Magistrates tried to ease their way into a planet's social structure without the consent of the people. And he'd done it well, so well the people practically worshiped him as a god.

A soft smile came to her tense face as she remembered Zadok Calas, the thin little man with the bulbous nose and twinkling eyes. A god. Her father. And her heart ached so terribly she could barely stand it.

She ran the rest of the way down the hall.

CHAPTER 19

Jeremiel weaved through the maze of ruby red caves, glancing repeatedly at the map Rathanial had given him. He turned right, then a short while later, stepped left down a descending staircase. At the bottom, he veered right at the split in the corridor. Blocked passageways and dead ends often met him when he took a wrong turn. At other times, a chaos of makeshift wooden steps thrust up like jagged teeth from massive holes knocked into the floor. Had they closed up so much of their underground world? Why?

From somewhere behind him came faint stirrings of sound and, turning, he heard the deep melodious voices of monks chanting their evening prayers. Their song twined like smoke through the underground passageways. He'd always found something warm and soothing in religious music.

Lifting his lamp higher, he studied the map again. "I've got to be close," he murmured in frustration. His eyes darted over the next series of openings. "Okay," he sighed, "left at the second chamber."

Striding forward, he entered the first chamber, absently noting the sacred symbols of a dozen generations that etched the walls, then stepped into the next chamber. A brown curtain hung over an entry ahead of him. The golden halo penetrating around the curtain threw streaks of light across the red stone walls.

"Rachel?"

From inside, a patter of feet sounded. "Just a minute. I'm coming."

When she drew back the curtain, his eyes widened. He hadn't seen her in two days, not since the morning they'd arrived filthy and frightened to Rathanial's cool welcome. Oh, he'd known that beneath that mat of stringy hair and the tattered robe a beautiful woman lurked, but this was far more than he'd expected. She stood before him dressed in an ivory robe that clung to every curve of her body. Her hair draped in lustrous raven waves to her waist. Though her heart-shaped face with the full lips, enormous black eyes and perfect nose seemed a little gaunt, the overall impact was stunning. His gaze unconsciously lingered on the swell of her breasts.

"You're . . . looking better," he said admiringly.

She lifted a brow. "Did you plan on coming in, or do you want to stand out there and gawk some more."

"I can gawk just as well inside," he decided and ducked beneath the curtain. Her sleeping cave was large in comparison to his own. Stretching approximately twenty by forty feet, the ceiling loomed a good forty feet over his head. But it still had the same stark accoutrements. Two woven grass sleeping pads lay on the far side, one supporting a softly snoring Sybil beneath a mound of brown and green blankets. On the opposite side, a small table and four chairs nestled. A tiny fireplace and a stack of wood graced the middle of the back wall. How, he wondered, did the Desert Fathers manage to hide all traces of smoke ventilation from these caves? Some sophisticated sort of filtering system must be present.

"It took me a half hour to find this place," he said disbelievingly. "Do you think Rathanial is trying to keep us apart?"

"I think he's trying to keep Sybil and me separate from his chaste monks. We incite 'unclean thoughts,' he said."

"Um . . . yes."

Her eyes narrowed.

"How are you?"

She cocked her head curiously as though thinking the question a trite bit of subterfuge. Then she nodded abruptly. "Ah, I'd forgotten you're responsible for me. I'm fine, and to what do I owe this visit?"

"You're rested?"

"Mostly. What's—"

"They've been feeding you well?"

"If I say no, will you give the chef a good thrashing?"

A teasing note entered her voice. He smiled. She felt better, obviously. "Probably."

"Now what brings you here?"

"Are you always in such a blasted hurry? I thought maybe we'd just talk for a few minutes."

She heaved an irritated sigh and folded her arms tightly across her breast. "I *am* always in a hurry when I suspect my life and that of my daughter might still hang in the balance somewhere. Let's compromise, I'll 'just talk' if you'll finish the sentence. A few minutes, *before . . .?*"

"Before," he breathed in annoyance, "we have to meet with Rathanial to discuss his plan for overthrowing the Mashiah."

Her eyes widened, face slackening. "He works fast."

"Actually, he's been working out the details for months, watching Tartarus, keeping track of his aides' movements."

She nodded quickly, swallowing a lump in her throat. Turning away from him, she paced before the fireplace, ivory robe reflecting the sherry-colored light. Her smooth olive brow furrowed with thought. From the haunted look, he strongly suspected she was making a few tactical decisions herself.

"I've already told you," he said tartly, "I don't expect you to participate."

"I didn't ask you to repeat it."

"No, but I thought it might make you feel better."

"It doesn't."

He shifted uncomfortably. "All right."

"It's just that I . . . I don't . . ."

He waited for her to complete the sentence. When she only clenched a fist and glared at the floor, he offered, "I don't blame you for being frightened."

"It's not that!" she protested. "It's not that at all."

He lifted his chin, studying her. She wasn't lying. Something else motivated her anxiety. He sensed a bitterness in her, a sense of failure and a hurt so deep she could barely keep its visible impact below the surface. Her husband?

"Look," he said gently, spreading his arms. "I know what it's like to lose someone you love to the war effort. You need time to heal. I understand that. And I'm sure Rathanial does, too. Please, don't worry."

"You lost someone?" Her voice carried the strained frailness of twigs burdened by heavy snow.

That tender place inside him, the chasm left by Syene, ached. "A lover. We'd been together for three years."

"How long ago?"

"Two months. A battle in the Akiba system."

Their gazes held, his guarded and hurt, hers suddenly stripped of the stern aura. Her gaze darted to Sybil, then, absently, to the crackling fire. After a brief moment of indecision, she stepped toward him, her thin shadow looming monstrously on the firelit wall behind her.

"I'm sorry," she said softly. "You seem so . . . whole . . . I wouldn't have guessed."

"Do I?"

"Yes. Don't you feel that way?"

"No," he replied honestly and wondered just why he'd done that. But as her gaze softened, he knew. Sharing losses created a bond of vulnerability and labeled paths to be trod cautiously.

"Are you afraid? I mean of the Mashiah?" She dug fingernails into her arms, staring at him with unnerving intentness. "I realize you don't know him or the horrors he's capable of."

"Every battle scares me to death."

"I'd have thought that a man of your experience would get over fear."

"Never happens." He spread his legs a little wider, glancing at her out of the corner of his eyes. Despite her beautifully shaped woman's body, it seemed almost too willowy, too frail for the rigors of Horeb's deserts . . . or of revolution. Yet he knew she'd organized and served as one of the leaders of the opposition movement on the planet. Rathanial had filled him in completely, pulling a six inch file from a drawer and spreading the reports across eight feet of table. It created a strange dichotomy inside him. On the one hand, he felt the need to protect her from life's horrors and on the other, he knew she probably didn't need his protection . . . or anybody else's for that matter.

"I didn't figure anything would scare you," she said. "Especially after the sneak attack you pulled in the Safed system. I've heard the Magistrates still haven't recovered from that one. We heard they suffered nearly three thousand casualties compared to your one hundred and fifty."

Surprised by her knowledge, a small flush of pride and embarrassment went through him. "And I thought I endured in anonymity."

"Oh, we hear very little out here at the edge of the galaxy. Just the major triumphs." She suddenly looked very impatient, wringing her hands nervously. "Well . . . is that enough 'small talk'? I don't want to be rude, but—"

"But you'd like to hear Rathanial's ideas on killing this man you hate. Yes, I certainly understand that." With a wide sweep of his arm toward the cave opening, he added, "After you, m'lady."

She walked past him, then stopped. "Oh, wait. I need to leave Sybil a note in case she wakes up while we're gone." Trotting gracefully across the room, she pulled a sheet of paper from her pack and jotted a quick note, leaving it on the floor beside her daughter.

"She can read?"

"Of course," Rachel whispered as she swept back toward him. "We have very good schools here on Horeb."

"The Mashiah allows the schools to continue? I'm surprised. That's the first thing tyrants usually eliminate."

"He's a . . . different sort."

Jeremiel gave her a quick speculative glance. Her tone had changed, grown soft and tremulous. "So I'm learning."

They exited and trod softly down the corridor. "Does he

prescribe a particular curriculum? Or are teachers free to educate?"

"The only classes he demands be taught are human history, intergalactic lingua, Gamant religion . . . and the religion of Milcom."

Jeremiel cocked his head in reluctant approval. "Broad-minded of him, allowing the traditional systems of thought to be taught."

"He uses the 'errors' in the traditional systems as tools of conversion to the more 'sensible' religion of Milcom."

"Indeed? You must tell me more about his theology."

They halted a moment at a three-pronged interface of corridors. Checking his map again, they turned left and plodded in silence for a time, footsteps echoing dully from the red walls. Finally, he came to the door with the yellow curtain, marked on his map. "I think we're here," he said uncertainly, then called, "Rathanial?"

A voice from inside responded, "Come in, Jeremiel."

He held aside the curtain for Rachel to enter and followed, taking a deep breath of the air. It smelled sweet, like freshly gathered holiday spices. A round room measuring at least one hundred feet in diameter, it had multicolored throw rugs strewn across the red stone floor. Chairs lined the walls, encircling the main table in the center of the room, on which crystal goblets and plates shimmered in the soft candlelight.

Rathanial stood before a roaring fire, stroking his white beard. He looked kingly in his dark plum velvet robe. A tall black man stood beside him, dressed in the perpetual brown of the novices. Jeremiel scrutinized the monk. He had a round mahogany face with a flat nose and sharp black eyes. His kinky hair formed a six inch halo around his head.

"Thank you both for coming," Rathanial greeted and stepped forward. His eyes seemed remote, stern, for all their weariness. He bowed slightly, fingers shaping the sacred triangle. "Please be seated and help yourselves to the wine."

Jeremiel placed a hand lightly at Rachel's back and guided her to the long rectangular table capable of seating twenty. The far end had been set with small plates and goblets. Two bottles of Seba blush wine stood canted at an angle in the ice buckets, and a heaping plate of desert apples graced the table.

As he pulled out a high-backed chair for Rachel, she whispered, "Who's the novitiate?"

"I don't know. I guess we'll find out."

Rathanial and his monk came around the opposite side of the table and took chairs. Jeremiel retrieved one of the dripping bottles, expertly wiped it on the towel hanging from the bucket and poured glasses of wine all around, glancing suspiciously at the monk. Why a neophyte? He could have understood Rathanial including one of his high-level associates in strategy talks—but a mere newcomer to the order? It seemed a dangerous and unprofessional move.

"First," the Most Reverend Father said, "let me introduce Father Avel Harper. He's—"

"A novice," Rachel supplied bluntly.

Rathanial frowned. "Does that bother you, my dear? I didn't realize you were an expert on such matters?"

She flushed and lowered her eyes to stare into her wine glass. "I'm not, but I—"

"I invited Father Harper here for a special reason. Would you like to *guess*, or wait until the time when I'd planned on *telling* you?"

Rachel stiffened, as though girding herself for battle. When she opened her mouth to speak, Jeremiel grabbed her arm in a death grip and interjected, "What's this all about, Rathanial?"

Casting a harsh sideways look at Rachel, he said, "We find ourselves in a curious and unenviable position. Without the *Mea* we can no longer reach the Veil. Without the guidance of God, will we never again be able to separate for certain who is wicked and who is good. We must, consequently, discuss alternatives."

"What's the *Mea*?" Rachel asked, looking to Jeremiel.

"A device, a gateway to the seven heavens where the Veil stands."

"The *Shekinah*? The cosmic curtain that shields the throne of God?"

He nodded. "As you know, then, on the Veil are written all the major preexisting events of creation, including the identity of the True Mashiah." He exchanged a tense look with Rathanial. "Unfortunately, we lost the *Mea* on Kayan."

"Superstition," she muttered derogatorily.

"Maybe. Doesn't matter now."

Rathanial sat rigid, a wrinkled and worn manikin of a man, his gaze fixed on Rachel. Finally, leaning forward, he smiled perfunctorily. "I'd thought, Miss Eloel, that is, my information suggested, you were an Old Believer?"

"Your information is wrong."

"Indeed? Didn't you and your husband set up an underground worship society to preserve the ancient rituals? Didn't you establish a religious school for children to balance and correct the misunderstandings pounded into their heads in the Mashiah's classrooms?"

"I'm not a believer anymore."

"If I might ask, why not?"

A sullen look of despair and hopelessness creased her beautiful face. She fumbled clumsily with her wine glass, shaking it so that liquid sloshed onto the table. "Because only a wicked god could force us to endure the suffering we have. And I can't worship an evil deity."

Rathanial's face pinched. He slowly leaned back in his chair. "The acts of God are often mysterious. That doesn't mean—"

"They're not mysterious," she hissed, posture reminiscent of a tiger about to pounce. "When I see thousands slaughtered at God's whim, I don't think it's *mysterious*. I think God's intentions are quite clear. He hates us and is trying to destroy us. God sows strife!"

"Of course, He sows strife. How else can He test us to be certain we're sincere?"

"I don't need a god who's so blind he has to kill my family to *test* my faith." Tears blurred her dark eyes, but Jeremiel wasn't certain whether they were tears of pain or anger. The fierce look on her face suggested the latter.

"My dear Rachel. Obviously Epagael is trying to open you to—"

"To what? Hatred? He already has that from me."

"No. You see, you're locked in your own ego so that you're prevented from seeing the path God has set before you. When God wants to open you to a new way, He often seems terrible, but if you let yourself be opened, you'll see Ultimate Reality, God, as the beneficent being He is."

"The only reality I know is that life is a nightmare of pain and anguish. If God is Reality, then He's Despair."

An uneasy hush fell over the chamber, the only sound the crackling of the fire and popping of the candles. Jeremiel studied Rachel. Her gleaming dark eyes never left Rathanial's as though a silent tug-of-war progressed between the two. *Damned uncomfortable, but I'm too curious about the outcome to interfere.*

"You're very confused," Rathanial pointed out.

212

"On the contrary," Rachel responded with unnerving confidence, "my mind is quite clear. If God exists, He is a monster."

Rathanial took a breath, exhaling through his nostrils. "So you refuse to open yourself to God's path?"

"I refuse to be any demon's tool."

"Well, that resolves my question. What about you, Avel?"

The black monk who'd sat quietly throughout the tense exchange gave Rachel a kindly look. "I think perhaps you won't need my services, Reverend Father."

"Just a minute," Jeremiel decided to break in, eyes going over the faces around the table, Rachel's pained and defiant, Rathanial and Harper's tired with disappointment. "I'm missing something here. Perhaps you could enlighten me?"

Rathanial got to his feet to pace at the head of the table, fingers extended to his lips. His plum robe brushed softly against the carpet. "I'm afraid I was wrong. I called you here tonight to suggest a plan which would directly involve Rachel."

"Without consulting me," Jeremiel whispered hoarsely, casting Rachel a wary look. "I thought we'd agreed—"

"Yes . . . yes, we did. But after considering all the options, one utilizing her skills and knowledge of the palace seemed the wisest. I apologize for misjudging the situation in our original discussion."

Tension hung like a pall of carrion stench over the table. Jeremiel's heart pounded. *Blast you, Rathanial! I told you Rachel's too emotionally unstable for field duty. Oh, she'll do fine coordinating strategy and tactics from the safety of the caves, but I seriously doubt she can endure the terrible stress of nearness to the Mashiah. Every painfully taut line on her face says I'm right. Can't you see it?*

"What," Rachel demanded, "was your plan?"

"It doesn't matter now."

"Tell me."

"If you don't believe in our cause there's no reason to discuss it."

"If I don't . . .?" She straightened in her seat, bracing an elbow on the table and cocking her head indignantly. Long hair flooded over her shoulders to form a black mantle over her ivory robe. "I believe in the cause of saving the Gamant people, if that's what you mean. I'll fight to the death for my friends and family. But I won't lift a finger for God."

"You'll fight? Even if it means—"

"Wait!" Jeremiel commanded, then lowered his voice. "Rathanial, we've already discussed this. Rachel is *out*!" He gave her a tight-lipped look of regret at having to say such things. "We must have someone on the inside who is *reliable*. Rachel isn't. It's that simple. She's undergone too much trauma in the past weeks to be stable under pressure."

Beside him, she tightly clenched her fists as if taken unawares by the horrifying memories of the past fortnight.

"She'll be fine," he continued softly, "if we use her knowledge of the terrain and city and let her stay here where she's safe."

"No," Rathanial declared.

Jeremiel blinked, taken aback. "What do you mean, 'no'?"

"I mean either she's in completely, or she's out completely. We can't risk involving someone in the details of our plans who might break and run in the final instant. If she's too unstable for field duty, she's too unstable for any sort of responsibilities. We should send her back to Seir or—"

"Have you lost your mind? The Mashiah would kill her!"

"I don't think so."

"For God's sake, why not? She blew up his temple. She—"

"Yes, but he's always had a soft spot for her."

He shook his head as though he hadn't heard right. Casting a glance at Rachel, he saw her look at the table tiredly. "What are you talking about?"

"Oh, Rachel knows. Don't you, my dear?"

He turned to her, scrutinizing the distasteful twist of her lips, the hard glare in her eyes. "What do you know, Rachel?"

She shrugged. "I'm not sure. I always felt something, some warmth coming from him, but I thought everyone did. He's very charismatic. But, it's true that he . . . he never really punished me," she said, an odd tone in her voice. "He killed my followers, but he treated me very kindly. Almost—"

"Tenderly," Rathanial supplied with a vehement nod.

All eyes focused on Rachel. The fire flood her olive skin with rose-amber threads of light, highlighting the tiny lines etched about her taut mouth.

"Tell me more?" Jeremiel asked curiously. "The Mashiah has 'tender' feelings for you?"

"I didn't say that. I don't know what he feels for me."

"In your audiences with him, did he seem more compassionate, more gentle than with others who went before you?"

"Yes."

He sat back and thought about that for a moment as he watched her. Sweat shone on her bare forearms, a sheen that glistened in the dim light. She fiddled nervously with her fingers. She did know; Rathanial had been right about that. He could tell from the way her gaze darted over the room, searching, seeking to deny, but unable to do so.

"Rachel, do you suspect he's infatuated with you? In love? In lust? What?"

"I'm not a good judge of his feelings."

He shifted to look over her head. Rathanial held a hand to his white beard, staring piercingly. "Most Reverend Father, your assessment?"

"Hard to say for certain. Though, given Adom's naïveté, I'd assume infatuation." He paused. "It could be very useful."

"Indeed." *Indeed!* But would the Mashiah forgive her for the sins she'd committed? Leading the rebellion? Destroying his temple? If his feelings for Rachel were strong enough, he might. And the possibilities were staggering. A spy the Mashiah would embrace with open arms? A potential lover he'd want to believe without intensive checking to verify her words? A damned godsend. He propped his elbows on the table, hands folded before his chin. *But she couldn't do it!* Now he understood Rathanial and Harper's former disappointment that verged on despair.

"I want to know," Rachel said softly, "what your plan was?"

Rathanial waved a hand. "Oh, I wanted to send you back to the palace, to gain his confidence and keep him busy thinking of other things while we prepared our forces to battle his. Then, at the last minute, *if you'd done your job*, you could kill him cleanly and we'd lose very few lives. The war would be short and—"

"Lord above, of course." Jeremiel vigorously rubbed his forehead. "As soon as his forces knew he was dead, they'd lose heart, scatter like roaches under a flame. We could walk in and subdue the city with very little bloodshed."

"Yes, when the focal point of a faith vanishes, the religion dies."

"A dead Mashiah is a false Mashiah."

"Exactly."

"Are you saying," Rachel asked with a quaver in her

215

voice. "That if I were to go back . . ." She forced a swallow down her tightening throat. The remainder came out a bare whisper. "Go back and gain his confidence, whatever . . . whatever that means, then fewer of our people would die in the battle for the city?"

Jeremiel squinted, seeing her line of thought. "That's what he means, but forget it, Rachel. I won't have you in there. We'll find somebody else."

"There is nobody else." Her gaze sought his. The sorrow in her eyes stabbed him to the heart. She acted like a sacrificial lamb on a holy day.

"Rachel, we can't chance it."

With softness as excruciating as a mother's last good-bye, she murmured, "Let me go back."

"No! You're not able!"

"I can do it."

He shook his head sternly and looked away to grimace at the flickering candle on the table. It threw a pale glittering shawl over the ruddy desert apples, reflecting in the facets of the crystal goblets.

"It's our best gamble," Rathanial urged. "But first we'll need to prepare her."

"Prepare?" Rachel asked.

"Yes, we'll have to dress you fitly for his highness. Though, lord knows where we'll find those sort of female things around here, but we'll manage somehow. And with your permission, dear, we'll need to . . . um . . . etch the letters AKT into your forehead."

"His initials?" she asked indignantly. "Why? As a sign of ownership?"

"No, no, it's nothing like that. They exist on his own forehead, you see, but he doesn't believe they have anything to do with his name. Rather he sees them as a seal of God's approval. Milcom apparently told him that." Rathanial's face darkened. "And if we go through with this, you should remember that Adom claims—and has witnesses to verify— that a Man of Flame burned them into his forehead on the day of his birth. They're a symbol of anointing."

"I understand. All right, if it's necessary."

"It's not *necessary,"* Jeremiel enunciated severely.

"Let me go, Jeremiel." She touched his arm with cool, light fingers.

He shot her a wary look and saw her change. As though fleeting shadows of precious faces touched her memories, the midnight depths of her eyes took on a faraway look and a spun-silk courage hardened her features.

"Rachel, you can't."

"I'm going in," she said with finality.

"No, you're not," he half-laughed at her sudden audacity. "I won't work with somebody I can't trust."

She shoved to her feet, gritting her teeth as she glared defiantly at Rathanial. "You don't need Jeremiel. I'll go back to the palace if you'll find someone else to lead this mission."

Rathanial's eyes widened and he blinked thoughtfully. "My dear, he's the brains of the outfit. I hardly think—"

"Damn it, Rachel. You can't do it alone. You've got to have support personnel *in the palace* to get your reports out. You've got to have a system of people here to receive, process, and augment plans based on information you provide. You can't do it without me, sweetheart!" He pounded the table with a fist.

"Well?" she demanded. "Are you coming with me?"

Exasperated, he threw up his hands and wondered just how she'd managed to turn the situation around so quickly. "Rathaniel, this is your game. You called me here for advice."

"And your advice is?"

"*Don't use Rachel.* It's worth whatever time it takes to find someone we can depend on. Murdering the Mashiah won't be a task for somebody queasy about—"

"About *what*?" She lunged to place a hand on his chair back, glaring down with a mixture of resentment and anger. Yet he caught a hint of pleading, too, as though she silently implored him to take a chance he knew he shouldn't.

He clamped his jaw resentfully. "Don't do this to me, Rachel. I'm telling you, my life depends on my ability to judge people and their abilities. *I know people.* And we'll all regret it if you're the linchpin to this mission."

She stiffened, holding his gaze even though she spoke to Rathanial. "Reverend Father, who will take care of my daughter?"

"That, my dear, is why I brought Father Harper to this gathering. He has consistently refused all advancements I've offered him, so he can continue his research in child psychology. He has rather impressive credentials in teaching. If you find him acceptable—"

"I do."

Rathanial heaved a sigh of relief and nodded. "Very well. I'll send him by tomorrow to start getting acquainted with Sybil."

"We'll be waiting." As though the discussion were over, Rachel turned on her heel and started for the door.

Jeremiel lurched out of his chair, grabbing her arm and swinging her around. *"You're going to follow every order I give, is that right? No heroics, no innovations on my plans, no—"*

"Every order—to the letter."

He noticed even through his anger and worry that her arm trembled in his grip. He blinked, realizing the terrors that must be tormenting her soul. She'd just offered herself up to the demon who'd killed her husband and hundreds of her friends. Slowly, he relaxed his grasp and let her go, then shoved his hands deep in his pockets.

In a voice cast at a pitch only he could hear, she murmured, "What you said earlier? You'll be the one in the palace with me, won't you?"

He nodded. "Into the dragon's lair. You and me."

"I've been there, Jeremiel. It's more like the pit of darkness. It'll rob both of us of our souls."

"It always seems that way before the dawn." He cocked his head impudently and forced a smile he didn't feel. "But the dawn always comes."

Behind them, a sharp gasp sounded, a chair squealing to topple to the stone floor. They both whirled, hearts in their throats. Jeremiel fell into a crouch, pulling his pistol instinctively as his eyes searched the room.

"Dear God," Rathanial croaked, pointing a wavering finger at the dark rear of the cave. "How long has it been there?"

The huge shadow moved along the ceiling and walls, undulating over the lumpy stone to silently vanish in the ebony blackness of the far corner. Rachel let out a small cry.

Jeremiel straightened, his pulse pounding. Wiping the perspiration from his upper lip, he suggested, "Probably, long enough."

CHAPTER 20

Adom sat at the table in his Council Chambers, legs stretched out across the floor as he read the book propped in his lap. Sunlight glared through the open windows behind him, dyeing his hair and flaxen robe saffron and catching in the gold threads of the crimson carpet to burn like flame. An enormous rose agate statue of Milcom stood between the pillars of the door, watching, Adom felt, all that happened within. Only stone could do justice to God's chiseled features. It comforted him to see that perfect face staring down at him.

A rumble of dissenting voices and pounding steps invaded the hallway outside. He looked up from his book, frowning.

"Get away, you old fool! I'll thank you to let me manage the affairs of Horeb."

"You balloon brain! What do you know about spying anyway?" an elderly voice asked. Funk? "You need somebody to help you. Just like those plans for the light shield. Sheesh! You could . . ."

Boots scuffled against the carpets, a muffled voice slurring unintelligible words, as though a rough hand prevented the speaker from enunciating.

A few moments later, Ornias swept imperiously into the room, face contorted with rage. Dressed in a form-fitting sable robe that accentuated his broad shoulders, his beard hung unbraided, a light brown rounded mantle over his chin. Sweat beaded on his tanned brow.

"Adom! Have you taken leave of your senses?" he demanded as he strode haughtily to slam a sheet of paper down on the table and glare. "I thought using them was a temporary whim of yours, but this is too much!"

Adom blinked, lowering his eyes to the report bearing his signature. "It's necessary, Ornias."

"They're bumbling idiots! How could you make them your *personal aides*? Dear God, I shudder to think what will happen the first time you give them an emergency message to carry to me. We're liable to become our own greatest enemies."

"They're not as naive as they seem," he defended softly, mouthing Milcom's words as he folded his hands tightly over the book in his lap. He hated it when Ornias shouted at him. It made him feel stupid. The councilman knew nothing of the ways of Milcom. A prophet couldn't disobey the orders of his God.

"What?"

"If you'll give them a chance, you'll find they're very bright."

"Bright? *They're both senile!*"

Adom pursed his mouth and stared at the hem of his flaxen robe. "You don't understand. They're just simple souls."

"Do you know what Funk did yesterday? Has anyone told you?"

He shook his head.

Ornias put hands on his hips and paced irritably to stare out across the jagged wilderness of Horeb. He pressed his mouth into a disgusted pout. Dust swirled in the golden sunlight, throwing a hazy veil over him.

"I gave the fool a confidential message to carry to Engineer Lumon. Five hours later, I found Funk tasting the soup in the kitchen—and the message had vanished! I had to search out Lumon to make sure it hadn't been delivered, then I had to retrace every step with Funk to find the message before it fell into the wrong hands."

"Did you find it?"

Ornias' lime green eyes narrowed. He nodded severely, giving Adom an evil look. "Yes, your 'simple soul' had left it *in* the bath when he departed the women's servants quarters. I had to fish it out!"

A soft smile curled Adom's lips. "Was he . . . in the bath. I mean, with—"

"Oh, the women denied it, but I'm not so sure. I think the old coot is a lech."

Mirth bubbled up Adom's throat. Ornias' expression grew colder by the second, eyes icing over.

"You think it's amusing now," the councilman said and glowered, "but just wait until the Magistrates are attacking the planet and you send me a message through one of those old fools to muster forces."

"The Magistrates have no reason to attack us."

"Don't be foolish. Tahn is still sailing around up there in his battle cruiser. I'm sure if the Magistrates can find a reason they'll use it. And if Funk or Calas is needed to—"

"You think we'll find them tasting the soup in the kitchen after Horeb is a cinder?"

"It's quite likely."

Adom smiled at the irony, then gently laid his book on the table and got to his feet to stroll across the plush carpet. A hot wind penetrated between the red drapes to flood the room, tousling his blond hair. "You must understand, Councilman, Yosef Calas can be a great asset in our journey through the Gamant hierarchy of power. His name alone carries the influence of generations of leaders."

"Adom," Ornias murmured skeptically. "Have you been reading or something? Who did you steal that from? It's very astute. I'm embarrassed I didn't think of it myself." His eyes widened as they always did when Adom began speaking in deft terms of political realities. It irritated the Mashiah a little. Did the councilman think him a complete idiot?

"So you see, we—"

"But still, we could put him in some innocuous position, not a critical one like your aide."

"I like him as my aide. I can treat him especially well there, give him my personal attention."

Ornias scoffed, "I hardly think he's deserving."

"I like him."

"Yes, well . . ." He threw up his arms. "All right. How do you plan on utilizing Calas to our benefit?"

"I'd assumed we'd work that out as we went along."

"You mean use him as the need arises?"

Unsure of Milcom's plans, Adom paled a little, shuffling his feet nervously as he gazed at the rose agate statue. "Something like that."

Ornias scrutinized his insecure posture. "Well, at any rate, I think you're right. Calas is worth cultivating."

"And he's a good man."

"He's a clumsy fool. He forgets things the instant you tell him or repeats confidential information to the wrong people. But . . . *but*, you're right about the possibilities."

Adom held his tongue, folding his arms tensely and regarding Ornias from beneath golden lashes. He strongly suspected the councilman considered everyone a clumsy fool, except himself.

"Adom," Ornias spoke soothingly and smiled deprecatingly, moving closer and placing a hand on his shoulder. "Forgive my bluntness. I know you like Funk and Calas. It's just that you're such a gentle forgiving person, I feel it's my duty to explain fully my own feelings on such matters— harsh though they may be. It provides perspective for your decisions."

"I understand."

"I don't want to see you hurt. You know I've always done my best to take care of you."

"I know." The sickly-sweet paternal tone grated on Adom's nerves. The only person who had ever truly fought to protect him was Milcom. He pressed his lips tightly together and looked away. What Ornias really did was to shield him from the truth, spoon-feed him lies. He knew. God had revealed the councilman's partial truths time and again, advising him merely take note, but do nothing about the deceits. "Let God do God's work," Milcom said. "Justice will be meted out at the appropriate time."

Ornias ran a hand through his brown hair and gave Adom a searching look as though reading his mind. "What is it? You look anxious."

"I was just thinking of how we might utilize Yosef."

"I have some ideas on that."

"What are they?"

"Are you aware that Kayan and a dozen other Gamant planets are rioting against the Magistrates?"

"Because they think the government killed Zadok?"

"Yes, that and . . ." He waved a trifling hand. "You know how Gamants are. I imagine it seemed as good a time as any for a revolt. The fools, the Magistrates will squash them like flies."

"But maybe not. David took Goliath on the plain of—"

"Adom," Ornias responded disparagingly, "we have perhaps a million people left in the galaxy. Even if we could unify ourselves—and, God knows, that'll never happen—that would still only provide us with a half million soldiers. Government military forces alone number in the trillions."

Sunlight edged across the Council Chamber and glared in Adom's eyes. He watched it wink on the gold stitching of the carpet, then pass to illuminate the statue of Milcom. God's stone eyes seemed to flare as though alive. He studied them, gaining strength and confidence from the illusion.

222

"What do you suggest, then?"

Ornias' tanned face lit and he threw out a fist. "We should punch a hole in the hierarchy and ease our way in. Gamant civilization is vulnerable now, seeking leadership which we can provide."

"But we don't preach traditional Gamant theology. Why would they suddenly turn to us? I anticipated it would take years of preaching and teaching before—"

"Not if we do it correctly."

"Correctly?"

"Yes." Ornias rubbed his bearded chin and sidled closer, lime eyes gleaming. "If we present our religious teachings in the guise of a Revitalization Movement, that is, a return to the true ways of our forebears, we can—"

"The religion of Milcom *is* a return to the true ways. The most ancient texts talk of how our great forefather Solm built a temple to Milcom on the hills around Yershulim. It's just that in all the book burnings of the past few millennia, we've lost the original teachings. That's why Milcom came to me, to set Gamants on the right path again."

"Yes, of course," Ornias agreed impatiently, pacing the floor, plotting.

Adom frowned. Every time he spoke of Milcom or Milcom's visits with him, Ornias always greeted the news with irritation. Of course, God had never appeared in person to Ornias; but still, such hostility indicated the Councilman's faith wasn't what it ought to be. He'd been promising himself for three years that he'd have to tend to that, but somehow he hadn't had the time or inclination. In shame, he had to admit he didn't really like his second in command.

"Ornias—"

"Shh!" The Councilman lifted a hand sharply, not wanting his thoughts disturbed. Adom shut his mouth obediently and turned his attention to the pink marble arches glowing luminescently in the searing light of midday.

Unable to bear it any longer, Adom blurted, "Milcom filled the warehouses, you know. That food didn't just appear out of nowhere."

"Hmm?" Ornias blinked his annoyance.

"Milcom," Adom said tightly, "provided food when we were hungry."

"Don't be silly. It was my confiscation of every shred of food in Seir that filled the warehouses. Careful distribution of limited supplies is what fed people."

"'Where do you think the people got the food!" he defended, aghast. "Milcom gave every family a loaf of bread and milk for the children. He brought—"

"*Of course, Adom,*" Ornias cut him off rudely. "I didn't mean to imply God had no part in our success, only that prudent political measures often . . ." He shrugged as though shaking off an itchy cloak. "You know, *help* God."

"Your doubts make me shudder."

"I apologize, Mashiah." He caressed his brow expressively, as though enduring great trials. "I'm just tired is all. My words don't necessarily reflect my faith. It's been a difficult two weeks."

"I'm well aware of that."

"Are you? Good." Ornias pinned him with those cold green eyes. "Then surely you'll like my ideas about what to do with Calas' name. It'll take some covert activities on planets like Kayan, but we have enough talented, loyal supporters who are trained in the military arts to accomplish what I have in mind, I think."

"What do you have in mind?"

"As soon as I'm certain about the details, I'll notify you. Hmm? That way your precious time isn't taken up with meaningless bantering."

That wasn't what Ornias meant, but Adom didn't have the confidence to challenge the man. "All right."

Ornias turned to leave, but Adom's voice stopped him. "Councilman . . . any word on Rachel Eloel yet?"

"Are you getting impatient?"

"It's not that exactly. Milcom and I just have things we'd like to do."

"Well, don't worry. It shouldn't be long now. I'm working on getting her back."

"You—"

"Of course."

Adom surveyed the slit-eyed exultant look on the man's face and folded his arms, fearing to ask any more questions, not sure it mattered anyway. Milcom had said she'd be back. That's what mattered.

"Very well, Councilman. Proceed."

Ornias bowed slightly and turned in a whirl of sable robes to stride between the marble pillars and out into the corridor. His boots thudded dully over the plush carpets.

Adom turned back to the window to stare longingly out at the red peaks rippling in the heat of the day. He stared for a long time, blue eyes distant with thought, contemplating Rachel Eloel, Ari and Yosef, and the battle cruiser that undoubtedly saw the movements of every stone ant on Horeb.

He cocked his head, thinking he heard faint wailing notes from the trumpets of Judgment Day.

* * * * *

Jeremiel slouched in the uncomfortable chair in Rathanial's private quarters, watching the old man use a potholder to draw the taza pot out of the fireplace. A large chamber, it had few furnishings. A sleeping pad lay against the far wall, a lamp on a table beside it. Next to him, a tiny table barely two hands' breadth across nestled on a rectangular blue and gold rug.

Rathanial rose from the fire, striding carefully back with two cups of steaming liquid in his hands. His khaki robe swayed with his movements.

As the old man set the cups down and took the opposite chair, Jeremiel noticed the sheen of sweat on his forehead that dampened his white hair.

"Let's get down to business, Rathanial. We can't use her."

"Oh, but we must. Don't you see, without Rachel in the palace thousands more will be lost."

Jeremiel stroked his beard thoughtfully. Had senility struck this elderly father? "After the appearance of the 'listener,' surely you realize our battle plans have been compromised? Sending Rachel in now is like throwing her to the lions."

Rathanial propped an elbow on the table, sipped his taza, and then frowned. "We're not sure how much the listener heard of our conversation. We only saw it at the very end. Perhaps it heard nothing at all."

"Don't be foolish. We can't risk that."

"What other choice do we have?"

"A hundred choices," Jeremiel breathed disbelievingly. "We'll reorient our plans, circumvent the necessity of having someone in the palace. We can—"

"No we can't!" the old man said with sudden violence, cup trembling in his hand. Leaning across the table, his eyes glistened. "She's our best hope. Don't you see? Even if the listener reveals our plans, Adom still feels deeply for her. He won't kill her! And she needs only a few weeks to—"

"You've lost your mind. He'll slit her throat the first chance he gets."

We don't know the listener heard! And even if it did, we can't be certain that's *dangerous*. We've never seen any of our plans compromised after one of them overheard our discussions."

"Regardless, we can't—"

"Wait!" Rathanial pleaded, slamming his cup down unsteadily and putting his hands on either side of his head as though to steady reeling thoughts. "Let's discuss this rationally. Our emotions are carrying us away."

Your emotions are affecting you. Mine are fine. "I'm listening."

"We've spent three years trying to figure out what the shadowy creatures are. For a time, one seemed to be present every time we had a serious discussion, but now they come only sporadically. Maybe they don't even really exist." He hesitated, searching Jeremiel's face imploringly. "Zadok suggested that perhaps the creatures actually existed in another universe. That they looked into ours through some," he waved a hand, " 'portal,' their shadows the only visible sign of the opening of the door."

"You mean something like a *Mea*?"

"Zadok didn't say, but I suspect that's what he meant since the parallel is so close."

"I suppose it's possible, but why would another universe be interested in our problems?"

"I don't know. Except, well, maybe what happens here will affect all of creation. If Adom is truly the . . ." he stopped, fiddling nervously with his steaming cup as he glanced at Jeremiel. "Well, at any rate, perhaps there are powers in force here we don't understand."

"If one, or many, beings are watching from another universe, then surely you're right. But such speculation is no better than saying the listeners are tools of the Mashiah. And we must assume the worst or we're liable to cut our heads off to spite our faces."

"I know that, Jeremiel. Really I do. But we've never seen any negative effects from the listeners' appearances. That's why I don't think we should alter our plans."

Jeremiel rubbed his brow fiercely. Did the old man have no battle sense at all? The instant it seemed plans had been compromised, a good commander always flew like a bat from the pit of darkness. Unless he were trapped and had no choice. But they weren't trapped, not yet.

"No, Rathanial. I won't chance it."

"Please, Jeremiel. Let's . . . let's test it. At that last meeting we discussed many things, preparing our forces to battle the Mashiah's, for example. Surely, if the listener revealed our plans to Adom, he'll immediately began rallying his forces to stop us."

That made sense. The longer the Mashiah waited, the slimmer grew his chances of winning. He'd have to take action quickly to quell their efforts. "So?"

Rathanial heaved a tired breath. "Let's delay sending Rachel in for a few weeks, and watch Adom's movements in the city very carefully. If we see signs that he's massing forces, we'll go to a different plan."

Jeremiel's gut tightened. Some wrongness sent tendrils up to invade his stomach. "All right, but in that case, I'll be putting equal emphasis on three different strategies, just in case we have to shift at the last moment."

"Good. Yes, that sounds wise."

Jeremiel kept his face impassive as he studied the swell of relief reflected in the old man's posture. Rathanial slumped back into his chair and surreptitiously wiped perspiration from his brow—as though a terrible weight had been lifted from his shoulders.

"I'll need every scrap of information you have on the palace and its construction."

"I'll have Father Harper take you down to the documents room. We have thousands of books which list alterations over the past few centuries. Though, God knows, we've never found a vulnerability to exploit. But maybe you can."

"I plan on it."

CHAPTER 21

Sybil moped around the cavern, picking up rocks and slamming them against the floor, watching her mother and Jeremiel from the corner of her eye. They stood hunched over a table with maps spread across the top, talking in low ominous tones. Jeremiel, dressed in a gray robe, stood a good foot taller than her mother, who had an elbow braced on the table and was staring thoughtfully up at him. Her jade robe shone a dull green in the dim candlelight. Sybil bashed another rock into the floor and looked up hopefully. Neither even turned her way. No one cared about her frustration or the worry that made her ill with dread. *Her mother was going away!*

She weaved slowly toward the far wall where shadows clung to the stones like cool screens of protection. She squatted on the floor. The caves all sprouted cold and dust, though almost every room had a fireplace. She gazed up at the high ceiling where the flames cast odd flickering shapes across the stone and bit her lip. *Why couldn't she go with her?* She'd never been without her mother before, not on that terrible day in the ruined temple when her daddy was killed, or during the smothering days in the square. Why did it have to happen now?

Sybil traced a series of wavy lines in the sand by her thigh. Oh, they'd talked about it, how her mommy had to help Jeremiel and the Desert Fathers win the war against the Mashiah, but she didn't really understand why she couldn't go help, too. There were lots of things she could do and . . . and her mommy needed her. Sometimes in the night, when her mom cried, Sybil had to hold her and tell her not to be afraid or she couldn't sleep. What would she do alone for two months? Would she ever sleep? *Two months . . . Forever.*

"God damn it, Rachel!" Jeremiel cursed and Sybil looked up sharply. He stood irritably with a hand on his hip. "We can't do that and survive to tell anybody. And I, for one, plan on surviving. Don't you think—"

"Don't yell at my mommy."

Jeremiel and her mother turned to stare at her and Sybil felt like melting into the rocks to hide. Her mother's mouth tightened disapprovingly.

"Sweetheart? Why don't you go down to the botanical gardens to play."

"I can't. Avel is supposed to come here to teach me today."

Her mother ran a hand through her long black hair and sighed, "That's right. I'd forgotten. Well, maybe you could—"

"She could come over here and help us," Jeremiel suggested mildly. "Sybil, would you like to come and put pins in for us?"

A flicker of hope and happiness flashed in her. She got to her feet and ran across the room, climbing to stand on a chair and lean over the maps. "Where do you need one?"

Jeremiel smiled and leaned over, pointing to a bunch of tight squiggly lines. "Right about here. This is a cliff face."

Sybil's eyes darted over the pile of different colored pins. "Which color?"

"That should be a red one."

"What does that mean? Red?"

Jeremiel frowned and hesitated, lifting his brows uncomfortably. "It's . . . well . . ."

Sybil put the pins back into their pile. "I can keep a secret, Mr. Baruch."

"Can you?"

"Yes, my mommy taught me. Didn't you, Mommy?"

"I certainly did."

He shot her mother a soft look. "I've no doubt of that," he said and bent to separate out the pins. "Okay, you listening?"

"Yes." Sybil studied him intently, noticing that he looked tired. Dark circles smudged his eyes, lines deeply graven into his forehead.

He picked up a pin, "This is a blue pin and it stands—"

"Mr. Baruch, I may be just a kid, but I'm not a stupid one. I know my colors."

The corners of his mouth tucked in a suppressed smile and he nodded. "I apologize. Let me try again. Red are cannon emplacements. Blue are troop locations. Green are communications points. White are medical facilities."

Sybil nodded hurriedly, excited by being included in this grown-up affair. She touched a finger to several patches of blue on the maps. "So people will be here fighting when you go after the Mashiah?"

"That's right."

Quietly, she tried hard to memorize all the other markings, so she could talk to her mother about them later. "And where will my mommy be?"

Jeremiel waved a hand for her mother to take over. Sybil turned to her. "Where, Mommy?"

"I'll be in the palace, Sybil. See this purple dot on the map?"

Fear raced like acid through Sybil's veins. Why hadn't her mother told her that? Her heart thundered so that she could barely think. *"With the Mashiah?"*

229

"Yes, but don't worry, baby. Jeremiel will be there with me and we'll—"

"I don't want you to go!" She flung her arms around her mother's neck, holding Rachel as though she'd never let go. "Mommy, he hates you! He'll kill you like he did Daddy!"

Her mother picked her up and walked a short distance away from the table, stroking her back soothingly. It didn't help. The horrifying sensation of doom continued. Through the veil of her mother's hair, she saw Jeremiel fold his arms and lean tiredly against the table.

"Mommy, I don't want you to!"

"I know, sweetheart, but I have to. There's nobody else who can do what has to be done."

"What do you have to do? Blow up his palace like we did the temple?"

"Yes . . . yes, something just like that. But don't you worry about it. Jeremiel and I will take care of things as soon as we can and then I'll come back for you."

Sybil's heart slowed a little as she pressed her cheek against her mother's. "And where will we go then?" She'd been dreaming for days about going back to their old house, living together in the warm little rooms she loved.

"Then it'll be safe for us to go home to Seir."

"Back to our old house?"

"If it hasn't been destroyed, yes."

Sweet memories flooded back. She leaned her chin on her mother's shoulder and saw herself playing in the red dirt in the yard, building corrals for her toy mules and horses, creating roads from one side of the fence to the other. The rich smell of her mommy's cookies baking carried on the warm wind.

"Will my doll still be there?" she asked with sudden foreboding. Her grandfather had given her that doll. People, soldiers, would be running all over the city. Maybe they'd steal all her toys, or maybe they'd get blown up by cannons in the war. Just the thought made her stomach ache. "Will Jennie still be there, Mom?"

"I think so. But if she's not?" Her mother pulled back a little and lifted Sybil's chin to gaze into her eyes. She smiled. "We'll get you another doll, all right?"

"A new one won't be the same as Jennie."

"I know. It's hard to lose good friends like that, isn't it? I had a doll I loved when I was four, too."

"Did Grandpa give her to you, too?

"Yes, her name was Randa. She had blonde curls and—"

"Blonde? Like Mr. Baruch's hair?"

Her mother turned to look at Jeremiel and smiled faintly. He rested his chin on his hand and watched them patiently. "Randa's hair didn't have as much red. It was almost a white blonde."

"Like the Mashiah's hair."

"Yes," her mother whispered and swallowed hard. "Just like his."

"What happened to her?"

"Oh, she died."

"Dolls don't die, Mommy," Sybil reprimanded. "They just break."

"Well, okay. Actually her head fell off, but I buried her just as if she'd died. Now, don't you worry about Jennie. I'll bet she's fine."

"I love you, Mom."

"I love you too, baby."

A whoosh of air set the fire to crackling wildly as Avel Harper threw back the curtain and entered the room. His mahogany skin gleamed with a sheen of perspiration in the uncertain flames, as though he'd raced to get there on time. Light filtered through his kinky hair, making it look as though he wore a diamond studded black halo. "I'm terribly sorry I'm late."

"You're perfectly on time, Avel," Jeremiel corrected sternly.

"Am I? Good. The Reverend Father had me so busy time just seemed to slip away." He turned, calling, "Sybil?" in his deep smooth voice. "Are you ready for your lesson?"

She nodded and reluctantly slid down her mother's hip to the floor. Her mother knelt and kissed her forehead, smoothing brown curls away from her face.

"You learn as much as you can, all right?"

"I will." Sybil watched pensively as her mother went back to stand beside Jeremiel and Avel came forward to take her hand and lead her to the table and chairs sitting next to the fireplace.

Father Harper put two books on the table and handed her a pen and paper. She took them and held them solemnly in front of her. Glancing over his shoulder at Jeremiel and her mother, Avel leaned down and whispered, "What's wrong? You look sad."

Sybil's mouth turned down in a pout. "I'm okay."

He scratched behind his ear and braced an elbow on the table, leaning his temple to his fist as he studied her. Sybil didn't look at him, but took deep breaths of his scent. He always smelled of sweet spices and smoke from the fireplaces.

"Do you want to talk about it?"

"Nope."

"You worried about your mother?"

She nodded.

"I don't blame you. I'm worried about her, too."

She searched his face and saw warm concern there, but sometimes people could look like that when they wanted to and didn't really mean it. "Why are you?" she asked suspiciously.

He leaned back in his chair and thought about it before answering softly, "Because she has the hardest job of anybody in the war. She has to face the Mashiah every day. And I'm not sure she can do it."

"My mommy can do anything," Sybil defended, but her eyes fell. Could her mom stand it? It would be very hard.

"Come here," Avel said softly, spreading his arms. Sybil reluctantly climbed down from her chair and up into his lap. He cradled her in his arms, kissing her brown curls.

"Well, he whispered. "If your mother can just stand the Mashiah for a few weeks, nobody will ever have to suffer because of him again."

"I know."

"Do you?"

"Yes, because if she kills him, then people will be free again, like when I was little and he used to wander the streets in rags, preaching like a crazy man."

"You remember that long ago?' '

"Not very well. I was only five then, but my mommy's told me a lot about it."

He hugged her close to his chest. "Life was pretty good then, wasn't it?"

She ran a hand under her running nose. "It was good just a year ago. My daddy . . . my daddy used to play with me a lot. He helped me build sand castles with wet sand. We used weeds for roofs and pillars. And my mommy used to make us come in and take baths before we could eat dinner."

"Things will be just like that again. Only—"

"*Only my daddy's dead.*" She gazed up at him harshly. Perspiration still glistened across his flat nose, but his eyes had grown calm. "The Mashiah killed him."

"Your mother told me. That's one of the reasons she's going back into the palace," he whispered. "Did you know that?"

She glanced around his arm at her mother. She stood pointing to a bunch of blue pins on the map. Sybil concentrated on listening and heard her mother say, "This face is too steep for troops. They'll never be able to climb it in time."

Jeremiel frowned thoughtfully and pointed to a different place. "Well, what about over here?"

"That won't work either. There's a massive field of small boulders not shown on the map. It'll take twice as long to maneuver . . ."

Sybil snuggled back against Harper's strong arm. What if her mother died, too? She'd seen a dozen little girls' mommies die that day in the square when the sun blistered her face and her throat ached for water. And she'd seen funerals. She'd hung onto her daddy's leg as they watched men in prayer shawls carrying black caskets down the streets of Seir and heard her little friends sobbing in fear. She loved her mother so much that the thought of her dying was like a huge black blanket coming down to smother her.

"Avel," she breathed in torment, twisting the fabric of his robe in tiny fists. "My mommy won't die, will she?"

Silence descended over the room, the long table where her mother and Jeremiel worked going starkly quiet. Had she spoken so loudly? She wanted to look, but was afraid to. Instead she kept her eyes glued to Avel's smooth mahogany face.

He rocked her slowly back and forth, brow furrowed for a time, before he murmured confidentially, "No, Sybil. I don't think she will. Your mother—"

"*Your mother,*" Jeremiel blustered, "is too mean to die."

She jerked up to glare at him, but her anger faded as she saw her mother laugh and swat him with a piece of paper. A glow warmed her chest. It had been a long time since she'd heard her mother laugh. A soft tremor of relief went through her. Maybe everything would be all right, after all.

"My mommy," she murmured positively, "is going to stay alive so she can pay the Mashiah back for what he did to Daddy."

"Yes," Avel answered, "and to make sure no other little girls have to lose their fathers, like you did. She loves you more than anything in the world."

Sybil leaned her cheek against the warm wool over his chest and contemplatively pleated the fabric between her fingers. "'She's my best friend."

"I know she is."

As Sybil thought how sad the Mashiah had made her, her mommy, and all her friends, sudden anger welled hot within her. She gritted her teeth. "My mommy can do anything. You just wait, she'll blow up the Mashiah's palace."

"After talking to you, I think you're right. Maybe she can do it."

Sybil felt better. She smiled at Avel and heaved a relieved sigh. If he believed it, it seemed easier for her. Maybe, since she understood it all better, she could stand being away from her mother for two months. She squinted up at Harper. "Avel? Will you take care of me when my mommy's gone?"

"Sure, I will. And maybe we won't study as hard as I'd thought at first, either."

"We won't?"

"No, I don't think so. Like today. Maybe, instead of doing mathematics, we'll go to the aviary and watch the birds. Or maybe you can teach me how to make sand castles? How would you like that?"

A little spot of relief swelled in her heart. "We'll need lots of water and at least a handful of weeds."

"Okay, let's go find them."

As he started to lift her to the floor, she patted his chest affectionately. "Avel, you understand little girls, don't you?"

His eyes took on a faraway look. "Yes, I do. I used to have one—a long time ago."

"You did?" Where is she?"

His dark face fell into hard lines and his lips pressed tightly together. "She died."

Sybil's heart ached for him, for she knew deep down how he must feel—like she did about her daddy. "Did the Mashiah kill her, too?"

"No, but it happened in Seir."

"I'm sorry." For a moment fear came back to Sybil, but as she searched his forlorn face an idea occurred to her. She sat up straighter and brushed tangles out of her face. "Avel? I know it won't be exactly the same, but maybe while my mommy's gone, I could be your little girl and you could be my daddy?"

He looked at her intently for a long moment, eyes softening, then he gripped her tightly and kissed her forehead. "I'd like that, Sybil. I'd like that very much."

Rachel watched them walk out hand in hand, and glanced at Jeremiel. He stood like a lazy tiger, leaning against the table, eyes alert, guarded.

"I'm so glad Father Harper has become her friend. It makes things easier."

"Umm," Jeremiel grunted.

"What does that mean?"

"Huh? Oh, nothing." He turned quickly back to the map. "Let's get back to business. Tell me what this terrain over here is like. If we have to—"

"You don't like Harper, do you?"

He blinked seriously at her. Candlelight glistened off his gold-furred forearms as he gracefully folded them. "Like has nothing to do with it. I'm—uncomfortable—with anyone I can't 'read.' "

"You can't read him?"

"No. Can you?"

She shrugged, smoothing her jade sleeves. "No, but he seems nice enough and he's always so good to Sybil. Actions speak louder than words."

"Not always."

"Why not?"

"Oh, there's some truth to that, but often other things are far more important than actions. Like a person's eyes. Do you understand what I'm saying?"

"You mean that the eyes reveal inner thoughts."

"Exactly. All a person believes and feels, is reflected there. Unless they're making a valiant effort to hide those things."

"And Harper's eyes?"

Jeremiel speculatively caressed his beard, blue eyes focused on the door where Harper and Sybil had vanished. "Like a brick wall."

"Well," Rachel sighed and turned back to the map, fiddling with a handful of pins. "Don't be so conceited. Maybe your talents at reading people aren't as perfect as you imagine."

"I never said they were perfect."

"So if you know they're not perfect, why are you so worried about him?"

"I didn't say I was worried," he protested. "I merely said he made me uncomfortable."

"I thought in your profession everybody made you uncomfortable?"

"Recently," he sighed and smiled halfheartedly, "that's very true."

"Recently?"

He ran a hand through his blond hair, chin lifted severely. He kept silent for a long time as though debating within himself what could be said safely. "The last time my 'instincts' screamed at me this way, someone I trusted deeply betrayed me."

The utter somberness of his voice sent a tingle of foreboding through her. "Who? When?"

His eyes narrowed in obvious pain and his nostrils flared. "Two months ago."

"The same time the woman you—"

"Yes," he whispered and briskly started to move away from the table.

"Wait." She grabbed his hand to hold him still. The bones of his fingers felt large and strong in her grip. His eyes met hers vulnerably. "Jeremiel, tell me more. Harper will be my daughter's sole friend when I'm gone. If I have any serious doubts about his—"

"Don't." He exhaled, and glanced down at her fingers twined with his. His eyes darted quizzically over her face. "I'm not sure my 'instincts' are reliable. The battle in the Akiba system is still too close. So don't worry—"

"I'll worry," she said and released his hand. "Flawed or not, there's a part of me inside that trusts those blasted instincts of yours."

"Really? And the one I had about you going on this mission?"

"I thought we'd already established you're not perfect?"

"Ah, I'd forgotten."

He gave her a nervous grin and she found herself clutching up, muscles tightening for no apparent reason, heart pounding.

His eyes went over her suddenly stiff posture. "What's wrong?"

"I don't . . . want to trust you."

"I can understand that. You only *suspect* my flaws, I *know* them."

Hesitantly, he touched her shoulder, then pulled his hand back as though burned. Frowning, he abruptly leaned back over the series of maps. "Let's get back to work. We've only got a few days. What do you think about . . ."

He continued talking but Rachel barely heard. His voice had grown soft, caressing, a little frightened. She balked at the feelings it stirred. As though time slipped, her mind found itself in the bedroom with Shadrach, trusting, loving. And now she caught herself relying on and believing in Jeremiel against every precious instinct.

"I think it would be better," she responded half-consciously to his question, "if we put the gun emplacement here." She leaned over the table next to him, intensely aware of the warmth of his closeness as she pointed to a high rocky point. "Except I don't know how we'll get the cannon there. We'd be in plain sight for miles."

His eyes evaded hers. "Don't worry about that. I have a map of the caverns that crisscross beneath and around Seir. We'll get it there."

"There are caverns beneath Seir?"

"Thousands of them."

"Is that how we'll get into the city?"

"Yes, why don't you come to my chamber later and I'll show you . . ." As though realizing the intimate implications of what he'd said, he quickly amended. "I mean, we need to discuss the best route with Rathanial. Why don't we all three meet in my chamber after dinner?"

"All right."

Her gaze lingered on the lines tightening around his eyes.

Avel Harper quickly guided Sybil to an adjacent chamber. "Can you put the books and things in that cabinet while I go get my pack? That way we'll have a place to keep the sand and sticks."

She wiped a hand beneath her nose. "All right."

"Wait here for me. I'll be right back."

She nodded and took the books to the far cabinet cut into the red stone wall.

Harper backed out of the cave, checked the corridor for intruders, then slid along the wall, easing silently up beside the room where Rachel and Jeremiel talked. His brow furrowed deeply as he listened to their conversation about him—*and the caves beneath the palace.*

CHAPTER 22

Pines loomed like black spears against the dusk sky as Sarah trudged up the winding mountain path. *Come alone*, they'd said. *Alone and unarmed.* Towering cinnamon cliffs thrust up around her. Twilight came early to these high canyons, gloom deepening in the fissures of rock while the last rays of sunlight lingered in sheets of lavender on the peaks. She stopped a moment to rest and noted painfully how narrow the slit of brightness had grown over her head. How long had it taken? Three hours? Maybe four, to climb this high? She'd never make it back to her own camp at the base of the mountain tonight. A small tremor of fear shook her as she realized she'd end up sleeping near the leaders of the planetary rebellions, sharing their camp—if they'd let her after she told them what she'd come to.

She hiked up the hem of her mint colored robe and slid by a jagged edged boulder. A soft voice stopped her.

"Your name?"

"Sarah Calas."

She waited, unmoving, eyes focused straight ahead, lest they think she posed a threat. A scritching of boots against rock came to her along with the pine-scented muttering of wind through the canyons.

A moment later, a hand touched her lightly on the shoulder and she turned. A short stocky man with a round nose and a tangled chaparral of black beard appraised her from head to toe, amber eyes narrowing. She guessed his age at about forty. His gray livery and the ominous pistol tucked in his belt blended with the deepening light until he seemed one with the shadows.

"Where are the others?"

"Some wouldn't come," he responded blithely, as though understanding and sympathizing with their reasons. He snorted as he looked her up and down again. "Don't much blame 'em. You're a hell of a 'leader' of Gamant civilization."

Her jaw muscles jumped as she lifted a brow. "I'm

not particularly impressed with you, either, Mister . . .
Mister . . . ?"

"Shem Kowitz."

"Let's get on with this. Where's your camp?"

He extended an arm up the path, bowing nominally, a
glint of amused contempt in his eyes. Sarah swept by him
and tramped up through the narrow defile, cursing the extra
weight that made her legs tremble with fatigue. After Mikael's
birth, she'd never quite been able to lose that twenty pounds
that clung to her belly and made her thighs bulge. Now,
suddenly, it bothered her more than it ever had. Pretty
women at least had a man's attention if not his respect, but
a plain pudgy woman had to earn both the hard way.

As they worked through a series of pine groves, Sarah
spotted a faint gleam in the distance. Black shapes moved
lithely in the gold glow. And, suddenly, all around her, she
saw the guards posted, some on the high points, others
along the trail, many perched in trees overlooking the entire
canyon.

"How many came, Mister Kowitz?"

"Three of us leaders, missy, plus a few of our boys to
stand guard in case we're ambushed while we're up here—er—
chatting with you."

Sarah caught the distrust in his voice, but ignored it,
heading straight for the fire gleaming beneath the canopy of
trees. As she strode into the circle of its warmth, one man
stood, tall and lanky, with brown hair and graying temples.
Wary eyes flickered green in the dimness, his worn tan suit
showing the tortures of battle. Dried blood stained the
leather of his boots in splotched brown patterns.

"Miss Calas," he greeted, forming his hands into the
sacred triangle.

"Please," she said, returning the gesture and bowing
slightly. "Call me Sarah."

"Not Zaddik?" Kowitz taunted, knowing it a title her
father had won, that of holy man.

"Just Sarah."

"I'm Zebulon Yoma and this is Ezra Nahor." The other
man extended an arm to the bald skinny little leader who
refused to rise or offer any welcome at all. He merely
clutched a cup of taza in dirty hands and gazed at her
through slitted eyes. The fire crackled in the wind, sending
sparks flitting through the tree branches overhead and throw-

ing amber light across taut mouths and calculating eyes. Sarah's heart pounded.

"Which rebellions do you represent?"

"I lead the Desert faction. Nahor is in charge of the Valley people."

Sarah turned slightly to ask Kowitz, but glimpsed only his back, disappearing amid the black looming shapes of the trees. "And Kowitz?" she asked the others.

"The River people."

She met and held Yoma's tense gaze, seeing a buried stillness there that spoke of old pains poorly concealed beneath glimmers of hope. A sensitive man, she could tell, though cautious—very cautious.

"Pull up a log," he said, pointing to an old stump that huddled close to the fire. "Can we get you some taza?"

"Yes, I'd like that, Mist—"

"Zeb. Just call me Zeb."

"Thank you." She spread her mint colored skirts and sat on the stump.

He threaded quietly back into the shadows where Sarah noticed tents pitched in the sheltered niches of the rocks. A soft clashing of metal and petrolon sounded. She saw him pull a cup from a pack and tap out the dirt that lined the bottom. He used his tan shirttail to wipe it clean. Nahor, she couldn't help but notice, never took his beady pig eyes off her, though he threw another log on the fire and drank his taza as though dying of thirst.

"What'd ye come here for?" he asked in a low gravelly voice, squinting at her.

"To talk about the riots."

"We ain't gonna stop."

"I'm not asking you to." She refrained from adding, *I just want you to stop for a while until we can get reinforcements from the Underground.* But she didn't, knowing it best to wait. They were strong-willed men. She needed to manuever *them* into suggesting it.

He blinked and slowly straightened, eyeing her curiously. "Then why'd ye come?"

"To explain the Gamant situation here on Kayan and throughout the galaxy as best I know it."

"And then what? We don't care what facts ye've got. We're doing the right thing killing the damned Magistrates. No matter what ye say, we're—"

"Why don't you give her a chance to catch her breath,

240

Ezra?" Yoma interrupted as he stepped up to the flames and lifted a battered sooty pot from the coals, pouring Sarah's cup full of steaming black liquid. "She's been walking for hours to get here."

"I walked meself," Nahor argued, puckering his lips disdainfully. "And got here not more than an hour ago."

"Shut up, Ezra."

The little man scowled but pursed his lips tight. Why, Sarah wondered? Did Yoma have more power than Nahor? That didn't make sense. Though the Desert people had larger numbers, they divided themselves into clear ancestral lines. Living partially nomadic existences, they moved cyclically from dry farms, gathering areas, and hunting regions throughout the year. And those resource procuring centers were strewn across the sandy wastelands within distinct territorial boundaries. No group crossed the lines without inviting war. Getting even two lineages together to fight the same battle would be considered a miracle anywhere in the galaxy. But the Valley people congregated in bustling sedentary communities, where huge farms were cooperatively owned. Coalescing a fighting organism from such a staid community would have been far easier. But, perhaps Yoma had managed a miracle and his forces outnumbered Nahor's despite the odds?

He handed the cup to Sarah and she gratefully clutched it in stiff fingers. Cold wind blew across her face as she watched him kneel by the fire. Kowitz came silently out of the trees to join them, sitting on a rock across from her.

"Did you see anybody coming up?" Yoma asked Kowitz.

"No. She's alone."

"How about in the valley?"

"Nobody. She left her own people to camp down at the foot of the mountain. You know, by that big spring that sprouts from the side of the mountain and makes that little waterfall?"

"Yeah, I know."

Sarah spoke crisply. "I came in peace to speak to men I consider brothers. Of course, I obeyed your wishes."

"It's a right good thing, too," Nahor said contentiously, stabbing a crooked finger at her. "Elsewise, ye'd have found an empty camp when you arrived. *If* ye arrived."

A dagger of anger pierced her nervousness. "I don't take kindly to threats, Mister Nahor."

"You don't do ye? What are ye gonna do about it? Eh?

241

We've heard all about how ye've been sidling up next to the Magistrates. Gonna get your buddies to bring down the wrath of God from the skies?" He clutched a fist and shook it at her. "Well, ye'd better be ready for the consequences, if ye do."

Sarah stared coldly, taken aback by the accusation. "I'd never sell out Gamant civilization to the government. Where would you get an idea like that?"

"We hear more things than you'd guess. News comes from all over the galaxy."

A fierce gust of wind shivered the grove's bones. Trees clattered against each other, sending a few old pine needles whirling down over them. Yoma brushed them from his silver-flecked hair and Sarah noticed for the first time the gleaming amber earrings he wore. They sparkled as he turned his head to look inquiringly at her.

"You warm enough? We've got blankets in the tents."

"No, I'm fine. Thank you." She paused, noticing apprehensively that the guards had changed positions, tightening their circle of protection. One man, who earlier had been silhouetted like a black vulture on the cliff over her head now perched lower, facing toward the fire. Many of the others had disappeared, fading expertly into the darkening shadows. "Perhaps we should get down to—"

"To what?" Nahor interrupted in a thin cold voice. "If yer not here to tell us to quit fighting the damned Magistrates and their vermin soldiers, then why are ye?"

Yoma turned slightly and gave Nahor an abrasive look, before assuaging, "What he means, Sarah, is that through our efforts this past month, we've been able to keep the Magistrates off balance enough to take back some of the territory they usurped for their military installations. Thousands of square miles of land where we'll be able to grow crops next year to fight the hunger that plagued us last." He turned his cup thoughtfully in his hands and Sarah watched the firelight flicker from his silver temples. "We've lost some good people in those battles." He looked up with mild defiance in his eyes. "We plan on keeping that land."

"But I thought the riots were over my father's death?"

"Oh, some are," Yoma remarked and shrugged. "That's how it all started—in revolt against Zadok's murder. But the riots have pushed past that now."

"We're fighting for Kayan, missy!" Kowitz spat, leaning

forward. His beady eyes gleamed. "And we're gonna keep fighting until every last government soldier is either dead or gone. *This is our planet!*" His fist flailed in the firelit air. "You know the stories of how our ancestors fled the center of the galaxy so they could keep their own ways and beliefs. Kayan has been a sanctuary for us. We won't give her up!"

"We should have never let the Magistrates come here at all," Nahor agreed. "Those military installations give them a base for destroying us."

"My father," Sarah said tiredly, gripping her warm cup in both hands, watching the flames glint off the dark brew, "granted the Magistrates base facilities during the last Gamant Revolt in exchange for their signing of the Treaty of Lysomia. Which, as you'll recall, gives Gamants the right to absolute jurisdiction of their own planets unless . . ." she paused strategically, meeting each of their eyes in turn. "Unless we break galactic laws, request intervention, or planetary anarchy threatens Magisterial property."

"Like their installations," Yoma acknowledged, bushy brows raised. Firelight flickered over his tightening lips.

"Yes."

"So, you think they're going to call down the might of the military against us?"

"I spoke with Colonel Silbersay three weeks ago. He *guaranteed* me that's exactly what would happen."

Yoma stood to pace before the fire, a hand beneath his clean-shaven chin. "They've already declared military law, what more could they do?"

"They could call in the nearest battle cruiser and initiate a scorch attack," she said mildly and was rewarded when every man jerked his head up to stare aghast. Fear sparkled in their eyes.

"They wouldn't—"

"They would, and have every legal right to. According to the Treaty, they may take whatever action is necessary to protect themselves and their belongings."

"But . . ." Yoma glared at her. "A scorch attack would kill every living person. Surely that's unnecessary brutality? We're not animals!"

"Zeb, despite what Mister Nahor said earlier, I take it you're not as familiar with galactic news as we are here at the capital. Are you aware that Pitbon is gone?"

"Gone?"

"Completely destroyed."

Gasps sounded around the circle, each man looking anxiously at the other. Sarah knew none of them were aware of that news since she'd heard it only a week before and from confidential Underground sources. She studied their faces. Could they now see beyond their foolish male pride to grasp the gravity of the situation?

Yoma shifted uncomfortably. When he looked down, his eyes sparked like flint struck against granite. "Why?"

She sipped her taza, letting the rich flavor soak through her tired limbs. "Pitbon refused to allow the building of a Magisterial Right School, after agreeing to it in treaty several years earlier in exchange for energy assistance. You know Pitbon has no natural energy reserves; it's a wasteland nearly as barren as Horeb."

"They accepted the assistance and then broke the treaty?"

"Yes."

Nahor snorted, "The imbeciles. Why didn't they gather their forces before they announced they were breaking the treaty? We'd have gone to help them fight!"

"That, Mister Nahor, is precisely what the Magistrates expected, and why they attacked without warning. The government refuses to take chances that we'll unite into another full-scale Gamant Revolt. That would be disastrous for their 'redistribution' and 'education' programs. Their control of the far edges of space is teetering already.

"Redistribution," Yoma growled, pacing vigorously. "Food in exchange for freedom! They want us all dependent on them so they can—"

"Make us dance to their tune," Nahor finished. "Well they'll be hard put to get me and mine to knuckle under."

"None of us should knuckle under," Sarah said simply, ending what looked to be a tirade on Gamant rights. "My point is that the Magistrates *do* consider us animals. Animals to be tamed or killed. The slightest provocation, the smallest disobedience calls forth the maximum punishment."

"Then," Kowitz charged disbelievingly, "why haven't they already scorched Kayan? We've been hitting them pretty near as hard as we can."

"Silbersay doesn't want to kill us. Though why, I don't know. It would certainly be the easiest answer to his problems. He told me a few days ago, that he's been shelving reports on our violence. But he can't keep it up much longer. His soldiers are dying. Deaths must be reported."

"It's a trick!" Nahor roared and lurched to his feet to

244

stand like a thin shadow against the black of the trees and rocks. "Lies! She's setting us up for something. If they was gonna scorch us, they'd have already done it!"

Stars poked through the ebony blanket of the sky, casting a cold light over the peaks, and a hollowness abruptly invaded Sarah's stomach. Her focus of attention jerked from the circle of the fire to the darkness swelling beyond; it seemed to waver like a black velvet blanket in the wind. The glacial touch of terror halted her breathing. She couldn't speak.

"*Well, missy!* What's yer answer for why they haven't done it yet?"

With her eyes, she frantically searched the darkness. A familiarity haunted it. Familiarity? *Was* he *there?* She felt the presence, like a feathery touch of dust against her face.

"I—I don't know," she stammered and tried to divert the conversation to minor topics. "Mister Kowitz, how many do your forces number?"

He looked at her as though she'd committed the unforgivable sin of evading a critical tactical question on the very eve of battle. "What's that got to do—"

"*How many?*"

"About two thousand," he responded grudgingly.

"And you, Mister Nahor?"

"Four, maybe five if you count all the injured and sick."

Yoma folded his arms tightly across his breast and said, "I've got about ten organized, but another five are waging their own efforts out across the deserts. I think I can convince them to fight with me."

All eyes riveted on her and she felt a qualm of nervous dread. They expected guidance now, a put up or shut up routine. She took a long drink of her taza, eyes flitting around the still rippling black. Couldn't they see it? She scanned the taut hostile faces. No one noticed the black curtain that flapped like wings around them.

"Sarah." Yoma folded his hands behind his back, large hard hands, and looked at her inquiringly. His earrings glinted like liquid amber beneath a noonday sun. "We're listening."

"I . . . I want your advice," she stammered. "What should we do?" That wasn't at all what she'd planned on saying, but just at that moment her heart thundered so terribly she couldn't think straight. The darkness seemed to be closing in around her, the ripples growing wider. Was something coming through the darkness, or leaving . . . or was *he* the darkness itself? Memories of the night in the caves after her father died rolled over her. Terror made her flinch as though touched by a cold dead hand.

"Oh, what's the use?" Nahor demanded, running a hand over his perspiring bald head. "She doesn't know what she wants."

"No . . . I—I—"

"*She's no leader, for God's sake!* We've given her her chance, Yoma. That's all ye asked and she's left us high and dry. She didn't come offering salvation, she came asking *us* for it."

Kowitz leaned back on his rock and held up a hand. "I told you it would be a waste of our time. We should—"

"We should align with that new Mashiah on Horeb. He's got power, by God." Nahor fixed a blistering gaze on her.

"Who?" Yoma asked.

"Haven't you heard about Adom Kemar Tartarus?" Kowitz said disbelievingly. "I thought everybody had by now. He's performing miracles, making bread fall out of the sky and doing healings. Folks are saying he's the real leader of Gamant civilization, that old Yosef Calas yielded the leadership to Tartarus before he died. Only last week, we got a messenger from the Mashiah, bringing us news that He's willing to unite to attack the Magistrates."

"He *deliberately* sent you a courier?"

"Sure. Some fellow named Lumon. He says they're already working on some high-tech gizmos that'll give us the edge over the government if we're willing to join them."

"High-tech? You mean illegal weapons?"

"So he claims. Says they'll make us damn near invincible."

Yoma frowned suspiciously. "That kind of information is buried under a million tons of dirt and guarded by a trillion soldiers."

"Yeah," Nahor demanded gruffly. "Even Baruch has to steal his stuff because *he* can't—"

"Well," Kowitz said, staring at Sarah with hard, gleaming eyes. "He says the Mashiah gets scientific information from that God of his: Milcom."

Yoma grunted and waved a harsh hand. "You're a fool if you believe that. I'm as religious as the next man, but Epagael has never given any of our ancestors such advantages."

"Maybe Epagael isn't as powerful as Milcom."

Kowitz hushed and let the statement hang in the air like

246

the sword of Jekutiel. Men stared contemplatively at the flames, but Sarah didn't notice. A dim blue glow shone in the blackness, wavering like a man carrying a lantern through a sea of rough water.

"I don't know. I've always trusted Epagael to lead us in the right direction before. Going to a new—"

"It won't really be like converting. Tartarus is a Gamant, too. He just calls God by a different name. If God is God, then there's only one of Him."

"I suppose."

"That brings up another thing," Nahor blurted, pointing a finger at Sarah. "Tell us what happened to your sister."

Kowitz turned halfway round to stare and fear glinted in his eyes. "Yes, tell us."

"She died," Sarah whispered absently. The blue glow grew. Waves of white eddied across its surface, like white-caps on an azure sea.

"Yeah, but it's the way that counts," Nahor blustered. "She got torn to pieces. God sent a demon to punish her."

"What do you mean, punish?" Yoma inquired. "What did she do?"

"Well," Nahor responded irritably, waving both arms, "I don't know. If you ask me, it's a sure thing that God knew Zadok was going to get killed and didn't want any more in the line of Calas ruling us." He eyed Sarah, his chin lifting. "And there's some what say this girl is going to go the way of her relatives, too."

As though in a trance, Sarah only vaguely sensed the mixture of fear and curiosity pouring from the men. The vortex of black focused on a single marble-sized gem that cast an enormous cerulean aura. She cocked her head slightly, letting the feelings the image wrought penetrate her terror. She felt oddly as though she gazed through the rippling darkness to the blue sky of different world. Where had she felt that before? As though she stood on the threshold of the time-worn gate to eternity? Her mind jumped over memories and a flood of confusion and longing smothered her.

Instinctively, she pushed to her feet and ran to the edge of the swirling vortex. "Who are you? Tell me what you want of me!"

A soft murmur of harsh bewilderment went around the fire, men jerking to follow the direction of her gaze into the chiaroscuro of forest and stars.

"Who is it?" someone called. "An intruder? David, Sholem, get over there!" The sharp clatter of boots over logs and brush sounded. The zing of weapons drawn from holsters pierced the night.

"No." Yoma's calm commanding voice responded and the hustle halted. "She's not looking at the world we see."

"What are you talking—"

"Shut up and wait!"

"For what?"

"People—legends—say that old Zadok used to be able to climb through the seven heavens to talk to God."

"Hocus-pocus! You don't believe that, do you?"

"I ain't gonna sit around here and let her scare us into thinking she's got some weird powers that give her authority over us. I say we just leave!"

"By God," Yoma's voice rose to a crescendo, "you get up from that seat one more time, Ezra, and I'll—"

"All right, damn it! I'm sitting. But I think it's all a trick. You see anything out there?"

". . . No."

Tears welled hot in Sarah's eyes as a sound like the hissing of wind through dry grass came from the blue aura. In the depths of her mind, she thought she heard a voice struggling to speak to her, but she couldn't make out the words. She forced her trembling knees closer, until she stood on the very lip of a precipice that fell away into a whirlpool of onyx waters. "I—I can't hear you."

The hissing dwindled away, replaced by a silence so barrenly empty she felt her soul shrivel. Reaching out a quaking hand and concentrating on the blue gem, she choked, "Give me the *Mea*. It's mine. You'd no right to take it. My people need it!"

The darkness undulated and beyond it she thought she perceived the silken flash of a swirling robe as someone turned to walk back through. Through?

In an instant the vortex collapsed and nothing but dark whispering trees and tumbled rocks surrounded her. Behind, she heard Nahor blurt, "God almighty, the woman's teched! Maybe even possessed by one of those demons that killed her sister." A lengthy pause, then, "Yeah, maybe that's just what it is. Did either of ye think of that? That's why she hasn't been torn apart yet. She's on goddamned Aktariel's side! Let's get the hell out of here!"

She raised a trembling hand to her mouth as a sob welled

and caught in her throat. Had the demon in the darkness chosen this time to appear because he knew it would discredit her? What could she do now to pull these fragmented strands of Gamant civilization back together? Soft footsteps stirred the pine duff and she glimpsed Zeb Yoma working his way across the grove. Towering over her, he gazed fearfully in the direction she had been looking. Scents of sand and smoke, horses and tobacco clung to his tan livery.

He stood in silence a long moment, before whispering urgently, "What did you see out there?"

Sarah lifted her gaze to him, mouth ajar with inadequate words. His green eyes tensed, etching his plain face with more years than it deserved. Back at the camp, she noticed Nahor and Kowitz gruffly throwing belongings into packs. Men bustled around them, tents dropping in puffs of dust that swirled in the firelight.

"Forget about them," Yoma murmured softly. "I'll talk to them later. Tell me about the phantom you spoke to."

"I've met him before."

"Him?"

As she blinked up at the starry sky, she grappled with herself. How much could she reveal? These were simple men from the far reaches of Kayan. They understood little of Gamant philosophy. To them, her father had been more magician than man and the *Mea* spawned journey he followed more myth than fact. Yet . . . what would happen if she told them nothing?

"Who, Sarah?"

"He's a thief."

"A thief? What has he stolen?"

"The path to salvation."

Mikael Calas stood outside the tents set up in the valley and looked up the steep path his mother had taken. His throat was tight with the urge to cry. His aunt had died. Then his grandfather. Would he wake up tomorrow morning and have someone tell him his mother was dead, too?

He trotted out into the tall grass of the meadow to get another angle on the path, to see if he could still see his mother climbing. But she'd disappeared. A sharp pain pricked his stomach. He always felt so tired and frightened lately.

The Magistrates were to blame. Anger flared to cover his fears. Someday, *someday*, he would lead a war against them, just like his grandfather had done during the Gamant Revolt. And he'd kill them all, and then his people could rest. They wouldn't have to be exhausted and hungry anymore. They could live in peace.

"Mikael?"

He turned to see his uncle Mark standing by their tent. A tall dark-haired man, he had a full black beard. "Dinner's ready. Come and eat."

"I'll be right there, sir."

"All right, but don't take too long. We don't want the meat getting cold."

"Yes, sir."

He gazed longingly back at the mountains again. His heart throbbed agonizingly. "Someday," he promised himself and soothed his worries by thinking about the battles he'd fight. Already he could imagine the comforting weight of a rifle in his hands. He'd make the Magistrates afraid of him—just like his grandfather had done.

CHAPTER 23

Zadok plodded down the narrow dirt path past the ancient oak trees that led to the gate of the seventh heaven. A broad knitted canopy shaded him, the cool of evening suffusing the air. Through the laced branches, he could see the sunset sky had turned a dark cherry color.

"What did that arrogant angel mean?" he asked himself quietly. While the gatekeepers of the other heavens had passed him with an almost hurried amusement, Sedriel's words continued to haunt him. "What whirlwind has Aktariel set in motion? And who are his perfect dupes? Surely he hasn't fooled Yosef or Sarah?" No, he couldn't believe that. Everyone in his family knew Gamant history too well to allow themselves to be used as a tool by God's most persistent adversary. Aktariel's evil efforts had been drilled into each of their minds since birth.

He waved a hand in irritation. "And maybe Sedriel was wrong. Maybe he was just trying to get me so flustered I wouldn't be able to answer his questions." Hope sprouted, but quickly faded. If that speculation were true, he wouldn't now feel his chest tight with apprehension and longing for this quest to be over. He'd always cherished his visits to the seven heavens. Even more, he'd loved tramping through the seven crystal palaces of God within Arabot, the seventh heaven.

As he emerged from the trees, he saw the gate gleaming in the fading sunlight. Its enormous Ionic columns stretched into the sky to pierce the ruby and lavender clouds. A chorus of seraphim broke into song, each note of their voices weaving a stunningly beautiful harmony.

"Zadok?" a tired, rich baritone rumbled. "Hurry, patriarch. The mind of Epagael wavers."

The archangel Michael soared down from the clouds. His milky wings sparkled mauve in the fading light. Zadok craned his neck to watch the circular glide of the celestial being. Of all the angels, only Michael's beauty stopped the heart from beating.

"Over what does God waver?"

As the archangel floated to land before the gate, his golden robe draped around his feet. He carefully folded his eiderdown wings and turned. His crystalline face shone so brightly, Zadok had to struggle to keep his eyes on him.

"The impudence of man has wearied him. He toys with the *Reshimu*."

"The *Reshimu*? The residue of light that remained when God withdrew himself to spawn the void before creation?"

"Yes, like the residue that clings to the bottle when the wine is emptied. That light still pervades everything, rushing headlong for oblivion. Background radiation, if you will."

"Why does God toy with it, Lord Michael?"

"Because it's the source of all evil, Zadok. Surely you can see that."

He blinked, searching his thoughts. "No, I can't."

"Ah . . . Then that, Zadok," Michael said, tapping his crystal chin reflectively, "is the question you must answer to pass through the seventh gate and be on your way through the crystal palaces. *How is the Reshimu tied to the existence of evil?*"

"But, Michael, I thought Aktariel was responsible for evil? The Deceiver—"

"Oh, in a way that's true." He smiled faintly to himself, a gesture filled with regretful warmth. "As our leader, he shouldn't have been so blasted democratic. Had he insisted on his own will, none of this would have happened."

"But his will is to do evil! That's why suffering exists. He deceives people into straying from the path of righteousness."

"From Epagael's perspective, that's quite true. You've learned your lessons well, patriarch. But there are other perspectives."

"What?"

"Hurry, Zadok. You haven't much time if you want to save your universe. And without you, it's surely lost."

Fear brushed Zadok like a cold wind from the door to the pit of darkness. "Lost?"

"Yes, one way or another. Whether the act is Epagael's or Aktariel's."

"Please, Lord, *help me*. I haven't studied the ancient texts on the *Reshimu* in over a hundred years. Give me a clue?"

Michael's amber eyes gleamed and he lowered his gaze to the grassy knoll beside Zadok, speaking softly to himself. "For old times' sake, Akt? I don't know. If God knew, he'd—"

"Michael, please! You said time is short!"

The angel waved a hand harshly. "All right, Zadok, but it's not for you that I risk expulsion from heaven. Rather for an old friend with a blind and stubborn nature. A friend I once sided with in a clandestine meeting of supreme importance."

"Clandestine? Secret from whom?" The archangel couldn't mean a meeting of angels where God was not present? No, that would be blasphemous.

"Hush, you old fool!" he spat, looking fearfully over his shoulder at the seraphim who swayed in the darkening sky, their song stopped in mid-sentence. "Quickly, here's your clue. Listen very carefully, for I'll say it only once: Look deep in your memories. The answer lies waiting for you in Terran history. Who else believed that retracing the cosmic process to its ultimate foundations would provide redemption?"

"That's no clue, Lord, Terran history is filled with prophets who sought the cosmogonic starting-point: Abraham ben Eliezer Ha-Levi, Moses ben Jacob Cordovero, Arno Penzias, Robert Wilson."

"All right, but this is the final one: 'And these are the Kings that reigned in the land of Edom . . .' Not only from the *Reshimu* but from the dross of the primordial kings does the domain of evil arise. *Unde malum, Zadok? Unde malum?*"

* * * * *

They slowly wound along the diamond-shaped red tunnel, lamps throwing huge shadows over the walls. Rachel and Jeremiel brought up the rear, walking side by side through the somber and deathly quiet that seemed to ooze from the very stones. The monks studied her, fear, doubt and something else, something deeper, plain on their faces.

"I wish they wouldn't look at me that way," she murmured for Jeremiel's ears alone. "I feel like I'm on exhibition."

He smiled wanly. "I'm quite sure they can't help themselves. You look like every man's fantasy come true."

Rachel tried to laugh, but her ribs felt as ungiving as iron bars. Dressed exotically in a rose silk gown topped by an ebony cloak, jewels sparkled from her ears and wrists. She knew she looked beautiful, had verified it before a dozen mirrors in the past two hours. But she felt drained and strange to herself, like a pagan goddess adorned for sacrifice. Sybil had said as much at their tearful parting, "Mommy, you look like you're dressed up to go to a funeral."

"How are you doing?" Jeremiel whispered confidentially. He'd stayed no more than three feet from her all day, soothing, praising, helping her get ready.

She gazed up at him, seeing the concern on his handsome face. His forehead gleamed with a sheen of perspiration in the golden light. He looked starkly professional, dressed again in his black jumpsuit, pulse-pistol on his hip. "As well as can be expected."

"The closer we get, the more you look like you might bolt and run."

"That's encouraging."

"Are you feeling that way?"

"Of course. I'd like nothing better than to crawl into some warm dark hole and stay there forever."

"You can back out. Just say the word and I'll make other arrangements."

"No . . . no."

They passed beneath a series of arches cut into the stone and crossed a bridge spanning a trickle of water: the fifth such bridge they'd traversed. Curious, Rachel thought, that so much water existed beneath the surface and she'd never known before. Ahead, a brazier glared, lighting what Rachel strongly suspected was the final door, *the gateway to the pit of darkness*. A hard knot of terror formed in her stomach and her steps faltered.

"Jeremiel, I—"

"Yes, I know."

Gripping her hand, he gently pulled her to him. Cradling her shoulders in one arm, he walked her back the way they'd come, speaking in soft soothing tones. "Do you need more time? You've only had a month. That's barely enough for the pain of the square and the death of your husband to dim. We can give you another week. Just tell me and—"

"No, though I appreciate your saying so. If I don't go now, I'll never be able to muster the courage again. I'm sorry I'm acting like a fool."

"You're not a fool. Every soldier prays before battle." He lowered his voice still more and gave her a wry smile. "And since you and I don't have metaphysical solace, our best method is to contemplate the virtues of cowardice."

"Just now I can think of quite a few such 'virtues.' "

"Oh, there are several. I myself have counted at least five hundred and sixty two."

She gave him a skeptical look. "That many?"

"And I never had a chance to finish thinking. The enemy stopped me."

"With an attack?"

"A wave of attacks."

"Did you heed the five hundred and sixty-two and politely excuse yourself from the foofaraw?"

He smiled wanly. "Nobody'd let me. But I've always wished they had. That, Rachel, is why I'm giving you the opportunity."

"You think I should back out?"

"I think you should do what your gut tells you. That's the only reliable portion of a person's anatomy at such a time."

"You don't rely on your head."

"Certainly not."

"Nor your heart?"

"No."

She frowned, thinking about that. "My head tells me I'm insane."

"And your heart?"

A lump rose in her throat. She swallowed it with difficulty. "It just aches."

"That's why I never listen to mine. If I did, I'd never fight a single battle. The killing is all insane and it hurts. There's no way around those two facts."

"Then why do you do it?"

"Oh . . ." He took a deep breath and said through his

254

exhalation, "Because there's some tickle in my gut that tells me I'm doing the right thing." He squeezed her shoulders tightly and she felt the warmth of his side against her arm. "What's your gut tell you?"

Rachel stopped and stood in the protective circle of his arm, trying to overcome the terror of her head and heart to feel something deeper. That same tickle he'd spoken of stirred in her stomach, but it had less to do with a utilitarian 'right,' she knew, than with a suffocating personal need to hurt back, to give as she'd received. After a minute, she responded in a resentful whisper, "It tells me to do *quickly* what I must."

He nodded his acceptance. "Shall we turn back around, or keep going in this direction?"

"Turn around."

He did as she bid, whirling them both and heading back toward the door that led to the streets of Seir and, inevitably, to the Mashiah's palace.

"Are you ready?" Rathanial asked in trepidation as they approached—as though he feared she might blurt a hearty 'no.' His white hair and beard gleamed silver in the brazier's glow.

"Yes, please, let's hurry."

Jeremiel placed strong hands on Rachel's shoulders and stared into her eyes. She saw his face harden. "Don't," he instructed stiffly, "let the guards get you alone."

A prickle climbed her back, memories rising of the soldier's leer the day Shadrach had died. "No, I—I—"

"Listen," he interrupted sternly. "If it looks like they might take you anywhere but inside the palace and directly to the Mashiah, scream your head off. Make sure somebody in power hears you. Plead for the Mashiah's mercy. Understand?"

"I understand."

In the feeble wash of golden light, he dropped his hands and clenched them into fists. "Remember, to secure your legitimacy, everything you've ever believed in must be disavowed."

"That won't be hard, Jeremiel."

The corners of his mouth tucked in a sort of forlorn conspiratorial smile. "But that's not all. *Everyone* you've ever believed in must be abandoned. The Mashiah has to think you've given up all alliances with the rebel faction. You'll have succeeded if he finds you nothing more than a beautiful, completely vulnerable acolyte who's lost her way and is in desperate need of his guidance."

"I know."

In a sudden movement, he looked uneasily over his shoulder at the monks. Then she felt his muscular arm go around her waist in a gentle but firm hug. He dragged her away into the darkness. His breathing came fast.

"What is it?" she whispered, feeling his tension as a palpable thing.

"Rachel, I want you to understand that no matter how critical your side of this undertaking, you don't have to . . ." he paused, pursing his lips as though unsure how to put the difficult words. "You don't have to do anything you find—morally offensive."

"Jeremiel, I won't become his lover for you or for the Gamant people. I'll shoot myself in the head rather than face myself in the mirror every morning for the rest of my life." Yet, whispers sounded in the depths of her soul, *what about for your family? Your friends who still live in the shadow of his brutality?* "Providing I live through this."

"You'll live."

"You're an optimist."

"No, I'm not. I have all the odds carefully calculated."

"Really?"

He shot her a look and smiled. "Well, maybe not all of them, but the vast majority."

"That's what I figured. I imagine your chances and mine are the hazy ones?"

"You're a good guesser."

She smiled wanly. How could they banter like this when in only an hour she'd be trapped in the lair, face to face with the dragon himself?

He slowly started to back away. "I'll see you in a few days. Don't get worried about me. *I will be there.*"

"I know you will," she murmured and watched him walk back into the darkness.

In front of her, the massive stone grated back just enough for her to exit. Pulling her cloak tightly closed, she stepped out into the moonlight and hurried down the narrow dirt street. Cold wind gusted into her face, bringing with it scents of human wastes and the howling of dogs. As she gazed around, she wondered how they'd come so close to the palace? Were there subterranean exits that accessed all parts of the city?

The midnight moon cast cobalt shadows across the quiet homes, gleaming like liquid silver from tin roofs and broken windows. Curious, she thought, that very little had been repaired since the destruction of the temple. Adom hadn't even moved the victims from their war torn domiciles. These damaged houses remained occupied. She knew from the low whickering of horses and occasional cries of a baby that brushed the night wind.

Pressing her back against a stone wall, she cautiously peered around the corner. In the distance, the Temple stood like a gaping black wound against the moonlit background of desert and mountains. Blasted walls towered bleakly. Nothing remained of the crystalline Vault of Heaven except a glittering web of diamonds scattered erratically across the temple grounds. She stood weakly, seeing again the blood-spattered walls and red dust pommeled by a thousand desperate feet.

Rachel stretched her neck to see farther down the street and a swallow caught in her throat. The palace loomed up like a huge triangular beast, its skin gleaming a soft dove color in the moonglow. She stumbled, panting, against the wall, eyes squeezed closed. Why hadn't she known the fear would be this bad? That it would gnaw at her like a starving animal? Somehow in the past month of warmth and safety the wound shock of previous weeks had worn off and now, suddenly, her terror had reawakened, tingling powerfully to life this night.

"You have to. There's no one else."

Forcing her terrified body to round the corner, she walked with silent deliberateness, fists clenched so hard they ached. The light penetrating the buildings threw a pewter patchwork across her path.

She fixed her eyes on the palace and fought to control her breathing. A hundred windows stood open to the cold breezes and in at least a dozen, lamps glowed, flames wavering in the wind. She surveyed the heavens, seeing the midnight moon adorning the skies. Why would so many still be up and about?

Rachel frowned and wet her lips, struggling against a blinding premonition that the lights gleamed just for her. "Don't be a fool," she mouthed silently. "No one knows you're coming."

Sprinting down the street, cloak billowing out behind her, she slowed and sidled alongside the parapet, listening. The portcullis stood open. *Where were the guards?*

Edging around the corner, she dipped into the gardens and stopped in the shadow of a gazebo. Moonlight glinted from every sprig of dead grass, contrasting the blades in a shadow show of silver and onyx. Through the latticework of the roof, light dappled her face as she stared up at the pink marble steps stretching like a huge fan to the brass doors. *The mouth of the dragon's lair.*

But . . . where were the guards?

She squinted around the ugly rock sculptures, searching. *There were always guards.* Amidst the weave of black shadows, she caught a brief flash of the palest of golds. Time ceased as her heart stopped. She peered intently into the darkness, but for an eternity nothing stirred. The entire world seemed to have fallen into a silent silvered crypt. Only the wind moved, whistling around the gazebos.

Then, near the next stone statue, a prolonged glimmer of tousled golden waves slid through the shadows. Moonlight shone on the inverted triangle around his neck. He walked gracefully with his hands clasped behind his back, as though deep in thought. The silver light caught in his voluminous blue cloak as the wind whipped it about him in snapping folds.

Rachel pressed a hand hard to her mouth to stifle the cry that rose and with the other gripped the turnpost of the gazebo to steady herself. Hatred mixed with fear to fill her like a drug, paralyzing her trembling legs. She could only stare as he strolled nearer.

When no more than ten feet away, he stopped and looked up suddenly. She couldn't be sure in the darkness, but she thought a faint smile curled his lips. He spoke gently, "Rachel? Oh, I'm so glad you're here. God said you'd come. I've been waiting for hours."

"Adom, please, I must talk with you. Don't . . . don't hurt me."

He stepped closer and she could clearly see the distress on his handsome face. "No, of course, I won't. That's why there are no guards tonight. Milcom said I should meet you myself, to assure you that you're safe here. I won't let anyone hurt you."

His words sank in and a wave of nausea tormented her. "You knew I was coming?"

"Oh, yes, I've known for days. I've been making preparations."

"I don't understand. I only decided yesterday—"

"God knows things long before we ourselves do."

"God?"

"Yes, He came to me almost a week ago to tell me. He wanted me to keep your arrival secret from the High Councilman, though he said he suspected Ornias already knew." He frowned in confusion. "I don't know why he said that."

"And you . . . you sent the guards away?"

"I didn't want them to frighten you. Sometimes they do things I don't know about and I wanted to be sure no one hurt you."

"Hurt?" she asked tremulously. "Don't you want to *kill* me after what I've done?"

"I did for a time," he said ashamed. In the silver gleam of moonlight, she saw his jaw tremble. "I didn't understand then, that you needed me. God helped me see the truth. He wants you close to Him before the first motions of the destruction begin."

"Destruction? Of what?"

"Oh, everything." He smiled tenderly.

Rachel felt sick, her stomach threatening to empty itself. She knew suddenly that she walked into the lair of a *mad* dragon and she could no longer back out. Somehow, she had to carry on, complete her part of the mission. She shuddered, sucking in a breath, and he strode quickly to her, wrapping his arms around her protectively. His velvet cloak felt warm and smelled of hyacinths and coffee.

"Don't be afraid," he murmured softly. "Come. Let me take you inside where it's warm and we'll talk."

Rachel looked away to the lattice shadows dappling the dead grass. From a parchment dry throat, she forced the words, "Thank you, Mashiah."

He steered her through the garden with its looming shadows and up the pink marble steps. "I have a room prepared for you. I hope it meets your requirements. If not, tell me and I'll remedy the ills immediately. It may take weeks of discussions before I can show you the Truths of Milcom. I want you to be absolutely comfortable during that time."

She stared at him, understanding dawning like the blow of a fist. He wanted the cage to be gilded to her liking. And that's what it was, a cage, a prison—until she converted . . . or the attack came and she could gain freedom, either through his death or hers. Curious, she thought, that she'd never considered such a possibility. She'd spent days contemplating all the terrible compromises she might have to make to convince him to *let* her stay until that fateful day.

259

Now, it stood brutally clear that he planned on keeping her until he felt her "fit" for release among the masses.

He closed the huge doors with a clang and she flinched. The magnificence of his wealth and power spread before her, the plush carpets and arching ceilings. Gold inlay in the walls shimmered with fiery gleam in the soft candlelight, forming a maze of geometric patterns. And she had the horrifying feeling that things half-seen prowled the shadows, lurking, watching, waiting for his personal signal to stir to life. To bolster her failing courage, she concentrated on the echoes of Jeremiel's confident assurance, "You'll live . . . You'll live . . . You'll live."

"Rachel, I want you and me to be happy together." He dropped his gaze shyly and Rachel noticed the flush of mottled crimson staining his cheeks. "I—I didn't mean—"

"Adom," she said and physically forced herself to smile as she lightly touched his arm. "I know what you meant."

He gave her a timid and grateful smile, tenderly patting the fingers resting on his forearm. "I'd hoped you would."

As he patiently led her down the long hall, her strength ebbed, her stomach cramped and dizziness overwhelmed her. She had to clutch at his blue velvet sleeve to keep from staggering.

Jeremiel folded his arms tensely as he walked back toward the heart of the Desert Fathers' sanctuary. The lamps carried by the monks ahead of him flooded the walls with light, showing every crack and irregularity in the red stone. Rathanial strolled beside him, silent, elderly head bowed.

"She can do it. I know she can," the old man murmured tautly. "She must. For the survival of Horeb and all Gamant civilization."

Jeremiel frowned, unsure what the latter meant. Rathanial wasn't going to push the idea of Tartarus as the Antimashiah again, was he? He wasn't sure he could bear it just now, not when his stomach roiled painfully at letting Rachel out of his sight. "She's important, Rathanial, but I hardly think our entire culture depends on her."

"I haven't told you everything, Jeremiel. I couldn't while she was close." He looked up remorsefully. "I couldn't risk you revealing even an inkling to Rachel. So I held back some critical—"

"What critical details?"

They crossed a bridge and the pleasant scent of wet sandstone rose up like incense to fill the air. Cool moisture caressed his face.

"We've had word, you see."

The hesitation made Jeremiel's blood run cold. "Word?"

"Word from Tikkun and Kayan and—" He waved a hand. "And a dozen other Gamant planets. The Mashiah has sent evangelists to our brethren, to preach the truth of Milcom and condemn Epagael and the old ways. From what little we've heard, thousands are converting. You know how it is. Everyone wants to believe the true Mashiah has finally arrived to save us. Especially in these terrible times when the Magistrates are—"

"Yes, I know very well what the Magistrates are doing," he responded darkly, images of a hundred ravaged planets rising like smoke to twine through his mind. "Rathanial, are you trying to tell me the Mashiah is massing an army? That he plans on carrying his religious movement to the stars?"

"From the scant information I have, I'd say that's a good guess."

"So, his power base extends far more broadly than we'd ever have thought."

"Far more," Rathanial breathed tiredly. "And, Jeremiel, I'm afraid I've worse news yet." He looked up and Jeremiel saw the gravity of his expression.

"What?"

"There are reliable sources in the palace who report Ornias, the High Councilman, suspects we're mounting forces against him and has made secret overtures to the Magistrates."

"I seriously doubt Slothen would be interested in puny religious bickering."

"There's a Magisterial battle cruiser in orbit around Horeb right now and I understand the captain, a Cole Tahn, has been down to converse with Ornias."

"Tahn?" A dark dread numbed Jeremiel. Whirling images of Syene's—death—tangled with his rationality, smothering it. It stunned him that he could even now say that word in his mind, making the formal acknowledgment that she'd never again smile away his fears, never again touch him guardedly beneath a strategy table to ease his anxiety, never again gaze at him through the vulnerability of loving eyes.

"Yes. You know him?"

"Only from experience fighting against him. He's a brilliant commander."

"Oh," Rathanial muttered and his tone rang with anguish, as though he tasted defeat already on his tongue.

"It's not as bad as you think. Even if Ornias were to arrange some sort of alliance, we can beat Tahn. I'll need to contact my forces, of course. But Tahn has weaknesses," he offered encouragingly, then searched his memories seeking a shred of data to support that statement—finding none. The only reason he and his troops had escaped the trap Tahn laid around the planet of Silmar was through the feeblest of devices. He squeezed his eyes closed, unable to bear the thought. Why had he allowed Syene to use herself as bait? Why had he waited so long to go in after her? But he knew the answer to the last question. He'd trusted Neil Dannon, trusted him like a brother. The debacle was his own fault. Neil had been dropping clues for weeks that he'd gone over: a missed meeting here, a lame excuse there, *a change in his eyes*.

Jeremiel dropped his arms to hang limply at his sides, feeling as though someone had bludgeoned him. He'd just sent Rachel into a position equally as dangerous as the one Syene had faced. But Syene had been an experienced, shrewd combat veteran. Rachel . . .

"Rathanial, let's finish discussing this over dinner tonight. I have to hurry and get my things together." He started down the hall, but the old man's voice stopped him.

"Jeremiel, don't be so hasty. You have at least three or four days before you have to leave."

"No. I'm going in tomorrow."

Rathanial's eyes widened, mouth hanging ajar. "But that's not wise. We need to give Rachel a few days alone with the Mashiah. If you go in immediately, they'll become suspicious. It's too risky!"

"I'm going in tomorrow," he said with finality and shouldered through the monks, grabbing the closest lamp, before sprinting down the hall.

A black pit of despair had opened inside him, draining all life from the world. From that pit a silent voice screamed that even now, though she'd just left, he might be too late.

Just as he'd been at Akiba.

CHAPTER 24

A dream. Nothing but a dream. Yet still the blind breathless terror stalked him as he ran through the stormy streets of Silmar. The foreign architecture and spiny trees struck him again like bits of nightmare. The Akiba oaks dotting the empty spaces between opaque botanical and habitation domes drooped mournfully under the weight of snow, flailing white down with every gust of the icy wind. Ahead of him, the apartment building where Syene had been for ten hours rose over the next hill like a spear ready to slash his belly. He charged headlong for it.

"Jeremiel! We've got to get out of here!" Rudy Kopal yelled, firing blindly into the surging mass of soldiers that suddenly seemed to engorge the streets. They poured from dark doorways, clutching rifles as they ran, blending with the civilian crowd who fled, gasping in terror, from the ruined section of the city.

"Get out of here, Rudy!" he commanded, hitting the icy grass on his stomach and pulling himself over the next hill on his elbows. Sheltered by the trunk of a towering oak, he scanned the building with his scope.

A mother with five children scrambled up the hill in front of him, dragging sheets burdened with belongings. The little girl gripped her mother's torn gray skirt, sobbing. Jeremiel could see the blood clotting the blouse to her side and running in streaks down the front of her pants. Wounded. It sickened him. When had things gone so wrong? What had he missed? Something, something critical. If Syene had been able to delay the major only another hour, this would never have happened. Clearly . . . she hadn't.

Kopal hit the ground beside him, panting, rifle trained on the building below. "Jeremiel, for God's sake, she knew what she was doing! She's bought us time. We can get everybody still alive out if we go now! But it's got to be now. *You hear me?*"

He twisted to stare at his friend and saw familiar gray eyes boring into him, wild with fear. Blood streaked Rudy's olive skin, matting his dark hair to his temples and spattering his beige battle suit.

"I gave you a direct order, Kopal!" Jeremiel shouted roughly. "Get out of here!" Getting to his feet he raced down the hill, jumping the fence that surrounded the apartment complex and shouldering between terrified people who flooded out the main entrance.

Behind him, a burst of fire squealed and he whirled. Rudy dove through the door, crawling around frantic civilian feet. He motioned urgently with his rifle. "Go, I'll cover the entry. But they're coming fast, Jeremiel. *Hurry!*"

He spun, taking the stairs to the third floor three at a time, heart jamming against his ribs. Reaching the top landing, he kicked open the door and struck the floor rolling, coming up to see a barrenly empty white hallway. If the government had evacuated and everyone else could run . . . An iron band constricted around his chest.

He lunged to his feet and bolted for the last door on the right, shouting *"Syene?"*

He bashed a boot against the door and stood back, waiting for ambush, expecting it. But no fire came, no sound. Only the horrified shrieks of the crowd eddying through the streets outside penetrated the silence of the room.

He darted inside, rifle ready, and quickly surveyed the overturned furniture, broken glass and blood splashed carpet. A fierce battle had ensued. Had she . . . had she made it out? Was she even now waiting for him somewhere beyond the perimeter of the city? Momentary hope flashed and he gasped a deep breath, then raced through the kitchen and down a long hall, searching.

In the last room . . . he found her.

She lay naked, sprawled across the bed, hands extended limply out the open window. Had she been so desperate she'd meant to jump from the third floor? He could tell from the fluid stains running down the insides of her thighs what they'd used her for.

His legs went weak as he took in the massive spray of blood that soaked the bed and splattered the walls. He forced his feet to move. Reaching for her, he gently turned her over and saw her blasted chest rise and fall. *Alive!*

"Syene," he murmured gently. "Hold on. I've got to get you out of here."

As he got his arms beneath her to lift her, she groaned. Her dark eyes flickered open and a faint smile touched her lips as she saw him. "Love you," she whispered, barely audible. "Knew . . . knew you'd come."

"Save your strength, we've—"

"No," she said and shook her head weakly. Blood-matted locks of long brown hair fell over his arm. "No use. Listen . . ." She twined weak fingers in his black sleeve and seemed to be mustering her failing energy. "Dannon . . ."

Knowing Magisterial soldiers loomed just outside, he ignored her words, lifting her like a child and carrying her across the room, and down the long hall toward the door.

"Jere . . . Jeremiel. Dannon . . . Tahn. Betrayed . . . us. He was . . . was here. Half hour ago."

"I'll kill him, Syene. *I swear.*"

She went suddenly stiff, and he jerked his gaze to her body as the convulsions hit. She writhed in his arms, forcing him to drop to his knees and lay her on the cold floor.

Agony slashed his heart, tears burning his eyes. *A dream. It's only a dream. She's been dead for months.*

"Jeremiel?" Rudy's frantic voice yelled and he heard the terrible edge of fear in it. "Jeremiel, come on!" Pounding steps echoed down the hall and his friend came to a sudden halt when he saw Syene slumped on the floor, her beautiful face twisted in a mask of pain.

Jeremiel gathered her in his arms, pulling her tightly to his chest. Through her bloody hair, he murmured, "I need you, Syene. Don't leave me." But she was already gone. He felt the press of her dead weight against his trembling arms.

Rudy gave him ten seconds to mourn, then gripped his arm and roughly . . .

"Mister Baruch?" a sobbing little girl's voice penetrated his terror, coming from some great distance. "Are you awake?"

. . . jerked him to his feet. "You won't realize it for days, good friend. But I'm saving your life."

Together they ran down the hall and out into the storm. From behind a tree, Magisterial soldiers flooded. He heard Rudy's rifle whine and saw a group explode in a sea of red. The first soldier caught Jeremiel from behind, slamming the butt of his pistol into his temple. Dazed, he whirled and kicked the man hard in the stomach. He stumbled toward the second soldier before the first had even landed on the snow-covered grass.

"Jeremiel!" Rudy screamed. "This way. We've got—"

"Jeremiel!" a frail childish voice wailed. "I'm scared."

He felt himself being pulled up through the layers of consciousness. "What?" he questioned muzzily.

"I'm scared. Could you . . . could you pat me?"

He shook himself, sitting bolt upright in bed before he could shed the horrible dreamscape. Cold sweat drenched his body and in the coolness of the cave, he shivered. In the far corner, his fireplace still glowed faintly with red coals. Tiptoeing feet whispered near his door, punctuated by muffled sobs and sniffles and he made out a patch of filmy white where her nightgown swayed.

"Jeremiel?" the girl choked.

"Sybil?"

"Yes. I'm scared. I need somebody to pat me."

"Hold on, honey," he said shakily. "Let me light a candle. Then we'll—"

"No! I—I can see good enough to find you. Just keep talking?"

"Okay," he answered, sucking in deep breaths of the smoky air. "I'm right over here . . . right here. How are you doing?"

Her steps pattered quickly across the stone floor, muted in places by the throw rugs. "Where are you?"

"I'm right over here, Sybil. Follow my voice. There you go. You're almost here. Just a little further."

He felt her feet touch the sleeping mat and reached out, then stopped, knowing the terror of unknown hands touching you when you're frightened. "I'm going to pick you up, all right?"

"Yes."

He cautiously touched her arm, then lifted her into bed beside him and tucked the blankets around her. Fumbling in the darkness, he found and lit a candle. The glow of the flame refracted through his faceted water glass to land like a fistful of luminous cornsilk across the foot of his bed. Sybil's puckered face shone swollen and red in the light.

"You feel like ice. How long have you been running around?"

"I came straight here, but it's farther than I remembered."

"Yes," he said, hugging her close. "Especially when you're scared, twenty minutes in the darkness seems an eternity. How did you find your way around all the twists and turns?"

"I had to."

He smiled, running a hand through his soaked blond hair.

266

"Desperation lends special talents. I've experienced that myself a time or two. Now, what's wrong, sweetheart?"

She sobbed miserably, burying her face against his bare chest. "I had a bad dream."

"There, it's all right," he soothed, smoothing her tumbled hair. "We're a pair, you and me. I had one, too."

Sybil wiped her runny nose. "Do you need somebody to pat you?" Without waiting she stretched her tiny arm across his chest and patted his side comfortingly. "What did you dream?"

"Oh, it was a nightmare I've had before. About someone I loved very much."

Sybil swallowed her tears and looked up, dark eyes wide and afflicted. "Me, too. I dreamed about my mommy and my daddy."

His heart went out to her. A brave little girl, she was nonetheless a child abandoned to a fiendish new world where she knew almost no one. "Don't worry about your mother," he soothed. "She's fine."

"You mean because she's too mean to die?"

He smiled and stroked her back. "I don't really think that. I just said it because you were afraid and I didn't want you to be."

She got up on her elbows and blinked thoughtfully at him. "You did?"

"Yes."

"I didn't think you liked me."

"What would give you that bright idea?"

"You never play with me."

"Did you want me to?"

"Sure. That's how you show little kids that you like them. Didn't you know?" Her brow furrowed in puzzlement.

He contemplatively scratched his beard, eyeing her in amazement. "No, I guess I didn't."

"Haven't you ever been around kids?"

"Not much. Except when I was very small and in school, but that wasn't for very long. The Magistrates closed down my school when I was eight and built a Right School on Tikkun. My father wouldn't let me go. He taught me at home."

"Didn't your friends come over to see you?" A small glint of horror sparkled in her brown eyes.

He shook his head. "Most of the kids in my part of town went to the Right School and it wasn't very long until they wouldn't come over to my house anymore and my father wouldn't let me go to theirs."

"But you know why, don't you? Those schools tear up children's minds. They put needles in a kid's head and tell them what to think. And when they think the wrong things the needles send out fire to burn their brains." She nodded with utter gravity.

Jeremiel suppressed a smile. "I've never heard a better description of mind probes, but I'm surprised you know that."

"My mommy and daddy told me lots of things most kids don't know."

"I can see that," he responded, noting that her eyes were no longer wide with terror and the tears on her cheeks had stilled.

"Jeremiel, do you miss your friends?"

"Yes, very much," he answered truthfully. Visions of Rudy's face that last day on Silmar still lingered fresh in his mind. He could name on one hand the authentic friends he'd had in his life—including one who'd turned out to be no friend at all. "Do you miss yours?"

She croaked, "I miss David and Stella."

"They were good friends?"

"They came over to play every night after school. We'd build things in my backyard."

"Don't worry. You'll see them again. After your mother, Rathanial, and I get things straightened out here, you'll—"

"If they're still alive."

He let the words hang, not knowing how to respond. This little girl knew too much about life's hard side to tell quaint "everything works out" lies to.

He pulled her closer, cradling her against him and kissing her dark curls. "What was your nightmare about?"

Sybil sighed and snuggled her cheek against his chest. "I dreamed that Mommy and Daddy were together in the Mashiah's palace, but they couldn't find each other. Daddy was in a dark place and Mommy was up in the light. She hunted and hunted, but she couldn't find the dark place . . . and she was crying." Her pretty face puckered again as her shoulders shook. Hot tears stung his chest.

He stroked her back as he watched the flickers of candlelight dancing on the ceiling. "Dreams are strange things, aren't they?"

"Sometimes they're scary."

Too damn many times. "I know what you mean."

"Mommy says dreams are your mind's way of showing you things you don't really want to look at."

"Um . . . often that's true. There's a dark place inside your head called your unconscious where those things sort of lurk. You know what I think your dream was trying to tell you?"

"What?"

"That you miss your mom and dad so much you can barely stand it and you'd give anything to have them back together with you. And wanting that is a good thing—" he paused, debating whether to say what he felt, deciding she could take it—"even if it can never be again."

He felt her eyelashes blink against the blond hair covering his chest.

"You know what I mean?"

She nodded once.

"Do you want to stay here and try to sleep with me the rest of the night? I have to get up pretty early, but you can stay warm in the blankets while I get my things ready."

"You're going to see my mommy tomorrow, aren't you?"

He frowned, glancing speculatively down at her. "Yes, how did you know?"

"Avel told me."

He felt himself start to stiffen and commanded his muscles to relax. "Did he?"

She nodded and stretched her arm across his chest again, patting him gently. "Jeremiel, will you take care of my mom? Sometimes at night, she has bad dreams, too. She cries a lot."

"And needs to be patted?"

"Yes."

"I'll take care of her."

She heaved a small sigh of relief. "Thank you."

He kissed her hair again and cradled her against him. It seemed only moments before her breathing fell into the deep rhythms of sleep and her tiny arm went limp, inching, with every deep breath he took, back to rest against her own side.

Carefully reaching over his head, he snuffed the candle and stared longingly into the darkness.

He listened for hours to the broken fragments of conversation Sybil had with her father in her sleep, gazing tiredly at the red eyes of coals growing dimmer in the fireplace.

And wondering why Rathanial had revealed secret infor-

269

mation to a simple novice of his order, even though that novice was responsible for Rachel's daughter? It could not possibly have made an impact on Harper's duties. Could it? He and Rathanial had agreed that it was best for all concerned not to mention his early departure until after he was gone. Agreed that with the frightening new developments, security had to be tightened. The fewer who knew critical details, the better.

He gazed down at Sybil, eyes narrowing. Had she not suffered a bad dream, he'd never have known the breach had occurred. And he might have walked into . . . into . . . *what* without knowing?

His mouth pursed into a hard line. Imagination, he told himself. Rathanial had undoubtedly told Harper of his sooner than anticipated departure because he thought Sybil might need to take care of some final details with him before he left. You know, he told himself, last minute messages for her mother, or requests of him to take care of her—just like the one Sybil had made.

Damn you, stop it! There's no ambush out there. Rathanial is trustworthy!

And Dannon was.

His breathing stopped. Maybe Rathanial hadn't told Harper at all? That was purely an assumption on his part. Perhaps the man had found out in other ways? Listening devices abounded. A spy? For who? The Mashiah seemed the most logical, but a Magisterial spy couldn't be ruled out. *Lord, what if the man's working for Tahn?* But why would a spy tell a little girl secret information? Because he didn't expect her to see Jeremiel again? Ridiculous.

Or . . . could Harper have suspected Sybil would come to see him one last time? Had the slip been deliberate? *A warning?* A tip-off that the leak had occurred and he should be damned careful?

The final possibility was the one he dreaded the most. Had the "listeners" told Harper and, consequently, the Mashiah? He'd waited a month to send Rachel in, watching Seir constantly. Tartarus had made no moves at all. *None!* That's why he'd given in to Rathanial's frantic pleading and let her go.

I may have authorized her execution.

If she weren't already in the Mashiah's palace and her fate unknown, he'd back out of the whole damn thing and make a run for it. Of course, he could get a message to his forces, go in and grab her and take off. Sure, in maybe six months, and how would they extricate a live Sybil from the hands of the Desert Fathers?

He tiredly rubbed his forehead. This trap had been woven too neatly. Had someone known that his feelings for Rachel grew with every passing day? That her warmth, intelligence and independence reminded him of Syene? And he would not, could not, leave her alone in the lion's den?

The demanding instincts of fifteen years of war roiled so violently in his gut, he finally had to rise. Easing from Sybil's sleepy grasp, he slid out of bed and tucked the blankets snugly around her. She slept soundly, mouth slightly open, dark curls twisting across his pillow. He smiled down at her and patted her arm gently. "Don't worry," he whispered. "I'll get us out of this."

He dressed quickly, leaving his pistol on the table by the fireplace. No sense in having his favorite weapon confiscated. He frowned suddenly, picking it up and feeling it melt comfortably into his hand.

"Course, I might never see you again anyway," he murmured. Reluctantly, he put it back and stuffed a few clothes in his pack.

He jotted a quick note to Sybil, telling her not to worry, and left it propped against the nightstand leg where she'd be sure to see it when she awoke.

Exiting quietly, he slipped into the darkness of the tunnel, holding his small lustreglobe out before him to light his path down the winding corridors that led into the city.

CHAPTER 25

Cole Tahn leaned back in his command chair while he surveyed activity on the bridge. It was an oval room composed of two levels; nine people worked the monitors and consoles commanding the *Hoyer*. His chair with its massive array of buttons and computer access links occupied the upper level, giving him a complete view of every action on the bridge. On the lower level, officers sat in twos, stationed side by side at four niches around the oval. He gazed up at the three-hundred-and-sixty-degree screen which detailed the status of all major areas of the ship. At a glance, he could determine energy consumption and food reserves, monitor virtual pair production around the primordial black holes in the engines, determine Lamb shift and adjust photon bombardment, ascertain which segments of navigation or recreation were undergoing repair—anything he needed to know. Just now, his eyes lingered on the communications log of incoming messages.

"Macey?" he called to the skinny redheaded com officer who hunched over his terminal on the lower level.

"Yes, sir?"

"What's that latest message from Magistrate Slothen?" He grimaced a little as he mentioned the name. He'd met the creature once, and had yet to overcome the revulsion and horror he'd felt. The monstrous blue-skinned Giclasian politician had a puckered blood-red mouth and hair that squirmed like a tangle of snakes when his sophisticated brain worked.

"It was a simple acknowledgment of our former message on the status of Horebian politics, sir. But if you'd like to read it, I can pull it up."

"No, for God's sake," he grumbled more sharply than he'd intended. Dealing with Gamants did that to him, made him irritable. "I read fifteen billion computer screens a day. *Talk to me.* Tell me what it says."

"Just a moment, please, sir." He hit a series of buttons on his console and the electromagnetic com aura glowed golden around his head, feeding his brain the data.

While Tahn waited, he studied the quiet industry on the bridge. Officers bent over their terminals, monitoring the latest data on movements across the surface of Horeb and collating incoming information on other Gamant activities across the galaxy. He sighed gruffly. He'd missed midday mess and his stomach tied itself in knots to remind him. He gently patted the organ, silently promising: *soon.*

Behind him, the door snicked back and Lieutenant Carey Halloway entered, expertly surveying the bridge. In charge of navigation, she had a practiced ease of movement, a perfect body rippling with toned muscles beneath her form-fitting purple uniform. Her auburn hair hung straight over her brows and fell to her shoulders, accenting the emerald green of her eyes and her pearlescent complexion. Strikingly beautiful, she also possessed one of the most abrasive personalities onboard. He liked her.

"Sir," Macey said and the com aura died. "Magistrate Slothen responded: *Am in receipt of your transmission regarding overtures from Horeb. Tell the councilman that as soon as he can guarantee delivery of our payload, we will certainly negotiate. Inform him we have ample largess on standby.*

"What the hell do they think?" Halloway spat, putting hands on her shapely hips. "That we're stupid? How many times do they have to tell us that?"

Tahn smiled at her appraising. "You know how the Magistrates are. They assume all humans need to be told the same thing at least three times or we'll miss their point."

"Morons," she said under her breath and cursed, striding to her chair at the navigation center.

"What's the status on our next mission? Have we received course corrections yet?" he requested hopefully.

"Don't you like it here? Orbiting this barren ball of sand?" she asked.

"Are you being funny?"

"Not very, I guess."

He relented, chastising himself for taking out his frustrations on his crew. "Sorry, lieutenant."

"No apologies necessary, Captain. We all feel like we're walking a tightrope over a pit of insanity."

"*Gamant* insanity."

"Yes, sir."

Spewing a disgruntled exhale, he leaned back in his chair and let his mind fill with images of lush forests, scantily-clad females and quaint candlelit taverns. "I was thinking maybe we'd stop off at Lopsen for a week or so before our next mission."

"A little R and R? The crew would throw themselves at your feet. Especially after the past eight months straight of riding herd on these fanatics."

"Maybe in atonement for causing us so many headaches, that blasted Gamant god will condemn all their hell-raising souls to the pit. That would make me feel better."

Halloway gave him a quick look over her shoulder as she fiddled with the screen on her console. "I hear this new Mashiah preaches there is no metaphysical pit of darkness—that hell is being in the universe."

"What are you doing? Reading Gamant propaganda?"

"Reading it and finding it quite intriguing, sir."

"Well, stop it. I couldn't endure a convert on my ship."

"I didn't say I'd lost my mind, Captain. Only that I found it intriguing. Their system of belief has very little logic but a fascinating experiential basis."

He felt himself recoil at the very thought of discussing anything Gamant, but grudgingly asked, "What are you talking about?"

She swiveled in her chair to give him a cold-eyed challenging look. "It's based on the mystical presupposition that God is accessible."

"What does that mean?"

"It means that their leader has a device, known as a *Mea Shearim*, that supposedly serves as a direct gateway to the throne of the divine."

"So they slip through the gate and go talk to God, is that it?"

"Apparently."

"What is the device? Some sort of drug?"

"No. At least not so far as those of the religious studies experts who've researched it have been able to determine."

"Gamants allow study of holy artifacts?"

"Certainly not. But some academicians have gone in undercover, nonetheless."

"Well, what is it?"

"No one's sure. Though the effect of the *Mea* has characteristics similar to drug or mind probe imprint catatonia. For example, the person whose soul is traveling to God appears to be lifeless. Rumor has it that during the last Gamant Revolt, old Zadok stayed absent from his body for over a month. His military troops nearly went mad with worry. Some, apparently, really thought he was dead."

"But he returned, obviously. *Damn him.*"

"Returned and led them to a crushing victory over Magisterial forces on the plains of Lysomia."

"I remember the history lesson, lieutenant. No need to repeat it."

"Calas claimed God had shown him the strategy to use."

"Every fanatic claims divine authority. Mohammed, the Crusaders, Pleros of Antares, Kilne of Giclas Three—"

"Sure, a lot of leaders make their followers feel safer by claiming such guidance, but this *Mea* business is a little different."

"How so?"

She stood and paced contemplatively before him, tapping a laser pen against one palm. He tried to keep his mind off the sensations her lithe form stirred. Damn, when he started seriously thinking about his crew, he'd been locked in his ship too long.

"One rogue religious studies professor who managed to sink deeper into the Gamant structure than any other, claimed the *Mea* had null singularity qualities."

He laughed softly, squeezing the bridge of his nose. *"What?"*

"Oh, yes. His name was Kessler, and he was quite serious. I have the documents, if you'd like—"

"No, I wouldn't," he responded severely and glared.

"All right, but the implications are rather staggering."

He was rapidly losing interest in this preposterous conversation, but forced himself to ask, "Tell me the implications."

"Well," she threw her straight auburn hair over her shoulders and adopted an at ease position before him. He hated it when she did that. The posture accentuated the swell of her breasts and the flatness of her stomach and he had trouble concentrating on what she was saying. "Consider that we use primordial holes for power generation and time dilation, but it would certainly be feasible to construct a crude weapon."

"They don't have the technology."

"Maybe not, but they could get it. Raiding a Magisterial science colony would—"

"You think they'd blow up their gateway to God just to get us?"

"Given their personalities, sir, I'd say that's not too farfetched."

He squirmed uncomfortably in his chair. He'd seen Baruch do some things he thought no sane commander would do, like endangering his entire fleet by rushing a heavily armed prison planet to rescue *two* of his soldiers. Or the time they'd had him boxed tight in an asteroid belt around Antares Minor, outnumbered five to one. Rather than surrendering like any smart commander who knows he's lost, Baruch stationed four of his ships in strategic locations, evacuated his crews, then set his matter-antimatter engines on time-delay for merge and ran the rest of his fleet like bats out of hell for the light vault. They'd shot three of the bats out of the sky before they realized the stationary ships were decoys. The entire asteroid belt, including fifteen Magisterial vessels, vanished in the explosions. The man wasted six quality ships and two crews to get a remaining six out . . . and kill fifty thousand government soldiers. No one sane could predict what he'd do.

"Actually," Halloway interrupted his thoughts. "I don't think they'd destroy their only *Mea*, but let's say, for the sake of argument, that they have a spare. Maybe they'd use it for a bomb, tapping the mass and sending the temperature soaring until the hole gave up the remainder of its mass in one final catastrophic burst of gamma rays." She looked up and frowned. "Placed properly, such a device would pulverize Palaia Station. The Magistrates—"

"Would be scattered far and wide across the Giclasian system." He twisted at the tendril of satisfaction he got from the thought.

"But a bomb is rather wasteful when you consider the long-term potential of a singularity cannon. Just one primordial black hole of minimum size, say a few billion tons, could be easily concealed and would produce 10 MeV of energy. That's a concentrated burst of power equal to six old-style nuclear power plants."

"A weapon. Sure. Why is it that the concept of a benevolent God sets so many ignorant hearts on the path of murder?"

"It provides comfort during times of stress." She smiled sweetly.

"Uh-huh."

"Although the Gamant god is a rather capricious character. He's left them out in the cold every time they've needed him in the past few thousand years."

"*All gods do that.* You can't expect fuzzy illusions to be reliable."

"Fuzzy? Like the Heisenberg Principle, the Lamb Shift, the—"

"I get your meaning, lieutenant." He narrowed his eyes and glared at her. She grinned in return, striding back to sit at her console.

"Insubordination," he grumbled in a low voice. "I have to put up with lunatic Gamants and disrespectful officers."

"Though for the life of me," she said, ignoring his comment. "I can't understand why they continue to believe in Epagael after he's abandoned them so many times. Perhaps that's why this new Mashiah is striking such a chord across Gamant civilization."

"Probably."

"Incidentally, Captain . . ." She hesitated a moment, glancing sideways at Macey, then remarked, "Have you heard the dattran scuttlebutt about Silbersay and Kayan?"

Macey whirled in his chair, brow furrowed, as though she'd infringed on his area of expertise. Red crept up his freckled cheeks. "That's not confirmed," he pointed out indignantly.

"I wasn't usurping your position, Rich. I just wanted to know if anyone had informed the captain?"

"We've had no official confirmation on any of those fragments of hearsay! Things like that come across the tran all the time. I didn't feel the captain needed to be bothered until we knew for certain."

"I know, Richy," she sighed disgustedly and lifted a brow. "By the Book every time.

"How dare—"

"What *is* it?" Tahn demanded sternly, looking from Macey's offended blue eyes to Halloway's cool green ones. As anyone with experience knew, in a galaxy where information ran the gamut of controls before release, rumor often stood as the single warning beacon that something rotten stirred among the stars.

Carey gallantly gestured for Macey to give the response.

He answered tersely, "Sir, we're getting a number of conflicting reports from the Kayan region on low frequencies. Most discuss Colonel Silbersay's recent cannon attacks on obscure villages. Others speculate on when he *will* attack. And still others laud his nonviolent handling of Gamant affairs there. It's a confusing mess, sir. Not worthy of your attention at this time. Silbersay has sent no reports of punitive actions being taken."

Carey lounged lazily back, an arm draped unprofessionally over her chair back, a look of quizzical distaste on her lovely face. "And . . . ?"

"And?"

"Oh, come on, Rich. The captain wants to know, and since it might involve us, don't you think you ought to tell him?"

Tahn leaned forward in his command chair, that familiar clenching up of his stomach muscles tormenting him. "What do you mean 'involve' us?"

Macey threw Halloway a rough sideways glance. "Sir, there is *unverified* gossip that speculates Silbersay is on the verge of calling in a scorch attack. Since we're the nearest Magisterial battle cruiser, that would necessitate our—"

"What?" he breathed. A bad taste rose in his mouth. He swallowed it, feeling queasy. God damn, he couldn't bear to carry out another such order so soon. The waste and devastation sent something inside him reeling with revulsion. "Why? What could a planet of scattered vagabonds have done to warrant such terminal action?"

"Apparently," Halloway responded coolly, "they've got half his forces bottled up in a desert region known as the Kabah."

"Even if they got the drop on him," he hissed in disbelief, "Kayan is a planet of technologically backward barbarians who live in caves and clapboard lean-to's. Why doesn't he just initiate selective sterilizations?"

"Burning population centers is difficult when most of the people are constantly moving. They're a nomadic—"

"I know that!" he snapped, mind racing. A scorch attack? It seemed almost inconceivable—but not quite. The Magistrates saw partial or total obliteration as a clean safe method of handling dissent. "Why doesn't Silbersay make examples out of the few sedentary communities? That could go a long way toward dampening the violent ardors of the rest."

Halloway extended long legs across the gray carpet and crossed them at the ankles, staring at him through eyes as hard and sparkling as stone. "The blood of a single martyr is enough glue to weld a revolution."

"Depends on how many and which martyrs you kill. Dead *leaders* take a toll." He swiveled his chair to face Macey. "Lieutenant, open a tran to Silbersay. Let's find out what's really going on out there."

"Sir," Macey said with stiff professionalism, eyes focused on a distant point. "May I speak candidly?"

He grimaced. "Quit that, Rich. You look like you swallowed a ramrod. You know I despise such formality on the bridge. Speak your mind."

Macey relaxed only a little. "Sir, may I suggest that if such problems existed, the Colonel would have already contacted you. And if he hasn't, he probably has his reasons. It may be because he wants to keep the lid on until he feels the situation is beyond his ability to control."

"Are you trying to tell me he may not like us interfering in his affairs?"

"Yes, sir."

278

Tahn ran a hand through his brown hair. "That's a good point. I wouldn't want anyone butting in on one of our assignments until I requested assistance."

"On the other hand," Halloway noted astutely, drumming her fingers on her console. "If the people he's really trying to keep it from are the Magistrates, he might appreciate a friendly call on narrow beam asking how he's doing? You know, a casual chat with a fellow Magisterial officer locked in the Gamant mental ward?"

He held that hard green stare as he thought. She could be an enormous trial at times, but her mind was just clever enough to warrant commendation after commendation.

She added offhandedly, "If Silbersay admits to his difficulties? It might prove valuable to ask about the dissidents' organization, supply routes and leaders. In case we know any of them by name and can connect them with—"

"Kayan has been a model planet for years, why would we know any of their rabble-rousers?"

"Doesn't it seem odd to you, that suddenly a bunch of ignorant poverty-stricken herders would be able to bottle up hundreds of trained Magisterial soldiers?"

He filled his cheeks with air and squeezed his eyes closed. "You mean maybe we were wrong after all about Baruch leaving Kayan?"

"Exactly."

He ground his teeth, anxiously heaving a breath through his nostrils. "Carey, get Neil Dannon up here. He knows Baruch's strategies."

"Shall I personally search all the women's cabins to find him, sir? Or do you think he might be occupying himself with productive activities of late? Drinking, perhaps?"

He ground his teeth. *"Move!"*

"Aye, sir," she answered distastefully, striding for the door.

"Macey, open that dattran to Silbersay. I'll ask him about the weather and hope he brings up his problems—if he has any."

"Acknowledged, sir. Just a moment."

Tahn rubbed the knot in the back of his neck. Baruch on Kayan? He didn't believe it. He possessed a sort of sixth sense where the rebel was concerned. When he got near, he felt Baruch's presence like a stiff belt of Ngoro whiskey, his head got thick and his gut roiled. Though he'd never seen the man since Baruch refused all visual communications and the only known zolographs showed him as a young boy with dark hair and blue eyes, he knew what he *felt* like. And he felt him here on Horeb, so close he could almost reach out and touch him.

"Sir," Macey announced, "I have Colonel Silbersay on monitor four."

He whirled his chair just as the older man's face formed and gave Silbersay a wide flashing smile. "Garold, how the hell are you? Still chasing Gamant women?"

* * * * *

Avel Harper stood in the utter darkness of a maintenance cubbyhole adjacent to Rathanial's personal chamber. The room smelled of chemical cleaning fluids and petrolon brooms—but it was safe. No one used it except during the day. He fumbled through his pack, retrieving what he needed. Fixing one end of the listening device to the wall, he placed the other in his ear.

Rathanial's voice came through, irritated: *"Don't tell me about Baruch's warnings! I know them better than anyone!"*

"Yes, Reverend Father," an unknown man responded humbly. "I didn't mean to offend you. But Jeremiel specifically told me *not* to alter any segment of this plan or the entirety would crumble. Every movement, he said, is intimately connected."

A pause. Harper ground his teeth, waiting, fearing the worst.

Rathanial's voice again, authoritative: "Jeremiel and I discussed this thoroughly, Martin. I assure you, it's all right to change this one tiny element of the strategy."

"All right, Father. If you say so. Forgive my disobedience."

Harper leaned a shoulder against the wall, exhaling tiredly. He stared unblinkingly into the blackness. Things were farther along than he'd thought. He'd have to act soon, or all would be lost.

Quietly, he put the listening device back in his pack and slipped out of the cubbyhole into the dim rock corridor. He'd have to send a series of clandestine messages to gather his allies for a counteroffensive.

Turning a corner, he ran down the next hall and ducked into a dark bedchamber.

CHAPTER 26

Talo huddled in a shadowed doorway, chewing an Orion peach and looking out over the square. The streets around the gathering place stood heaped with debris. Broken boards and smashed stones, wrought from the body of the city by the marines' wild firing that horrifying dawn a month ago, were still scattered throughout the area. Down the street, he gazed longingly at the shattered yellow bakery where he'd sat and fed cooing doves. Bloating corpses filled the place of the birds now—corpses of those who'd tried to escape the holocaust; they lay in twisted, unrecognizable piles. In the distance, the red peaks of the mountains wavered with the blazing heat, hawks lilting in unfettered greatness on the wind currents.

Talo took another bite of his fruit. The blue flesh spurted with juice. With each bite, sticky rivulets coursed through his white beard to drip on his ragged brown pants. His face wore smudges of soot, dirt, and blood. Around him, workers staggered in the searing day, shoveling debris into carts. They'd been rounded up by the Mashiah's forces to form cleanup crews . . . how long ago? Two weeks? Three? He'd forgotten whole hours of the day the Mashiah's marines marched into his section of town, but his mind still burned with some memories. The soldiers whipped the people into following, blasting any home if one single member refused. Something had happened to him that day, his mind had gotten fuzzy, as though cotton stuffed the depths of his skull. He remembered the beatings. But not very well, and anyway, it didn't matter. Just work and eat, that's all he had to do to stay alive. And so today, for yet another day, they staggered beneath the fiery sun.

He shielded his eyes against the glare and looked up to see Sima struggling to shovel the blackened body of a child into an already overloaded cart. When she got the gruesome prize over her head, it abruptly split open and a writhing mass of white feeders slithered down over her arms. She let out a

281

gasp of horror, dropping the shovel to wipe frantically at her arms, as though slapping away the acidic venom of a monster.

Talo lowered his eyes. His heart throbbed. From the alley behind him, he heard the sweet voice of his niece, Myra, whisper, "Uncle, lunch was over a half hour ago. Why are you still here? You know what they'll do if they find you."

"My heart aches," he said, glancing back to where Sima suppressed sobs as she leaned heavily against the stinking cart.

Myra walked over to stand beside him and he smelled her sweat, saw her hair flutter in the roasting wind. She wore a ragged blue dress and a head rag. Her pretty face had gone gaunt, the cheekbones sticking out like a skeleton's.

"I—I feel poisoned," he moaned softly.

"We've all been poisoned," she murmured, eyes focused on the battered street. "Each time we touch the dead, they shoot their poison into us."

He frowned, not certain he'd heard right. Sometimes, now, that happened. He would hear people talking to him, could even watch their lips moving, but his mind couldn't decipher the words. They seemed to be speaking a foreign language. "What?"

Myra tenderly patted his shoulder. "I meant that it's a poison that strikes at the heart, making it pound and ache."

"Oh, yes. I know."

"Another wound to our souls, another reason for living lost."

"We still have eternity," he murmured thankfully, licking the juices of the peach from his fingers. A warm hope spread through his limbs. He looked up at her and smiled reassuringly.

Her jaw muscles tightened. "I know you believe that and I pray to God you always will. But for me—for most of us, the soldiers have killed eternity."

Lost in his comforting reverie, he didn't quite grasp what she'd said. "Epagael will take care of us. He won't let them kill us."

"We cannot expect relief, Uncle. Until we bring it ourselves."

"Bring it?"

In front of them, Sholmo waved a hand frantically, motioning at them. Myra slapped his shoulder, whispering "Hurry!" before hastily sprinting into the street. She retrieved a shovel and began attacking a precarious pile of stones with a vengeance. Sholmo waved again, more urgently. The young man had been scraping at an avalanche of boards that heaped the wall along one side of the square. A green uniform glinted in Talo's peripheral vision, but he took another bite of his peach. They got two a day and he relished each as though it would be his last. Just a few moments of huddling in the cool shadows, finishing his fruit, wouldn't matter. His fingers stuck together with the fragrant juices.

"You! Lazy old fool!" a short red-haired marine with huge freckles yelled. "Why aren't you working?"

"I—I . . ." A small shudder of fear touched him. Talo dropped his precious peach and stood wide-eyed, pointing to it as though that explained everything.

The marine kicked it with his black boot and it made a soft squishing sound when it hit the burned-out building. Talo looked at the ruined fruit and tears rose to his eyes. Such waste, and for nothing. The marine jerked the heavy petrolon bar from his belt and lifted it suddenly, smashing it against Talo's head. He fell to the filthy street, crouching under the blows.

Hot blood trickled into his eyes, but Talo could see the other workers standing around, watching without moving. Some wrung their hands. Most looked angry, as though they were mad at him for not avoiding the marine's wrath. And he knew that often when one member of the work team got a beating, all the others suffered, too. A week ago, the marines had gone wild, using their bars to kill twenty in ten minutes. Blood had run like a river down the street.

"Stop it!" Myra screamed finally. "He lost his mind after your last beatings. He probably didn't understand what you said to him!"

The marine whirled, chest puffing out indignantly. "You want to be next, girly? Want me to break your teeth out with my fist?" He listed the huge hand and shook it at her. She recoiled a step, crying.

Talo tried to rise, to get up before anyone else got hurt because of him, but dizziness overwhelmed him and he vomited wretchedly into the street. He heard the clicking of boots as another marine trotted up.

"What did he do?" the new man asked.

"He won't work! He's a lazy old imbecile."

Then they both laughed and the new man tormented,

"Filthy, brainless old man. Don't you remember what we do to people who won't carry their weight?"

Talo looked up pleadingly. "I—I remember . . ." he whispered valiantly.

But the marine didn't hear. He drew back his foot and kicked Talo brutally in the stomach. He tumbled sideways, feeling as though some organ had split inside him; a fiery pain swelled like a black balloon in his gut. But in spite of the agony, he forced himself to try to rise again, and managed to get to his knees. A prayer rose in his heart, a prayer to the great God of goodness who would, he knew . . . *he knew*, press him to His blessed bosom when the marines were finished this day. *Epagael, Lord of the Universe, give me strength*.

"Get back to work!" the redheaded marine shouted at the crowd that grew by the second, waving his arms insanely. But no one moved. They all stood riveted, watching in horror.

"You won't work either, eh? You want a good show before you go back? I'll give you a good show!"

The marine lifted his heavy bar again and again, beating Talo unmercifully. The other marine joined in after a few blows, shattering his legs and pounding his spine. They laughed at him while a gray haze rose. In the background he thought he heard someone utter a bare whisper of, "We'll kill them. It won't be long. Rachel is back. Sholmo says his mother saw her go into the palace last night. Wait until she . . ."

Talo awoke to see stars gleaming through a fissure in a roof. But his eyes wouldn't quite focus; the world heaved in a sickening blur. Peroxide and other pungent smells filled the air of the battered building and he heard soft footsteps threshing through clutter. In a flood of panic he thought they must be marines.

"Don't hit me!" he wept, trying feebly to cover his head with his single arm. "Don't . . . don't hit me!"

Myra leaned over him, the ends of her blue head rag touching his cheek. He gazed up blindly for a moment, then made out the massive bruises and disfiguring wounds that marred her once pretty face. He put his arm over his eyes and sobbed. They'd hurt her for trying to help him. The knowledge tore at his soul, for he knew he still needed help badly.

"Uncle Talo," she whispered lovingly. "Quiet! Hush! You mustn't weep so loudly. They'll hear! It'll only make things worse." She glanced nervously over her shoulder. He followed her glance toward the dark socket of an empty doorway. Were they through there? The marine guards they assigned to the work crews each night?

Still, he couldn't stop the tears that wracked his very soul. He should shove her away, force her to let him die, he thought numbly.

"Shut up!" someone shouted. "Keep him quiet. They'll kill us all if he wakes them!"

Talo clutched weakly at her blue sleeve, shrieking, "Go away! Don't . . . don't help me."

"Quiet!" she hissed fearfully, clapping a hand over his mouth.

Through the hard fingers, he gasped. "Rachel . . . ?"

Myra reluctantly released her hands, glancing at the doorway. "Keep your voice down, Uncle. What about her?"

"Did I hear right? Is it true? She's back?" He felt the same aching hope he did when he spoke of the coming of the Redeemer.

"We're not sure. You know Sholmo's mother, Martha, isn't in her right mind anymore. Maybe she just mistook a sliver of moonlight for Rachel. She's also been babbling about the coming of the true Mashiah for a week straight. Day and night, no one can stop her constant muttering."

"He *is* coming," Talo assured warmly. "He is."

"I believe you, Uncle," she said softly, but he could tell by the tone she didn't. She hesitated, then whispered, "I'll tell you something else, if you promise to just lie quietly and listen."

He nodded feebly.

"We've heard rumors from other sources that Rachel is inside the palace. One person said she'd been alone all day with the Mashiah. But no one knows what's happening."

He felt suddenly feverish, his whole body searing hot. "She's telling him to save us."

"Or she's gone over."

He stared madly into her blurry, bruised face. In the background, stars glimmered like huge fuzzy torches. "No! Don't even think that! She'll . . . she'll take care of us," he rasped frantically. "You'll see. She's the tool of Epagael!"

"For the sake of God!" someone whispered shrilly. "Shut him up! The rest of us have to work tomorrow!"

"Shhh! Uncle, don't . . ." Her voice trailed into nothingness, eyes widening in terror.

285

He followed her gaze and through the dark doorway, saw the marine. The man stood silhouetted, a black form against the dark gray background of night. In Talo's distorted vision, he seemed to float forward like a ghost.

"Water?" he croaked at Myra. "Niece, give me some water before they forbid it. I'm so hot."

She backed away from his bed, her whole body trembling. The redheaded marine stared down and Talo felt his soul shrivel. The hate in those cold blue eyes flooded over him like the poisoned oceans in the north.

"Water?" he asked the soldier. "I'm dying from fever. Just a little water to cool my throat."

"Didn't you hear the girl? She said be quiet!"

"But please, just a little. I only need—"

"Shut up!"

"Just a sip to wet—"

The marine bashed him violently on the head and Talo heard his skull crack. It seemed as though in that instant his brain oozed from its shell, for he felt a slimy wetness against his head.

He gasped, body going numb, but still he forced himself to murmur one final time, "Wa . . . water . . ."

The marine whirled in military fashion and strode haughtily through the room, screaming as he exited, "You filthy fools had better not lay a finger on him. If we find out any of you has helped him tonight, you'll all suffer for it!"

A hum of murmuring voices laced the darkness, but in a few short moments, he saw Myra lean over him again. Her lips trembled and tears streaked her bruised cheeks. "Uncle . . ."

"My—Myra." He tried to say the name lovingly, but his voice rasped like sand against stone.

His energy drained away like water through a hole in a rickety bucket. But he felt only a sense of freedom, a peaceful floating into oblivion. He let himself go, relaxing in the sweet chill of the night, dreaming.

And he found himself walking the old streets. Candles lit the windows and scents of fresh baked muffins lingered on the morning wind. Happiness touched him as he rounded the corner and saw again the stone doves who gathered before the bakery. They strutted and cooed, racing to encircle his feet, waiting for the bread they knew stuffed his jacket pockets.

* * * * *

Mikael snuggled under his blue plaid blanket, pulling it up around his ears. Cold fingers seemed to creep from every part of his chamber, twining out of the rock to stroke his warm body greedily. He shivered, watching his mother wearily pull a box that contained extra blankets from beneath his bed. She looked very tired, the light that used to gleam in her eyes dead and gone. Black hair hung in dirty strands over her shoulders. He hadn't seen her in a long time. She spent most of her days, and sometimes long into the nights, talking with grown-ups. Lately, she'd taken to speaking sharply to him, "Can't you see I'm busy, Mikael? Go outside and play." "Are you crying again? Won't you ever grow up to be a man?" Loneliness and fear haunted him.

"Mama?" he asked bravely. "Are we going to die, like Grandfather and Aunt Ezarin?" He'd heard people talking and knew something very bad was happening. Cousin Shilby said that big ships might come and rain violet fire down on them that would melt the rocks into pools like water.

In a violent motion, she shook out a blanket and flung it over him. "We'll be fine, Mikael. Go to sleep. It's awfully late."

But Mikael couldn't sleep. He hid beneath his covers, only his eyes showing. His breathing against the plaid blanket came back warm, filtering through his nightshirt to touch his cold chest. He felt only half convinced by his mother's words. She'd said them with a shakiness in her voice that made his insecure world totter.

"Mama, why won't the men leading the riots in the deserts and valleys help us?"

"I don't know."

"Don't they like us?"

"They don't like me."

"Why not?"

"Because I'm not your grandfather," she blurted and slapped a fist into the brown stone wall.

He jumped, appraising her through dark glistening eyes. "What difference does that make?"

"To them . . . a lot."

"Mama, why don't we—"

"Stop it, Mikael! I don't want to talk about it."

He nervously pleated the corner of his blanket between his fingers. When she looked back at him, tears shone in her eyes. But something else glimmered there, too. Something he didn't understand, a feeling like when his weabit—his

287

best friend—had been crushed under a rock slide. His chest had ached and felt hollow for days.

"Are you sad, Mama?"

She paced unsteadily and in a savage voice whispered, "You're being a bad boy, Mikael. Don't ask me things like that. Go to sleep."

He snuggled a little deeper beneath the blankets. The words about him being bad hurt. He'd tried very hard these past few weeks to be especially good. He never made loud noises anymore and he only played in his chamber, picking up his toys every night. He felt as though a heavy sack of grain had been laid on his chest. He couldn't breathe very well. He searched his thoughts for something to make her feel better.

"Mama?" he blurted and suddenly sat up. The blankets coiled around his waist. "Why don't you take me with you to talk to those men? After you, I'm the next leader of Gamant civilization. Maybe if we both went, they'd listen to us and then the Magistrates would leave us alone?"

"The leaders of the riots won't talk to us anymore. I've been trying to arrange meetings for weeks. They refuse."

"Why, Mama?"

"Because they think I'm crazy!"

He flinched at the harshness, murmuring defensively, "I love you, Mama."

She glared at him, but soon her hard look softened and she came back to sit on the side of his bed. Brushing dirty hair behind her ears, she took his hand in hers and said softly, "I'm sorry, Mikael. I've been mean, haven't I?"

"No, Mama. You've just been worried."

She pulled him to her chest and hugged him fiercely. "You're my best friend," she murmured. "Did you know that? You're my best friend and I've been rushing around so much I'd almost forgotten you existed."

"I know, Mama, but it's all right. Now we'll be better."

"I don't know, Mikael. The whole world is falling down around our ears and I've nowhere to turn for guidance."

"What about God?"

"No, I can't—"

"Because the shadow man stole the *Mea*?"

She pushed him away suddenly. "Where did you hear that?"

"Shilby told me. He said it happened the night Grandfather was killed."

She blinked, lips trembling as she looked away. "Yes, it did. I'm sorry. I should have been the one to tell you. But I've been so busy."

"It's all right."

"It was yours, you know? Papa said to give it to you after his death."

"So I could go talk to God."

"Yes."

Mikael lowered his eyes and picked a piece of lint from his blanket, rolling it in his fingers. He'd been very sad when he first heard. Sad and disbelieving and angry.

"Mama, I hit Shilby when he told me."

"Did you?"

He nodded, ashamed. The worst thing in the world to his mother was fighting. She hated it and had punished him throughout his life when he accidentally had to do it. But the battle with Shilby had been different. He'd hit his cousin with a stick because he wanted to—wanted to hurt Shilby as badly as his cousin had hurt him by the news. Mikael remembered painfully the dozens of times his grandfather used to dangle the object in front of his eyes. He'd watched in awe as blue light poured from the globe. He'd felt God calling him those times, like a prickle of ant feet at the back of his neck. God wanted to talk, needed to. But now he knew he'd never be able to answer the call.

"Mama? Who's the shadow man?"

"I don't know."

"Maybe it's Aktariel? The Deceiver. He can come in any shape he wants. Maybe he wants all the *Meas*!"

"I don't think the devil would—"

"Remember Grandfather's story about *Indra's Net*? Remember how he said that in the old times *Meas* filled the skies, sparkling like gems across the celes . . ." He concentrated. "The celestial vault and how our ancestors used to be able to take their own *Meas* and follow the gems in the net anywhere in the universe they wanted to go?"

"Yes," she said and smiled wanly. "I remember that funny story."

"But when the Magistrates came, they started plucking all the *Meas* from the net and putting them in a big hole at Palaia."

She yawned tiredly, putting a hand to her mouth and nodding. He could tell she listened only out of politeness, but it had been so long since he'd had a chance to really talk with her, that he couldn't bear the thought she might leave. He kept talking.

"Only certain *Meas* led to God, remember, Mama? Grandfather said our ancestors had to experiment to find which ones."

"And there were only forty."

He nodded vigorously.

"Yes, honey, but what does that have to do with anything?"

"Don't you see?" he said excitedly, clutching her hand. "Grandfather said once that Aktariel ruled the Magistrates, so maybe he has most of the *Meas* in the hole at Palaia, but—"

"He didn't have ours, you mean?"

"So he came and stole it! And once he throws them back in the sky, he can go through any door in the net again."

"Yes, I see, Mikael." She gave him a kindly smile and tucked the blankets around him. "You must go to sleep now, all right?"

"But, Mama—"

"It's late, son. And I need to go to bed. I have a big meeting tomorrow with Colonel Silbersay in Capitol."

"To ask him not to hurt us?"

"Yes, that and other things."

He reached up and patted her hair, then nodded quickly, seeing how tired she looked. "I love you, Mama."

"I love you, too, Mikael. More than anything in the world." She smiled down at him and stroked his dark hair like she used to. Obediently, he rolled to his stomach and closed his eyes.

A little while later, he heard his mother rise and tiptoe to the candle, blowing it out before she left. Mikael opened his eyes and stared into the cold darkness, thinking about Indra's net and the sparkling web of *Meas* that used to fill the skies like tiny stars.

"Aktariel's the thief, Mama," he whispered to the darkness. "If he has all the *Meas* that lead to God, maybe he can close all the gates. Then he can tell people anything he wants and nobody will be able to ask God if his stories are true."

A stab of fear tormented him. Anxiously, he gazed heavenward. "Epagael? What will you do when nobody can come see you anymore? Will you be lonely?"

Suddenly he ached desperately inside himself. He'd been very lonely these past weeks, crying into his pillow at night, and it tortured him to imagine anyone else feeling the same way. Especially God. God had lots of other hard things to do, like taking care of the universe. He didn't need to be lonely, too.

Mikael blinked at the ebony night. His neck prickled and he shivered. Was God calling again? Calling and calling and no one in the universe could answer?

Tears welled in his eyes. "What will you do, God? I'm afraid."

CHAPTER 27

Wind moaned faintly through the candlelit arches of the palace, penetrating cracks around windows to chill Rachel's skin. She walked slowly down the marble hallway, noting the gleam of the gold threads in the rich carpets. Why were the passageways on this floor always empty? Were the servants forbidden entry to certain sections? Or just the Mashiah's private section?

Her steps echoed hollowly as she stepped off the rugs and onto the stone floor to turn a corner. Before her stretched a long hallway, brightly lit by the flickering lamps that lined the walls. Rose agate statues of the saints adorned niches in the marble, stony eyes watching her coldly.

She stopped, sucking in a halting breath. Adom's bed-chamber lay behind that final door gleaming golden at the termination of the corridor. *Come to dinner in my room*, he'd invited. *We'll talk of Milcom and Horeb.*

"Milcom and Horeb?" she whispered to herself, sensing her feet going cold, heart pounding. Was that all he wanted tonight? Her memories glossed over the chamber he'd prepared for her. Filled with magnificent gowns, scented bath soaps and bejewled combs and brushes, it seemed he curried her for his own special needs. And she played the game like a professional courtesan, selecting, *for his pleasure*, to wear a gorgeous flame-colored gown. Made of luminescent taffeta, the billowing sleeves and low-cut bodice glimmered with amber beads, as though drips of resin had fallen and glued themselves to the fabric. Handfuls of diamonds sparkled like ice crystals in the thick waves of raven hair hanging to her waist.

"And if he wants more than talk?"

The possibility had been rotting in her mind for days, yet still she'd made no decisions regarding it, preferring to deny the reality until the time came.

Girding herself as though for a final battle, she strode quickly toward his door. Her hand trembled as she lifted it to knock. Lowering it, she wiped her clammy palm on the skirt. *He hasn't hurt you, has he? In fact, he's like a stranger, not at all the Mashiah who's haunted your dreams for years.* Lifting her hand again, she quickly knocked, calling softly, "Adom?"

A patter of steps sounded within and in only a moment he opened the door wide and smiled, eyes going over her admiringly. "You look beautiful. Please come in. Dinner will be here in half an hour."

She stepped across the threshold and felt her heart throb painfully. The chamber spread sixty feet across, resembling nothing so much as the great baroque cathedrals of legend. Pink marble arches rose in dramatic brilliance along every wall, creating countless niches of shadow and light where desks and tables piled high with toppled stacks of books nestled. Overhead, in the glorious trompe-l'oeil fresco of the dome, a golden crystalline god soared, radiant, through a star-studded black heaven.

Her mouth opened as she took another step gingerly across the plush red and gold carpet, whispering in awe, "Mashiah . . ." but stopping when her own voice reverberated so ethereally in her rib cage that she felt her knees go weak. It took her breath away, as though the structure were built on top of the highest Horebian peak and she couldn't quite fill her lungs with air.

"It's lovely, isn't it?" he asked in a soft contralto.

"Beyond anything I could have imagined."

"They tell me some Terran architect designed it a thousand years ago for one of the original Horebian kings. Edom, somebody or other—a real rogue as I understand it. I never paid much attention. Supposedly there are hundreds of secret passageways twining throughout the palace, just in case Edom had to escape quickly."

"From a much-deserved retaliation, no doubt."

"I suspect so."

She turned to him, gazing up. Dressed in a coffee colored

satin robe fringed across the chest with strings of opals, his blond hair shimmered like sunshine on snow.

"I can now understand why you speak so softly most of the time," she whispered and listened to her voice echo hauntingly.

He smiled, his whole pure soul revealed in his blue eyes. She felt buffeted by that gaze, as though he'd crept inside her and pressed her very soul against his, *Charismatic . . . so charismatic.*

"I suppose living here does do things to my behavior," he said and with a gentle hand, he guided her across the carpet to a table and chairs huddled in front of two enormous open windows. The flame of the candle lamp on the table wavered in the cool breeze that flooded the room, rustling the papers cluttering his desk.

Pulling out a chair for her, he asked. "May I get you a glass of wine. We have some very good alizarins or—"

"Alizarin is fine, thank you," she responded, letting herself drop easily to the chair.

He bowed and went to a tall carved cabinet that looked very much like a reliquary. When he pulled back the double doors, she saw the lines of dusty brandy and wine bottles. Crystal decanters and goblets lined a lower shelf.

While he gathered them, she examined the room more carefully and found herself frowning, confused. To her right a huge brass bed sprawled, the crimson spread hastily tugged up over the pillows. Beneath the edges of the spread, old cups of liquid sat half-hidden, moldering. As she peered closer, she noticed a velvet thick green culture creeping up over the lip of one glass to drool down the side.

She gave him a curious sideways glance as he came back and set two glasses and a bottle of wine on the table.

"Is something wrong?"

"Adom, don't you ever let anyone clean this place?"

A blush crept into his cheeks and he smiled awkwardly, lifting one of his broad shoulders. "Not if I can talk them out of it."

"You have a hundred servants in the palace. Don't you trust them?"

"Oh, I trust them, It's just that . . . well, you see, I can never find any of my books once they've cleaned." He pointed shyly to a crammed marble bookcase cut into the wall. Gold engraved leather bindings gleamed. "They always put them back and it takes me hours to hunt them down again.''

"But you could let them in just to clean up dishes and make the bed.''

"I suppose,'' he said in embarrassment and poured their crystal goblets full of wine. "But they'd change the sheets every day and I . . .''

He squirmed like a child caught with his hand in the cookie jar. Pulling his chair closer to her, he sat down gracefully. His bushy blond brows drew together and he pursed his lips uncomfortably. *A curious man, so innocent, so frail. Like a child, his manner makes me want to protect him from life's harshness. Remember the square!*

"You don't want them to change the sheets?''

"It's not that—exactly. It's just that in my position, I'm alone most of the time, locked here in the palace—for my own good,'' he hastily clarified.

"What does that have to do with the sheets.''

"I have some personal quirks, I guess.''

"You like dirty sheets?''

He glanced painfully up at her, a boy afraid of punishment. "I like coming to bed at night and—and—smelling . . . human scents on the sheets.'' In a quick flood as though he feared he'd lose his courage, he continued, "I think I'd go mad if I came back after a long day and smelled only soap. I never get to be close to people, you see. My world is sterile. And I need to feel human—at least in my own bedchamber.''

She'd started to smile at his puerile fears, but the smile ran away from her face as his meaning dawned. Loneliness tormented him. And she knew about loneliness. After Shadrach's death, she thought for a time her heart would break with the weight of it. Were it not for Sybil, she might have gone mad herself. "Being a god on a pedestal must be very difficult. I can understand your need to just be a man with yourself.''

"Sometimes I feel almost as though there's nothing warm in the world. I find myself empty and aching and I feel terrible, until . . .''

"Until you come home to dirty sheets?''

He smiled timidly. "Yes. They make me feel better.''

"I understand.'' Her mind drifted painfully to the pleasant, comforting scent of Shadrach's side of the bed. When she napped during the day, she always slept on his side, letting his scent wrap her, promising safety and love. She could understand now, if a person had no one else, even his own scent would be comforting—reminding him he was indeed human and, if nothing else, he had himself.

"Do you understand? Really?"

"Yes." She lifted her crystal goblet, watching the golden light spark from the maroon surface.

"Mostly, I have to try very hard to be perfect, but here in my room I can relax."

"Yes, and retreat to that place inside that always listens."

"Listens," he murmured and gazed up in a kindly way, "and tells you it's okay to have moldy cups of tea under your bed."

Despite herself and the prickle of danger that tormented her stomach, she laughed. He joined her, looking down bashfully. She sipped her wine, relishing the rich earthy flavor as she thought about that place inside. She knew it well, had gilded it with iron bars and mirrors so she could strip herself naked and glare at her soul in privacy. An unbreachable sanctuary, it represented the only truly safe place in the universe.

A gust of wind whistled through the windows, slapping at the candle and setting her flame-colored sleeves to dancing. He looked up and she caught his gaze and held it. For a long time, he remained still, his childish expression deepening into that of a man. A deep vulnerability glistened in his eyes.

"I have a gift for you," he whispered suddenly.

"What?"

"Let me get it." He sprang gracefully to his feet and trotted across the floor, pulling a small box from his dresser drawer. Smiling, he ran to bring it back. "It's very rare." He gave her a sweeping bow like some medieval knight and gently laid it in her hands.

"What is it?"

"Open it."

She glanced warily from the carved box to Adom's delighted expression. He sat on the edge of his chair, waiting in barely endurable excitement.

"Open it!"

"All right." Rachel pulled up on the lid. The box made a soft velvet-against-wood scratching as she opened it. She cocked her head strangely, staring at the blue ball on the gold chain. "It's beautiful. But what is it?"

"A necklace."

"I can see that, Adom. What's it made of?"

He blinked, smiling as he shrugged. "I haven't the slightest idea."

"Where did you get it?"

His smile faded and he stared uncomfortably at her boots. "That's a secret." He quickly went on, "But you must wear it."

She lifted it out of the box by the chain and held it up to the candlelight. A very curious object, white froth, like that of turbulent waves, undulated across the surface. It seemed, as well, to have an inner source of light, not a reflected one.

"You don't know what it is?"

"No, but don't you like it? I thought it was very interesting."

"Yes, it is Adom. But it . . . I'm not sure what to think about it."

He reached for the chain and she released it. Then he leaned forward to slip it around her neck. Rachel shuddered when the blue globe came to rest against her bare chest. Warmth oozed from it.

"You can't touch the globe with your hands," he instructed patiently, but an uncertain expression pinched his face. "At least, I don't think you can. That's what *I* was told."

"Why can't I touch it with my hands?"

"I don't know, really."

"Why is it so bright?" She looked down to where it rested against her olive skin, glowing brighter by the second. A small fear trickled through her. She felt almost as though it were alive, feeding off her own energy.

"I—it didn't do that when I wore it. Maybe the necklace has some special affinity for you."

"Maybe it likes women born under the House of Ephraim."

"Are you?"

"Oh, that's what my father used to say, but I never quite believed it."

"Well, maybe that is why the globe casts that brilliant aura when you wear it."

"I'm not sure that makes me comfortable."

"Oh, don't be worried. I'm sure it's quite safe. Mil . . . You wouldn't have gotten it if it weren't."

"Mil . . . ? Milcom, what?" She watched the red climb his cheeks, as though he'd ineptly revealed a secret and now silently chastised himself for it.

"What I meant is that God watches over us. I'm sure He wouldn't let something like that hurt you."

"I don't trust gods very much. Particularly when it comes to protecting me from harm."

"God loves us, Rachel. He spends enormous amounts of time traveling around the universe trying to get our future worked out."

"Does He?"

"Oh, yes. Every time I see Him lately, He looks worn out to the point of exhaustion."

"He comes to you physically?"

"Usually. Though sometimes I just hear his voice or feel his power."

"What does He look like?"

His chin tipped and his eyes fixed reverently on the frescoed dome. Rachel followed his gaze upward to the crystalline god soaring through the blackness of space. Tiny pinpoints of light twinkled like a glimmering net around him.

"Like that?"

He nodded, heaving an expressive sigh, as though Milcom's image touched him deeply.

"How often does He come to you?"

"Not as often as He used to. He's very busy, you see." Lines appeared around his eyes, betraying some inner struggle. Finally, he straightened in his chair and swallowed hard. "Rachel, there's something else I must tell you."

"About the necklace?"

"No."

"What, then?"

"Milcom came to see me last night." Utter seriousness pierced his voice. He swirled his wine nervously, gazing at her from beneath his lashes.

"What did He say?"

"He said I can't let you go back to the caves of the Desert Fathers—ever."

She recoiled as though someone had bashed her in the stomach with a blunt beam. He knew about the Desert Fathers? Knew she'd been there? What else did he know? That they'd planned to overthrow his government? *That she was supposed to . . . ?* She squeezed the fingers around her goblet hard to keep them from trembling. "Why?"

"Because you'd be in danger there. I—I don't understand how exactly. He didn't say. But He commanded me to keep you here until He came for you."

297

"Came for me?"

"He said when the time arrived, He'd show you the way to the River of Fire." He tilted his head in confusion. "Do you know where that is?"

"No."

"Don't worry. He'll show you. He's shown me many places and things I'd have never believed possible."

She nodded once, trying desperately to keep her breathing even. A river of fire and a blue globe powered by some mysterious energy source? "Adom, what do you know of the Desert Fathers?"

He shrugged unconcernedly. "Oh, not very much. Just that they're part of a secret religious sect and hide in the caves of the desert."

"Do you know anyone there?" She tried to sound detached, just mildly curious, but she felt unable to breathe as she waited for the answer.

"No, not directly, at least I don't think so. Though sometimes, one of their monks comes into the palace—"

"What for?" Terror wound like fire through her veins. Did Jeremiel know that *someone* in the Desert Fathers' group had ties to the palace?

"Mostly to see some of our servants, who are family, I presume. I don't really know, but I think I talked to him once and he seemed nice enough.

"You know they believe in Epagael?"

"I know."

"Why haven't you tried to destroy them."

He smiled curiously, frowning. "Why would I do that?"

"Because they won't convert."

"In time, they will," he said gently, nodding confidently to himself. "When Milcom decides to bring them into the fold."

"What do you mean?" She felt as though a chasm had opened inside and she teetered on the edge, staring down into eternal darkness. Sounds from the square paralyzed her: night birds flapping their wings and tearing at dead flesh. Babies choking on their own tears. Muffled moans of people who'd never rise from beneath the terrible tangle of dead.

"Why . . ." she moaned and stifled her voice, forcing a swallow down her constricted throat.

"What is it, Rachel?"

"I—I don't . . ."

"Tell me and I'll fix it," he whispered imploringly, reaching across the table to tenderly clutch the hand knotted into a fist in her lap. Holding it tightly, he repeated very softly. "Tell me? I'll make it better. If I can."

She stared breathlessly at him. Who was this timid man with the innocent blue eyes? A Mashiah who preferred to be surrounded by moldering cups and dirty sheets? Could this be the same tyrant who'd slaughtered her people by the thousands for refusing to give up their trust in an ancient god?

"Why do you punish some and not others?"

In shame, he squeezed her hand and let it go, turning to frown at the flickering candle on the table. "You mean the rebels you organized?" A hurt timbre shook his voice.

"Yes."

"Sometimes people have to be set back on the right track, and it isn't always painless. We—"

"You murdered thousands!"

He turned sharply, eyes darting over her face. "What are you talking about?"

"Don't . . . don't play games with me, Adom. You ordered the deaths of thousands of the Old Believers. My family and friends!" In the back of her mind, Jeremiel's words wailed like a siren: *To secure your legitimacy, everything you've ever believed in must be disavowed . . . Everyone you've ever believed in must be abandoned.* Dear God, what had she just done?

His face slackened, mouth hanging slightly ajar. Fear touched his eyes. "I remember you saying something like that in the temple. But I don't know what you're talking about. I would never order such a thing. Oh, I might sentence a rebel to work the salt mines, or plow one of the city farms, but I'd never sentence anyone to death."

The discussion had gone too far. She decided to follow her instincts. "I saw them die—*I was with them, for God's sake!*" she shouted and slammed a fist into the table. Her glass of wine rocked to spill across the shiny wood. "In the square a month ago. Ornias came in the *samael* and told us to witness *your* power, then he ordered the marines to fire into the crowd." Tears rose in her eyes and a sob caught in her throat.

"Rachel," he whispered in terrible fear. His face contorted. "I was locked in consultation with Milcom that entire week. I knew nothing about . . . But I can't believe it."

"You did it! Don't try and deceive me!"

"No."

"I don't believe you!"

She lifted her chin and examined him like an eagle circling a mouse, hatred and anguish plain on her face. He gazed at her pleadingly, anxious lungs puffing his chest in shallow breaths.

"Rachel, I would never do such a thing."

"Then who did?"

"I don't . . . *Please*, tell me every detail of what's happened the past few weeks?"

In a flood, she recounted the beatings, rapes, raids, confiscations, the horrors of living under his rule. As she spoke, his face blanched more and more until he looked like a sickly apparition.

When she'd finished, she sat still, staring at his downcast eyes. He clamped his trembling jaw tightly. She wiped tears from her cheeks. Had she been mistaken? Had all her efforts at murder been directed at the wrong man? She felt numb and half-drowned by the implications pouring over her dazed mind. Ornias had always been the one present when the orders were carried out. What if Adom hadn't known? If Ornias were the true demon?

He gazed at her feebly. "If you thought me such a monster, why did you come to the palace?"

"To beg you to stop."

He fiddled nervously with the fringe of beads draping over his broad chest. "Consider it stopped. I'll get to the bottom of this, I promise you."

Lies! All lies! Despair and confusion rose like a tidal wave to crash over her. Yet his every expression reeked of honesty. Anguish rose in a sob. She jerked her hands up to cover her face.

"Rachel," his soft voice begged. After a few moments, she heard him rise from his chair and felt a timid hand on her shoulder. "Rachel? Please, look at me."

She mustered her courage and dropped her hands, meeting his frightened eyes. He knelt on the floor beside her, the soft wavering light accentuating the hollows of his smooth cheeks.

"Adom, what about Ornias? Could he have acted without your knowledge?"

He lowered his gaze. "If so, why didn't Milcom tell me? He always tells me."

"Maybe He didn't know, either?"

"God knows everything."

"Why wouldn't He want to tell you?"

"Maybe He feared I'd do something stupid. Sometimes I do." Ashamed, he glanced up at her, then got to his feet to pace thoughtfully.

"Why would Ornias command that the Old Believers be wiped out?"

"I don't know. But he's always saying his methods of containing the rebellion are 'clean.' I never questioned what he meant by that. The outside world is his jurisdiction, you see. I handle the spiritual affairs and he handles the mundane ones."

"He's handled them all right," she said in a savage voice. "People on the far side of the city are still running in terror from his marines."

Numbly, she watched the candles throw his tall form in multiple shadows across the towering pink arches. Every line of his wounded face said he truly hadn't known. *But what difference did that make now? Ornias was obviously the true power of Horeb. Could Adom do anything to stop the orders for more mass murders that the High Councilman had already given?*

"Rachel, are you still hungry?"

She shook her head, too upset and empty to eat.

"Could you . . . Would you walk with me a while in the garden? Perhaps if you tell me what's been happening these past few months on your side of the city, I'll be able to understand better."

She got unsteadily to her feet. "Yes, I—I'd like to." Though she hadn't the vaguest idea what good it would do and discussing the horrors would be a lance in her soul. "Let me get my cloak. I'll meet you—"

"No, here," he said hurriedly and went quickly to his own closet, pulling a magnificent ivory cloak from the hanger. Amethysts studded the wide collar and sleeves, sparkling as he held it up. "Please, take mine."

"Thank you."

Rushing back with the garment, he wrapped it around her shoulders and with an unthinking intimacy, thoughtfully fastened the collar and the top two buttons. Not meeting her eyes, he asked softly, "Will you be warm enough?"

She looked down. The cloak spread behind her in sculpted

301

waves of the purest velvet. "I'll ruin the hem in the dew-soaked grass."

"I don't care."

Pulling out an ebony velvet cloak for himself, he swirled it over his shoulders. "Come. We'll cancel dinner on our way past the kitchen."

* * * * *

Sybil sat on the brown rug in Avel's personal chamber. The blaze in the fireplace crackled behind her, warming her back. He stood by his sleeping mat, searching through a box for a book on ancient fairy tales. She waited impatiently, tying and untying her shoes.

"Avel?"

"Hmm?" he said without looking up.

"Someday I'm going to have a funny necklace."

He found the book he'd been hunting for and came back to her. Sitting down cross-legged beside her, he put it in her lap. "There you go. *Grimlin's Tales.* You'll love them."

"Have you ever seen a necklace that looks like a lustreglobe, Avel?"

He cocked his head, frowning. "No, but it sounds like the infamous *Mea.* Where did you hear about it?"

She smoothed her fingers over the colorful cover of the book. In the picture a boy and girl played beside a stream. "Oh, I had a dream about it last night. My mom will give it to me when I get old enough."

"I pray you're right. That means there's still a *Mea* in existence."

"What does the palace look like, Avel? In my dream I saw my mom there, wearing the necklace."

"I'm sorry, Sybil. I've never been in the palace. I don't know."

"I think it has pink walls and big statues."

He drew up his knees and folded his long arms around them as he watched her closely. "From what I've heard, that's right. What else did you dream?"

"Oh," she said shyly, feeling strange telling him about one of her "funny" dreams. "That was mostly it."

"Mostly?"

"Yes, just about the necklace and the palace." But in her mind the dream replayed and she could see the young man with curly black hair putting the necklace against his forehead. She pressed her forehead to the opposite side and they kissed. His lips had felt warm and soft, making her tingle deep inside. And the necklace had glowed so brilliantly between them she'd had to close her eyes.

"Can you read me a fairy tale now, Avel?"

He nodded contemplatively. "Sure. And maybe later we can talk more about your dream?"

"Maybe."

She handed him the book and tied her shoes again, avoiding his eyes.

CHAPTER 28

Adom clenched his fists as he rounded the corner which led to Ornias' office. A burly guard stood outside, straightening abruptly when he saw him.

"Good morning, Lieutenant Dally," he greeted. Fear twisted in his stomach. Ornias would be enraged by the intrusion. He'd chastised Adom often for appearing without warning. "Would you tell the Councilman I'd like to speak with him immediately?"

"Mashiah . . ." Dally's voice floundered. "Ornias said I wasn't to let nobody disturb him."

Adom pursed his lips tightly. "Please tell him I'm here."

"I—I can't sir. He'd have me flayed if I so much as knocked on his door. You know how he is about his privacy. He—"

"Lieutenant, I order you to—"

"*Don't*, Mashiah, I beg you," Dally said pleadingly. Sweat had erupted on his nose. He looked at Adom through wide frightened eyes. "The last time I interrupted him after he gave me orders not to, he sent my six-year-old daughter to work the potato fields. She got real sick from the heat. She hasn't been right in the head since. *Please*, I couldn't bear it if—"

"I'm sorry, Dally. I didn't know he . . . Just—just give the councilman a message when he comes out that I want to see him as soon as possible? Could you do that?"

Dally heaved a relieved breath. "Yes, sir. Thank you, sir. I'll tell him."

Adom turned and walked briskly away. In his head, the words, *Oh no, oh no, ohno*, echoed. He broke into a run, racing down the hall.

Rachel's stories must be true if Ornias had done something so terrible to Dally's child. He'd prayed she'd simply misunderstood and Ornias could explain everything. But now he felt as desperate as a hunted fox.

He *had* to talk to Milcom. God would tell him how to make it better.

* * * * *

Jeremiel dodged back into the alley as a horse-drawn carriage loomed out of the darkness, clattering by him and away down the street. Voices shouted from the line of battered apartment buildings and he heard metal clashings from a kitchen. Somewhere, a baby wailed.

The perilously narrow cobblestone street wound down a hill overlooking the palace. He'd spent most of the day scouting the structure, checking each door and window in the likely event that in the near future he'd have to use one as an escape route. Bracing a shoulder against the stone wall, he peered at one of the points of the massive triangular structure. The palace had obviously been constructed a millennia or more ago by someone afraid of his own populace. The lowest windows hung at least thirty feet above the ground and most external doors sported crisscrossing wooden fortifications. Iron bars completely encompassed the balcony on the top floor, making it more a cage than a place for viewing Horeb's rocky wilderness. Guards seemed to be everywhere, gray suits melting into the night as they prowled the gardens or stood with hands extended over braziers of red glowing coals. Laughter and the scents of smoke and whiskey rode the wind.

He'd made a particular study of the guards, watching each go through his daily routines, noting when they changed stations, or took breaks. He'd identified the captains, listened surreptitiously to fragments of their conversations, knew which ones had streaks of brutality and which were basically decent human beings. The man lingering at the corner in front of the dim light of the brazier, tall with red hair and a full round face, seemed the most devoted to the faith of Milcom. He'd heard him discuss several times this day the intricacies of the Problem of Evil, speaking in depth about the hierarchy of demons and God's purpose in allowing them to exist. Except when the man spoke in terror of the powers of darkness, he had a kind voice, soft and unassuming. A gentle person at heart, Jeremiel guessed. Once that morning, this captain had found a guard secretly napping in the towering shadows of the palace. Instead of screaming rage and recriminations, he'd merely kicked the negligent underling's foot until he woke, then stared down in silent reproof.

Elaysin was his name.

Wiping grimy hands on his brown robe, Jeremiel moved like mist down the alley, clinging to the shadows until he reached the street which fronted the palace. Looking out across the high parapet, his gut twisted. Since his conversation with Sybil, he'd been unable to shake the terrible premonition of a trap. He felt vaguely as though a hooded figure stood at his shoulder, guiding his fateful path to destruction.

"Doesn't matter," he whispered tightly and adjusted the small pack on his back. "Rachel's in there."

Sucking in a deep breath, he wondered briefly why someone of his experience couldn't think up a more impressive plan, then he let out a bloodcurdling scream and dashed madly for the sentry in the gatehouse. Guards sprang to their feet, rushing toward the gate to look. The courtyard echoed with a babble of voices and pounding boots.

"Help me!" Jeremiel shrieked, casting terrified glances over his shoulder as he threw himself headlong on the locked portcullis, twining his fingers in the grate and shaking it ferociously. "They're coming! They're coming! Dear God, let me in before—"

"What's coming?"

"The Beliels! They've been chasing me for—"

"Demons?" one man gasped and stepped back from the gate, peering frantically into the darkness behind Jeremiel. "Like those from the plague?" He licked his lips anxiously and stared at the men around him.

"I must speak with the Mashiah," Jeremiel pleaded, sobbing. "They've been tormenting me for days and I—"

"Go on, get away from here!" a squint-eyed sergeant commanded and kicked the grate hard to throw Jeremiel off, but he clung desperately.

"Elaysin! Who's named Elaysin here?"

The captain stiffened, but said nothing as all eyes sought him.

Feverishly, Jeremiel continued, "The demons are mounting an attack against the palace. They've got in mind to capture Elaysin and use him as bait. I must tell the Mashiah. We're all in grave danger!"

A clamor of uncertain voices rose. "Blessed Milcom, maybe another plague is on the way!" "He's crazy. Don't believe a thing he says." "Demons? My Lord, how can we fight them? Our weapons are useless. We'll be crushed . . ."

Captain Elaysin pushed through the crowd, eyeing Jeremiel severely. His red hair glimmered light threads of copper in the crimson glow of the brazier. "Beliels?" he asked fearfully. "They're bad ones. They . . . they mentioned my name?"

"You're Elaysin," Jeremiel whispered unsteadily, swallowing hard. "Dear God, did you know they were after you?"

"No, I—sometimes, I've thought, but I never knew."

"Captain, please, I beg you. I must speak with the Mashiah before it's too late."

"Raise the portcullis," Elaysin ordered quickly. "We need to interrogate this man."

The grate squealed as it rose and men anxiously clutched their weapons, pointing them at the darkness beyond. Jeremiel jumped to the ground and slid beneath on his stomach, hissing, "Close it! Hurry!"

The sentry slapped the appropriate lever and the portcullis dropped to the ground with a loud clang. Iron arms seized him from all sides, dragging him to his feet and ripping his pack from his back before throwing him brutally against the stone wall. He lifted his arms over his head, letting them search him.

That logical part of his brain that could calculate battle strategy at three in the morning, determine energy expenditure ratios without even concentrating and fly through the complexities of navigation and not break out in a sweat, *wondered what in the hell he was going to do next.*

A half hour later, he slumped in a chair in a stone chamber stretching maybe ten feet by ten. Sparsely furnished with four chairs and a table, the banked glow of the hearth threw ruby reflections across the walls, revealing the stern suspicion in the eyes of two guards who stood before him.

"He's lying, El!" a young dark-haired sergeant charged, glaring at Elaysin. "Don't waste any more time on him. I say we shove him back out the gate and forget this whole thing."

"And what if he really knows about an attack the demons are planning? Eh? You want to be the one to tell the Councilman *we* threw him out?"

"How would he find out?"

"Beliels pick and choose their prey, Tony."

"This is blasted foolishness, El. If the Beliels were waiting out there, the Mashiah would have told us! Remember before the plague? He came and gave an hour long speech, telling people to bar their doors and windows."

Elaysin shuddered visibly. "Course, I remember. But maybe this time—"

"I don't believe it!"

The captain folded his arms uncomfortably, gazing sideways at his subordinate. "You're not in charge here, are you, Tony?"

"Damn it, no."

"Then maybe you should let me do the questioning and make the decisions?"

The sergeant's nostrils flared. He jerked a nod and tramped across the room to stand stiffly before the door.

Elaysin rubbed his stubbly jaw, green eyes troubled as he turned to Jeremiel. "The papers we found in your pack say your name is Jere Lansford and you're from Pitbon. What are you doing here?"

He heaved a disgusted breath. "I told you. I came to worship the Mashiah, but before I had a chance to—"

"The Beliels attacked you."

"That's right."

The captain strolled to the hearth and extended his hands to the warmth, glancing warily around as he considered the story. "What did the demons tell you?" he asked in a hushed voice, as though he feared the beasties might hear. "About me, I mean?"

"Only that they knew you were a good god-fearing man and figured they could use you to gain leverage with the Mashiah."

"Aye, that's probably true. The Mashiah holds me in pretty high regard. I've never missed one of his public worship sessions. Everybody knows my faith. They just plan to capture me?"

Jeremiel lowered his eyes, not having to feign fear. "No, I'm—I'm afraid they mentioned one other possibility."

"What? Tell me, man! I've a right to know."

"You know the demons can assume different forms? They'd planned on infiltrating the Mashiah's ranks using your—"

"Hush!" Elaysin whispered urgently, peering to where Tony stood. "If my men hear that, they're liable to balk at their own shadows when I'm around."

"I understand. That's why I *must* speak with the Mashiah. They're planning to attack soon."

"When?" Elaysin shuddered visibly, eyes darkening.

"I don't . . . I'm not sure."

"Did they speak to you in Belielon?"

Belielon? Was that the wicked creatures' ancient tongue? Jeremiel shook his head and felt suddenly uneasy about the story he'd concocted. He knew only the barest details of the Mashiah's teachings on demonology. One mistake and they might think he came from the realm of darkness himself.

"What language did they use?"

"My own home planet's. Pitbonese."

"Ah." Elaysin nodded sagaciously and wiped clammy hands on his gray pants. "The old books talk about how they can make Belielon sound like any tongue they want. They're crafty."

Some of the tension went out of Jeremiel's shoulders. So far so good. "While we sit here bantering, Captain, they could be massing their forces beyond the parapet. *I have things I can reveal only to the Mashiah! Let me see him!*"

Elaysin gave him a hard look then turned to the sergeant. "Tony, go see if Shassy can find the Councilman? See if he has a moment to spare?"

The man darted through the door. Jeremiel heard his fast steps echoing down the hall. *Shassy.* A name to remember. She had an inside track to Councilman Ornias.

Elaysin ran a hand through his damp red hair, holding Jeremiel's gaze. "Have you ever been to Horeb? Haven't I seen you before?"

"No."

"You look awfully familiar. Were you ever on Thelma in the Akiba system?"

"No." He stopped breathing. He'd waged a desperate battle on that forbidding planet a dozen years ago. The Magistrates had slashed his forces to pieces, leaving dead piled ten feet high in the streets. He'd been young and inexperienced. The memories of his errors stung something deep inside. Had this man seen him? *Did he recognize him?*

"But you're a believer in the Mashiah? I didn't know we'd sent missionaries to Pitbon."

"Missionaries are everywhere, Captain."

"I'm glad to hear it. We need to spread the good news of the coming of the true Redeemer," he whispered reverently. His eyes lit with adoration when he spoke of the Mashiah. "We're going to squash the Magistrates as soon as we get enough converts. Just wait."

He tried to look surprised. "Our missionaries didn't tell us the Mashiah planned on battling the government. Where will we get the ships and weapons?"

"I suspect Milcom will provide them when the time comes. He's always taken care of us in the past."

"I see."

"What did the Beliels look like?" Elaysin brought the subject back suddenly, eyes narrowed.

Jeremiel sat perfectly still. He hadn't the slightest idea. He let himself shiver. "I remember most their glowing eyes. In the darkness they appeared like a thousand tiny flames."

"There were that many?"

"Hundreds."

"My God, what will we do? If they attack like they did during the plague, we're liable to lose the rest of the city."

"Plague?"

"Yes, a few months ago, the Samas, those are the lesser demons, attacked under cover of darkness. They'd find people walking the streets alone and jump them, tearing huge chunks of flesh from their bodies. Toward the end, they got so bold they crashed through doors to get at the people hiding in houses. We found caches of skeletons littering the alleys of the far side of the city, not a speck of flesh left on them. They killed thousands."

"Why did they stop?"

Elaysin swallowed convulsively and steepled his fingers against his lips. "Nobody knows. From what you've been saying, maybe they were just regrouping to hit us harder. If the Beliels are involved now, there's no telling what we're up against. The old books say they command legions of lesser creatures."

Jeremiel nodded, noting that the captain's jaw muscles had tensed with fear. A sheen of sweat covered his face, gleaming in the candlelight.

"Maybe once the Mashiah knows, he can stop them."

"I doubt it," Elaysin whispered hoarsely. "He couldn't stop the last attack. Some folks—the backward and uneducated—speculated the plague was sent by Epagael to kill the new believers. But lots of the Old Believers died, too. Other people said maybe the plague was just the beginning of a battle between Epagael and Milcom."

"Horebians admit the possibility that both Milcom and Epagael exist?"

"Admit? We *know* both exist. They're locked in constant battle. Milcom fighting for us, Epagael against us. The Mashiah's teachings are very clear." His expression changed; a soft look touched his freckled face. "Have you seen him yet? I mean, even from afar?"

"The Mashiah? No."

"He's the kindest man in the world."

Jeremiel nodded sympathetically, remembering the horror stories Rachel told of senseless murder and calculated holocaust. "I'm looking forward to having an audience with him."

"He'll shock you," Elaysin said, smiling as though the subject brought him great pleasure. "You'll think he's just a young boy he's so innocent and pure, but when Milcom overtakes him, he changes completely. Almost like he becomes someone different; he gets a thousand years older in a second."

"I've heard stories like that. About how his face goes slack and he . . ."

Hurried steps sounded in the hallway outside and Jeremiel held his breath, watching the sergeant enter, leading a tall white-robed man into the room. Even at this late hour, he looked regal, reeking with authority and the power of command. His light brown hair and lime green eyes shimmered in the glow of the hearth.

"Councilman," Elaysin said apologetically, "I'm sorry to disturb you at this hour, but we've got a special case here. Papers we found say his name's Jere Lansford. He threw himself against the portcullis, sir."

"He's a crazy fool," the sergeant supplied. "Tried to talk us into believing Beliels were chasing him. But nobody's seen anything out there."

"Yet," Elaysin murmured ominously.

"Interesting," Ornias said, giving Jeremiel a curious evaluative stare. A hush descended over the room. Only the popping of the candle disturbed the quiet.

"Lansford, eh?"

"Yes, I'm from Pitbon and I . . ."

The Councilman laughed from the depths of his stomach. "Indeed? How long has it been since you were there?"

"Months. Why?"

"The Magistrates scorched it, that's why."

"When?" Jeremiel asked, feeling a chasm develop in his stomach. Where had his own forces been? Surely Rudy Kopal had received intelligence regarding the possibility? Why hadn't he been there to protect them?

"Last week."

Still smiling, the Councilman strolled closer and Jeremiel could smell the sweet scent of roses seeping from his swaying robe. The man's calm knowing expression grated on his nerves.

"You've been with the demons, I understand?"

"Yes, they came out of—"

"And you want to tell the Mashiah of an impending attack?"

"He's the only one I can reveal the details to."

"Uh-huh."

Ornias' green eyes narrowed and for a long minute, he paced quietly across the room, watching Jeremiel in the glimmer of the candle. His gaze seemed to trace every line of Baruch's face, studying, weighing. Finally, he bent forward and whispered in a voice so low Jeremiel knew the guards couldn't hear, "I've a special place arranged for you. I assure you, we'll make you comfortable until the last minute." A small gloating smile twisted his lips.

"What?"

"You know very well what I mean."

As he held the man's cold eyes, his muscles clenched tight. He sensed the councilman not only knew his identity, but had been eagerly anticipating his arrival. *I've got to get the hell out of here.*

Seeing him stiffen, the Councilman chuckled softly and waved to the guards. "Captain, you know the guest chamber on the second floor?"

Elaysin nodded. "Yes, sir. The one with no windows?"

"Yes. Take Mister *Lansford* there, please. Secure him in the shackles, and make absolutely certain the exit is barred. But under no circumstances are you to kill him. Understood?"

"Yes, sir, I wouldn't let my men—"

"Good. I want two guards posted outside the door at all

311

times and a special regiment assigned to guard that side of the palace."

"An entire regiment?" He whirled to look dubiously at Jeremiel. "For one man?"

"Don't question my orders, Captain!"

"No, I—I didn't mean to, sir." Elaysin looked confused. "I'll obey, of course, but what about the demons? Don't you think we should send troops to the parapet to guard against them?"

"In due time, Captain," Ornias smiled maliciously. "Now, hurry, take him."

I have to try now, while the forces near the gate are still ignorant of who I am.

The sergeant grabbed one of Jeremiel's arms and pulled him to his feet. With a violent wrench, he twisted free and struck out with his knee, slamming the sergeant in the groin. Whirling he pounded a fist into Elaysin's solar plexus, shoved the councilman to the floor and made a desperate run for the door.

He didn't get five steps before the guards who'd been standing unseen in the hallway rushed him. They fell on him like wolves, throwing him to the stone floor. A pulse pistol flashed from a holster and the man brought the butt down hard against his head. Dazed, Jeremiel flailed out with his fists, trying to get to his knees to crawl, but the butt landed again at the base of his skull and he sank to the floor, half-conscious.

He heard the Councilman order in a stern voice, "Drag him if you have to, *but don't hurt him severely.*" Chill hands rolled him over and locked onto his arms, tugging him from the room.

CHAPTER 29

Zadok grunted as he lowered himself to sit cross-legged and stare up at the infinitely high columns of the seventh gate that stretched to the stars. Though night had touched Arabot, Michael's radiance cast a soft golden glow across the meadow where Zadok sat.

"I know part of the puzzle, Michael," he said tensely. He'd wasted three days already, dredging his memories for the answer, heart pounding all the time. How many days did he have left to save his universe? Two hundred or two?

"Do you, Zadok?"

"Yes, I know the answer lies in the writings of Issac Luria, better known as Ari the Saint. Luria likened the 'deaths of the primordial kings' to the 'breaking of the shells of light,' from which the creation emanated, but I—"

"Ari the Saint, yes. Aktariel's very clever with name synchronicity."

Zadok grimaced. "Don't complicate this further, Michael. I'm already long overdue."

"Uh—sorry, patriarch. It would help, perhaps, if you tried a different perspective. A different metaphor. Say, for example, we conceive of each shell, *sephira*, as a cell from God's brain."

Zadok cocked his head, watching Michael's face glow brighter, piercing the blanket of darkness like a beacon. "You mean the death of the primordial kings can be likened to the bursting of bits of God's mind—the breaking of the shells?"

"Yes."

"So, if we follow the analogy, from those cells all things in my universe are created. But you said the 'dross,' dirt, of those kings relates to the *Reshimu*. How could pure cells from God's mind have any taint whatsoever?"

Michael's amber eyes narrowed and he fluttered his wings gently. A cool wind brushed Zadok. "How could they not?"

"What?"

"Oh, Zadok, must I *give* you the answer?"

"That would help, Lord."

Michael bowed his head and smiled. "You know I can't do that. But let me guide you just a little more."

Michael's golden brow furrowed as he thought and Zadok knew the result would be another cryptic response, but he'd accept any help just now. His thoughts drifted constantly to Yosef and Sarah, Kayan and Horeb, where he knew war probably raged. People might be dying while he sat here bantering with angels in the cool grasses of heaven.

"Perhaps wine is a bad analogy. Try this? When you pour milk from a bottle, what do you have left?"

"The dregs. A—"

"Given time, what happens to the dregs?"

"After a few days it's nothing but a foul-smelling residue."

"Yes, it actually changes its nature, becomes a sour shadow of the original sweet substance."

"Yes, but what does that have to do with—"

"My God, Zadok!" Michael chastised severely, pursing his golden lips in disdain. "The apocalyptic abyss yawns before you and you can't grasp the *obvious!* It might be a good thing your universe is doomed. Natural selection." He crossed his arms, leaning a shoulder heavily against one of the enormous Ionic columns.

Zadok dropped his gaze to the grass. In the archangel's glow, the blades glimmered a soft saffron color. Thoughtfully, Zadok tugged them, breaking some. Their sweet scent surrounded him like a soothing blanket. *What happened when you added fresh milk to sour? A microbial metamorphosis occurred, the fresh picking up the taint and bursting forth in foul reduplication, progressively getting worse, until the entirety had gone bad.*

"Lord," Zadok said mildly, looking up into Michael's brilliant face. "Are you trying to tell me that *Reshimu* is like the residue left by milk? That without the fullness of God, it soured and when Epagael cast the bits of himself into the cosmic Void— "

"I'll accept that as an answer, Zadok!" Michael interrupted, glancing cautiously around the starry night sky as though for eavesdroppers. "Now, get up, patriarch, and run as fast as your human legs will carry you." He thrust an arm toward the dark path beyond the columns.

Zadok pushed to his feet and rushed through the gate, hurrying to the seventh crystal palace of God, heart throbbing miserably in his bony chest.

CHAPTER 30

Yosef pushed his spectacles up higher on his nose and squinted at the dark empty hallway, watching Ari duck behind a statue. His old friend stood tall and lanky in a spear of silver light, wearing a black silk robe that highlighted his bony frame and mop of gray hair. Moonlight streamed through the windows above them, falling in glowing sheets across the marble walls. In the darkness, the colors of the rich carpets faded to mottled shades of cream and charcoal.

Yosef looked around cautiously, then whispered, "Will you let me lead!"

"You're too slow," Ari hissed back. Darting from behind his statue, he crept quickly down the hall.

Yosef pursed his lips in disgust, watching his friend's willowy shadow weave inexpertly around dark obstacles. "If you don't slow down, you're going to—"

A thud sounded, followed by a loud gasp. He saw Ari tumble to the floor. The vase that had been sitting on top of the pedestal he'd bumped, tottered and fell with a crash. "Blast it!" Ari cursed.

"Did you break that vase?"

"Forget about the vase. Worry about my brain. It smashed my skull."

"Agnes told me that's the only part of your body that stays hard. I'm not worried."

"You can't believe anything that old maid says! She doesn't know the difference between—"

"That proves my point! I don't know why I take you anywhere. You made enough noise to wake the entire floor!" Yosef waddled down the hall, grabbing Ari's arm and roughly helping him up.

"We're going to kill ourselves trying to find this locked room in the dark. Why can't we go look during the day?"

In the shaft of dove-colored light, Yosef scowled. "You bozon. The maid called that room the Councilman's private 'Chamber of Horrors.' "

"I'm not stupid," Ari defended. "I know if Ornias finds us prying our way inside, we're dead ducks."

Yosef blinked, taken aback. "Wait a minute. I didn't say we were going to pry our way inside!"

"So?"

"So? What do you mean so? I thought we'd just go down and see if we could hear anything."

"Don't be an idiot. If we're going to risk our necks going down there, we may as well find out for sure what's inside."

"But if we try to open it, somebody's sure to hear us and catch us."

"What's the matter with you?" Ari heaved a gruff breath and limped down the hall like a great awkward stork, arms outstretched for balance. Yosef followed grudgingly. Ebony statues loomed out of the darkness as they passed, their disapproving faces gleaming like ghostly sentries in the moonlight. "If that ugly councilman keeps the chamber locked all the time and forbids anyone to go near it, he's hiding something important inside."

"I'm well aware of that, you old fool. Why do you think I suggested going?"

"I thought you suggested it because you suspected *somebody* was in there? You didn't?"

Yosef stopped beside Ari at the top of a descending staircase. They both looked apprehensively down the spiraling black maw. "Sure, I did. But I figured we'd try and find out by listening and asking around before we started hunting for a crowbar."

"There's a prisoner in that room. You know it. Would you lock it if it was filled with beets?"

"Around you, yes."

Ari's eyes narrowed. "Too bad we ate the last can. I could use a few more just now." He patted his abdomen and shook his head bleakly.

"I thought you were regular?"

"Regular what?"

"Regular stupid!"

Ari ignored him. "So, we're going to go break the prisoner out, right?"

"Okay!" Yosef threw up his hands. "They'll kill us either way if they find us, so we may as well have something to show for our idiocy."

A broad smile split Ari's face, teeth gleaming in the moonlight. "Sure."

They carefully descended the staircase to the second floor and stood at the apex of the triangular structure with dark corridors branching in every direction. "Which way now?"

"The next staircase that leads down is straight ahead as I remember. On the left."

"You've been this way before?"

"Of course. You and me together! We came this way three days ago. Don't you remember? Going to the Mashiah's room?"

Ari squinted, peering down the marble hall. "Are you sure? I don't remember that big painting up there. Or that funny horse tapestry."

"Come on, I'll show you."

Yosef smacked him hard on the shoulder as he passed,

disappearing into the moonlit darkness. Suddenly, he heard Ari's steps quicken and his friend gripped him by the arm, jerking him back.

"Shhh!"

"What? What are you . . ."

Ari brutally shoved Yosef back against the wall, pushing him around a tall statue and into the dark wall niche behind. Ari crowded in beside him, trying to stuff his tall body into the cramped hollow.

"Have you lost your senses?"

"Shut up! Are you deaf? *Can't you hear them?*"

Yosef trained his ears on the darkness. The thudding of booted feet came up a staircase no more than thirty feet away, punctuated by harsh commanding whispers. Panic flooded his veins. He twisted Ari's arm. "We've got to get out of here!"

"There's no time. Be still!"

They struggled against each other, Yosef trying to push past his friend, Ari forcibly pressing him to the wall. But they stopped, falling deathly quiet, when lamplight flickered over the marble walls, glowing from the white and red swirls in the rugs and throwing huge shadows across the arching coral ceiling.

A middle-aged redheaded captain appeared on the second floor landing and held his lamp higher, calling, "Come on!" to people still climbing the stairs. "I've got to get back outside and alert our forces to watch for the Beliels."

The erratic pounding of tired footfalls, grunts and gasps, echoed from below, as though the guards carried a heavy load. Yosef exchanged a curious look with Ari, hoping the tiger shadows would cloak them from view if the men passed their way, praying they'd choose to go the other direction down the dark hall.

Yosef stiffened as the guards half-dragged their burden to the top of the stairs and roughly threw him onto the plush carpet, then staggered backward to lean panting against a pillar. Sweat chilled Yosef's throat and went clammy against his bald head. *What was Baruch doing here!*

"God damn," the young blond guard gasped. "He must weigh two hundred and twenty pounds. Carrying him up three flights is sheer agony."

"Shut up. We've got to get him to the guest room. He must be a dangerous character if the councilman wants him shackled," a dark-haired sergeant panted.

317

"He's not dangerous," the captain defended. "Just confused. He's been tormented for days by demons. What do you expect?"

"Well, he's sure as hell valuable. I've never heard Ornias order us to 'take good care' of anybody before. Usually he wants us to rough 'em up the best we can."

The blond shook the sweaty ends of his hair out of his eyes and puffed a breath. "Maybe he's from that battle cruiser that's been orbiting for a month."

Yosef tried to swallow, his throat suddenly dry. Captured by the Mashiah, a cruiser within shouting distance, Jeremiel was in terrible danger.

"A Magisterial spy? He's got a hell of a talent for subtlety. Throwing himself on the portcullis and screaming his head off."

"He wanted in bad."

"Yeah. Wonder why?"

"Because the Beliels have been after him!" the captain insisted, fists clenched.

"Yeah, sure, El."

"Maybe he's suicidal, huh?" the blond laughed and kicked his prisoner in the side. A soft groan sounded and Yosef saw Jeremiel's eyes flutter open, but he quickly shut them again. "I wouldn't offer myself up on a silver platter to the Councilman. He's got a mean streak as wide as the Shamba Desert."

The captain pursed his lips tightly. "He's waking up. Less we want to fight him again, we'd better get him to the guest room so we can get him shackled."

As the captain knelt on one side and the private on the other, Jeremiel whirled, lashing out with his powerful arm, knocking the private down the stairs. The captain lunged for him, wrestling frantically.

"Hit him, Tony! *Hit him!*"

Jeremiel brought up a knee and slammed it into the captain's back. The man folded in agony as Jeremiel shoved out from beneath him and scrambled feebly away on his stomach. As he neared Ari and Yosef, he saw them, jerking up his head and squinting, as though he didn't believe they were real. Yosef touched a finger to his lips. Frightened, Jeremiel glanced back over his shoulder and struggled to get on his feet to run in the opposite direction, but he fell to his knees, holding his head and gasping in agony.

The captain staggered to his feet, yelling, "Tony! For

God's sake! Get up! We've got to get him!" He slapped the sergeant, who seemed to wake from a daze. They both pulled their saps from their belts and fell on Jeremiel, bashing him first in the spine and then repeatedly in the head. The terrible cracks made Yosef's stomach heave. Blood soaked Jeremiel's blond hair where he lay limply against the thick rug, arms and legs sprawled.

"That's enough. He's out again." The captain wiped his mouth and straightened up. "Loma?" he called toward the stairs just as the blond private came sprinting up. "You all right?"

"Just got the wind knocked out of me," the blond answered, trudging up the stairs. "He's sure as hell a stubborn bastard, isn't he?" He glared at Jeremiel, then drew back his foot and booted him hard in the head.

"Don't hurt him anymore!" the captain shouted, shoving the blond away. "He'll be no trouble now."

Yosef flinched and felt Ari's hand close on his wrist, urging stillness and quiet. If Jeremiel survived the vicious blows undamaged, it would be a miracle.

"Come on, El, help me get him up." The sergeant knelt and lifted one of Jeremiel's shoulders, while the captain took the other.

"Loma, you take the lamp."

"I've got it," the private said, leading the way down the hall.

Hefting their prisoner to his feet, they dragged him the opposite direction from the niche behind the statue. Yosef heaved a sigh of relief, watching the men disappear around a corner. Jeremiel's black boots made a hideous sound against the rugs, a scraping like an executioner's knife being sharpened against a strap.

Yosef waited a while longer, then he shoved Ari hard, pushing him out of the niche and into the middle of the corridor.

"Come on," Ari whispered, "we have to find out where they'll be holding him."

He started down the hall at a run, but Yosef caught his collar, halting him. "What do you think you're—"

"Quit that! We don't want to get too far behind!"

"You want them to see us?" Yosef asked. "Give them another minute. Their lamp will be like a beacon. We'll be able to follow in the darkness and they'll never know."

Ari relented, wetting his lips nervously. "Okay."

They stood in the shadows, breathing hard, listening intently for several seconds before Yosef whispered, "The guards don't know who he is, but do you think—"

"Yes, Ornias must." A tremor shook Ari's voice and Yosef looked up to see wide gray eyes staring back, pained. "He ordered Baruch shackled, didn't he? He knows."

"Looks that way."

"I guess we'll have to break Jeremiel out first. Then we'll get to whoever's in the basement."

Yosef didn't answer, knowing in his heart that Ornias would undoubtedly order Jeremiel held in the most secure, impenetrable place he could find. And if he did realize that he could obtain the billion offered by the Magistrates for Jeremiel's capture, armed guards would be posted and perhaps this entire wing of the palace shut off with a battalion moved into the corridors.

Yosef's heart sank. He took a deep breath and murmured shakily, "Come on, let's follow them."

CHAPTER 31

A furious gust of wind whistled shrilly through the palace's marble halls as Adom walked. Tugging up the collar of his lavender robe, he clasped the small gift tightly in his hand, pressing it safely to his chest. He barely saw the ornate statues or beautiful rugs he passed on his way to Rachel's chamber. He'd told her he wanted to discuss Milcom, but religion was just his excuse. His mind whirled with thoughts of her, as it had for a week, not sparing even his dreams from her sweet image. The knowledge filled his stomach with butterflies, making his heart pound. What he really wanted was to be near her.

She feared him. He knew it, felt it every time they sat across from each other over dinner, and he wasn't sure what to do about that. In his entire life, he'd never known anyone to fear him. Many had disdained him when he'd roamed the streets preaching a few years ago. Many adored him now. But fear? It made his heart ache. He sensed that her face was turned as stonily against him as granite and he wanted anything but that. He wanted to comfort her, to pet her, to soothe all the pains she'd suffered as a result of his administration's cruelties.

Anger rose to sizzle in his chest. *Ornias!* When he'd again demanded to see the Councilman several days ago, Ornias had sent a messenger back saying he was simply too busy to be disturbed. However, if Adom thought it necessary, he'd squeeze in a few moments after dinner on Saturday.

"Crumbs from your table, Councilman?"

He tried to pretend supreme indifference to the treatment, but found it lurking sourly beneath the surface of his growing affection for Rachel. *Rachel, Rachel, Rachel.* She'd told him in detail about the terrifying death of her husband and, try as he might, he couldn't suppress the welling of hope that engendered. Milcom would chastise him for such insensitivity to her pain, but he couldn't help it. He'd never felt this way about another human being. It seemed to him that every moment away from her was wasted time, even when the moments dealt with critical problems of Horeb or Gamant civilization. He'd have abandoned everything for a single moment of the inner glow he experienced from her smile.

"Not everything," he hastened to correct himself. "Not Milcom or His path of goodness and righteousness." But almost anything else.

He rounded a corner and headed down the long pillared hall leading to her chamber. Sunlight filtered through the high windows overhead to land in patches of luminous gold across the pink marble arches. He could see her door at the end and felt his stomach muscles tense, lungs involuntarily sucking in a deep breath of the palace's sandalwood scented air.

He gently knocked. "Rachel? It's Adom."

From within he heard the rustle of fabric and, in a few moments, her door opened. He smiled, touched by her beauty. She was dressed in a saffron colored gown which drew attention to her tiny waist and the curve of her hips, and her raven hair draped in thick waves to her waist. The *Mea Shearim* lay glowing brilliantly between the breasts swelling over the low-cut neckline. His throat tightened.

"I'm sorry I'm late. A servant caught me just before—"

"You're not late, Adom," she corrected, opening the door wider. "Please, come in."

"I brought you this," he said nervously, handing her the gift. "I hope you like it."

"Adom, you mustn't bring me so many gifts. They make me feel— "

"But it makes me happy to see your eyes sparkle. Open it."

Rachel sighed resignedly and ran her hands over the carved box before lifting the lid. Her lips parted slightly as she took the jewel-encrusted hair comb from its blue velvet bed. "It's beautiful, Adom. Are those Lytalion sapphires?"

He nodded. The robin's-egg color was unique, priceless. "I'd hoped it would match the *Mea*, but I see it's a little darker."

"It'll complement the *Mea*. See?" Lifting one side of her raven waves, she secured the wealth over her ear with the comb. The gems glimmered brilliantly.

He smiled approvingly and took a step into her chamber, noting appreciatively that his servants had done a very good job preparing it. The huge brass bed against the far wall sat in a shaft of brilliant yellow streaming through the windows. The intricately woven lace bedspread highlighted the emerald tones of the plush carpet. The table and chairs before the stone hearth boasted a crystal decanter of brandy and a vase of fresh flowers. They were grown, he knew, under artificial lights in the moist caverns beneath the palace.

"How—how are you?" he stammered awkwardly. "Is everything all right? Are the servants tending your needs adequately? I want everything to be—"

"The servants are perfect, Adom. I feel like a princess."

"That's just how I want you to feel."

She dropped her gaze uneasily and started across the room for the table, as though she were anxious to be away from him. A twinge of hurt touched him.

"Can I get you a glass of brandy?"

"Yes," he answered softly, "I'd like that."

He followed her and gracefully dropped into one of the chairs, watching her pour the crystal goblets full. She handed him one and as his fingers warmly brushed hers, their gazes caught and held. Warmth flushed him. He lowered his eyes, fearing he'd frighten her if she grasped even a hint of the emotions that roiled tumultuously inside him.

"Have you been getting enough sleep? I told the kitchen maids not to wake you for breakfast, but to wait until you rang. I hope they've obeyed."

"I haven't had breakfast before ten this entire week, Adom. I guess I'm catching up for the past few months."

Her brow furrowed. "Though God alone knows how I can sleep here at all."

As she sat down, he studied her tense posture. An overwhelming urge to touch her, to comfort her, tormented him. He folded his arms across his chest, tucking his fingers beneath his flowing lavender sleeves. "Don't you want to feel safe?"

"It's not a question of want, it's one of training. I haven't been safe on Horeb in three years. Now, every time I feel myself relaxing, a part of me deep inside screams."

He fumbled with his glass. "I'm so sorry. I'd hoped—"

"When is Ornias supposed to meet you?"

"Tomorrow. Unless something more important comes up."

"What could be more important than the *brutal* murders of Horeb's citizens?"

The hostility in her voice made him go rigid. "Nothing. I agree with you. I just don't know how to force him to attend a meeting."

"You're the ruler of Horeb. Ornias has no right to treat you this way. You mustn't let him."

"I'm not very good at commanding people to do things." The admission stung. Leaders were supposed to be great commanders, but he knew he wasn't and never would be. He wanted to be easy and gentle with everyone. That was what gave him pleasure.

"Because you're a kind man, Adom," Rachel whispered, sitting back in her chair. Lustrous raven waves fell over her saffron robe. "But Ornias takes advantage of you because of it. You have to stand up to him."

"Like you said earlier, about training? It's hard to change old patterns. He's always taken care of the business end of the movement. And, so long as I don't interfere, things seem to go smoothly. But when I . . . I do, they don't." He clumsily sipped his brandy, a trickle spilling down his chin. Wiping it quickly on his sleeve, he cringed, knowing she'd noticed. Could he never do anything right?

"Adom," she said through a tense exhalation. "Ornias enjoys using you as a front for his cruelty. It's your position as Mashiah that gives him his power."

"I know."

"You *must* take action quickly, before he kills a thousand more."

"I will, Rachel. On Saturday when he comes to—"

"Can I be there?"

He pulled in a breath, straightening in his chair. Her eyes gleamed like dark jewels. Ornias wouldn't want her present, he knew that without asking. For three years, the Councilman had prohibited everyone else from participating in their strategy sessions.

"I can help you, Adom. Let me be there."

"But, Rachel, that will anger him and I hate to do that."

"You're going to throw a wrench into his carefully planned terrorist campaign. He'll be angry regardless." She reached across the table to take his hand. The feel of her flesh against his soothed him, but he gazed at her timidly, worried that she, too, would reprimand him as Ornias did so often. "I promise not to say anything unless you need my support. I *trust* you to stop him from murdering your people."

"Do you? Or are you just saying that?"

"I trust you, Adom. Though, Lord knows, every instinct in my soul cries out against it."

"I—I trust you, too, Rachel."

Her eyes softened and she lightly squeezed his hand. "Then you'll let me come to the meeting?"

"Yes, I'll let you come, Rachel. I just won't tell him in advance. I'll let him find out when he arrives at the council chambers."

She nodded and heaved a relieved sigh. They sat in silence a few moments, sipping their brandy, then he asked in a sudden desire to change the subject to one more enjoyable, "Did you have a chance to read the books on Milcom I brought?"

A tiny upright line formed between her brows. "Yes, I found them very interesting."

"I'd hoped you would. God wants you to thoroughly comprehend His teaching. We don't—I . . . I don't—force conversions. *Not ever.* Milcom wants only those who willingly give themselves to Him."

Rachel glanced at him over the rim of her glass. "I'm curious about Milcom's teachings on the Problem of Evil. The notion that Epagael is a wicked deity fascinates me."

"Yes, once you've suffered severely, the truth seems obvious, doesn't it?"

"Oh, I didn't say it was obvious, just intriguing."

"You'll see," he answered patiently, "once you understand better. It's a hard thing to accept at first, especially after all your life you've been taught that Epagael loves and watches over you."

324

"It is hard to accept. Especially the concept of creation *ex nihilo*, from nothing, and how evil begins there. Can you tell me more about it?"

Adom smiled, joy rising inside him. *She wanted to know!* "Milcom says that in the beginning Epagael was all that existed. In order to create the universe, he had to withdraw Himself, empty out a part of his presence."

"He contracted himself? All right. And Milcom?"

"Milcom was created to serve as Epagael's voice in a universe He could not enter." Adom lifted a hand, waving it expressively. "Epagael could not enter the Void because if He had it would have ceased to exist, melted into Oneness again."

"The dichotomy of God and not-God would have vanished. I understand. So the Creation is absent Epagael, but if that's so, of what are we and all 'this' created?"

He smiled, applauding softly. He'd never had anyone to seriously discuss God's teachings with. Ornias refused and he saw so few other people. Rachel's interest excited him. "A good question. And one Milcom explains in this way: We know that consciousness has an epiphenomenal basis, that is, it's spawned by the physicochemical processes of the brain, correct?"

"You don't believe in a soul?"

He shook his head politely. "No. The concept of a soul is a quaint fiction. Everything in our universe has a physicochemical basis." He shrugged. "Though the energy that composes what we are certainly continues. So, if you want to call that a soul, you can, I suppose."

"No. I don't and I don't think very many other Old Believers would." She leaned back, lifting both brows. "I'm surprised you weren't burned at the stake years ago.'"

"Oh, Milcom protects me."

"I see. And what does epiphenomenalism have to do with Creation?"

"Milcom uses the following example: If you took a minute clump of cells from your brain, you would continue to function unimpaired. Your consciousness would remain intact. But if the severed cells were prodded into mitosis, who's to say the growing tissue mass wouldn't develop a consciousness of its own?'"

"Milcom teaches that Epagael cut out a part of His brain and threw it into the Void to form the foundation of the universe?"

"That's the analogy he uses, but actually the cells were

vessels, shells, filled with light. When they broke, the light spilled forth."

"And developed a consciousness of its own?"

"Yes. Epagael hadn't the slightest idea that would happen. It fascinated Him, He—"

"I can understand that. It's vaguely analogous to bringing up a child. You know they're part of you, but they develop so very differently."

Adom smiled in embarrassment. "I wouldn't know. Is chaos the key factor in childhood development?"

"Unquestionably."

"Well, then it is analogous. Because God loves the chaotic patterns spun by universal consciousness."

Rachel braced an elbow on the table and leaned forward, studying him intently. Her breasts pressed tighter against her saffron robe. He tried not to notice, holding her gaze, drowning in the warmth he felt there.

"It's the chaos that fascinates God?"

"Oh, yes. In fact, the more the better, so far as He's concerned. He destroyed the first two universes for lack of it."

She laughed softly, frowning. "Like the ancient myths say? Only the third survived his judgment?"

"They aren't myths. The third survived only because the other angels in heaven were too cowardly to side with Milcom that it, too, should be destroyed."

"So we exist because Milcom failed to convince God that more chaos was bad?"

"Exactly."

She grunted disbelievingly and Adom felt a twinge of pain. "Chaos is related to evil, I take it?"

He tried harder to be clear and persuasive. "Yes, don't you see? The very nature of the universe is to struggle chaotically against itself. We experience the struggle as suffering."

Rachel toyed with her brandy glass and he studied her contemplative features. Her heart-shaped face and straight nose could not have been more perfect if Milcom himself had designed them with Adom's likes and dislikes in mind.

"But there's a logical flaw, Adom."

He frowned. Was there? Milcom had never mentioned one. "Is there?"

"Yes. What catalyst set the cells of Epagael's brain to dividing in the first place? What caused the shells of light to break?"

326

He grabbed a lock of his blond hair and tugged at it aimlessly. "I remember once Milcom spoke sarcastically about something called the *Reshimu* kicking off creation, but I never asked what it was."

"Hmm. Well, there's something else bothering me. If Epagael can't enter the universe, how can He know we suffer? If he doesn't know, how can He be evil?"

"Oh, He knows. Milcom has told him over and over."

"Epagael knows and allows the suffering? Is He powerless to stop it?"

"He's not powerless. He just has to kill the consciousness in this universe that spawns chaos."

She shivered visibly. "How would he do that?"

"I don't know. Milcom has never discussed it with me."

"Well, for the sake of argument, let's say Epagael could 'kill' chaos and stop our suffering. Why doesn't He?"

Adom lifted his glass, sipping his brandy, feeling it warm his stomach. "Milcom says it entertains Him."

"That's cruel."

"That's why Milcom hates Him so."

"Can *we* ever end the suffering, by ourselves, I mean?"

"Milcom teaches that the purpose of existence is to return the universe to Epagael. Only then will suffering end."

Striped bandit shadows crept across her face, accenting her sparkling eyes. Behind her, through the window, he saw the rooftops had been dyed crimson by the deepening fires of Horeb's midday sun. Soft voices climbed up to him on the warm wind, people moving about in the streets below.

"Adom, that sounds suspiciously like Milcom means we need to destroy the universe."

"That's right."

She laughed softly. "Surely, you're joking. There's a great deal of beauty and joy in the universe, too. How could he want to—"

"Beauty exists only because there's ugliness. Goodness exists only because there's evil. Dichotomy is the source of everything. God and not-God. Tell me? Which is more prevalent in life, happiness or suffering?"

She clenched her goblet so tightly the brandy washed the sides of the glass. "Suffering."

An ache touched his breast. He knew where her thoughts must be lingering. "Yes. The produce cart was upset long, long ago. There hasn't been a balance between good and evil for billions of years. And for every moment the Creation continues to exist, evil grows. Chaos spreads through the body of the universe like a malignancy."

She smiled vaguely. "Entropy?"

"You can call it that if you like."

"But won't the natural culmination of entropy end the suffering?"

"No," he breathed tiredly. It always hurt him to think about this part of Milcom's teachings. "The ultimate dichotomy will still exist: Epagael and the Void. He'll be able to use the emptiness to regenerate suffering whenever it pleases Him. We have to make Him *feel* the misery of the universe."

"And we do that by returning it to Him?"

"Yes."

She drained her brandy glass dry. "And just how do we slap Epagael in the face with our universe?"

Adom lifted his shoulders sheepishly. "Milcom's never told me precisely, except that it has to do with the naked singularity. He says I'm not far enough along to understand."

She contemplatively rose from her chair and strolled to the window. Standing in the tawny afternoon light, her dark wavy hair shimmered like strands of silk.

He got up, shoving his hands deep in his pockets, before uncomfortably going to stand beside her. Did she believe the teachings? Butterflies attacked his stomach. Glancing at her, he saw her face darken. She stared at a line of children moving wearily through the windblown streets.

"They're going to the potato fields," Adom whispered.

"I know. I've seen them working until midnight every night this week." A terrible bitterness filled her eyes.

"I can't help it, Rachel. We're in a famine. Everyone has to work."

"At three lirot a month? When they're paying the adults ten?"

"The children don't have the same strength or endurance. They produce less."

Her eyes hardened. "Then maybe it would be better for all of us if you released half your kitchen staff and guards and sent them to the fields to replace the children. They could do three times the work. The harvest would be so much greater."

Watching a woman lead a donkey through the streets, he considered the idea. The woman tugged her tattered skirts up and knotted them around her waist, revealing deeply tanned legs. She looked gaunt and tired. The rickety cart behind the animal lay empty to the harsh sun. Had she found no food at the market this day? But Ornias had said they'd closed the distribution center because the economy was back on its feet—the fields producing again. Worry twined through him. He breathed tightly, "I'll reassign my staff immediately."

From below, he heard the gruff voice of a water-seller piercing the quiet, but he closed his ears to it, letting himself sink into the dark depths of her eyes.

"And if Ornias won't let you?"

He grimaced, clenching his fists and turning away from the window to look at the thick emerald carpet. Odd, he'd never felt a prisoner until her coming. But now he felt as though the pink marble walls weighed on his chest, suffocating him. "I'll do it anyway."

"Be careful, Adom. Ornias has less scruples than a Giclasian. I wouldn't put it past him to murder you if you got too out of hand and then tell the people you were alive and in deep consultation with Milcom."

"Oh, I don't think he'd . . ."

They both jumped as an urgent rapping came at Rachel's door. Exchanging a confused look, she asked, "Are you expecting someone?"

"No, though the servants sometimes chase me down when I'm needed." He ran gracefully to the door and opened it. Ari and Yosef stood outside, wrinkled faces strained. "What's wrong?"

"Oh, nothing major, Mashiah," Yosef soothed. The little man's round belly protruded through his white robe as though he were pregnant. "It's just that Ari and I wanted to go to the rare books section of the library to read more of Milcom's teachings, but we found the room is locked and guarded. We—"

"Yes, we had one stolen once," Adom acknowledged reluctantly. He thought every bookshelf should be open to the entire populace of Horeb, but Ornias had convinced him otherwise, reprimanding, "Dear God, Adom! Don't you want to have a single volume left for yourself?"

"We're sorry to disturb you, Mashiah, but could you sign this authorization form?" Yosef extended the crystal sheet and a laser pen.

Adom took it, his glance tugged to Ari's face. The tall old man leered appreciatively at Rachel. In that instant, Adom remembered Milcom's words about making sure the two liked each other. He quickly signed the sheet without so much as reading the first word, thrust it back into Yosef's hand and reached out, forcefully dragging Funk into the bedchamber. The elder looked a little surprised, but pleased.

"Rachel?" Adom called. "I want you to meet Ari Funk. He's one of my personal aides. Yosef Calas is the other. If you ever need anything, you can call on them and they'll see it gets done."

She formed her hands into the sacred triangle. "Mister Funk, Mister Calas, it's a pleasure to meet you."

Ari wiped sweaty palms on his gray robe and gave her a broad flashing smile, almost dashing, Adom thought with mild amusement. "You look like my type," Ari crooned. "Want to run away with me?"

"I beg your pardon?"

"Sure. I'm all the man you'll ever need. I can do anything you want."

Rachel frowned. "Uh-huh. That's interesting."

"Oh, I—I'm sure Ari meant that—pleasantly," Adom intervened, feeling the tension rise.

Rachel looked the old man up and down. "Besides, you're too skinny and I prefer blondes." She winked at Adom. Startled, he shifted uncomfortably, embarrassment and gladness swelling in his chest. Did she mean it, or was she just embellishing her banter with Funk?

"He's too shy," Ari said. "You need somebody bold and brash. Like me."

"Thanks anyway."

"You'll regret it. I'm in big demand around here."

"It's your subtle charm, I'm sure."

Adom laughed and turned to grin at Yosef to see if he'd enjoyed the show, too. The bespectacled elder looked irritated, squinting at Funk disapprovingly.

"Ari!" Yosef hissed. "Quit bothering these people. We have *reading* to do."

Funk scowled in confusion, then, as if a flame of memory flickered to life, he blurted, "Oh, I'd forgotten!"

"You'd forgotten," Yosef accused indignantly. "You idiot. Come on!"

Adom patted Ari gently on the back as he passed. "Let me know if you have any more problems with the library guard?"

"We will, Mashiah," Yosef assured, bowing slightly. When Ari got within reach, he gripped his friend's sleeve and jerked him out the door. "Good day to both of you."

"Good day, Yosef."

The pudgy elder closed the door gently and Adom heard them burst into argument, snarling at each other as they walked away down the hall. He smiled in delight.

"Curious, aren't they?" he asked, turning to Rachel.

"Funk is an old lech. Where did you find him? I've never seen him on Horeb."

"They're both from Tikkun. They came to worship Milcom. You didn't . . . didn't like Ari?"

"He might be tolerable in small doses."

"He's really a wonderful man. You need to get to know him better. Feel free to call on him whenever you need."

"Adom . . ." A haunted look came into her eyes. She squared her shoulders. "Yosef's last name is Calas?"

"Yes, he's Zadok's brother, if that's what you're thinking."

Her beautiful face slackened and she looked piercingly at the door where the pudgy little man had vanished. "You mean I just met the leader of Gamant civilization?"

Adom blinked. He'd never thought about it, but, of course, that would be true, if Yosef had accepted the authority. Obviously, he hadn't, since he'd freely delivered himself to Milcom. "Legally, I suppose so. But he's converted to the religion of Milcom, prostrating before me."

Rachel looked up at him speculatively. "Does that mean he's yielded to you? That *you're* the new leader?"

He shrugged uneasily, unsure how to answer the dark question. He didn't want to be, but maybe he was. If so, he'd simply yield to someone else. But no, *he couldn't!* Milcom had spoken of how he *needed* to rise in the Gamant hierarchy of leadership to bring salvation to the universe.

He felt himself pale and stammered, "I—I guess so."

CHAPTER 32

A small sound woke Jeremiel, someone setting a cup on a stone table. He kept his eyes closed, listening to learn as much as he could before revealing himself. His head throbbed so violently he felt sick. Though he knew his arms were chained over his head, he couldn't feel them; they felt like dead meat. How long had he hung here unconscious? Hours? Days? Had his capture endangered Rachel or the Desert Fathers?

Someone shuffled papers, murmuring, "The Councilman said to inform him of the prisoner's condition at half past the hour. Run and tell him the man's still out, Loma."

"Sure, El. You want me to bring you another cup of taza when I come back?"

"Bring a whole pot. I'll stoke up the fireplace and we'll set it in the coals."

The patter of footsteps echoed from the walls and a door opened. The frigid gush of air made Jeremiel shiver involuntarily.

"Whoa up, Loma. I think he's coming around. Tell the Councilman maybe he'd better come down."

"He won't like it. He just took Shassy into his bedchamber."

"I don't care! He said to tell him, so tell him!"

Jeremiel opened his eyes to see a man exit through the door. Captain Elaysin turned and frowned at him. Sweat stained his gray suit in dark patches beneath his arms. His red hair shimmered in the light from the single candle on the table near the fireplace. Only a few red coals still glowed.

"You're awake, are you?"

"As awake as could be expected after the beating you gave me." He struggled to get his weak legs under him, relieving some of the strain from his arms. The chains around his wrists and ankles tinkled. Groggily, he surveyed the room. Spreading about forty by twenty feet, it had none of the opulence of the marble hall he remembered. Huge gray stones formed the high walls, the floor bare except for a tiny rug beneath the table and chairs where Elaysin had been having taza. A plank bed with a straw mattress was shoved against the far wall. He stood chained to a pillar in the center of the room.

" 'Bout time you came around. The Councilman's been hot to talk to you. He chewed my head off the last time I told him you still weren't awake." Going to the fireplace, he sprinkled kindling over the coals and threw a log in on top. Blowing gently, he set the fire jumping to life, flames licking up around the tinder.

"How long have I been out?"

"Two godforsaken days. We feared for awhile we'd hit you too hard."

"Given my headache, I'd say you did."

332

"Well, you didn't give us any choice, trying to escape like that. What else could we do? Who are you that you'd fear capture so much?"

Jeremiel tightened his legs muscles, keeping himself standing despite the fatigue and the wretched nausea that made him want to vomit. Voices chattered softly in the hall, boots clacking on bare stone. The door to his chamber opened and the Councilman stepped in. A cruel glow lit his tanned face.

"Elaysin," he commanded. "Get out."

"Aye, sir. I'll wait in the hall." The captain quickly exited, closing the door behind him.

In the warming air, Jeremiel could smell the flowery stench of the politician's perfume as Ornias leaned against the pillar opposite him. Dressed in a frost colored robe, he seemed a ghost from the mists.

"Didn't mean to disturb your foreplay with Shassy," Jeremiel murmured, trying to wiggle his nerveless fingers.

The lines of sleeplessness showed clearly as the man's face tensed. He studied Jeremiel by the ruddy glare of the fire, then a bare smile touched his lips. "She's there whenever I call. I might even order her to service you if you cooperate to my liking."

"Thanks, but I don't take seconds."

"Don't be so cocky, Baruch! Make me too angry and I might throw you to Tahn before it's most advantageous."

A bitter cold stirred his soul. So Rathanial had been right. Another piece of the puzzle fell into place. "Yes, I heard you were prostrating before him, selling out Gamant civilization."

"I prostrate before no one!" Ornias insisted angrily. His chill green eyes narrowed. "Bargaining is different than—"

"Uh-huh, but tell me, doesn't it bother your conscience to know that selling me to the Magistrates will result in the deaths of millions?"

"Not at all, since I won't be one of them."

"Spreading Milcom's religion means that much to you?"

Ornias laughed loudly, throwing his head back. Firelight flickered over his light brown hair and beard. "Who told you something so foolish? I could care less about religion. Adom and his quaint delusions have simply been a means to an end."

"Ah, I see. And what have the Magistrates promised you? Certainly the billion for my reward, but you don't look dull-witted enough to have stopped at that. Let's see, what else could they give a power-monger that would make it worth his while? Rank? No, you don't look like the military type. A planet of your own? A civilization to enslave?"

Ornias chuckled smugly. "Not exactly, but something like that. I assure you, if you live, you'll know my name. As will everyone in the galaxy."

He forced himself to smile, though he felt brittle and vulnerable. "So what's stopping you? Why don't you send a dattran to Tahn and get this over with?"

"There are too many obstacles left to be taken care of. I insist on 'neatness,' you see. Besides, you arrived long before I expected."

Jeremiel shook his head, the fatigue weighing him down, sapping what little strength he had left. *So, I left too abruptly for your spy to get the information out. There are limits to your network in the caves.* "Tahn doesn't know I'm here?"

"Not yet. But don't worry, your meeting is near at hand. I understand you know each other?"

"No."

"Indeed? He spoke of you like a brother."

Jeremiel quietly responded, "Well, you'd know better than I. We haven't been on speaking terms for a while."

Ornias smiled callously as he ambled over to the fire, a manicured hand caressing his bearded chin. His head jerked up as a disturbance sounded in the hall, a woman cursing, "I have the right to see him, damn you!"

Elaysin's voice apologetically explained, "The Councilman said no one was allowed inside, ma'am. I can't be going against—"

"Get out of my way!"

Ornias' face tensed, a brow lifting threateningly. He started for the door as it thrust open, slamming back against the wall with a dull thud. Jeremiel gazed at a beautiful black woman silhouetted against a background of frightened male faces. Her amber satin robe flattered every curve of her tall body, highlighting her mahogany skin.

Elaysin pushed up behind her, shouting, "I told her, Councilman, but she wouldn't listen."

"It's all right, Captain. Return to your duties." Then to the woman he cooed with poorly concealed irritation, "Shassy, dear, please shut the door."

Her dark eyes stayed glued to Jeremiel as she pushed it closed behind her. He felt like a side of meat in a marketplace. "Is it him?" she asked breathlessly, searching Ornias' face. *"Is it?"*

"Of course, darling, but I thought I asked you to stay in my chamber?"

"My life in exchange for his . . . that's what you said. Let me go now! Ornias, please," she pleaded, wringing her hands as she hurried across the room. In the firelight, Jeremiel could see her shaking. "You have what you want, let me—"

"Not quite yet, Shassy. But soon, I promise."

The marmalade light of the flames glittered against the fabric of her robe, outlining her breasts as she drew a deep, shuddering breath, struggling between rage and tears. "How soon? I can't go on like this. You know how *cooperative* I've been."

"Yes," Ornias chuckled, reaching up to stroke her smooth cheek. "You've been very cooperative. And I'll release you just as I said I would, but you must wait a few more days."

She said nothing for a time, standing with fists clenched. Reflected firelight danced in her golden earrings as she turned to stare hollowly at the cold stone floor. Then she glanced regretfully at Jeremiel, and looked back to Ornias, desperation haunting her dark eyes. "A few days. That's all?"

"Yes, dear. That's all."

"On your word of honor?" Her voice broke suddenly, cracking like a branch under the weight of heavy snow. She lifted a hand to cover her trembling lips. "As if you had any."

"Don't be insulting, Shassy. I've given you the truth."

Jeremiel pushed up again, straining against the chains to relieve some of the unbearable pain in his shoulders. At the jingling of his shackles, Shassy turned, staring. He met her frightened gaze with equanimity, feeling nothing, no hatred, no anger—only a sublime sense of curiosity. Obviously her situation was little better than his, a prisoner for a price. But who bargained for her? Who in the caves of the *chaste* Desert Fathers waited for her return?

"All right," she whispered. She ran from the room, flinging the door wide and dashing into the hall. The guards peered into the chamber anxiously. Elaysin stepped forward and started to gently pull the door closed again, but the Councilman's curt voice stopped him.

"Captain, please come in and unlock our guest's chains. I'm sure he'd appreciate a night's rest in a prone position."

"Yes, sir." Elaysin hurried in, his lips pressed tightly together. Fumbling with the jingling key ring at his waist, he selected one and lifted it to Jeremiel's wrists. "There."

Jeremiel felt dead weight slap against his sides and he dropped to his knees. Elaysin knelt beside him to unlock his ankles, softly saying, "Don't worry. You'll be fine in an hour or so. It'll hurt like Hob, but you'll pull through."

From the corner of his eyes, Jeremiel saw Ornias' white teeth gleam briefly before he strode for the door.

"Councilman?" he called, pain clear in his voice. Ornias stopped, tilting his head inquiringly. "Just one thing before you go. I can't hurt you now. I think you owe it to me to tell me who your contact is in the caves."

"You mean, who sold you out?"

He nodded haggardly. They held each other's eyes for a long minute, Ornias' face dark and impassive. Striding for the door again, the councilman cast over his shoulder, "I owe you nothing, Baruch."

Elaysin quickly followed Ornias out and Jeremiel heard the door slam and a bar drop across it outside. Falling sideways, he rolled to his back, gasping at the agony tormenting his shoulders and ankles. Unable to feel or move his arms, he did his best to ensure they stretched at the proper angles at his sides.

"Rudy . . ." he moaned faintly, his friend's image filling his mind. "Damn it, Rudy. You were right again."

He stared at the flickers of the fire dancing over the stone ceiling, listening to his heart throb.

* * * * *

The long cigar-shaped cavern smelled dry and sweet with the scent of dust. But underlying it, the metallic tang of freshly cleaned weapons caught in Harper's throat. He swallowed hard and gazed absently at the spiderwebs that covered the ceiling; they glistened in the dim candlelight.

"I'm sorry," he said. "I'd have given you more notice if I could have."

"Oh, hell, Harper," Janowitz, a short stocky blond responded. He sighted down his rifle at the far wall, fingering the trigger. "We knew the score decades ago. We've always been ready."

Harper warmly clapped the man on the shoulder. "I knew you would be. Abba picked the best."

Walking down the line of assembled men, he stared each one in the eyes, trying to project a confidence he didn't feel. Their anxious faces gleamed with a sheen of sweat. When they'd finally dressed in the gray uniforms of the Mashiah's personal guards, he'd start praying. There weren't very many of them, but, by God, they were better trained than anyone else on Horeb. If they could blend in with the palace staff for fifteen minutes, they'd make a hell of a close-quarters assault team.

When he finished his inspection, he heaved a tense sigh. "Any questions?"

"Just one," Janowitz said. "When are we going to hit 'em?"

"I don't know yet. I'm waiting for one more signal from Rathanial. Be prepared to go at any time."

Men nodded and fell out of line, drifting to the tables to collect small packs and stuff as many extra magazines into their pockets as they could hide.

* * * * *

Dreams of Shadrach tormented Rachel's sleep.

She walked anxiously through the kitchen of their old house, winding toward their bedroom, touching the still warm timbers that lay like charred human limbs across the floor. All her dishes had been smashed and strewn over half the house; she could see colored fragments of the floral pattern beneath the rubble.

"Shadrach?" she shouted into the stillness, fear welling to flutter in her stomach. Something deep in her soul told her he'd been hurt, but she couldn't remember where or how. Her heart ached with the need to find him. Had he been here when they burned the house?

She clawed at a web of smoking boards that blocked entry to their bedroom. "I—I have to get inside."

An urgency built in her chest, demanding, violent. She pounded fists into the web, loosening a board; it groaned miserably as she pried it out of the way and edged through into the darkness. The stench of smoke and melted petrolon stung her nose.

"Shadrach?"

Her foot struck a fallen chunk of wall. A dull thud rang out. Feeling her way, she stepped around the obstruction and gingerly worked deeper into the room and the black curtain that draped the silence.

A soft rasping came from the far corner and Rachel's heart stopped, the sound echoing like an earthquake in her soul. It was him, she knew it! The closet? *Had he hidden in the closet?*

"*Shadrach?*" she screamed, thrusting things out of her path as she stumbled forward. "Answer me!"

A shaft of searing light penetrated a rent in the roof like a dagger, stabbing the broken closet. She raced forward, gasping as she worked to jerk the crushed door open. Pounding it with her shoulder, she shouted, "Are you in there, Shadrach? *Where are you?*"

When the door finally dislodged, tears streaked her face. She peered inside, eyes drawn magnetically to the place the finger of light pointed. Her heart went cold and dead in her chest.

Her husband hung in shackles against the wall, his once muscular body emaciated from starvation. Lifeless eyes stared back, covered with flecks of ash.

She jerked awake, panting, to stare blindly at the opulence of the Mashiah's palace. The emerald tones of her plush carpet gleamed in the subdued light cast by the still glowing hearth.

"Oh, Shadrach," she choked out. Rolling to her side, she buried her face in her pillow.

A chill breeze crept through her open window, silver moonlight falling in a long rectangle across her tousled bed. She clumsily grasped for her blanket and pulled it up to her throat. Curling into a fetal ball, she unknowingly snuggled her forehead against the warm *Mea*, barely perceiving the brilliant cerulean glow that built to fill her entire room. "Epagael," she murmured in soft agony to the god she no longer believed in. "Why is this happening to me?"

In a sudden rush, a new dream washed over her. She found herself in a long tunnel; dark mists wavered as though alive. She shook her head incredulously, feeling as though she stood in the eye of Time's hurricane. Nothing but a whirl of blackness supported her feet. "What is this place?"

A soothing whisper echoed from the all around. "You asked 'why?' Come to me. Let me tell you."

Adrenaline flushed hotly through her veins. She stepped backward. *God?* She didn't voice the question, but an answer came regardless.

"Yes. Come?"

What sort of dream is this that reawakens the old and powerful emotions I used to feel for Epagael? Images of the square flooded her mind and she railed, "I don't want to talk to you! You're a monster. You torture us with suffering!" Sobs rose in her throat and her shoulders heaved. She lifted a fist to shake it . . .

And woke in the palace again, the *Mea* glowing so brilliantly it nearly blinded her.

CHAPTER 33

"Sybil!" Avel's harsh voice stabbed through her sleep.

She shoved her blankets off and crawled frantically toward him before asking breathlessly, "What?"

He jerked her up by one arm, throwing warm clothes at her. "Get dressed. Quickly!"

She flew out of her nightgown and tugged the sweater over her head, pulling on her pants and diving to retrieve her shoes. "What's the matter, Avel? Are we attacking the Mashiah?"

"Don't ask questions now, Sybil."

Before she'd finished tying her left shoe, he dragged her off the bed and out of her room, nearly running down the diamond-shaped tunnel. The candle he carried cast glimmering golden designs across the walls. She watched them in frightened silence. If it wasn't the attack, what could be happening that would scare Avel so much?

The farther they walked the more tightly he clutched her hand until finally it ached miserably. She squirmed, trying to tear it free. Didn't he know his grip strangled her fingers?

"Avel, where are we going?"

"To a safe place."

She clamped her jaw tight, watching three monks in brown robes approach, heading toward the surface. Harper nodded tersely to them, his halo of black hair shining in their candles as they passed.

She looked up when they were alone again, seeing the

tight lines that etched the mahogany skin around his mouth. "Why? Why, Avel? Wasn't I safe in the upper caves?"

"Not any more. Things aren't going the way we'd thought. The Mashiah has forced us to change our plans."

"Is my mom all right?" she blurted, fear stabbing her. "Has the Mashiah hurt her? Tell me!"

"Hush!"

She swallowed her next words. Avel's dark eyes narrowed. He tugged her around a corner and stepped out so fast, she had to run to keep from stumbling. The new corridor seemed very old, the sandstone a blood red. Dust grew in velvet thick veils along the walls and floor, as though all the tramping feet in the upper caves, sent it down here where no one ever stirred it. Sybil coughed at the cloud that sprang from their headlong rush.

"Avel?" she pleaded quietly. "Is my mom—"

"She's fine, Sybil." Looking around surreptitiously, he whispered, barely loud enough for her to hear, "Don't worry. I'm taking you to a place I've had prepared for years. It's filled with food and water and there's even some books to read. You'll be safe."

Sybil shuddered. *You, not WE!* "But you'll be there, too, won't you?"

"Not for a while. I have business to take care of that's very dangerous. I can't risk having you hurt while I'm organizing— "

"But, Avel, I don't want to be alone. Don't leave me alone! You said you'd take care of me just like I was your own little girl!"

Brushing damp curls from her sweating forehead, she saw his lips tighten. "I am, Sybil. It just won't seem like it for a time."

Sybil stared wide-eyed at the next corridor, her ragged breathing sharp in her ears. She wanted to believe him, but couldn't. The way he hurtingly hauled her down the long winding halls terrified her. Her heart longed agonizingly for her mother. Tears threatened to ooze from her eyes. She blinked them away, forcing herself to be brave.

"What's the Mashiah done, Avel?"

"He's mounting his forces secretly, in the caves just below the city."

"So you're going to attack him sooner than you'd planned?"

He took a deep breath, stopping before a descending staircase hacked into the stone. Cold air boiled up from the blackness. "I don't know, Sybil. We may not attack at all. I have to try and fix things."

"How would we *not* attack? *My mommy's waiting for you to come rescue her! She can't blow up the Mashiah's palace until you—*"

"I know, Sybil. I'm working on it. I promise."

"Let me help you! I watched Mommy and Jeremiel make plans. I can help!"

Lifting her to his hip, he almost ran down the stairs. When they reached the bottom, he lowered her to the frigid floor and reached for a seemingly solid block of stone. A small crawl space opened. Searching the staircase for shadows, he urged, "Hurry, Sybil. Go inside."

Fear choking her, she hesitated. "I—I don't want to."

He brutally grabbed her and shoved her through the opening into black, dusty darkness. Getting on his stomach, he crawled through with the lamp. Sybil backed away from him, scrambling to a far corner stacked high with boxes. She eyed him worriedly, keeping quiet. The cave stretched only about ten by fifteen feet, with a ceiling no more than four feet high. She could stand up, but he couldn't. Was this a safe place or a prison—like the square? Had she done something bad to deserve this punishment? Had her mommy?

"I'm sorry if I hurt or frightened you, Sybil. I just can't waste time right now explaining everything," he said, hurried anxiety in his voice. "Here, let me show you where things are."

Crawling around the small cavern, he pointed. "Food is here. Petrolon bottles of water are here. Candles are here."

"Books. You said there'd be books," she stalled, trying to keep him with her longer. Though she feared him, she feared being alone more.

He smiled weakly, patting a box with his hand. "They're in here."

"Avel, why can't you tell me what's wrong? I'm scared and it would make me feel better to know."

He closed his eyes briefly, pursing his lips as though knowing she were right, but not wanting to say anything. His broad nostrils flared erratically. "You mustn't ever repeat what I tell you. You understand? Not to anyone."

She nodded hurriedly. "I'm good at keeping secrets."

"I know you are, Sybil. All right. There's someone here who wants to stop the war. He—"

"And leave my mommy stuck alone in the palace? *The Mashiah will kill her!*"

"Shhh, I won't let that happen. But there are other people to consider, too. The Mashiah is holding hostages, good people. We have to try and save them, too, don't we?"

"Yes, Avel. But—"

"Saving them won't be easy. I have a lot to do and not much time." His gaze fell and Sybil's throat ached.

"You're going away now, aren't you?"

"Yes, but I'll be back. Don't be afraid."

"I—I won't," she whispered courageously, lifting her trembling chin. "Go help my mommy, Avel."

He leaned forward, kissing her forehead and hugging her tightly for a few seconds. She snuggled her face against his scratchy robe, smelling the spicy scent that always clung to his clothing. It comforted her some.

"When will you be back?"

He patted her shoulder tenderly. "As soon as I can. Trust me, will you?"

"Yes," she croaked.

Releasing her abruptly, he crawled for the opening and threw her one final warm look before scrambling out on his stomach.

The stone door grated shut and a haze of red dust rose, swirling slowly back to the ground in a pattern that indicated there was some hidden opening through which air entered the chamber. Sybil coughed, staring at the flickering candle he'd left. After a few minutes, her hard breathing turned to soft cries, tears streaking her dirty face. She wiped her nose on her sleeve and blinked fearfully around. Through blurry eyes, she took in the numbers of boxes tucked all around the edges of the cave. There had to be enough supplies to last for a half a year. Had he planned on hiding here for that long? *Did he plan on leaving her here for months?*

Sudden horror overcame her. She dove for the door, clawing at it unmercifully, seeing if she could dig beneath it and escape. Only cold stone met her frantic fingers, tearing her nails until sharp pain shot up her arms and blood covered her hands.

Sinking down against the gritty wall, she dropped her forehead to her knees and wept.

* * * * *

Cole Tahn pressed a fist to his lips as he listened. The Councilman was visible in the forward monitor, his ivory robe shimmering wildly against the brilliant background of candles.

"I have him here in my possession, Captain. When will the Magistrates be willing to barter?"

Tahn eyed him coldly. The manicured prissiness of the man irritated him beyond reason. As he thought about his answer, he studied the bridge. His officers perched on the verge of exuberant celebration, whirling in their chairs to stare at him. Everyone except Halloway. She sat stiff-backed at the navigation console, hard green eyes on the Horebian politician, calculating. He wished he could tell this conniving power-monger to take a hike while he talked to her privately. What the hell was she thinking? He knew what he was thinking, that all this "bartering" damned well made him sick to his stomach.

"When will you be willing to deliver Baruch?"

"As soon as I've been assured by Director Slothen that he'll meet my demands."

"And those are?"

Ornias smiled smugly. "There's a small planet near Palaia Station called Grinlow. *I want it.* As well, I—"

"Don't be presumptuous. There are five million people living on Grinlow. You can't have it."

A hot expression of anger creased the man's tanned face. "I didn't realize you had veto power over Magisterial decision, Captain? Shall we ask Slothen?"

Tahn's eyes narrowed. "We'll need to see Baruch before we deal. *I want to talk to him.*"

The Councilman paced leisurely. "Certainly, Captain. Once *I've* been assured the Magistrates are earnest about this business propostion."

Surreptitiously, Halloway reached over and hit the audio button on Macey's console, quelling the sound. Then, behind her hand, suggested, "He may have the goods, Captain, but we have *him.* Maybe we should jog his memory that Magisterial anger can be most unpleasant?"

Tahn lifted a brow. "I was getting to that, Lieutenant."

"Just thought I'd remind you." She hit the audio button again. Macey glared at her.

Tahn exhaled through his nostrils. "Councilman, the Magistrates have more important things to worry about than you and your offers. There will be no more discussion on this topic until you let me personally speak to Baruch so that *we* may verify *your* earnest intentions. And . . ." He lifted a brow, glaring piercingly. "I shouldn't think it would be necessary after the recent debacle on Pitbon, but may I remind you that the government acts speedily and harshly when it comes to foul-dealing."

Ornias straightened indignantly. "I don't take well to threats, Captain."

"Nor do I. Make it fast, Councilman. I won't have Baruch enduring any more waiting than is absolutely necessary. He knows what's ahead." Rising from his chair before Ornias could respond, he ordered, "Cut the tran, Macey."

The screen went dead and a brief instant of absolute silence hung before a whoop of exultation and flying pens undulated across the bridge. People ran to hug each other. He watched curiously, feeling Halloway's penetrating eyes on him. He ignored her. They'd been after Baruch for a long time. Too many loyal friends had died because of his genius, his tricks. . . . *So why do I feel nothing but damned cursed sadness—like what awaits him is less than he deserves?*

Tahn shoved his hands deep in his pockets and quietly walked off the bridge, leaving the sounds of triumph behind.

* * * * *

Ornias strolled toward Adom's private council chamber, idly fingering the lacy sleeves of his turquoise robe. Kayan sapphires studded the hem and the v-shaped neckline. His light brown hair had been freshly washed and scented with sandalwood, his beard braided neatly.

Turning the corner, his eyes lingered on the broad expanse of glass overlooking Horeb. Dusk fell in smoky veils, shadows dying the peaks indigo. The last remnants of sunset, dark purple clouds, drifted lazily eastward. Such a beautiful night, he hated to waste it on Adom, especially since he expected Tahn to be placing an urgent call to him any moment—apologizing, making counter offers. Oh, he loved the games! As well, Adom had been pestering him for days. Pestering him so badly, he'd more than once ordered the irritating messengers locked up so Adom couldn't send them back again.

He felt nearly invincible now. It wouldn't be long until he could culminate his deal with the Magistrates and leave the barren wasteland of Horeb forever—in style.

He slapped the face of a saint as he swept by the statue, going to stand before the council chamber door. Knocking lightly, he called, "Mashiah? It's Ornias."

"Come in."

The stiff tone of voice instantly set him on edge. What had gotten into Adom? Eloel's influence? The woman had been there only a few days. Had she already used her feminine wiles to seduce the poor innocent Mashiah into favoring her rebel cause? He'd been apprehensive that would happen, but Eloel had been essential to his plans. *A tool too good to waste, given Baruch's vulnerabilites.* Besides, he'd have no problem undermining whatever influence she'd gained. He'd been dealing with Adom for far longer than she. While her attempts at coercion had to be experimental, his were expert. He knew all of Adom's weaknesses.

Opening the door, Ornias stepped into the softly lit room. His face hardened at the sight that met his eyes. Standing before the fireplace in a golden brocaded robe, Adom had his arms folded, a look of utter fright on his childish face. Close beside him, Rachel sat, a glass of cognac before her. Dressed in a sage-colored gown with a high neckline, her flowing hair draped in glistening waves over her swelling breasts.

Ornias smiled. How clever of Adom to pull something like this. But no, it couldn't have been the guileless mad-man's idea. Eloel must have convinced him. He toyed for a moment with *how* she might have done that, then dismissed the idea. Adom was too naive to know what to do if she had made advances.

"Rachel, what a pleasure to see you. I'd been informed of your presence here. I hope you've been treated well?"

She met his gaze with such a hate-filled look it nearly made him laugh out loud. Instead, he averted his gaze and moved across the plush red and gold rugs to take the chair opposite her. "What did you want to see me about, Adom?"

The Mashiah swallowed hard and frowned at the floor. "Ornias, Rachel has brought it to my attention that you've been tormenting the Old Believers."

"Tormenting?" he chuckled, glancing sideways at her. "Not at all."

Adom looked up inquiringly. "You . . . you haven't been?"

"No. And, as well, I've had a very difficult week. If we're going to discuss political realities before an audience," he sighed, waving a hand at Rachel, "I'd like to help myself to

345

the Ngoro whiskey first." Without waiting for an answer, he strode across the room and pulled a dusty hundred-year-old bottle from the cabinet. Grabbing a glass, he walked back to the table. Adom and Rachel, he noticed, exchanged a tense look.

Sitting again, Ornias removed the petrolon cork and poured himself a stiff amount, noting with pleasure the rich amber color. "Now, back to business," he said curtly, fixing Adom with his most honest expression. "I don't torment. You've known me long enough to realize that. If I have a problem, I *eliminate* it. To prolong any conflict is counterproductive."

Adom ran a pale hand through his blond hair, licking his lips as though he feared Ornias. A healthy attitude. "What have you been doing to subdue the rebels? Rachel said that the last time I was in deep consultation with Milcom you—"

"Oh, some of the marines got out of hand without my knowing it. You know how that goes. You can't watch everybody all the time. But I assure you, the ruthless men have been duly punished." He sipped his whiskey. The robust flavor slid smoothly down his throat to build a fire in his stomach. *Umm, blessed whiskey.*

"You punished them? The ones who killed the rebels?"

"Of course, Adom. I demand justice. I would never—"

"You're a *filthy* liar!" Rachel accused hotly, half standing up. "You ordered the holocaust! It was only after you flew over in the *samael* that the marines started firing!"

"It didn't happen while I was there, did it?"

"No, but—"

"Well, there you have it. After I'd gone, the men took measures into their own hands." He turned mournful eyes on Adom, lowering his voice to a sympathetic coo. "Mashiah, you know how the people hate anyone who opposes Milcom's loving rule. Your followers despise the rebels. I've been *restraining* the faithful in every way I know how, but sometimes things get out of hand. Like the pathetic accident in the square."

Adom's boyish face tensed. "Yes, the people do hate the rebels. It's a terrible thing, but true." He glanced sheepishly at Rachel.

"Adom," she murmured, dark eyes widening in fear. "He's a clever liar. Not a word of what he says is true!"

"But, Rachel, Ornias is right about the sentiments of the people. I know myself they screamed for your murder after the temple destruction."

"Don't be foolish, Adom! Ornias rules the marines with an iron fist. They wouldn't dare disobey him! He orders the mass murders!"

Ornias heaved a breath, shaking his head in defense. Adom's eyes went back and forth between them, not knowing precisely what to think. But then he never did. He had to be told. Perhaps the time had come to smash the Mashiah's faith in his newfound confidante?

"Adom?" Ornias murmured, pinning Rachel with a cold glare. "Did Rachel also tell you that her friends, the Desert Fathers, are mounting a tremendous attack against us? They want to kill you and all your followers and reestablish the old religion again. Did she mention she's one of their tools?"

"What?" Adom whispered unsteadily, whirling to stare at her. Every line in his face gleamed with hurt. She paled, staring up speechlessly.

"Oh, yes, they sent her here specifically to keep you distracted while they organized their forces."

"It's not true," she insisted. "I came here to beg you to have mercy on the Old Believers. I know nothing about any attack plans. I would never betray you, Adom!" At the still, ravaged expression on his vulnerable face, she paused. Seeming to come to a difficult decision, she stood and went to stand beside the Mashiah, laying a hand intimately on his arm. "Please," she whispered, eyes imploringly searching his face, "don't let Ornias ruin the feelings growing between us."

His blue eyes widened, breathing quickening. "Do you—have feelings for me?"

"Yes. And he's trying to push us apart just as we're getting close. I need you, Adom."

He smiled down at her. "I need you, too, Rachel."

Ornias squeezed the bridge of his nose, frowning distastefully. He had the uncomfortable feeling he'd been outmaneuvered. "Really, Adom, you must get over your puerile infatuation for this woman. She's using your emotions against you. Can't you see that?"

A flicker of anger froze the man's face. "It's not your concern, Ornias. If Rachel says she knows nothing of any war plans, then she doesn't. I trust her and I won't have you—"

"All right," Ornias said and laughed, throwing up his hands. It didn't matter anyway. "Well, I've been preparing the polar chambers for you in case the attackers strike sooner than we anticipate. Shall I instruct the servants to

347

prepare the chambers for *two?*" He gave Rachel an oily smile. She'd made her nest, he'd certainly let her sleep in it, help her, in fact.

Adom glanced warmly at her, squeezing the hand resting on his forearm. "Will you go with me? If the time comes?"

"I don't . . ." she began in terror, then halted as though through physical effort. "Yes. Yes, Adom. I'll go."

Ornias bowed his head, lips curling in a suppressed smile. He took another sip of his whiskey, relishing the richness. "I'll see to it, then."

"What are the polar chambers?" she asked Adom.

"They're hundreds of years old. No one really knows who built them, but they're a sophisticated network of underground rooms. We think they were originally built to protect the Kings of Horeb from celestial attack." Gently, he added. "I've seen them. They're very comfortable. Don't worry."

She jerked a nod and Ornias noted with amusement that the hands she clenched into fists trembled like leaves in the wind.

"Well, if there's nothing else, Adom, I still have many duties to carry out tonight." He drained his glass and leaned forward expectantly.

The Mashiah shook his head slowly. "No, Ornias. I have nothing else. Rachel, do you want to ask the Councilman any more questions?""

He turned to Rachel as though hanging on her next words. "Please ask. I'm at your disposal."

She lifted her chin, dark eyes sparkling with moisture and near hysterical defeat. He smiled in anticipation. Had she really thought she could present the truth and it would stand against his manipulation of the facts? The silly little fool. She knew nothing about him or his talents.

"No," she finally whispered.

"Good, then I'll be on my way." Bowing, he turned and strode happily for the door. As he exited, he caught a final glimpse of Adom staring in childish delight at the woman destined to cut his throat. *Well, I warned, you, you imbecile. I'd planned on having it happen accidentally when the cause would most benefit from a blessed martyr, but perhaps this is more poetic. And if you're both at the polar chambers, I can still hold the announcement of your murder and use it to maximum benefit when it's most advantageous.*

Ornias hummed gaily as he headed back for his bedchamber and a night with Shassy. There wouldn't be many more. He wanted to rend as much as he could from those remaining.

Adom gazed joyously down at Rachel. She'd said her feelings for him were growing. Lifting a hand to caress her silken hair, his heart pounded so loudly in his ears, he could barely hear himself speak. "Rachel, would you . . . Could we be together tonight?" Shocked at his boldness, he hastily amended, "if you want to. I'll understand if you don't."

"Yes . . ."

At the answer, he stopped breathing. Fear glimmered in the magnificent ebony depths of her eyes. Almost instinctively, he wrapped his arms around her and pulled her close against him, stroking her hair tenderly.

"It's all right, don't be afraid. I won't hurt you."

"I know, Adom. Forgive me—my nerves. It's just—my husband's death is so recent, I—I'm not sure how I'll—"

"Are you sure you want to be close to me? We don't have to."

"Yes," she said almost sternly. "I want to."

Her arms hesitantly went around his waist and he felt her hands resting softly against his back. He tightened his hold on her, the warm feelings of her breasts against his chest causing his pulse to race. A flush taunted him.

Slowly, he released his grasp and guided her toward the door and down the hall to his bedchamber.

CHAPTER 34

Jeremiel wandered absently around his prison, occasionally throwing logs onto the dwindling fire to fight the night's chill. The gray stone walls and high ceiling seemed to suck all his warmth away, leaving him bone-cold and weary.

Folding his arms, he paced before the mirror hanging over his plank bed, staring at himself. He looked like hell, bruised and battered. Worse, he sensed something growing in the dark silence, some malignancy without form.

"How long do I have to wait, Ornias?" he gritted, fingers digging into his arms as he paced. "Tahn, damn it, you know what this must be like. *Call his hand! Force him to turn me over!*"

Surely Tahn knew by now that the Councilman had him. How many days would this torture of waiting continue? Silently, he cursed himself. He ought to break that damned mirror and slit his carotid artery with a shard. They only checked on him once every half hour. He'd be dead long before they came again.

"If it comes to the that, I will," he backtalked his conscience. "But I've been in far worse traps than this and managed to get out. I just haven't thought of every possibility yet. I have to . . ."

Voices filled the hallway outside. He spun. They'd checked on him only ten minutes ago, who could be coming to see him at this late hour?

Had Tahn heard him? A tingle of adrenaline went through him.

* * * * *

Yosef peered around the corner, spying the two guards in front of the door. Easing back, he nodded to Ari who waved his stolen pulse pistol confidently. Crouched behind a rose agate statue of Saint Broglie, his friend's mop of gray hair seemed to sprout from the statue's armpit.

"Go!" Ari hissed, waving an arm erratically.

Yosef took a deep breath, brushed absently at the sleeves of his lavender robe and rounded the corner. The guards stiffened as he waddled unhurriedly toward them, the blond's hand dropping to the gun on his hip. Yosef felt a little like a field mouse under those piercing hawklike gazes. *A captain, sergeant and private. Weren't they the same men who'd dragged Jeremiel up the stairs that night when he and Ari had hidden in the hall?* He pushed his spectacles up higher on his nose and squinted. Yes! What were their names? Loma was the private, he remembered. Anger built in Yosef's chest. The little brute had made a point of hurting Jeremiel. Maybe he ought to let Ari shoot him? *Back to business—what was the captain's name? Think you old fool! El? Something like that.*

As he neared, the captain ordered, "Halt. State your name and business." He examined Yosef severely. His gray suit looked like he'd slept in it, wrinkles creasing the arms and legs in spidery patterns.

"Are you . . . El?" Yosef asked in a kindly way, smiling.

350

The captain blinked, glancing uneasily at his companions. "I am."

"You're one of the Mashiah's favorites, did you know that? He considers your heart to be of the purest quality." Yosef adopted a serene and glowing expression, trying to mimic the one Adom used when he spoke like that.

The captain's hard face softened. A bare smile curled his lips. "Wait a minute, don't I know you? Aren't you one of his personal aides?"

"Oh, yes. I'm Yosef Calas. The Mashiah told me to be sure and give this to *you*, El." Yosef waddled forward, heedless of the guns the other two guards slipped from their holsters. He handed the captain the crystal sheet, and held his breath.

El unfolded it, brow furrowing as he read aloud: "Yosef Calas and Ari Funk are acting under orders from me. Please allow them access to your area and follow their instruction." The captain glanced up suspiciously at Yosef. "Tony? Take a look at this."

Yosef smiled mildly under their scrutiny. Had he known Adom would sign the authorization without reading it, he'd have made it more specific, but the words were designed to be vague enough that he could defend it as a library pass. It had been Ari's idea to interrupt Adom while he was with Rachel, figuring he'd be less inclined to question the wording. Though they hadn't met the woman at the time, they'd seen her with the Mashiah, seen his eyes light when he looked at her. Obviously the gangly boy had a crush on her. Yosef looked back to the sergeant. *Blessed Epagael, let them buy it as easily as Adom did.*

The dark-haired officer lifted his brows. "It's certainly the Mashiah's signature, El. I've seen it a thousand times. Nobody could forge that flowing scrawl." He handed the note back to Yosef.

"But maybe we ought to send Loma to make sure. The Councilman would—"

"Don't even think about it! Ornias said he was going to meet with the Mashiah on a matter of grave importance and *nobody* was to disturb them. I won't be responsible for—"

"What could it hurt anyhow?" Loma said gruffly, shaking shaggy blond hair out of his eyes. "Let the old man go inside and talk to the prisoner."

"Interrogate," Yosef corrected politely. The guards scowled at him.

"You're interrogating the prisoner for the Mashiah?" El asked.

"Yes. You see he thinks that perhaps this man has information on the . . ." Yosef tried to remember the term he'd heard in the hall that night. "The Beliels." Then, more creatively, "Adom has felt the mounting of evil power. He *must* find out what this man knows. But, as I'm sure you're aware, he's very busy. As a result, I'm here in his stead."

El's ruddy face paled, freckles standing out starkly. "I told the Councilman," he whispered confidentially to no one in particular. "I told him the prisoner wasn't making that up."

"Don't start in again, El," the sergeant chastised. "Let's get this over with."

"Um?" the captain grunted, lost in some frightening inner world. His face had gone grim. "Oh, yes . . . I hope you don't mind, but we'll have to search you."

"That's fine, Captain. I expected as much." Yosef lifted his arms and spread his legs, waiting patiently. The captain knelt to pat him down thoroughly, then stood again.

"You take as long as you need, Mister Calas. Do you want one of us in there with you," he asked hopefully.

"I'm sorry, but this is confidential. You understand."

"Sure. The Beliels are serious business, I know that. Well, we'll be right out here. Just holler if you need us and we'll come running."

Yosef smiled in gratitude, nodding. "Thank you, Captain."

El gestured for the sergeant to help him. Together, the two guards lifted the heavy bar over the door and set it against the wall.

"Go on, Mister Calas."

He waddled forward, twisting the knob and opening the door just enough to squeeze through. Once inside, he pushed it closed and fell against the wall, panting. Sweat poured like rain down his chest and sides. Looking to his right, he saw Jeremiel standing stiffly before a crackling fire, a startled look on his face.

Yosef's heart went out to him. Beneath his torn black jumpsuit, his biceps and pectorals bore shocking bruises and abrasions. But his skull had endured the worst injuries. The entire left side of his head had swollen to form a massive knot.

"Yosef?"

"Hurry, son. This isn't going to be easy."

Jeremiel strode toward him and Yosef saw the deep gashes left in his wrists by the cutting shackles. A small pain pierced him. For the protector of Gamant civilization to be treated so on a Gamant planet seemed beyond belief. He pursed his lips and wrapped his arms around Jeremiel's waist, embracing him tightly. Jeremiel pounded his back warmly, then shoved back to stare.

"Yosef, what the hell are you doing here? How'd you get in?"

"It's a long story. Let's sit down for a few minutes." Taking Baruch's arm, Yosef led him back to the table beside the warm hearth and helped him sit down in the chair. Though the man didn't feel frail, it made Yosef feel better to show his concern in this paternal way.

Dropping to the other chair, he asked, "Are you all right, son?"

Jeremiel blinked in disbelief at the question. "Not particularly, but as well as can be expected given the circumstances. *Yosef, what are you doing here?*"

"I came to break you out. Ornias and Adom are in consultation and it seemed the perfect time."

"*To break me out?* Don't be crazy, there's no way you can do that." He thrust out an arm to point at the door. "How many guards are in the hall at this very minute?"

"Three. That makes us even, but I'm afraid they might be sticky. Getting in was easy, but walking out with you at my side will probably be tougher."

"*Probably?* Have you lost your mind? I assure you, they won't just let me traipse out of here."

"But I'm afraid we'll have to try, Jeremiel. You see, Ornias has recently shifted the locations in the caves—or so the palace servants' rumors say—so the regiment that used to be guarding this side of the palace has been temporarily reassigned to the parapet. But I don't think that will last for long. As soon as a trained regiment is ready to—"

"I get the idea," Jeremiel breathed, leaning back in his chair and thoughtfully caressing his beard. His gaze wandered over the high ceiling and down the gray stone walls, resting painfully on the shackles attached to the pillar in the center of the bare room. He massaged a wrist reflexively. "Well, small talk aside, I have some questions. How do you plan on getting me out?"

"Ari's waiting in the hall with a gun. He—"

"Oh, dear Lord," Jeremiel murmured tightly. "Funk is

353

armed? Pray he doesn't shoot one of us when we make our break."

Yosef nodded. "I reminded him I was the one in lavender. Not certain what you'd be wearing I couldn't cue him on that one."

"I'll wave my arms expressively." Jeremiel nervously drummed his fingers on the tabletop. In the flickers of firelight, the bruises on his face glowed a mottled blue and purple. "If we survive the guards and Funk, is there a way to get out of the palace? To the streets of Seir?"

"I don't know if it'll work, but Ari appropriated a large guard's uniform from the storehouse near the women's bath downstairs—the same place he got the gun. We thought you might need it."

"Yes, it might work." He vigorously rubbed the back of his neck. "Especially if Ornias is shifting personnel around. I might be able to blend in with a flow going outside into the city. But I'll need a place to hide in the meantime."

"Oh," Yosef waved a hand. "There are plenty of places in the palace to hide. Both above and below ground, the area is honeycombed with secret passageways."

"Yes, I know . . . But how do *you* know?"

"We've been exploring for the past several weeks. There are a large number, as a matter of fact, leading from the women's quarters to the food storerooms. We figured maybe in the past the women stole food or something."

"Makes sense. But you haven't located any tunnels connecting the palace to the underground cave system that leads into the desert?"

Yosef shook his head. "No. We didn't know there was such a system."

"Not many do, thank God. Unfortunately, I couldn't find a connection either. I'll have to go back and thoroughly search the doc room. There must be one."

"Do you want us to look? We might—"

"No, don't waste your time. I have to get back to the caves of the Desert Fathers immediately. If I don't make it in five days, it won't matter."

Yosef frowned, his heart thumping suddenly, as though his body knew something his mind didn't yet grasp. "Who?"

"A secret religious sect located in the desert regions. They've been here on Horeb for millennia."

"Yes, of course. I remember Zadok mentioning them.

354

They're monks, aren't they? Following the old ways of chastity and purity?"

"Yes."

"Of course, years ago, Zadok mentioned he had spies amongst them." He chuckled. "Men who complained heartily about the privations they were forced to endure."

Jeremiel leaned across the table. "*Who?* Do you remember any names?"

Yosef searched his memory, feeling awkward. He didn't recall things too well anymore and it always pained him to be reminded of it. "No, Jeremiel. I remember only that he mentioned one of his latest recruits had been recently widowed, his wife and child killed in a freak accident."

Water filled Baruch's eyes, but not in sorrow, Yosef could tell. A flush of adrenaline?

"Dear God," Jeremiel whispered. "I've been wrong all along." In a violent gesture, he slammed a fist into the table. "How could I have been so blind?"

"About what?"

"Never mind," he said hurriedly. "What else do you remember, Yosef? Tell me anything that comes to mind, any detail, no matter how frivolous it may seem." His blue eyes gleamed like cold sapphires.

Yosef's mind drifted back to that conversation with Zadok. They'd been sitting around the dinner table at his home on Tikkun, sharing the last bottle of beer in his cooler, laughing. But what else had he said? "Something about not fully trusting someone, but I don't recall who. I'm sorry, Jeremiel. Is something happening with the Desert Fathers I should know about?"

Jeremiel hesitated, as though weighing seriously whether or not to answer. "Yosef, how did you manage to get into the guards' storeroom and in here to see me?"

Yosef blinked, taken aback. Did Jeremiel doubt whose side he was on? "Oh, I'm sorry. I should have shown you this." He took the crumpled crystal sheet from his pocket and handed it over. Jeremiel took it and smoothed it out on the table, tilting it to the firelight to read it.

When he'd finished, he stared hard at Yosef. "*How did you get this?*"

"Ari and I caught the Mashiah when he was alone with his girlfriend and he signed it without even reading it. I think he was anxious to get back to . . . Well, anyway, we've been using it on different guards ever since. But I think maybe its usefulness is nearly at an end. Stories go around quickly in this palace."

"They do in all small, closely organized units. Battleships are the same way." Then suddenly Jeremiel jerked around. "What's his girlfriend's name?"

"Rachel. She's a real beauty. Came here just after—"

"So she's in."

"In what?"

"Yosef, can you arrange for me to see her? Maybe, if we live through the next hour, bring her to wherever I'm hiding?"

"I suppose so. Do you know her?"

"Yes, but that's confidential information. She's part of the clandestine attack force set up to lay siege to this palace in a few days."

Yosef's mouth dropped open. "How long do we have?"

"I don't know for sure. That's why I have to get out of here. That and other reasons. And just in case I miss Rachel, tell her *I specifically ordered* she is to go through with our original plans.

"I'll see she gets that message. But if you have plans set up, why do you need to go back to the Fathers? Maybe we could get you off Horeb if we could find a way to the spacedock."

"No, not yet." Jeremiel ran a hand through his blond hair and exhaled tiredly. "There's a—a traitor—in the midst of the Fathers. I know his motives for wanting to sell me to the Magistrates, but I don't know if he intends to undermine the attack forces or not. My guess is, since he thinks me safely in the Councilman's hands, he does. I have to find out."

"Is it necessary to attack Seir? The Mashiah is really a fine boy. He's very immature but not a bad person."

"Don't you care that Tartarus wants to stamp out the old religion?"

Yosef shrugged apologetically. "I haven't had any religious convictions in years, Jeremiel. Now, Ari, he's as devout as they come, but to me one religion's as good as another."

Jeremiel lowered his eyes, nodding slowly. "I understand. However, the attack must go through, for the sake of Horeb in general, believers and nonbelievers. I'm certain Ornias plans on destroying all of his enemies."

Yosef nodded forlornly. "Well, Ari's waiting. Perhaps we could continue this later? I'm afraid if we wait too long, he'll get fidgety."

"Fidgety? That's scarier than the thought of facing those guards."

Yosef placed a hand against his chair arm and pushed up to stand, stretching his aching back. "I thought you'd agree. Shall we go, then?"

Jeremiel stood, heaving an anxious breath. Wind battered the palace, whistling through the corridor outside. "Anything's better than waiting for Tahn to call."

Yosef nodded his understanding. Tahn hadn't seemed at all the type to treat Jeremiel kindly. He waddled toward the door, opening it wide and stepping out, Jeremiel at his heels.

"Hey!" the sergeant shouted, leveling his pistol. "Get back in there before I blow a hole in you so big they'll be able to drive a damned starship through it!"

"Captain?" Yosef called as El whirled, slapping at his own gun. "I need to take this man to the Mashiah. His information is far too valuable for me to present it second-hand. Could you assign a guard to accompany us?"

"You need to take him? But Mister Calas, my orders from the councilman are that he is to stay here under lock and key. I have no authority to release him to you."

Yosef frowned mildly, taking the note from his pocket again and handing it to El. "If you'll please reread that last line, I'm sure you'll see that the Mashiah asked you to follow my instructions. It will greatly displease him if you don't."

The captain shoved Yosef's message back to him. "I recall the wording, sir, but I can't just disobey the Councilman."

"Do you work for Ornias, Captain, or the Mashiah?"

El anxiously scratched behind his ear, red hair glistening as he tilted toward the lamp on the wall. "Both. But I've never had their orders conflict before. To be honest, the Mashiah's never given me one."

"And so on this first, you'll disobey him?" Yosef asked in disappointment, hoping to make the convert feel guilty. It always worked with Ari. Whenever his friend suggested something absolutely outrageous, Yosef had but to ask what Epagael would think to get him to settle down.

"No, no, I didn't mean to say that. It's just that, well, I need to verify this. Loma? Go ahead and disturb . . ."

Jeremiel kicked out with lightening speed, boots slamming the captain in the chest and hurling him to the wall. The blond private swung around, aiming at Jeremiel's head, finger tightening on the trigger. A shrill whine rent the air and a violet bolt of light slashed across the private's abdomen, then shifted to lance the sergeant's chest.

Yosef stumbled backward, hot blood spattering him. Horror flooded his veins. He saw Ari trot down the hall, pistol held tightly in both hands, pointed at the captain, who now stood with his hands up, whimpering.

"Don't kill me, please, I've got a family, a little boy!"

"Shut up!" Jeremiel commanded. Leaping over the mangled sergeant, he tore the pistol from his still warm hand. Spinning on his heel, he leveled it at the captain.

Yosef screamed, "NO!" as the shot went off, taking the man square in the chest, exploding his body and sending fragments to slam the walls.

Yosef wailed in horror. A hundred years from now in his grave, he knew he'd still hear that arrhythmic thudding of flesh against cold stone. He stared uncomprehendingly at Jeremiel. "How could you . . . he was . . . a good— good—"

"Stop it, Yosef. We haven't time. Did you want someone alive who could tell Ornias *you* helped me escape? This way your cover's intact, you can keep operating here."

"I—I don't want to. I can't bear—"

"Yosef," Ari said soothingly, running to his side and slipping a lanky arm over his shoulders. "Come on. We'll talk about it later. Right now, we have to get away. Lean on me. I'll help you."

Yosef braced his shoulder against Ari's side, listening only vaguely as his friend gave Jeremiel instructions: "Hurry! Straight ahead, then take a left down those stairs. There's a secret entryway behind the statue of Archangel Michael wielding his sword."

Jeremiel sprinted silently forward, gun sweeping the darkness. He disappeared around the corner.

"Yosef," Ari whispered tenderly, supporting him as they marched. "There was nothing else to be done. It's not your fault."

"But I—I lied to—get the—the captain to let me—"

"That doesn't make it your fault. Jeremiel and I pulled the triggers—and for good reasons, to protect all Gamants. Sometimes terrible choices have to be made."

Yosef nodded, but in his mind, he saw again the captain's smile when he told him he was one of the Mashiah's favorites. A good man. A man with a family. A little boy. Dead.

His stomach heaved suddenly and he pushed out from beneath Ari's arm to vomit on the floor.

CHAPTER 35

Mikael huddled in the corner, heart pounding. His mother and Uncle Mark shouted at each other by the door. They'd been fighting for hours. It had begun right after dinner when his uncle had rushed in and started whispering in a strained voice. In the firelight cast by the roaring hearth, his face still twisted with anger and fear. Mikael glanced at his mother. Her tan robe was wet beneath the arms and around her throat.

"Damn it, Sarah!" his uncle yelled. "They've tricked you! This diplomatic bantering has all been a stall until they could get Bogomil here!"

"We can't just go in and blast their main base, Mark. For God's sake, *think!* If their minds are wavering at all, such action will leave them no choice."

Mikael's knees shook so badly he had to brace his back against the cold wall to keep himself standing. *No choice about what? Killing them?*

His uncle made a strangled sound and slammed a fist repeatedly into the wall. "Sarah, *please!* Don't force me to defy you. That will split the people in two! And we need unity now if we're going to survive."

"Don't you think I know that? That's why I've been talking to Silbersay, trying to keep the lid on."

"The man is lying to you, and you can't see it!" He pointed a finger threateningly. "Why do you think Bogomil is here, *huh?* For a pleasant chat about the weather on Kayan? *Silbersay called him in!*"

Sarah ran her sweating hands over her robe. "The fact is, we don't know why he's here. Give me another day, Mark. Let me go in and ask Silbersay."

Uncle Mark straightened, taking a deep breath. Mikael saw his black beard vibrate as he ground his teeth. "All right, Sarah. Another day, but that's it. *You hear me?* After that, I'm going to take control and join our forces with the rebels in the desert. By God, we'll make them regret that they ever set foot on Kayan!"

"You'd go behind my back? You'd circumvent Gamant tradition?"

"To keep us alive? Hell, yes!"

Her voice quaked. "You and your kind will be the death of us, Mark."

"Maybe. But we won't walk into their arms like sheep the way you want us to. We'll die fighting. *Your father fought, Sarah! Why in hell won't you?*" He whirled and stamped away.

Mikael blinked back the tears that stung his eyes. His mother clenched her fists and bowed her head.

"Mama," he said softly. "Mama, don't cry."

"Go to your room, Mikael."

A log broke in the fire behind him. The resulting flash cast his shadow in multiple images on the far wall. "Mama? Let's fight like Uncle Mark says. You and me. Together, we could lead another Gamant Revolt and kill all the Magistrates. Then we wouldn't have to worry anymore that they'll come and hurt us for no reason."

"I said go to your room!"

His mouth quivered as tears filled his eyes. He ran with all his might, racing across the cave and down the hall for his room. Throwing himself on his bed, he pulled the pillow over his face to smother the sound of his sobs.

If he just had a *Mea*, he could go to God and ask Him what to do. Someday . . . someday, he would. And then God would give him ships out of whirlwind, like He'd done Jekutiel. And Mikael would kill everyone who'd ever hurt his mother.

* * * * *

Adom woke suddenly in the middle of the night. Rachel stretched softly across his arm, her hair spilling like a raven veil over the satin sheets. Moonlight flooded the room, glowing brilliantly in the frescoed dome where Milcom soared through the stars.

Why had he awakened? Yawning, his gaze drifted over the coral arches, bookcase, chairs, table. Through the open windows, he saw the mountain peaks silhouetted darkly against the silvered sky. His gaze returned to Rachel and his heart warmed. Lying on her stomach, the olive skin of her back gleamed, exposed to her hips. Deep emotions stirred within him. Ornias had called his feelings "puerile infatuation." Were they? He didn't know; nor did he care. The only thing that mattered was that she seemed to share them and his joy threatened to burst his soul. He reached out, raising a lock of her hair and drawing it across his face in a glistening web, inhaling the subtle floral scent. Her gentle hands had set his body afire earlier. He had the urge now to wake her and begin it all again, but she seemed to be sleeping so soundly.

Before he could decide, a hiss sounded and he turned back to the window. A black whirling vortex blotted the moon. He tensed, realizing that he'd undoubtedly awakened because Milcom had called. He gently eased his arm from beneath Rachel and sat up, tugging the sheet over his nakedness.

In a moment, Milcom stepped through and the dark whirlwind vanished. He stood regally, crystalline body shimmering wildly. Throwing back the ebony hood of his cloak, he strode forward. Adom started to rise, to dress, so they could speak.

"No, don't get up, Adom. This won't take long."

"What is it, Lord?" he whispered, not wanting to wake Rachel.

"Just a moment," Milcom murmured, lifting a hand toward Rachel and slowly closing his fingers on air. "There, she won't awaken. We can speak normally."

God put a hand on his hip and paced before the windows. "The polar chambers, I need you to go there as soon as possible. Can you do that?"

"Yes. I don't know if they've been readied completely, but we can go anyway."

"Good. Make sure the chambers have a graphics capability. The people in Seir must be able to see you while you're gone."

"To bolster their courage during the battle, you mean?"

"Exactly."

"So the Desert Fathers are going to attack," he said softly, casting a sideways glance at Rachel. "Lord, Ornias said Rachel was their tool. Can you tell me—"

"Don't listen to Ornias," Milcom sighed deeply, rubbing his amber brow. "He's an idiot."

"Yes, Lord."

"But you need reassurance, don't you? Well, I should have shown you before." God strode briskly to the opposite side of the bed where Rachel lay and with a feathery touch, brushed back the hair covering her brow. "Come and look, Adom."

He quietly eased over to peer at the place Milcom indicated. In the glistening light cast by God's body, Adom read the letters AKT on her brow and his mouth gaped. "Lord, I—I thought I was the only one who—"

"You two, you're the only people in this universe with my seal."

Confusion and rapture struck Adom at once. "Then Rachel and I are meant to be together?"

"Fated since the beginning of time," Milcom said tiredly. He stared out across the rocky ridges for a time before continuing. "You and Rachel, without you, I'd never be able to end the suffering here."

"Then she believes? I wasn't sure."

"Not yet. Right now she's working very hard to convince herself Epagael doesn't exist at all. In a few days, however, I'm betting she'll be convinced not only that He exists, but that He's the monster she's suspected these past few weeks." In a reverent gesture, he reached inside his cloak and pulled out a brilliantly gleaming *Mea*. Adom stared in awe, he didn't know Milcom owned one. "In fact, I've been meaning to do this for a week, but just haven't gotten around to it. I mistakenly thought He might call me to talk." Pain etched his deep voice. "But now I know He'll never call again. So . . . I don't need this anymore." In a violent motion, he ripped the *Mea* from around his neck and went to kneel beside Rachel, gently lifting her head to remove the one he'd given her earlier and draping his own around her throat. "There," he whispered warmly, intimately to her, "a direct route. Now you won't have to go through the seven heavens. Though Epagael would have passed you anyway—*knowing who you are.*"

"Does he know her?"

"Oh, yes. He's known since the day I erected the Veil. I told Him all the major events I could foresee—even chaos has decipherable patterns. I'd hoped He'd end the game after He knew the wretchedness ahead."

"But He refused. That's why we suffer."

Milcom nodded slowly. "Yes and now He thinks by playing

with the *Reshimu* He can stop me. He doesn't realize His actions advance my cause. The increase in suffering is throwing species who were formerly indifferent over to my side."

Adom perked up, remembering that Rachel had asked about the *Reshimu*. "What is that, Lord? The *Reshimu?*"

"It's the faint remnant of His effulgence—gone wild now, spinning in infinite chaos."

"But," Adom murmured, struggling with the logic. "How can He play with it if it's in our universe? I thought He couldn't enter into this realm?"

Restrained emotion glazed Milcom's face. "He doesn't have to enter to send the *Reshimu* into convulsions. He merely has to change the shape of the container, flex His muscles around the perimeter of the Void. Like a tidal wave, the warping sends galaxies crashing into each other— rips the fabric of space and spawns myriad singularities. Whole universes have been swallowed into others, thrown through the gaping holes breached around them." He put hands over his ears, face contorting in agony. "I hear the screams of billions dying even now."

Adom winced, eyes glued to God's anguished features. He'd never seen Milcom so distraught. Fear soured in his stomach. "Can Epagael stop you that way? By changing the shape—"

"Not if we act quickly. But given time, He could merge all the matter and antimatter universes—cleansing the Void without ever having to face the terrors within. In the blink of an eye, He could start it all over again."

"What can Rachel and I do to help?"

"Just get to the polar chambers as quickly as you can."

"Yes, Lord."

Milcom hesitated, eyes going minutely over Adom, as though trying to fix his features in his memory. A pitiable expression of grief creased his amber face. "Adom," he said in soft anguish. "Forgive me for what I must do in the days ahead. But nothing—*no one*—is sacred in this battle. Do you understand? The goal we strive for supersedes all other things."

"Of course, Lord. I've always known that when the final battle between you and Epagael began, suffering would seem to increase for a time. Don't worry. I trust you completely. I . . ." He halted when God's crystalline face contorted. What had he said that caused such pain? . . .Trust? A tendril of apprehension wound through his chest. "Lord?"

"What is it?"

"I'm afraid."

Moonlight outlined the edges of Milcom's fluttering ebony cloak like liquid silver, landing sharply on his quivering jaw. "So am I, Adom," he whispered.

"But, Lord, you can't . . ."

God closed his eyes and lifted a hand to the night. The vortex whirled outward, consuming him in a black cyclone before it vanished.

Adom leaned back, anxiously pulling the sheet up over his chest as he stared at the place where God had stood. So the day he'd feared for years had come. They hung over the precipice of the final battle of Light and Dark.

"Please, Milcom," he prayed softly. "Help the powers of Darkness triumph."

God had explained long ago that darkness far exceeded light in our universe. Therefore the forces of the Void were "dark" in comparison to the stark brilliance of Epagael. Absently, he creased the sheet between nervous fingers, wondering why human beings had gotten it wrong for so long, thinking they should be fighting on the side of the Light. But Epagael had awesome abilities to deceive and coerce.

Quietly, Adom threw back the sheet and rose. Going to his dresser, he pulled the small pack from beneath it and stuffed it full of clothes. How long would they be at the Pole? For good measure, he threw in another pair of underwear.

Dressing in a maroon robe, he quickly brushed his blond hair and went to kneel beside the bed.

"Rachel?" he called softly. When she didn't answer, he put a hand against her bare shoulder and shook gently. "Rachel? You can wake up now."

She stiffened, lying perfectly still.

"It's all right," he murmured, stroking her back tenderly. "It's me."

She pulled herself to a sitting position and gave him an anxious smile. "It's still dark. What's—"

"Yes, I'm sorry to wake you, but we have to go to the polar chambers now. The battle has begun."

Her beautiful face slackened in terrible understanding.

* * * * *

Garold Silbersay stood abruptly, pacing his small white office, arms crossed tightly. Captain Brent Bogomil sat uneasily in the chair before his desk, twisting his purple hat in large hands. A short, stocky man, the captain had piercing jade eyes and curly red hair, clipped close to the head.

"Colonel, I realize you're timid about—"

"It has nothing to do with being timid!" Silbersay defended. Damn the Magistrates. How dare they send in someone to "help reorganize" his military operations. Just because he'd suffered a few setbacks was no reason to think him incompetent. Outsiders had no grasp of Gamant psychology. "Brent, with all due respect, you've no idea what sort of dragon you'll unleash if you order a full-scale attack here. Gamants are a peculiar lot. The harder you hit them, the harder they fight you. They'll die to the last warrior just to prove a point about justice."

"You give them too much credit. Gamants are nothing but a bunch of partially civilized hoodlums. You've let them get away with—"

"Nothing!" Silbersay raged, whirling to face his accuser. "You don't understand. After a few months of fighting, they'll grow tired of the mud and blood. We've seen similar situations all over the galaxy! All we have to do is appear to make a few minor concessions, like turning back some of the territory, then those 'hoodlums,' as you call them, will be perfectly happy again. They'll settle back down to herding their goats and growing their pathetic crops. We do not—"

"Colonel," Bogomil interrupted, heaving an exasperated breath as he ran a hand through his red hair. He shifted positions, making his chair creak. "Do you realize Yorkcaster, Sifre, and a hundred other planets are screaming because most of our cruisers are tied up circling Gamant worlds? Without a Magisterial presence in non-Gamant sectors, pirate activity has increased twentyfold. Trade has virtually stopped in the Wecgin area. The Magistrates want something done—and fast—so we can get back to normal operations."

Silbersay clenched a fist, lightly kicking at a stack of crystal sheets piled in the corner. "How many other Gamant planets are rioting? I've heard some scuttlebutt, but—"

"Too many. That new Mashiah on Horeb has sent missionaries all over the damned galaxy, telling the people that *we* killed Zadok—of all the blasted stupid notions—and that they must rally behind this Tartarus and fight back or we'll exterminate them all."

"Our actions against Pitbon certainly lend credence to that philosophy."

Bogomil looked up sharply. "We didn't have any choice and you know it! The fools broke the treaty, then proceeded to attack Magisterial installations. They're all suicidal lunatics!"

Silbersay ground his teeth, waiting until most of the red drained from Bogomil's cheeks. "Brent, what are your orders, *specifically*?"

"Slothen didn't send a dattran to tell you?"

"No."

The captain shook his head regretfully. "Garold, I thought you knew. I'm sorry."

"Tell me."

"Slothen has ordered me to take over military command here, though you'll still handle domestic affairs, of course."

"And what actions are you authorized to take?"

Bogomil hesitated, twisting his hat in his big hands. "Any necessary, though we'll begin with selective sterilizations, but if that doesn't work—"

"It won't work, damn it! Don't those idiots read any of my reports? You kill a few leaders and their followers, who are mostly disorganized and disinterested currently, will mass together into the biggest revolt the Magistrates have ever seen!"

"Then the planet will be scorched, Garold!"

Silbersay closed his eyes, listening to his heart pound. "When will the Magistrates get it through their tri-brains that such brutal measures don't work. How long did he give you to resolve the issues?"

"Seven days, your time."

"Have you told Tahn?"

"Yes. He called me some names I'd rather not repeat. He doesn't like the idea any better than you or I do, but if those are the final orders . . ."

Silbersay nodded tautly. He felt like shouting in rage, but restrained himself. He'd do it later, when he got back to his private quarters and could get reeling drunk. "Yes, of course."

* * * * *

Mikael ran, bursting through the dense underbrush, gibbering to himself in terror. The stormy night crowded round him, rain drenching his thin gray nightshirt. Darkness had

366

fallen so heavily, he could barely make out the forms of trees ahead. He squinted miserably, searching for the path he knew existed.

"The burrows . . . th—the burrows." He'd be safe there. He veered sharply left, falling to his knees to crawl. Behind him an explosion shredded the night, violet light reflecting like wavering fire from the overcast sky. He watched it through the tangle of trees.

"Mama! Mama, run!" he sobbed. She'd told him she couldn't. She had to stay, to try and talk Colonel Silbersay out of it. He knew now, that whatever she'd said—if the soldier had given her a chance to say anything—hadn't worked. Had she run, then? *Yes, she ran away as fast as she could. She's hiding somewhere . . . just like me.*

Scrambling up the slope, he found one of the weabit burrows he'd been searching for and slithered into it on his stomach. The dense weave of vines overlooked the caves. Through the branches, he could see patches of his home, the cinnamon cliffs hanging in wounded patterns, gouged by the violet lances. He huddled in the darkness, panting.

A scream echoed up the slope, someone shouting, "Oh, my God, there they are!"

Mikael's eyes went to the tangle over his head where a dark shape floated soundlessly. Red and blue lights around the edges outlined the huge ship. He held his breath, unable to take his eyes from it.

"No! No!" he heard his mother shriek, her voice echoing over the rain-drenched slopes.

He struggled to see, catching a glimpse of her standing with her arms out, her blue robe clinging to her body, before the mouth of the caves. Desperately, he slithered out of the burrow, emerging into a meadow as another beam of violet lashed from the ship. Chunks of rock tumbled through the sky, flashing in the lights of the ship like meteors. He fell to the ground, covering his head, whimpering.

Horrible silence descended and he saw the ship ease away, gliding over the cliffs. Rain ran in rivulets from the trees to soak his head and shoulders. He shivered, listening to the brittle wails that began softly, but quickly built to a deafening roar.

He got to his feet to run headlong down the slope, slipping on the wet grass. Through breaks in the forest, he saw people crowding around the entrance to the caves. *"Mama?"*

An avalanche of boulders had toppled under the ship's fire to fill the valley. People climbed over this mound of rocks like ants, trying to find a way into the caverns. They'd left the old and sick behind, knowing they couldn't run.

Mikael stopped at the bottom of the slope, breathing deeply of the dust-laced air. A few lamps glowed in the darkness, lighting faces twisted with fear. At the outskirts of the boulders, he saw his cousin Shilby. The boy cried raggedly, eyes swollen and red. In front of his cousin, a group of people shouted, digging frantically beneath a huge rock. A tendril of blue fabric caught Mikael's eye.

"Karl!" a man shouted. "We've found her. Oh, dear God. Tell . . . tell Doctor Smythe not to—to bother."

"Mama?" he whispered, stumbling sightlessly toward the scene. *"Mama!"*

People turned as he approached, the lamplight flickering over their hollow eyes. Like still, lifeless ghosts they all stared at him.

"Mikael," his uncle Mark shoved through the crowd. "Come here."

"No!" He threw himself at the group, shouldering past his friend Halan's father who tried to grab him, but he dropped to his knees, crawling frantically.

"My mama," he shouted. "Did you see her?"

Cries for help twined through the jumbled rocks, driving him to near madness. "My mama!" he screamed. "Where is she?"

As he neared the place, a man grabbed him by the arm and jerked him up, struggling to keep him back. "Let me go! I have to find my . . ." The words stilled in his mouth. Around the man's leg, he saw a tangle of blue fabric and bloody flesh.

"The filthy murderers!" Halan's father screamed, tears streaking his dark face as he stumbled through the boulders. "They've left us no choice now! We tried to stay peaceful. We have to protect ourselves!"

Mikael listened numbly to the shouts of agreement that sounded from various parts of the avalanche. Lamps sparkled like amber jewels over the rain-drenched rocks, moving, searching.

"War!" someone wailed. "That's what they've wrought!"

From his right, Uncle Mark emerged, black hair hanging in a wet stringy mass over his face. "Geol, let me have my nephew."

Mikael let himself be handed into different arms. When he felt the warmth of the man's chest touch his, he whispered, "That's my mama—isn't it?"

His uncle hugged him tightly. "Yes, Mikael. Don't cry. You're our leader now. You have to be strong for the people."

He leaned his head on his uncle's wet shoulder and tucked a finger in his mouth, sucking softly. He felt numb.

A cold black pit opened in his tiny chest.

CHAPTER 36

Rachel's knees shook as she hurriedly dressed in a white polar jumpsuit, then worked her hair into a single braid that hung to the middle of her back. Adom had said the battle had begun and she should meet him back at his room before sunrise. From there they'd fly to the polar chambers. But no sounds of gunfire met her ears, no waves of soldiers boiled over the parapet outside. Maybe he'd meant it was *about* to begin?

She hadn't the time to wonder. A faint lavender glow lit the horizon out her window. Striding purposefully across the room, she caught her image in the mirror and stopped. Empty black eyes stared back at her. *A time for tears, this day after betraying yourself.*

"But I secured my legitimacy, Jeremiel," she murmured, pretending the hollow eyes were his. "When you said I didn't have to, you didn't know the situation Ornias would place me in. *I did. I did have to.*"

Tugging her gaze away, she sprinted to her closet and pulled out dresses, throwing them on the bed, heedless of their expensive fabrics. Adom haunted her thoughts like a pale ghost. The fragile look in his eyes left her floundering, his innocent words of love piercing her soul. A boy, such a boy. Yet, throughout their lovemaking she'd felt he held himself back, like a *man* riding his passions with a curbed bit, for fear of hurting or frightening her.

"What happened to the hatred that used to fuel your efforts? *Damn you!*" she shouted at herself. "What happened to the promises of revenge you made in the square?"

She suddenly felt dazed and sick, ashamed of the answer: Her animosity had melted beneath Adom's gentleness.

"Jeremiel, where are you? You promised you'd come. I need you! *I . . . I can't kill Adom.*"

Clenching her fists, she squeezed her eyes closed. What would happen if she failed to carry out her part of the battle plan?

"I don't even know if the plan is still in action," she justified hostilely. "Maybe the whole thing's been called off and I haven't been notified because Jeremiel couldn't breach Ornias' security around the palace." She blinked, sucking in a sudden breath. *Yes, and maybe the sun won't rise tomorrow either. This is Baruch you're talking about. If he didn't come it was for another reason—strategic probably. You can't just arbitrarily change plans! Stop tormenting yourself! War takes many innocent victims.*

But Adom . . . *Adom . . .*

"Think of the Old Believers who still suffer on the far side of the city." She forced her memories to call up their faces. Talo appeared, eyes gleaming with stubborn faith on the day of the holocaust; he reproached her indecision. Others appeared. Each silently asked how she could even hesitate.

"He's not to blame!"

Retrieving her pack from the near the hearth, she slammed it on the bed and began shoving dresses and her black cloak inside. Unfastening the side pocket to stuff in socks, she saw the silver gleam of the knife she'd stolen from one of her plates days ago. She jerked her hand away involuntarily, as though from the fangs of a poisonous snake.

Heart pounding, she wiped sweaty palms on her jumpsuit. *Pick it up. Pick it up, damn you!*

With quaking fingers, she pulled it from the pocket and tucked it in her black boot.

Glancing out the window, she noticed the horizon had changed to a deep purple. A mauve glow slipped between the buildings in the merchants' section of town, dappling the red streets. In the distance, the peaks stood like lone sentinels, silently guarding the secret passageways of the Desert Fathers. A frail sense of hope rose.

Grabbing her pack she ran out of her room and down the long hall, passing the rich tapestries without looking. When she reached Adom's door, tears pressed against her lashes.

"Adom?"

Footsteps sounded within and he opened the door, stepping out into the hall, his pack in one hand. His ebony cloak covered most of the white jumpsuit he wore beneath. Blond hair hung over his chest, shimmering like pale gold in the morning light. He smiled affectionately, eyes going over her. "You look beautiful. I hope I didn't rush you too much. It's just that we have to hurry."

"It's all right. I'm ready." She met and held his warm gaze. Inside, a voice shouted at her: *Now! Kill him now. You may never have another chance so perfect.* The knife blade pressed coldly against her calf, beckoning.

He turned to close his door, back to her. She stared at the place between his shoulders where the blade would be certain to puncture a lung. Sweat broke out on her brow, and her heart thundered. She dropped her hand to her boot . . . and froze, unable to force her fingers to touch the instrument of his death. *She couldn't do it!*

"There's a *samael* waiting at the spaceport," he said softly. Turning back, he clasped her hand fondly. "Ornias has arranged for a regiment of guards to escort us there."

"A regiment?"

"Oh, at least. He's afraid someone from the Desert Fathers might try to assassinate me before we can get to safety." He laughed, shaking his head in genuine amusement as they walked down the hall.

"You think that's funny?"

"Only because I've told the councilman several times that God promised me I wouldn't die in Seir."

Rachel swallowed hard. She could prove his god wrong. "He doesn't believe Milcom?"

"No, but it doesn't matter now."

"Why not?"

"Because the end is almost here. If Milcom wins the war ahead, none of this will exist. So, you see, whether Ornias has faith or not is unimportant."

They turned a corner and descended a staircase. At the bottom, Rachel saw the huge brass doors looming darkly. Over three dozen guards crowded them, gray suits and silver helmets donned. Yosef and Ari stood on the last step, waiting.

Yosef licked his lips nervously, watching the Mashiah and Rachel descend the steps. He hastily climbed to meet them. "Forgive me, Mashiah," he said politely. "The palace is humming with the news of your departure. Would you mind if I talk with Rachel before you go?"

Adom frowned slightly, but shrugged. "Please, say your good-byes." He squeezed Rachel's hand affectionately, then trotted down the steps to meet Ornias, who paced nervously before the doors, whispering with the guards.

Rachel stared at Yosef. He smiled in a kindly way, seeing the shine of sweat across her beautiful face. She glanced repeatedly at Adom, pain and something else in her eyes, longing? Regret?

"What is it, Mister Calas?"

"I have a message for you."

"From who?"

"Jeremiel Baruch."

Her face paled, eyes widening. She put an insistent hand on his arm. "Quickly, what is it?"

"He says you are to carry out the original plan."

She flinched, dropping her hand limply to her side. "Does . . . does he?"

"Yes."

"Tell him, I—I . . . can't."

Tears filled her eyes as she looked back at Adom. She clearly cared for the gentle boy. Were they lovers? Yes, Yosef suspected they were. The poor girl, her heart must be breaking. After the deaths of the guards outside Jeremiel's chamber, he knew the horror of murder. "I know it's a terrible duty, Rachel."

"You don't understand. Adom's as much a victim of Ornias' scheming as we are!"

"Yes, I know that. And so does Jeremiel. Ari and I told him last night. He understands what the situation is here. But he said that changes nothing. You must—"

"Last night? Where is he?"

"Down there, dressed as a guard. He'll be with you most of the way to the spaceport."

"Where?" Desperately she searched the gray-clad men, taking a step down the staircase. "Which one?"

"On the far right, beneath the wall lamp."

Her eyes flitted wildly across the room, recognition dawning at sight of the reddish blond beard protruding from beneath the half-closed helmet visor. Lamplight illumined the small smile that touched Jeremiel's lips. She smiled back, tears of relief welling. "Please, Yosef, I must talk to him. I must explain that Adom isn't to blame."

She lurched down another step and Yosef gripped her arm tightly, jerking her back. She stared at him pleadingly, a look that made Yosef's heart ache. "You can't. If anyone sees you talking with him, you'll both be compromised."

"But I must. *I must!* There's something he doesn't understand!"

"He does understand, my dear," Yosef repeated miserably. Her arm trembled in his grip. "Ari and I told him everything we know. He won't change his mind about the plan. As Jeremiel says, the Mashiah is still the figurehead. *You have to take the heart out of his followers, or ten times more will die needlessly.* I'm so sorry."

She swallowed, obviously struggling with the urge to cry. Bitterly, she shook off his hand and gave Jeremiel a tormented look. Yosef grimaced, watching Baruch. He seemed startled, posture stiffening. Yosef spotted Ornias peering at Rachel curiously, trying to follow her line of sight through the weave of bodies.

Yosef harshly jerked her sleeve and she dropped her gaze to her boots. "Ornias is getting suspicious. We must hurry."

"Yes. All right."

Yet he could tell every fiber of her being screamed at her to run to Baruch and beg mercy for Adom. Yosef pushed the spectacles up on his nose and his gray bushy brows drew together. "Is there anything you want to tell Jeremiel?"

"Yes, tell him I'm going to the northern ice cap. I don't know where exactly. Tell him . . . tell him to take care of Sybil if I don't . . ." Her voice faltered. "If I don't make it back."

"I'll let him know. Take care of yourself, Rachel. *We need you. All of us.*" He stepped down the stairs to stand next to Ari.

Rachel stood hesitantly, shame tightening her face. Her gaze landed on Adom and he lifted a hand, urging her to hurry. Warmth and love filled his eyes. She took the steps two at a time, running to him.

Yosef looked away, unable to bear the tortured expression on her face. Wild guilt must have stormed like a beast inside her.

"I don't know how she can do it," he whispered miserably to Ari.

His friend's face creased. He studied Rachel through hard gray eyes. "I just hope she *can*."

CHAPTER 37

Slowly, Jeremiel worked through the crowd of guards to get closer to Rachel. The look on her face when she'd stood on the stairs with Yosef had sent a chill down his spine. She seemed near panic. What the hell had happened? She knew the stakes. Surely she understood she couldn't back out now? Inside, his own voice mocked, *I told you not to use Rachel. She's too emotionally unstable to be reliable under pressure.*

Trying not to call attention to himself, he stepped around a laughing circle of gray-clad men, winding toward her. As he neared, he heard Adom murmur, "Rachel, you're trembling." The Mashiah turned so he shielded her from prying eyes and asked softly, "Are you cold?"

"Y–Yes."

Jeremiel gritted his teeth. He couldn't see her face, but her voice sounded like she was on the verge of shattering into a million pieces. *Damn it, Rachel. Things are too desperate! You can't fall apart now!*

Adom spread his ebony cloak so that it enclosed both of them and hugged her tenderly. "Is that better?"

She nodded, squeezing his hand. "Yes, Adom. Hurry, let's go."

The Mashiah nodded to Ornias and the councilman opened the huge brass doors. The fires of sunrise splashed into the palace, bands of lavender streaking the coral arches.

"Form up!" the captain of the guards shouted, motioning. Men milled for a moment, pulling visors down, shoving each other to get to their proper places. Jeremiel fell in line at the end, wanting to be as far from Ornias as possible. When the troop marched, he marched with them, methodically

374

descending the pink fan stairs to stand in the garden. Dead grass crackled beneath his boots.

"How come Neelam's in charge today?" the black-haired man in front of him whispered to his blond friend.

"The councilman said Elaysin's been assigned more important duties."

"More important than protecting the Mashiah? What could—"

"I don't know, Jonqui, but I've heard rumors we're going to be attacked. Maybe El's coordinating forces."

"*Attacked?* By who? I thought we'd shoved the rebels into the dirt? All their leaders are dead. By Milcom, we made sure of that! And we're continuing to punish anyone who so much as mentions Epagael's name. Who could possibly—"

"There's that battle cruiser," the blond murmured, motioning at the sky with his head. "Don't forget them."

The black-haired guard swallowed hard, nodding. "Aye."

Jeremiel's heart pounded. When Tahn found he'd slipped through Ornias' fingers, and battle had broken loose on Horeb, he'd have every legal right to descend on the planet with massive forces. Instinctively, his hand dropped to the pistol hanging from his belt. Ari had "loaned" it to him. A gesture of support for the Underground, he'd explained. *Tahn.* If only he hadn't forced Rudy away, he'd have had someone here he could depend upon. But now, every key person in the scenario seemed as stable as quicksilver.

Jeremiel forced his thoughts back to the next few minutes. He had to find a moment when everyone's attention was elsewhere so that he could get away unnoticed. Perhaps somewhere along the route? He concentrated on the dust devils that wound across the desert in the distance, swirling to touch the turquoise sky. A few feathery clouds drifted over the red peaks.

Near the portcullis, Ornias shouted something unintelligible and the guards reformed in an awkward circle around Rachel and the Mashiah. Searing wind blasted them, whipping sand into their eyes as they flooded into the street. Jeremiel worked around until he stood closer than anyone else, no more than fifteen feet from Rachel. Maybe if he could catch her attention he could at least bolster her courage by his presence.

"You!" the captain of the guards shouted and casually

375

Jeremiel turned. The dark-haired man waved at him. "Who are you? Move farther back! We need more in the rear."

Nodding obediently, Jeremiel quickly retreated, pulse racing. If they found him out now, it would truly be over. He could only kill so many before they overpowered him.

Tall buildings lined the streets, apartments for the most part. People pressed eagerly against thin panes, waving at the Mashiah as he passed. Jeremiel frowned at the love in their trusting eyes. Did none of them care what his lackeys did to their cousins across town? A flame of anger flickered to life. Jonqui had said the Old Believers still endured punishment. How many more had died since Rachel fled the capital city? And these adoring fans didn't care?

It took almost no time to walk the seven blocks through the herringbone streets to the spaceport. Black *samaels* lined the fenced pad in neat rows. All but one. It sat in the center, gangplank down, pilot standing in the entryway. Behind his ship, a red and gray ridge twisted like a serpentine chain across the desert.

As Ornias unlocked the gate to the fenced area, Adom stopped and turned, waving affectionately at the guards and the people who stared from the surrounding buildings. A cheer went up, people waving back, shouting good wishes, promising to take care of the city for him. Rachel stood painfully stiff at his side, eyes darting through the crowd, as though searching for Jeremiel. The raging anxiety on her pale face made his belly ache. Despair lay in every feature of her posture, the hunched shoulders, the clenched fists. And when she looked at Adom, an intense warmth and sorrow filled her eyes. *God damn . . . does she care about him? Can she still carry out her duty?* Desperation pushed him to lift a hand.

She jerked around, staring. He gave her a smile, nodding confidently, trying to reassure her. They held each other's gazes for a long moment, and he sensed her terror and aching heart. Obviously, she longed to talk to him. The agonized set of her mouth told him that much. But such a thing would get them both killed and lose Horeb as well.

He shook his head sternly and started backing away, searching for the best place to edge out of the crowd. As the guards pushed forward, following the Mashiah onto the pad, he slowed, drifting to the periphery, then dodged onto a side street.

She followed Adom up the gangplank to the *samael*, looking over her shoulder, dark eyes glistening with tears.

Jeremiel ducked out of sight, throwing himself against the wall of a bakery. The sweet scent of bread curled around him. "You have to, Rachel," he whispered, licking dry lips. *"God damn it, don't let me down now!"*

He turned and ran headlong up the street, trying to reach the entrance to the caves that rested just above the palace.

* * * * *

Ornias watched the *samael* lift off, shooting toward the pole and then strode hurriedly away from the spaceport, leading the guards, who formed a disorganized herd behind him. The pistol on his belt slapped uncomfortably against his hip. Blast! When he felt he had to carry a weapon rather than having someone else do it, things were getting too tense for comfort. Wind set the hem and sleeves of his mauve robe to flapping. He yawned irritably. Adom had wakened him at three o'clock, jerking him from Shassy's reluctant arms, and he'd barely had time to breathe since. Getting the protective forces, ship, and necessary equipment organized had kept him running for the past three hours. But at least Adom was out of his way. Now he'd have the freedom to culminate his deal with Tahn without worrying about the Mashiah and his delusions.

He turned up the street that led to the palace. People waved to him and he resentfully waved back. The idiots, why weren't they at work in the fields? Then it occurred to him that it was only six. They had another hour before they had to go. That didn't sooth him much. They were up, they ought to be producing! *He* was up and had been producing for hours.

The parapet loomed large before him, guards crowding around, peering out as he approached. "Lift the portcullis," he ordered shortly.

"Sir," a sergeant whispered from within as the grate rose. "You'd best hurry. Shassy's been driving us mad. She tried to climb the walls while you were gone, and nearly tore off Lieutenant Rangon's head when he pulled her down. We had to lock her in the palace for fear she'd—"

"What? Get out of my way!" he growled, ducking beneath the still lifting portcullis. He ran across the garden. If she'd tried to escape, something was terribly wrong. "What's

377

the matter, precious?" he asked through gritted teeth. She knew it would mean her husband's and his religious order's lives if she failed to carry out her part of the bargain. Of course, he'd planned on crushing them anyway, but she didn't know that. *Did she?*

He raced up the fan steps, throwing back the brass doors. Shassy hit him like a frightened cat, clawing and screeching. Her black hair jutted out at odd angles, as though she'd torn at it with frantic fingers. Her silver robe had crimson stains hugging the hem. Blood?

"Ornias! For god's sake, you incompetent fool, he's escaped!"

"What are you talking about?"

Her wild eyes narrowed and she slapped him across the face with all the force she could muster. He staggered backward, enraged by the stinging ache in his jaw. "I could have you killed for that, precious."

"Go ahead. We're all going to die now! The Magistrates will think you've been lying to them and they'll scorch us!" She broke into sobs.

"Tell me what you're—"

"I went to see Baruch to ask him about my husband," she blurted. "And I found the guards dead, splattered across the hall! And he was gone!"

Adrenaline flushed Ornias' system. He shoved her out of his way and took the stairs to the second floor three at a time. *Baruch gone?* His entire future crumbled before his eyes. It had to be Shassy's husband. The man had double-crossed him! Who else would help the Underground leader escape? But it didn't make any sense! Damn them! He'd pound their caves until nothing but rubble remained!

Panting, he darted around the final corner, sliding to a halt at the carnage that met his eyes. Baruch's door swung wide open and in the hall beyond, arms and legs twisted at hideous angles from a bloody mass of dead. Elaysin's green eyes stared sightlessly at him, accusing, just as Shassy's had done.

"You fools!" he screamed, on the verge of wrathful hysteria. "It's your fault! You let him escape!"

He pulled the pistol from his belt and fired into the dead bodies, watching them explode. A severed hand slammed the wall beside his head. He stumbled sideways, but he kept firing . . . until no eyes could accuse.

He had to get Baruch back. He *would* get him back. If

Shassy no longer worked as a tool, he'd have to throw the weight of his military might against the caves. He'd planned on doing that on a lesser scale anyway, but now he'd have to hurry. Before Tahn demanded he turn Baruch over and he couldn't comply.

Idly, he noticed that a river of blood coursed over his boots. He kicked it, letting the coppery scent ease his frenzy. Heaving a deep sigh, he holstered the pistol and walked briskly back down the hall, glaring at the statues of the saints.

Most of his forces were training in the caves beneath the palace. The time had come for them to take to their ships.

CHAPTER 38

Zadok plodded tiredly across the open field. Cool grass reached to his knees, brushing against his coarse robe. Wind blew over the wildflowers, rustling their white and yellow heads. But amidst the beauty, his skin tingled painfully. The few gray hairs still dotting his head stood on end, teased by the powerful presence of Epagael.

"The *Reshimu*," he whispered to himself, "is the source of Evil in the universe? Then what role does the Deceiver, Aktariel, play? And why are all the angels in heaven eagerly awaiting the outcome of his plan to destroy my universe?"

He pondered the conundrum, knowing the simple solution was to ask Epagael when he reached the Veil. But he'd rarely accepted simple solutions, preferring to reason them out first.

As he climbed over a soft swell in the land, his breathing quickened. At the foot of the snowcapped blue mountains ahead, the seventh crystal palace gleamed, its faceted surface reflecting a rainbow of colors. Four towers jutted up like spears to pierce the clouds. Round-faced cherubim hung from them playfully, laughing and pointing at the wheels of fire that tossed and reeled through the sky above.

"Zadok?" a rich heavenly voice called. Anapiel, the last gatekeeper, stepped out of the crystalline palace doors. Clad in a deep blue robe cinched around the waist by a golden sash, the creature flapped his wings lazily. "You're early. I thought Michael would keep you longer."

"No, Lord," he answered, hurrying down the path. "Michael and I got along amiably this time."

"I'm surprised. I'm sure his bet is *for*."

"For *what*?"

Anapiel rubbed his golden chin, laughing softly as he leaned a shoulder against the shimmering wall. "Never mind. Suffice it to say, Michael's a rank sentimentalist. He still harbors loyalties that should have died millennia ago."

Zadok frowned. *Loyalties to whom?* The same tendrils of doubt that had taunted him when he stood before the archangel returned. *Not Aktairel?* All the old books spoke of how the wicked creature had once been Epagael's chosen, leading all lesser angels, but surely Michael knew that since the Fall from heaven Aktariel had gone bad. *Just like the Reshimu.*

"Anapiel," Zadok said shortly, plodding toward the open door. "Forgive me, but I desperately need to talk to Epagael."

Anapiel stepped in front of Zadok, blocking the door. "Not yet, patriarch. Epagael said he'd let me know when He was ready to receive you."

"He's never kept me waiting before. What's the delay?"

"Oh, some final ploy of Aktariel's," the angel responded nonchlantly, but his amber eyes gleamed like flames. "So you might as well sit down, Zadok. I've no idea how long this will take. But believe me, if I could hurry you along I would," he added, smiling deprecatingly. "My bet is *against*."

* * * * *

Cole Tahn ran briskly up the white corridor, passing saluting crew members without responding. Pounding the access button to the transportation tube, he panted, "Bridge." He'd been sleeping soundly for the first time in weeks when Halloway's urgent call blared through his quarters. "God damn Gamants! What the hell have they done now?"

He burst through the bridge door and ran into the midst of a holographic display. The surface of Horeb spread ethereally across the bridge, his officers visible beneath it. A massive array of spiny sandstone ridges, bleak deserts, and chunky houses gleamed.

"Point it out, lieutenant," he ordered, eyes going over the image.

Halloway got lithely to her feet, striding to the hilly location outside of Seir. Her auburn hair glinted coppery in the harsh lights. "Here, sir. Though the location is camouflaged you can see the cannon emplacement. As well, the men emerging from below ground, here and here, are certainly scattered troops. They— "

"Damn them!" he cursed incredulously. "Have they lost their minds?" Slipping around his chair, he walked to her side, studying the suspect location more carefully. The holo display could pick out an ant at five hundred miles and trace its invisible trail back to its hole. How had they missed the initial operations? "Yes, those are definitely troops." Each soldier carried a rifle and pistol. The packs on their backs indicated they'd probably be involved in ground movements, away from supply centers for at least several days, maybe even a week. "The fools. Don't they know what a war will force me to do?"

"I distinctly recall you telling them, sir."

He spun, shouting, "Get me that blasted councilman, Macey!"

"Captain," Halloway said, emerald eyes boring into him. "You should also be aware that the Mashiah and an unknown woman left Seir four hours ago. His ship landed in the polar region just before I disturbed you."

"Disturbed, hell. You pulled me out of the first satisfying dream I've had in weeks."

"Satisfying?" she murmured knowingly. "It didn't involve Gamant politics, I take it?"

"Not hardly." He walked to drop uneasily into his command chair. "Do we have any idea why the Mashiah would chose to leave the city at this particular moment?"

Hands on her shapely hips, she paced before the navigation console. "We can only assume that he's fleeing the coming battle."

"Uh-huh. All right. Cut the holo, Halloway, and get on the com. Dannon knows Baruch's strategies. Get him up here! If all this 'bartering' has been a trick to buy time so Baruch could organize a full-scale revolt, I'll—"

"Sir," Macey's clipped voice interrupted. The young officer swung around in his chair to face Tahn. The com aura snapped on, a golden halo flaring around his head. "Clandestine *One* message coming in from Kayan. Bogomil demands to speak with you immediately."

Tahn squeezed his eyes closed. "What now? Put him on screen."

He tried valiantly to straighten the wrinkles of his purple

uniform which he'd thrown over a chair only five hours ago, but the effort was clearly hopeless. He settled for sucking in a tense breath before the captain's face formed. Sweat beaded Bogomil's broad brow, and damp curls of red clung to his temples. In the background, Tahn saw Silbersay sitting rigidly, face turned away from the screen.

"You look like an Orillian havelina's been after you, Brent. What's up?"

"Cole, thank you for acknowledging so quickly. Life on Kayan is not going well. We've—"

"Don't tell me you've got a battle in the making there, too?"

"Too?"

"Yes, we've just discovered Horeb is ready to burst at the seams. What's happening on other Gamant planets? Heard any scuttlebutt? Are these isolated events, or do they form a pattern? We're not facing another Gamant Revolt, are we?"

"Rioting is coming in waves on nearly every Gamant planet, but no organization seems to be present. Except here on Kayan. And we've got a full-scale war on our hands, Tahn." Bogomil hesitated, tapping a waser pen on the desk before him and glancing uncomfortably at Silbersay. The colonel kept his back to the screen. "The Magistrates have authorized a Prime Mover Two maneuver, Cole. How soon can you comply?"

His stomach muscles clenched tight. He lowered his gaze, massaging his forehead. Halloway whispered in a low savage voice, "Bogomil always opts for absolute solutions. What is he, Slothen's hit man?"

Tahn exhaled tautly, *"Prime Mover, Brent?* I can't believe there are no alternatives. Did you try selective sterilizations?"

"We've tried everything. Nothing's worked," he defended, as though he resented Tahn's suggestion that he might have missed something. "At this very moment, we're deep underground because the enemy is pounding the installation over our heads. Yesterday they bombed two field camps."

"Bombed? Where would a planet full of backward barbarians get bombs?"

"They made them from the native elements. Crude things, but they work. Over six hundred of our forces died in the blasts yesterday."

Tahn sank back into his chair, rubbing his chin thoughtfully. Desperation always served as the mother of invention, but how could a bunch of uneducated cave dwellers pose such a severe threat to Magisterial forces? "Garold? What's your analysis of the situation?"

Silbersay heaved a disgruntled sigh and turned to the screen. He looked haggard, gray hair matted to his head, eyes dull. "I told them strong-arm techniques wouldn't work, Cole. But you know how the Magistrates are. They—"

"The order," Bogomil interrupted, glaring at Silbersay, "has already come down. Discussion is spurious at this point. How soon can the *Hoyer* be here, Tahn?"

"Carey, calculate minimum time to Kayan."

She threw Bogomil a disgusted look and pensively examined her console. "Forty-seven hours, sir."

"Got that, Brent?"

A look of relief spread over his face. "Yes. Is there anything we can do on this end to help you?"

"Just get everybody the hell off that planet. You know how it works; we'll commence firing as soon as we make orbit."

"Acknow—" Bogomil began, but behind him Silbersay lurched to his feet, his elderly face twisted in anguish.

"I told them! I told them what would happen, but they wouldn't listen to me! Now we'll have more innocent blood on our hands and all because the Magistrates are too stupid—"

"Shut up!" Bogomil hissed, staring wide-eyed. "They'll be reading this tran, Garold. For God's sake, you don't want to— "

"I don't care! Somebody should know what we've done here. We can't continue blasting children for no reason!"

"Silbersay!" Bogomil lunged to his feet, his bulk blocking the screen.

"Garold? Garold!" Tahn shouted, thrusting up from his chair. "Let him talk, Brent. God damn it! What's going on there?" He watched impotently as Bogomil whirled the colonel around and shoved him out the nearest door.

Tahn's gut knotted. He felt his entire bridge crew go tense. Shoulders stiffened, eyes narrowed. Obviously Silbersay had been relieved of command. Halloway glanced speculatively at him, murmuring, "I suppose the Rule of Law established at the ancient Narmber trials doesn't apply anymore, huh?"

Tahn glared at her. "Have you been present at a Magisterial court-martial, Lieutenant?"

"No, sir, but—"

"Well, I have. My longings to join the ranks of the 'Glorious Dead' haven't been the same since. Not only that, I won't betray my duty to those men and women on Kayan."

"Um. Ohlendorf would be proud, Captain."

His anger flamed at her knowing tone. "Who the hell's Ohlen— "

"Tahn," Bogomil called urgently, leaning over his monitor so that his perspiring face filled the screen. "I'll begin evacuations immediately. Get here as quickly as you can. We need you."

"I'm on my way, Brent."

The screen went dead and a heavy silence fell over the bridge. No one so much as moved. He glanced at each stiff back in turn, a bad taste rising in his mouth. They hated it as much as he did. Maybe more. He just had to give the order. They had to carry it out, making sure no inhabited part of the planet remained unsterilized.

"Halloway, input course corrections for Kayan. I'm—"

"What about the military movements on Horeb, sir? Do you still want me to wake Dannon?"

"No, belay that. But order Lieutenant Talworth to take the shuttle and remain in orbit around this godforsaken planet. I want constant updates on troop movements. And forget about the Councilman, Macey. It looks like the fools on Kayan have just given their Horebian relatives a brief reprieve."

He started for the door. "I'm going back to my quarters. Don't disturb me unless it's urgent."

The door snicked shut behind him and he found himself alone in the tube, staring hard at nothing. "Fourth level." He paced the cramped tube a few times, then slumped against the wall and slammed a fist into the white petrolon.

*   *   *   *   *

Mikael slept fitfully, dreaming of his grandfather. They sat on the floor of his bedchamber, playing yarrow by the light of a single candle. His mother shook her head, eyes warm as she gazed lovingly at both of them, laughing. Even in slumber, tears filled his eyes, his heart tight with longing for them. *Lonely. So lonely.*

"Mikael?" a soft, soothing voice penetrated his dreams.

He yawned and rolled to his side, blinked hazily at the golden light that gleamed from his cinnamon walls. But he remembered blowing out the candle . . . Turning, he shot up in bed, gasping in fear. A man of glowing glass knelt beside him wearing a green cloak with the hood pulled up.

384

The *Mea* swung slowly from the chain in his hand, its blue glow like a beacon of comfort.

"I believe this is yours, isn't it?" the man asked in a kind voice. He extended the blue ball. Mikael's eyes widened, but he felt too much surprise to reach for it.

"Don't be afraid," the man said, tenderly patting his exposed foot. "I won't hurt you."

"Are you . . . are you an angel from God?"

"Yes."

"What's your name?"

"You can call me Metatron."

"The Prince of the Divine Presence? I remember studying about you," he said proudly. Metatron had taken Ezra to heaven to talk to Epagael.

"Yes, you studied very hard. I've watched you. Mikael, there's something very important God and I need you to do. Will you help us?"

"What is it?"

"You'll need the *Mea*." He held the globe out again and this time Mikael took it, putting it around his neck and patting it lovingly. His heart thumped as the ball glowed to life, blue light mixing with the yellow of the angel to stain his walls a pale green.

"I'll do anything Epagael needs me to."

"You're a good boy. God knew He could count on you. Listen carefully, Mikael. As the new leader of Gamant civilization, you're responsible for saving the people. Did you know that?"

"Oh, yes, sir. I know."

The angel smiled and laid a gentle hand on Mikael's shoulder. The warmth sent a tingle through him. "Before you can do that, you need to save yourself. I've come to help you."

"What's happening? Are the Magistrates going to hurt us again?"

"I'm afraid so. God needs you to get out of bed and get dressed, then put some clothes in your pack. You must run down the mountain to Capitol as quickly as you can."

Mikael threw off his blanket and jumped to the floor. Grabbing his brown robe from his chair, he slipped it over his head and fell to his stomach to pull his pack from beneath his bed. "Can I tell Uncle Mark where I'm going?"

"No, I'm sorry. This has to be a secret."

"I understand. Sometimes Grandfather told me secrets,

too," he said breathlessly as he stuffed socks and underwear in his pack.

The angel stood up, his glowing body casting eerie shadows across the walls as he strolled around the small cave. "You must find Colonel Silbersay in Capitol. Can you say that name?"

"Oh, yes—Silbersay. I've heard it many times. Mama used . . . used to go talk to him a lot." Pain cramped his stomach. He swallowed his tears, knowing instinctively it wouldn't be good to cry in front of an angel. He stuffed another robe in his pack.

Metatron bent over to stroke his brown hair softly. "It's all right, Mikael. You can cry if you want to. I know how much you've been hurt. I'm trying to make sure nobody else has to hurt the way you do."

"By helping God to save us?"

". . . Yes."

"What should I say to Colonel Silbersay when I see him?"

"Tell him who you are and that your mother was killed in his last attack. *Tell him you want an audience with Director Slothen.* By the Treaty of Lysomia, it's your right as the new leader. Demand it."

Mikael nodded, fastening his pack and standing up. Breathing hard, he gazed intently at the beautiful angel. "What should I say to Slothen?"

The angel exhaled heavily, then smiled and extended a hand. "That's a good question. Let me walk you to Silbersay's office. We'll discuss it on the way."

Mikael gripped the golden fingers tightly, shuddering at the warmth that crept through him. The look on the angel's face reminded him of his grandfather, gentle and wise. He had that same pinched look of sadness around his eyes, too.

Mikael let Metatron lead him through the dark hallway, the angel's body casting the light of fifty candles.

When they finally stepped out into the misty rain drenching the mountains, pine-scented winds lashed them.

"Cold?" the angel asked softly. His voice seemed to echo from the cliffs.

"No, sir."

Metatron nodded, but spread his green cloak and enfolded Mikael in it anyway, shielding him from the darkness and the storm.

CHAPTER 39

Silent as a shadow, Jeremiel slid through a nightmare of dark caverns, feeling his way by memory and luck: The hollow thud of bridges beneath his boots, the scent and sound of water trickling over stone.

And in the distance far ahead, a soft chanting caressed the sandstone.

In the eternity of black quiet, he found himself falling into the trap of weariness; he couldn't yield to the sweet whispers of his body that he should just sit down for a while and rest. His bruises ached and his head was fuzzy from exhaustion, but ten minutes might make the difference between life and death for Rachel. He couldn't risk it.

A flash of gold in the hall ahead made him fall back against the wall. Two monks dressed in brown robes strolled hurriedly through a perpendicular passageway, speaking in hushed tones.

"But the Mashaih has stopped his attacks."

"Stopped? Surely you don't believe that? Tartarus has just halted to confuse us. While we're arguing ethics, he's probably readying his military forces. I think . . ."

They disappeared down the hall and strain as he might, Jeremiel couldn't make out any more of their conversation. He drew his pistol and gripped it in sweating palms. Slipping from his hiding place, he silently followed them, letting the glow of their lamps guide him.

For fifteen minutes, he dogged their steps, twisting down a series of diamond-shaped tunnels, until finally he found himself at a three-pronged interface of corridors he recognized. He faded back into the shadows, barely breathing as he listened for other footsteps. Hearing none, he wiped perspiration from his forehead and eased left around the corner, studying the long hall. At the end, a brazier of red coals glowed, casting a bloody halo over the stone. Holding his pistol with the barrel pointed at the ceiling, he silently ghosted toward the yellow curtain fluttering on the left.

The earthy scents of crushed herbs drifted out to him,

along with soft sounds of movement. Pressing his back against the wall, he lifted the curtain a slit and peered inside. The multicolored throw rugs had been rearranged, but the long table and chairs sat in the same place in the center of the large room. And near the fireplace, Rathanial stood, arms crossed tautly, flaxen robe shimmering like liquid gold in the flickers of flame.

Jeremiel surreptitiously checked the rest of the room through his slit, insuring that the Most Reverend Father was alone, then he slipped inside, casually whispering, "I met your wife. Quite a beauty."

Rathanial whirled, horror twisting his elderly face. "Je—Jeremiel. We—we heard you'd been captured! I'm so glad to see you're all right."

"I'm sure. Tahn probably doesn't accept damaged merchandise." Aiming the pistol at Rathanial's heart, he crossed the room to stand next to him before the fire. After the cold of the caves, the warmth seeping through his gray suit made him shiver.

"I don't know what you mean. Tahn—"

"Oh, I think you do."

"No, I—"

"Sit down, *good friend.*" He pointed to the chair beside the fire with his pistol barrel. "I've got most of it figured out, but there are still a few details I'm hazy about."

Rathanial swallowed hard, studying the gun, then wisely dropped into the chair. The fire crackled, threading his panicked face with glimmers of orange. "Jeremiel, let—let me explain."

"I intend to. I've rarely killed anyone before extracting all the relevant information. First, let's discuss Kayan. You said that Zadok never received any of your messages about Horeb—that all your messengers had been killed en route. I wondered how you'd made it to and from the planet so easily. If *somebody* was out to keep Zadok in the dark about Horebian politics, you should have been their primary target. But there never were any messengers, were there?"

Sweat beaded on the father's face. He twisted his hands in his lap. "Yes, of course, I sent at least five. I—"

"This charade is over, Rathanial. Either you answer my questions straight or I kill you right now. Your only value to me at this moment is as a source of information. There never were any messengers, *were there*?"

"Don't shoot! I—I'll answer your questions. . . . No."

"And after I responded to your message, saying I wanted Zadok's opinion, you panicked? Decided you had to cover your tracks? Is that when you suggested I report to Zadok first?" He laughed softly at his own stupidity, pacing slowly before the crackling flames. "Then you hotfooted it to Zadok with the same story about Horeb that you'd fed me?"

Rathanial leaned forward suddenly and Jeremiel instinctively leveled the pistol at his heart. The Desert Father sat back, slowly. "Please, Jeremiel, the story about Horeb was true! Surely you've gathered that much?"

"You just left out the part that your wife was being held hostage by the Mashiah's henchman. And the fact you needed a billion note prize to exchange for her freedom. Clever, Rathanial." He smiled appreciatively. "Obviously it became necessary to kill Zadok, but Ezarin?"

"I didn't kill Ezarin! And Zadok," he murmured painfully, "Zadok's death wasn't my plan. Ornias feared he'd actually come to test Adom—people here were clamoring for it—and discover he wasn't the promised Redeemer. That would have ruined his whole plan."

"But you didn't see fit to tell Zadok an assassin had ridden to Horeb in *your own ship*. You—"

"Ornias would have killed Shassy! I couldn't risk it!"

"Let me get this straight. You sold out the leader of Gamant civilization and the leader of the Underground movement to save your wife. Right?"

"Jeremiel, you don't understand. I had no choice."

"Uh-huh. Did you ever really plan on attacking the Mashiah, or did you assume that once I'd been delivered, Shassy would be returned and the whole annoying affair would be over?"

Rathanial clutched fistfuls of his flaxen robe, closing his eyes momentarily. When he spoke, a quaver touched his voice. "No. I didn't plan on continuing the attack. My order is filled with inexperienced boys for the most part. I wouldn't have risked them if I'd known Shassy was safe."

"Compassionate of you." He waved his pistol expressively. "And all the Old Believers? You didn't care that Ornias was slaughtering them by the thousands?"

"Of course, I cared! That's how I got into this mess! Shassy went into Seir to consult with the leaders of the rebellion. We desperately wanted to help them, to offer advice on how they could accomplish their goals nonviolently. Our order preaches *ahimsa*, Jeremiel. Violence is inconceivable, except as a last desperate resort. But—Shassy was captured and I—I couldn't think straight." He ran a quaking hand through his gray hair.

"You thought straight enough to plan several efficient murders. I hardly—"

"What would you have done?" he asked pleadingly, anguish twisting his aged face. "What?"

"I wouldn't have risked thousands to save one."

"*Wouldn't you?* If the woman you loved had been captured by your enemy and you—you knew she was in terrible danger unless you complied with the letter of his demands. If you knew she was probably being abused and . . ."

Rathanial continued, but Jeremiel didn't hear. His ears rang with different sounds: Rudy screaming at him—fleeing people shrieking—gunfire. Snow whirled through the towering Silmar oaks as he ran headlong for the apartment building. Syene, naked, sprawled across the bed. "Love you . . ." her frail whisper echoed through him like a sword slash. "Knew . . . knew you'd come."

A taloned claw constricted around his chest, making it difficult to breathe. He stared at the old man before him, seeing the agony in his dark eyes, hearing the terrible fear in his voice.

"I love her, Jeremiel. We've been married for fifteen years, clandestinely meeting in a series of small caves near the city. I couldn't let Ornias hurt her. Don't you understand?"

The pistol in his hand trembled. He gripped it tighter, reaiming at the elder's chest as he exhaled haltingly, "And Rachel?"

"Purely accidental. I knew about her, of course. She and her husband were two of the people Shassy was supposed to talk to, but—"

"Why did you decide to use her after I objected?"

"When Ornias discovered I had her, he *ordered* me to send her to him. He wanted to use her as a lure. You see he . . . he knew about Syene Pleroma and he thought . . ."

Jeremiel's jaw muscles hardened, his heart pounded sickeningly. "So you sent her in as a sacrificial lamb."

"If there'd been another way, if I could have refused, I'd have . . ."

"Traitor." The word echoed. Time seemed to do a flip-flop. Scenes from Horeb transposed over those of Silmar. *I'll kill him, Syene. I swear.*

Rathanial's voice faltered, eyes widening as Jeremiel's finger tightened on the warm trigger.

He said nothing for a time, but their eyes held. Blood surged so powerfully in his ears, he didn't hear the soft footsteps behind him, but he caught the frail look of relief that crossed Rathanial's face.

"Baruch?"

Jeremiel's spine went rigid. Had the old man set this up, too? No, Ornias wouldn't have had the time to send an informant with the information that he'd escaped. Would he? He slowly turned to see Harper standing tall, his black halo of hair shimmering in the firelight, the rifle in his arms held expertly.

"God damn," Jeremiel breathed. "I'm glad to see you're alive."

A faint smile curled Harper's dark lips. "Glad you made it out, too. I was afraid I might have to pull off the war by myself."

"You have the forces trained?"

"As trained as they'll ever be. They're rusty, but they'll do, I think."

He nodded once. "Sorry I didn't realize earlier you were Zadok's agent. If I'd known—"

"What?" Rathanial paled, eyes darting from one man to the other. "What do you mean, Zadok's agent?"

"There are about thirty of us, Reverend Father," Harper said nonchalantly. "The Patriarch took few chances—not even with you." Then he turned back to Jeremiel and his dark eyes tightened. "Is Rachel still with us? How many casualties can we expect?"

Jeremiel heaved a sigh. "Rachel is an unknown at this point. The last time I saw her she seemed on the verge of collapse. Whether she'll carry out her mission or not is in question."

"Then we have to assume she'll fail and plan accordingly."

"Yes, I think that's wise. Our first target should be Ornias. Perhaps a small guerrilla force could penetrate—"

"Let me help?" Rathanial pleaded. The collar of his flaxen robe gleamed darkly with sweat. "Please, the only way I can get Shassy out now is to help win the battle."

"No."

"But I know the palace. I can tell you—"

"*No*," Jeremiel murmured savagely, gripping the pistol so tightly his hand ached. He wanted to kill, needed to. Even though a part of him cried out in understanding, he couldn't forgive Rathanial's treachery—any more than he could forgive Dannon's. His damp finger caressed the trigger. "Harper, do we need this traitor for anything? Will he be useful?"

"He might. Especially if Ornias still believes *you* trust him."

Jeremiel frowned. Then, as understanding dawned, he smiled grimly and reluctantly lowered his pistol. "I get your meaning. And I'm willing."

"Good, we'd better hurry. I'm nearly certain Ornias plans to attack tomorrow. If he hits us first, we're—"

"Yes." Jeremiel reached out and gripped Rathanial's arm, roughly shoving him toward the door. "If he strikes first and Rachel fails, we're going to have a hell of a time."

Harper nodded, running for the door.

"Where are you going?" Jeremiel shouted, disturbed by the man's sudden retreat.

"I'll meet you in the upper council chambers in a half hour. I've got a little friend to rescue."

*   *   *   *   *

Halloway set the controls to initiate light vault and leaned back in her chair, staring at the forward screen. A tunnel of luminescent yellow formed, purple wavering around the edges. They hurtled headlong down it, going faster and faster. The ship lurched slightly as the stars disappeared.

"Vault attained," she announced and checked her readouts to make sure the *Hoyer*'s status was stable. "Secure from blue alert."

The bridge went through a brief flurry of activity, then grew ominously quiet as officers returned to their former tasks. She scanned the three-sixty monitors. Everything appeared perfectly normal, nothing out of the ordinary was happening anywhere—*except in her goddamned gut*, which felt like it was being lacerated by broken glass.

"I'm off duty, Richy," she said and stood up. "Let me know if anything unusual happens."

"Aye, Lieutenant," he responded blandly without so much as looking at her.

She gave him a disgusted glance and headed for the transport tube. When the doors snicked shut, she ordered, "Level four."

Doubts ate at her insides. What the hell were they doing?

She used to have a clear idea of her mission with the Service. But now, she felt like nothing more than a moving piece on a government chessboard. No, *worse*. At least with chess she knew the game.

The tube stopped and she exited into the brightly lit hallway, eager to reach her room. Her steps slowed, however, when she rounded the corner and stood beside Tahn's cabin.

He'd said he didn't want to be disturbed. She folded her arms and paced quietly back and forth, considering. Finally, she hit the com button. "Captain? It's Halloway."

A pause.

"Just a minute, Lieutenant. Unless you want to see me stark naked."

"I wouldn't mind, Cole. But you know how people talk."

Silence stretched. She paced again, her nervousness increasing as the seconds swept by.

Finally, his door slid back. Dressed casually, he braced a hand against the wall and gave her a questioning look. "What can I do for you, Lieutenant?"

She kept her eyes from straying to his broad shoulders. The black silk shirt revealed every muscle. "I want to talk to you. Alone."

"You're off duty?"

"Yes."

"Come in."

He stepped aside and she entered. The door slipped shut behind her. His cabin was larger than hers. About twenty feet square, with a table and four chairs near the entry. A set of three bookshelves adorned the niche above them. His unkempt bed crowded against the far wall, beside his desk. The lights were turned low.

"I'm sorry to disturb you. I know you said—"

"Forget it, Carey. I couldn't sleep anyway. I was on the verge of getting up and pouring a stiff scotch." He crossed to the cabinet on the far wall. "Shall I pour two?"

"Damn well better."

His brows drew together, eyes narrowing as he gave her a speculative look. "You're subtle tonight."

She watched him take down the bottle and two glasses, filling each with amber liquid. He moved with the controlled strength of a tired lion. Brown hair fell around his face in soft curls, as though damp. He must have showered before going to bed. As he turned back, she caught the curious glint in his blue-violet eyes. *Damn those eyes.* She'd always felt like she was being tugged down into a whirlpool when she looked into them.

He walked back and handed her a glass, then pulled out a chair for her and took one himself. She sat, sipping quietly as she gazed around the dim room.

After a minute, he said, "You just came by to drink?"

"No, I came by to complain."

"I see." He stretched his long legs out and crossed them at the ankles, then took a healthy swig of his scotch. "I'm listening."

"What the hell are we doing, Cole?"

"I'm obeying orders. I'm not sure what you're doing anymore."

"Goddamn it! We've just been ordered to kill another planet! How can you sit there so calmly?"

He massaged his forehead. "It's only a level two attack, Carey. We'll destroy all the known habitation centers. The planet's resources will be intact. Some of the people might even survive. But the nuisance factor will be completely eliminated."

"And you can live with that?"

"Carey . . ." He sighed heavily and shook his head. For a long moment he evaded her eyes. When he looked back, a deep and aching regret strained his expression. She'd never seen him drop the *Iron Captain* mask; it worried her a little. She looked again at his casual clothes. He wouldn't have had time to grab them just for her—they must have already been laid out. What had he been doing? Pretending what civilian life would be like?

"Are you all right, Cole?"

"No." He drank deeply of his scotch. When he spoke again, his voice was lower, softer. "I've been thinking about the Service."

"I can see why that would depress you. If you've come to any conclusions that might heal my mangled stomach, I'd be interested in hearing them."

He frowned darkly at his glass. "Why did you join, Lieutenant?"

"I couldn't bear the thought of working as a planet-bound mathematician for the rest of my life. Why did you?"

The curve of his mouth tightened. He finished his scotch and set his glass on the table. "How much do you know about the history of the Delphinus sector?"

She grimaced, remembering the frightening holos they'd showed in history courses at Academy. "I know you lived through the Carina invasion, if that's what you mean."

"Do you know that I watched my parents die? I was six."

She lowered her gaze. "No, I didn't."

"Carinans have a curious custom of cutting open their captives and ripping out their internal organs to demonstrate conquest. I hid in the bushes and listened to my mother's screams. A week later, when the Magisterial battle cruisers came in and drove the Carinans out, they found a half-mad little boy still clinging to his parents' corpses." He ran a hand through his hair and stared grimly at the floor. "Captain Moreno of the *Quillon* talked softly to me for two hours to convince me they were dead. I still fought like a tiger when he dragged me away."

He paused and glanced uncomfortably at her. She'd seen that same look once before, the morning they stepped out of the shuttle to examine what remained of the planet Jumes after their attack. Shocked bewilderment—the bewilderment of a man who's certain he knows himself completely, yet is suddenly overwhelmed by raw emotions he didn't realize he was capable of—and scorns the revelation.

"You regret telling me that?" she asked.

He shook his head. "No. It's just that not many know and I'd rather keep it that way."

"I'm trustworthy." She studied her scotch for a moment, watching beads of moisture form on the glass, then turned back to the conversation. "So you joined the Service because you wanted to be like Moreno? To save—"

"No, I joined because I wanted to kill Carinans. Fortunately, I grew out of it."

"Did you?"

He gave her a faint grin. "Mostly."

Their gazes held and both their smiles vanished like dust in the wind. "Cole . . . isn't there some way we could—"

"*Don't say it, Carey.* There's not a damn thing I can do about the orders and you know it." He stood tiredly and carried his glass back to the bottle of Scotch, refilling it. Over his shoulder, he asked, "Can I get you another?"

"No."

"Are you sure?" He studied her pensively over the rim of his glass as he took another sip.

She got to her feet and stiffly stood at attention, fixing him with a cool glare. "Captain Tahn, according to manual

7118, it is my duty as your second in command to inform you of any and all conditions which have arisen that might adversely affect my ability to carry out—"

"What the hell are you doing?" he demanded distastefully. "Stop that! If you've got something to say—"

"Then hear me out, damn it!"

"Carey, I know what's bothering you. But I can't . . . What do you *want* me to do?"

"I don't know!" She threw up her hands and paced his cabin. "I just feel like we're doing the same thing to Gamant planets that the Carinans did to Delphinus. And the Magistrates are to blame! *I've got the terrible feeling that all humans may be at risk under the current administration.*"

His dark brows drew together and he eyed her severely for a moment. "I don't like Slothen either, Carey. But let's not exaggerate. The Magistrates have been protecting humans and all other species for centuries."

"Going blind in your old age?"

"I don't think so. Maybe you should try finding your objectivity. You lost it somewhere."

"Oh, I see," she sighed, feeling her heart thud hollowly. "Well, since I can tell you're on the verge of righteously preaching government policy to me, I'll leave. Thanks for the drink."

She stood and started for the door. He lunged for her hand, gripping it tightly. She stopped and looked up at him. Fear creased his handsome face.

"Carey, be careful. You know what being 'corrected' does to the human brain. *You don't want to end up like Garold, do you?*"

For a moment she concentrated on the warm feel of his fingers twined with hers, letting herself drown in his eyes.

"Did it ever occur to you, Cole, that the populace of Delphinus may have been better off dead?"

The color drained from his handsome face and his grip relaxed. She hit the exit button, leaving quickly.

CHAPTER 40

A frigid gust of polar wind shoved at Rachel. She leaned into the gale to steady herself, watching Adom and the pilot of the *samael* unload supplies, setting them in a storage room inside the polar chambers. Though they'd slipped into thick weather-suits and helmets before landing, tendrils of the eighty-below-zero temperatures penetrated her suit like frosty fingers. She shivered, squinting out across the dark wilderness. Stars twinkled overhead, their light throwing deep blue shadows across massive snowdrifts.

"Rachel?" Adom shouted against the hurricane roar. "Please, go inside. I don't want you out here in this."

She stared feebly into his tender eyes, heart aching. He cocked his head curiously at her silence and set down the crate he'd been lifting to come to her. Putting gentle hands on her shoulders, he smiled, searching her face. Wind whipped the frozen ends of his blond hair up around his silver helmet.

"Don't be afraid. I know this seems very forbidding, but it'll only be for a short time. We'll be back in Seir soon."

"I'm sorry, Adom," she shouted wearily. "This is all so strange."

He smiled, a glimpse of sunshine in the glacial landscape. "I know. Come, let me help you inside." Wrapping a strong arm around her shoulders, he guided her through the entry and down the steps into the harsh white light of a small anteroom. Doors lined the walls, all storage compartments, she guessed.

"We'll be on the eleventh level down," he said. "The captain already delivered our packs there. If you want to go inspect our living quarters, just call up the vator and punch in the number." Hugging her affectionately, he trotted back up the steps and outside into the dark expanse of ice and wind.

She milled aimlessly for a few minutes, gazing at the antique lustreglobes and low ceiling. Finally anxious frustration overtook her. She went to the vator and placed her hand over the key-patch. When it opened, she climbed inside the narrow chamber and punched the right button. The lights dimmed, a soft whir marring the silence. A bitter flush went through her—as though her descent led to the fabled reaches of the pit of darkness. She smiled to herself, recalling Adom's words that Milcom preached we were already in the pit, that the universe contained more dark than light. She believed. Yes, there could be no hell worse than the suffocating guilt and despair she endured.

When the door opened, she stepped out into a long white corridor. Lustreglobes lined the ceiling, casting a brilliant white glow over the white walls. Almost blinding, she thought as she ambled down the hall, past dozens of numbered doors. Separate passageways jutted off from the main one she followed, seemingly extending into infinity.

"A honeycomb," she murmured to herself. The control panel in the vator had indicated forty floors. "There must be thousands of rooms."

Picking room number six hundred and thirteen, she jarred open the door, coughing at the dust that plumed out into the hall. Waving it away, she pushed harder, until she could look inside. A velvet-thick layer of dust covered everything: the collapsed couch to her left, the sagging bookcase on her right, the tiny black table and chair shoved against the far wall. Stacks of precariously piled ancient paper books encircled the table.

"Are all the chambers like this? A treasure trove of antiquities?"

Interest pricked, she started inside, but Adom's soft voice stopped her. "Our chambers are down this passageway."

She turned, struggling to close the door. "Good, this room isn't fit for man or beast."

He laughed, eyes sparkling. "Ornias didn't have time to prepare the entire level as he'd originally planned. I'm afraid we'll have to make do with ten rooms." He lifted a map, pointing to the location amidst the blue lines. "Come on, we'll find them together."

"All right."

He extended a hand and she reached out to meet it. Tipping the map so she could see it, too, he said, "I think we're supposed to walk down this hall to get there. Is that what it looks like to you?"

"Yes."

They opened the door to the first room on the right. Rachel's mouth gaped. A large room spreading about thirty by forty feet, delicately embroidered tapestries covered the walls, colors of jade and rose dominating the forest scenes. Strange animals pranced across the weaves.

Adom smiled at the awestruck look on her face. "Apparently King Edom wanted to make up for the lack of windows. Ornias said this chamber was particularly beautiful. The maids left it exactly as it was, just cleaning and straightening."

She released his hand and stepped into the room, studying the ornately carved high-backed chairs made of ruby red wood that were pushed back against the wall to her left. Straight ahead sat a bed made of the same wood. Its pink velvet canopy gleamed in the harsh lustreglobe light, the curtains pulled back to reveal intricately designed pillows and quilts.

"Edom had a passion for red and pink, it would seem. Just like in the palace."

Rachel nodded, inhaling deeply of the sandalwood scented air. Obviously the maids had thought of everything. She walked to one of the tapestries, studying the horselike creature that leaped over the fence in the autumn forest. "What do you suppose this is?"

Adom came to stand beside her. "I don't know. Ornias said something about finding some old books that talked of Horeb looking like this at one time. A paradise, they said, filled with an abundance of animals and trees."

She frowned, her heart beginning to thump for no apparent reason. "I wonder how long ago and what happened to turn the planet into a barren desert?"

He shrugged his broad shoulders. "Something terrible, I'd imagine."

"Yes. I wonder what other surprises await us?"

"We need to find the communications room soon. I have to tell Ornias we're here safe and sound and ask what's happening in Seir. The Desert Fathers may have begun their attack."

A dark dread coursed through her, Jeremiel's orders echoing like distant cannon fire in her mind: *The instant we strike, you are to kill him. The announcement of his death will take the fight out of his followers. Horeb will lose far fewer lives.*

Her knees trembled suddenly as she met Adom's kind blue eyes. "Yes, let's find out what's happening."

They stepped out of the room and he looked at his map

again, pointing as they strode down the hall. "It's the second door ahead on the left."

Pushing it open, a huge screen greeted them. Towering to the ceiling, it curved two-thirds of the way around the room. Adom went ahead of her, studying the control panel before pushing a particular button. The screen sprang to life, a cold-eyed young corporal swinging around in his chair. His gray uniform hung in wrinkled patterns, as though he'd been manning the communications center all night. He ran a hand abruptly through his sandy hair.

"Good afternoon, Mashiah."

"Hello, Corporal Sanders. How are you?" Adom said. "How's your new baby son?"

"We're all fine, sir. Councilman Ornias said to patch you through to him as soon as you called. Please hold on."

"Holding."

Adom smiled at her, whispering conspiratorially. "I hate them to think I don't want to talk to them. They're just as important to me as Ornias is."

"I know."

As though in a daze, she realized her flesh felt hot. Unfastening her weather-suit, she stepped out of it, draping it over a chair. Then she opened her white jumpsuit to the middle of her chest and nervously stroked her sweating throat. The weight of the knife in her boot pressed heavily against her calf—an iron shackle to purpose. *Will this torture never pass?*

She clenched her fists as Ornias' image filled the screen. The councilman was dressed in a regal purple robe. He stood in a cave, the trappings of wealth cluttering the red walls: paintings, rose agate statues. "Adom, I see you made it all right. Good."

"Yes, how are things going there?"

"Interesting. I've moved underground, to the chambers beneath the palace."

"Into the gardens? With the flowers?"

Ornias gave the Mashiah a disgusted look. "I had the flowers removed. However, yes, that same location. The most important news I have for you is that Tahn's ship sailed out of orbit only an hour ago, heading for God knows where, but at least he's out of our hair for a few days."

"And the Desert Fathers?"

"We've already endured the first wave of attacks, but we're retaliating—pushing them back."

"Casualties?"

"Around three hundred."

Rachel's soul screamed in agony. *Now! Jeremiel is depending on you. You must do it now!*

Adom stared forlornly at the white tile floor. Rachel noticed his hands were clenched into tight fists. "Tell . . . tell the people not to worry. Milcom watches over all of us. He'll protect them."

"I'll tell them, Adom," Ornias replied blandly. "You just stay warm. I'll contact you as soon as it's necessary."

The screen went blank and Adom blinked in surprise, exhaling irritably. He turned around and smiled timidly at Rachel. "Well, I guess that's it for now. Are you tired? We could sleep for awhile, or just lie in bed and talk about the tapestries."

She stood stiffly. The battle had begun. It was her duty to *take the heart out of his followers.* Yet she couldn't move.

"We don't have to," he said gently, red rising into his pale cheeks. He flapped his muscular arms helplessly. "We could go explore. Tell me what you want to do?"

He took a step toward her, opening his arms, baring his vulnerable chest and every fiber of her body hummed, *now! now!*

She stepped unsteadily forward—hesitating a long moment before falling into the circle of his arms. She slid her hands around his waist, burying her face against his chest.

"Are you all right?" he whispered in concern, kissing her hair and stroking her back. "Are you ill? You've been pale all day. Perhaps I should call a doctor from Seir? He could be here in a few hours."

"I'm just tired."

"You have every right to be. It's been a terrible day and we didn't get much sleep last night. I woke you so early. I'm sorry. it's just that everything is happening so fast and Milcom—"

"Let's go and rest for an hour. Maybe when we get up, I'll feel better." *Perhaps when he's asleep and I can't see the love in his eyes, maybe then I can do what has to be done.*

They walked back to the king's bedchamber. Closing the door behind them, he went to turn down the quilts while she undressed. He watched her growing nakedness with shy intensity, a look of warm adoration on his handsome face.

"Aren't you going to rest, too?" she asked, gesturing at his clothing.

"Oh! Yes." He laughed at himself and peeled off his jumpsuit.

While he finished the process, she unbraided her hair and fluffed it around her shoulders, then picked up her boots and set them beside the bed, within easy reach. A glint of silver caught her eye as she slipped beneath the sheet and tugged it up to her throat to shield her forced breathing. Even her lungs burned with her anxiety. She gazed at Adom, engraving his image onto her soul: the high cheekbones and patrician nose. He stood naked, tall, blond hair cascading in waves over his broad chest. His deeply set blue eyes sparkled as he crawled into bed beside her.

"Rachel," he murmured tenderly as he slid across the bed. She tensed and he stopped of a sudden, hesitating to put his arm around her. He lowered his eyes fearfully. "Rachel, we don't have to do anything. I know you're tired. I've just been alone for so long that feeling you warm beside me soothes something deep inside. I just want to be close to you. Is that . . . all right?"

Rachel looked into his boyish eyes, and for a moment she fought despair. "I want to be close, too, Adom," she whispered, holding out her arms. He hurried into them, pressing tightly against her bare chest and rubbing his chin over her thick wealth of hair. Sighing, he playfully stroked her foot with his toes.

"You make me very happy, did you know that?" His voice was startlingly beautiful, filled with tender emotion.

She forced her hand to caress his shoulder. "You make me happy, too, Adom. Let's sleep now? And maybe when we wake, we'll *do* something anyway."

He smiled suddenly, then his eyes went seriously over her face and he kissed her gently. "I . . . I love you, Rachel."

She started to say something but he put fingers softly against her lips. "No, I know you don't yet," he said understandingly. "But maybe soon. If everything on Horeb works out. When we have more time together."

"Yes."

He snuggled his cheek against her hair and closed his eyes. The feel of his ribs against her breasts, the rhythm of his breathing, all slashed at her heart like a dagger.

After several minutes, he shifted, graceful even in his sleep, rolling to his back. Pink and green quilted pillows framed his innocent face.

Rachel studied his exposed chest. One quick thrust to the heart—that's all it would take. He'd barely know what had happened.

And then no more would die in Seir.

She quietly leaned sideways, hand drifting unsteadily toward the knife. She touched it, but the cold blade burned like fire. Dropping it back into her boot, she pressed hands over her face. Shudder after silent shudder of grief racked her. Curling into a fetal ball, she hugged herself, trying to force all the tears, all the terror and guilt back inside.

Time alone, that's what I need.

Moving silently, she threw her legs over the edge of the bed and rose, casting a long look at Adom's peaceful face. The man who needed dirty sheets and moldering cups beneath his bed, slept soundly in the king's bedchamber. His blond hair spread over the pillows like a web of pale gold. Unconsciously, he moved a hand to her side of the bed, fingers searching unknowingly for something he sensed had vanished.

Rachel tiptoed to her pack and pulled out her ebony cloak. Swinging it around her shoulders, she quickly opened the door and stepped into the stark white light of the hall. The hem of the robe billowed out behind her as she walked unsteadily away, trailing like a perverse bridal veil in the harsh glare.

"Jeremiel," she whispered miserably, "do you know I can't do it? He's innocent. He doesn't *deserve* to die."

Turning the corner, she found herself before room number six hundred and thirteen. She stood awkwardly, wringing her hands, then shoved it open and stepped inside. Perhaps the books would distract her, take her mind from the horrifying feelings of culpability and failure.

She closed the door, coughing at the dust that fogged around her with each movement. Her gaze was drawn to the bookcase. It sagged balefully, its ancient leather-bound volumes caked with what seemed the loam of millennia. She ambled toward it, cloak hem sweeping the dirt into swirling patterns.

"You'll win, Jeremiel, I know you will. And, without Ornias, Adom will fade into the shadows again—a saint without a marketing genius. He won't hurt anyone."

Ancient paper volumes were scattered on the dusty floor. She knelt, carefully turning one over. Many of the pages had crumbled to dust; others were only partially intact. She frowned as she struggled to read the fragments of sentences still visible:

> . . . *blue beasts came in droves . . . took us to . . . Lord only knows what would have happened if we hadn't . . . the secret lay in their energy source. We stole . . . took our scientists three years to discover a way to contain the primordial . . . the Gate has set us free . . . and they don't even know we escaped by their own . . .*

Rachel shook her head in bewilderment and eased the book back to the floor, then picked up another. The pages were made of some strange sticky substance. Over time, mostly of them had melted together. But the text on the first page was clear.

> The Secret History of the Great Halls of Giclas
> . . . *During the month of Uru, First Magistrate Mastema lectured to the Hall of Science on "Phase Transition Dynamics in Clouds of Trapped Ions," relating working theories to the construction of the containment chamber on newly completed Palaia. He said the only possible weaknesses might be associated with temperature or frequency control, since the chamber required constancy or the ions broke apart into disordered . . .*

"Phase transition dynamics?" she repeated, wondering what that meant. She put the book down and searched the array on the floor, looking for one that seemed whole. A black leather-bound volume caught her eye. She picked it up and stood, walking to the table. Blowing dust from a chair, she sat down and gingerly brushed off the first page. Her heart stopped at the words:

> *January 11, 4412.*
> *Dear God, I don't know what to do. I've ordered all my family and critical staff here to the polar chambers, but I know . . . I know we're not safe. Jekutiel's forces are massed on our borders, and Milcom says her army numbers over a billion.*

Rachel's blood raced. She gently turned the volume back to the first page. "Edom Middoth's personal journal? Not the Middoth of the Exile? The tyrant who forced Gamants to endure terrible suffering in his labor camps?"

It seemed a bizarre impossibility. None of the old teachings had spoken of him coming from Horeb. But try as she might, she couldn't remember them ever speaking of his planet of origin at all. In a flood of excitement, she flipped through the pages.

> *March 31, 4413*
>
> *He won't come in the day any more. But at night, He touches me, His ghostly fingers gliding like electricity over my flesh to wake me. I think . . . but I shouldn't write this, if He chances to read . . . No, He doesn't care so long as I continue massing my army of slaves for His bidding. No . . . I—I'm safe. And this journal is my only refuge from Him. I must at least write.*
>
> *I think he's Aktariel, hiding behind the name of Milcom. Though, God help me, He's so persuasive. I can't disbelieve his horror stories about Epagael. When I look around me, all I see is suffering.*
>
> *If I only knew for certain. Blessed Lord, where are all the Meas? I'd challenge Epagael myself if I could, demand He answer the terrible questions about human suffering that Milcom poses.*
>
> *But all the Meas have vanished. And I've wondered in the depths of my soul if Milcom didn't take them. For if the gates are gone, God can't defend Himself.*

Rachel blinked, leaning back in her chair. Her eyes sightlessly landed on the dilapidated couch with the broken legs. "Jeremiel and Rathanial talked about a *Mea* that Zadok had." She looked back at the haunting page. "So—they really existed. Exist? And lead to the sacred Veil?"

She thumbed another page.

> *July 7, 4414*
>
> *My daughter is dead. My beautiful Pyran, torn to pieces by some mad demon. My heart aches so that I can barely force my hand to write. Milcom says it's Epagael's work.*
>
> *I don't believe it.*
>
> *I told Him yesterday she hated the war, that she'd*

stormed into my chamber after the Rensin disaster vowing when she became leader of Gamant civilization she'd stop the bloodshed and free the slaves— His army of destruction.

Dear Pyran, forgive me, I didn't know how insanely desperate He'd become.

Now, I fear He'll do anything to keep me on his hook.

Almost hypnotized by fascination, she flipped to the last page of Middoth's journal.

September 12, 4414

Yea, though I walk through the valley of the shadow of death . . . The final attack has come. Horeb lies a barren waste. Thirty-two million dead. Milcom— Aktariel, I'm sure now—says we must press ahead.

I haven't the heart. The slaves have revolted. We're being torn apart from the inside now, too. Jekutiel owns the only Mea left. I can't fight someone who can talk to God face to face. Doubt consumes me.

I have only a questionable source . . . a fallen angel of immense beauty with a soothing voice and the power to convince frail humans of anything.

I can't go on.

Tikkun, Tikkun, where is the promised Mashiah? Broken shells, Kings of Edom, I am finished. Rachel, last of the Sefirah, you must return it all to the original root. Don't let Him take your substance!

We cannot bear it.

She sat frozen. *Him?* Epagael or Milcom? An inner voice chastised, "He means the mother of the people, not you." Yet she couldn't get the words out of her mind. Clutching the ebony robe tightly around her, she stared at the passage again. "So, Adom is not the first to be approached by Milcom—*Aktariel?*" She'd been taught the evil acts of the wicked angel since birth. The Deceiver. *How could Middoth have believed?* Couldn't he see the effects of Milcom's actions were devastating? Billions died in his war with Jekutiel.

The deep roots of her former belief in Epagael stirred, prodding like the tip of a sword, beckoning.

A soft creak made her jump. She turned. Adom stood in the doorway, a sleepy look of anguish on his face. "Rachel,

Ornias is on the monitor. The war is . . ." He squeezed his eyes closed, reaching out for her pleadingly. "Ten thousand have died."

"Ten . . ." Numbly, she rose from her chair and ran past him, sweeping out the door and down the long hall to the communications room.

CHAPTER 41

Cole Tahn sat rigidly in his command chair, watching as the lush blue-green world of Kayan swelled on the forward screen. Clouds swirled across the surface.

"How much time until we attain orbit?"

Halloway struck a button on her console, looking like someone had kicked her in the belly. "Thirty seconds."

"Macey, any further messages from Silbersay?"

The redhead switched on the com, twitching slightly as the golden aura flared around his skull. "No, sir. But we have one from Bogomil."

"What is it?"

"His dattran reports: Full evacuation completed. We are also in possession of the latest leader of Gamant civilization. Will be transferring him as soon as your mission is completed. Hope you have toys aboard."

Tahn heaved an irritated sigh. "What the hell did he mean by that?"

"Unknown, Captain."

Halloway swung around in her seat, staring at him contemptuously, her purple uniform stretched tight across her breasts. He could see that her breathing fluctuated erratically. "Orbit."

He held that frigid gaze, feeling empty inside. What did she want? He couldn't disobey a direct order from the Magistrates. *Even if he wanted to—it would be suicide.* Every officer on the bridge turned to stare at him, waiting. Oddly, he felt as though his own conscience accused him through their eyes. A sinking sensation invaded his stomach.

"How many of these have we performed in the past

standard year, Captain?" Halloway taunted. "Three? Or do we count the half measure on Nuja to make four?"

He glared at her. Did she think he liked this? That he enjoyed the silent screams of the billions that filled his nightmares?

He massaged his brow, hollowly ordering, "Commence Prime Mover. Then tran Talworth and give him an estimated time of our return."

Clattering sounded across the bridge, officers checking status reports, taking energy readings, sucking in a final breath before unleashing the fiery apocalypse. Everyone except Halloway.

She sat sternly still, examining him with mutiny in her cool green eyes. A mutiny his gut agreed to. But his head rebelled.

"I suggest you calculate orbit fluctuations resulting from energy surges, Lieutenant," he said stiffly.

"Aye, sir." She exhaled distastefully, swinging back to her console.

In a few moments, broad beams lanced out from his ship, slashing the lush forests in carefully calculated patterns of devastation.

A haze of dust and smoke belched into the moist atmosphere.

*   *   *   *   *

Jeremiel sat deathly still, watching the battle scenes blaze across the monitor. A troop of monks rushed a hill held by Ornias' forces. A web of violet death spun briefly. When the dust cleared, moonlight glimmered from contorted faces as man after man fell, torn bodies sliding down the slope to rest in a mangled mass at the bottom.

"Blessed God, what's happening?" He squeezed his eyes closed, blindly striking the button to request an update on casualty figures. Squinting at the dim screen, his eyes hardened. "Twenty-two thousand?"

Bracing his elbows on the table, he steepled fingers over his mouth and stared at the long copper designs cast by the faceted decanter before him: Akiba rye whiskey. Candlelight awoke dancing reflections of flame in the amber liquid.

Reaching for a glass, he poured it full and slumped in his chair. Maybe if he'd never gone to the palace, never tried to provide support for Rachel, maybe he could have properly trained the Fathers. "Nothing but green boys," he muttered to himself, feeling bitterly tired, desperate with the idleness of waiting. "Harper did the best he could, but . . ."

He swirled the whiskey in his glass, then drank deeply. The rye burned a path down his throat, bringing tears to his eyes.

He leaned his head back against the chair and stared sightlessly at the red ceiling. From somewhere deep in his mind his father's choking voice welled: "You know, don't you, son, that if—if you decided not to be a Gamant anymore, I'd understand. Ours is not an easy life. We're always in trouble. Promise me you'll never forget this talk? When I'm gone, I want you to remember I gave you . . . permission . . . to—to become the kind of man you think you must. Not the kind you think I want."

He lifted his glass and drained it dry. Sweet memories of his father encircled him. Shabbat evenings of songs and warm hugs. "I'm still a Gamant, Papa. But I've never felt more like backing out. We're in worse trouble now than we've ever been."

Getting to his feet, he paced the small chamber, stroking his beard. His tired mind seemed incapable of figuring a way out of the impending debacle. Even if Harper succeeded in killing Ornias, he strongly suspected the Mashiah's followers would keep fighting, fired by loyalty to their savior. *Rachel.* Obviously, he'd been right in the beginning. Making her the linchpin had been a grave error—one that twenty-two thousand had already paid for.

"So many mistakes, Baruch. Oh, Syene . . . I'm glad you can't see me now."

A beep sounded on his belt com. He pulled it off and hit the switch. "Baruch here."

"Jeremiel," Rathanial's voice intoned. His shoulder muscles tightened. "We've picked up a tran from Tahn. He'll be on his way back in roughly three hours. I think we'd better set operation 'bait' in motion."

He squeezed the bridge of his nose. He didn't relish relying on known traitors, but Rathanial's position with Ornias might be his only ace right now. "Are you ready?"

"Yes. I'll do whatever you say, just so long as once we're in the palace I can try to save Shassy."

"We've already agreed you only have to take me there. Then you're free to do as you wish. Do you have data on Kayan's status yet?"

A pause.

"Tahn scorched the planet, Jeremiel. All habitation centers have been obliterated."

He'd been expecting as much, still, the news struck him like a blunt beam in the stomach. Poor Sarah. She'd never been meant for leadership. And Tahn's cold efficiency left no room for considerations of human frailty; the man never hesitated once the order had been given—not even if the planet pleaded wildly. That meant, in all probability, the primary threat on Horeb had shifted. The wrath of the Magistrates stood only a breath away unless he took quick action. "Have we intercepted any messages between Tahn and Slothen?"

"None."

So we don't know whether he's been ordered to take full-scale measures here or not. Silently he did the calculations in his head. "We've got about fifty hours to get things set up, then. In the miraculous event that Tahn is returning to do more diplomatic negotiations, I'll spend the next few hours concentrating our attacks on Ornias' weak spots. Maybe we'll have won this war before Tahn even gets close."

"And if not?"

"I'll be ready for operation 'bait.' "

"Jeremiel . . . I know we've had difficulties, but I hope we don't have to use you—"

"Baruch out," he said shortly and clipped his com back on his belt. Propping hands on his hips, he stared hollowly at the floor. If Tahn came in under Prime Mover orders, the only thing that might stop Horeb's destruction would be a trade.

He poured himself another glass of rye.

* * * * *

The light of Kayan's sun filtered through the debris clouding the atmosphere to create a gruesome mauve halo around the planet. Now that they were almost finished with their maneuver, the halo grew a deeper purple with each passing minute. Tahn watched in wretched fascination.

"Captain?" Macey said, swinging around in his chair, eyes wide as the aura snapped on. "Message coming in from Bogomil."

"Put him on screen."

"Aye, sir."

Bogomil appeared on the forward screen, green eyes

pinched and tired. "Cole, how are things going?" The man forced a smile.

Tahn growled, "Just lovely, Brent."

"I . . . sorry. I know you hate these things. I called to ask if it's all right if we transfer the new leader of the Gamants to your ship? He's getting frustrated here. He won't eat. I think it's because our ship's cramped and too busy for a seven-year-old. He needs—"

"Seven?"

"Yes, his name is Mikael Calas, Zadok's grandson apparently. A persistent little beggar. Keeps quoting the Treaty of Lysomia, demanding his right to an audience with Slothen."

"It is his right—regardless of his age. Yes, Brent, transfer him over. We'll take care of him."

"He's on his way. Oh, and, Cole . . ." Bogomil fiddled aimlessly with a sheet of paper in front of him. "Thanks for getting here so quickly when I called. Your efficiency probably saved over a thousand of my crew's lives."

"No problem, Brent. Just doing our duty."

"Well, thanks anyway. Dependability in the fleet is going the way of most old traditions. I'm relieved to find it still exists on the *Hoyer*. If you ever need me," he said sincerely, "call and I'll come running."

"I appreciate that." Tahn hesitated. "How's Garold?"

"In the hospital. Complete breakdown. He'll be all right once we can get him corrected at the nearest neurophysiology center."

Tahn's gut writhed. "Sure. Right. Send him my regards. Tell him I know how he feels."

Bogomil frowned, chin going up. "I'm not sure that sort of encouragement is good for him. He's—"

"Just tell him, damn it!"

Bogomil eyed him disapprovingly for a moment, then nodded. "I will."

The screen went blank.

"Sir?" Macey said tautly, looking a little like a kicked puppy.

Tahn grimaced. "What?"

"When you were talking with Bogomil, Talworth sent a dattran on Horeb."

"And?"

"They're in full-scale civil war."

Before he could stop himself, he slammed a fist into his chair arm. Every eye on the bridge turned his way, waiting.

Halloway got up from her seat, stretching her arms over her head like a cat in the sun, then she paced toward the transportation tube. She stopped by his chair, gazing down seriously. "I'm going to go and greet Mikael Calas. Why don't you come? I think it would be fitting, considering what we just did to his planet."

He rose from his chair, following her to the tube. When the door snicked shut, he ordered, "Level nineteen."

"Feel better?" Halloway asked.

"No."

"Too bad. I'd hoped getting you off the bridge would—"

"And what was that mutinous look you gave me earlier? I ought to have you court-martialed for that!"

"I didn't know they did that for 'looks.' "

"I may start a new trend." He glared at her.

The corners of her mouth tucked in a repressed smile. "Sometimes I almost think you're human. Not usually, but—"

"Good."

Silence descended and he surreptitiously studied the beauty of her face, the smooth curve of her jaw, the pale translucence of her skin, the calculating look in her green eyes. Why the hell did that attract him? He rubbed his forehead briskly. *Too long without a vacation.*

The door zipped back on level nineteen and he waved an arm for her to exit. She bowed slightly and strode out. He followed, watching the grace of her movements as they hurried toward Transportation.

"What," she asked, eyeing him as though she were the captain and he a subordinate officer, "do you plan on doing if the Magistrates order you to scorch Horeb?"

"I'll scorch Horeb."

"No discussion? No attempt to change their minds?"

"I'm an officer in the Magisterial fleet, Lieutenant. I don't question orders."

She nodded tersely, back stiffening. "I see."

Together they walked through the door to Transportation. A small dark-haired boy whirled as they entered, utter fright on his face. Dressed in a brown robe, he looked cadaverously thin.

Tahn stopped, feeling queasy at that haunted look. He put out a hand for Halloway to stand aside, then went to the boy and knelt in front of him.

"I'm Captain Tahn," he said softly, watching the boy's eyes widen. *Had he looked so wretchedly terrified when*

412

Moreno found him? "You don't have to be afraid here. I won't let anybody hurt you."

The boy's mouth quivered, tears filling his dark eyes. "Will you take me to Magistrate Slothen? I need to talk to him."

"I'll take you. Don't worry."

The boy's gaze darted over Tahn's face, as though searching for untruths. He smiled, trying to project as much honesty as he could, given the circumstances.

After a few moments, Mikael reached out a hand and put it on Tahn's shoulder, patting gently. "Thank you, sir. Can I—can I go somewhere and sleep now?"

Tahn frowned. "Yes, I'll take you to our guest quarters on level seven. But don't you want to eat first, or talk some more? I'd be happy to—"

"No, sir, please. When I sleep, the bad times go faster."

Tahn dropped his chin to rest on his chest, exhaling heavily. The boy had been through hell, no wonder he wanted to sleep as much as possible.

He stood. "Come on. I'll take you to your quarters." He started to walk away and heard the boy's quick steps, felt a tiny hand slip inside his, the fingers going tight around his thumb. A vulnerable part of him came alive—a part he hadn't felt in years. Like shocked nerves awakening, he tingled, feeling a need to protect the boy from any more trauma.

"Captain, let me—" Halloway started.

"I'll take care of our guest, Lieutenant. Please get to the bridge and set course for Horeb. Notify the Magistrates of the situation there. I'll be in my quarters if anything important comes up."

She reluctantly started to back away, then asked suddenly, "Will you be all right?"

"I have all sorts of strange talents, Carey. Don't worry."

"Aye, sir." She hesitantly backed out of the room.

He squeezed Mikael's hand and led the boy down the long white hall, thinking of how Bogomil said he hadn't been eating.

"Mikael, I have to go my cabin first. Have you ever been inside a captain's cabin?"

"No, sir."

"Would you like to? I have some fancy things in there. Games and a galactic stamp collection. Even some—"

"Do you want me to?"

He looked down into those wide, pained brown eyes and his heart melted. "Yes, I do. Maybe we could even have some sandwiches and soup brought in while we look at things."

"I'm not very hungry. My stomach doesn't work too well any more. It hurts a lot."

Tahn nodded understandingly. They passed several crew members who saluted. He returned the gestures perfunctorily. "I've felt that way myself recently. Maybe we can—"

"Did the Magistrates hurt you, too?" Mikael's face darkened and he lowered his eyes to the floor. "Oh, I'm sorry. I guess you wouldn't feel that way since you work for them."

"Well, I may work for them, but they hurt me sometimes, too."

"They do? But don't you like them?"

Tahn flinched at the question, imagining Slothen's blue hair writhing as the alien thought. "No, can't say that I do."

"Then why do you work for them?"

They walked to a transportation tube and he palmed the entry. Leading Mikael inside, he slumped back against the white wall. *Leave it to a kid to go to the heart of things.* "I'm not sure anymore. I used to know. But things have gotten hazy lately."

The boy tucked a finger in his mouth and squeezed Tahn's hand comfortingly. "Sometimes things get like that."

He smiled faintly. "I guess so."

CHAPTER 42

Rachel stood beside Adom in the communications center, watching his handsome face contort in agony. He gripped her hand like a life raft in a turbulent ocean as he spoke lovingly to the populace of Seir:

"My people, take heart. I know the trials ahead seem terrible and terrifying, but we must rise to meet them. Milcom fights for us even now, fights to conquer the horrors of suffering wrought by Epagael. We will all triumph if we stay together and help each other. The chambers here are cold and I—I miss you very much. As soon as I can, I'm coming home to you. In the meantime, love everyone who fights at your side, serve everyone, and remember God."

The screen went dead for a second, a gray static filling the expanse, then Ornias' tanned face appeared, a gloating smile on his lips. In the background a series of red and blue tapestries glowed in a golden halo of candlelight. "Perfect, Adom. I'm sure they'll gain heart again. We're projecting your face all over the city."

"How many," Adom choked out, swallowing hard. He clenched Rachel's hand hard. "How many have we lost?"

"I haven't checked casualty figures lately."

"Well, please do so."

Rachel blinked at the commanding tone of voice. It didn't sound like Adom, but he was distraught, vividly feeling every pain he witnessed occurring on the streets of Seir.

Ornias eyed Adom deprecatingly, but leaned over and punched a key on his computer. "As of three a.m. the total losses of both sides approximate thirty thousand."

Adom shuddered violently, so violently Rachel stepped between him and screen, whispering, "There's nothing you can do about it. It's not your fault. Don't torture yourself."

"But they're my people, Rachel." He opened his eyes and tears clouded the blue depths. "I know Milcom will save them all eventually, but I can't bear to see them suffer more."

"Adom?" Ornias called gruffly, clearly disgusted by the display. "Last time you requested to see scenes of the war, do you still—"

"Yes!" he ordered sharply. "I want to know what's happening. Let me—*us*—see."

"Very well."

The screen switched to show an overview of the far section of the city. Rachel sucked in a breath. Her home stood not more than two blocks from the focal point of the lens. The bakery she'd frequented, the meat merchant's shop, the dress shop, filled the screen in toppled devastation. She put a trembling hand over her mouth. Had Ornias planned it? To torment her? Hatred rose.

Adom jerked, stepping back as a bolt of violet splashed the screen. Buildings crumbled with a deep-throated roar. And from the broken debris a child, a little girl, darted, running headlong toward them. She clutched a green-spotted toy horse to her breast.

"Oh, my God," Adom murmured, watching in horror. "Ornias?" he cried raggedly. "There's a child in the streets! Send someone to—"

A shrill whine split the air and the child's head jerked around, staring in horror at the sky. Her mouth opened in a scream and she clutched the horse tightly, but the sound disappeared in the thunder of beam cannon fire, her body exploding like a ripe melon dropped from a great height. Blood and bits of flesh slammed the walls of toppling buildings.

Rachel faded back, Sybil's face—for a terrible, terrible instant—replacing that of the unknown girl. Her shoulder thudded hard against the wall and she slid to the floor, stunned, barely noticing Adom's sobs or his fist repeatedly slamming the control console—though the sharp thuds seemed to echo through the entire vast complex.

Jeremiel told you—he told you ten times more would die if you failed to carry out your mission. Every moment you sit here and waste time weeping, another child perishes miserably.

She drew up her knees and buried her face in the velvet folds of the ebony cloak.

"No . . ." Adom murmured.

Rachel looked up to see a group of seven women running through the streets, dragging crying children by the hands. They rounded a corner, hurrying as much as they could through the smoking rubble. Her heart stopped. She studied the faces. Wasn't that Myra in the lead? Talo's niece? She remembered her from those eternal hours in the square where time stopped; only thirst and terror existed. The stench of death. The night birds tearing. The whimper of buried children who would never be found. Sybil's still body against her legs.

Yes, it was Myra, she recognized the long thin hair and large eyes. Rachel watched with sick hope as they rounded another corner, running straight at the lens.

A coherent beam lashed through the already torn buildings and a huge stone wall crumbled, enormous chunks tumbling down onto the street. Rachel clutched her throat, watching the stones roll over the fleeing group.

"Wait! One's still alive," Adom sobbed, wringing his hands.

Myra dragged herself from beneath the debris to lie in a broken heap beside a mound of fragmented gray stones. In a hopeless gesture, she extended a hand toward the screen, pleading inaudibly, as though she could see Rachel's pale ravaged face.

And Rachel understood.

Kill him. Kill him! For all of us. Do what you promised that terrible day in the square!

"Adom?" Ornias' face replaced Myra's on the screen. "The troops are fading again. Stragglers have gathered outside the palace. Can you speak to them?"

"Yes. I—I can."

The monitor filled with the hollow eyes of thousands, each staring pleadingly at the screen before them, yearning for the Mashiah's reassurance that everything would be all right. Dressed in rags and bloodstained uniforms, they appeared ghoulish.

Through great effort Adom pulled himself together, raising his arms to the multitudes, a look of terrible suffering on his face.

"Friends, I grieve with you, I . . ."

Rachel rose as though in a dream, her heart numb, legs moving forward leadenly. *"Adom?"*

He turned and all the color drained from his face when she drew the knife from her boot and lifted it over her head. Sweat popped out across his forehead as he backed away, stumbling into the screen. In the background Rachel could see people screaming in horror as they watched.

"No," he said softly, "Rachel, no."

She lunged, thrusting the knife into his broad chest. Blood splattered his ivory robe, an irregular crimson starburst. He clutched his heart, closing his eyes as he sank to the floor.

Then the horrified rage of thousands blared across the audio system and Rachel's knees went weak. The image faded abruptly, Ornias' angry face swelling to fill the monitor like an enraged beast.

"You fool!" he screamed. "It wasn't time! Now the forces will fall apart. I'll kill you for this. *You stupid FOOL!*"

She slammed a fist against the switch, turning it off. The room grew breathlessly quiet, the only sound, the soft sucking of the hole in Adom's chest.

"Rachel . . ." He coughed, sliding in slow motion to his side. A red froth bubbled at his lips. "Hold me?"

She dropped to her knees, gathering him in her arms and pulling him tightly to her breast. "Adom, forgive me."

"But," he said quietly, desperation edging his words, "Milcom said you . . . you wouldn't . . ."

"Milcom is Aktariel, Adom!" she cried in anguish. "He'd do anything, say anything to get you to help him!"

"Oh," he whispered, eyes looking lovingly into hers. "I know. I've known . . . for a long time. But he . . . he's right. We have to . . . to end the suf . . ."

He fell into a coughing fit and Rachel expertly held his head sideways, her soul shriveling at the amount of blood he spit up on the floor.

He gazed up at her. In his eyes she saw all the tenderness, the boyish innocence that had ravaged her heart in past weeks. She bowed her head and wept silently, tears running down her face to drop on his chest. He reached a trembling hand up to stroke her cheek.

"It's . . . all right, Rachel. I know you just wanted to . . . end the suffering . . . too."

His robe rustled as he tried to move, then fell silent. His body went limp in her arms and she hugged him blindly, crying into his blond hair.

In agony, she looked up and saw her reflection on the blank screen. Her wide eyes accused. Nothing she could say would be defense enough. She'd murdered the only gentleness in the universe that could soothe the agony.

Slowly, she lowered his slack body to the floor, and pulled her arms from beneath him. Ornias had promised revenge. A *samael* undoubtedly flew north even now, filled with marines whose orders she dared not think about.

She started to rise but couldn't, her legs shook too hard to hold her. Leaning forward, she tenderly kissed Adom's pale forehead and for a moment snuggled her cheek against his. "Adom, I . . ."

In the harsh glare of the lustreglobes, his wide blue eyes stared out, strangely calm, as though relieved that the horrors of the universe no longer concerned him.

Rachel forced herself to get to her feet.

"I've got to get out of here." She ran, stumbling down the hall, to the vator. Palming the entry, she rode to the surface anteroom in a trance of deadly quiet.

When it stopped and the door clacked back, she lunged for the storage room where Adom had told her the *samael* pilot had hung extra weather-suits. She found two hanging in perfect order, helmets on the shelf above.

Stepping into one of the suits, she fastened it all the way

up and fixed the helmet on her head. She hit the door button and a blast of glacial wind flooded over her. Even through the suit, she felt the tendrils of fatal cold.

Darkness spread like a black velvet blanket outside. Wind whipped fingers of snow high into the heavens and sent a white haze rippling close to the ground.

Rachel walked out into the waste wilderness of ice and ran toward the windblown snowdrifts, seeking a place to hide from the *samaels*. Through the snow caking her visor, she studied the indigo shadows clinging to the cliffs, striving to follow the lee of the ice wall.

She tramped for a timeless eternity, until her feet and hands ached miserably from cold. Stars glittered like frost crystals above, but still no *samaels* dove through the night. How long had she been wandering? Two hours, maybe three? If Ornias had dispatched them immediately, they'd still be an hour away. A flicker of hope warmed her. She picked up her leaden legs and ran with all the frail might she could muster for a cleft in the icy cliff ahead. A series of black dots marred the white. Overhangs? She'd passed hundreds in the past hours, but they'd all been too close to the polar chambers.

As she neared the location, she recognized the dots as caves. Bending over, she lumbered inside one. Blackness enveloped her, but at least the wind no longer tormented. Waving hands over her head, she searched the expanse to find its limits. The ceiling stretched too high for her fingers to touch, but the walls seemed no more than ten feet in any direction. She edged as far back as she could and slumped to the floor, staring out the entry. In the fainter gray beyond, wind hurled snow against the cliffs, shrieking mournfully.

Rachel clumsily unfastened her helmet and set it on the floor beside her, taking a deep breath of the sharp air. Her exhale plumed whitely. *What you just did is suicide.* But as she leaned her head back against the wall, she knew she didn't care. *I'll put it back on soon*, she promised, blinking around at her shelter. Without the helmet blocking her view, she could see the brilliance of the *Mea* splashing her collar. *Light.* She tugged on the chain, pulling it out. A cerulean halo illuminated the cave, reflecting darkly from the irregular surface of the walls.

She dropped it against her white suit, where it flared insistently. Dear God, had it been only a few hours ago that Adom had nestled against her like a frightened child? All her memories of him seemed vivid, crystalline. Adom in his long robes, smiling shyly, brushing blond hair from his handsome face to expose eyes wide with innocent longing.

Tears welled, freezing on her lashes as silent sobs racked her body. "I didn't want to kill him. Why did I have to kill him, God?" Unconsciously, she gripped the warm *Mea* and pressed it to her forehead, burying her face against her drawn up knees.

* * * * *

Night covered the spiny ridges, wind carrying the damp pungency of blood and resin smells from explosions. Harper slithered on his stomach to the hill overlooking Seir. Four monks in gray uniforms crawled up behind him, faces grim. The city glowed golden with flames. Rifle fire burst in the darkness, forming a glittering necklace along the streets.

"Janowitz, you go first, we'll fan out behind you."

"On my way, Harper." The short stocky blond scrambled down the hill. Hitting the street, he dodged into the shadows of blasted buildings.

"Bromy . . ." Harper began, but a shrill whine stopped him. "Take cover!" He jerked his arms over his head as the whine grew to a deafening roar. The ground shook violently, cascades of dirt raining down. In the distance, he saw the violet beam of the cannon panning another hill, slashing the tor to nothingness.

"They're hitting all the high spots," he rasped. "Go, get into the city! We'll regroup at the corner of Izhar Street."

Men flooded around him. He waited until their dark forms disappeared amidst the avalanche of tumbled walls. Casting a look over his shoulder, toward the faraway caves of the Fathers, he saw a red glow flame and burst like a forest fire, sweeping the hills. "Direct hit. Does that mean Jeremiel's plan is working?" *Once you get to the city,* he'd said, *we'll lower the defenses here. That should draw them like vultures to a dying weabit. While they're pounding us, you'll have fewer ships and troops to worry about in the city.*

He cringed as another blast flared, fear forcing him to hurry down the hill to find the madman who gave those pilots their orders. Running onto the street, he pounded toward the corner, glimpsing fleeting shadows congregating there.

"Harper."

The whisper came from an alley to his right. Adrenaline flooded through his veins. He veered in that direction, edging into a deep well of blackness. Four faces gleamed faintly.

"Janowitz, who's on the corner?"

"We don't know, but there's about a dozen of them, dressed in rags, carrying clubs for the most part."

Harper gripped his rifle tighter. Part of Rachel's old rebel faction? They could use all the people they could recruit. But what if they were Mashiah devotees? Armed civilian fanatics would tear them to pieces more zealously than Ornias' marines. "Go! Head down the alley. The way into the palace underground is from Eleventh Avenue."

Hugging the steep banks of rubble, they silently drifted out onto the next street and raced through a still smoking section of merchant shops. Signs hung mournfully, canted at awkward angles. Roof debris was scattered along the road and overhead billows of smoke glowed like marmalade from still raging fires.

"Left or right, Harper?" Janowitz whispered.

"Right."

Somewhere a horse screamed, a sobbing woman shouting at it; the sound of a whip on flesh cracked sharply.

It took nearly an hour to work their way to the narrow streets of the residential section that overlooked the palace. Clenching his teeth, Harper studied the massive triangular structure. One entire side had collapsed under Jeremiel's cannon blasts, throwing jagged splinters of marble into the nearby hillsides; they protruded like pink lances. No guards lined the parapet. No lights shone.

"Abandoned?" Janowitz asked suspiciously. In the glow of the fires, Harper saw the sweat beaded on his long pale nose, the lines etched tightly around his green eyes.

"The staff probably retreated underground with the councilman. I'd guess that's where the majority of guards are stationed, too."

"Where are the entryways?"

"Jeremiel drew a detailed map for us. He knows the palace and its enclaves better than the Mashiah himself."

"How the hell did he find something none of us knew about? I know he sifted through thousands of those musty documents in the records room, but—"

"Apparently, *he* knew what he was looking for." *Passageways with the fewest intersecting corridors—the straightest, safest routes to the heart of the caverns directly beneath the palace.* That's *where Ornias will be,* he'd said.

Taking the map from his pocket, he examined it in the dim light. Janowitz came to lean over his shoulder, staring.

"There are two possible entrances. See? Here and here? The third can only be reached from inside the palace. I don't think we want to try that."

"I don't either."

"Bromy?" Harper waved the gray-haired man over and pointed out the entrance. "You take Mipas and Uriah and hit this inlet. Janowitz and I will strike this one." He looked up, nervously licking his lips. "We haven't got much time. If we're lucky our paths will intersect in the garden directly beneath the palace kitchens."

Bromy nodded anxiously, gray brows drawing together. "Will Ornias be there?"

"Baruch thinks so. It's the safest place in the city. But we're not sure."

"Okay. We're on our way." He led Mipas and Uriah up through the burned-out buildings. Harper's breathing quickened as he watched them disappear around a corner.

Janowitz glanced sideways at Harper. "How come you didn't tell me this was a suicide mission?"

"Would you have backed out?"

"Might have."

Harper switched his rifle to full charge and sucked in a deep breath, "That's why I didn't tell you." *Nor am I going to tell you about Baruch's insane contingency plan—until I have to, that is. Damn, how could Jeremiel think the Magistrates might scorch Horeb and the only way to stop them would be to . . .* He shuddered, not even wanting to think about what might happen if he found Jeremiel with Ornias when they reached the gardens.

Janowitz shook his head, lips curling into a smile. A brilliant beam of violet limned the drifting clouds, reflecting from the fragmented windows of the palace. They both froze, watching the bolt explode out in the desert.

"Well," Janowitz sighed, "let's get it over with." He dashed headlong down the street and fired a short burst into a seemingly solid part of the road. "Are you sure this is it? If it won't yield to rifle fire—"

"Wait." Harper ran to join him, looking again at the map and comparing it with their location on the street. "This is it. Baruch suspected the passageway hadn't been used in years since it doesn't appear on later diagrams of the caverns. Let's try concentrating our fire simultaneously. Just a short burst." They both aimed at the spot and violet light streamed out, lashing the road. In less than a second, the entry caved.

Harper jumped down into the darkness. He switched on a tiny handglobe and carefully examined the passageway. It looked old beyond anything he would have believed. Cobwebs filled the tunnel like white veils and the bones of some animal lay strewn across the red floor as though mauled by a now long-dead predator.

Janowitz thudded behind him and they stared at each other apprehensively. Neither could say anything for a moment, then Janowitz remarked, "Well, I guess we don't have to worry about anybody being ahead of us."

"No, not for a while anyway."

"You lead. I'll guard our backs."

Harper nodded, ripping down webs with his rifle barrel as they slid silently toward the center of the caverns. Curious runes covered the walls. Dust outlined their strange linear patterns. He had the eerie feeling this passageway may have been a sacred path, used for millennia by the Milcomworshiping kings in the line of Edom.

"Almost like mathematical symbols, aren't they?" Janowitz whispered behind him.

"It's no math I've ever seen."

They walked in silence for what seemed an eternity, then Harper checked his map again. "We should be coming to an intersecting corridor. Look sharp."

As they neared it, the cave blew cold gusts over them and Harper could see a tall metal door of ancient origin blocking their path. *It wasn't on the map. Had they sealed this corridor for some unknown reason?* He reached out and touched the handle, feeling it icy beneath his fingers. Forcing down the handle, he was surprised when the door unlatched. He gestured for Janowitz to stand still, then he eased up and checked the passageway outside. Empty. Quiet. Not nearly as old as the one they'd been following. Only a few cobwebs clung to the ceiling. He motioned Janowitz forward.

"Which way now?"

"Straight ahead."

They closed the door and trotted across the corridor, racing down the new hall. They ran through the blackness, the sound of their steps echoing from the walls. Then they stopped dead in their tracks, staring in panic at the huge landslide of rocks and debris that filled the tunnel.

"Holy Father," Janowitz breathed. "Is that on the map?"

"No."

"What the hell do we do now? We haven't got very goddamned much time!"

Harper's pulse raced. This was one thing Baruch couldn't have anticipated. He was on his own now. "We can't blast it. That might bring the whole palace down on us. We'll have to go back to that other corridor and work our way around. Come on, for God's sake, let's hurry."

* * * * *

Ornias paced frantically, glaring at the marine captains he'd ordered to assemble in his strategy cave. They stood stiffly, candlelight reflecting oddly from their sweaty faces. "Renon, what's the status outside?"

The tall bald man grimaced. "Bad. Many of the common worshipers broke and ran when they heard about the Mashiah's death. They're hiding—"

"Well, find them! I don't care if you have to kill every coward in the city to keep the rest of the masses fighting. *Do it!*" He had to get Baruch back and quickly or the past four years of planning and sacrificing would have been for nothing. "Anyone who won't fight the Desert Fathers' forces is guilty of treason. You will immediately execute such traitors. Is that clear?"

Panbo, a short man with bad teeth smiled grimly. "You bet, Councilman. Me and my men have been wanting to slaughter the bloody demon worshipers for years. We'll handle it."

"But, sir," Renon said uncomfortably. "If we take our men into the streets, will you have enough protection here?"

"Yes, yes! Get out!"

The captains quickly turned and left.

CHAPTER 43

Cole Tahn lay quietly, staring absently at the dark light panel on the ceiling. His blanket coiled around his waist, exposing the dark mat of hair covering his chest. The soft green glow from the com unit on his bedside desk cast an aquamarine halo over the cabin, highlighting its stark simplicity. His gaze lingered on his books shelved so neatly in the niche over the table.

"Damn it, why can't I sleep anymore? Punitive attacks never used to bother me so much."

But really he knew why. The number had begun to weigh on him. *Carey had begun to weigh on him.* Had the Magistrates given up on diplomacy? Or had all their true diplomats, like Garold Silbersay, been driven mad with frustration? He shuddered to think how Mikael, an innocent boy, would react to the horror of standing face-to-face with Slothen. The Giclasian beast set even his skin to crawling. Would the child be a malleable tool in the government's hands, used to carve the foundation away from Gamant civilization? Probably. Though that might well be a good thing. Someday Gamants had to assimilate into galactic civilization. Better now than later—because there might not be a later.

"Captain?" Macey's voice whispered over the com unit.

He looked at the computer, wanting suddenly to smash it with his fist. Gruffly, he answered, "What is it, Lieutenant?"

"Special message from Magistrate Slothen. It's classified under *Captain's Seal.* Shall I pipe it through, or do you want me to send it on com aura?"

"You know I hate the aura. Pipe it through."

Words sprang into existence on his screen. Sighing deeply, he threw back the blanket and swung his legs over the side of his bed. The cool air chilled his naked body as he leaned forward to read the message.

> *Greetings, Captain Tahn:*
> *Congratulations on a job well-done on Kayan. We are in receipt of your report on Horeb. You are to*

proceed there immediately and initiate sterilization procedures. First, however, contact Councilman Ornias. Inform him we have considered his request and decided to make a counteroffer. In exchange for Baruch, we'll be willing to increase the reward to five billion notes. Grinlow, however, is not available. Regardless of whether he accepts or rejects, proceed with Prime Mover One. Gamants must learn we will allow no deviation from our treaties. While Baruch's knowledge is invaluable, his death will be adequate. We cannot afford another day of useless "bartering." Both Tikkun and Lechud are in violent upheaval. Magisterial installations have been devastated. Trade is at a standstill. Starvation threatens quadrant seven.

Please advise immediately after consulation with the High Councilman.

Magistrate Slothen

Tahn deleted the message and reached for his pants. Stepping into them, he turned back to the com, switching on the visual. The bridge appeared, officers sitting obediently at their consoles.

"Halloway?"

She turned, green eyes glinting. "Bad news, I presume?"

"How long to Horeb?"

"About four hours."

"Contact Doctor Iona. See to it he administers a sedative to Mikael Calas. I want the boy sleeping for the next twelve."

"Why? What are we—"

"Did you get that, Lieutenant?"

"Aye, sir," she responded curtly. "Anything else?"

"Yes, tran Talworth and tell him to get the hell out of orbit by at least 0:1500 hours."

"Cole," Halloway said softly, color draining from her beautiful face. "Surely, we're not—"

"We'll argue about it over a dark ale on Lopsen, Carey. This isn't the time."

He flicked off the com and wearily reached for his shirt.

*   *   *   *   *

"Jeremiel," Rathanial said tightly as he rushed into the council chambers accompanied by his five guards—part of

426

Zadok's contingent. His maroon robe shone blackly in the firelight. He sprinted for the monitor on the table.

"What is it?"

"Quickly, we're not sure when this happened. Our analysts just brought it to me. We've so many 'eyes' on the city and so few people keeping track—since the rest are involved in the battle—that sometimes it takes a while to sift the data."

Jeremiel leaned against the table as the monitor flickered to life. *Scenes from the polar chambers.* Rachel sat against the wall in the background, face pale, chest rising **and** falling as though she'd run a hundred miles.

"Friends, I grieve with you . . ." The Mashiah said in an agonized voice.

Jeremiel gripped the table edge hard as he watched Rachel rise and walk forward, hand dropping to her boot. A glint of silver sparked across the screen. "Come on!" he urged through gritted teeth. "You can do it."

Rachel lifted the knife, beautiful face contorted in grief, then thrust it deep into Adom's chest. A roar of adulation went up from the guards next to Jeremiel as the Mashiah staggered and fell.

Rathanial stared at him. "Now that she's fulfilled her mission, we must get to the palace. Shassy will be in danger. I can't—"

"Shut up!"

The transmission from the caves went dead, but the monitor on the city continued to send. The masses before the palace shrieked in fear, tearing their hair as they ran wildly through the battered streets. Flickers of cannon fire lit the night.

"Get out of my way, Rathanial," Jeremiel said gruffly, shoving the old man aside and switching the monitor to casualty figures. His heart thumped as he read them. "On one side of the city there's been a substantial decrease in deaths. Around the palace, however, casualties have increased sevenfold. Looks like Ornias' marines have gone on a blood rampage. They must be trying to whip those who've lost heart into shape to keep them fighting. Some of it is probably the civilian populace, too, taking out their wrath on anyone who looks like one of our soldiers. Regardless, Rachel must have killed the Mashiah only a short time ago and the news is just now spreading. But it'll take hours for it to reach the troops in the field. The most isolated positions won't find out until this is all over."

"If we have the time to tell them."

He glanced at Rathanial. The elder stood with his arms folded tightly.

"What do you mean? Tahn should still be five—"

"We've been monitoring the transmissions of that small ship he left in orbit. The pilot there was just notified the *Hoyer* is less than two hours away. We—"

"God damn. He's been pushing his engines to the limit. What else? Did Tahn say how he was coming in? What kind of orders he's received?"

"No, we've heard nothing about his orders. But he did tell Talworth, the pilot in the shuttle, to quote: 'be out of orbit by 0:1500 hours.'"

Jeremiel's gut crawled. He sank down on the tabletop. "Well, that's it then."

"What? What does that mean?"

"It means," he said through a tense exhale, "that you need to contact Councilman Ornias. Operation 'bait' is in motion as of this instant."

"Oh," Rathanial lowered his gaze, gray hair gleaming in the flickers of firelight. "Jeremiel, forgive me. I'm so sorry. I—"

"One last thing."

"What is it?"

"Rachel is still at the pole—somewhere. If Tahn calls off the attack, you'd damned well better get up there and find her!"

"I don't think there's any way—I mean . . ." The old man looked up guardedly, as though he feared Jeremiel might kill him.

"What are you talking about?"

"I meant to tell you earlier, but in the flurry over the Mashiah's death, it slipped my mind. You see, Ornias has already dispatched four *samaels*. So even if I could get there once you're—off—I doubt—"

"For God's sake," he whispered, squeezing his eyes closed. The councilman would have undoubtedly given his pilots the same kind of orders he'd been giving his marines for the past three years. Scenes of Syene's dead body ravaged his mind. "Do it anyway, Rathanial. You owe it to her to hunt."

Red climbed the old man's cheeks, he nodded. "Yes, if I can."

"Give me fifteen minutes." Jeremiel shoved to his feet and strode across the room, heading for his chamber to ready the few personal things he'd need.

He made it almost to his room before he doubled over, sick to his stomach.

*   *   *   *   *

Rachel ran, stumbling through the eye of a black cyclone. She'd had the dream before, but this time it seemed even more real and terrifying, as though she'd walked into a trap from which she'd never escape.

Had she died? Had the bitter polar cold killed her body and now her soul searched aimlessly for heaven? The old teachings flooded over her, heaven and hell, Epagael and Aktariel.

Rachel gasped as a woman on horseback rode down on her, sword gleaming as she waved it over her head and shouted angrily in an unknown tongue. She dove out of the way, falling through the bottomless blackness. Getting on hands and knees, she scrambled frantically ahead. "Epagael! Let me go home? Please, I beg you. My little girl needs me. Don't take me away yet!"

A brown splotch wavered to her right. She blinked, trying to bring it into focus, but it rippled as though a wall of water separated her from it.

"Epagael? I believe. I believe! I'm sorry I ever doubted."

A fiery wheel dove out of the blackness, hurtling down at her. She covered her head, screaming, "Let me go home!"

Then a soft, elderly voice penetrated her terror. "Follow the light," it urged. "That's the way to God."

"Who are you?"

"An experienced friend."

The brown splotch moved methodically ahead of her, fading into a brighter gray in the distance. Was that the light? The way?

Rachel got to her feet and ran with all her might, panting as the spot grew brighter and brighter. A curious scent like ozone stung her nose. Her steps faltered.

"Rachel," a deep voice called. "It's not much farther. Step through the gate."

A shiver tingled up her spine. All her life she'd dreamed

429

of talking to God. Stirrings of a fragile childish faith rose. *He'd* explain. *He'd* tell her why so much pain tormented the universe. She longed to run to him and bury her face in his legendary robe, knowing his kind embrace would drive out her fear. "Epagael?"

"Yes. I've been waiting a long time to talk with you. Stars have been born and died in the interim."

Her spirits soared. She sprinted forward. The gray changed to orange and she strode out into a magnificent crystalline palace.

Ten feet in front of her, a wide River of Fire ran, the heat nearly suffocating. Bridges spanned the fiery furnace.

"Rachel?"

She peered across the river. A white veil stood before a massive spinning well of darkness. The voice hurled from out of the black whirlwind.

"Has he deceived you?"

"W–who?"

"Milcom?"

She slowly lowered her arms to her sides and took a deep breath. "You mean Aktariel? No, I—"

"Ah, so you know who he is. Good. His wickedness grows like a cancer in the body of your universe."

Rachel stood silent for a moment, her body trembling. Was this dream or real? The roar of the fiery waves. The gaping black hole. The brilliance of the marmalade walls. They seemed more real at this moment than the icy wilderness of the pole where she knew she must be sleeping . . . or—maybe she really was dead. She felt so tired, so weary. If she could only lie down and sleep and wake to feel Shadrach kissing her face and teasing, "My sweet darling, you've the laziest bones I know. I thought we'd planned on getting up early to go dig radi roots." But she'd never hear his voice again. And she longed to have someone unwearied and wiser on whose shoulders she could rest her heavy burdens.

She looked pleadingly into the whirlwind. "Lord, help me. I don't understand what's happening."

"No, of course, not. Poor Rachel. Aktariel makes everything seem so difficult."

"Why, Lord? You have all the power in the universe. Why do you let him torment us?"

"Sometimes, it's necessary. Faith has to be proven before it can be rewarded."

430

She winced, feeling a small pain in her heart. *The square . . . Talo's words.* She had all the rest of her life to ache, she couldn't succumb just now.

"But if you're all-knowing, Lord, you wouldn't need proof. You'd know."

"It's not as simple as you think. The wickedness of your universe shrouds my eyes."

"Don't speak to me of wickedness!" She shuddered, Edom Middoth's aching journal entries darting through her memories. "My people have died by the thousands praising your name! And where were you? *Absent!* In your convenant with our forebears you promised to protect us. But all you've done is *test our faith* through murder and misdirection!"

"I haven't abandoned the Gamant people. It only seems so from your limited perspective."

"I just murdered . . ." A sob caught in her throat. "I just murdered an innocent man to stop the slaughter of thousands on Horeb. *Why didn't* you *stop it?*"

"Ummm, yes, Adom. Actually, hope killed him. Has Aktariel given you your thirty pieces of silver yet?"

"What? Thirty—"

"Never mind. It happened a long time ago. Another of his plots gone awry."

She shook a fist at the whirlwind. "Do you know how terribly we suffer? Are you omniscient?"

"I know."

"Do you care? If you were really omnibenevolent like the sacred books say, you'd care and you—"

"I care. But, Rachel, you must understand, I'm not—"

"Are you omnipotent?"

"I have absolute power over creation and destruction, if that's what you mean."

"You're a liar! If you were truly all knowing, all good, and all powerful, you could stop the suffering and you'd want to! *Innocent children wouldn't be dying right now on Horeb and across the universe if you were as perfect as the Old Books say!*"

For a time only the roar of the river responded and Rachel found herself on the verge of terrible tears. She clenched her fists. Memories tore at her like the beaks of the night birds.

"Perfection is a matter of perspective."

"You *monster!* You could stop it and you won't. You *enjoy* the starvation and disease. The wars—"

"The spinning patterns of chaos are beautiful. Yes. Watching them gives me great pleasure."

Her knees trembled, heart throbbing. "You're like the plantation master who loves to see the barns fill with cotton regardless of how the field hands suffer beneath the hot sun to put it there."

"The field hands can't appreciate what happens to the cotton once it's gleaned, Rachel. They see only their puny labors, not the magnificent works of art woven from their toil."

"Oh, no . . . *no* . . ." Her lungs heaved as though she'd run to the end of her endurance. "Aktariel is right."

"*He is* not *right!*" Epagael thundered, shaking the crystal floor beneath her boots until she staggered. "Your perceptions are too limited to understand the vastness of the universe. The—"

"I understand suffering! *Do* you? I know how horrifying it is to watch your parents die slowly from disease. I know the agony of having a husband die fighting for righteousness. I've watched my friends brutally slaughtered. I know—"

"*You know nothing.* Where were *you* when I laid the foundations of the universe? Where were *you* when I threw the stars into the heavens and set them to singing? Answer!"

"I—I don't . . . that's a ridiculous question. What does that have to do with suffering?"

"Everything. Can you bind the sweet influences of the Pleiades, or loose the bands of Orion?"

Hatred swelled suffocatingly in her chest. "I'm human. Of course, I can't!"

"When you can, then you'll have the right to argue with Me. Until that time—"

"I'll never stop arguing with you! It would have been better that we were never born, than to endure in misery all our lives!"

"Don't be foolish. Aktariel has deceived you into believing all of existence is suffering. Have you never seen a sunset? Have you never counted the wildflowers in the deserts in the spring? Do you wish your beautiful daughter had never been born?"

Rachel's heart ached. Her mind filled with images of dark tousled curls, wide brown eyes and joyous smiles. She knew now that God offered no infinite solace for her aches. Only in the arms of her little girl would the pain ease. "Adom said Milcom told him the suffering would progressively get worse. Will it?"

"Chaos becomes more intricate as time passes, yes. It's fascinating to observe the wealth of new patterns that have burst into existence in just the time we've been talking."

Despair swept her. "I hate you. *I hate you, Epagael!*"

"So . . ." he murmured. "So."

And for a long time, she stood, glaring across into the black whirlwind. Then the floor went out from under her feet. She was falling, falling, falling.

CHAPTER 44

Yosef and Ari wandered down the cluttered hall, the lamp in Ari's hand trembling so that it was a menace to what remained of the palace. Candlelight flickered eerily over shattered rose agate statues and crushed furniture. Marble pillars leaned precariously, supported by walls that sagged inward.

"A death trap," Ari muttered, eyes focused on the dark ceiling. "There could be anything up there waiting to fall on us and we wouldn't know."

Dressed in a tattered gray robe, his friend's face shone with sweat. He nervously fiddled with the pistol hanging from his belt. Yosef had one, too, though he didn't like to think about it. They'd taken them from dead palace guards yesterday, just in case they had to "shoot their way out," Ari had suggested.

"Such a shame. The building used to be so beautiful."

"I wonder why the cannon blasts have stopped? You think maybe the war's over?"

Yosef shrugged. He desperately hoped so, but dared not believe yet. "Maybe it's just a lull in the firing while Jeremiel gets into a better position."

"Maybe."

"Let's hurry and get to the lower levels, just in case."

"Sure." Ari reached over and patted Yosef's shoulder tenderly, as though sensing the depths of his fear.

They descended a staircase to the dark basement level

and found an intact hall. Breathing easier, Yosef trudged ahead. Perhaps they could find a sanctuary to hide in for the next few days?

"You think Baruch's winning?" Ari asked as they turned a corner.

"Who knows? It seems like the entire world has gone up in flames in the past few hours. No one wins a war. Everybody loses."

"But we will have to fight, Yosef. If we fight enough, maybe we can prove to our enemies we're not going to lie down and die just because they say so."

He pursed his lips and stared at the floor. Zadok had said something like that to him after the first Gamant Revolt. In his mind, he heard his brother's vehement voice again: "If they think they can step on us, they will! We have to prove we bite back. *Or our people will cease to exist!*"

Ari threw out a hand to stop him from turning the next corner. Yosef, deep in thought, hadn't noticed the faint glow of other lamps that penetrated the darkness. He stopped abruptly, holding his breath.

"Hear them?" Ari whispered.

Yosef strained to hear and caught the murmur of low voices. A deep baritone hissed, "I don't know. Some folks are saying he's that leader of the Underground, Baruch. But I'm not sure I believe it."

"Baruch?" another voice spat disbelievingly. "Brought in at gunpoint by an old man? I don't buy it, either. Besides, you saw how the councilman treated him. A blow like that across my chops would have laid me down for an hour. If he was really Baruch, why wouldn't the councilman be sidling up to him for help? We're all Gamants, for God's sake."

Ari gave Yosef a worried look, shaking his shaggy gray head. He breathed, "The *snake?*"

Yosef nodded. Had Jeremiel returned to the caves and been captured by the very traitor he sought? The thought set Yosef's heart to throbbing. He cupped a hand to his ear to see what else he could hear.

"But what if he is Baruch?" the baritone asked.

"What difference would it make now?"

"Maybe a lot. Suppose these fellas we've got shackled in here are his cohorts? Maybe his army is waiting just over the hill to come riding down on us."

"Baruch, betray Gamants? I don't believe it."

"We're not true Gamants, though. We believe in a different god. Milcom—"

"Don't talk about it, Sam! I can't bear the thought of the Mashiah being dead. It—it makes my belly ache."

Yosef squeezed his eyes closed, grief swelling to fill him. So that's why the firing had stopped? Rachel had taken the heart out of Adom's followers? Were Ornias' forces breaking and running even now? *Blessed Epagael, he hoped so and yet, what a price to pay.*

He gazed at Ari. His friend hung his head, staring at the candlelit floor. When he looked up, a strange fire glowed in his ancient eyes. He whispered, "We've got to break into that room and free those men."

"But what if they're not Jeremiel's forces? What if—"

"Doesn't matter," Ari insisted. "Anybody that ugly councilman would shackle in his Chamber of Horrors deserves to be rescued."

A swallow bobbed uncomfortably in Yosef's throat. "How?"

Ari's face darkened. He drew the pistol from his holster and held the barrel pointed toward the ceiling.

Yosef looked down. He touched his own gun, but jerked his hand away, unable to bear the thought of killing another human being. "Ari, I—I don't know if I can—"

"You don't have to, Yosef. You stay here. Cover the hall for me."

"No," Yosef said softly, shaking his head. "I won't let you go out alone." Forcing his hand down, he pulled the pistol and held it inexpertly pointed at his foot. He pushed his spectacles up on his nose. "Come on. Let's go."

Together, they rounded the corner. The guards leapt up from their seats, chairs squealing to slam into the wall as they grabbed for their weapons.

"Don't!" Ari shouted, aiming at the tall corporal's stomach. The men halted, raising their hands.

"Aren't you the Mashiah's aides?" the redheaded corporal asked, licking his lips nervously.

"Yes. Open that door."

"I don't get it, old man. Did you decide to go turncoat when you found out he'd been murdered? Goddamn, now's the time we've got to stick together. The councilman says the Mashiah's been speaking to him from beyond the grave."

"Open that door!"

"All right. Don't get jumpy." The corporal lifted his key

ring and jiggled it in the lock, then swung the door open. The private stood rigidly still, eyes fixed on Ari's gun.

"Yosef," Ari ordered gently. "Go see who's in there. I'll stand in the door and keep an eye on these two."

Quickly, he trotted ahead, gingerly going down the steps. He saw Ari enter and stand rigidly in the doorway behind him. A horrifying sight met his eyes. Four men hung a foot off the ground, shackled to the long wall. One had been dead for weeks. The man's shrunken face twisted in terrible agony, mouth open, eyes staring wide and horrified at the ceiling. Yosef gazed forlornly at him. Probably he'd been a handsome man. Who was he? Some other innocent victim of this terrible war? Would the man have been alive today if he and Ari had made it down the night they'd planned? The night they'd seen Jeremiel dragged up the stairs? His heart ached, wishing they could have saved him.

He tugged his gaze back to the living. "Are you part of Jeremiel's forces?"

"Yes," the captive nearest, a gray-haired man said. "Did he send you to save us?"

"No, we . . ."

In the hallway, a shrill blast of rifle fire erupted. Ari lunged backward, knocking Yosef to the floor. He covered his head. Bedlam let loose outside, soldiers screaming, shouting, violet flashes shredding the corridor . . . and then it all went silent. Yosef got to his feet and ran to look out the door. Both marine guards were dead, slumped over each other on the floor, and two men in gray uniforms crouched in the hall.

"Come out of that room!" the tall black man ordered.

Yosef eased out with his hands up, but Ari mysteriously stayed behind.

"Who are you?"

Yosef locked his trembling knees. "We're loyal followers of the Mashiah. We came down here to—"

"Harper?" the gray-haired man in the Chamber of Horrors shouted and Yosef whirled. "Harper, for God's sake, get us out of here!"

"Bromy?" The black man ran forward. "How the hell did you get captured?"

"Jeremiel's plan was working great until we took a wrong turn and ran into a mess of guards."

Yosef smiled at the short blond who still had his pistol aimed at Yosef's pudgy stomach. "You're part of Jeremiel's forces?"

"I am. Who are you?"

"I'm Yosef Calas. My friend, Ari Funk, is—"

"Right here," Ari said. He pushed out of the room, his gun shoved in Harper's chest. "How do we know these guys are working for Baruch?" he questioned suspiciously.

Yosef blinked, going back and forth between Ari's pistol and the blond's. If Ari killed Harper, the blond would certainly kill him. It didn't look good. "Well . . . let's test them," he suggested. "What planet is Baruch from?"

Harper blinked incredulously. "Tikkun."

"What was his mother's maiden name?"

"I . . . I haven't the vaguest idea. But, excuse me, what did you say your name was?"

"Calas."

The man's gaze softened, a smile touching his lips. "Zadok's brother from Tikkun. Yes, I remember. He spoke of you often. I'm Avel Harper."

"You knew my brother?"

"Yes, please, Mister Calas, Zadok recruited me years ago to serve as his eyes and ears here on Horeb. I must find Councilman Ornias. We are all in very great danger."

"If you knew my brother, you'd know his wife's name."

"Nelda. She died during the last revolt after having been captured and held by the Magistrates. She—"

"That's good enough. We'll have to take the chance. Jeremiel's in trouble. He needs help badly."

Harper's face slackened in horror. "He's *here?*"

"That's what the guards said when we sneaked up on them. He's been captured. He's with the councilman."

"Oh, God, then we've got to hurry. Even if we rescue Jeremiel, we've got a long day left."

"Cut off these irons!" The men inside the chamber shouted.

Harper dodged past Ari and the sound of metal squealing under rifle fire sounded. In only moments, all four men emerged from the chamber.

"Where's Baruch being held captive?" Harper asked.

"In the old gardens. We need to go down this hall and descend the stairs, then go straight ahead, past the ivory statue of Milcom. It's the first door on the right. But it'll be heavily guarded. You might want to—"

Ari interrupted. "Let us go first. We know the way and we were the Mashiah's personal aides. Many of the guards know us." Dragging Yosef forward, he pressed between the gray-clad men and headed down the hall.

Zadok braced his shoulder against the wall of the seventh crystal palace of God, gazing out over the beauty. Sunset fired the skies, splashing drifting clouds with bands of mauve and crimson. He yawned, watching an elk cow and calf graze in the viridian meadow that spread along the dirt trail back to the sixth heaven. The cool breeze carried the sweet scents of wildflowers and pines.

"Zadok?" Anapiel's heavenly voice called.

He straightened, rushing for the doors to the palace. The huge angel appeared, his dark blue robe glimmering purplish in the sunset.

"Will Epagael see me now?"

"Yes. Come in."

Zadok hurried through the entry, sucking in a deep breath at the wild orange sparkles of the crystal walls. Fluttering shadows danced across his brown robe as though alive.

"I've never seen Arobot look so beautiful," he murmured as he raced down the long hall. Ahead, he could see the waves of heat rising from the River of Fire.

Anapiel kept pace at his side. "Perhaps it's just for you, Zadok?"

"Why would that be, Lord?"

"To impress you, of course."

"I hardly think Epagael needs to work at that."

Anapiel laughed, giving him a thorough appraisal. "Really?"

"Is there something you're trying to tell me?"

"Me? No. Not I. One of my goals in life is to tell you as little as possible, Zadok."

"I've noticed that before."

Anapiel smiled, lazily flipping the ends of the golden sash around his waist. "Well, you won't have to worry about it much longer. But I do wonder how Epagael's going to manage getting you out of here. You being dead and all."

"A minor point, I'd think, for God."

"Oh, no, I assure you, it's a major point, Zadok. While the energy that defines you can travel unhindered through the gate, you have no receptacle to return to. *I wonder where Epagael's going to* put *you?*" Anapiel chuckled gleefully. "Then again, maybe he'll leave you 'in-between,' eh? Your own private purgatory? I'd pay to see that."

"You irritate me to death, Anapiel, did you know that? You're almost as bad as Sedriel."

The angel flapped his wings indignantly. "Don't be insulting, patriarch."

Zadok forced his ancient legs to move faster. The roar of the River of Fire grew louder with each step and he could faintly glimpse the shimmering white of the Veil.

"Anapiel, why don't you go find something productive to do? There must be a latrine somewhere that needs your personal attention."

The angel glowered. "You're lucky I'm not God, Zadok."

"We're *all* lucky you're not God."

Anapiel sighed and bowed jauntily. "Very well. I'll let you go alone to Mount Moriah. But Avram took companions, if you'll recall."

"He had people around that he trusted."

Anapiel chuckled. "Well, then . . ." He turned and strode back toward the doors of the palace, his soft laughter echoing eerily from the orange walls.

Zadok clenched his fists, trotting forward as quickly as he could. Moriah? The place at which Epagael tested Avram's faith? The Father of the people had faced four great crises in his life, each involving the surrender of something precious.

Zadok steeled himself for the worst—*the loss of his people.* His knees trembled by the time he reached the River of Fire.

"Lord? Lord, I've come. Please, let me see the Veil?"

From out of the black whirlwind, God's soothing voice issued. "Zadok, blessed servant, of course. Cross."

The searing heat from the river turned to a cool breeze and Zadok rushed across the bridge to stand awkwardly on the white tiles before the curtain that shielded the throne of God. His skin prickled with the energy of God's presence.

"The Veil." It stretched like a long satin sheet, fluttering gently in the cool breeze sweeping the crystal palace. He hurried for the end.

"The time is at hand, Zadok. The final battle of Light and Dark threatens even at this moment. Aktariel's forces are poised for attack."

"So I've gathered from your arrogant angels, Lord." Zadok dropped to his knees to read the tiny words written at the base of the Veil. His eyes widened involuntarily, throat constricting as he read. He scrambled, crawling to read the remainder. "No. Epagael, No! *You mustn't let this happen!*"

"You may be able to avert it, Zadok. I don't know."

He got to his feet, bracing a hand against the cool white Veil to steady himself. "Tell me what I must do."

"Zadok, Zadok, it will require a great sacrifice on your part. For I cannot send you back to your universe."

My Mount Moriah. "Then how can I help, Lord?" He shouted, spreading his arms wide. "Surely you won't let my people die because I can't go home?"

The black whirlwind churned violently, God's voice resounding like thunder. "What will you give to save your universe—your people?"

"Anything!"

"Indeed, patriarch? *Good.*"

CHAPTER 45

Sybil stood anxiously, spreading her feet across the sandstone to brace herself against the cold wind. Far below, raging fires rolled over Seir, starlight glowing from billowing clouds of smoke. Fifty or more monks crowded around her, murmuring in fear to each other. She studied them cautiously. If they were so frightened, maybe things weren't going as well as Petran had told her? The short bald monk, Harper's friend, patted her head uneasily. He didn't really like little girls, she could tell. He never held her warmly or played with her.

"Petran?" she shouted into the wind. "When can I go see my mom?"

He leaned down, timidly squeezing her hand. "Soon."

She searched his pale face, catching the hesitation, the tightly pressed lips, and knowing of a sudden that he'd lied to her. He had no idea when she'd get to see her mother . . . or . . . or if she would.

She jerked a nod and, brushing brown hair from her eyes, looked back to the city. Inside her chest, a hollow place grew.

*　　*　　*　　*　　*

"Captain," Macey informed. "I have the councilman."

"On screen, Lieutenant."

Ornias' tanned face formed, a gloating smile creasing his

440

lips. Dressed regally in a gold silk robe, he stood in an underground chamber, red stone gleaming darkly in candlelight. "Greetings, Captain. I understand the Magistrates have considered my offer?"

Tahn rubbed his chin. At her console, Halloway made a small noise that sounded like a subvocal curse. The rest of his bridge crew sat rigid, eyes glued to the screen, some with fists clenched.

"Let's get this on the table quickly, councilman. The Magistrates say no to your request for Grinlow. However, they will up the reward for Baruch to five billion notes. Do you accept or reject?"

The councilman's face tensed, lime green eyes going hard. "Five billion is hardly enough to—"

"*Yes, or no.*"

"You don't mind if I think about for a short time, do you, Captain?"

"I'll give you five minutes. In the meantime, *put Baruch on. I want to see him.*"

Ornias inclined his head cooperatively and waved a hand. Tahn's stomach muscles went tight as a tall muscular blond with fierce blue eyes was shoved in front of the screen. Two men in gray suits clutched his arms. Bound with his hands behind his back, the blond lifted his bearded chin defiantly. A sheen of sweat matted his hair to his forehead and temples.

"Baruch."

"Tahn."

They stared at each other, taking one another's measure. A curious sensation tormented Tahn. He'd often dreamed of sitting down with the man over a few glasses of rye and talking strategy—or landing a few fists. "You'll be treated well, Baruch. I give you my word."

"Until you get me to the next neurophysiology center."

"Nonetheless—"

"Did you give your word to the innocent victims on Kayan? Or Pitbon?"

The hostile tone rankled, the words like salt in his wounds. "I wasn't at Pitbon."

"No? How about Jumes or Wexlen? I *know* you were there."

Tahn looked up slowly, adrenaline flooding his system. Baruch had pulled brilliant maneuvers at both, slipping through his fingers before he knew what had happened.

441

"Councilman?" he called, indicating the discussion with Baruch was over.

The two guards tried to drag Baruch out of range of the monitor but he struggled violently, shouting, "Tahn! *Tahn, damn you!* What are your orders for Horeb? You told your shuttle pilot to get out of orbit. If these people turn me over, *what are you going to do?*"

The guards succeeded in hauling him away. Ornias stepped in front of the screen, smiling insincerely. He opened his mouth to speak and Tahn growled, "Get off screen, Councilman. I've decided I'm not finished with Baruch."

"How dare you—"

Tahn leaped from his seat, shouting in rage, "Get off screen!"

Ornias ground his teeth but he bowed stiffly, giving the monitor back to Baruch. The Underground leader's bearded face showed strain and fear, his breathing shallow.

"Baruch . . . I have Prime Mover orders."

"Level two? Or one?"

"One."

Baruch exhaled haltingly. "This planet is composed of red sandstone. Do you know you're going to raise a wave that looks like a sea of blood?"

"Irrelevant."

". . . Time until initiation?"

"Carey?"

She pinned him with cold green eyes, slapping a button on her console. "Fifty minutes."

"Copy, Baruch?"

"Tahn . . ." The man's blue eyes glimmered imploringly, though his voice stayed hard, steady. "There are a few ships here that might be able to sustain systems until help arrives. If they—"

"I won't attack fleeing refugees. My orders are for the planet alone."

"Thanks for the crumbs from the Magistrates' table. I'll inform the people here."

Tahn anxiously tapped his thumb against his arm. "Councilman? What is your decision regarding our offer."

The manicured politician appeared again, face filling the screen. He glanced uncomfortably at Baruch, then back to Tahn. "What, Captain, is Prime Mover?"

"*Yes or no,* Councilman. Be quick about it."

"Well, under the curious circumstances, I accept. But I want it known I object to the heavy-handed—"

"I'll notify the Magistrates. Prepare Baruch for transport. One of our shuttles will be at your spaceport to retrieve him in exactly thirty minutes." He sighed, "Cut it, Macey."

The screen blanked and he clamped his jaw hard. Halloway swung around in her chair, cocking her head like an eagle with a mouse in sight.

"What is it, damn it?" he asked brusquely.

"Request permission to send wide-beam dattran regarding status of Horebian survivors, sir."

"*Wide-beam*? Have you lost your mind?"

"No, sir. I want to alert any merchant vessels in the vicinity to alter their course. It might just save—"

"You're developing suicidal tendencies, Lieutenant."

"Aye, sir." Her fingers drummed an irregular staccato against the white console. "The message?"

God damn it. A wide beam signal might bring Baruch's own forces down on the Hoyer. *And she knew it just as well as he did. It might also save thousands of Gamant lives.*

"Macey," he ordered, still holding Halloway's challenging gaze. "Send wide-beam dattran regarding status of Horeb, then notify Defense to have a full contingent in Transportation immediately. I want Marc Simons at the helm of the shuttle going for Baruch. Tell him to expect *anything*."

Carey lowered her eyes, swinging back around to her console.

Macey glanced sideways at her and asked, "Shall I inform the Magistrates of Councilman Ornias' decision, too, sir?"

"Yes. And tell them . . ." He filled his lungs with air, staring hollowly at the blank screen. "Tell them I earnestly request two weeks off-duty time on Lopsen."

"Yes, sir." A smile curled his communications officer's mouth. Instantly, the com aura glowed around his head.

Tahn walked toward the door, feeling hot from the adrenaline still searing his veins. "Halloway," he said almost as an afterthought. "Please accompany me to Transportation to meet Baruch."

"On my way."

She got up quickly and followed him into the tube. Once inside, she gave him a level look. "Thanks for the wide-beam authorization. And I appreciate the way you freed us from firing on fleeing civilians."

"Did you think I did it for you?"

Her eyes narrowed, gaze going through him like a coherent beam. "No. I thought you did it in penance for the guilt that's suffocating you."

He shoved his hands deep in his pockets and leaned heavily against the wall. "Damn you, Carey."

* * * * *

Jeremiel strained against the cuffs around his wrists, panic making his hands tremble. He'd seriously thought the Magistrates might call off the attack if it looked like Horeb was cooperating by turning him over. *Fool. Damn fool. They want the death of your civilization. They'll take every opportunity they can to kill Gamants.*

How long did he have left? Fifteen minutes? Where the hell was Harper?

"Councilman. You haven't much time. A Prime Mover Level One attack means complete devastation of the central portion of a planet down to a depth of one hundred feet. If you expect anyone to—"

"You mean a scorch attack?" Ornias whispered, eyeing his guards anxiously.

"Yes. Tahn will make sure nothing survives."

The six guards shifted nervously, standing stiffly at intervals along the red cave walls. Without Harper, he could do nothing. If he made a break for the door, would they kill him? In the corner, Rathanial and Shassy shared a tearful reunion, murmuring softly to each other. They'd be in the line of fire if the guards missed. He contemplated that fact briefly, but decided their lives weren't worth the number of people in his forces who'd die if the Magistrates probed his mind. He edged for the door.

"Don't even think about it, Baruch," Ornias said sternly, stopping in mid-stride before a long table stacked high with priceless vases. His gold robe shimmered in the candlelight. "My guards have orders *not* to kill you under any circumstances, but they can certainly maim you and the Magistrates will still have your brain to play with."

Jeremiel glared. "In a half hour, this planet will be a molten ball. *Get on your pan-city screens and tell the people!*"

"Are you giving me orders, Baruch?"

"Looks like somebody's got to."

"Don't be presumptuous."

"Ah, I see. You're afraid the people will riot and make a

444

dash for the *samaels*, shoving you out of the way in the panic. Hear that, men?" Jeremiel smiled at the guards. "How many of you do you think he plans on taking with him? What about your families?"

The guards eyed each other in abrupt uncertainty, shifting back and forth.

Ornias' eyes hardened. "I'll take every loyal member of my staff and their families. These men know that."

"They think you're *reliable*?" He laughed deprecatingly. "So you haven't told them you killed Zadok Calas? Or that by selling me to the Magistrates, the Underground Movement will go through a reshuffling of leadership and *thousands* of Gamants will probably die during the interim?"

"Your lies will get you nowhere, Baruch. My people are loyal. I've always rewarded them for . . ."

In the hallway, pounding boots sounded and the door slammed open, violet lances of light shredding the room. Jeremiel hit the floor rolling. Screams echoed in his ears as he slithered for cover.

"Put down your weapons!" someone shouted.

Jeremiel looked up to see Harper and his team of assassins spreading out over the room, turning over dead guards, searching those still alive. Ornias leaned unsteadily against the far wall, hands high over his head. Behind Harper, Funk peered anxiously through the door, gray hair sticking out at odd angles.

"Harper!" Jeremiel ordered, sitting up. "Quickly, get these cuffs off me."

The tall black monk ran across the room, slicing the iron bands with two pistol shots. "Good to see you're in one piece. We'd feared—"

"*Later.* Tahn's expecting to transport me to his ship in about ten minutes. Then he's going to scorch Horeb."

Harper's mahogany face slackened in terror. "So it's happened. I guess that means Operation Abba is in effect."

"I'm afraid so." Jeremiel lurched to his feet, rubbing his wrists to get the circulation flowing again. He met Harper's dark eyes with frantic seriousness. "The first thing we have to do is get a *samael* to your caves. Put Calas and Funk in it, pick up Sybil and anybody else you can fit—"

"Janowitz," Harper ordered sharply. The blond monk looked up. "Get on the Councilman's com unit and find out how many ships our forces have captured, then immediately dispatch two to the caves."

"Contact those *samaels* over the polar cap, too," Jeremiel added. "Counteract all previous orders. Tell them if they can find Rachel Eloel to pick her up *unharmed*. And if not, to get out to orbit within thirty minutes."

"Got it." Janowitz ran for the com on the far table.

Harper turned back to Jeremiel, chest rising and falling quickly. "And after that?"

"Have Janowitz get on the screens and tell the people of Seir. Get them moving for the spaceport. We won't be able to save everybody, but—"

"Jeremiel, Horeb . . . It's lost, isn't it?"

"Not necessarily." He gave the monk a smile, that insane feeling of hope that always accompanied desperation flooding him. "I've always had the insane urge to *try* Operation Abba. Rudy, my second in command, had a lunatic belief in it."

Harper shifted uncomfortably. "Has anyone ever tried it before?"

"No. At this point, it's pure theory. Listen, now. Tahn will be expecting me to transport in the company of guards—to insure the councilman's investment, of course. Pick two of your best people and get ready."

He ran across the room, jerking a gun from a dead guard's warm hand.

* * * * *

Rachel woke bitterly cold, unable to move her legs. Ice covered her weather-suit. She tried to flex her fingers, but found them too stiff. Leaning her head back against the icy wall, she gazed upward through frost-encrusted lashes. The blue glow of the *Mea* had dimmed to nothingness—a gate locked.

"*I'm d–dying.*" The empty sound of her voice frightened her. She sucked in a breath of the glacial air, feeling it bite in her lungs. She just wanted to sleep.

She closed her eyes.

A soothing voice penetrated her numbness. "*Ah, there you are.*"

Weakly, she blinked. A dark shadow undulated over the irregularities in the walls. Then a brilliant flash fired the ice cave and a man of crystalline beauty appeared. Terror ravaged her as she looked into the face of a frescoed god come to life. He stared down at her with heartrending sorrow in his amber eyes. Throwing back his blue velvet hood, he knelt, gaze going over her concernedly.

"Who . . . who are you?"

He bowed his head. "Adom knew me as Milcom. But you know my real name is Aktariel."

She forced her head to nod. Frosty black waves cascaded over her shoulder. She rested her head against the wall again, meeting his eyes. Odd, the warmth, the hurt there, made her feel as though she'd known him all her life, as though they shared a pain too deep for words.

"Ep—Epagael . . ."

"Yes, I'm sorry I had to put you through that. Forgive me. I had no choice. Only by facing Him could you understand my desperation."

Rachel's gaze drifted aimlessly over the cave. In the soft golden light cast by his body, the icy walls sparkled like a million diamonds.

"Rachel, please, let me hold you? I know you're frightened of me, but—"

"You killed Adom."

Tears glistened in his eyes. "Not I. Epagael."

"He . . ." A sob shook her. "God doesn't—care—about us."

"No. But I do."

He reached out and pulled her against him, cradling her tenderly. Warmth seeped into her extremities, tingling painfully in her toes and fingers. She shuddered and he nuzzled his cheek against hers. The overwhelming need to sleep rolled over her. Unwillingly she sank deeper into the warm blanket of his arms.

"Sleep, Rachel," she heard him say soothingly, as he gently stroked her hair. "The moment you wake, the universe changes. Sleep all you can."

His voice seemed to echo in the frigid stillness. "And don't worry. I won't let anyone hurt you. Not even God."

*　　*　　*　　*　　*

Darkness shrouded the caves, dust splashing into Sybil's eyes as the *samael* landed. A huge black beetle, it hissed like a serpent. Monks ran headlong for it, pushing each other and whispering frantically.

"Hurry, Sybil!" Petran shouted, shoving her toward the ship.

"Are we going to find my mommy?"

"Blast you, child! This planet's going to be a molten ball in a few minutes. Move!"

He tried to grab her but she dodged his hand. "If the Magistrates are going to scorch us, somebody has to find my mommy! Where is she? She was going with the Mashiah—"

"We don't have time to fight, Sybil!"

He jerked her up, twisting her hand so hard it ached, and carried her beneath his arm for the ship. Sybil sank her teeth into his thumb. He cried out, dropping her and she ran across the dark rocky plateau. In the distance, fires still dotted Seir, smoke billowing to blot the stars.

"Get her!" Petran shouted.

From all sides, monks closed in, surrounding her.

She clenched her fists, shouting at the top of her lungs, *"Where's my mommy?"*

Two monks lunged for her, clutching her arms and hauling her up the steps and into the waiting *samael*.

* * * * *

Harper stood stiffly beside Jeremiel at the spaceport, eyes going over the charred rubble of Seir. The third moon rose over jagged peaks, flooding the city with milky light. Apartment buildings loomed black in silhouette, shattered walls leaning precariously. People crowded the streets, clubs or stolen rifles clutched in their hands. Here and there a filthy bandage wrapped an arm or leg. And all shoved violently toward the ships that were loading just beyond the fence.

An awesome panic had gripped Horeb. Near the gate, Janowitz and Uriah stood, hands on pistols.

Jeremiel wet his lips and bent down, drawing pictures in the dirt. Sweat stained the arms of his black jumpsuit, but a curious vitality invaded his eyes, as though the life and death tightrope that stretched before him only hardened his resolve to win.

Harper sighed. Gamants. They'd suffered crushing misfortunes for millennia, yet they'd never succumbed to the crashing of empires, the brutality and confiscation of arrogant conquerors. Fate had broken their backs, but never their spirits. Ghostly ancestors seemed to move quietly in the moonlit shadows around him. Men and women who'd seen the worst life could offer and who'd struggled from the mire to shake bloody fists at defeat. They hadn't bemoaned fortune, they'd fought back.

He looked contemplatively at Jeremiel. In the past few minutes, an unsettling calm had gripped the Underground leader.

"Come here, Avel. I want to make sure you understand this."

"You mean the ship's design?"

"Yes. One more time. This is the transportation center on Tahn's ship. This is the closest transport tube. Remember?"

He nodded. "Yes."

"We'll take the shuttle first. The hard part comes when we hit Tahn's landing bay. I'll go for him. You'll—"

"What makes you think he'll be there?"

Jeremiel's eyes glittered as hard and brilliant as sapphires. "Oh, he'll be there—just as I would were the situation reversed."

"Uh-huh." He blinked anxiously. "You know, even though the element of surprise will be on our side, this is insane."

"Of course." Jeremiel gave Harper a broad, flashing smile. "You don't think we should give up just because it'll be four against three thousand, do you?"

"If we had a choice—"

"We don't. Not if we want to save Horeb. Besides, this isn't nearly as insane as the stunt I pulled in the Scholem system. We were outnumbered a thousand to one. Tahn had us boxed tight in a—"

"You've been in worse situations."

"Oh, much worse."

Overhead, a hum broke the silence, *Hoyer*'s shuttle diving from the dark star-limned skies like a deadly lance.

Baruch stood, slapping red dirt from his jumpsuit as he watched the craft descend. He turned, gazing confidently at Harper, a glint of amusement in his eyes. A slow smile curled his lips. "Ready?"

Avel massaged his brow, a desperate laugh bubbling up. "Let's go."

* * * * *

Ornias put his feet up on the white control console of the ship, gazing out the window at the spiny ridges of Horeb so far below. A bottle of Kayan sherry sat beside him. He watched as the planet rolled from light to dark. The lights of

Seir passed beneath him. He chuckled and uncorked the bottle.

"How long to Palaia Station, Corporal?" he asked the brown haired boy at the controls.

"About three days, sir."

He smiled and poured his glass full, then lifted the crystal goblet to the battle cruiser floating in the black depths beyond. "A toast to your efficiency, Tahn. I hope you can hold him."

CHAPTER 46

Tahn uneasily paced the gray carpet in Transportation. The room was small, twenty by thirty feet, with stark white walls and a single com terminal. The security team hadn't arrived yet and he felt so tense he wanted to scream. Preferably at somebody—anybody.

Halloway took a deep breath and braced a shoulder against the wall. Her gaze followed his every movement.

He stopped pacing and glowered at her. "You got something to say to me? *Say it!*"

She fixed him with one of those superior looks. "What good would it do?"

"What is it!"

She ground her teeth a moment. "Cole, after we scorch Horeb, are you going to deliver Baruch to a neurophysiology center?"

"I'll follow orders, whatever they are."

"Even if it means destroying one of the most brilliant military minds in the galaxy?"

"Damn it, Carey!" He slammed a fist into the white wall. His nerves hummed, strung tight as catgut fiddle, and she damn well knew it! "What do you want me to do? Set Baruch *free*? Let him go back and lead his Underground against us again? How many friends have you lost to his *brilliance*?"

She didn't look like she was breathing, but she gave him look for look. "Too many, but—"

"That's answer enough."

"No, it's not. What's past is past. You could intervene on his behalf. Plead his case to the Magistrates. If you—"

"You want me to put *my* career on the line for a man who's been my enemy for over fifteen years? What the hell's the matter with you?"

Hostilely she folded her arms. "Not a damn thing a new job wouldn't fix. Just think about taking the chance, Cole. Turning Baruch into a vegetable will be a loss for all of us. The Magistrates won't reprimand you for bringing up the possibility of saving him. And you know I'll back you till kingdom come if it's necessary."

He shook his head, laughing contemptuously. "You'll stand up with me at my court-martial?"

"They won't court-martial you. You're too valuable."

"You're a hell of an optimist. Aiding the enemy is still considered treason in this part of the galaxy and Slothen frowns on things like that."

"I'm not asking you to 'go over' to the other side. But you know as well as I do that the orders we've been getting lately reek of political gamesmanship. We can't keep obeying . . ."

The door snicked back and Carey went forebodingly silent, though her eyes leveled a bitter indictment. Six security officers strode in, saluting crisply. Tahn returned the gesture and absently straightened the sleeves of his purple uniform in preparation for the event that seemed destined to turn him inside out. Without giving Halloway a second look, he hit the button to open the doors to the landing bay foyer.

"Sergeant?" he called to the young brown-haired bay officer. "What's the status of the shuttle?"

"Simons reports he has Baruch in custody. No problems, ETA is two minutes, sir."

A desperate hollowness invaded his chest. He clenched his fists, ordering, "Notify the bridge to commence Prime Mover One."

"Aye, sir."

He glanced up at the planet monitor, watching numbly as broad violet beams lanced the surface of Horeb. Red dust boiled into the atmosphere. Unable to contain his anxiety, he started pacing again. He was acutely aware his security team watched him intently. He refused to check on what Halloway was doing.

"Shuttle docked, sir. Simons reports, 'all clear.' "

He nodded. "Open the doors."

They pulled back and he strode out into the bay. From

the corner of his eye, he thought he caught movement. He stopped abruptly, whirling to stare at the far wall. His heart pounded, but only a gleam of white tiles met his scrutiny.

"What is it?" Halloway asked pensively. Her hand had dropped to the butt of her holstered pistol.

"Nothing . . . I—I thought I saw a shadow. Something black . . . moving over the walls. I'm just skittish, I guess."

"Materialized guilt," she whispered so low no one but him could hear.

He glared sharply. "Remind me to prosecute you for insubordination."

"Aye, sir."

The lanceolate shuttle sat like a black spear on the white tiles. His stomach muscles tightened as the side doors parted. Baruch stepped out first, hands cuffed behind him. His black jumpsuit glimmered with red dust. He looked worn beyond exhaustion. Simons came out next, prodding the Underground commander with his rifle. Three more men stepped out after Simons, undoubtedly part of the security team. Tahn didn't recognize them, but that wasn't unusual. With over three thousand people on his ship, it was impossible to know every face. Faintly, he heard someone order, "Move."

Baruch started walking, back painfully straight, until he spied Tahn. His steps faltered and he lifted his chin defiantly. The security personnel spread out behind him, weapons aimed at his broad back. Baruch checked their positions and a hint of a smile curled his lips as he walked forward again. Almost unconsciously, Tahn's hand slid to his own pistol; it felt cool and comforting beneath his sweaty palm.

Baruch stopped no more than three feet in front of him and greeted his nemesis, "Tahn."

"I keep my promises, Baruch. You'll be well treated."

"You're a butcher. Have you initiated the scorch attack yet? How many babies do you think you've already murdered?"

Tahn barely had time to open his mouth when the ship lunged sideways, g-force making him stagger.

"What the hell . . ."

"Cole! *Look out!*" Carey screamed.

Several things seemed to happen simultaneously. Baruch's hands flashed from behind his back and he expertly slammed Tahn in the temple with the heavy butt of a pistol. Dazed, he hit the floor hard, rolling, hand awkwardly slipping from the polished grips of his gun. A shrill whine erupted. Simons and his security team slumped to the tiles in pools of blood. More shots rang out, echoing thunderously from the walls.

"Harper, *GO!*" Baruch shouted and lunged for Tahn.

They struggled against each other, kicking, punching, panting. Baruch smashed him again and again with the pistol. From the corner of his eye Tahn saw the three shuttle officers he'd assumed to be his race for the transport tube. *God damn! What the hell was happening?*

A split second later Carey's wild shot flashed off the floor beside him and Baruch made a mad dive, rolling to his feet and running for the tube.

Tahn crawled weakly to his knees. Nausea overwhelmed him and he vomited repeatedly onto the white tiles. *Concussion.* He could feel the shock wave jostling the electrochemical environment of his brain; memories flashed, thoughts misfiling, fading. Carey's cool hand touched his arm and she pulled him up.

"Lean on me. Cole? Cole! We've got to get out of here!"

He clung to Halloway, vaguely surprised at her strength as she supported him to the other side of the bay toward the doors that led to Defense.

Fuzzy images taunted his injured mind—snatches of thoughts roiling together, faces coming close and melting into nothingness. Time scurried out of sequence, events mixing, haunting . . .

"*Cole?*" Maggie Zander called, laughing. He saw her beautiful face, blonde hair draping in thick waves down her back. "Hey, love, get a load of this cream puff cake." Orillian spice pastry. Columba 3, twenty years ago.

"*Maggie?*" He reached out pleadingly, needing her, wanting her.

"*Cole! For God's sake, hold on!*" Carey's frantic voice demanded.

"What?" Voice thick. Eyes fuzzy. He looked around. He didn't remember getting into the Defense bay. *Oh, God. This is bad.*

Carey locked the entry and let him down to the floor easy, then raced to the com on the wall. "Security, this is Lieutenant Halloway. Trace the paths of the men who just left landing bay four via transport tube nineteen-two. They are hostile. Stop them. *Use full force if necessary.*"

Tahn feebly got to his feet and suddenly had no idea where he was. Somewhere in the back of his foggy mind he heard the first alert sirens wailing. Leaning against the wall, his stomach cramped again. He suppressed the welling sourness, looking at Halloway hostilely. Somewhere, he'd lost hours. Were they still orbiting Kayan? "Carey, what the hell's . . . going on?"

"You're all right. Don't—"

"But what . . . *Baruch*," he remembered in a staggering flash. The rest of the scene flooded back. "Damn it, Carey. You were only ten feet away! *Why the hell did you miss?*"

She whirled, roasting him with her gaze. "I thought it would be poor form to shoot through you to get to Baruch!"

"Damn you! You could have—"

"Shut up!" She shoved him hard against the wall and ripped open his shirt to stare at his chest. Surprised, he yielded, watching the expression on her beautiful face go from scared stiff to momentary relief. "Must be Simons' blood. You're all right. But I've still got to get you to Iona."

Only then did he realize his shirt clung to his skin in sticky red folds. The world whirled around him. "*Tahn! Listen up, buddy! Get the hell out of the Service! I'm telling you, friend. It'll kill you in the end . . . in the end . . . in the . . .*" The voice replayed over and over.

"Wirth? Jonny?" Paris, Old Earth. Pegasus Invasion. Spring rain misted through the bloody streets, bodies piled ten feet high against the walls of the old cathedral of Notre Dame. "*Jonny,*" he said weakly, watching as his friend went down under a shrill blast of fire. He drove. . . .

"Goddamn it, Cole," Carey intruded. She grabbed his arm hard, draping it over her shoulders. "Stay alert! *Run a count!*"

"Ten, nine, eight, se . . . seven . . . four . . ." Lost it. What . . .

"I've got to get some steroids into you."

"Get me . . . get me to the bridge."

She gave him a doubtful look, but nodded, supporting him down a short corridor where they caught a tube going up. Sweat beaded on his brow, an overwhelming headache pressing behind his eyes. He leaned his cheek against the cool wall.

"Why the hell are we alive? Why didn't—"

"Baruch was between us and them. They couldn't risk shooting you, but our security team was out in the open like sitting ducks. Baruch positioned his people perfectly. That wrestling match was a diversion so they could get away."

"Then why didn't he kill me once they were gone?"

"Maybe he likes you."

Absurdly, he started to laugh, but his vision clouded suddenly, balance wavering. Carey grabbed him, wrapping her arms around him before he hit the floor. He took deep breaths, struggling against the stunning aftereffects of the head blows Baruch had delivered with such expertise.

"Cole?" Carey said in his ear and he could hear the fear in her voice. "You're fading. I'm going to take you straight to the infirmary."

"No. I—I just need a minute." He forced himself to think. Think! He went over every moment of the attack, cataloguing each with an intensity that kept him here, *here* on the *Hoyer*. "What was that . . . that lurch we suffered?"

"I don't know. It was like the fabric of space heaved."

He looked at her sharply, realizing that's exactly what it had felt like. *Phase change.* A prickle of unreasoning terror climbed his spine.

*　　*　　*　　*　　*

Harper licked his lips nervously, wondering when the sirens would go off. Jeremiel had said they'd have thirty seconds maximum. He stared at Uriah and Janowitz. "You know the plan. Full-scale attack. No prisoners."

Janowitz eyes glowed. "We're ready."

Uriah, a skinny black-haired boy of twenty merely jerked a nod and wet his lips.

Harper gripped his rifle tightly as the tube came to a stop and the door slipped open. They lunged into the hall, sweeping the corridor with their weapons. Four people fell dead before they could even scream.

Then they charged the big bay doors. All C-J class battle cruisers, Jeremiel had explained, had the same design. The control section of engineering was a tri-level round chamber manned at any given time by about twenty people. Duty stations perched like wire birds' nests on each level—making it damned easy shooting if you surprised the crew from below.

They burst through the doors and opened fire just as the First Alert blared.

Jeremiel pressed back against the tube wall, panting, excitement flooding hotly through his veins. The sound of rifle fire keened through the corridor outside. "Goddamn, let that be Harper."

Screaming people fled madly by him. He waited until the flood passed, then cautiously glanced outside. The doors to engineering stood open.

He ran with all his might, leaping the dead that littered the corridor and sliding to a halt just outside. Harper's irrationally calm voice drifted out: "Get away from those controls, mister."

"Who—who are you? You can't just walk in here and—"

A rifle blast shredded the air, blending with the sporadic bursts of fire that still sounded from other areas. Jeremiel eased through the doors, pistol leveled, and took in the blood spattered interior. Mangled bodies dangled from the wire duty stations.

Harper stood on the far side, his rifle aimed at the belly of a dead red-haired lieutenant. Jeremiel raced to the control console near Harper and began hitting the appropriate buttons.

"What are you doing?" Harper asked, glancing sideways as the doors snapped closed and the alert sirens ceased.

"Rerouting control of the ship. Sealing off this section, level seven, and the bridge and decompressing every other level."

"Decompressing? You're . . . You're going to kill thousands of people?"

"You want them in here with us?"

Harper closed his eyes, lowering himself into a chair. "No."

"Every Magisterial soldier who lives is another chance we'll be defeated. I'm not taking any chances."

"What's on level seven?"

"About five hundred scientists who know this ship inside and out. We might need them. Where are Janowitz and Uriah?"

"On cleanup duty. Seeing if we missed anyone in the initial attack."

"Uh-huh. Good," he muttered absently as he canceled the commands for the scorch attack. The energy output readings on his monitor spiraled down and he allowed himself a brief moment of solace. "I don't know how much damage has already been done, but Horeb's safe for the time being."

Harper smoothed his halo of black hair and sighed. "Thank God."

"Avel, get over there on that panel." He pointed to the console five feet down from him. "That's communications.

It works basically the same way the units on the planet did. Open a channel to the *samaels* filled with your old comrades. We'll need the best technical people and make sure you find Yosef Calas. Whether he likes it or not, he's the new leader of Gamant civilization. Find out—"

Harper frowned. "The best technical people? What for?"

"In about five minutes this ship is going to be dead in space. We can hold orbit almost indefinitely, but if we're going to get to a Gamant planet and take this ship as ours, we'll need loyal crew."

"You're going to use Gamants?"

"Damn right. I doubt Tahn will like it, but—"

"You didn't kill him?" Harper asked incredulously.

"I don't know, I may have. I gambled he'd head straight for the bridge. If he didn't, I lost my ace in the hole and we'll have a thousand-armed headless monster in the Technoscience division. If Tahn survived, he's still their captain, even if he's lost his ship. He can be very useful in convincing them to be cooperative."

"You think he'll help us?"

Jeremiel looked up, meeting Harper's dark brooding eyes. "I think people will do almost anything when you hold a gun to their heads."

"Makes sense."

"Get on the com. I'm opening all the bay doors so the *samaels* can land."

"I'm on it." Harper sprinted away.

Jeremiel felt weak suddenly. He braced his hands against the console, staring sightlessly at the dials. Twenty-five hundred dead, he estimated. In the dark depths of his soul, a pain welled, trying to hook up with his brain to form a scream. Almost as clearly as if that dreadful day had returned, he felt the bitter chill of Silmar's snow, heard the desperation in Rudy's voice, felt his despair when he found Syene. He remembered how he'd hated Tahn that day . . . prayed he'd get his hands on him so he could torture him to death. But now, the truth sank in, filtering to the deepest recesses of his mind. *He had Tahn.* And he damn well didn't want him. They'd all done what they had to do in the battle for survival—even Tahn. But his people in the Underground would try to force him to make an example of the man who'd killed so many of their families and friends.

He straightened, irresolute, frightened, and looked around at the blood spattered room. Crimson streams streaked the walls, still pouring from the dead hanging precariously out of their wire duty stations.

He searched his soul intently, hunting, hunting desperately for some shred of triumph.

* * * * *

By the time Halloway hauled him onto the bridge, his headache had grown to a smashing misery that left him trembling. He was on the verge of passing out.

"Tahn!" Neil Dannon whirled as they entered, face stark with terror. "What's happening?"

Carey let him down easily into his command chair and ran for her navigation console.

"Ship's status, Lieutenant?" he asked. The words echoed agonizingly in his head.

Macey stuttered. "We—we don't know, sir. We can't—"

"Is it true?" Dannon lunged for him, bracing hands on his chair arms to stare wild-eyed into his face. *"Is Baruch aboard?"*

Tahn gritted his teeth, trying to focus his eyes. Dannon's jet-black hair hung in damp strands over his pale face. "What the hell are you doing here? Get off my bridge!"

"I want to know if he—"

The alert sirens went deathly silent and Tahn felt his gut go tight. A pestilent stillness gripped the bridge. "No . . . he can't have—"

"Captain!" Macey yelled shrilly. "I've—I've got decompression readings from all over the ship. We—"

"Gas engineering!"

Halloway's fingers fluttered over her console. Her voice came out quiet. "Can't. He's rerouted control."

"Bypass!"

". . . Can't."

"Oh, God!" Dannon wailed hysterically. *"He's taken your ship. You fool! You let him take your ship!* You should have *known* he'd—"

Tahn used his last strength to stand and slam a powerful right cross into Dannon's mouth. The man staggered into a chair and sobbed insanely before crawling for the nearest suit locker. Someone screamed and Tahn fell back into his seat. His gaze landed numbly on the forward screen. Bodies tumbled from his ship, scattering into the blackness of space like bloody eggs spewed from a huge fish.

He felt suddenly as though he weren't really there, that he walked in some terrible, terrible nightmare from which he couldn't awaken. He numbly saw that his crew watched the screen in mute horror, moisture glistening in their eyes.

"Halloway . . . *Carey*, estimate casualties."

As she reached for her monitor, he saw her hand quake. "Approximately two thousand seven hundred fifty."

Tahn closed his eyes, listening to the thunderous silence. "Which level did he seal? Seven?"

"Aye, sir."

Seven . . . Seven . . . The sweet scent of Giclasian apple blossoms. Academy. "Private Tahn," Major Kersten's voice grated. The man stared him in the eyes, stabbing a hard finger against his chest. He stiffened. "You couldn't even score *eight* on a simple astrophysics test? You'll never make it son. Never make it . . . never . . ."

"Captain?" Macey's voice intervened, on the verge of tears. "What's happening?"

He fought to straighten up from where he'd slumped in his chair. *Sick, so sick.* He couldn't think, couldn't sift through the tangled web in his mind. He felt as though cloth stuffed his head to the bursting point. He'd lost his ship—he remembered. The implications drowned him like a tidal wave. His thoughts kept revolving around a single sentence, *"What the hell are we doing, Cole? What the hell are we . . . Whatthehell . . ."* And he knew deep down that Carey'd been right. He should have done something, tried talking to the Magistrates, relinquished his command on ethical grounds, *something*. Then he'd have been the only one lost. Not . . .

On adjacent screens, he saw the planetary ships surging toward the *Hoyer* and abruptly knew Baruch's plan.

Forcing a deep breath, he ordered, "Macey, get me engineering."

*　　*　　*　　*　　*

Jeremiel tensed as the visual monitor flared to life on the com console. Tahn looked haggard, ill, the fire in his blue-violet eyes dulled. He met that gaze with equanimity. Why was it he never felt exultation anymore? Victory always seemed two-edged, a dagger that just twisted one way or the other. He straightened a little, arms folded, heart hammering.

"Baruch . . . let's talk."

"I'm listening."

"I should think . . . telling you we surrender is a little redundant, but if you need to hear it—"

"I don't."

Tahn nodded tiredly, respect in the gesture—and hatred. "What can I do to save the lives of the rest of my crew?"

"I want your cooperation. The people I'm bringing aboard are able, but not trained. Tell your science division to school my people and I guarantee I'll put you off alive and well on the nearest Gamant planet."

"I'm not sure that'll be doing us a favor . . . but we'll manage. Is there anything else I can do to assure our comfort?"

"Negative. We'll give as we receive."

Tahn hesitated a moment. "I've got one other request."

"What is it?"

"When you're finished repressurizing the decks, I've . . . I've got a bottle of hundred-year-old rye whiskey in my cabin. Let's sit down . . . just you and me. There are some other things I want to discuss with you."

In the long silence that followed, Jeremiel debated with himself. A trap? No, he doubted it. The time for ploys was long past. A sincere request from one commander to another—even though they'd been enemies for years? Or, perhaps, *because* they had? He nodded slowly. "Name the time."

"Tonight. 2100 hours?"

"I'll be there." His hand hovered over the switch which would cut the transmission. He said nothing for a time, but held Tahn's gaze. The man looked so shaken, so emptied of all his usual fire. He couldn't help himself, he asked, "Are you all right, Tahn? I hit you pretty hard."

'That's another thing I'd like to . . . 'discuss' . . . with you. Once I get back in shape. For the moment, I just need some drugs and . . . and sleep. I'll see you tonight."

"Affirmative."

He flicked off the monitor and turned to Harper. The man sat rigidly in his chair, a deep frown furrowing his forehead. Sweat glimmered from his mahogany face.

"Avel, I have to go meet the incoming *samaels*. There are two things I need you to do. First, I've set the ship's scanners on maximum. All you have to do is use this board to search the polar ice cap for life. If you get confused, ask the ship, she'll help guide you. *I want to know if Rachel's still alive.*"

"I understand. If she is, I'll dispatch a *samael* immediately to get her."

"Good." *Please, Epagael? Let her be all right.* "Second . . ." A warm hollowness filled him. He bowed his head and propped a fist on the console. "Use a narrow beam transmission. Aim for somewhere around Pitbon. See if you can contact my fleet. If so, tell Rudy Kopal we've got another battle cruiser for him. Ask him to meet us at Tikkun."

"I will."

Jeremiel turned and headed for the vacuum-suit locker. Though most decks had enough air to allow survival now, it would take another two hours to completely restore the life systems of the ship. In the meantime, he wanted to feel safe.

He hadn't felt safe in a long, long time.

And he knew it would only be a brief reprieve. When the Magistrates learned he'd taken the *Hoyer*, they'd hit him with everything they had.

Fastening his helmet down, he shoved his hands in his pockets and walked toward the rear lock.

CHAPTER 47

Sybil crouched in the corner of the *samael's* command cabin. She wanted to be out of the way, where no one could see her crying. Men raced around, flicking switches on the table, talking fast. She watched them through blurry eyes, wiping her nose with her sleeve.

"Get Calas up here," the captain said. "Baruch wants to talk to him."

"Aye, sir." The other man left at a run.

Sybil drew up her knees and put her forehead against them, staring down at her untied right shoe. Her mom and dad had given her those shoes for her eighth birthday. She remembered her dad's warm smile at her party as he watched kids playing around her feet, and her mother whispering, "Try not to hit Moshe today. He's supposed to be here having fun."

She didn't like Moshe. He used to shove her down in the playground at school . . . but, just now, she wished she knew if he was all right. She wished she knew if her mom . . .

A darkness like a huge black monster grew inside her. It watched, waiting. She wiped wet cheeks on her sleeve and closed her eyes, trying not to think about what life would be like without her mom.

The door opened and she heard new voices. She opened one eye. Two old men, one very tall and one short and a little fat, stood in front of her talking to the captain.

"Hey," the tall one said, "I can fly this thing. You need a copilot? Watch this. I know all about weapons and shields and things." He started for the empty seat in front of the controls.

"You imbecile!" the short one said. He grabbed his friend's belt loop and jerked him back. "We want to *get* to the *Hoyer*. Go stand in the corner over there." He pointed to where Sybil crouched. Putting a funny ring around his head, he acted like he was listening to someone on the other end. "Yes," he said unhappily, "I understand, Jeremiel." And then, "Oh, thank God. I'm so glad."

The tall man looked at her, cocking his head curiously. Sybil stiffened, sitting up straighter. He smiled broadly, and walked over to kneel in front of her. "You look like my type," he said. "Want to run away with me?"

"I don't think so. My name's Sybil, what's yours?"

"I'm Ari and that's Yosef over there. He's not as good looking as me, but he has other—"

"Sybil?" the short man said. He pulled the ring off his head and handed it to the captain. His gray brows drew together. "Are you Rachel's daughter?"

Hope burst wide in her chest, making her voice tremble. "You know my mom?"

He smiled warmly. "Yes, I do. And Jeremiel says to tell you she's all right. He just sent a ship to pick her up."

Sybil felt like her heart would break. Sobs puffed her chest as tears poured hotly down her face.

"Hey," Ari said, "Come here." He reached out and lifted her to his lap. "I should have known you were Rachel's girl. She turned me down, too."

Sybil buried her face in his shirt and cried.

CHAPTER 48

Mikael groggily rolled to his side. He felt so tired it was hard to breathe. His gaze drifted over the white cabin. Captain Tahn had tucked him into bed, patting him. That had eased some of the hurt that swelled like a black bubble in his chest. But a doctor had come and given him a shot. His arm still hurt.

He stared blankly at the far wall, seeing the way the darkness welled in the corner.

"Mikael?"

He lay still, frightened. The voice trickled from the *Mea* that Metatron had given him. "Grandfather?"

"Yes, I miss you terribly, Grandson."

"Where are you?"

"Here. Inside the *Mea*."

Mikael feebly pushed up on his elbows, staring down at the brilliantly glowing ball around his neck. A blue gleam spread like fire over the walls.

"Can you come out, Grandfather? I need you here with me."

"I know, Mikael. But to be close to you, I have to stay here. This way, at least you can hear me."

"Grandfather? Did you know the Magistrates killed Mama? A big ship came and shot into the cliffs. Rocks rolled down on her." A sharp pain throbbed in his tiny chest. He wiped his nose.

"No. I—I didn't know."

There was a long pause and Mikael heard a sound like the roar of putting a seashell to his ear.

". . . I love you, Mikael."

"I love you, too. I wish I could hold you."

"I do, too, Grandson. Maybe soon. It's hard, I know, to go on and do what you have to, but I need you to listen. Can you?"

He pulled himself up in bed, exhaling tiredly as he shoved his pillow behind his back. "Yes."

"A man named Jeremiel Baruch has just come aboard the ship with you. You have to tell him something."

"What, Grandfather?"

"The Antimashiah has come."

Mikael's heart pounded sickeningly. All his life, he'd heard stories of the wicked being who would try to destroy the universe. "Who is he, Grandpa?"

"Tell Jeremiel he'll know the evil one by the initials AKT branded into her forehead."